D1565667

A SHAKESPEARIAN GRAMMAR

An Attempt to Illustrate Some
of the Differences Between
Elizabethan and Modern English

E. A. ABBOTT

Dover Publications, Inc.
Mineola, New York

Bibliographical Note

This Dover edition, first published in 1966 and republished in 2003, is an unabridged republication of the work originally published by Macmillan and Company, London, in 1870. As such, it is the complete text of the third revised edition.

Library of Congress Cataloging-in-Publication Data

Abbott, Edwin Abbott, 1838–1926.
    A Shakespearian grammar : an attempt to illustrate some of the differences between Elizabethan and modern English / E.A. Abbott.
        p. cm.
    Originally published: London : Macmillan, 1870.
    Includes index.
    ISBN 0-486-43135-5
    1. Shakespeare, William, 1564–1616—Language. 2. English language—Early modern, 1500–1700—Grammar. I. Title.

PR3075.A4 2003
822.3'3—dc21

2003053173

Manufactured in the United States of America
Dover Publications, Inc., 31 East 2nd Street, Mineola, N.Y. 11501

CONTENTS.

CONTENTS.

PROSODY.

PREFACE TO THIRD EDITION.

THE success which has attended the First and Second Editions of the "SHAKESPEARIAN GRAMMAR," and the demand for a Third Edition within a year of the publication of the First, has encouraged the Author to endeavour to make the work somewhat more useful, and to render it, as far as possible, a complete book of reference for all difficulties of Shakespearian syntax or prosody. For this purpose the whole of Shakespeare has been re-read, and an attempt has been made to include within this Edition the explanation of every idiomatic difficulty (where the text is not confessedly corrupt) that comes within the province of a grammar as distinct from a glossary.

The great object being to make a useful book of reference for students, and especially for classes in schools, several Plays have been indexed so fully that with the aid of a glossary and historical notes the references will serve for a complete commentary. These Plays are, *As You Like It, Coriolanus, Hamlet, Henry V., Julius Cæsar, Lear, Macbeth, Merchant of Venice, Midsummer Night's Dream, Richard II., Richard III., Tempest, Twelfth Night.* It is hoped that these copious indexes will meet a want, by giving some definite work to be prepared by the class, whether as a holiday task or in the work of the term. The want of some such distinct work, to give thoroughness and definiteness to an English lesson, has been felt by many teachers of experience. A complete table of the contents of each paragraph has been prefixed, together with a Verbal Index at the end. The indexes may be of use to students of a more advanced stage, and perhaps may occasionally be found useful to the general reader of Shakespeare.

A second perusal of Shakespeare, with a special reference to idiom and prosody, has brought to light several laws which regulate many apparent irregularities. The interesting distinction between *thou* and *you* (Pars. 231—235), for example, has not hitherto attracted the attention of readers, or, as far as I am aware, of commentators on Shakespeare. The use of the relative with plural antecedent and singular verb (Par. 246); the prevalence of the third person plural in *-s* (Par. 333), which does not appear in modern editions of Shakespeare; the "confusion of proximity" (Par. 412); the distinction between an adjective before and after a noun; these and many other points which were at first either briefly or not at all discussed, have increased the present to more than thrice the size of the original book. I propose now to stereotype this edition, so that no further changes need be anticipated.

It may be thought that the amplification of the Prosody is unnecessary, at all events, for the purpose of a school-book. My own experience, however, leads me to think that the Prosody of Shakespeare has peculiar interest for boys, and that some training in it is absolutely necessary if they are to read Shakespeare *critically*. The additions which have been made to this part of the book have sprung naturally out of the lessons in English which I have been in the habit of giving; and as they are the results of practical experience, I am confident they will be found useful for school purposes.* A conjectural character, more apparent however than real, has perhaps been given to this part of the book from the necessity that I felt of setting down *every difficult verse of Shakespeare* where the text was not acknowledged as corrupt, or where the difficulty was more than slight. Practically, I think, it will be found that the rules of the Prosody will be found to solve most of the difficulties that will present themselves to boys—at least, in the thirteen Plays above mentioned.

Besides obligations mentioned in the First Edition, I must acknowledge the great assistance I have received from MÄTZNER'S *Englische Grammatik* (3 vols., Berlin, 1865), whose enormous collection of examples deserves notice. I am indebted to the same author for some points illustrating the connection between Early and Elizabethan English. Here, however, I have received ample assistance from Mr. F. J. Furnivall, Mr. R. Morris, and others, whose kindness I am glad to have an opportunity of mentioning. In particular, I must here acknowledge my very great obligation to the Rev. W. W. Skeat, late Fellow of Christ's College, Cambridge, whose excellent edition of *William of Palerne* (Early English Text Society, 1867), and whose *Mœso-Gothic Dictionary* (Asher, London, 1866), have been of great service to me. Mr. Skeat also revised the whole of the proof-sheets, and many of his suggestions are incorporated in the present work. I may add here, that in discussing the difference between "thou" and "you" (231–5), and the "monosyllabic foot" (480–6), I was not aware that I had been anticipated by Mr. Skeat, who has illustrated the former point (with reference to Early English) in *William of Palerne*, p. xlii.,

---

* The somewhat grotesque name of "amphibious verse" (Par. 513) sprang in this way from class-teaching. I have retained it, as answering its purpose, by communicating its meaning readily and impressively.

and the latter in his *Essay on the Metres of Chaucer* (vol. I., Aldine Edition, London, 1866). The copious *Index to Layamon*, edited by Sir Frederick Madden, has also been of great service. I trust that, though care has been taken to avoid any unnecessary parade of Anglo-Saxon, or Early English, that might interfere with the distinct object of the work, the information on these points will be found trustworthy and useful. The Prosody has been revised throughout by Mr. A. J. Ellis, whose work on Early English Pronunciation is well known. Mr. Ellis's method of scansion and notation is not in all respects the same as my own, but I have made several modifications in consequence of his suggestive criticisms.

I have now only to express my hope that this little book may do something to forward the development of English instruction in English schools. Taking the very lowest ground, I believe that an intelligent study of English is the shortest and safest way to attain to an intelligent and successful study of Latin and Greek, and that it is idle to expect a boy to grapple with a sentence of Plato or Thucydides if he cannot master a passage of Shakespeare or a couplet of Pope. Looking, therefore, at the study of English from the old point of view adopted by those who advocate a purely classical instruction, I am emphatically of opinion that it is a positive gain to classical studies to deduct from them an hour or two every week for the study of English. But I need scarcely say that the time seems not far off when every English boy who continues his studies to the age of fifteen will study English for the sake of English; and where English is studied Shakespeare is not likely to be forgotten.

E. A. A.

30*th May*, 1870.

PREFACE TO FIRST EDITION.

THE object of this work is to furnish students of Shakespeare and Bacon with a short systematic account of some points of difference between Elizabethan syntax and our own. The *words* of these authors present but little difficulty. They can be understood from glossaries, and, even without such aid, a little reflection and attention to the context will generally enable us to hit the meaning. But the *differences of idiom* are more perplexing. They are more frequent than mere verbal difficulties, and they are less obvious and noticeable. But it need hardly be said, that if we allow ourselves to fancy we are studying Shakespeare critically, when we have not noticed and cannot explain the simplest Shakespearian idiom, we are in danger of seriously lowering our standard of accurate study, and so far from training we are untraining our understanding. Nor is it enough to enumerate unusual idioms without explaining them. Such is not the course we pursue in Latin and Greek, and our native tongue should either not be studied critically at all, or be studied as thoroughly as the languages of antiquity.*

The difficulty which the author has experienced in teaching pupils to read Shakespearian verse correctly, and to analyse a metaphorical expression, has induced him to add a few pages on Shakespeare's prosody and on the use of simile and metaphor.

---

* Of course it is possible to study Shakespeare with great advantage, and yet without any reference to textual criticism. Only, it should be distinctly understood in such cases that textual criticism is not attempted.

A very important question in the study of English is, what should be the amount and nature of the assistance given to students in the shape of notes. It is clear that the mere getting up and reproducing a commentator's opinions, though the process may fill a boy with useful information, can in no sense be called a training. In the Notes and Questions at the end of this volume I have tried to give no more help than is absolutely necessary. The questions may be of use as a holiday-task, or in showing the student how to work the Grammar. They have been for the most part answered by a class of boys from fourteen to sixteen years old, and some by boys much younger.

In some of the sections of the Prosody I must acknowledge my obligations to Mr. W. S. Walker's work on Shakespeare's Versification.* Other obligations are acknowledged in the course of the work; but the great mass of the examples have been collected in the course of several years' close study of Shakespeare and contemporaneous authors. I am aware that there will be found both inaccuracies and incompleteness in this attempt to apply the rules of classical scholarship to the criticism of Elizabethan English, but it is perhaps from a number of such imperfect contributions that there will at last arise a perfect English Grammar.

REFERENCES.

The following works are referred to by the pages :—

Ascham's Scholemaster . (Mayor) . London, 1863.

The Advancement of Learning . . Oxford, 1640.

Bacon's Essays . . . (Wright) . London, 1868.

Ben Jonson's Works . . (Gifford) . London, 1838.

North's Plutarch . . . . . . London, 1656.

Florio's Montaigne . . . . . London, 1603.

* In correcting the proof-sheets I have gained much from consulting Mr. Walker's " Criticisms on Shakespeare."

Wager, Heywood, Ingelend, &c., and sometimes Beaumont and Fletcher, are quoted from "The Songs of the Dramatists," J. W. Parker, 1855.

WORKS REFERRED TO BY ABBREVIATIONS.

Some of the plays of Shakespeare are indicated by the initials of the titles, as follow:

A. W.	All's Well that Ends Well.
A. and C.	Antony and Cleopatra.
A. Y. L.	As You Like It.
C. of E.	Comedy of Errors.
J. C.	Julius Cæsar.
L. L. L.	Love's Labour Lost.
M. for M.	Measure for Measure.
M. of V.	Merchant of Venice.
M. W. of W.	Merry Wives of Windsor.
M. N. D.	Midsummer Night's Dream.
M. Ado	Much Ado about Nothing.
P. of T.	Pericles of Tyre.
R. and J.	Romeo and Juliet.
T. of Sh.	Taming of the Shrew.
T. of A.	Timon of Athens.
T. A.	Titus Andronicus.
Tr. and Cr.	Troilus and Cressida.
T. N.	Twelfth Night.
T. G. of V.	Two Gentlemen of Verona.
W. T.	Winter's Tale.

(The quotations are from the Globe edition unless otherwise specified.)

Asch.	Ascham's Scholemaster.
B. *E.*	Bacon's Essays.
B. and F.	Beaumont and Fletcher
B. J.	Ben Jonson.

B, J.	*E. in &c.* .	Every Man in his Humour.
„	*E. out &c.* .	Every Man out of his Humour.
„	*Cy.'s Rev.* .	Cynthia's Revels.
„	*Sil. Wom.* .	Silent Woman.
„	*Sejan.* . .	Sejanus.
„	*Sad Sh.* . .	Sad Shepherd.
L. C.		Lover's Complaint.
N. P.		North's Plutarch.
P. P.		Passionate Pilgrim.
R. of L.		Rape of Lucrece.
Sonn.		Shakespeare's Sonnets.
V. and A. . . .		Venus and Adonis.

Numbers in parentheses thus (81) refer to the paragraphs
of the Grammar.

INTRODUCTION.

ELIZABETHAN English, on a superficial view, appears to present this great point of difference from the English of modern times, that in the former any irregularities whatever, whether in the formation of words or in the combination of words into sentences, are allowable. In the first place, almost any part of speech can be used as any other part of speech. An adverb can be used as a verb, "They *askance* their eyes" (*R. of L.*); as a noun, "the *backward* and abysm of time" (*Sonn.*); or as an adjective, "a *seldom* pleasure" (*Sonn.*). Any noun, adjective, or neuter verb can be used as an active verb. You can "happy" your friend, "malice" or "foot" your enemy, or "fall" an axe on his neck. An adjective can be used as an adverb; and you can speak and act "easy," "free," "excellent:" or as a noun, and you can talk of "fair" instead of "beauty," and "a pale" instead of "a paleness." Even the pronouns are not exempt from these metamorphoses. A "*he*" is used for a man, and a lady is described by a gentleman as "the fairest *she* he has yet beheld." Spenser asks us to

> "Come down and learne the little *what*
> That Thomalin can sayne."—*Calend. Jul.* v. 31 (Nares).

And Heywood, after dividing human diners into three classes thus—

> "Some with small fare they be not pleased,
> Some with much fare they be diseased,
> Some with mean fare be scant appeased,"

adds with truly Elizabethan freedom—

> " But of all *somes* none is displeased
> To be welcome." *

In the second place, every variety of apparent grammatical inaccuracy meets us. *He* for *him, him* for *he; spoke* and *took,* for *spoken* and *taken;* plural nominatives with singular verbs; relatives omitted where they are now considered necessary; unnecessary antecedents inserted; *shall* for *will, should* for *would, would* for *wish; to* omitted after " I *ought,*" inserted after " I *durst;*" double negatives; double comparatives ("more better," &c.) and superlatives; *such* followed by *which, that* by *as, as* used for *as if; that* for *so that;* and lastly, some verbs apparently with two nominatives, and others without any nominative at all. To this long list of irregularities it may be added that many words, and particularly prepositions and the infinitives of verbs, are used in a different sense from the modern. Thus—

> " *To* fright you thus methinks I am too savage,"—
>   *Macb.* iv. 2. 70.

does not mean " I am too savage to fright you." " Received *of* the most pious Edward " (170) does not mean "*from* Edward," but "*by* Edward;" and when Shakespeare says that "the rich" will not every hour survey his treasure, "*for* blunting the fine point of seldom pleasure," he does not mean "for the sake of," but "for fear of" blunting pleasure.

On a more careful examination, however, these apparently disorderly and inexplicable anomalies will arrange themselves under certain heads. It must be remembered that the Elizabethan was a transitional period in the history of the English language. On the one hand, there was the influx of new discoveries and new thoughts requiring as their equivalent the coinage of new words (especially words expressive of abstract ideas); on the other hand, the revival of classical studies and the popularity of translations from Latin and Greek authors

---

* Compare " More by all *mores.*"—*T. N.* v. i. 139.

suggested Latin and Greek words (but principally Latin) as the readiest and most malleable metal, or rather as so many ready-made coins requiring only a slight national stamp to prepare them for the proposed augmentation of the currency of the language. Moreover, the long and rounded periods of the ancients commended themselves to the ear of the Elizabethan authors. In the attempt to conform English to the Latin frame, the constructive power of the former language was severely strained.

The necessity of avoiding ambiguity and the difficulty of connecting the end of a long sentence with the beginning, gave rise to some irregularities, to the redundant pronoun (242), the redundant '*that*' (285), and the irregular '*to*' (416).

But, for the most part, the influence of the classical languages was confined to single words, and to the rhythm of the sentence. The *syntax* was mostly English both in its origin and its development, and several constructions that are now called anomalous (such as the double negative [406] and the double comparative [409]) have, and had from the earliest period, an independent existence in English, and are merely the natural results of a spirit which preferred clearness and vigour of expression to logical symmetry. Many of the anomalies above mentioned may be traced back to some peculiarities of Early English, modified by the transitional Elizabethan period. Above all, it must be remembered that Early English was far richer than Elizabethan English in inflections. As far as English inflections are concerned the Elizabethan period was destructive rather than constructive. Naturally, therefore, while inflections were being discarded, all sorts of tentative experiments were made: some inflections were discarded that we have restored, others retained that we have discarded. Again, sometimes where inflections were retained the sense of their meaning and power had been lost, and at other times the memory of inflections that were no longer visibly expressed in writing still influenced the manner of expression. Thus Ben Jonson writes :—

"The persons plural keep the termination of the first person singular. In former times, till about the reign of King Henry VIII. they were wont to be formed by adding *en* thus :—Lov*en*, say*en*, complain*en*. But now (whatsoever is the cause) it is quite grown out of use, and that other so generally prevailed that I dare not presume to set this on foot again."

He appears to be aware of the Midland plural in *en* (332) which is found only very rarely in Spenser and in *Pericles of Tyre*, but not of the Northern plural in *es* (333), which is very frequently found in Shakespeare, and which presents the apparent anomaly of a plural noun combined with a singular verb. And the same author does not seem to be aware of the existence of the subjunctive mood in English. He ignores it in his "Etymology of a Verb," and, in the chapter on "Syntax of a Verb with a Noun," writes as follows :—

"Nouns signifying a multitude, though they be of the singular number, require a verb plural :

" ' And wise men rehearsen in sentence,
  Where folk be drunken there is no resistance.' "—LYDGATE, lib. ii.

And he continues thus :— "This exception is *in other nouns also very common, especially when the verb is joined to an adverb or conjunction:* ' It is preposterous to execute a man before he *have* been condemned.' " It would appear hence that the dramatist was ignorant of the force of the inflection of the subjunctive, though he frequently uses it. Among the results of inflectional changes we may set down the following anomalies:—

I. *Inflections discarded but their power retained.* Hence (*a*) "spoke" (343) for "spoken," "rid" for "ridden." [*] (*b*) "You ought not walk" for "You ought not walk*en* " (the old infinitive). (*c*) The new infinitive (357) "to walk " used in its new meaning and also sometimes retaining its old gerundive signification.[†] (*d*) To "glad" (act.), to "mad"

---

[*] It should, however, be stated that the *n* is often dropped in Early English.

[†] Morris, "Specimens of Early English," p. xxxiii. Inf. "loven." Gerund, "to lovene."

(act.), &c. (290) for to "gladd*en*," "madd*en*," &c. (*e*) The adverbial *e* (1) being discarded, an adjective appears to be used as an adverb : "He raged more *fierce*," &c. (*f*) "Other" is used for "other(e)," pl. "other men," &c. (*g*) The ellipsis of the pronoun (399) as a nominative may also be in part thus explained.

II. *Inflections retained with their old power.*

(*a*) The subjunctive inflection frequently used to express a condition—"*Go* not my horse," for "*If* my horse *go* not." Hence (*b*) *as* with the subj. appears to be used for *as if, and* for *and if, but* (in the sense of *except*) for *except if,* &c. (*c*) The plural in *en ;* very rarely. (*d*) The plural in *es* or *s ;* far more commonly. (*e*) *His* used as the old genitive of *he* for *of him. Me, him,* &c. used to represent other cases beside the objective and the modern dative : "I am appointed *him* to murder you."

III. *Inflections retained but their power diminished or lost.*

(*a*) Thus '*he*' for '*him*,' '*him*' for '*he ;*' '*I*' for '*me*,' '*me*' for '*I*,' &c. (*b*) In the same way the *s* which was the sign of the possessive case had so far lost its meaning that, though frequently retained, it was sometimes replaced (in mistake) by *his* and *her.*

IV. Other anomalies may be explained by reference to the *derivations of words and the idioms of Early English.*

Hence can be explained (*a*) *so* followed by *as ;* (*b*) *such* followed by *which* (found in E. E. sometimes in the form *whuch* or *wuch*) ; (*c*) *that* followed by *as ;* (*d*) *who* followed by *he ;* (*e*) *the which* put for *which ;* (*f*) *shall* for *will, should* for *would,* and *would* for *wish.*

The four above-mentioned causes are not sufficient to explain all the anomalies of Elizabethan style. There are several redundancies, and still more ellipses, which can only be explained as follows.

V. (*a*) *Clearness was preferred to grammatical correctness,* and (*b*) *brevity both to correctness and clearness.* Hence it was common to place words in the order in which they came uppermost in the mind without much regard to syntax, and the result was a forcible and perfectly unambiguous but ungrammatical sentence, such as :

(*a*) "The prince that feeds great natures they will sway him."
                                                    B. J. *Sejanus.*

(*b*) As instances of brevity :—

"Be guilty of my death since of my crime."—*R. of L.*
"It cost more to get than to lose in a day."—B. J. *Poetaster.*

VI. One great cause of the difference between Elizabethan and Victorian English is, that the latter has introduced or developed what may be called the *division of labour.* A few examples will illustrate this.

The Elizabethan subjunctive (see VERBS, SUBJUNCTIVE) could be used (1) optatively, or (2) to express a condition or (3) a consequence of a condition, (4) or to signify purpose after "that." Now, all these different meanings are expressed by different auxiliaries—"*would* that !" "*should* he come," "he *would* find," "that he *may* see,"—and the subjunctive inflection is restricted to a few phrases with "if." "To walk" is now either (1) a noun, or (2) denotes a purpose, "in order to walk." In Elizabethan English, "*to* walk" might also denote "*by* walking," "*as regards* walking," "*for* walking;" a licence now discarded, except in one or two common phrases, such as "I am happy *to* say," &c. Similarly, Shakespeare could write "*of* vantage" for "*from* vantage-ground," "*of* charity" for "*for* charity's *sake*," "*of* mine honour" for "*on* my honour," "*of* purpose" for "*on* purpose," "*of* the city's cost" for "*at* the city's cost," "*of* his body" for "*as regards* his life," "made peace *of* enmity" for "peace *instead of* enmity," "we shall find a shrewd contriver *of* him" for "*in* him," "did I never speak *of* all that time" for "*during* all that time." Similarly "by" has been despoiled of many of its powers, which have been divided among "near," "in accordance with," "by reason of," "owing to." "But" has been forced to cede some of its provinces to "unless" and "except." Lastly, "that," in Early English the only relative, had been already, before the Elizabethan times, supplanted in many idioms by "who" and "which;" but it still retained its meanings of "because," "inasmuch as," and "when;" sometimes under the forms "for *that*," "in *that*;" sometimes without the prepositions. These it has now lost, except in a few colloquial phrases.

As a rule, then, the tendency of the English language has been to divide the labour of expression as far as possible by diminishing the task assigned to overburdened words and imposing it upon others. There are, of course, exceptions to this rule—notably "who" and "which;" but this has been the general tendency. And in most cases it will be found that the Victorian idiom is clearer but less terse than the corresponding Elizabethan idiom which it has supplanted.

VII. The character of Elizabethan English is impressed upon its pronunciation, as well as upon its idioms and words. As a rule their pronunciation seems to have been more rapid than ours. Probably the greater influence of spoken as compared with written English, sanctioned many contractions which would now be judged intolerable if for the first time introduced. (See 461.) This, however, does not explain the singular variation of accent upon the same words in the same author. Why should "exile," "aspect," "confessor," and many other words, be accented now on the first, now on the second syllable? The answer is, that during the unsettled Elizabethan period the foreign influence was contending with varying success against the native rules of English pronunciation. The English rule, as given by Ben Jonson, is definite enough. "In dissyllabic simple nouns" (by which it is to be supposed he means un-compounded), "the accent is on the first, as 'bélief,' 'hónour,' &c." But he goes on to say, that "all verbs coming from the Latin, either of the supine or otherwise, hold the accent as it is found in the first person present of those Latin verbs." Hence a continual strife over every noun derived from Latin participles : the English language claiming the new comer as her naturalized subject, bound by English laws; the Latin, on the other hand, asserting a partial jurisdiction over her emigrants. Hence *accéss* and *áccess, precépt* and *précept, contráct* (noun) and *cóntract, instínct* and *ínstinct, relápse* and *rélapse.* The same battle raged over other Latin words not derived from participles : *commérce* and *cómmerce, obdúrate* and *óbdurate, sepúlchre* and *sépulchre, contráry* and *cóntrary, authórize* and *aúthorize, perséver* and *persevére, cónfessor* and *conféssor.* The battle terminated in a thoroughly English manner. An arbitrary compromise has been effected between the combatants. *Respéct, relápse, succéss, succéssor,* were ceded to the Latin: *áspect, cóllapse,* áccess, sépulchre,* were appropriated by the English. But while the contest was pending, and prisoners being taken and retaken on either side, we must not be surprised at finding the same word ranged now under native, now under foreign colours.

VIII. *Words then used literally are now used metaphorically, and vice versâ.*

The effect of this is most apparent in the altered use of prepositions. For instance, " by," originally meaning " near," has supplanted " of " in the metaphorical sense of *agency,* as it may in its turn be supplanted by "with" or some other preposition. This is discussed more fully under the head of prepositions (138). Here a few illustrations will be given from other words. It is not easy to discover a defined law regulating changes of metaphor. There is no reason why we should not, with Beaumont and Fletcher, talk of living at a " *deep*† rate " as well as a " *high* rate." But it will be found with respect to many words derived from Latin and Greek, that *the Elizabethans used them literally and generally ; we, metaphorically and particularly.* Thus " metaphysical" was used by Shakespeare in the broader meaning of " supernatural ; " and " fantastical " could be applied even to a murder, in the wide sense of " imagined." So " exorbitant " was " out of the path," " uncommon ; " now only

---

* *Collapse* is accented on the last syllable in most dictionaries.

† " How brave lives he that keeps a fool, although the rate be *deeper,*
But he that is his own fool, sir, does live a great deal cheaper."

applied to that which is uncommonly "expensive." So *extravagant* ("The *extravagant* and erring spirit," *Hamlet*, i. 1) has been restricted to "*wandering* beyond the bounds of economy." "To aggravate" now means, except when applied to disease, "to add to the mental burdens of any one," hence "to vex ;" but in *Sonn.* 146 we find "to aggravate thy store" in the literal sense of "to add to the weight of" or "increase." So "journall" meant "diurnal" or "daily ;" now it is restricted to a "daily" newspaper or memoir. The fact is that, in the influx of Greek and Latin words into the English language, many were introduced to express ideas that either could be, or were already, expressed in the existing vocabulary. Thus we do not require "metaphysical" to express that which is supernatural, nor "fantastical" to express that which is imagined ; "exorbitant" is unnecessary in the sense of "uncommon ;" "extravagant" (though it has a special force in "the *extravagant* and erring spirit," *Hamlet*, i. 1) is not in most cases so obvious as "wandering ;" "increase" is simpler than "aggravate," and "daily" more English than "diurnal." Similarly "speculation" is unnecessary to express the power of seeing, "advertised" useless in the sense of "warned" or "informed" (*Lear*, iv. 6. 214), "vulgar" in the sense of common. Such words, once introduced into the language, finding the broader room which they had been intended to fill already occupied, were forced to take narrower meanings. They did this, for the most part, by confining themselves to one out of many meanings which they had formerly represented, or by adopting metaphorical and philosophical instead of literal and material significations ; and as the sense of their derivation and original meaning became weaker, the transition became easier. This is not merely true of words derived from Latin and Greek. "Travail," for example, finding itself supplanted in its original sense by "work" or "labour," has narrowed itself to a special meaning : the same is true of "beef," "pork," &c.

On the other hand, some Latin and Greek words that

express technicalities have, as the sense of their exact meaning was weakened, gradually become more loosely and generally used. Thus, "influence" means now more than the mere influence of the stars on men; "triumph," "preposterous," "pomp," "civil," "ovation," and "decimate," have lost much of their technical meaning. Of these words it may be said, that Shakespeare uses them more literally and particularly than we do. Thus, "triumph" is used for a show at a festival; "civil" is used for peaceful; "preposterous ass" (*T. of Sh.* iii. 1. 9) is applied to a man who put music *before* philosophy; "decimation" (*T. of A.* v. 1. 31) is used in its technical sense for "a tithed death."

One cause that has affected the meaning of Latin-derived words has been the preference with which they have been selected in order to express depreciation. This has narrowed some words to an unfavourable signification which they did not originally possess. Thus, "impertinent" in Elizabethan authors meant "not to the point;" "officious" could then mean "obliging," and a clever person could be described as "an admirable conceited fellow" (*W. T.* iv. 4. 203).

A classical termination (446) may sometimes be treated as active or as passive. Hence "plausibly" is used for "with applause" actively.

"The Romans *plausibly* did give consent."—*R. of L.*
"A very *inconsiderate* (inconsiderable) handful of English."
　　　　　　　　　　　　　　　　N. P. Appendix 31.

Thus, on the one hand, we have "flux*ive* eyes" (eyes flowing with tears : *L. C.* 8), and on the other the more common passive sense, as "the inexpres*sive* she" (the woman whose praises cannot be expressed).

With respect to words of English or French origin, it is more difficult to establish any rule. All that can be said is that the Elizabethan, as well as the Victorian meaning, may be traced to the derivation of the word. Why, for instance, should not Ben Jonson write—

"Frost fearing myrtle shall *impale* my head."—*Poetast.* i. 1.

i.e. "take in within its pale, surround," as justifiably as we use the word in its modern sense of "transfixing?" Why should not sirens "train" (*draw* or decoy—*trahere*) their victims to destruction, as well as educators "train" their pupils onward on the path of knowledge? We talk of "a *world* of trouble" to signify an infinity; why should not Bacon (*E.* 38) talk of "a *globe* of precepts?" Owing to the deficiency of their vocabulary, and their habit of combining prepositions with verbs, to make distinct words almost like the Germans, the Elizabethans used to employ many common English words, such as "pass," "hold," "take," in many various significations. Thus we find "take" in the sense of (1) "bewitch;" (2) "interrupt" ("You *take* him too quickly, Marcius," B. J. *Poetast.*); (3) "consider" ("The whole court shall *take* itself abused," B. J. *Cy.'s Rev.* v. 1); (4) "understand" ("You'll *take* him presently," *E. out &c.* i. 1); and (5) "resort to" ("He was driven by foule weather to *take* a poor man's cottage," N. *P.* 597). With prepositions the word has many more meanings. "*Take* out"="copy;" "*take* in"="subdue;" "*take* up"="borrow;" "*take* in with" (Bacon)="side with;" "*take* up"="pull up" of a horse. And these meanings are additional to the many other meanings which the word still retains. To enter further into the subject of the formation and meaning of words is not the purpose of this treatise. The glossaries of Nares and Halliwell supply the materials for a detailed study of the subject. One remark may be of use to the student before referring him to the following pages. The enumeration of the points of difference between Shakespearian and modern English may seem to have been a mere list of irregularities and proofs of the inferiority of the former to the latter. And it is true that the former period presents the English language in a transitional and undeveloped condition, rejecting and inventing much that the verdict of posterity has retained and discarded. It was an age of experiments, and the experiments were not always successful. While we have accepted *copious, ingenious, disloyal,* we have rejected as useless *copy* (in the sense of "plenty"), *ingin*, and *disnoble*. But for freedom, for brevity and for vigour, Elizabethan is superior to modern English. Many of the words employed by Shakespeare and his contemporaries were the recent inventions of the age ; hence they were used with a freshness and exactness to which we are strangers.* Again, the spoken English so far predominated over the grammatical English that it materially influenced the rhythm of the verse (see Prosody), the construction of the sentence, and even sometimes (460) the spelling of words. Hence sprung an artless and unlaboured harmony which seems the natural heritage of Elizabethan poets, whereas such harmony as is attained by modern authors frequently betrays a painful excess of art. Lastly, the use of some few still remaining inflections (the subjunctive in particular), the lingering *sense* of many other inflections that had passed away leaving behind something of the old versatility and audacity in the arrangement of the sentence, the stern subordination of grammar to terseness and clearness, and the consequent directness and naturalness of expression, all conspire to give a liveliness and wakefulness to Shakespearian English which are wanting in the grammatical monotony of the present day. We may perhaps claim some superiority in completeness and perspicuity for modern English, but if we were to appeal on this ground to the shade of Shakespeare in the words of Antonio in the *Tempest*,—

" Do you not hear us speak ?"

we might fairly be crushed with the reply of Sebastian—

" I do ; and surely
It is a sleepy language."

---

* Exceptions are "eternal" used for "infernal" (*O.* iv. 2, 130 ; *J. C.* i. 2. 160 ; *Hamlet*, i. 4. 21) ; "triple" for "third" (*A. W.* ii. 1. 111) ; "temporary" for "temporal" (*M. for M.* v. 1. 145) ; "important" for "importunate" (*Lear*, iv. 4. 26) ; "expiate" for "expired" (*Rich. III.* iii. 3. 23) ; "colleagued" (*Hamlet*, i. 2. 21) for "co-leagued ;" "importing" (*ib.* 23) for "importuning." The Folio has "Pluto's" for "Plutus" (*J. C.* iv. 3. 102).

GRAMMAR.

ADJECTIVES.

1. Adjectives are freely used as Adverbs.

In Early English, many adverbs were formed from adjectives by adding *e* (dative) to the positive degree : as *bright*, adj.; *brighte*, adv. In time the *e* was dropped, but the adverbial use was kept. Hence, from a false analogy, many adjectives (such as *excellent*) which could never form adverbs in *e*, were used as adverbs. We still say colloquially, "come *quick;*" "the moon shines *bright*," &c. But Shakespeare could say:

> "Which the false man does *easy*."—*Macb.* ii. 3. 143.
> "Some will *dear* abide it."—*J. C.* iii. 2. 119.
> "Thou didst it *excellent*."—*T. of Sh.* i. 1. 89.
> "Which else should *free* have wrought."—*Macb.* ii. 1. 19.
> "Raged more *fierce*."—*Rich. II.* ii. 1. 173.
> "Grow not *instant* old."—*Ham.* i. 5. 94.
> "'Tis *noble* spoken."—*A. and C.* ii. 2. 99.
> "Did I expose myself *pure* for his love."—*T. N.* v. 1. 86.
> "*Equal* ravenous as he is subtle."—*Hen. VIII.* i. 1. 159.

We find the two forms of the adverb side by side in:

> "She was *new* lodged and *newly* deified."—*L. C.* 84.

The position of the article shows that *mere* is an adverb in:

> "Ay, surely, *mere* the truth."—*A. W.* iii. 5. 58.

So "It shall *safe* be kept."—*Cymb.* i. 6. 209.

> "Heaven and our Lady *gracious* has it pleas'd."
> > 1 *Hen. VI.* i. 2. 74.

> "(I know) when the blood burns how *prodigal* the soul
> Lends the tongue vows."—*Hamlet*, i. 3. 116.

Such transpositions as " our lady gracious," (adj.) where "gracious" is a mere epithet, are not common in Shakespeare. (See 419.) In

"My lady sweet, arise,"—*Cymb.* ii. 3. 29.

"My-lady" is more like one word than " our lady," and is also an appellative. In appellations such transpositions are allowed. (See 13.)

Sometimes the two forms occur together :

"And she will speak most *bitterly* and *strange.*"
M. for M. v. 1. 90.

2. Adjectives compounded. Hence two adjectives were freely combined together, the first being a kind of adverb qualifying the second. Thus :

"I am too *sudden-bold.*"—*L. L. L.* ii. 1. 107.
"*Fertile-fresh.*"—*M. W. of W.* v. 5. 72.
"More *active-valiant* or more *valiant-young.*"
1 *Hen. IV.* v. 1. 90.
"*Daring-hardy.*"—*Rich. II.* i. 3. 43.
"*Honourable-dangerous.*"—*J. C.* i. 3. 124. See *ib.* v. 1. 60.
"He lies *crafty-sick.*"—2 *Hen. IV.* Prol. 37.
"I am too *childish-foolish* for this world."—*R. III.* i. 3. 142.
"You are too *senseless-obstinate,* my lord."—*R. III.* iii. 1. 44.
"That fools should be so *deep-contemplative.*"—*A. Y.* ii. 7. 31.
"*Glouc.* Methinks the ground is even.
Edg.   *Horrible-steep.*"—*Lear,* iv. 6. 3.

In the last example it is hard to decide whether the two adjectives are compounded, or (which is much more probable) "horrible" is a separate word used as in (1) for "horribly," as in *T. N.* iii. 4. 196. In the West of England "terrible" is still used in this adverbial sense.

There are some passages which are only fully intelligible when this combination is remembered :

"A strange tongue makes my cause more *strange-suspicious.*"
Hen. VIII. iii. 1. 45.
Erase the usual comma after " *strange.*"

"Here is a *silly-stately* style indeed."—1 *Hen. VI.* iv. 7. 72.
Perhaps "He only in a *general-honest* thought."—*J. C* v. 5. 71.

3. Adjectives, especially those ending in *ful, less, ble,* and *ive,* have both an active and a passive meaning.; just as we still say, "a *fearful* (pass.) coward," and "a *fearful* (act.) danger."

> "To throw away the dearest thing he owed,
>   As 'twere a *careless* trifle."—*Macbeth,* i. 4. 11.

"Such *helpless* harmes yt's better hidden keep."—SPEN. *F. Q.* i. 5. 42.

"Even as poor birds deceived with painted grapes,

. . . . . .

Like those poor birds that *helpless* berries saw."
  V. and A. 604; *Rich. III.* i. 2. 13.

"Upon the *sightless* couriers of the air."—*Macbeth,* i. 7. 23.

"How dare thy joints forget
To pay their *awful* duty to our presence?"—*Rich. II.* iii. 3. 76.

"*Terrible*" is "frightened" in *Lear,* i. 2. 32; "*dreadful,*" "awe-struck," *Hamlet,* i. 2. 207; "*thankful*" is "thankworthy," *P. of T.* v. 1. 285. So "*unmeritable*" (act. *Rich. III.* iii. 7. 155; *J. C.* iv. 1. 12); "*medicinable*" (act. *Tr. and Cr.* iii. 3. 44); "*sensible*" (pass. *Macb.* ii. 1. 36; *Hamlet,* i. 1. 57); "*insuppressive*" (pass. *J. C.* ii. 1. 134); "*plausive*" (pass. *Hamlet,* i. 4. 30); "*incomprehensive*" (pass. *Tr. and Cr.* iii. 3. 198); "*respective*" (act. *R. and J.* iii. 1. 128; pass. *T. G. of V.* iv. 4. 200); "*unexpressive*" (pass. *A. Y. L.* iii. 2. 10); "*comfortable*" (act. *Lear,* i. 4. 328); "*deceivable*" (act. *R. II.* ii. 3. 84; *T. N.* iv. 3. 21).

"*Probable,*" "*contemptible,*" and "*artificial,*" are active in—

"The least of all these signs were *probable*."—*2 Hen. VI.* iii. 2. 178.

"'Tis very probable that the man will scorn it, for he hath a very *contemptible* spirit."—*M. Ado,* ii. 3. 188.

"We, Hermia, like two *artificial* gods
Have with our needles created both one flower."
  M. N. D. iii. 2. 204.

Hence even "The *intrenchant* air."—*Macbeth,* v. 8. 9.

"Unprizable" (*T. N.* v. 1. 58) means "not able to be made a prize of, captured."

"Effect" (*Rich. III.* i. 2. 120) seems used for "effecter" or "agent" if the text is correct.

4. Adjectives signifying effect were often used to signify the cause. This is a difference of *thought.* We still say "pale death," "gaunt famine," where the personification is obvious; but we do not say—

" Oppress'd with two *weak* evils, age and hunger."
                                                A. Y. L. ii. **7. 182.**

" Like as a sort of hungry dogs ymet
    Doe fall together, stryving each to get
    The greatest portion of the *greedie* pray."
                                        SPENS. *F. Q.* vi. 11. 17.

" And *barren* rage of death's eternal cold."—*Sonn.* 13.

Nor should we say of the Caduceus—

" His *sleepy* yerde in hond he bare upright."—CHAUC. *C. T.* 1390.

Compare also   " Sixth part of each !
        A *trembling* contribution !"—*Hen. VIII.* i. 2. 95.

Here "trembling" is used for "fear-inspiring."

So other Elizabethan authors (Walker) : "idle agues," "rotten showers," "barren curses."

5. Adjectives are frequently used for Nouns, even in the singular.

" A sudden *pale* usurps her cheek."—*V. and A.*

" Every Roman's *private* (privacy or private interest)."
                                                B. J. *Sejan.* iii. 1.

" 'Twas caviare to the *general.*"—*Hamlet,* ii. 2. 458.

" Truth lies open to all.   It is no man's *several.*"—B. J. *Disc.* 742 b.

" Before these bastard signs of *fair* (beauty) were born."—*Sonn.* 68.

So "*fair* befal," *Rich. II.* ii. 1. 129 ; *Rich. III.* i. 3. 282.   But see 297.

" Till fortune, tired with doing *bad,*
    Threw him ashore to give him *glad.*"—*P. of T.* ii. Gower, 37.
                          " That termless (indescribable) hand
Whose *bare* outbragg'd the web it seem'd to wear."—*L. C.* 95.

" In *few*" = "in short."—*Hamlet,* i. 3. 126 ; *Temp.* i. 2. 144.

" *Small* (little) have continual plodders ever won."
                                                L. L. L. i. 1. 86.

" By *small* and *small.*"—*Rich. II.* iii. 7. 198 ; *Rich. III.* i. 3. 111.

" Say what you can, my *false* o'erweighs your *true.*"
                                                M. for M. ii. 4. 170.

" I'll make division of my *present* (money) with you."
                                                T. N. iii. 4. 380.

If the text were correct, the following would be an instance of an adjective inflected like a noun :

" Have added feathers to the learned's wing."—*Sonn.* 78.

But probably the right reading is "learned'st."

"Wont," the noun (*Hamlet*, i. 4. 6), is a corruption from "woned," from the verb "wonye" E. E., "wunian" A.-S., "to dwell." Compare ἦθος.

6. Adjectives comparative. The inflection *er* instead of *more* is found before "than."

"Sir, your company is fair*er* than honest."—*M. for M.* iv. 3. 185.

The comparative "more wonderful" seems to be used, as in Latin, for "more wonderful than usual," if the following line is to be attributed to Cicero as in the editions :

"Why, saw you anything *more wonderful ?*"—*J. C.* i. 3. 14.

In *Hamlet* iv. 7. 49, "my sudden and *more strange* return," means "sudden, and even more strange than sudden."

7. The comparative inflection-*er* was sometimes used even when the positive ended in-*ing,-ed,-id,-ain,-st,-ect*. These terminations (perhaps because they assimilate the adjective to a participle by their sound) generally now take "more."
"Horr*ider*," *Cymb.* iv. 2. 331 ; "cur*ster*," *T. of Sh.* iii. 2. 156 ; "perf*ecter*," *Coriol.* ii. 1. 91 ; "cert*ainer*," *M. Ado*, v. 3. 62.

8. Superlative. The superlative inflection *est*, like the Latin superlative, is sometimes used to signify "very," with little or no idea of excess.
"A little ere the might*iest* Julius fell."—*Hamlet*, i. 1. 114.

"My mut*est* conscience" (*Cymb.* i. 6. 116) may perhaps mean "the mutest part or corner of my conscience," like "summus mons."

9. The superlative inflection *est* is found after-*ent,-ing,-ed, -ect*. Thus, "viol*entest*" (*Coriol.* iv. 6. 73) ; "curs*edst*" (*M. of V.* ii. 1. 46); "ly*ingest*" (*T. of Sh.* i. 2. 25); "perf*ectest*," (*Macb.* i. 5. 2).
This use of -*est* and -*er* (see 7) is a remnant of the indiscriminate application of these inflections to all adjectives which is found in Early English. Thus, in *Piers Plowman*, we have "avarous*ere*" (B. i. 189), "merveillous*est*" (B. viii. 68).

10. The superlative was sometimes used (as it is still, but with recognized incorrectness) where only *two* objects are compared.

" Between two dogs which hath the deeper mouth,
    Between two blades which bears the better temper,
    Between two horses which doth bear him *best*,
    Between two girls which has the merr*iest* eye."

I *Hen. IV*. ii. 4. 15.

" Not to bestow my *youngest* daughter
    Before I have a husband for the elder."—*T. of Sh.* i. 1. 50.

" Of two usuries, the *merriest* was put down, and the worser
allowed."—*M. for M.* iii. 2. 7.

Here it seems used for variety to avoid the repetition of the comparative.

11. Comparative and superlative doubled.—The inflections
-er and *-est*, which represent the comparative and superlative degrees
of adjectives, though retained, yet lost some of their force, and
sometimes received the addition of *more, most*, for the purpose of
greater emphasis.

" A *more larger* list of sceptres."—*A. and C.* iii. 6. 76.
    " *More elder*."—*M. of V.* iv. 1. 251.
    " *More better*."—*Temp.* i. 2. 19.
    " *More nearer*."—*Hamlet*, ii. 1. 11.
    " Thy *most worst*."—*W. T.* iii. 2. 180.
    " *More braver*."—*Temp.* i. 2. 439.
    " With the *most boldest*."—*J. C.* iii. 1. 121.
    " *Most unkindest*."—*J. C.* iii. 2. 187.
    " To some *more fitter* place."—*M. for M.* ii. 2. 16.
    " I would have been much *more a fresher* man."

Tr. and Cr. v. 6. 21.

Ben Jonson speaks of this as " a certain kind of English atticism,
imitating the manner of the *most ancientest and finest* Grecians."—
B. J. 786.   But there is no ground for thinking that this idiom was
the result of imitating Greek.   We find Bottom saying :

" The *more better* assurance."—*M. N. D.* iii. 1. 4.

Note the anomaly : " *Less happier* lands."—*R. II.* ii. 1. 49.

12. The Adjectives all, each, both, every, other, are sometimes interchanged and used as Pronouns in a manner different
from modern usage.

All for *any* :

" They were slaine without *all* mercie."—HOLINSHED.
    " Without *all* bail."—*Sonn.* 74.

"Without *all* reason."—ASCH. 48.

(Comp. in Latin "sine omni, &c.") Heb. vii. 7 : Wickliffe, "withouten *ony* agenseiyinge ;" Rheims, Geneva, and A. V. "without *all* contradiction."

This construction, which is common in Ascham and Andrewes, is probably a Latinism in those authors. It may be, however, that in "things *without all* remedy," *Macb*. iii. 2. 11, "without" is used in the sense of "outside," "beyond." See **Without** (197).

All for *every* :

"Good order in *all* thyng."—ASCH. 62.

"And *all* thing unbecoming."—*Macb*. iii. 1. 14.

We still use "all" for "all men." But Ascham (p. 54) wrote : "*Ill* commonlie *have* over much wit," and (p. 65) "*Infinite* shall be made cold by your example, that *were* never hurt by reading of bookes." This is perhaps an attempt to introduce a Latin idiom. Shakespeare, however, writes :

"*What* ever *have* been thought on."—*Coriol*. i. 2. 4.

Each for "all" or "each one of :"

"At *each* his needless heavings."—*W. T.* ii. 3. 35.

So **every** (*i.e.* "ever-ich," "ever-each ") :

"Of *every* these happen'd accidents."—*Temp*. v. 1. 249.

And "none :" "*None* our parts."—*A. and C.* i. 3. 36.

Each for "both :"

"And *each* though enem*ies* to *either's* reign
Do in consent shake hands to torture me."—*Sonn*. 28.

"*Each* in her sleep *themselves* so beautify."—*R. of L.* 404.

"Tell me
In peace what *each* of them by the other *lose*."—*Coriol*. iii. 2. 44.

This confusion is even now a common mistake. Compare

"How pale *each* worshipful and rev'rend guest
Rise from a Clergy or a City feast."—POPE, *Imit. Hor.* ii. 75.

Each for "each other : "

"But being both from me, both to *each* friend."—*Sonn*. 144.
(*i.e.* both friends each to the other.)

Both seems put for "each," or *either* used for "each other," in

"They are both in *either's* powers."— *Temp*. i. 2. 450.

There may, however, be an ellipsis of *each* after *both :*

> " They are both (each) in either's powers."

Compare   "A thousand groans . . . .
            Came (one) on another's neck."—*Sonn.* 131.

It is natural to conjecture that this is a misprint for "one or other's." But compare

> " I think there is not half a kiss to choose
> Who loves *another* best."—*W. T.* iv. 4. 176.   (See 88)

Every one, Other, Neither, are used as plural pronouns :

> " And *every one* to rest themselves *betake.*"—*R. of L.*

" *Every one* of these considerations, syr, *move* me."—ASCH. Dedic.

> " *Everything*
> In readiness for Hymenæus *stand.*"—*T. A.* i. 1. 325.

> " Smooth *every* passion
> That in the nature of their lord *rebel.*"—*Lear,* ii. 2. 82.

"Every " is a pronoun in

> " If *every* of your wishes had a womb."
> > *A. and C.* i. 2. 38 ; *A. Y. L.* v. 4. 178.

> " Thersites' body is as good as Ajax'
> When *neither* are alive."—*Cymb.* iv. 2. 252.

> " *Other* have authoritie."—ASCH. 46.

> " And therefore is the glorious planet Sol
> In noble eminence enthron'd and spher'd
> Amidst the *other.*"—*Tr. and C.* i. 3. 89.

Other is also used as a singular pronoun (even when not preceded by "each") :*

> " Every time gentler than *other.*"—*J. C.* i. 2. 231.

" With greedy force each *other* doth assail."—SPENS. *F. Q.* i. 5. 6.

i.e. "each doth assail *the* other."—*Rich. II.* i. 1. 22.

> " We learn no *other* but the confident tyrant·
> Keeps still in Dunsinane."—*Macb.* v. 4. 8.

> " He hopes it is no *other*
> But, for your health and your digestion's sake,
> An after-dinner's breath."—*Tr. and Cr.* ii. 3. 120.

> " If you think *other.*"—*Othello,* iv. 2. 13.

> " Suppose no *other.*"—*A. W.* iii. 6. 27.

---

* It is used as a singular adjective, without the article, in *Cymb.* iii. 4. 144:

> " You think of *other* place."

In the two last passages "other" may be used adverbially for "otherwise," as in *Macbeth*, i. 7. 77, which may explain

"They can be meek that have no *other* cause."—*C. of E.* ii. 1. 33. *i.e.* "no cause *otherwise* than for meekness."

The use of *all(e)* and *other(e)* as plural pronouns is consistent with ancient usage. It was as correct as "omnes" and "alii" in Latin, as "alle" and "andere" in German. Our modern "*others* said" is only justified by a custom which might have compelled us to say "*manys*" or "*alls* said," and which has induced us to say "our better*s*," though not (with Heywood) "our bigger*s*." The plural use of *neither*, "not both," depends on the plural use of *either* for "both," which is still retained in "on *either* side," used for "on both sides." This is justified by the original meaning of *ei-ther*, i.e. "every one of two," just as *whe-ther* means "which of two." "Either" in O.E. is found for "both." Similarly we say "*none were* taken" instead of "*none (no one) was* taken." We still retain the use of *other* as a pronoun without *the* in such phrases as "they saw each *other*," for "they saw each *the other*." *Many* is also used as a noun. (See 5.) Hence we have :

" In *many's* looks."—*Sonn.* 93.

Beside the adjective "mani," "moni" (*many*), there was also in Early English the noun "manie" or "meine" (multitude, from Fr. "maisgnée," Lat. "minores natu"). But it is doubtful whether this influenced the use just mentioned.

13. The possessive Adjectives, when unemphatic, are some- times transposed, being really combined with nouns (like the French *monsieur, milord*).

"Dear *my lord*."—*J. C.* ii. 1. 255.
" Good *my brother*."—*Hamlet*, i. 3. 46.
" Sweet *my mother*."—*R. and J.* iii. 5. 200.
" Oh ! poor *our sex*."—*Tr. and Cr.* v. 2. 109.
" Art thou that *my lord* Elijah ?"—1 *Kings* xviii. 7.
"Come, *our queen*."—*Cymb.* ii. 3. 68.

So probably, vocatively :

"Tongue-tied *our queen* speak thou."—*W. T.* i. 1. 27.
Compare "Come on, *our queen*."—*Rich. II.* i. 2. 222.
" Good *my knave*."—*L. L. L.* iii. 1. 153.

"Good *my friends.*"—*Coriol.* v. 2. 8.
"Good *your highness,* patience."—*A. and C.* ii. 5. 106.
"Good *my girl.*"—1 *Hen. VI.* v. 4. 25.
Hence, by analogy, even
"Good *my mouse* of virtue."—*T. N.* i. 5. 69.
The emphatic nature of this appellative "good" is illustrated by
"*Good* now, sit down."—*Hamlet,* i. 1. 70:
where the noun is omitted. So *W. T.* v. 1. 19 ; *Tempest,* i. 1. 16.
"Gunnow" (good now) is still an appellative in Dorsetshire.
Sometimes, but very rarely, the possessive adjective used voca-
tively is allowed to stand first in the sentence :
"*Our* very loving sister, well be met."—*Lear,* v. 1. 20.
It is possible that this use of "my," "our," &c. may be in part
explained from their derivation, since they were originally not
adjectives, but the possessive cases of pronouns. Thus, "sweet my
mother," = "sweet mother of me," or "sweet mother mine."
Similar vocatives are
"*The last of all the Romans,* fare thee well."—*J. C.* v. 3. 99.
"*The jewels of our father,* with wash'd eyes,
Cordelia leaves you."—*Lear,* i. 1. 271.
So Folio, "Take that, *the likeness of this railer here.*"
3 *Hen. VI.* v. 5. 38 (Globe "thou").

14. The Adjectives just, mere, proper, and very were
sometimes used as in Latin.

Just = exact. "A *just* seven-night."—*M. Ado,* ii. 1. 375.
"A *jus!* pound."—*M. of V.* iv. 1. 327.
Whereas we retain this sense only in the adverbial use, "*just* a
week." Compare "justum iter."

15. Mere = "unmixed with anything else :" hence, by inference,
"intact," "complete."
"The *mere* perdition of the Turkish fleet."—*O.* ii. 2. 3.
i.e. the "complete destruction."
"Strangely-visited people,
The *mere* despair of surgery."—*Macbeth,* iv. 3. 132.
i.e. "the utter despair." So *Rich. III.* iii. 7. 263.
The word now means "unmixed," and therefore, by inference,

"nothing but," "bare," "insignificant." But, in accordance with
its original meaning, "not *merely*," in Bacon, is used for "not
entirely." So *Hamlet*, i. 2. 137.

16. Proper = "peculiar," "own."

"Their *proper* selves."—*Temp.* iii. 3. 60.
" With my *proper* hand."—*Cymb.* iv. 2. 97; *T. N.* v. 1. 327.
i.e. " with my own hand," as in French. So *J. C.* i. 2. 41, v. 3. 96.

Very = "true." " My *very* friends."—*M. of V.* iii. 2. 226.

17. More (*mo-re*) and most (*mo-st*)

(comp. E. E. *ma* or *mo* ;
mar or *mor* ; *maest, mast,* or *most*) are frequently used as the comparative and superlative of the adjective "great." [*Moe*, or *mo*, as
a comparative (*Rich. II.* ii. 1. 239 ; *Rich. III.* iv. 4. 199), is contracted from *more* or *mo-er.* Compare "bet" for "bett-er," "leng"
for "leng-er," and "streng" for "streng-er," in O. E. See also
"sith," 62.]

" At our *more* leisure."—*M. for M.* i. 3. 49.
" A *more* requital."—*K. J.* ii. 1. 34.
" With *most* gladness."—*A. and C.* ii. 2. 169.
" Our *most* quiet " (our very great quiet).—*2 Hen. IV.* iv. 1. 71.
" So grace and mercy at your *most* need help you."
Hamlet, i. 5. 180.

Hence we understand :

" Not fearing death nor shrinking for distress,
But always resolute in *most* extremes."—*1 Hen. VI.* iv. 1. 38.
i.e. not " in the majority of extremities," as it would mean with us,
but " in the *greatest* extremes."

Hence :

" *More* (instead of *greater*) and less came in with cap and knee."
1 Hen. IV. iv. 3. 68.
" And *more* and less do flock to follow him."
2 Hen. IV. i. 1. 209.
" Both *more* and less have given him the revolt."
Macbeth, v. 4. 12.

That "less " refers here to rank, and not to number, is illustrated by
" What *great* ones do the *less* will prattle of."—*T. N.* i. 2. 33.
So Chaucer :

" The grete giftes to the *most* and leste."—*C. T.* 2227.

18. One is used for "above all," or "*alone,*" i.e. "*all-one,*" in Elizabethan English with superlatives.

> "He is *one* the truest manner'd."—*Cymb.* i. 6. 164.
> "*One* the wisest prince."—*Hen. VIII.* ii. 4. 49.
> "Have I spake *one* the least word."—*Ib.* 153.

But in Early English *one* is thus used without a superlative:

> "He *one* is to be praised."
> "I had no brother but him *one.*"
> "He was king *one.*"

(Here Mr. Morris conjectures that the O. E. "ane" stands for A.-S. dative "an-um.")

So in Latin "justissimus unus;" and in Greek μόνος is similarly used. So "alone" = "above all things."

> "That must needs be sport *alone.*"—*M. N. D.* iii. 2. 119.
> "I am *alone* the villain of the earth."—*A. and C.* iv. 6. 30.
>   "So full of shapes is fancy
> That it *alone* is high fantastical."—*T. N.* i. 1. 15.

None. See 53.

19. Right (which is now seldom used as an adjective, except with the definite article, as the opposite of "*the* wrong," *e.g.* "*the* right way," not "*a* right way"), was used by Shakespeare, with the indefinite article, to mean "real," "down-*right.*"

> "I am a *right* maid for my cowardice."—*M. N. D.* iii. 2. 302.

Compare *A. and C.* iv. 12. 28, "a *right* gipsy." It means "true" in

> "A *right* description of our sport, my lord."—*L. L. L.* v. 2. 522.

20. Self (*se* = *swa* [so]; *-lf.* = Germ. *leib,* "body:" Wedge-wood, however, suggests the reciprocal pronoun, Lat. *se,* Germ. *sich,* and he quotes, "Et il *ses cors* ira," *i.e.* "and he *him self* will go," Old French, and still retained in Creole patois) was still used in its old adjectival meaning "same," especially in "one *self,*" *i.e.* "one and the same," and "that *self.*" Compare the German "selbe."

> "That *self* chain."—*C. of E.* v. 1. 10.
> "That *self* mould."—*Rich. II.* i. 2. 23.
> "One *self* king."— *T. N.* i. 1. 39.

Compare 3 *Hen. VI.* iii. 1. 11; *A. and C.* v. 1. 21; *M. of V.* i. 1. 148.

Hence we can trace the use of *himself*, &c. The early English did not always use "self," except for emphasis; their use was often the same as our modern poetic use :

"They sat *them* down upon the yellow sand."—TENNYSON.

In order to define the *him*, and to identify it with the previous *he*, the word *self* (meaning "*the same*," "the aforesaid") was added : "He bends him*self*." *Thyself* and *myself* are for *thee-self*, *me-self*. "One *self* king" may be illustrated by "one *same* house."—MON-TAIGNE, 228. We also find the adjectival use of "self" retained in

"The territories of Attica *selfe*."—N. *P.* 175.
"The city *selfe* of Athens."—N. *P.* 183.

"Itself" is generally, if not always, written in the Folio "it selfe."

There is a difficulty, however, in such a phrase as "I *myself* saw it." Why do we not find "I-self," "he-self," in such cases? Why, even in A.-S., do we find the rule that, when *self* agrees with the *subject* of the sentence, the pronoun has to be repeated in the *dative* before *self*: "he (him) *self* did it," but when the noun is in an oblique case *self* is declined like any other adjective, and agrees with its noun : "he hine *seolfne* band," *i.e.* "he bound himself?" The fact is, that in the second case "self" is an ordinary adjective used as an adjective : "he bound *the same* or *aforesaid* him." But in the former case "himself" is often an abridgment of a pre-positional expression used as an adverb : "he did it by himself," "of himself," "for himself," and, being a quasi-adverb, does not receive the adjectival inflection.* It follows that "my," "thy," in "myself" and "thyself," are not pronominal adjectives, but represent inflected cases of the pronouns. Thus "ourself" for "our-selves" is strictly in accordance with the A.-S. usage in

"We will *ourself* in person to this war,"—*Rich. II.* i. 4. 42.

though of course Shakespeare only uses it for "myself" in the mouth of a dignified personage. Similarly in *Piers Plowman* (B. viii. 62) we have "*myn* one" (= "*of me* one," *i.e.* "*of me* alone" [see One]) used for "by myself," and "him one" (William of Palerne, 17) for "by himself;" and here "myn" is the genitive of "I," and "him"

---

* *Myself* seems used for our "by myself" in
"I had as lief been *myself* alone."- *A. Y. L.* iii. 2. 269.

the dative of "he," and "one" is an adjective. This is also illustrated by the Scottish "my lane," *i.e.* "*my,* or *by me,* alone."
Hence, instead of "ourselves" we have in Wickliffe, 2 *Cor.* x. 2,
"but we mesuren us in *us silf* and comparisownen *us silf* to us,"
and, a line above, "*hem silf* " for "themselves."

Very early, however, the notion became prevalent that the inflected pronoun was a pronominal adjective, and that "self" was a
noun.   Hence we find in Chaucer, "*myself hath* been the whip,"
"and to prove *their selfes*" in Berners' Froissart; and in Shakespeare, *Temp.* i. 2. 132, "thy crying *self.*" Hence the modern
"ourselves," "yourselves."

The use of "self" as a noun is common in Shakespeare: "Tar-
quin's self," *Coriol.* ii. 2. 98 ; "my woeful *self,*" *L. C.* 143.   Hence
the reading of the Folio may be correct in the first of the following lines :

> "Even so *myself bewails* good Gloucester's case,
>   With sad unhelpful tears and with dimm'd eyes
>   *Look* after him."—*2 Hen. VI.* iii. 1. 217.

But the change to the first person is more in accordance with Shakespeare's-usage, as :

> "This love of theirs *myself have* often seen."
>   *T. G. of V.* iii. 1. 23.

So *T. G.* iii. 1. 147 ; *ib.* iv. 2. 110.

So "himself" is used as a pronoun, without "he," in

> "Direct not him whose way *himself* will choose."
>   *Rich. II.* ii. 1. 29.

"*Self*-born arms" (*Rich. II.* ii. 3. 80) seems to mean "divided
against themselves," "civil war."

21. Some, being frequently used with numeral adjectives qualifying nouns of time, as "*some* sixteen months" (*T. G. of V.* iv. 1.
21), is also found, by association, with a singular noun of time.

> "*Some hour* before you took me."—*T. N.* ii. 1. 22.
> "I would detain you here *some* month or two."—*M. of V.* iii. 2. 9.
> "*Some* day or two."—*R. III.* iii. 1. 64.

It would seem that in such expressions "some" has acquired an
adverbial usage, as in the provincialisms, "It is *some* late," "Five
mile or *some*" (MÄTZNER, ii. 253).   Compare

> "I think 'tis now *some* seven o'clock."—*T. of Sh.* iv. 3. 189.

"Sum" is, however, found in Early English and Anglo-Saxon in the sense of "a certain." Compare A.-S. "*Sum* jungling hym fyligde," *Mark* xiv. 51. So Wickliffe, where A. V. has "A certain young man followed him." "Other-*some*" (*M.N.D.* i. 1. 226), see p. 6.

22. The licence of converting one part of speech into another may be illustrated by the following words used as adjectives:

"The fine point of *seldom* (rare) pleasure."—*Sonn.* 52.

"Each *under* (inferior) eye."—*Sonn.* 7.

"This *beneath* (lower) world."—*T. of A.* i. 1. 44.

"The orb below
As *hush* (silent) as death."—*Hamlet*, ii. 2. 508.

See also *still*, below (22).

"Most *felt* (palpable) and open this."—B. J. *Sejan.* i. 2.

"Most *laid* (plotted) impudence."—B. J. *Fox.*

As still with us, any noun could be prefixed to another with the force of an adjective: "*water*-drops," "*water*-thieves," "*water*-fly," &c.

This licence, however, was sometimes used where we should prefer the genitive or an adjective. Thus, "the *region* kites" (*Hamlet*, ii. 2. 607,) for "the kites of the region;" and "the *region* cloud," *Sonn.* 33. So perhaps, "a *moment* leisure," *Hamlet*, i. 3. 133. We say "heart's ease," but Shakespeare, *Hen. V.* ii. 2. 27, says "*heart*-grief;" "*heart*-blood," *Rich. II.* i. 1. 172, &c.; "*faction*-traitors," *ib.* ii. 2. 57. Again, a word like "music" is not commonly used by us as a prefix unless the suffix is habitually *connected with* "music:" thus "music-book," "music-master," &c., but not "music" for "musical" as in

"The honey of his *music* vows."—*Hamlet*, iii. 1. 164.

Compare "*venom* mud," *R. of L.* 561; "*venom* clamours," *C. of E.* v. i. 69, for "venomous;" "*venom* sound," *Rich. II.* ii. 1. 19; "venom tooth," *Rich. III.* i. 3. 291.

This licence is very frequent with proper names.

"Here in *Philippi* fields."—*J. C.* v. 5. 19.

"Draw them to *Tiber* banks."—*J. C.* i. 1. 63.

"There is no world without *Verona* walls."—*R. and J.* iii. 3. 17.

"Within rich *Pisa* walls."—*T. of Sh.* ii. 1. 369.

"To the *Cyprus* wars."—*O.* i. 1. 151.

"*Turkey* cushions."—*T. of Sh.* ii. 1. 355, as we still say.

" From *Leonati* seat."—*Cymb.* v. 4. 60.

" *Venice* gold."—*T. of Sh.* ii. 1. 366.

The reason for this licence is to be found in an increasing dislike and disuse of the inflection in '*s*. Thus we find, "sake" frequently preceded in 1 *Hen. IV.* by an uninflected noun : " for *recreation* sake," 1 *Hen. IV.* i. 2. 174; *ib.* ii. 1. 80; *ib.* v. 1. 65; "for *fashion* sake," *A. Y. L.* iii. 2. 271.

ADVERBS.

23. It is characteristic of the unsettled nature of the Elizabethan language that, while (see 1) adjectives were freely used as adverbs without the termination *ly*, on the other hand *ly* was occasionally added to words from which we have rejected it. Thus : "fastly" (*L. C.* 9) ; "youngly" (*Coriol.* ii. 3. 244).

24. Adverbs with prefix a-: (1) Before nouns. In these adverbs the *a-* represents some preposition, as "in," "on," "of," &c. contracted by rapidity of pronunciation. As might be expected, the contraction is mostly found in the prepositional phrases that are in most common use, and therefore most likely to be rapidly pronounced. Thus (*Coriol.* iii. 1. 261-2) Menenius says : "I would they were *in Tiber*," while the Patrician, "I would they were *a-bed*." Here *a-* means "in," as in the following :

"*3d Fisherman.* Master, I marvel how the fishes live *in the sea.*
1st Fisherman. Why, as men do *a-land*."—*P. of T.* ii. 1. 31.

A- is also used where we should now use "at." Compare, however, O. E. "*on* work."

" Sets him new *a-work*."—*Hamlet*, ii. 2. 51 ; *Lear* iii. 5. 8.

So *R. of L.* 1496. And compare *Hamlet*, ii. 1. 58, "There (he) was a' gaming," with

" When he is drunk, *a*sleep, or *in* his rage
   At gaming."—*Hamlet*, iii. 3. 91.

Sometimes "of" and "a-" are interchanged. Compare "*a*-kin" and "of kind," "of þurst" and "a-thirst," "of buve" and "a-bove." Most frequently, however, "a-" represents our modern "on" or "in." Compare "*a*-live" and "on live."

"Bite the holy cords *a-twain.*"—*Lear,* ii. 2. 80 ; *L. C.* 6.

Compare "That his spere brast *a-five,*" *i.e.* "burst in five pieces." (HALLIWELL.) So

"*A-front.*"—1 *Hen. IV.* ii. 4. 222. "*A-fire.*"—*Temp.* i. 2. 212.
"Look up *a-height*" (perhaps).—*Lear,* iv. 6. 58.
"Beaten the maids *a-row.*"—*C. of E.* v. 1. 170.
"And keep in *a-door.*"—*Lear,* i. 4. 138.

Thus, probably, we must explain

"Thy angel becomes *a fear.*"—*A. and C.* ii. 3. 22.

i.e. "*a-fear.*" The word "a-fere" is found in A.-S. in the sense of "fearful" (Mätzner, i. 394). And in the expressions "What *a* plague?" (1 *Hen. IV.* iv. 2. 56,) "What *a* devil?" (1 *Hen. IV.* ii. 2. 30,) "*A* God's name" (*Rich. II.* ii. 1. 251,) and the like, we must suppose *a* to mean "in," "on," or "of." There is some difficulty in

"I love a ballad in print *a life*" (so Folio, Globe, "o' life").
W. T. iv. 4. 264.

It might be considered as a kind of oath, "on my life." Nares explains it "as my life," but the passages which he quotes could be equally well explained on the supposition that *a* is a preposition. The expression "all *amort*" in 1 *Hen. VI.* iii. 2. 124, and *T. of Sh.* iv. 3. 36, is said to be an English corruption of "à la mort."

"To heal the sick, to cheer the *alamort.*"—NARES.

The *a* (E. E. *an* or *on*) in these adverbial words sometimes for euphony retains the *n :*

"And each particular hair to stand *an* end."—*Ham.* i. 4. 19.*

So *Hamlet,* iii. 4. 122, *Rich. III.* i. 3. 304 ; and compare "*an* hungry," "*an* hungered" below, where the *an* is shown not to be the article. So

"A slave that still *an end* turns me to shame,"—*T. G. of V.* iv. 4. 67. where "*an* end" (like "run *on* head" (Homilies), *i.e.* "run *a*-head") signifies motion "on to the end."

These adverbial forms were extremely common in earlier English, even where the nouns were of French origin. Thus we find : "*a*-grief," "*a*-fyn" for "en-fin," "*a*-bone" excellently, "*a*-cas" by chance. Indeed the corruption of *en-* into *a-* in Old French itself

---

* Compare "Shall stand *a* tip-toe."—*Hen. V.* iv. 3. 42.

is very common, and we still retain from this source "*a*-round" for
"en rond" and "*a*-front" for "en front."

(2) Before adjectives and participles, used as nouns.

When an adjective may easily be used as a noun, it is intelligible
that it may be preceded by *a*-. Compare "*a*-height," quoted above,
with our modern "on high," and with

> "One heaved *a-high* to be hurled down below."
>
> *Rich. III.* iv. 4. 86.

It is easy also to understand *a*- before verbal nouns and before adjectives used as nouns, where it represents *on :*

> "I would have him nine years *a-killing.*"—*O.* iv. 1. 188.

i.e. "on, or in the act of killing." So

> "Whither were you *a-going ?*"—*Hen. VIII.* i. 3. 50.

i.e. "in the act of going."

> "The slave that was *a-hanging* there."—*Lear*, v. 3. 274.
>
> "Tom's *a-cold.*"—*Lear*, iii. 4. 59.

i.e. "*a*-kale," E. E. "in a chill."

Some remarkable instances of this form are subjoined, in which
nouns are probably concealed.

> "I made her weep *a-good.*"—*T. G. of V.* iv. 4. 170.

i.e. "in good earnest;" but "good" may be a noun. Compare
"*a*-bone" above.

> "The secret mischiefs that I set *abroach.*"—*R. III.* i. 3. 325 ;
>
> *R. and J.* i. 1. 111.

where *a* is prefixed to "broach," now used only as a verb. "On
broach" and "abroach" are found in E. E. Compare

> "O'er which his melancholy sits *on* brood."
>
> *Hamlet,* iii. 1. 173.

Compare "That sets them all *agape.*"—MILTON, *P. L.* v. ;
which is to be explained by the existence of an old noun, "gape."

(3) As the prefix of participles and adjectives.

In this case *a*- represents a corruption of the A.-S. intensive *of.*
Thus from E. E. "*of*feren," we have "*a*fered" or "afeared ;"
from A.-S. "*of*-gán," "*a*-gone." The *of* before a vowel or *h* is
sometimes changed into *on* or *an*. See ON, 182. And indeed the
prefixes *an-, on-, of-, a-,* were all nearly convertible. Hence "of-
hungred" appears not only as "*a*fingred," but also "*an*-hungered,"
as in *St. Matthew* xxv. 44, A. V.: "When saw we thee *an* hungered

or *a*thirst?" It would be a natural mistake to treat *an* here as the article : but compare

" *They* were *an* hungry,"—*Coriol.* i. 1. 209.

where the plural "they" renders it impossible to suppose that *an* is the article.

Perhaps, by analogy, *a*- is also sometimes placed before adjectives that are formed from verbs. It can scarcely be said that weary is a noun in

"For Cassius is *a*-weary of the world."
J. C. iv. 3. 95; 1 *Hen. IV.* iii. 2. 88.

Rather " *a*-weary," like " *of*-walked," means " *of*-wery," *i.e.* " tired out."

25. Adverbs ending in " s " formed from the possessive inflection of Nouns. Some adverbs thus formed are still in common use, such as " needs " = " of necessity."

" *Needs* must I like it well."—*Rich. II.* iii. 2. 4.

" There must be *needs* a like proportion."—*M. of V.* iii. 4. 14.

But we find also in Shakespeare :

" He would have tickled you *other gates* than he did."
T. N. v. 1. 198.

i.e. " in another gate or fashion."

In this way (compare "sideways," "lengthways," &c.) we must probably explain

" Come a little nearer *this ways*."—*M. W. of W.* ii. 2. 50.

And " Come thy *ways*."— *T. N.* v. 2. 1.

Compare also the expression in our Prayer-book :

" *Any ways* afflicted, or distressed."

Others explain this as a corruption of " wise."

" Days " is similarly used :

" 'Tis but early *days*."—*Tr. and Cr.* iv. 5. 12.

i.e. " in the day," as the Germans use " morgens." Compare " now-a-days," and N. *P.* 179, " *at noondaies.*"

A similar explanation might suggest itself for

" Is Warwick *friends* with Margaret ?"
3 *Hen. VI.* iv. 1. 115 ; *A. and C.* ii. 5. 44.

But " I am *friends* " is not found in E. E., and therefore probably it is simply a confusion of two constructions, " I am friend to him " and " we are friends."

26. After was used adverbially *of time:*

> "If you know
> That I do fawn on men, and hug them hard,
> And *after* scandal them."—*J. C.* i. 2. 76.

Now we use *afterwards* in this sense, using *after* rarely as an adverb and only with verbs of motion, to signify an interval *of space,* as "he followed *after.*"

27. The use of the following adverbs should be noted :

Again (radical meaning "opposite") is now only used in the *local* sense of *returning,* as in "He came back *again,* home *again,*" &c. ; and *metaphorically* only in the sense of *repeating,* as in "*Again* we find many other instances," &c. It is used by Shakespeare *metaphorically* in the sense of "on the other hand." Thus—

> "Have you
> Ere now denied the asker, and now *again* (on the other hand)
> Of him that did not ask but mock, bestow
> Your sued-for tongues?"—*Coriol.* ii. 3. 214.

"Where (whereas) Nicias did turne the Athenians from their purpose, Alcibiades *againe* (on the other hand) had a further reach," &c.—*N. P.* 172. So *Rich. II.* ii. 9. 27.

It is also used *literally* for "back *again.*" "Haste you *again,*" *A. W.* ii. 2. 73, does not mean "haste a second time," but "hasten back."

Again is used for "*again* and *again,*" *i.e.* repeatedly (a previous action being naturally implied by *again*), and hence intensively almost like "amain."

> "For wooing here until I sweat(ed) *again.*"—*M. of V.* iii. 2. 205.
> "Weeping *again* the king my father's wreck."
> > *Tempest,* i. 2. 390.

For omission of *-ed* in "sweat" (common in E. E.), see 341.

28. All (altogether) used adverbially :

> "I will dispossess her *all.*"—*T. of A.* i. 1. 139.
> "For us to levy power is *all* unpossible."—*Rich. II.* ii. 2. 126.

In compounds *all* is freely thus used, "*All*-worthy lord ;" "*all*-watched night ;" "her *all*-disgraced friend," *A. and C.* iii. 12. 22. Sometimes it seems to mean "by all persons," as in "*all*-shunned." So, "this *all*-hating world," *Rich. II.* v. 5. 66, does not mean "hating all," but "hating (me) universally."

All used intensively was frequently prefixed to other adverbs of degree, as "so."

> "What occasion of import
> Hath *all so* long detain'd you from your wife?"
>
> *T. of Sh.* iii. 1. 105.

The connection of *all* and "so" is perpetuated in the modern "also." Still more commonly is *all* prefixed to "too."

> "In thy heart-blood, though being *all too* base
> To stain the temper of my knightly sword."
>
> *Rich. II.* iv. 1. 28.

> "Our argument
> Is *all too* heavy to admit much talk."—*2 Hen. IV.* v. 2. 24.

So *Cymb.* v. 5. 169 ; *T. G. of V.* iii. 1. 162 ; *Sonn.* 18, 61, 86 ; *R. of L.* 44, 1686.

There are two passages in Shakespeare where *all-to* requires explanation :

> "It was not she that called him *all to* nought."—*V. and A.* 993.
> "The very principals (principal posts of the house) did seem to rend
> And *all to* topple."—*P. of T.* iii. 2. 17.

(1) In the first passage *all-to* is probably an intensive form of "*to*," which in Early English (see **Too**, below) had of itself an intensive meaning. Originally "to" belonged to the verb. Thus "to-breke" meant "break in pieces." When "all" was added, as in "all to-breke," it at first had no connection with "to," but intensified "to-breke." But "to" and "too" are written indifferently for one another by Elizabethan and earlier writers, and hence sprang a corrupt use of "all-to," caused probably by the frequent connection of *all* and *too* illustrated above. It means here "altogether."

(2) In the second passage some (*a*) connect "to-topple," believing that here and in *M. W. of W.* iv. 4. 57, "to-pinch," "to" is an intensive prefix, as in Early English. But neither of the two passages necessitates the supposition that Shakespeare used this archaism. (See *M. W. of W.* iv. 4. 5 below, **To omitted and inserted,** 350.) We can, therefore, either (*b*) write "all-to" (as in the Globe), and treat it as meaning "altogether," or (*c*) suppose that "all" means "quite," and that "to topple," like "to rend," depends upon "seem." This last is the more obvious and probable construction.*

---

* Or, adopting this construction, we may take *all* to mean "the whole house." "The principals did seem to rend, and the whole house to topple."

From this use of "all too" or "all to," closely connected in the sense of "altogether," it was corruptly employed as an intensive prefix, more especially before verbs beginning with *be-* : "*all-to-bequalify*," B. J.; "*all-to-bekist*," *ib.*; and later, "he *all-to be-*Gullivers me," SWIFT ; "*all-to-be-*traytor'd," NARES.

29. Almost, used for *mostly, generally* :

"Neither is it *almost* seen that very beautiful persons are of great virtue."—B. *E.* 163.

Our modern meaning *nearly* is traceable to the fact that anything is *nearly* done when the *most* of it is done.

Almost (see also **Transpositions**) frequently follows the word which it qualifies.

"I swoon *almost* with fear."—*M. N. D.* ii. 3. 154.
"As like *almost* to Claudio as himself."—*M. for M.* v. 1. 494.

Hence in negative sentences we find "not-almost" where we should use "almost not," or, in one word, "scarcely," "hardly."

"You can*not* reason (*almost*) with a man."—*Rich. III.* ii. 2. 39.
The Globe omits the parenthesis of the Folio.

" And yet his trespass, in our common reason,
Is *not almost* a fault . . . to incur a private check."—*O.* iii. 3. 66.

i.e. "is *not* (*I may almost say*) fault enough to," &c. or "is *scarcely* fault enough to," &c.   So

"I have *not* breath'd *almost* since I did see it."—*C. of E.* v. 1. 181.

It was natural for the Elizabethans to dislike putting the qualifying "almost" before the word qualified by it.   But there was an ambiguity in their idiom.   "Not almost-a-fault" would mean "not approaching to a fault ;" "not-almost a fault," "very nearly not a fault."   We have, therefore, done well in avoiding the ambiguity by disusing "almost" in negative sentences.   The same ambiguity and peculiarity attaches to interrogative, comparative, and other conjunctional sentences.

"Would you imagine or *almost* believe ?"—*Rich. III.* iii. 5. 35.

i.e. "Would you suppose without evidence, or (I may *almost* say) believe upon evidence?" &c.

" Our aim, which was
To take in many towns ere *almost* Rome
Should know we were afoot."—*Coriol.* i. 2. 24.

Alone, see **One, 18.**

30. Along is frequently joined to " with " and transposed, as :

" With him is Gratiano gone *along.*"—*M. of V.* ii. 8. 2.

Hence the " with me " being omitted, " along " is often used foɪ " along with me."

" Demetrius and Egeus, go *along,*
I must employ you in some business."—*M. N. D.* i. I. 123.

Note, that here, as in *T. of Sh.* iv. 5. 7 ; 2 *Hen. IV.* ii. I. 191 ; *O.* i. I. 180 ; "go" is used where we should say "come." The word is used simply to express the motion of walking by WICKLIFFE : *Acts* xiv. 8. MONTAIGNE, *Florio,* 230.

Sometimes the verb of motion is omitted, as in

" Will you *along* (with us)?"—*Coriol.* ii. 3. 157.

" Let's *along* " is still a common Americanism.

Sometimes the ellipsis refers to the *third* person.

" Go you *along* (with him)."—*A. and C.* v. I. 69.

Perhaps we ought (to the advantage of the rhythm) to place a comma after *along,* in

" Therefore have I entreated him *along,*
With us to watch the minutes of this night."—*Ham.* i. I. 26.

30 a. Anon. The derivative meaning of *anon* (an-ane) is "at one instant," or " in an instant," and this is its ordinary use. But in

"Still and *anon.*"—*K. J.* iv. I. 47.

" Which ever and *anon* he gave his nose."
 1 *Hen. IV.* i. 3. 38.

anon seems to mean " the moment after," a previous moment being implied by "still," "ever." Compare our " now and *then.*"

31. Anything, like **Any ways,** is adverbially used :

" Do you think they can take any pleasure in it, or be *anything* delighted ?"—MONTAIGNE, 31.

" *Any ways* afflicted, or distressed."—*Prayer-book.*

" Ways" is, perhaps, genitive. See 25.

32. Away.

" She could never *away* with me."—2 *Hen. IV.* iii. 2. 231.

i.e. " she could not endure me." A verb of motion is probably

omitted.   Compare our " I cannot get on with him," "put up with
him," and the provincial " I cannot do with him."

"I could not do *withal.*"—*M. of V.* iii. 2. 72.

So "she could never away with me" = "she could not go on her
way," *i.e.* "get on with me."   For the omission of the verb
of motion compare

"Will you along !"—*Coriol.* ii. 3. 157.

33. Back, for "backward."

"Goes to and *back* lackeying the varying tide."
A. and C. i. 4. 46.

Where we should say "to and *fro.*"

34. Besides = "by the side of the main question," *i.e.* "in other respects," "for the rest."

"This Timæus was a man not so well knowne as he, but *besides*
(for the rest) a wise man and very hardy."—N. *P.* 174.

Similarly *besides* is used as a preposition in the sense "out of."

"How fell you *besides* your five wits?"—*T. N.* iv. 2. 92.

35. Briefly = "a short time *ago,*" instead of (as with us) "*in* a short space of time."

"*Briefly* we heard their drums.
How couldst thou . . . bring thy news so late?"
Coriol. i. 6. 16.

Similarly we use the Saxon equivalent "shortly" to signify futurity.

36. By (original meaning "near the side."   Hence "*by* and *by*" = "very near," which can be used either of *time* or, as in Early English, also of *place*) is used for "aside," "on one side," "away," in the phrase

"Stand *by,* or I shall gall you."—*K. J.* iv. 3. 94.

Whereas, on the other hand, "to stand *by* a person" means "to
stand *near* any one."

37. Chance appears to be used as an adverb :

"How *chance* thou art returned so soon ?"—*C. of E.* i. 2. 42.

But the order of the words "thou art," indicates that Shakespeare treated *chance* as a verb.   "How may it *chance* or *chances*

that," as *Hamlet*, ii. 2. 343, "How *chances* it they travel?" Compare—

"How *chance* the roses there do fade so fast?"

M. N. D. i. 1. 129.

So *Tr. and Cr.* iii. 1. 151; *2 Hen. IV.* iv. 4. 20; *Rich. III.* iv. 2.
103; *M. W. of W.* v. 5. 231; *P. of T.* iv. 1. 23.

Compare, however, also—

"If *case* some one of you would fly from us."—3 *Hen. VI.* v. 4. 34.

where "case" is for the Old French "per-case."

This use of *chance* as an apparent adverb is illustrated by

"*Perchance* his boast of Lucrece' sovereignty
Suggested this proud issue of a king:
Perchance that envy of so rich a thing
Braving compare, disdainfully did sting."—*R. of L.* 39.

Here "perchance" seems used first as an adverb, then as a verb,
"it may chance that." So Shakespeare, perhaps, used *chance* as
an adverb, but unconsciously retained the order of words which
shows that, strictly speaking, it is to be considered as a verb.

38. Even. "*Even* now" with us is applied to an action that
has been going on for some long time and *still* continues, the
emphasis being laid on "now." In Shakespeare the emphasis is
often to be laid on "even," and "*even* now" means "*exactly* or
only now," *i.e.* "scarcely longer ago than the present:" hence
"*but* now."

"There was an old fat woman *even* now with me."

M. W. of W. iv. 5. 26.

Often "but *even* now" is used in this sense: *M. of V.* i. 1. 35.
On the other hand, both "*even* now" and "*but* now" can signify
"just at this moment," as in

"But now I was the lord
Of this fair mansion;... and *even now, but now,*
This house, these servants, and this same myself
Are yours."—*M. of V.* iii. 2. 171.

We use "*just* now" for the Shakespearian "*even* now," laying
the emphasis on "just." *Even* is used for "even now," in the sense
of "at this moment," in

"A certain convocation of politic worms are *even* at him."

Hamlet, iv. 3. 22.

So "*even* when" means "just when" in

> "(Roses) die, *even* when they to perfection grow."
> *T. N.* ii. 4. 42.

39. Ever (at *every* time) freq. :

> "For slander's mark was *ever* yet the fair."—*Sonn.* 70.

The latter use is still retained in poetry. But in prose we confine "ever" (like the Latin "unquam") to negative, comparative, and interrogative sentences.

Ever seems contrary to modern usage in

> "Would I might
> But *ever* see that man."—*Temp.* i. 2. 168.

"But," however, implies a kind of negative, and "ever" means "at *any* time."

40. Far, used metaphorically for "very."

> "But *far* unfit to be a sovereign."—3 *Hen. VI.* iii. 2. 92.

So 2 *Hen. VI.* iii. 2. 286.

41. Forth, hence, and **hither** are used without verbs of motion (motion being implied) :

> "I have no mind of feasting *forth* to-night."—*M. of V.* ii. 2. 37.
> "Her husband will be *forth*."—*M. W. of W.* ii. 2. 278.
> "By praising him here who doth *hence* remain."—*Sonn.* 39.
> "From *thence* the sauce to meat is ceremony."—*Macb.* iii. 4. 36.
> "Methinks I hear *hither* your husband's drum."—*Coriol.* i. 3. 32.
> "Prepare thee *hence* for France."—*Rich. II.* v. 1. 31.

Forth, "to the end :"

> "To hear this matter *forth*."—*M. for M.* v. 1. 255.

Forth, as a preposition : see **Prepositions.**

42. Happily, which now means "by *good* hap," was sometimes used for "haply," *i.e.* "by hap," just as "success" was sometimes "good," at other times "ill."

> "*Hamlet.* That great baby you see there is not yet out of his swaddling-clouts.
> *Ros.* Happily he's the second time come to them."—*Hamlet*, ii. 2. 402.

> "And these our ships, you *happily* may think,
> Are like the Trojan horse (which) was stuffed within
> With bloody veins."—*P. of T.* i. 4. 29.

> " Though I may *fear*
> Her will recoiling to her better judgment
> May fall to match you with her country forms,
> And *happily* repent."—*Othello*, iii. 3. 238.

It means "gladly" in *Macbeth*, i. 3. 89.

43. Here is used very freely in compounds: "they *here* approach" (*Macb.* iv. 3. 133); "*here*-remain" (*ib.* 148). Perhaps *here* may be considered as much an adjective, when thus used, as "then" in " our *then* dictator " (*Coriol.* ii. 2. 93). So in Greek.

44. Hitherto, which is now used of time, is used by Shakespeare of space:

> " England from Trent and Severn *hitherto*."
> 1 Hen. IV. iii. 1. 74.

45. Home. We still say "to come *home*," "to strike *home*," using the word adverbially with verbs of motion, but not

> " I cannot speak him *home*," *i.e.* completely.
> Coriol. ii. 2. 107.

> " Satisfy me *home*."—*Cymb.* iii. 5. 83.

> " (Your son) lack'd the sense to know her estimation *home*."
> A. W. v. 3. 4.

> " That trusted *home*
> Might yet enkindle you unto the crown."—*Macbeth*, i. 3. 121.

46. How (adverbial derivative from *hwa* = *hwu*, O. E.) used for "however:"

> " I never yet saw man
> *How* wise, *how* noble, young, *how* rarely featured,
> But she would spell him backward."—*M. Ado*, iii. 1. 60.

> " Or whether his fall enraged him or *how* 'twas."
> Coriol. i. 3. 69.

How is perhaps used for " as " in *V. and A.* 815:

> " Look, *how* a bright star shooteth from the sky,
> *So* glides he in the night from Venus' eye."

This, which is the punctuation of the Globe, is perhaps correct, and illustrated by

> " Look, *as* the fair and fiery-pointed sun
> Rushing from forth a cloud bereaves our sight,
> Even *so*," &c.—*R. of L.* 372.

So *V. and A.* 67 ; *M. of V.* iii. 2. 127.

Similarly, GASCOIGNE (Mätzner) has :

> " *How* many men, *so* many minds."

47. Howsoe'er for " *howsoe'er* it be," "in any case."

"*Howsoe'er*, my brother hath done well."—*Cymb.* iv. 2. 146.

So **However.** See 403.

48. Last. Such phrases as "at the last," "at the first," are common, but not

"The *last* (time) that e'er I took her leave at court."
A. W. v. 3. 79.

Merely, completely. See **Adjectives, Mere,** 15.

More, Most. See **Adjectives,** 18.

49. Moreabove = "moreover."—*Hamlet,* ii. 2. 126.

50. Moreover precedes "that," like our "beside that."

"*Moreover* that we much did long to see you."
Hamlet, i. 2. 2.

51. Much, More, is frequently used as an ordinary adjective, after a pronominal adjective, like the Scotch *mickle,* and the E. E. *muchel.** (So in A.-S.)

"Thy *much* goodness."—*M. for M.* v. 1. 534.

"Yet so *much* (great) is my poverty of spirit."
Rich. III. iii. 7. 159.

Much was frequently used as an adverb even with *positive* adjectives.

"I am *much* ill."—2 *Hen. IV.* iv. 4. 111.

So *Tr. and Cr.* ii. 3. 115 ; *J. C.* iv. 3. 255.

"Our too *much* memorable shame."—*Hen. V.* ii. 4. 53.

So *Rich. II.* ii. 2. 1.

More is frequently used as a noun and adverb in juxtaposition.

"The slave's report is seconded and *more*
More fearful is deliver'd."—*Coriol.* iv. 6. 63. Comp. *K. J.* iv. 2. 42.

"*More* than that tongue that *more* hath *more* express'd."—*Sonn.* 23.

"If there be *more, more* woeful, hold it in."—*Lear,* v. 3. 202.

We sometimes say "*the* many" (see 12), but not "the most," in the sense of "most *men.*" Heywood, however, writes—

"Yes, since *the most* censures, believes and saith
By an implicit faith."—*Commendatory Verses on* B. J.

---

* Compare "A noble peer of *mickle* trust and power."—MILTON, *Comus.*

Needs. See 25.

52. Never is used where we now more commonly use "ever" in phrases as :

> "And creep time *ne'er* so slow,
>   Yet it shall come for me to do thee good."—*K. J.* iii. 3. 81.

So 1 *Hen. VI.* v. 3. 98 ; *Rich. II.* v. 1. 64.

There is probably here a confusion of two constructions, (1) "And though time creep so slow as it never crept before," and (2) "And though time never crept so slow as in the case I am supposing." These two are combined into, "And though time creep— (how shall I describe it ? though it crept) never so slow." Construction (2) is illustrated by

> "*Never so* weary, *never so* in woe,
>   I can no further crawl, no further go."—*M. N. D.* iii. 2. 442.

Here, strictly speaking, the ellipsis is "*I have been,*" or "having been ;" "I *have never* been *so* weary." But it is easy to see that "never so weary" being habitually used in this sense, Hermia might say, "I *am* never-so-weary," or still more easily, "though I were *never-so-weary.*"

In such phrases as "*never* the nearer," *never* seems to mean "nought." So Wickliffe, *John* xix. 21 :

> "But how he now seeth we wite *nere,*" *i.e.* "we know *not.*"

53. None seems to be the emphatic form of "no," like "mine" of "my" in the modern idiom :

> "Satisfaction (there) can be *none* but by pangs of death."
>   *T. N.* iii. 4. 261.

For we could not say "there can be *none* satisfaction." This emphatic use of the pronoun at the end of a sentence is found very early. *None* seems loosely used for "not at all," like "nothing" (55), "no-whit," *i.e.* "not." And this may, perhaps, explain :

> "*None* a stranger there
>   So merry and so gamesome."—*Cymb.* i. 6. 59.

Here either *none* means ".not," "ne'er," or a comma must be placed after *none:* "*none,* being a stranger," which is a very harsh construction.

The adverbial use of "none" may be traced to Early English and Anglo-Saxon. Under the form "nan," *i.e.* "ne-an" (compare

German "nein"), we find "nan more," and also "*none* longer," "whether he wolde or *noon*" (CHAUCER, Mätzner). "Nan" was used as an adverbial accusative for "by no means" even in A.-S. (Mätzner, iii. 131.) In *Rich. II.* v. 2. 99, "He shall be *none*," the meaning is, "he shall not be one of their number." "None" is still used by us for "nothing," followed by a partitive genitive, "I had *none* of it ;" and this explains the Elizabethan phrase

"She will *none* of me."—*T. N.* i. 3. 113.

i.e. "She desires to have (321) nothing from, as regards to do with, me." So

"You can say *none* of this."—*T. N.* v. 1. 342.

54. Not is apparently put for "*not* only" in the two following passages :

"Speak fair ; you may salve so
Not what is dangerous present, but the loss
Of what is past."—*Coriol.* iii. 2. 71.

"For that he has
Given hostile strokes, and that *not* in the presence
Of dreaded justice, but on the ministers
That do distribute it."—*Coriol.* iii. 3. 97.

55. Nothing, like "no-way," "naught," "not," (A.-S. nȧht, *i.e.* "no whit,") is often used adverbially.

"And that would set my teeth *nothing* on edge."
1 *Hen. IV.* iii. 1. 133.

"I fear *nothing* what may be said against me."
Hen. VIII. i. 2. 212.

where "what" is not put for "which."

56. Off (away from the point) :

"That's *off*: that's *off*. I would you had rather been silent."
Coriol. ii. 2. 64.

To be *off* = to take *off* one's hat :

"I will practise the insinuating nod and be *off* to them most counterfeitly."—*Coriol.* ii. 3. 107.*

57. Once ("once for all," "above all") :

"*Once*, if he require our voices, we ought not to deny him."
Coriol. ii. 3. 1.

---

* "Stands *off*" is used for "stands *out*, i.e. in relief."—*Hen. V.* ii. 2. 103.

> " 'Tis *once* thou lovest,
> And I will fit thee with the remedy."—*M. Ado*, i. 1. 320.

Hence "positively."

"Nay, an you be a cursing hypocrite, *once* you must be looked to."—*M. Ado*, v. i. 212.

"Nay, an you begin to rail on society, *once* I am sworn not to give regard to you."—*Timon*, i. 2. 251.

The Folio and Globe place the comma after *once*

Once is sometimes omitted :

> "This is (*once*) for all."—*Hamlet*, i. 3. 131.

Once sometimes "in a word:"

> "*Once* this—your long experience of her wisdom,
> Her sober virtue, years, and modesty,
> Plead on her part some cause to you unknown."
> *C. of E.* iii. 1. 90.

At once is found in this or a similar sense :

> "My lords, *at once;* the cause why we are met
> Is to determine of the coronation."—*Rich. III.* iii. 4. 1.
> "My lords, *at once;* the care you have of us
> Is worthy praise."—*2 Hen. VI.* iii. 1. 66.

Once seems to mean "at some time (future)" in

> "I thank thee, and I pray thee, *once* to-night
> Give my sweet Nan this ring."—*M. W. of W.* iii. 4. 103.

But the word may be taken as above.

58. Only, i.e. *on(e)ly*, is used as an adjective. See **But** (130), and **Transpositions** (420).

> "The *only* (mere) breath."—SPENS. *F. Q.* i. 7. 13.
> "It was for her love and *only* pleasure."—INGELEND.
> "By her *only* aspect she turned men into stones."—BACON, *Adv. of L.* 274.

We have lost this adjectival use of only, except in the sense of "single," in such phrases as "an *only* child."

Only, like "alone" (18), is used nearly in the sense of "above all," "surpassing."

> '*Oph.* You are merry, my lord.
> *Ham.* Who? I?
> *Oph.* Ay, my lord.
> *Ham.* O God, your *only* jig-maker."—*Hamlet*, iii. 2. 131.
> "Your worm is your *only* emperor for diet."—*Ib.* iv. 3. 22.

58 a. Over means "*over* again" in

"Trebles thee *o'er*."—*Tempest*, ii. 1. 221.

i.e. "repeats thy former self thrice."   Compare

"I would be trebled twenty times myself."—*M. of V.* iii. 2. 154.

59. Presently = "at the present time," "at once," instead of, as now, "soon, but *not* at once."

"*Desd.*   Yes, but not yet to die.
Othello.   O yes, *presently*."—*Othello*, v. 2. 52.
So *Rich. II.* iii. 1. 3 ; 2. 179.

60. Round, used adverbially in the sense of "straightforwardly." "Round," like "square" with us, from its connection with "regular," "symmetrical," and "complete," was used to signify "plain and honest."   Hence

"I went *round* to work."—*Hamlet*, ii. 2. 139.

means just the opposite of "circuitously."

61. Severally ("sever," Lat. *separo*), used for "separately." So

"When *severally* we hear them rendered."—*J. C.* iii. 2. 10.

And "Contemplation doth withdraw our soule from us, and *severally* employ it from the body."—MONTAIGNE, 30.

Thus, "a *several* plot" (*Sonn.* 137) is a "separate" or "private plot" opposed to "a common."

62. Since (A.-S. *sith* = "time," also adv.* "late," "later ;" "*sith-than*" = "after that") adverbially for "ago."

"I told your lordship a year *since*."—*M. Ado*, ii. 2. 13.

This must be explained by an ellipsis :

"I told your lordship (it is) a year *since* (I told you)."

Compare a transitional use of "since" between an adverb and conjunction in "Waverley ; or, 'tis Sixty Years *since*." Omit "'tis," and *since* becomes an adverb.

So *since* is used for "since then," like our "ever since" in

'And *since*, methinks, I would not (do not wish to) grow so fast."—*Rich. III.* ii. 4. 14.

Since, when used adverbially as well as conjunctionally, fre-

---

* *Sith* for *sither*, like "mo" for "mo-er."   (See 17.)

quently takes the verb in the simple past where we use the complete *present:*

> "I did not see him *since.*"—*A. and C.* i. 3. 1.

This is in accordance with an original meaning of the word, "later," ("sith.") We should still say, "I never saw him *after* that;" and *since* has the meaning of "after."

We also find the present after "since," to denote an action that *is* and *has been* going on *since* a certain time. (So in Latin with "jampridem.")

> "My desires e'er *since pursue* me."—*T. N.* i. 1. 23.

See **Conjunctions,** 132.

63. So (original meaning "in that way") is frequently inserted in replies where we should omit it:

> "*Trib.* Repair to the Capitol.
> *Peop.* We will *so.*"—*Coriol.* ii. 3. 262.
> "*T.* Fortitude doth consist, &c.
> *D.* It doth *so* indeed, sir."—B. J. *Sil. Wom.* iv. 2.

Here *so* means "*as* you direct, assert." "As" is, by derivation, only an emphatic form of *so.* See 106.

64. So is sometimes omitted after "I think," "if," &c.

> "*G.* What, in metre?
> *Luc.* In any proportion or language.
> *G.* I *think,* or in any religion." —*M. for M.* i. 2. 24.
> "Will the time serve to tell? I do not *think* (so)."
>   *Coriol.* i. 6. 46.
> "Haply you shall not see me more; or *if,*
> A mangled shadow."—*A. and C.* iv. 2. 27.

"Not like a corse; or *if,* not to be buried."—*W. T.* iv. 4. 131.

"Do not plunge thyself too far in anger, lest thou hasten thy trial, which *if,* Lord have mercy on thee for a hen."—*A. W.* ii. 3. 223.

Compare

> "What *though;* yet I live like a poor gentleman born."
> *M. W. of W.* i. 1. 287; *Hen. V.* ii. 1. 9; *A. Y. L.* iii. 3. 51.
>   "O, if it *prove,*
> Tempests are kind and salt waves fresh in love."
>   *T. N.* iii. 4. 418.

65. So is put for the more emphatic form, al-*so*.

"Demetrius, thou dost over-ween in all,
And *so* in this, to bear me down with braves."
T. A. ii. 1. 80.

"It is a cold and heat that does outgo
All sense of winters and of summers *so*."—B. J. *Sad Sh.* ii. 1.

"Mad in pursuit, and in possession *so*."—*Sonn.* 129.

"Good morrow, Antony.
    Ant. So to most noble Cæsar."—*J. C.* ii. 2. 117.

So approaches "also" in

"Cousin, farewell ; and, uncle, bid him *so*."
Rich. II. i. 3. 247.

So that ; so as. (See **Pronouns, Relative,** 275, 276.)

66. So (like the Greek οὕτω δή) is often used where we should use "then." "In this way" naturally leads to "thus," "on this," "thereupon," "then."

"And when this hail some heat from Hermia felt
So he dissolved."—*M. N. D.* i. 1. 245.

So is, therefore, sometimes more emphatic than with us, as in (arrange thus, not as Globe)—

"   *Olivia.* To one of your receiving enough is shown ;
A cypress, not a bosom, hides (Fol.) my heart—— (*pauses*)
So (*i.e.* after this confession) let me hear you speak.
    Vio.   I pity you."
T. N. iii. 1. 133.

So in conditional clauses. See **Conjunctions,** 133.

67. So was often, and correctly, used (where we use the adverbial "such" or "so" with "a") before an adjective, *e.g.* "*so* great faith" where we say "*such* great faith," "*so* long time" where we say "*so* long *a* time." We seem to feel that "so" (being an adverb, and therefore more liable to transposition than the adjective "such") requires to be attached to the word which it qualifies, either (1) by introducing the article which necessarily links together the words thus : "so-great a-loss ;" or else (2) by placing "so" in a position where its effect is equally unmistakeable : "a-loss so-great."

When the noun is in the plural we cannot use the former method ; we are, therefore, driven to the latter, and instead of saying

"*So* hard termes."—N. *P.* 176.

we say "*terms so* hard."

"In *so* profound abysm I throw all care."—*Sonn.* 112.
> " My particular grief
> Is of *so* flood-gate and o'erbearing nature."—*O.* i. 3. 55.

" And I will call him to *so* strict account."—1 *Hen. IV.* iii. 2. 149.

" With *so* full soul."—*Temp.* iii. 1. 44.

" Of *so* quick condition."—*M. for M.* i. 1. 54.

But note that in these instances the "so" follows a preposition. After prepositions the article (see **Article,** 90) is frequently omitted. Shakespeare could have written

> " My grief is of nature so floodgate," &c.

> " I will call him to account so strict that," &c.

Our modern usage was already introduced side by side with the other as early as Wickliffe. Compare

> "So long time."—*St. John* xiv. 9.

with   "So long a time."—*Hebrews* iv. 7.

68. Something used adverbially, like "somewhat."

> " A white head and *something* a round belly."
> > 2 *Hen. IV.* i. 2. 212.

We should say " a *somewhat* round," placing the adverb between the article and the adjective so as to show unmistakeably that the adverb qualifies the adjective. "Something" may possibly be so taken (though "somehow" would make better sense) in

> "This *something*-settled matter in his breast."—*Ham.* iii. 1. 181.

68 a. Sometimes, like "sometime," is used by Shakespeare for "formerly" in

> "Thy *sometimes* brother's wife."—*Rich. II.* i. 2. 54.

So probably
> "*Sometimes* from her eyes
> I did receive fair speechless messages."—*M. of V.* i. 1. 163.

Compare "olim" in Latin.

69. Still used for **constantly,** in accordance with the derivation of the word, "quiet," "unmoved." It is now used only in the sense of "even now," "even then." The connection between "during all time up to the present" and "even at the present" is natural, and both meanings are easily derived from the radical meaning, "without moving from its place." Comp. the different meanings of *dum, donec,* ἕως, &c.

" Thou *still* hast been the author of good tidings."
Hamlet, ii. 2. 42.

" But this thy countenance *still* lock'd in steel
I never saw till now."—*T. and C.* iv. 5. 195.

i.e. " because it was *constantly* lock'd in steel."

And this is the best, though not the most obvious, interpretation of

" But *still* the house affairs would draw her hence."
Othello, i. 3. 147.

It is used as an adjective for *constant* (though some suggest
" silent") in

" But I of thee will wrest an alphabet,
And by *still* practice learn to know the meaning."
T. A. iii. 2. 44.

This interpretation is corroborated by

" But that *still* use of grief makes wild grief tame,
My tongue should to thy ears not name my boys."
Rich. III. iv. 3. 229.

70. Than is used for *then :*

" And their ranks began
To break upon the galled shore and *than*
Retire again."—*R. of L.* 456.

Then for than, freq. in North's *Plutarch*, Ascham, &c.

In O. E. the commonest forms are " thanne" = *then ;* " then "
= *than.*

Then and *than* (like *tum* and *tam*, *quum* and *quam* in Latin) are
closely connected, and, indeed, mere varieties of the same word.
They were originally inflections of the demonstrative, and meant " at
that (time)," " in that (way)." As " that " is used as a relative,
" than " has the signification of " in the way in which " (*quam*),
just as *then* (71) is used for " at the time at which" (*quum*). It is
usual to explain " He is taller *than* I " thus : " He is taller ; *then*
I am tall." This explanation does not so well explain " He is
not taller than I." On the whole, it is more in analogy with the
German *als*, Latin *quam*, Greek ἤ, to explain it thus : " *In the way
in which* I am tall he is taller." The close connection between
" in that way," " at that time," " in that place," &c., is illustrated
by the use of *there* for *thereupon*, or *then*.

" Even *there* resolved my reason into tears."—*L. C.* 42.

71. Then apparently used for "when." So in E. E. See
That, 284.

> " And more more strong, *then* lesser is my fear,
> I shall endue you with ; meantime but ask," &c.
>
> *K. J.* iv. 2. 42.

72. To-fore, which was as common in E. E. as "be-fore" and
"a-fore," is found in

> " O would thou wert as thou *to-fore* hast been."
>
> *T. A.* iii. 2. 294.

73. Too, which is only an emphatic form of "to" (compare
πρός in Greek, used adverbially), is often spelt "to" by Elizabethan
writers (*Sonn.* 38, 86) ; and conversely, "too" is found for "to"
(*Sonn.* 56, 135).

Too seems used, like the E. E. "to," for "excessively" in
Spenser, *Shepheard's Calendar, May :*

> " Thilke same kidde (as I can well devise)
> Was *too* very foolish and unwise."

Perhaps, also, in

> " Lest that your goods *too* soon be confiscate."—*C. of E.* i. 2. 2.

though the meaning may be " the goods of you *also.*"

> " Tempt him not so *too* far."—*A. and C.* i. 3. 11.

And there is, perhaps, an allusion to the E. E. meaning in "too-too,"
which is often found in Elizabethan English.

Too is often used in the phrase, " I am *too* blame" (Folio)

> " I am much *too* blame."
>
> *O.* iii. 3. 211, 282 ; *M. of V.* v. 1. 166; *Rich. III.* ii. 2. 13.

This is so common in other Elizabethan authors, that it seems to
require more explanation than the confusion between "to" and
"too" mentioned above. Perhaps "blame" was considered an
adjective, as in

> " In faith, my lord, you are *too wilful-blame.*"
>
> 1 *Hen. IV.* iii. 1. 177.

and "too" may have been, as in E. E., used for "excessively."

Too seems used for "very much," or "too much," in

> " Tell him that gave me this (wound), who lov'd him *too,*
> He struck my soul and not my body through."
>
> *B. and F. F. Sh.* iii. 1.

The context will hardly admit of the interpretation, "Me who *also* lov'd him."

The transition from the meaning of progressive motion to that of "increasingly" or "excessively," and from "excessively" to the modern "to excess," is too natural to require more than mention.

73 a. What, when. *What* and *when* are often used as exclamations of impatience :

> " *What*, Lucius, ho !"—*J. C.* ii. 1. 1.
> " *When*, Lucius, when ?"—*Ib.* 5.

Some ellipsis is to be supplied, "What (is the matter)?" "When (are you coming)?" So in

> " *Gaunt.* Throw down, my son, the duke of Norfolk's gage.
> *K. Rich.* And, Norfolk, throw down his.
> *Gaunt.* When, Harry, *when ?*"—*Rich. II.* i. 1. 162.

See also **What,** 253.

74. Whilst. " The *while*" is often used in accordance with the derivation of the word for "(in) the (mean) time." The inflected forms *whiles* and *whilest* are generally used as conjunctions. But we have

> " If you'll go fetch him
> We'll say our song *the whilst.*"—*Cymb.* iv. 2. 254.

75. Why (instrumental case of E.E. *hwa*, "who"), used after "for," instead of "wherefore." Like the Latin "quid enim ?" it came after a time to mean "for indeed," as

> " And send the hearers weeping to their beds ;
> *For why*, the senseless brands will sympathise."
> > *Rich. II.* v. 1. 40.

i.e. "wherefore ? (because) the senseless," &c. The provincialism "whyfore" still exists. "For" does not correspond to "enim," but is a preposition by derivation. Later writers, however, and possibly Shakespeare, may have used "for" in "for *why*" as a conjunction. Some, however, maintain that the comma should be removed after "for *why*," and that "for *why*" (like ἀνθ' ὧν) means "for this that," "because," the relative containing an implied antecedent.

A distinction seems drawn between "why" and "for what" in

> " *Why*, or *for what* these nobles were committed
> Is all unknown to me, my gracious lady."—*Rich. III.* ii. 4. 48.

Why, perhaps, refers to the past cause, *for what* to the future object.

> " *Ant. S.* Shall I tell you *why ?*
> *Drom. S.* Ay, sir, and *wherefore ;* for they say every *why* hath a *wherefore.*"—*C. of E.* ii. 2. 43–45.

i.e. " every deed said to be done owing to a certain cause is really done for a certain object."

Compare

> " Say, *why* is this ? *Wherefore ? What shall we do ?* "
> > *Hamlet,* i. 4. 57.

" Why " and " how " are both derivatives of the relative, and are sometimes interchanged in A.-S. " Why " seems to have been the ablative of instrument, and " how " the adverbial derivative of manner, from " who."

76. Yet (up to this time) is only used now *after* a negative, " not *yet,*" " never *yet,*" &c. Then it was also used *before* a negative.

> " For (as) *yet* his honour never heard a play."—*T. of Sh.* Ind. I. 96.
> > " *Yet* I have not seen
> > So likely an ambassador of love."—*M. of V.* ii. 9. 92.

> " *Yet* (up to this time) they are *not* joined."—*A. and C.* iv. 12. 1.

" I will make one of her women lawyer to me, for I *yet not* understand the case myself."—*Cymb.* ii. 3. 80.

The following is a remarkable passage :

> " *Hel.*   You, Diana,
> Under my poor instructions *yet* (still) must suffer
> Something in my behalf.
> > *Diana.*   Let death and honesty
> > Go with your impositions, I am yours
> > Upon your will to suffer.
> > > *Hel.*   *Yet* (*i.e.* for the present) I pray you ;
> > > But with the word the time will bring on summer," &c.
> > > > *A. W.* iv. 4. 30.

i.e. " a little longer I entreat your patience, but," &c.

Yet is also used in this sense without a distinct negative :

> " *Solan.* What news on the Rialto ?
> *Salar.* Why *yet* it lives there unchec̈k'd that Antonio," &c.
> > *M. of V.* iii. I. 1.

77. The adverbs **backward** and **inward** are used as nouns.

> "In the dark *backward* and abysm of time."—*Temp.* i. 2. 50.
> "I was an *inward* of his."—*M. for M.* iii. 2. 138.

So   " Thou losest *here* a better *where* to find."—*Lear*, i. 1. 264.
"Nor can there be that deity in my nature
  Of *here-and-everywhere.*"—*T. N.* v. 1. 235.

i.e. "the divine attribute of ubiquity."

Then, as with us, was used as an adjective.

"Our *then* dictator."—*Coriol.* ii. 2. 93.

So   "Good *sometime* queen."—*Rich. II.* v. 1. 37.
"Our *here* approach."—*Macb.* iv. 3. 133. See **Compounds.**

78. Adverbs after "is." We still say "that is *well;*" but, perhaps, no other adverb (except "soon") is now thus used. Shakespeare, however, has

"That's *verily.*"—*Tempest*, ii. 1. 321.
"That's *worthily.*"*—*Coriol.* iv. 1. 53.
"Lucius' banishment *was wrongfully.*"—*T. A.* iv. 4. 16.

Some verb, as "said" or "done," is easily understood. "In harbour" has the force of a verb in

" *Safely* in harbour
Is the king's ship."—*Tempest*, i. 2. 226.

ARTICLES.

79. An, A, (Early Eng. An, Ane, On, One, a, o,) our indefinite Article, is now distinguished from our Numeral "one." In Early English, as in modern French and German, there was no such distinction. Hence, even in Elizabethan English, *a* (since it still represented, or had only recently ceased to represent, "one") was more emphatic than with us, a fact which will explain its omission where we insert it, and its insertion where we should use some more emphatic word, "some," "any," "one," &c.

80. An and **one,** pronunciation of. The connection between "an" and "one" appears more obvious when it is remembered that "one" was probably pronounced by Shakespeare, not as now "won," but "un." This is made probable by the constant elision of "the" before "one" in "th' one" as in "th' other :" compare "th' one" in

" *Th' one* sweetly flatters, t' other feareth harm."—*R. of L.* 172.

---

* The verb "hear" may be supplied from the context.

So *Rich. II.* v. 2. 18. Ben Jonson (783) mentions as authorized contractions, "y'once" for "ye once" along with "y'utter." Compare also the pun in *T. G. of V.* ii. 1. 3 :

> "*Speed.* Sir, your glove.
> *Val.* Not mine; my gloves are *on*.
> *Speed.* Why, then, this may be yours, for this is but *one*."

This will explain the rhyme :

> "So thanks to all at once and to each *one*
> Whom we invite to see us crowned at Scone."
>
> *Macbeth*, v. 8. 74–5.

In the dialect of the North of England and of Scotland, the "w" is still not sounded.

"An" was always used in A.-S. and mostly in E.E. before consonants as well as vowels: "ane kinges . . . dohter" (STRATMANN). I have not found an instance in Shakespeare of "an" before an ordinary consonant, but it occurs before "w":

> "Have *an* wish but for't."—*P. of T.* iv. 4. 2.

81. A was used for *one* in such expressions as "He came with never *a* friend," &c.

> "He and his physicians are of *a* mind."—*A. W.* i. 3. 244.
> "'Fore God, they are both in *a* tale."—*M. Ado*, iv. 2. 33.
> "An two men ride of *a* horse one must ride behind."
>
> *Ib.* iii. 5. 44.
> "For in *a* night the best part of my power
> Were in the Washes . . . devoured."—*K. J.* v. 7. 64.

So "The Images were found in *a* night all hacked and hewed."

> *N. P.* 172.
> "We still have slept together,
> Rose at *an* instant, learn'd, play'd, eat together."
>
> *A. Y. L.* i. 3. 76.
> "Myself and a sister both born in *an* hour."—*T. N.* ii. 1. 20.
> "You, or any living man, may be drunk at *a* time, man."
>
> *Othello*, ii. 3. 319.

i.e. "at *one* time," "for once."

> "These foils have all *a* length."—*Hamlet*, v. 2. 277.

We find "one" and "a" interchanged in

> "Hear me *one* word :
> Beseech you, tribunes, hear me but *a* word."
>
> *Coriol.* iii. 1. 266.
> "But shall we wear these honours for a day?
> Or shall they last?"—*Rich. III.* iv. 2. 5.

We never use the possessive inflection of the unemphatic *one*
as an antecedent ; but Shakespeare writes :

" For taking *one's* part that is out of favour."—*Lear*, i. 4. 111.

We also find in Early English :

" Thre persones in *a* Godhede."—HALLIWELL.

where *a* is for *one*. Compare Scotch " ae" for " one."

It seems used for " any," i.e. *ane-y*, or *one-y*, in

"There's not *a* one of them."—*Macb.* iii. 4. 131.

"Ne'er *a* one to be found."—B. J. *E. in &c.* iii. 2.

So *Cymb.* i. 1. 24.

And emphatically for "some," "a certain," in

" There is *a* thing within my bosom tells me."

2 *Hen. IV.* iv. 1. 183.

' I should impart *a* thing to you from his majesty."

Hamlet, v. 2. 92.

" Shall I tell you *a* thing?"—*L. L. L.* v. 1. 152.

" I told you *a* thing yesterday."—*Tr. and Cr.* i. 2. 185.

" And I came to acquaint you with *a* matter."

A. Y. L. i. 1. 129.

82. A and The omitted in archaic poetry. In the infancy
of thought nouns are regarded as names, denoting not classes but
individuals. Hence the absence of any article before nouns.
Besides, as the articles interfere with the metre, and often supply
what may be well left to the imagination, there was additional
reason for omitting them. Hence Spenser, the archaic poet, writes

" Fayre Una—whom *salvage nation* does adore."

F. Q. i. 6. Title.

" And seizing *cruell clawes* on *trembling brest.*"—*Ib.* i. 3. 19.

" *Faire virgin*, to redeem her deare, brings Arthure to the
fight."—*Ib.* i. 8. Title.

" From *raging spoil* of *lawlesse victors* will."—*Ib.* i. 3. 43.

" With *thrilling point* of *deadly yron* brand."—*Ib.* i. 3. 42.

Shakespeare rarely indulges in this archaism except to ridicule it:

" Whereat *with blade*, with bloody blameful blade,
He bravely broached his boiling bloody breast ;
And Thisby, tarrying *in mulberry shade*,
His dagger drew and died."—*M. N. D.* v. 1. 147.

Somewhat similar is

" *In* glorious Christian *field.*"—*Rich. II.* iv. 1. 93.

" When *lion rough* in wildest rage doth roar."
M. N. D. v. 1. 224.

" Ah ! Richard with the eyes *of* (*my* or *the*) *heavy mind.*"
Rich. II. ii. 4. 18.

" So, *longest way* shall have the longest moans."
Ib. v. 1. 90.

In antitheses, as

" And with no less nobility of love
Than that which *dearest father* bears his son,"
Hamlet, i. 2. 111.

the omission of *the* is intelligible, since the whole class is expressed. But it appears not uncommon to omit the article before superlatives :

" *Best safety* lies in fear."—*Hamlet,* i. 3. 41.

This is, perhaps, explained by the double meaning of the superlative, which means not only " *the* best of the class," but also "very good." See 8.

83. A and **The** are also sometimes omitted after *as, like,* and *than* in comparative sentences :

" *As falcon* to the lure away she flies."—*V. and A.* 1027.

" The why is plain *as way* to parish church."
A. Y. L. ii. 7. 52.

" More tuneable *than lark* to shepherd's ear."
M. N. D. i. 1. 184.

This is, however, common both in early and modern English. In such sentences the whole class is expressed, and therefore the article omitted. It might be asked, however, why " *the* lure " on this hypothesis ? *The* is put for its. So in E. E. (MÄTZNER, iii. 195) " *ase hound* doth (chase) *the* hare," *i.e.* " *its* prey the hare."

A is still omitted by us in adverbial compounds, such as " snail-like," " clerk-like," &c. Then it was omitted as being unnecessarily emphatic in such expressions as :

" Creeping *like snail.*"—*A. Y. L.* ii. 7. 146.

" Sighing *like furnace.*"—*Ib.* 148.

" And *like* unletter'd *clerk.*"—*Sonn.* 85.

" Like snail " is an adverb in process of formation. It is intermediate between "like a snail" and "snail-like."

84. A being more emphatic than with us, was sometimes omitted where the noun stands for the class, and might almost be replaced by the corresponding adjective. " If ever I were *traitor,*" *Rich. II.* i. 3. 201 = traitorous. Similarly

' And having now shown himself open *enemy* to Alcibiades."
                                    N. *P.* 176.

So, though we find " never *a* master " in the sense of " not *one*
master," yet where the " never " is emphasized and has its proper
meaning, " at no time," the *a* is omitted :

"Those eyes which *never* shed remorseful tear."
                                    Rich. III. i. 2. 156.
" In war was *never* lion rag'd so fierce."—*Rich. II.* ii. 1. 173.
" *Never master* had a page so kind."—*Cymb.* v. 5. 85.
" Was *ever king* that joy'd an earthly throne."
                                    2 *Hen. VI.* iv. 9. 1.
" 'Twas *never* merry world since," &c.—*T. N.* iii. 1. 109.

On the other hand, in contrast to the example first quoted, when the
" never" is omitted and *an* is emphatic, almost like *one*, it is inserted :

' My manly eyes did scorn *an* humble tear."
                                    Rich. III. i. 2. 165.

A is also omitted before collective nouns, such as " plenty,"
" abundance," &c., and therefore before " great number " in

" Belike you slew *great number* of his people."—*T. N.* iii. 3. 29.

85. A inserted after some adjectives used as adverbs :

" It was upon this fashion bequeathed me by will but poor *a*
thousand pounds."—*A. Y. L.* i. 1. 2.

This usage is found in the earlier text of LAYAMON (A.D. 1200):
" *Long a* time (longe ane stunde)," ii. 290, &c., where the adjective
appears merely to be emphasized, and not used adverbially. In the
later text the adjective is placed, here and in other passages, in its
ordinary position. The adjectives " each," " such," " which,"
(used for " of what kind,") and " many" were especially often thus
used. " At *ich a* mel " = " at each meal," *Piers Plough. Crede.*
109. (So in Scotch " ilk*a*.") " *Whiche a* wife was Alceste,"
CHAUCER, *C. T.* 11754 = " *what a* wife." " On *moni are* (*later
text*, mani ane) wisen," LAYAMON, i. 24 ; "*monianes* cunnes," *ib.* 39 ;
" of *many a* kind (*l. t.* of *manian* erthe)," " of *many an* earth."

The last-quoted passages render untenable the theory (Archbishop Trench, *English Past and Present*) which explains "many
a man" as a corruption of " many of men." In these passages,
e.g. " moni *anes* cunnes" (" of many a race "), the article or numeral

ARTICLES. 61

adjective "an" is declined like an adjective, while "moni" is not.
The inference is, that "moni" is used adverbially. In the same
way the Germans say "mancher (adj.) mann," but "manch (adv.)
ein mann," "*ein* solcher (adj.) mann," but "solch (adv.) *ein* mann."
In A.-S. the idiom was "many man," not "many a man." The
termination in *y*, causing "many" to be considered as adverbially
used, may not perhaps account for the introduction of the *a* into
E. E., but it may account for its retention in Elizabethan and
modern English. Nor can it escape notice that most of the
adjectives which take *a* after them end in *ch*, or *lic* ("like"), an
adverbial termination. So beside the adjectives enumerated above,
"thellich" (modern Dorsetshire, "thilk" or "thick"), "the like,"
answering to "whilk" ("which"), is followed by *a*. So after the
adverb "ofte," we have "a day" in

"Ful *ofte* a day he swelde and seyde alas!"

CHAUCER, *Knighte's Tale*, 498.

It is perhaps some such feeling, that "many" means "often," which
justifies the separation of "many" and "a" in the following:

"I have in vain said *many*
A prayer upon her grave."—*W. T.* v. 3. 144.

Perhaps in this way (as an adjective used adverbially) we must
explain (compare "*none* (adj.) inheritance," *Acts* vii. 5):

"Exceeding pleasant; *none* (adv.) *a* stranger there
So merry and so gamesome."—*Cymb.* i. 6. 59.

like "ne'er a stranger," unless after "none" we supply "who
was."

A is pleonastically used in

"I would not spend *an*other such *a* night."—*R. III.* i. 4. 5.

In "What poor *an* instrument" (*A. and C.* v. 2. 236), "what"
is used for "how."

86. A was sometimes omitted after "what," in the sense of
"what kind of."

"Cassius, what night is this?"—*J. C.* i. 3. 42.

(*A* has been unnecessarily inserted by some commentators.)

"I'll tell the world
Aloud *what* man thou art."—*M. for M.* ii. 4. 153.

"Jove knows *what* man thou mightst have made."

Cymb. iv. 2. 207.

" *What* dreadful noise of waters in mine ears."
Rich. III. i. 4. 22.

" *What* case stand I in? " (*W. T.* i. 2. 352) = In what *a*
position am I ?
" *What* thing it is that I never
Did see man die ! "—*Cymb.* iv. 4. 35.

We omit the article after " what " before nouns signifying a collective class, saying " what wickedness ! " but " what *a* crime ! "
" what fruit ! " but " what *an* apple! " Hence the distinction in the
following : " *What a* merit were it in death to take this poor maid
from the world ! *What* corruption in this life that it will let this
man live ! "—*M. for M.* iii. 1. 240.

A is omitted after " such :"
" Showers of blood,
The which, how far off from the mind of Bolingbroke
It is *such* crimson tempest should bedrench," &c.
Rich. II. iii. 3. 46.

Here " such " probably means " the aforesaid," referring to the
" showers of blood."

After " such " in this sense the indefinite article is still omitted ;
naturally, since " such " is used in a defining sense.

A is omitted after " many" in " *Many* time and oft " (2 *Hen. VI.*
ii. 1. 93). Here " many-time," like " some-time," " often-times,"
" many-times" (MONTAIGNE, *Introduction*), seems used as one word
adverbially.

A is omitted before " little," where we commonly place it in the
sense of " some:"
" O, do not swear ;
Hold (*a*) *little* faith, though thou hast too much fear."
T. N. v. 1. 174.

It is perhaps caused by the antithesis which assimilates the use of
" little " to the use of " much." " In (a) *little* time " (*V. and A.*
132) is to be explained as a prepositional phrase approximating to
an adverb : see 89.

87. A was frequently inserted before a numeral adjective, for the
purpose of indicating that the objects enumerated are regarded
collectively as *one.* We still say " a score," " a fo(u)rt(een)-night."
But we also find :

" *An* eight days after these sayings."—*Luke* ix. 28.

" *A* two shilling or so."—B. J. *E. in &c.* i. 4 *ad fin.*

"'Tis now *a* nineteen years agone at least."—B. J. *Case is altered.*

Also in E. E. :

" *An* five mile."—HALLIWELL.

This usage is not common in Shakespeare, except after "one."

" But *one* seven *years.*"—*Coriol.* iv. 1. 55.

The *a* is omitted in

" But this our purpose now is *twelve-month* old."
1 *Hen. IV.* i. 1. 28.

Compare " *This three mile.*"—*Macbeth*, v. 5. 37.

The *a* in " *a* many men," " *a* few men," is perhaps thus to be explained. Compare " *This* nineteen *years* " (*M. for M.* i. 3. 21), with " *This* many *summers* " (*Hen. VIII.* iii. 2. 360). So

" *A many* merry men."—*A. Y. L.* i. 1. 121.
" *A many* thousand warlike French."—*K. J.* iv. 2. 199.

So *Hen. V.* iv. 1. 127; iv. 3. 95. And still more curiously :

" But *many a many foot* of land the worse."—*K. J.* i. 1. 183.

Some explain " *a* many " by reference to the old noun " many," " *a* many men," for " *a* many (of) men." And the word is thus used :

" *A many* of our bodies."—*Hen. V.* iv. 3. 95.
" O thou fond *many*, with what loud applause
Didst thou beat heaven."—2 *Hen. IV.* i. 3. 91.
" In *many's* looks."—*Sonn.* 93.

So perhaps *A. W.* iv. 5. 55. Add "their *meiny*," *Lear*, ii. 4. 35.

Nor can it be denied that in E. E. " of " is often omitted in such phrases as " many manner (of) men," " a pair (of) gloves," &c. just as in German we have " diese Art Mensch." But we also say " *a* few men" (an expression that occurs as early as Robert of Brunne), and "few " seems to have been an adjective.

It is probable that both the constructions above-mentioned are required to explain this use of *a*. Thus " *a* hundred men" is for " *a* hundred (of) men," but in " *a* twelvemonth," " *a* fortnight," "twelve" and "fourteen" are not regarded as simple nouns, but as compound nouns used adjectively. Compare the double use of " mille," " millia," in Latin.

88. An-other. A is apparently put for *the* in

"There is not half a kiss to choose who loves *an* other best."
W. T. iv. 4. 176.

This is, however, in accordance with our common idiom : "they love one an other," which ought strictly to be either "they love, the one the other," or "they love, one other." The latter form is still retained in "they love each other;" but as in "one other" there is great ambiguity, it was avoided by the insertion of a second "one" or "an," thus, "they love one an-other." This is illustrated by *Matt.* xxiv. 10 (TYNDALE) : "And shall betraye *one an*other and shall hate *one the* other;" whereas WICKLIFFE has, "ech other." So 1 *Cor.* xii. 25 : WICKLIFFE, "ech for other;" the rest "for one another." "One another" is now treated almost like a single noun in prepositional phrases, such as, "We speak to one another." But Shakespeare retains a trace of the original idiom in

"What we speak *one to an other.*"—*A. W.* iv. 1. 20.

89. The was frequently omitted before a noun already defined by another noun, especially in prepositional phrases.

"*In number* of our friends."—*J. C.* iii. 1. 216.
"*Since death of* my dearest mother."—*Cymb.* iv. 2. 190.
"*At heel of* that defy him."—*A. and C.* ii. 2. 160.
"*In absence of* thy friend."—*T. G. of V.* i. 1. 59.
"*To sternage of* their navy."—*Hen. V.* iii. Prol. 18.
"*To relief of* lazars."—*Ib.* i. 1. 15.
"*For honour of* our land."—*Ib.* iii. 5. 22.
"Thy beauty's form *in table of* my heart."—*Sonn.* 24.
"Some beauty peep'd *through lattice of* sear'd age."
L. C. st. ii.
"Forage *in blood of* French nobility."—*Hen. V.* i. 2. 110.
"*In cradle of* the rude imperious surge."—*2 Hen. IV.* iii. 1. 20.
"Proving *from* world's *minority* their right."—*R. of L.*
"On *most* part of their fleet."—*Othello,* ii. 1. 24.

So 1 *Hen. VI.* i. 2. 77 ; 2 *Hen. VI.* i. 2. 36, 79; *Rich. II.* i. 3. 136. We could say "in season," but not

"We *at* (the right) time of (the) year
Do wound the bark."—*Rich. II.* iii. 4. 57.

So even in Pope :

"Alas, young man, your days can ne'er be long ;
In *flower* of age you perish for a song."
POPE, *Imit. Hor.* i. 102.

90. The is also omitted after prepositions in adverbial phrases.

> " *At door.*"—*W. T.* iv. 4. 352 ; *T. of Sh.* iv. 1. 125.
> " *At palace.*"—*W. T.* iv. 4. 731.
> " *At height.*"—*Hamlet,* i. 4. 21.
> " Ere I went *to wars.*"—*M. Ado,* i. 1. 307.
> " *To cabin.*"—*Tempest,* i. 1. 17.
> " The grace 'fore meat and the thanks *at end.*"
> > *Coriol.* iv. 7. 4.
> " You were *in presence* then."—*Rich. II.* iv. 1. 62.

i.e. "in the presence-chamber."

> " And milk comes frozen home *in pail.*"—*L. L. L.* v. 2. 925.
> " With spectacles *on nose* and pouch *on side.*"
> > *A. Y. L.* ii. 7. 159.
> " This day was viewed *in open* as his queen."
> > *Hen. VIII.* iii. 2. 405.
> " He foam'd *at mouth.*"—*J. C.* i. 2. 256.
> " Sticks me *at heart.*"—*A. Y. L.* i. 2. 254.
> " Exeunt *in manner* as they entered."—*Ib.* ii. 4. 242.
> " Than pard or cat-*o'-mountain.*"—*Tempest,* iv. 1. 262.

And with adjectives :

> " *In humblest* manner."—*Tempest.* ii. 4. 144.
> " *In first* rank."—*Tr. and Cr.* iii. 3. 161.

" In pail " is as justifiable as " in bed," except that the former, not being so common as the latter, has not the same claim to the adverbial brevity which dispensed with the article. Both are adverbial phrases, one of which has been accepted, the other rejected. Thus in

> " Stealing unseen *to west* with this disgrace."—*Sonn.* 33.

" to-west " is as much an adverb as " west-ward."

Sometimes a possessive adjective is thus omitted :

> " Not Priamus and Hecuba *on knees.*"—*Tr. and Cr.* v. 3. 53.

So in E. E. "a-knee."
Compare our " I have *at hand.*"
Perhaps this may explain the omission of " the " after " at " in

> " We are familiar *at first.*"—*Cymb.* i. 4. 112.

where " at first " is not opposed to " afterwards " (as it is with us), but means " at *the* first," or rather " from *the* first," " at once."

The omission of " the " in

> " On *one* and *other* side Trojan and Greek
> Sets all on hazard."—*Tr. and Cr.* i. i. 21.

is in accordance with our idiom, " one another " and " each other. "

On the other hand, where " the " is emphatic, meaning " that " or " the right," it is sometimes inserted before " one."

> " *Morocco.* How shall I know if I do choose the right ? "
> *Portia.* *The* one of them contains my picture, prince."
> *M. of V.* ii. 7. 11.

91. The was inserted in a few phrases which had not, though they now have, become adverbial. " At the length " (N. *P.* 592), " At the first," " At the last," &c.

> " There in *the* full convive we."—*Tr. and Cr.* iv. 5. 272.
> " In *the* favour of the Athenians."—N. *P.* 177.

92. The used to denote notoriety, &c. Any word when referred to as being defined and well known may of course be preceded by the article. Thus we frequently speak of " *the* air." Bacon (*E.* 231) however wrote, " *The* matter (the substance called matter) is in a perpetual flux."

The is sometimes used (compare Latin " ille ") for " *the* celebrated," " *the* one above all others," occasionally with " alone," as

> " I am *alone the* villain of the earth."—*A. and C.* iv. 6. 30.

Or with a superlative :

> " He was *the wretched'st* thing when he was young."
> *Rich. III.* ii. 4. 18.
> " The last (prayer) is for my men : they are *the poorest ;*
> But poverty could never draw 'em from me."
> *Hen. VIII.* iv. 2. 148.

But also without these :

> " Am I *the* man yet ? "—*A. Y. L.* iii. 3. 3.
> " Smacks it not something of *the* policy ? "—*K. J.* ii. 1. 396.
> " For their dear causes
> Would to *the* bleeding and *the* grim alarm
> Excite the mortified man."—*Macbeth,* v. 2. 4.

The ellipsis to be supplied is added in

> " Are you *the* courtiers and *the* travell'd gallants ?
> *The* spritely fellows *that the people talk of ?* "
> B. and F. *Elder Brother,* iv. 1.

The seems to mean "the same as ever" in

"Live you *the* marble-breasted tyrant still."—*T. N.* v. 1. 127.

It is not often that "the" is used in this sense before English proper names. In

"The Douglas and *the* Percy both together."

1 *Hen. IV.* v. 1. 116.

the second *the* may be caused by the first, which, of course, is still used, "*the* Bruce," "*the* Douglas," being frequent, and explicable as referring to *the chief of the Douglases and Bruces.* But we also have

"To leave *the* Talbot and to follow us."—1 *Hen. VI.* iii. 3. 20, 31.

and so in Early English "the Brute," "the Herod."

The is seldom used, like the article in French, for the possessive adjective:

'The king is angry: see, he bites *the* lip."

Rich. III. iv. 2. 27.

The word "better" is used as a noun, and opposed to "the worse," (compare the French proverb, "le mieux est l'ennemi du bien,") in

"Bad news, by'r lady; seldom comes *the* better."

Rich. III. ii. 3. 4.

"Death," the ender of life, seems more liable to retain the mark of notoriety than "life." Hence

"Where they feared *the death*, they have borne *life* away."

Hen. V. iv. 1. 81; *Rich. III.* i. 2. 179; ii. 3. 55.

So "Dar'd to *the* combat."—*Hamlet*, i. 1. 84.

i.e. "the combat that ends all dispute." French influence is perceptible in these two last instances, and in

"To shake *the* head."—*M. of V.* iii. 2. 15.

The which (see Relative), 270.

93. The frequently precedes a verbal that is followed by an object:

"Whose state so many had *the* managing."—*Hen. V.* Epilog.

"You need not fear *the* having any of these lords."

M. of V. i. 2. 109.

"*The* seeing these effects will be
Both noisome and infectious."—*Cymb.* i. 5. 25.

"*P.* Pray, sir, in what?
D. In *the* delaying death."—*M. for M.* iv. 2. 172.
　　"Nothing in his life
Became him like *the* leaving it."—*Macb.* i. 4. 8.
"*The* locking up the spirits."—*Cymb.* i. 5. 41.

So *Lear*, iv. 4. 9 ; *Hen. VIII.* iii. 2. 347 ; *M. for M.* iii. 2. 126 ;
M. of V. iv. 1. 309 ; *M. Ado*, ii. 2. 53 ; *O.* iii. 4. 22 ; *T. N.* i. 5. 84.

The question naturally arises, are these verbals, "locking," &c.
nouns? and, if so, why are they not followed by "of,"—*e.g.* "the
locking *of* the spirits"? Or are they parts of verbs? and in that
case, why are they preceded by the article? The fact that a verb in
E. E. had an abstract noun in -*ing* (A.-S. -*ung*)—*e.g.* "slaeten," to
hunt ; "slaeting," hunting—renders it *a priori* probable that these
words in -*ing* are nouns. Very early, however, the termination -*ng*
was confused with, and finally supplanted, the present participle
termination in -*nde*. Thus in the earlier text of Layamon (iii. 72)
we have "heo riden *singinge*," *i.e.* "they rode *singing* ;" and in the
later text the proper participial form "*singende*." An additional
element of confusion was introduced by the gerundial inflection *enne*,
e.g. "singenne," used after the preposition "to." As early as the
twelfth century "to singenne" (Morris, *E. E. Specimens*, p. 53)
became "to singende," and hence (by the corruption above mentioned) "to singinge." Hence, when Layamon writes that the
king went out "an-slaeting" (ii. 88), or "a-slatinge" (iii. 168), it is
not easy to prove that the verbal *noun* is here used : for the form
may represent the corruption of the gerund used with the preposition
"an" instead of with "to." And as early as Layamon we find the
infinitive "to kumen" side by side with the present participle "to
comende" (i. 49) ; and the gerund "cumene" side by side with the
verbal "coming" (iii. 231) ; and the noun "tiding(s)" spelt in the
earlier text "tidind" or "tidinde," the present participle (i. 59).
The conclusion is, that although "locking" is a noun, and therefore
preceded by "the," yet it is so far confused with the gerund as to
be allowed the privilege of governing a direct object. The "of"
was omitted partly for shortness, as well as owing to the confusion
above mentioned.
　It is easy to trace a process of abridgment from

　　"For *the* repealing *of* my banish'd brother,"—*J. C.* iii. 1. 51.

to (2) " Punish my life for (89) tainting *of* my love,"

T. N. v. 1. 141.

down to our modern (3) "for tainting my love." And hence the E. E. (William of Palerne, edit. Skeat), "for drede of descuverynge *of* that was do," l. 1024, "of kastyng *of* lokes," l. 942, are abbreviated in modern English into "disclosing that which was done" and "casting looks." This abbreviation is also remarkably illustrated by Bacon in his third Essay. He first uses the abbreviated form, and then, with a verbal noun that could not so easily have a verbal force, he adopts the full form : "Concerning the Means of *procuring Unity*. Men must beware that in *the Procuring or Muniting of Religious Unity*, they do not dissolve and deface the Laws of Charity." It is perhaps this feeling that the verbal was an ordinary noun, which allows Shakespeare to make an adjective qualify it even though *of* is omitted after it.

"He shall have *old turning* the key."—*Macbeth*, ii. 3. 2.

The substantival use of the verbal with "the" before it and "of" after it seems to have been regarded as colloquial. Shakespeare puts into the mouth of Touchstone :

"I remember *the kissing of* her batlet and . . . *the wooing of* a peascod instead of her."—*A. Y. L.* ii. 4. 49–51.

"Did these bones cost no more (in) *the* breeding?"

Hamlet, v. 1. 100.

94. The (in Early Eng. *thi, thy*) is used as the ablative of the demonstrative and relative, with comparatives to signify the measure of excess or defect.

This use is still retained. " *The* sooner *the* better," *i.e.* "*By how much* the sooner *by so much* the better." (Lat. "*quo citius, eo* melius.")

It is sometimes stated that "the better" is used by Shakespeare for " better," &c.: but it will often, perhaps always, be found that *the* has a certain force.

"The good conceit I hold of thee
Makes me *the* better to confer with thee."— *T. G. of V.* iii. 2. 19.

" *The* rather
For that I saw."—*Macb.* iv. 3. 184.

In both passages "the" means "on that account." In

" Go not my horse *the* better
I must become a borrower of the night,"—*Macb.* iii. 1. 25.

Banquo is perhaps regarding his horse as racing against night, and

" *the* better " means " *the* better of the two." The following passage has been quoted by commentators on the passage just quoted,
to show that "the" is redundant. " And hee that hit it (the
quintain) full, if he rid not *the faster*, had a sound blow in his
neck, with a bag full of sand hanged on the other end."—STOWE'S
Survey of London, 1603. But the rider is perhaps here described
as endeavouring to anticipate the blow of the quintain by being
" *the* faster " *of the two.* Or more probably, " *the* faster " may
mean *the* faster *because* he had struck the quintain, which, if struck,
used to swing round and strike the striker on the back, unless he
rode *the* ("on that account ") *faster.* In either case it is unscholar-
like to say that *the* is redundant.

CONJUNCTIONS.

95. And (in old Swedish *æn* [Wedgewood] is used for "and,"
"if," and "even") emphatically used for "also," "even," "and
that too." We still use "and that" to give emphasis and call
attention to an additional circumstance, *e.g.* "He was condemned,
and that unheard." This construction is most common in participial phrases. The "that " is logically unnecessary, and is omitted
by Shakespeare.

" Suffer us to famish *and* their storehouses crammed with grain."
—*Coriol.* i. 1. 82.

> " And shall the figure of God's majesty
> Be judged by subject and inferior breath,
> *And* he himself not present ?"—*Rich. II.* iv. 1. 129.

> "When I have most need to employ a friend,
> *And* most assured that he is a friend,
> Deep, hollow, treacherous, and full of guile
> Be he unto me."—*Rich. III.* ii. 1. 37.

In the last two passages an ellipsis of "be" or "to be" might be
understood, but scarcely in the following :

> ' So may he ever do and ever flourish
> When I shall dwell with worms, *and* my poor name
> Banish'd the kingdom."—*Hen. VIII.* iv. 2. 126.

> " The friends thou hast, *and* their adoption tried,
> Grapple them to the soul with hoops of steel."
> > *Hamlet.* i. 3. 62.

Compare 3 *Hen. VI.* i. 2. 47 ; *Tr. and Cr.* i. 3. 51.

So perhaps *Hamlet*, iii. 3. 62; *T. N.* i. 1. 38; and in the following irregular sentence :

"But a man that were to sleep your sleep, *and* a hangman to help him to bed, I think he (redundant pronoun : see 243) would change places with his officer."—*Cymb.* v. 4. 179.

i.e. "*and* that too a hangman being ready to help him to bed."

96. And. This use, though most frequent with participles, is also found without them :

"Here comes a spirit of his, *and* to torment me."
Temp. ii. 2. 15.
"He that has *and* a little tiny wit."—*Lear*, iii. 2. 74.

i.e. "a little and *that* a very little." So

"When that I was *and* a little tiny boy."—*T. N.* v. 1. 398.

97. And is frequently found in answers in the sense of "you are right and" or "yes and," the "yes" being implied.* Hence the "and," introducing a statement in *exact* conformity with a previous statement, comes almost to mean "exactly." It is frequently found before "so."

"*Hamlet.* Will the king hear this *piece of* work ?
Pol. (Yes) *And* the queen too."—*Hamlet*, iii. 2. 53.
"*Cass.* This rudeness is a sauce to his good wit.
Brut. And so it is."—*J. C.* i. 2. 307.

i.e. "you are right, *and* so it is ;" or "just so," "even so."

"*Pompey.* I'll try you on the shore.
Antony. And shall, sir."—*A. and C.* ii. 7. 134.

i.e. "You say well, *and* you shall," or "So you shall," "that you shall," emphatically.

"*Sir M.* And there's . . . a head of noble gentlemen.
Archbishop. And so there is."—1 *Hen. IV.* iv. 4. 27.
"*Parolles.* After them, and take a more dilated farewell.
Bertram. And I will do so."—*A. W.* ii. 1. 60.

i.e. "that is *just* what I will do."

"*Mayor.* But I'll acquaint our duteous citizens
With all your just proceedings in this cause.
Glouc. And to that end we wish'd your lordship here."
Rich. III. iii. 4. 67.

i.c. "To that very end," "even to that end."

---

* So γάρ in Greek.

98. And is often found in this emphatic sense after statements implied by ejaculations, such as "faith," "sooth," "alas," &c. Thus

> " *Catesby.* Your friends at Pomfret, they do need the priest.
> *Hastings.* Good faith (it is so), *and* when I met this holy man
> Those men you talk of came into my mind."
>
> Rich. III. iii. 2. 117.

> " Faith, *and* so we should."—1 *Hen. IV.* iv. 1. 52.

This use is found in A.-S.

99. "And" emphatic in questions. When a question is being asked, "and," thus used, does not express emphatic assent, but emphatic interrogation :

> "Alas ! *and* would you take the letter of her ?"—*A. W.* iii. 4. 1.

i.e. "is it so indeed, and further would you *actually* &c.?" So

> "*And* wilt thou learn of me ?"—*Rich. III.* iv. 4. 269.

i.e. "do you indeed wish to learn of me ?"

Hence Ben Jonson, who quotes Chaucer :

> "What, quoth she, *and* be ye wood?"

adds that

> "*And*, in the beginning of a sentence, serveth for admiration."—B. J. 789.

It is common in ballads, and very nearly redundant :

> " The Perse owt of Northumberlande,
> *And* a vow to God made he."—*Percy* (MÄTZNER).

(Mr. Furnivall suggests "an *avow*," the original form of the word "vow.")

100. "And" for "also" in Early English. We find "and" often used for "also," "both," &c., and standing at the beginning of a sentence in earlier English. Wickliffe has, 2 *Cor.* xi. 21, 22 :

> "In what thing ony man dare, *and* I dare. Thei ben ebreus, *and* I."

"And" is used for "even" or "also" in *Acts* xiv. 15 :

> "*And* we ben deedli men like you."

In "I almost die for food, *and* let me have it,"

A. Y. L. ii. 7. 104.

"I pray you" may perhaps be understood after *and*, implied in the imperative "let."

101. And or **an** (= if). (The modern *and* is often spelt *an* in E. E.) This particle has been derived from *an*, the imperative of *unnan*, to grant. This plausible but false derivation was originated by Horne Tooke, and has been adopted by the editors of the Cambridge Shakespeare. But the word is often written *and* in Early English (Stratmann), as well as in Elizabethan authors.*

"For *and* I shulde rekene every vice
Which that she hath ywiss, I were to nice."—CHAUC. *Squire's Prol.*

"Alcibiades bade the carter drive over, *and* he durst."—N.P. 166.

"They will set an house on fire *and* it were but to roast their eggs."—B. *E.* 89.

"What knowledge should we have of ancient things past *and* history were not?"—Lord BERNERS, quoted by B. J. 789.

102. "And" with the subjunctive. The true explanation appears to be that the hypothesis, the *if*, is expressed not by the *and*, but by the subjunctive, and that *and* merely means *with the addition of, plus*, just as *but* means *leaving out*, or *minus*.

The hypothesis is expressed by the simple subjunctive thus:

"*Go* not my horse the better
I must become a borrower of the night."—*Macb.* iii. 1. 25.

This sentence with *and* would become, "I must become a borrower of the night *and* my horse go not the better," *i.e.* "*with*, or on, *the supposition* that my horse go not the better." Similarly in the contrary sense, "*but* my horse go the better," would mean "*without or excepting the supposition* that my horse, &c." Thus Chaucer, *Pardonere's Tale*, 275:

"It is no curtesye
To speke unto an old man vilonye
But he trespas."

So also Mandeville (*Prologue*):

"Such fruyt, thorgh the which every man is saved, *but* it be his owne defaute."

103. And if. Latterly the subjunctive, falling into disuse, was felt to be too weak unaided to express the hypothesis; and the same tendency which introduced "more better," "most unkindest," &c., superseded *and* by *and if*, *an if*, and *if*. There is nothing remarkable in the change of *and* into *an*. *And*, even in its ordinary sense, is often written *an* in Early English. (See Halliwell.)

* So almost always in the Folio. See Index to Plays.

And or *an* is generally found before a personal pronoun, or "if," or "though ;" rarely thus :

"*And* * should the empress know."—*T. A.* ii. 1. 69.

In the Elizabethan times the indicative is often used for the subjunctive.

The following is a curious passage :—

"*O.* Will it please you to enter the house, gentlemen?
D. And your favour, lady." —B. J. *Sil. Wom.* iii. 2. med.

Apparently, "*And* your favour (be with us)," *i.e.* "if you please."

104. An't were was wrongly said by Horne Tooke to be put for "as if it were."

"*Cress.* O ! he smiles valiantly.
Pand.   Does he not ?
Cress. O yes ; *and* * 'twere a cloud in autumn."
                    Tr. and Cr. i. 2. 139.

"He will weep you *an't* were a man born in April."
                    Ib. i. 2. 189.

"I will roar you *and* * 'twere any nightingale."—*M. N. D.* i. 2. 86.

"'A made a fairer end and went away, *and* * *it* had been a Christom child."—*Hen. V.* ii. 3. 10.

Some ellipsis is probably to be understood. "I will roar you, *and* if it were a nightingale (I would still roar better)."

The same construction is found in E. E.

"Ye answer *and* ye were twenty yere olde."
                    Cov. Myst. p. 80 (MÄTZNER).

It is illustrated by the use of "ac," "atque," after "similis," "pariter," &c. thus :

"(Homo) qui prosperis rebus æque *ac* tu ipse (gauderes) gauderet."—CIC. *De Amicitia,* vi. 1.

i.e. "a man who would rejoice at your prosperity, *and* you yourself (would rejoice as much and no more)." "You answer in such and such a way, *and* were you twenty years old you would answer similarly."

105. And if represents both "even if" and "if indeed" (*i.c.* both καὶ εἰ and εἰ καί).

And if is used emphatically for "even if" in

"It dies *and* * *if* it had a thousand lives."— 1 *Hen. VI.* v. 4. 75.

So 1 *Hen. IV.* i. 3. 125.

* So Folio.

> "What *and* * *if*
His sorrows have so overwhelm'd his wits." —*Tit. And.* iv. 4. 10.

"He seems to be of great authority, give him gold. *And* though authority be a stubborn bear, yet he is oft led by the nose with gold."—*W. T.* iv. 4. 831.

On the other hand, *and if* seems to mean "if indeed" in the following passages:—

> "*Percy.* Seize it if thou darest.
> *Aum. And* * *if* I do not, may my hands rot off!"
> > *Rich. II.* iv. 1. 49.

> "Oh father!
> *And if* you be my father, think upon
> Don John my husband."—MIDDLETON *and* ROWLEY (Walker).

> "*Prince.* I fear no uncles dead (419).
> *Glou.*   Nor none that live, I hope.
> *Prince. And* * if they live, I hope I need not fear,"
> > *Rich. III.* iii. 2. 148,

where the Prince is referring to his maternal uncles who have been imprisoned by Richard, and he says, "*if indeed* they live I need not fear."

Thus probably we must explain:

> "O full of danger is the duke of Gloucester!
> And the queen's sons and brothers haught and proud;
> *And* were they to be ruled, and not to rule,
> This sickly land might solace as before."—*Rich. III.* ii. 3. 29.

Here, at first sight, "but" seems required instead of "and." But "*and* were they" means "*if indeed* they were."

It is not easy to determine whether *and though* is used for "even though" or for "though indeed" in the following—

> "I have now
> (*And* though perhaps it may appear a trifle)
> Serious employment for thee."—MASSINGER (Walker).

In all these passages *an* or *and* may be resolved into its proper meaning by supplying an ellipsis. Thus in the passage from *Rich. II.* iv. 1. 49, "*And* if I do not," &c. means, "I will seize it, *and*, if I do not seize it, may my hands rot off."

106. As† (A.-S. "*eall-swa*," with the sense "just *as*") is a contraction of *al(l)-so.* In Early English we find "*so* soon *so* he came." The *al(l)* emphasized the *so*, "*al(l)-so* soon *al(l)-so* he

---

* So Folio.   † Comp. ὡς, ὥστε, for the various meanings.

came." Hence through different contractions, *alse, als, ase,* we get
our modern *as.* (Comp. the German *als.*) The dropping of the
l is very natural if *alse* was pronounced like "half." The broad
pronunciation of *as* may throw light upon the pun in

> "*Sir And.* And your horse now would make him an ass.
> *Mar. Ass* I doubt not."—*T. N.* ii. 3. 185.

It follows that *as* originally meant both our modern *so,* "in that
way," and our modern *as,* "in which way." The meaning of *so*
is still retained in the phrases "*as* soon as" and "I thought *as*
much," &c., but generally *as* has its second meaning, viz. "in
which way."

107. As, like "an" (102), appears to be (though it is not) used
by Shakespeare for *as if.* As above (102), the "if" is implied in
the subjunctive.

> "To throw away the dearest thing he owed
> *As* 'twere a careless trifle."—*Macb.* i. 4. 11.   So v. 5. 13.

i.e. "*in the way in which* (he would throw it away) were it a
careless trifle." Often the subjunctive is not represented by any
inflection :

> "One cried, 'God bless us,' and 'Amen' the other,
> *As* they had seen me with these hangman's hands."
> *Macbeth,* ii. 1. 28 ; *Rich. III.* iii. 5. 63.

Sometimes the *as* is not followed by a finite verb :

> "As gentle and as jocund *as* (if I were going) to jest,
> Go I to fight."—*Rich. II.* i. 3. 95.

108. As, like "who," "whom," "which" (see below, **Relative**),
is occasionally followed by the supplementary "that."

> "Who fair him 'quited *as that* courteous was."
> Spens. *F. Q.* i. 1. 30.

109. As for "that" after "so." ("In which way;" "As the
result of which.") This is a consequence of the original connection
of *as* with "so."

> "You shall be so received
> *As* you shall deem yourself lodged in my heart."
> *L. L. L.* ii. 1. 174.

> "Catesby . . . finds the testy gentleman so hot
> *As* he will lose his head ere give consent."
> *Rich. III.* iii. 4. 41.

After "*such :*"

> "Yet *such* deceit *as* thou that dost beguile
> Art juster far."—*Sonn.*

This occurs less commonly without the antecedent *so :*

> "My lord, I warrant you we'll play our part
> *As* he shall think by our true diligence
> He is no less than what we say he is."—*T. of Sh.* Ind. i. 68.

This points out an important difference between the Elizabethan and modern uses of *as.* We almost always apply it, like "because" (117), to the past and the present; Shakespeare often uses it of the future, in the sense of "according *as.*"

> "And, sister, *as* the winds give benefit
> And convoy is assistant, do not sleep,
> But let me hear from you."—*Hamlet*, i. 3. 2.

Here a modern reader would at first naturally suppose *as* to mean "since" or "because;" but the context shows that it means "according *as.*"

110. As, in its demonstrative meaning of *so,* is occasionally found parenthetically = "for *so.*"

> "This Jacob from our holy Abraham was
> (*As* * his wise mother wrought in his behalf)
> The third possessor."—*M. of V.* i. 3. 73.

> "Who dares receive it other—
> *As* we shall make our griefs and clamours roar
> Upon his death?"—*Macb.* i. 7. 78.

i.e. "*so* did his mother work;" "*so* will we make our griefs roar."

> "The fixure of her eye has motion in 't,
> *As* we are mock'd with art."—*W. T.* v. 3. 68.

There seems some confusion in the difficult passage

> "Speak truly, on thy knighthood and thy oath,
> *As* so defend thee heaven and thy valour."
> *Rich. II.* i. 3. 15.

In the similar line 34 *as* is omitted. This would lead us to conjecture "and." But perhaps the marshal was beginning to say "speak truly *as* may heaven defend thee," but diverged into the more ordinary "so," which was the customary mode of invocation. In that case the meaning will be "*as* thou wouldst desire the fulfilment of thy prayer, 'so help me heaven.'"

* Comp. οἶον ἐξαρτύεται γάμον γαμεῖν.—ÆSCH. *Prom. Vinct.* 908.

So in

> "*Duke.* If this be so (*as*, yet, the glass seems true)
> I shall have share in this most happy wreck."
>
> > *T. N.* v. 1. 272.

The Duke has called the appearance of the twins "a natural perspective that is and is not" (*ib.* 224), *i.e.* a *glass* that produces an optical delusion of two persons instead of one. He now says: "it they are two, brother and sister (*and indeed*, spite of my incredulity, the perspective or glass seems to be no delusion), then I shall," &c. The curious introduction of the "wreck" suggests that the *glass* called up the thought of the "pilot's glass." (*M. for M.* ii. 1. 168.)

An ellipsis must be supplied in

> "Had I but time (which I have not)—*as* this fell sergeant,
> Death,
> Is strict in his arrest."—*Hamlet*, v. 2. 347.

111. As = "as regards which," "though," "for," was sometimes used parenthetically in a sense oscillating between the relative "which," "as regards which," and the conjunction "for," "though," "since." It is used as a relative in

> "But say or he or we, (*as* neither have [pl. see **12, Neither**],)
> Received that sum."—*L. L. L.* ii. 1. 133.

As is used in a transitional manner for "as regards which" or "for indeed," in

> "Though I die for it, *as* no less is threatened me."
>
> > *Lear*, iii. 3. 19.
>
> "When I was young, *as*, yet, I am not old."
>
> > 1 *Hen. VI.* iv. 4. 17.
>
> > "If you will patch a quarrel
> *As* matter whole you've not to make it with."
>
> > *A. and C.* ii. 1. 53.

Here in the second example, "When I was young *as* I yct, or still, am," would have retained the relatival signification of *as*, but the addition of "not old" obliges us to give to *as* the meaning not of "which," but "as regards which" or "for."   So in

> "She dying, *as* it must be so maintained."
>
> > *M. Ado*, iv. 1. 216.

112. As, owing to its relatival signification, is sometimes loosely used for "which."   This is still usual with us, but rarely except when preceded by "such" or "the same."

" *That* gentleness *as* I was wont to have."—*J. C.* i. 2. 33.
" Under *these* hard conditions *as* this time
  Is like to lay upon us."—*J. C.* i. 2. 174.

This is still common in provincial language.   See 280.
  As is used for " where " in

" Here *as* I point my sword the sun arises."—*J. C.* ii. 1. 106.

113. As is frequently used (without *such*) to signify " namely :"

" And that which should accompany old age,
  As honour, love, obedience, troops of friends."
                                    Macb. v. 3. 25.
" Tired with all these for restful death I cry,
  As to behold desert a beggar born
  And needy nothing trimm'd in jollity
  And, &c."—*Sonn.* 66.

So *C. of E.* i. 2. 98; *Hen. VIII.* iv. 1. 88; *M. of V.* iii. 2. 109.

" Two Cliffords, *as* the father and the son."
                                    3 *Hen. VI.* v. 7. 7.

So *A. Y. L.* ii. 1. 6; *Rich. II.* ii. 1. 18; and *Hamlet*, i. 1. 117,
where however a line has probably dropped out between 116
and 117.

114. As is apparently used redundantly with definitions of time
(as ὡς is used in Greek with respect to motion).   It is said by
Halliwell to be an Eastern Counties' phrase :

" This is my birth-day, *as* this very day
  Was Cassius born."—*J. C.* v. 1. 72.
" One Lucio *as* then the messenger."—*M. for M.* v. 1. 74.

The *as* in the first example may be intended to qualify the statement that Cassius was born on " this very day," which is not
literally true, *as* meaning " *as* I may say." Here, and in our Collect
for Christmas Day, " *as* at this time to be born," *as* seems appropriate to an *anniversary.* In the second example the meaning of
"*as* then" is not so clear; perhaps it means " *as far as regards* that
occasion." Compare

" Yet God at last
  To Satan, first in sin, his doom applied,
  Though in mysterious terms, judg'd *as then* best."
                            MILTON, *P. L.* x. 173.

where "*as* then" seems to mean "for the present." So " as yet "
means "*as far as regards* time up to the present time." So in

German "*als* dann" means "then," and "als" is applied to other temporal adverbs.

As in E. E. was often prefixed to dates :

"*As* in the year of grace," &c.

"*As* now" is often used in Chaucer and earlier writers for "as regards now," "for the present :"

"But al that thing I must *as* now forbere."
CHAUC. *Knighte's Tale*, 27.

In "Meantime I writ to Romeo
That he should hither come *as* this dire night,"
R. and J. v. 3. 247.

as perhaps means "*as* (he did come)."

115. As was used almost but not quite redundantly after "seem" (as it is still, after "regard," "represent") :

"To prey on nothing that doth seem *as* dead."
A. Y. L. iv. 3. 119.

and even after "am :"

"I am but *as* a guiltless messenger."—*A. Y. L.* iv. 3. 12.

"I am here *in the character of*," &c.

As is also used nearly redundantly before participles to denote a cause, "inasmuch as :"

"If he be now return'd
As checking at his voyage."—*Hamlet*, iv. 7. 63.

116. As, like "that" (see 287), is used as a conjunctional suffix : sometimes being superfluously added to words that are already conjunctions. In the case of "when as," "where as," it may be explained from a desire to give a relative meaning to words interrogative by nature :

"(I am) one that was a woeful looker-on
When as the noble duke of York was slain."
3 *Hen. VI.* ii. 1. 46 ; i. 2. 75.

So "Where*as*."—2 *Hen. VI.* i. 2. 58, for "where."

117. Because ("for this reason that") refers to the *future* instead of, as with us, to the past, in

"The splitting rocks cower'd in the sinking sands
And would not dash me with their rugged sides,
Because thy flinty heart, more hard than they,
Might in thy palace perish (act. 291), Margaret."
2 *Hen. VI.* iii. 2. 100.

i.e. "*in order that* thy flinty heart might have the privilege of destroying me."

118. But (E. E. and modern northern English "bout") is in Old Saxon "bi-utan," where "bi" is our modern "by," and "utan" means "without." Thus *but* is a contraction for "by-out," and is formed exactly like "with-out." Hence *but* means *excepted* or *excepting.* This use of *out* in compounds may be illustrated by " *outstep* (except) the king be miserable." *

> "It was full of scorpyones and cocadrilles *out-takene* in the fore-said monethes." *
>
> "Alle that y have y grant the, *out-take* my wyfe." *

The two latter passages illustrate the difficulty of determining whether *but* is used as a passive participle with nominative absolute, or as an active participle with the objective case. In the same way we find "excepted" and "except" placed (*a*) after a noun or pronoun, apparently as passive *participles,* and (*b*) before, as prepositions. Thus—

    (*a*)   "Only you *excepted.*"—*M. Ado*, i. 1. 126.
        "Richard *except.*"—*Rich. III.* v. 3. 242.

Then, on the other hand,—

    (*b*)   "Always *excepted* my dear Claudio."—*M. Ado*, iii. 1. 93.
        "*Except* immortal Cæsar."—*J. C.* i. 2. 60.

(For the confusion between "except" and "excepted" compare "deject" for "dejected," &c. See below, 342.)

The absence of inflections, however, in the above instances leaves us uncertain whether "except" is a preposition or participle. But "save" seems to be used for "saved" and "he" to be the nominative absolute in

        "All the conspirators *save* only he." †—*J. C.* v. 5. 69.
So   "*Save* thou."—*Sonn.* 109.
                "Nor never none
    Shall mistress be of it *save* I alone."—*T. N.* iii. 1. 172.
    "What stays had I *but* they."—*Rich. III.* ii. 2. 76, iv. 4. 34 ;
        Cymb. ii. 3. 153 ; *Macbeth*, iii. 1. 54 ; *R. and J.* i. 2. 14.

On the other hand, Shakespeare does not agree with modern usage in the inflections of the pronouns (see 206—216).

---

  * Halliwell's Dictionary.
  † Similarly "sauf" was used in French in agreement with a noun placed in the nominative absolute.

119. But is almost always used in Layamon for "unless" or "without" (prep.), or "without" (adv.) in the sense of "outside." Thus (i. 159): "that a queen should be king in this land and their sons be *buten*," (l. t. *boute*), i.e. "*without* (the land)." So (i. 215) "buten laeve," i.e. "*without* leave." It occurs adversatively in (i. 353) a passage which illustrates the transition, "If thou wilt receive his reconciliation, it will be well; *but*, he will never deliver Evelin to thee." Here *but* is the preposition "without," used adverbially as "otherwise."

120. But, in all its uses, may be explained from the meaning of "out-take" or *except*. It is sometimes used (like *and*, see above) to *except* or "out-take" a whole clause, the verb being occasionally in the subjunctive.

> "And, *but* thou love me, let them find me here."
>
> *R. and J.* ii. 2. 76.

i.e. "*except* or *without* thou love me."

> "And, *but* I be deceived, Signior Baptista may remember
> me."—*T. of Sh.* iv. 2. 2.

Compare 1 *Hen. VI.* iii. 1. 34 : "*Except* I be provoked."

So   "Not *without* the prince be willing."—*M. Ado*, iii. 3. 86.

We now use "unless" in this sense, and by a comparison of Wickliffe with Tyndale and Cranmer it will be seen that *but* was already often superseded by "except."

But with the subjunctive is, however, more common in Early than in Elizabethan English.   Sometimes without the subjunctive—

> "And, *but* she spoke it dying, I would not
> Believe her lips."—*Cymb.* v. 5. 41.
> "And, *but* he's something stain'd
> With grief that's beauty's canker, thou might'st call him
> A goodly person."—*Tempest*, i. 2. 414.
>   "The common executioner
> Falls not the axe upon the humbled neck
> *But* first begs pardon."—*A. Y. L.* iii. 5. 5.
> "And, *but* infirmity hath something seized
> His wish'd ability, he had himself
> The lands and waters 'twixt your throne and his
> Measured, to look upon you."—*W. T.* v. 1. 141.

121. But.   Transition of meaning. These last passages illustrate the transition of *but* from *except* to "on the contrary," "by way of prevention." The transition is natural, inasmuch as an *exception* may well be called *contrary* to the rule. The first passage is a blending of two constructions: "*if* she *had not spoken* it dying I would not believe," and "I would not believe, *but* she spoke it dying." Similarly: "*Except* infirmity *had* seized—he had (would have) measured," and "He had (would have) measured, *but* (by way of prevention) infirmity *hath* seized."

The different usages of *but* arise, (1) from its variations between the meaning of "except," "unless," and the adversative meaning "on the other hand;" (2) from the fact that the negative before *but*, in the sense of "except," is sometimes omitted and at other times inserted. Thus "*but* ten came" may mean "ten *however* came," or "(none) *but* ten, i.e. *only* ten, came." *But* is now much more confined than it was, to its adversative meaning. We still say "it never rains *but* it pours" (where the subject is the same before and after but); and, even where a new subject is introduced, we might say, "I did not know *but* you had come," "You shall not persuade me *but* you knew," &c.; but this use is colloquial, and limited to a few common verbs. We should scarcely write

"I never saw *but* Humphrey duke of Gloucester
Did bear him like a noble gentleman."—*2 Hen. VI.* i. 1. 83.

122. "But" signifying prevention. The following passages illustrate the "preventive" meaning of *but:*

"Have you no countermand for Claudio yet
But he must die to-morrow?"—*M. for M.* iv. 2. 97.

i.e. "to prevent that he must die." If "but" were the ordinary adversative, it would be "but must he die?"

"That song to-night
Will not go from my mind: I have much to do
But (to prevent myself) to go hang my head all at one side
And sing it, like poor Barbara."—*Othello,* iv. 3. 32.

"Have you no wit, manners, nor honesty *but* to gabble like tinkers at this time of night?"—*T. N.* ii. 3. 95.

i.e. "to prevent you from gabbling," or, as Shakespeare could write, "to gabble." See 349.

After verbs of "denying" and "doubting" which convey a notion of hindrance, *but* is often thus used:

"I doubt not *but* to ride as fast as York."—*Rich. II.* ii. 5. 2.

"I have no doubt (*i.e.* fear) about being prevented from riding.'

So 1 *Hen. IV.* ii. 2. 14 :

> " It must not be denied *but* I am a plain dealing villain."
>   *M. Ado,* i. 3. 32.

" There must be no denial to prevent my being supposed a plain-dealing villain." In the last passage, however, *but* is used transitionally, almost as an adversative. Compare

> " It cannot be *but* I am pigeon-livered,"—*Hamlet*, ii. 2. 605.

which approximates to " It cannot be (that I am otherwise than a coward)," *i.e.* " it cannot be that I am courageous ; on the contrary (*but* adversative), I am pigeon-liver'd."

The variable nature of *but* is illustrated by the fact that " believe not *but*," and " doubt not *but*," are used in the same signification :

> " We doubt not *but* every rub is smoothed."—*Hen. V.* ii. 2. 187.

i.e. " we have no doubt of a nature *to prevent* our believing that," &c. So *Rich. II.* v. 2. 115. But, on the other hand,

> " I'll not believe *but* they ascend the sky."—*Rich. III.* i. 3. 287.

i.e. " I'll not believe anything *except* (or ' otherwise than ') that they ascend."

In the first of these passages *but* is semi-adversative.

>   " She is not so divine
> *But* with as humble lowliness of mind
> She is content to be at your command."—1 *Hen. VI.* v. 5. 18.

i.e. " not so divine as to prevent that she should be content."

" *But* " and " *but* that " are still thus used.

123. But (in phrases like " there is no man *but* hates me," where a subject immediately precedes *but*) often expels the subject from the following relative clause. This perhaps arose in part from a reluctance to repeat a subject which was already emphatically expressed. See 244. For the same reason the relative is omitted in such expressions as

> " There is no creature *loves* me."—*Rich. III.* v. 3. 200.

In such cases we still sometimes omit the subject, but perhaps not often where *but* is separated from the preceding subject, as in

> " There is no vice so simple *but* assumes
> Some mark of virtue in its outward parts."
>   *M. of V.* iii. 2. 81.

On the other hand, this omission is not found in the earliest stages of the language (Mätzner, iii. p. 469), and thus we find the subject frequently retained in Shakespeare :

> " I found no man *but he* was true to me."—*J. C.* v. 5. 35.
> " There's ne'er a villain dwelling in all Denmark
> *But he's* an arrant knave."—*Hamlet,* i. 5. 124.

Less frequently *but* expels the object in the relative clause :

> "No jocund health that Denmark drinks to-day
> *But* the great cannon to the clouds shall tell."
> *Hamlet,* i. 2. 126.

124. But meaning *except* may apply to an *expressed* contingency, as (1)

> "God defend *but* I should still be so."—1 *Hen. IV.* iv. 3. 38.

i.e. " God forbid everything *except* (I should, &c.) "

> " *But* being charged we will be still by land."
> *A. and C.* iv. 11. 1.

i.e. " *Excepting* the supposition of our being charged."

(2) Sometimes the contingency is merely *implied.*

> " I should sin
> To think *but (except* I should think) nobly of my grandmother."
> *Temp.* i. 2. 119.

> "Her head's declined and death will seize her, *but*
> Your comfort makes her rescue."—*A. and C.* iii. 11. 48.

i.e. " *only* your comfort."

The last passage illustrates the connection between *but* meaning *only,* and *but* used adversatively.

125. But thus varying between an adversative and an exceptional force causes many ambiguities.   Thus :

> ' Whenever Buckingham doth turn his hate
> On you and yours, *but* with all duteous love
> Doth cherish you and yours, God punish me."
> *Rich. III.* ii. 1. 33.

Here *but* means " without," or " instead of, cherishing you."

> " You salute not at the court *but* you kiss your hands."
> *A. Y. L.* iii. 1. 50.

i.e. " without kissing your hands."

126. But is not adversative, but means " if not," after " beshrew me," &c. :

"Beshrew my soul *but* I do love," &c.—*K. J.* v. 4. 51.

So 3 *Hen. VI.* i. 4. 150.

"The Gods rebuke me *but* it is tidings
To wash the eyes of kings."—*A. and C.* v. 1. 27; *ib.* 103.

Thus we explain:

"I'll plead for you myself *but* you shall have him."
                              T. of Sh. ii. 1. 15.

i.e. "I'll plead for you myself *if* you shall *not* have him otherwise;" but it must be admitted that the above construction may be confused with "I may have to plead for you myself, *but* (adversative) in any case you shall have him." So

"I should woo hard *but* be your groom,"—*Cymb.* iii. 6. 70.

is, perhaps, a confusion between "*if* I could *not* be your groom otnerwise" and "*but* in any case I would be your groom." In the last example, however, it is possible that there is an additional confusion arising from the phrase: "It would go hard with me *but.*"

127. But in the sense of *except* frequently follows negative comparatives, where we should use *than.*

"*No more but* instruments."—*M. for M.* v. 1. 237.

Here two constructions are blended, "*Nothing except* instruments" and "*only* instruments; *no more.*" So—

"*No more* dreadfully *but* as a drunken sleep."
                              M. for M. iv. 2. 150.

"The which *no sooner* had his prowess confirm'd,
But like a man he died."—*Macbeth*, v. 8. 42.

"I think it be *no other but* even so."—*Hamlet*, i. 1. 108.

"*No more but* that."—*A. W.* iii. 7. 30.

"With no worse nor better guard *but* with a knave."
                              Othello, i. 1. 126.

"Thou knowest *no less but* all."—*T. N.* i. 4. 13.

Sometimes *but* follows an adjective qualified by the negative with "so."

"Not so dull *but* she can learn."—*M. of V.* iii. 2. 164.

So Chaucer:

"I *n*am *but* dede,"—*Knighte's Tale.*

where, omitting the negative *n*, we should say "I am *but* dead."

128. But passes naturally from "except" to "only," when the negative is omitted. ("No-but" or "nobbut" is still used provincially for "only.") Thus :

"No more *but* that,"—*A. W.* iii. 7. 30.

becomes "*but* that."

> "*Glouc.* What, and wouldst climb a tree ?
> *Simple. But* that in all my life."—2 *Hen. VI.* ii. 1. 99.

i.e. "no more but that one tree," or "*only* that one tree."

> "*Cleo.* Antony will be himself.
> *Ant. But* stirr'd by Cleopatra."—*A. and C.* i. 1. 142.

i.e. "not except stirr'd," "only if stirr'd."

> "*But* sea-room, and (*if* Fol.) the brine and billow kiss the
> moon, I care not."—*P. of T.* iii. 1. 45.
> "Where Brutus may *but* find it."—*J. C.* i. 3. 144.

i.e. "Where Brutus can (do nothing) *but* find it," *i.e.*, as we say, "cannot *but* find it." Possibly, however, *but* (see 129) may be transposed, and the meaning may be "Brutus only," *i.e.* "Brutus alone may find it."

> "He that shall speak for her is afar off guilty
> *But* that he speaks."—*W. T.* ii. 1. 105.

i.e. "simply in that he speaks," "merely for speaking."

The effect of the negative on *but* is illustrated by

> "*But* on this day let seamen fear no wreck."—*K. J.* iii. 1. 92.

Here, at first, *but* might seem to mean "only," but the subsequent negative gives it the force of "except."

But perhaps means "only" in

> "He boasts himself
> To have a worthy feeding : *but* I have it
> Upon his own report, and I believe it."—*W. T.* iv. 4. 169.

i.e. "I have it *merely* on his own report, and I believe it too."

There is, perhaps, a studied ambiguity in the reply of Hamlet :

> "*Guild.* What should we say, my lord ?
> *Hamlet.* Anything *but* to the purpose."—*Hamlet,* ii. 2. 287.

The ellipsis of the negative explains "neither" in the following difficult passage :

"To divide him inventorily would dizzy the authentic of memory and yet *but* yaw *neither* (*i.e.* do *nothing but* lag clumsily behind neither) in respect of his quick sail."—*Hamlet,* v. 2. 120.

"Neither" for our "either" is in Shakespeare's manner, after a negative expressed or implied.

But means "setting aside" in

"What would my lord, *but* that (which) he may not have,
  Wherein Olivia may seem serviceable."—*T. N.* v. i. 104.

Such instances as this, where *but* follows not a negative but a superlative, are rare :

"*Pistol.* Sweet knight, thou art now one of the greatest men in this realm.
Silent. By're lady, I think 'a be, *but* goodman Puff of Barson."
                                            2 *Hen. IV.* v. 3. 93.

But seems used for "*but* now" in

"No wink, sir, all this night,
  Nor yesterday : *but* (*but* now) slumbers."—B. J. *Fox,* i. i.

129. But (like *excepted* and *except*) varies in its position. Similarly "only" varies with us : we can say either "one *only*" or "*only* one."

"This very morning *but.*"—B. J. *Sad Sh.* ii. 2.
i.e. "*only* this morning."

"Where one *but* goes abreast."—*Tr. and Cr.* iii. 3. 155.
for "*but one*" or "one *only.*"

"*But* in these fields of late."—*Tr. and Cr.* iii. 3. 188.
for "*but* of late."

"A summer's day will seem an hour *but* short."—*V. and A.*
"Betwixt them both *but* was a little stride."
                                            SPENS. *F. Q.* ii. 7. 24.
"And when you saw his chariot *but* appear."—*J. C.* i. i. 48.
i.e. "his chariot merely" or "*but* his chariot."

"Your oaths are words and poor conditions *but* unseal'd."
                                            A. W. iv. 2. 30.
i.e. "merely unsealed agreements."

130. The same forgetfulness of the original meaning of words which led to "more better," &c., led also to the redundant use of *but* in "*but* only," "merely *but,*" "*but* even," &c.

"*Merely but* art."—*L. C.* 25.
"He *only* lived *but* till he was a man."—*Macbeth,* v. 8. 40.

"My lord, your son had only *but* the corpse."
                    2 Hen. IV. i. 1. 192.
" Even *but* now " for " *but* now."
                    M. of V. v. 1. 272; *A. Y. L.* ii. 7. 3.
" *But* a *very* prey to woe."—*Rich. III.* iv. 4. 106.
                    " Augustus,
In the bestowing of his daughter, thought
But even of gentlemen of Rome."—B. J. *Sejan.* iii. 2.

Probably like " *merely but.*"

So   "Even just."—*Hen. V.* ii. 3. 12.

" *But* now," like "even now" (38), is capable of different meanings : "a moment ago" and "at the present moment."

                    " *But* now I was the lord
Of this fair mansion, and even now, *but now*
This house, these servants, and this same myself
Are yours."—*M. of V.* iii. 2. 171.

For. See 151.

131. Or (before). *Or* in this sense is a corruption of A.-S. *ær*
(Eng. *ere*), which is found in Early English in the forms *er, air,
ar, ear, or, eror.*

      " *Or* (before) he have construed."—ASCH. 95.

As this meaning of *or* died out, it seems to have been combined
with *ere* for the sake of emphasis.   Thus :

      "Dying *or ere* they sicken."—*Macbeth,* iv. 3. 173 ;
                    K. J. v. 6. 44 ; *Temp.* v. 1. 103.

We find in E. E. "erst er," "bifore er," "before or" (Mätzner,
iii. 451).

Another explanation might be given.   *Ere* has been conjectured
to be a corruption of *e'er, ever,* and "or ever" an emphatic form
like "whenever," "wherever."   "Ever" is written "ere" in
Sonn. 93, 133.   And compare "*Or ever* your pots be made hot with
thorns."—*Ps.* lviii.

Against the latter explanation is the fact that "ever" is much
more common than "ere."   It is much more likely that "ever"
should be substituted for "ere" than "ere" for "ever."   For
Or . . . or, see 136.

132. Since* seems used for *when* in—

> " Beseech you, sir,
> Remember *since* you owed no more to time
> Than I do now."—*W. T.* v. 1. 219.

" Remember *the time past when* you," &c.

> " We know the time *since* he was mild and affable."
>
> 2 *Hen. VI.* iii. 1. 9.
>
> "Thou rememberest
> *Since* once I sat upon a promontory."—*M. N. D.* ii. 1. 149.
>
> " This fellow I remember
> *Since* once he play'd a farmer's eldest son."
>
> *T. of Sh.* Ind. i. 84.

So 2 *Hen. IV.* iii. 2. 206.

This meaning of *since* arises from the omission of " it is " in such phrases as " it is long *since* I saw you," when condensed into " long *since*, I saw you." Thus *since* acquires the meaning of " ago," " in past time," adverbially, and hence is used conjunctively for " when, long ago."

Since (like the adverb) is found connected with a simple present where we use the complete present (so in Latin) :

" *Since* the youth of the count was to-day with my lady, she is much out of quiet."—*T. N.* ii. 3. 144.

More remarkable is the use of the simple past for the complete present :

> " I was not angry *since* I came to France
> Until this instant."—*Hen. V.* iv. 7. 58.

Note

> " Whip him . . .
> So saucy with the hand of she here,—what's her name?
> *Since* she was Cleopatra."—*A. and C.* iii. 13. 99.

Perhaps the meaning is " Whip him for being saucy with this woman, *since* (though she is not now worthy of the name) she once *was* (emphatical) Cleopatra." Else " What is her new name since she ceased to be Cleopatra?" If *since*, in the sense of " ago," could be used absolutely for " once," a third interpretation would be possible : " What's her name? *Once* she was Cleopatra."

---

* The old form *sith* occurs several times in Shakespeare, and mostly in the metaphorical meaning "because." *Sith* in *Hamlet*, ii. 2. 12, is an exception. *Sith* in A.-S. meant "late," "later;" "*sith-than*," "after that." *Sithence* (Chaucer, "sethens," "sins") is found once in Shakespeare.

133. So is used with the future and the subjunctive to denote "provided that."

"I am content *so* thou wilt have it so."—*R. and J.* iii. 5. 18.

"*So* it be new, there's no respect how vile."—*Rich. II.* ii. 1. 25.

So seems to mean "in this way," "on these terms," and the full construction is "be it (if it be) *so* that." "Be it" is inserted in

"*Be it so* (that) she will not."—*M. N. D.* i. 1. 39.

"That" is inserted in Chaucer, *Piers Ploughman*, &c.

"(Be it) *So that* ye be not wrath."—CHAUCER, *C. T.* 7830.

means "provided you will not be angry." So

"Poor queen! *So that* thy state might be no worse
I would my skill were subject to thy curse."
Rich. II. iii. 4. 102.

So, thus meaning "on condition that," is sometimes used where the context implies the addition of "even."

" *Messenger.* Should I lie, madam?
Cleopatra. O, I would thou didst
So (even if) half my Egypt were submerged."—*A. and C.* ii. 5. 94.

Sometimes the subjunctive inflection is neglected and "*so as*" is used for "*so* that."

"*So as* thou livest in peace, die free from strife."
Rich. II. v. 5. 27.

We must distinguish the conditional "*so* heaven help me" from the optative "*so* defend thee heaven" (*Rich. II.* i. 3. 34), where the order of the words indicates that "be it . . . that" cannot be understood. Here *so* means "on the condition of my speaking the truth," and is not connected with defend. Compare *Rich. III.* ii. 1. 11, 16. See also 275–283.

That. See **Relative.**

That omitted before the subjunctive. See 311.

134. Where is frequently used metaphorically as we now use *whereas.*

"It (the belly) did remain
I' the midst o' the body idle and unactive
 . . . . . *where* the other instruments
Did see and hear, devise," &c.—*Coriol.* i. 1. 105.

for "whereas the other instruments did," &c. Comp. *Coriol.* i. 10. 13. So *Lear,* i. 2. 89 ; *Rich. II.* iii. 2. 185.

135. Whereas, on the other hand, is used for *where* in

"Unto St. Alban's
Whereas the king and queen do mean to hawk."
2 Hen. VI. i. 2. 58.

"They back returned to the princely place ;
Whereas . . . a knight . . . they new arrived find."
SPENS. *F. Q.* l. 4. 38.

So "*where-that.*"—*Hen. V.* v. Prologue, 17. Probably both "as" and "that" were added to give a relative meaning to the (originally) interrogative adverb *where.* See 287.

136. Whether is sometimes used after "or" where we should omit one of the two :

"*Or whether* doth my mind, being crown'd with you,
Drink up the monarch's plague, this flattery?
Or whether shall I say mine eye saith true," &c.—*Sonn.* 114.
"Move those eyes?
Or whether riding on the balls of mine
Seem they in motion?"—*M. of V.* iii. 2. 18.
"*Or whether* his fall enraged him, or how it was."
Coriol. i. 3. 69.

The first example is perhaps analogous to the use of "or . . . or," as in

"Why the law Salique which they have in France
Or should *or* should not bar us in our claim."
Hen. V. i. 2. 12 ; *T. N.* iv. 1. 65.

There is, perhaps, a disposition to revert to the old idiom in which the two particles were similar : "other . . . other." (The contraction of "other" into "or" is illustrated by "whe'r" for "whether" in O.E. and the Elizabethan dramatists.) Perhaps, also, additional emphasis is sought by combining two particles. We find "*whether* . . . *or whether?*" to express direct questions in Anglo-Saxon. In the second example a previous "whether" is implied in the words "move those eyes?"

137. While (originally a noun meaning "time"). Hence "a-*while,*" "(for) a time;" "the *while,*" "(in) the (mean) time;" "*whil*-om" ("om" being a dative plural inflexion used adverbially), "at a (former) time;" "*while*-ere" (*Temp.* iii. 2. 127), "a time before," *i.e.* "formerly."
So *whiles* (genitive of *while*) means "of, or during, the time."

The earliest use of *while* is still retained in the modern phrase "all *the while that* he was speaking." "The *while* that," from a very early period, is used in the condensed form "the *while*," or "*while* that" or *while;* and *whiles* was similarly used as a conjunction.

While now means only "during the time when," but in Elizabethan English both *while* and *whiles* meant also "up to the time when." (Compare a similar use of "dum" in Latin and ἕως in Greek.)

> "We will keep ourself
> Till supper-time alone. *While* (till) then, God be with you."
> > > *Macbeth,* iii. I. 43.

"I'll trust you *while* your father's dead."
> > > MASSINGER (Nares).

> "He shall conceal it
> *Whiles* you are willing it shall come to note."—*T. N.* iv. 3. 28.

> "Let the trumpets sound
> *While* we return these dukes what we decree.
> > > [*A long flourish.*
> Draw near, &c."—*Rich. II.* i. 3. 122.

PREPOSITIONS.

138. Prepositions primarily represent local relations; secondarily and metaphorically, agency, cause, &c. A preposition (as *after,* see below) may be used metaphorically in one age and literally in the next, or *vice versâ.* This gives rise to many changes in the meaning ot prepositions.

The shades of different meaning which suggest the use of different prepositions are sometimes almost indistinguishable.

We say, "a canal is full *of* water." There is no reason why we should not also say "full *with* water," as a garden is "fair *with* flowers." Again, "a canal is filled *with* water," the verb in modern English preferring *with* to signify instrumentality, but "filled *of* water" is conceivable; and, as a matter of fact, Shakespeare does write "furnished *of,* provided *of,* supplied *of,*" for *with.* Lastly the water may be regarded as an agent, and then we say, "the canal is filled *by* the water." But an action may be regarded as "*of*" the agent, as well as "*by*" the agent, and "*of*" is frequently thus used in the A. V. of the Bible and in Elizabethan authors, as well as

in E. E.   For these reasons the use of prepositions, depending
upon the fashion of metaphor in different ages, is very variable.
It would be hard to explain why we still say, "I live *on* bread,"
but not "Or have we eaten *on* the insane root?" (*Macb.* i. 3. 84);
as hard as to explain why we talk of a "high" price or rate,
while Beaumont and Fletcher speak of a "deeper rate."

139. Prepositions: modern tendency to restrict their meaning.

One general rule may be laid down, that the meanings of the prepositions are more restricted now than in the Elizabethan authors:
partly because some of the prepositions have been pressed into the
ranks of the conjunctions, *e.g.* "for," "but," "after;" partly
because, as the language has developed, new prepositional ideas having
sprung up and requiring new prepositional words to express them,
the number of prepositions has increased, while the scope of each has
decreased.   Thus many of the meanings of "by" have been divided
among "near," "in accordance with," "by reason of," "owing
to;" "but" has divided some of its provinces among "unless,"
"except;" "for" has been in many cases supplanted by "because
of," "as regards;" "in" by "during."

140. A.
Ben Jonson in his Grammar, p. 785, writes thus:—
"*A* hath also the force of governing before a noun—'And the Protector had layd to her for manner's sake that she was *a* council
with the Lord Hastings to destroy him.'—Sir T. MORE."

"Forty and six years was this temple *a* building."
St. John ii. 20.

The present text is *in*, but Cranmer and Tyndale had "*a.*"
This *a*, which still exists in *alive, afoot, asleep,* &c. is a contraction of A.-S. *on* or the less common form *an.*   We find in Early
English "on live," "on foot," "on hunting," "on sleep;" "*a*
morrow and eke *an* eve," for "by morning and also by evening;"
"*a* land and *a* water," *Piers Pl.* (where some MSS. have *on*),
"*a* (for in) God's name," "*an* end" for "on the (at the) end."
In the Folio we sometimes find *a* where we write *o':*

"What is 't *a* clocke?"—*Rich. III.* v. 3. 47.

See Adverbs, 24

141. After ("following," Latin "secundum," hence "according to ").

> "Say, you chose him,
> More *after* our commandment than as guided
> By your own true affections."—*Coriol.* ii. 3. 238.
> '*After* my seeming."—2 *Hen. IV.* v. 2. 128.

Compare "Neither reward us *after* our iniquities," in our Prayer-book.

After is now used only of space or time, except in " *after* the pattern, example, &c.," where the sense requires the metaphorical meaning.

142. Against used metaphorically to express time. This is now restricted to colloquial language :

> "I'll charm his eyes *against* he do appear."—*M. N. D.* iii. 2. 99.

i.e. " *against* the time that he do appear." Any preposition, as " for," " in," can thus be converted into a conjunction by affixing " that," and the " that" is frequently omitted.

> " *Against* (the time that) my love shall be as I am now."—*Sonn.* 63.
> "'*Gainst* that season comes."—*Hamlet*, i. 1. 158.
> "As *against* the doom."—*Ib.* iii. 4. 50.

i.e. "as though expecting doom's-day."

143. At. The use of *a* mentioned in 140 was becoming unintelligible and vulgar in Shakespeare's time, and he generally uses *at* instead. The article is generally omitted in the following and similar adverbial forms.

> "All greeting that a king *at friend* can send his brother."
> *W. T.* v. 1. 140.
> "The wind *at help.*"—*Hamlet*, iv. 3. 46.
> "*At shore.*"—MONTAIGNE. "At door."—*W. T.* iv. 4. 352.
> "(A ship) that lay *at rode.*"—N. *P.* 177.
> "As true a dog as ever fought *at head.*"—*T. A.* v. 1. 102.
> "Bring me but out *at gate.*"—*Coriol.* iv. 1. 47.
> " *At point.*"—*Coriol.* v. 4. 64; *Cymb.* iii. 6. 17.

But "When they were fallen *at a point* for rendering up the hold."
> HOLINSHED, *Duncane.*

The *at* of price generally requires an adjective or article, as well as a noun, after it, except in " *at* all." We have, however,

> "If my love thou hold'st *at aught*,"—*Hamlet*, iv. 3. 60.

i.e. "at a whit."

In Early English *at* does not seem to have been thus extensively used. It then was mostly used (Stratmann) in the sense of "at the hands of" (πρός with gen.) : "I ask *at*, take leave *at*, learn *at* a person," &c.

At is used like "near" with a verb of motion where we should use "up to :"

> "I will delve one yard below their mines,
> And blow them *at* the moon."—*Hamlet*, iii. 4. 209.

In "Follow him *at* foot,"—*Ib.* iv. 3. 56.
at is not "on" but "near," as in "*at* his heels."

144. At, when thus used in adverbial expressions, now rejects adjectives and genitives as interfering with adverbial brevity. Thus we can say "*at* freedom," but not

> "*At honest* freedom."—*Cymb.* iii. 4. 71.
> "At *ample* view."—*T. N.* i. 1. 27.
> "*At a mournful* war."—*Sonn.* 46.
> "*At heart's* ease."—*J. C.* i. 2. 207.

We say "*at* loose," but not
"Time . . . often *at his very loose* decides
> That which long process could not arbitrate,"—*L. L. L.* v. 2. 752.
where "loose" means "loosing" or "parting."

So we say "aside," but not

> "To hang my head all *at* one side."—*Othello*, iv. 3. 22.

We say "*at the* word," but, with the indefinite article, "*in a* word," not

> "No, *at a word*, madam."—*Coriol.* i. 3. 122.

It is, perhaps, on account of this frequent use of *at* in terse adverbial phrases that it prefers monosyllables to dissyllables. Thus we have "*at* night" and "*at* noon," and sometimes "*at* eve" and "*at* morn," but rarely "*at* evening" or "*at* morning," except where "*at* morning" is conjoined with "*at* night," as in

> "*At morning* and *at* night."—*M. of V.* iii. 2. 279.

London was not so large as it now is when Shakespeare wrote

> "Inquire *at* London."—*Rich. II.* v. 3. 51.

145. By (original meaning "near"). Hence our "to come *by* a thing," *i.e.* "to come near" or "attain."

> "(How) cam'st thou *by* this ill tidings ?"—*Rich. II.* iii. 4. 80.
> "I'll come *by* (*i.e.* acquire) Naples."—*Temp.* ii. 1. 292.

By is used in a manner approaching its original meaning in

> " Fed his flocks
> *By* (on) the fat plains of fruitful Thessaly."
>
> B. and F. *Fair Sh.* i. 1.

" At a fair vestal throned *by* the west."—*M. N. D.* ii. 1. 58.

So Wickliffe: "*By* (on) everi Saboth," *Acts* xiii. 27. Somewhat similar is our present colloquial "*by* this" of time ; an expression which is found in

> " Of the poor suppliant who *by this* I know
> Is here attending."—*A. W.* v. 3. 134; *Lear,* iv. 6. 45.

This is illustrated by the play on "*by* your favour," where favour means also "complexion," "face," in

> " *Duke.*   Thine eye
> Hath stay'd upon some favour that it loves,
> Hath it not, boy?
> *Viola.*   A little, *by* your *favour.*"—*T. N.* ii. 4. 26.

Compare also the puns in *T. N.* iii. 1. 2–10.

Hence "about," "concerning."

> " How say you *by* the French lord?"—*M. of V.* i. 2. 60.
> "Tell me, sirrah, but tell me true, I charge you,
> *By* him and *by* this woman here what know you ?"
>
> *A. W.* v. 3. 237.

> " I would not have him know so much *by* me."
>
> *L. L. L.* iv. 3. 150.

> " I know nothing *by* myself," 1 *Cor.* iv. 4 (no harm *about* myself).
> " Many may be meant *by* (to refer to) the fool multitude."
>
> *M. of V.* ii. 9. 25.

Compare B. J. *Poetast.* v. 1 :

> " *Lupus.* Is not that eagle meant *by* Cæsar, ha ? . . . .
> *Cæsar.* Who was it, Lupus, that inform'd you first
> This should be meant *by* us ?"

Hence from *near* came the meaning *like, according to.*

> " It lies you on to speak
> Not *by* your own instruction, nor *by* the matter
> Which your own heart prompts you."—*Coriol.* iii. 2. 52.

> " And him *by* oath they duly honoured."—*R. of L.* 410.

i.e. " according to their oath."

> "Not friended *by* his wish, to your high person
> His will is most malignant."—*Hen. VIII.* i. 2. 40.

i.e. " in accordance with his wish," " to his heart's content."

"If my brother wrought *by* my pity it should not be so."
M. for M. iii. 2. 224.

"I will believe you *by* the syllable
Of what you shall deliver."—*P. of T.* v. 1. 170.

So, where we say "*to* the sound of:"

"Sound all the lofty instruments of war,
And *by* that music let us all embrace."

By seems to mean "near," hence "with," in

"(My daughter) hath his solicitings,
As they fell out *by* time, *by* means and place,
All given to mine ear."—*Hamlet*, ii. 2. 127.

Perhaps we may thus explain:

"I'll trust *by* leisure him that mocks me once."—*T. A.* i. 1. 301.

i.e. "in accordance with, to suit, my leisure."

The use of *by* in

"The people . . . *by* numbers swarm to us,"
3 *Hen. VI.* iv. 2. 2.

is the same as in

"*By* ones, *by* twos, *by* threes."—*Coriol.* ii. 3. 47.

By, in the sense of "near," like our "about" (*Acts* xiii. 21, Wick. "*by* fourti yeeris," the rest "about"), Greek κατά, was used from the first in rough distributive measurements in E. E.: "He smote to the ground *by* three, *by* four," "*by* nine and ten," "*by* one and one." So

"I play the torturer *by small and small*
To lengthen out the worst that must be said."
Rich. II. iii. 2. 189.

i.e. "*in* lengthening out *by* little and little." Hence, perhaps, from "*by* one *by* one" sprang our shorter form, "one *by* one," "little *by* little;" though it is possible that "one *by* one" means "one *next to* or *after* one."

By is used as a noun in the expression "on the *by*" (as one passes by).—B. J. 746.

We still use *by* as an adverb after "close," "hard," &c., but we should scarcely say,

"I stole into a neighbour thicket *by*."—*L. L. L.* v. 2. 94.

146. By ("near," "following close after," hence "as a consequence of").

> "The bishop of York,
> Fell Warwick's brother, and, *by* that, our foe."
> > *3 Hen. VI.* iv. 4. 12.

> "Lest, *by* a multitude
> The new-heal'd wound of malice should break out."
> > *Rich. III.* ii. 2. 124.

> "So the remembrance of my former love
> Is *by* a newer object quite forgotten."—*R. and J.* ii. 4 194.

> "Fear'd *by* their breed and famous *by* their birth."
> > *Rich. II.* ii. 1. 52.

Hence sometimes it seems to be (but is not) used instrumentally with adjectives which appear to be (but are not) used as passive verbs. *By* does not mean "by means of," but "as a consequence of," in

> "An eagle *sharp by* fast."—*V. and A.* 55.

> "Oh how much more does beauty *beauteous* seem
> *By* that sweet ornament which truth doth give."—*Sonn.*

> "*Laer.* Where is my father?
> *King.*   Dead!
> *Queen.*   But not *by* him."
> > *Hamlet*, iv. 5. 128.

147. For (original meaning "before," "in front of"). A man who stands in front of another in battle may either stand as his friend *for* him or as his foe *against* him. Hence two meanings of *for*, the former the more common.*

148. (I.) **For**, meaning "in front of," is connected with "instead of," "in the place of," "as being."

> "Or *for* the lawrell he may gain a scorne."
> > B. J. *on Shakespeare*

i.e. "instead of the laurel."

> "See what now thou art,
> *For* happy wife, a most distressed widow,
> *For* joyful mother, one that wails the name,
> *For* queen, a very caitiff crown'd with care."
> > *Rich. III.* iv. 4. 98.

> "Thyself a queen, *for* me that was a queen."—*Ib.* i. 3. 202.

Between this and the following meanings we may place

> "Learn now, *for* all."—*Cymb.* ii. 3. 111.

> "This is *for* all."—*Hamlet*, i. 3. 131.

i.e. "once instead of, or in the place of, all."

---

* Comp. ἀντί, which in composition denotes *against*, and at other times *instead of, for.*

> " I abjure
> The taints and blames I laid upon myself
> *For* (as being) strangers to my nature."—*Macbeth*, iv. 3. 125.

"Conscience . . . is turned out of all towns and cities *for* a dangerous thing."—*Rich. III.* i. 4. 146.

> " How often have I sat crown'd with fresh flowers
> *For* summer's queen !"—B. and F. *Fair Sh.* i. 1.

Hence *for* is nearly redundant in

> " Let the forfeit
> Be nominated *for* an equal pound."—*M. of V.* i. 3. 150.

There is a play on the word in

" On went he *for* a search, and away went I *for* (packed up in a basket and *treated like*) old clothes."—*M. W. of W.* iii. 5. 100.

> " Three dukes of Somerset three-fold renown'd
> *For* hardy and undoubted champions."—3 *Hen. VI.* v. 7. 6.

(Where probably hardy means Fr. *hardi*, "bold;" and "undoubted" means "not frightened," "doubt" like "fear" being used for "frighten.")

Perhaps *for* comes under this head in

" What is he *for* a fool that betroths himself to unquietness."
M. Ado, i. 3. 49.

i.e. " What is he, as being a fool." It is more intelligible when the order is changed: "*For* a fool, what is he," *i.e.* "considered as a fool—it being granted that he is a fool—what kind of fool is he?"

So　" What is he *for* a vicar?"—B. J. *Sil. Wom.* iii. 1. med.

So in German "was für ein?"

149. For is hence loosely used in the sense " as regards."

" It was young counsel *for* the persons and violent counsel *for* the matter."—B. E. 75.

Very commonly this *for* stands first, before an emphatic subject or object, which is intended to stand in a prominent and emphatic position :

> " *For* your desire to know what is between us,
> O'er-master it as you may."—*Hamlet*, i. 5. 39 ; 2. 112.

" Now, *for* the taking of Sicily, the Athenians did marvellously covet it."—N. *P.* 171.

> " *For* your intent,
> It is most retrograde to our desires."
> *Hamlet*, i. 2. 112 ; *Rich. II.* v. 3. 137.

"*For* a certain term," "*for* seven days, a day" (or even "*for* the day" where one day is meant), is still customary, but not

> "Doom'd for a certain term to walk the night,
> And *for the day* confined to fast in fires."—*Hamlet*, i. 4. 11.

150. For, from meaning "in front of," came naturally to mean "in behalf of," "for the sake of," "because of."

> "Yet I must not (kill Banquo openly),
> *For* certain friends that are both his and mine."
> > *Macbeth*, iii. 1. 120.

i.e. "*because of* certain friends."

This use was much more common than with us. When we refer to the past we generally use "because of," reserving *for* for the future. Compare, on the other hand :

> " O be not proud, nor brag not of thy might,
> *For* mastering her that foil'd the God of fight."
> > *V. and A.* 114.

> " He gave it out that he must depart *for* certain news."
> > *N. P.* 179.

> " No way to that, *for* weakness, which she enter'd."
> > 1 *Hen. VI.* iii. 2. 25.

i.e. " no way can be compared *for* weakness with that," &c.

" Of divers humours one must be chiefly predominant, but it is not with so full an advantage but, *for* the volubilitie and supplenes of the mind, the weaker may by occasion reobtaine the place again." —MONTAIGNE, 116.

For is similarly used with an ellipse of " I lay a wager " in

> " Now, *for* my life, she's wandering to the Tower."
> > *Rich. III.* iv. 1. 3.

151. For, in the sense of "because of," is found not only governing a noun, but also governing a clause :

> " You may not so extenuate his offence
> *For* I have had such faults."—*M. for M.* ii. 1. 28.

i.e. " *because* I have had such faults."

> " ('Tis ungrateful) to be thus opposite with heaven,
> *For* (because) it requires the royal debt it lent you."
> > *Rich. III.* ii. 2. 95.

So *Othello*, i. 3. 269; *Cymb.* iv. 2. 129. And parenthetically very frequently :

> " The canker-blossoms have as deep a dye
> As the perfumed tincture of the roses,
> But *for* their virtue only is their shew,
> They live unwoo'd, and unrespected fade."—*Sonn.* 54.

> " Oh, it is as lawful,
> *For* we would give much, to use violent thefts."
>   *Tr. and Cr.* v. 1. 21.

i.e. to rob, " *because* we wish to be generous."

With the future, *for* meant "in order that."

> " And, *for* the time shall not seem tedious,
> I'll tell thee what befel me."—3 *Hen. VI.* iii. 1. 11

The desire of clearness and emphasis led to the addition of *because.*

> " But *for because* it liketh well our eyes."—N. *P.* Pref.

> " And *for because* the world is populous."—*Rich. II.* v. 5. 3.

Comp. " *but only*," " *more better*," &c.

For, when thus followed by a verb, like *after*, *before*, &c. ("*after* he came," "*before* he went"), is called a conjunction. It is often, like other prepositions (287) thus used, followed by "that." *Coriol.* iii. 3. 93, &c. The two uses occur together in the following passage, which well illustrates the transition of *for* :

> " I hate him *for* he is a Christian,
> But more *for that* . . . he lends," &c.—*M. of V.* i. 3. 43.

152. For to, which is now never joined with the infinitive except by a vulgarism, was very common in E. E. and A.-S., and is not uncommon in the Elizabethan writers. It probably owes its origin to the fact that the prepositional meaning of " to" was gradually weakened as it came to be considered nothing but the sign of the infinitive. Hence *for* was added to give the notion of motion or purpose. Similarly in Danish and Swedish (Mätzner, ii. p. 54) "for at" is used. Both in E. E. and in Elizabethan writers the *for* is sometimes added to the latter of two infinitives as being, by a longer interval, disconnected from the finite verb, and therefore requiring an additional connecting particle :

> " First, honour'd Virgin, to behold thy face
> Where all good dwells that is ; next *for to* try," &c.
>   B. and F. *Fair Sh.* v. 1.

For the same reason :

> " Let your highness
> Lay a more noble thought upon mine honour
> Than *for to* think that I would sink it here."—*A. W.* v. 3. 181.

From the earliest period "for to," like "to," is found used without any notion of purpose, simply as the sign of the infinitive. So in Shakespeare:

"Forbid the sea *for to* obey the moon."—*W. T.* i. 2. 427.

153. For, variable. The following passage illustrates the variableness of *for* :

"Princes have but their titles *for* (to represent) their glories,
An outward honour *for* (as the reward of) an inward toil,
And *for* (for the sake of gaining) unfelt (unsubstantial) imagination
They often feel a world of restless cares."—*Rich. III.* i. 4. 78-80.

154. (II.) **For** (in opposition to) : hence "to prevent."

"And over that an habergeon *for* percing of his herte."
CHAUCER, *Sire Thopas*, 13790.
"*Love.* Is there an officer there?
Off. Yes, two or three *for* failing."—B. J. *Alch.* v. 3.
"The which he will not every hour survey
For blunting the fine point of seldom pleasure."—*Sonn.* 52.
"We'll have a bib *for* spoiling of thy doublet."
B. and F. (Nares).

So it is said of Procrustes, that if his victim was too long for the bed, "he cut off his legs *for* catching cold."—*Euphues* (Malone).

It can be proved that Sir T. North regarded *for* as meaning "in spite of," since he translates "Mais, nonobstant toutes ces raisons," by "But, *for* all these reasons," (N. *P.* 172); where the context also shows beyond dispute that *for* has this meaning. On the other hand, in

"All out of work and cold *for* action,"—*Hen. V.* i. 2.

for seems to mean "*for* want of," unless "out of work and cold" can be treated as equivalent to "eager," which would naturally be followed by *for*.

For is found in E. E. in this sense, but perhaps always with the emphatic "all."

For in this sense is sometimes used as a conjunction:

"*For* all he be a Roman."—*Cymb.* v. 4. 109.

i.e. "Despite that he be a Roman."

For may either mean "against" or (149) "for what concerns" in

"I warrant him *for* drowning."—*Temp.* i. 1. 47.

We still retain the use of *for* in the sense of *in spite of*, as in "*for all* your plots I will succeed." Such phrases, however, frequently contain a negative, in which case it is difficult to ascertain whether *for* means *because of* or *in spite of*.

> "My father is not dead *for* all your saying."
> > *Macbeth*, iv. 2. 36.

> " (The stars) will not take their flight
> *For* all the morning light."—MILTON, *Hymn on the Nativity*.

It is a question how to punctuate

> "To fall off
> From their Creator and transgress his will
> *For* one restraint lords of the world besides."
> > MILTON, *P. L.* i. 32.

If a comma be placed after "will," and not after "restraint," then "besides" should be treated as though it were "except" or "but:" "Lords of the world but *for* one restraint."

155. For is sometimes *ready for*, *fit for*. (See 405.)

> "He is *for* no gallants' company without them."
> > B. J. *E. in &c.* i. 1.

> "Your store is not *for* idle markets."—*T. N.* iii. 3. 46.

Compare our "I am *for* (going to) Paris."

Some ellipsis, as "I pray," must be understood in

> "(I pray) God *for* his mercy."—*Rich. II.* ii. 2. 98 ; v. 2. 75.

156. Forth is used as a preposition (from) :

> "Steal *forth* thy father's house."—*M. N. D.* i. 1. 164.
> "Loosed them *forth* their brazen caves."
> > 2 *Hen. VI.* iii. 2. 89, and 1 *Hen. VI.* i. 2. 54.

Sometimes with "of" or "from :"

> "That wash'd his father's fortunes *forth of* France."
> > 3 *Hen. VI.* ii. 2. 157.

So *Rich. II.* iii. 2. 204–5 ; *Temp.* v. 1. 160. The "of" in itself implies motion from. (See 165.)

> "From *forth* the streets of Pomfret."—*K. J.* iv. 2. 148.

So *Rich. II.* ii. 1. 106.

Forth, being thus joined with prepositions less emphatic than itself, gradually assumed a prepositional meaning, displacing the prepositions. *Forth* is not found as a preposition in E. E. See also **Prepositions omitted.**

157. From is sometimes joined with *out*, to signify outward motion, where we use *out of*.

"In purchasing the semblance of my soul
  From out the state of hellish cruelty."—*M. of V.* iii. 4. 20.
"*From out* the fiery portal of the East."—*Rich. II.* iii. 3. 64.

158. From is frequently used in the sense of "apart from," "away from," without a verb of motion.

"*From* thence (*i.e.* away from home) the sauce to meat is
  ceremony."—*Macbeth,* iii. 4. 36.
"I am best pleased to be *from* such a deed."—*K. J.* iv. 1. 86.
"Which is *from* (out of) my remembrance."—*Temp.* i. 1. 65.
"They run themselves *from* breath."—B. J. *Cy.'s Rev.* i. 1.
"Clean *from* the purpose."—*J. C.* i. 3. 35.
"This discourse is *from* the subject."—B. and F. *Eld. B.* v. 1.
"This is *from* my commission."—*T. N.* i. 5. 208.
"Anything so overdone is *from* the purpose of playing."
  Hamlet, iii. 2. 22.
"This is *from* the present."—*A. and C.* ii. 6. 30.

Hence " differently from : "

"Words him a great deal *from* the matter."—*Cymb.* i. 4. 16.
i.e. "describes him in a manner departing *from* the truth."

"This label on my bosom whose containing
  Is so *from* sense in hardness."—*Cymb.* v. 5. 431.
"Write *from* it, if you can, in hand and phrase."
  T. N. v. 1. 340.
"For he is superstitious grown of late
  Quite *from* the main opinion he held once."—*J. C.* ii. 1. 196.
"So *from* himself impiety hath wrought."—*R. of L.*
"To be so odd and *from* all fashions."—*M. Ado,* iii. 1. 72.
    "Particular addition *from* the bill
That writes them all alike."—*Macbeth,* iii. 1. 100.

This explains the play on the word in

"*Queen.* That thou dost love thy daughter *from* thy soul."
  Rich. III. iv. 4. 258.
"I wish you all the joy that you can wish,
  For I am sure you can wish none *from* me."
  M. of V. iii. 2. 192.

i.e. "none differently *from* me," "none which I do not wish you."
This is probably the correct interpretation of the last passage. So
Othello, i. 1. 132.

" If aught possess thee *from* me."—*C. of E.* ii. 2. 180.

Also " apart from : "

" Nay, that's my own *from* any nymph in the court."
B. J. *Cy.'s Rev.* ii. 1.

" *From* thee to die were torture more than death."
2 *Hen. VI.* iii. 2. 401.

159. In, like the kindred preposition *on* (Chaucer uses "*in* a hill" for "on a hill"), was used with verbs of motion as well as rest. We still say " he fell *in* love," " his conduct came *in* question."

" He fell *in* a kind of familiar friendship with Socrates."
N. *P.* 192.

" Duncane fell *in* fained communion with Sueno."
HOLINSHED.

" *In* so profound abysm I throw all care."—*Sonn.* 112.

" Cast yourself *in* wonder."—*J. C.* i. 3. 60.

" Sounds of music creep *in* our ears."—*M. of V.* v. 1. 56.

" They who brought me *in* my master's hate."
Rich. III. iii. 2. 56.

" But first I'll turn yon fellow *in* his grave."
Ib. i. 2. 262; 3. 88.

" And throw them *in* the entrails of a wolf."—*Ib.* iv. 3. 23.

" If ever ye came *in* hell."—UDALL.

In (for " into ") with " enter," *Rich. II.* ii. 3. 160 ; *Rich. III.* v. 3. 227.

Into is conversely sometimes found with verbs of rest implying motion. " Is all my armour laid *into* my tent ? "—*Rich. III.* v. 5. 51.

" Confin'd *into* this rock."—*Tempest,* i. 2. 361.

" To appear *into* the world."—MONTAIGNE, 224.

And earlier " Hid *into* three measures of meal."—WICKLIFFE, *Luke* xiii. 21.

160. In for *on :*

" What *in* your own part (side) can you say to this ? "
Othello, i. 3. 74.

So in the phrase " *in* the neck," where we should say " *on* the neck " or " *on* the heels."

" Soon after that depriv'd him of his life
And, *in* the neck of that, task'd the whole state."
I *Hen. IV.* iv. 3. 92.

The same phrase occurs *Sonn.* 131; MONTAIGNE, 17; N. *P.* 172.
"*In* pain of your dislike."—2 *Hen. VI.* iii. 2. 257.

161. In for "during" or "at." *In* has now almost lost its
metaphorical use applied to time.   As early as the sixteenth century
"*In* the day of Sabbath" (WICKLIFFE, *Acts* xiii. 14) was replaced
by "on."   It is still retained where the proper meaning of "in,"
"in the limits of," is implied, as with plurals, "Once *in* ten days"
or "for once *in* my life," or "he does more *in* one day than others
in two."   Thus A. V. *Gen.* viii. 4, "*In* the seventh month, *on* the
eighteenth day."   We also find frequently in the A. V. "*In the
day* of the Lord, *in the day* when*," &c. "*in the day* of judgment."
This may in part be due to a desire to retain the more archaic
idiom, as being more solemn and appropriate ; but perhaps the
local meaning of *in* may be here recognized.   We still say "in
this calamity, crisis," &c. where we mean "*entangled in, sur-
rounded by* the perils of this calamity ;" and some such meaning
may attach to "in" when we say "*In* the day of tribulation,
vengeance," &c.   Occasionally, however, we find "at the day of
judgment" (*Matt.* xi. 22), as also in Shakespeare in the only passage
where this phrase occurs.   Shakespeare frequently uses *in* for "at"
or "during."
>"How ! the duke in council
In this time of the night."—*Othello*, i. 2. 93.
"*In* night."—*V. and A.* 720.
"*In* all which time."—*Rich. III.* i. 3. 127.
"*In* such a night as this."—*M. of V.* v. 1. 1, 6, 9.
>"This is, sir, a doubt
In such a time as this, nothing becoming you."
>*Cymb.* iv. 4. 15.
"Nay, we will slink away *in* supper-time."—*M. of V.* ii. 4. 1.

162. In metaphorically used for "in the case of," "about," &c.
"Triumph *in* so false a foe."—*R. of L.*
"*In* second voice we'll not be satisfied."
>*Tr. and Cr.* ii. 3. 149.
>"Almost all
Repent *in* their election."—*Coriol.* ii. 3. 263.
"Our fears *in* Banquo stick deep."—*Macb.* iii. 1. 49.
"(We) wear our health but sickly *in* his life
Which *in* his death were perfect."—*Ib.* iii. 1. 107.

We say "*in* my own person" or "*by* myself," not

"Which *in* myself I boldly will defend."—*Rich. II.* i. 1. 145.

So   "But I bethink me what a weary way
    In Ross and Willoughby . . . will be found."—*Ib.* ii. 2. 10.

i.e. "in the case of Ross," equivalent to "by Ross."

In is used metaphorically where we should say "in the thought of" in

"Strengthen your patience *in* our last night's speech."
    Hamlet, v. 1. 317.

163. In. We still say "it lies *in* your power." But we find also—

"And the offender's life lies *in* the mercy
    Of the duke only,"—*M. of V.* iv. 1. 355.

where we now should use *at*. This example illustrates the apparently capricious change in the use of prepositions.

We should now use *at* instead of *in* and *of*, in

"*In* night and on the court and guard of safety."
    Othello, ii. 3. 216.

and   "What! in a town *of* war."*—*Ib.* 213.

"*In*-round" (O. Fr. "en rond") is used for the more modern "a-round" in

"They compassed him *in round* among themselves."—N. *P.* 192.

But probably "round" is for "around." Compare "compassed him *in*."—A. V. 2 *Chron.* xxi. 9.

164. In is used with a verbal to signify "in the act of" or "while."

"He raves *in* saying nothing."—*Tr. and Cr.* iii. 3. 247.

"When you cast
Your stinking greasy caps *in* hooting at
Coriolanus' exile."—*Coriol.* iv. 6. 131.

"Mine eyes, the outward watch
Whereto my finger like a dial's point
Is pointing still, *in* cleansing them from tears."—*Rich. II.* v. 5. 54.

"The fire that mounts the liquor till't run o'er,
In seeming to augment it, wastes it."—*Hen. VIII.* i. 1. 145.

"And may ye both be suddenly surprised
By bloody hands *in* sleeping on your beds."—1 *Hen. VI.* v. 3. 41.

* But "towns of war," *Hen. V.* ii. 4. 7, means "garrisoned towns," and so probably here, like our "man *of* war."

" As patches set upon a little breach
Discredit more *in* hiding of the fault."—*K. J.* iv. 2. 30.

It is probable, as the last example suggests, that these verbals are nouns after which " of" is sometimes expressed.   Hence " *in* sleeping" may simply be another form of " a-sleeping."   But the *in* brings out, more strongly than the *a-*, the time *in* which, or *while,* the action is being performed.   It is also probable that the influence of the French idiom, " *en disant* ces mots," tended to mislead English authors into the belief that *in* was superfluous, and that the verbals thus used were present participles. (See also 93.)   *In* is used thus with a noun :

" Wept like two children *in* (during) their deaths' sad stories."
Rich. III. iv. 3. 8.

" (These blazes) giving more light than heat, extinct in both,
Even *in* their promise, while it is a-making."
Hamlet, i. 3. 119.

165. Of (original meaning " off" or " from ").   Comp. ἀπό ; " ab," Mœso-Gothic " af."

In Early English *of* is used for " from," " out of," " off," as in " He lighted *of* his steed, arose *of* the dead," " The leaves fall *of* the tree."   This *strong* meaning of motion was afterwards assigned to "*off* " (which is merely an emphatic form of *of*), and hence *of* retained only a *slight* meaning of motion, which frequently merged into causality, neighbourhood, possession, &c.

Off is, perhaps, simply *of* in

" Over-done or come tardy *off.*"*—*Hamlet,* iii. 2. 28.

i.e. " fallen short *of.*"   Compare ὑστερεῖν.   Otherwise " come off " is a passive participle, 295.

Of retains its original meaning in

" Overhear this speech
Of vantage."—*Hamlet,* iii. 3. 33.

i.e. " from the vantage-ground of concealment."

" Therefore *of* all hands must we be forsworn."
L. L. L. iv. 3. 219.

i.e. " from all sides," " to which ever side one looks ;" hence " in any case."

" Being regarded *of* all hands by the Grecians."—N. *P.* 176.

* Compare "Too late *of* our intents."—*Rich. III.* iii. 5. 69

So our modern "off hand," applied to a deed coming *from* the hand, and not from the head. Hence "*of* hand" is used where we use "on" (175) in

"Turn *of* no hand."—*M. of V.* ii. 2. 45.

Of also retains this meaning with some local adjectives and adverbs, such as "north *of*," "south *of*," "within fifteen hundred paces *of*" (*Hen. V.* iii. 7. 136). We could say "the advantage *of*," but not   "You should not have the eminence *of* him."
Tr. and Cr. ii. 2. 266.

'There is a testril *of* (from) me too."—*T. N.* ii. 3. 34.

166. Of used for "out of," "from," with verbs that signify, either literally or metaphorically, depriving, delivering, &c.

"We'll deliver you *of* your great danger."—*Coriol.* v. 6. 14.

"I may be delivered *of* these woes."—*K. J.* iii. 4. 56.

This use of *of* is still retained in the phrase "to be delivered *of* a child."

"Heaven make thee free *of* it."—*Hamlet*, v. 2. 342.

"To help him *of* his blindness."—*T. G. of V.* iv. 2. 45.

"Unfurnish me *of* reason."—*W. T.* v. 1. 123.

"Take *of* me my daughter."—*M. Ado*, ii. 1. 311.

"Rid the house *of* her."—*T. Sh.* i. 1. 150.

"Scour me this famous realm *of* enemies."—B. and F.

"That Lepidus *of* the triumvirate
Should be deposed."—*A. and C.* iii. 6. 28.

"His cocks do win the battle still *of* mine."—*A. and C.* ii. 3. 36.

"Get goal for goal *of* youth."—*A. and C.* iv. 8. 22.

"I discharge thee *of* thy prisoner."—*M. Ado*, v. 1. 327.

In virtue of this meaning, *of* is frequently placed after *forth* and *out*, to signify motion.

Hence, metaphorically,

"He could not justify himself *of* the unjust accusations."—N. *P.* 173.

Of is also used with verbs and adjectives implying *motion from*, such as "fail," "want," &c. Hence—

"But since you come too late *of* our intents."—*Rich. III.* iii. 5. 69.

167. Of thus applied to time means "from." So still "*of* late."

"I took him *of* a child up."—B. J. *E. in &c.* ii. 1.

i.e. "*from* a child, when a mere child." So in E. E. "*of* youth."

" *Of* long time he had bewitched them with sorceries."

Acts viii. 11.

" Being *of* so young days brought up with him."

Hamlet, ii. 2. 11.

168. Of, meaning "from," passes naturally into the meaning " resulting from," " as a consequence of."

" *Of* force."—*M. of V.* iv. 1. 421 ; 1 *Hen. IV.* iii. 2. 120.

" *Of* no right."—1 *Hen. IV.* iii. 2. 100.

" Bold *of* your worthiness."—*L. L. L.* ii. 1. 28.

" We were dead *of* sleep."—*Temp.* v. 1. 221.

" And *of* that natural luck
He beats thee 'gainst the odds."—*A. and C.* ii. 3. 26.

Hence "What shall become *of* this ?" *M. Ado,* iv. 1. 211; *T. N* ii. 1. 37, means "what will be the consequence of this ?"
So "by means of:"

" And thus do we *of* wisdom and of reach
By indirection find direction out."—*Hamlet,* ii. 1. 64.

While *by* is used of external agencies, *of* is used of internal motives, thus:

" Comest thou hither by chance, or *of* devotion ?"

2 *Hen. VI.* ii. 1. 88.

" The king *of* his own royal disposition."—*Rich. III.* i. 3. 63.

" *Of* purpose to obscure my noble birth."—1 *Hen. VI.* v. 4. 22.

" Art thou a messenger, or come *of* pleasure ?"

2 *Hen. VI.* v. 1. 16.

Sometimes "out *of*" is thus used:

" But thou hast forced me,
Out *of* thy honest truth, to play the woman."

Hen. VIII. iii. 2. 431.

Of, "as a result of," is used as a result for "with the aid of," "with," or "at."

" That . . . she be sent over *of* the King of England's cost."

2 *Hen. VI.* i. 1. 61.

" *Of* the city's cost, the conduit shall run nothing but claret wine."

Ib. iv. 6. 3.

Hence the modern phrase "To die *of* hunger."

169. Of hence is used in appeals and adjurations to signify "out of."

" *Of* charity, what kin are you to me ?"—*T. N.* v. 1. 237.

Hence, the sense of "out of" being lost, = "for the sake of," "by."

> "Speak *of* all loves."—*M. N. D.* ii. 2. 154.

This explains

> "Let it not enter in your mind, *of* love."—*M. of V.* ii. 9. 42.

Similar is the use of *of* in protestations:

> "*Leon.* We'll have dancing afterwards.
> *Ben.* First, *of* my word."—*T. N.* v. 4. 123.

> "A proper man, *of* mine honour."—2 *Hen. VI.* iv. 2. 103.

170. Of meaning "from" is placed before an agent (*from* whom the action is regarded as proceeding) where we use "by."

> "Received *of* (welcomed *by*) the most pious Edward."
>   *Macb.* iii. 6. 27.

> "Like stars ashamed *of* day."—*V. and A.*

i.e. "shamed *by* day."

Of is frequently thus used with "long," "'long," or "along." —LAYAMON.   "Along *of*" = "from alongside of" (παρά with gen.).

> "The good old man would fain that all were well
> So 'twere not *'long of* him."—3 *Hen. VI.* iv. 7. 32.

> "'*Long* all *of* Somerset."—1 *Hen. VI.* iv. 3. 46, 33.

> "I am so wrapt and throwly lapt *of* jolly good ale and
>   old."—STILL.

171. Of is hence used not merely of the agent but also of the instrument. This is most common with verbs of construction, and of filling; because in construction and filling the result is not merely effected *with* the instrument, but proceeds out *of* it. We still retain *of* with *verbs* of construction and *adjectives* of fulness; but the Elizabethans retained *of* with *verbs* of fulness also.

> "Supplied *of* kernes and gallow-glasses."—*Macb.* i. 2. 13.

> "I am provided *of* a torch-bearer."—*M. of V.* ii. 2. 24.

> "You are not satisfied *of* these events."—*Ib.* v. 1. 297.

> "Mettle—where*of* thy proud child arrogant man is puffed."
>   *T. of A.* iv. 3. 180.

> "Mixt partly *of* Mischief and partly *of* Remedy."—*B. E.* 114.

Hence   "Flies
> Whose woven wings the summer dyes
> *Of* many colours."—B. and F. *Fair Sh.* v. 1.

Of with verbs of construction from "out *of*" sometimes assumes the meaning of "instead of."

"Made peace *of* enmity, fair love *of* hate."—*Rich. III.* ii. **1. 50.**
And with "become : "

"(Henry) is *of* a king become a banish'd man."—3 *Hen. VI.* iii. 3. 25.

172. Of is hence used metaphorically with verbs of construction, as in the modern

"They make an ass *of* me."—*T. N.* v. 1. 19.

But *of* is also thus found without verbs of construction, as .

    ' *Apem.* Or thou shalt find—
    Timon.   A fool *of* thee.   Depart."
                              T. of A. iv. 3. 232.
         "E'en such a husband
    Hast thou *of* me as she is for a wife."—*M. of V.* iii. 5. 89.
"We should have found a bloody day *of* this."—1 *Hen. VI.* iv. 7. 34.
            "We shall find *of* him
    A shrewd contriver."—*J. C.* ii. 1. 157.
    "We lost a jewel *of* her."—*A. W.* v. 3. 1.
    "You have a nurse *of* me."—*P. of T.* iv. 1. 25.
    "You shall find *of* the king, sir, a father."—*A. W.* i. 1. 7.
i.e. "*in* the king."

173. Of is hence applied not merely to the agent and the instrument, but to any influencing circumstance, in the sense of "as regards," "what comes from."

             "Fantasy,
    Which is as thin *of* substance as the air."—*R. and J.* i. 4. 99.
    "Roses are fast flowers *of* their smells."—B. *E.* 188.
    "A valiant man *of* his hands."—N. *P.* 614.
"But *of* his cheere did seem too solemn-sad."—SPEN. *F. Q.* i. 1.

Under this head perhaps come :

    "Niggard of question ; but *of* our demands
    Most free in his reply."—*Hamlet,* iii. 1. 13.
    " *Of* his own body he was ill, and gave
    The clergy ill example."—*Hen. VIII.* iv. 2. 43.
    "That did but show thee, *of* a fool, inconstant
    And damnable ungrateful."—*W. T.* iii. 2. 187.
i.e. "as regards a fool," "in the matter of folly."

This may almost be called a locative case, and may illustrate the

Latin idiom "versus animi." It is common in E. E. We still say, in accordance with this idiom, "swift *of* foot," "ready *of* wit," &c.

174. Of passes easily from meaning "as regards" to "concerning," "about."

> "Mine own escape unfoldeth to my hope
> The like *of* him."—*T. N.* i. 2. 21.

"You make me study *of* that."—*Temp.* ii. 1. 81.

"'Tis pity *of* him."—*M. for M.* ii. 3. 42 ; *A. and C.* i. 4. 71.

"'Twere pity *of* my life."—*M. N. D.* iii. 1. 44.

"I wonder *of* there being together."—*Ib.* iv. 1. 128.

"Wise *of* (informed *of*) the payment day."—B. *E.*

> "He shall never more
> Be fear'd *of* doing harm."—*Lear*, ii. 2. 113.

"The same will, I hope, happen to me, *of* death."
> MONTAIGNE, 36.

i.e. "with respect to death."

"I humbly do desire your grace *of* pardon."
> *M. of V.* iv. 1. 402.

"I shall desire you *of* more acquaintance."
> *M. N. D.* iii. 1. 183 ; *A. Y. L.* v. 4. 56.

For this use of "desire" compare A. V. *St. John* xii. 21, "they *desired* him saying," where Wickliffe has "preieden," "prayed."

"I humbly do beseech you *of* your pardon."—*O.* iii. 3. 212.

"The dauphin whom *of* succours we entreated."
> *Hen. V.* iii. 3. 45.

> "Yet of your royal presence I'll adventure
> To borrow *of* a week."—*W. T.* i. 2. 38.

"We'll mannerly demand thee *of* thy story."—*Cymb.* iii. 6. 92.

"Enquire *of* him."—*Rich. II.* 3. 186.

i.e. "*about* him."

"Discern *of* the coming on of years."—B. *E.* 105.

"Having determined *of* the Volsces and," &c.—*Coriol.* ii. 2. 41.

"I'll venture so much *of* my hawk or hound."
> *T. of Sh.* v. 2. 72.

> "Since *of* your lives you set
> So slight a valuation."—*Cymb.* iv. 4. 48.

In   "No more can you distinguish *of* a man
> Than *of* his outward show,"—*Rich. III.* iii. 1. 9, 10.

the meaning seems to be, "you can make no distinctions *about* men more than," *i.e.* "except, *about* their appearances."   So

"Since my soul could *of* men distinguish."—*Hamlet,* iii. 2. 69.

In the following passages we should now use "for :"—

"France where*of* England hath been an overmatch."—B. *E.* 113.

"I have no mind *of* feasting." —*M. of V.* ii. 5. 37.

"In change *of* him."—*Tr. and Cr.* iii. 3. 27.

"*Of* this my privacy I have strong reasons."
Tr. and Cr. iii. 3. 190.

"In haste where*of,* most heartily I pray
Your highness to assign our trial day."—*Rich. II.* i. 1. 150.

As we say "what will become *of* (about) me !" so

"What will betide *of* me."—*Rich. III.* i. 3. 6.

We say "power *over* us," not

"The sovereign power you have *of* us."—*Hamlet,* ii. 2. 27.

"I have an eye *on* him," not

"Nay, then, I have an eye *of* you."—*Ib.* 301.

175. Of signifying proximity of any kind is sometimes used *locally* in the sense of " on." The connection between *of* and *on* is illustrated by *M. of V.* ii. 2, where old Gobbo says : "Thou hast got more haire *on* thy chin than Dobbin my philhorse has *on* his taile ;" and young Gobbo retorts, "I am sure he had more haire *of* his taile than I have *of* my face."

"*Gra.* My master riding behind my mistress—
Cart. Both *of* one horse."—*T. of Sh.* iv. 1. 71.

Of is sometimes used *metaphorically* for " on."

Compare "A plague *of* all cowards !"—1 *Hen. IV.* ii. 4. 127.

with "A plague *upon* this howling."—*Temp.* i. 1. 39.

"Who but to-day hammer'd *of* this design."—*W. T.* ii. 2. 49.

"I go *of* message."—2 *Hen. VI.* iv. 1. 113.

A message may be regarded as a motive *from* which, or as an object *towards* which, an action proceeds, and hence either *of* or " on " may be used.

Compare "He came *of* an errand."—*M. W. of W.* i. 4. 80.

with "I will go *on* the slightest errand."—*M. Ado,* ii. 1. 272.

"Sweet mistress, what your name is else I know not,
Nor by what wonder you do hit *of* mine."—*C. of E.* iii. 2. 30.

Add also— "And now again
Of him that did not ask, but mock, bestow
Your sued-for tongues."—*Coriol.* ii. 3. 215.

"I shall bestow some precepts *of* this virgin."

A. W. iii. 5. 103 ; *T. N.* iii. 4. 2.

"Trustyng *of* (comp. "depending *on*") the continuance."

ASCH. *Ded.*

176. Of, signifying "coming from," "belonging to," when used with time, signifies "during."

"These fifteen years : by my fay a goodly nap!
But did I never speak *of* all that time?"—*T. of Sh.* Ind. 2. 84.

"There sleeps Titania sometime *of* the night."—*M. N. D.* ii. 1. 253.

i.e. "sometimes during the night."

"My custom always *of* the afternoon."—*Hamlet,* i. 5. 60.

"And not be seen to wink *of* all the day."—*L. L. L.* i. 1. 43.

"*Of* the present."—*Tempest,* i. 1. 24.

So often "*Of* a sudden."

177. Of is sometimes used to separate an object from the direct action of a verb : (*a*) when the verb is used partitively, as "eat of," "taste of," &c. ; (*b*) when the verb is of French origin, used with "de," as "doubt," "despair," "accuse," "repent," "arrest," "appeal," "accept," "allow;" (*c*) when the verb is not always or often used as a transitive verb, as "hope" or "like," especially in the case of verbs once used impersonally.

(*a*) "*King.* How fares our cousin Hamlet?
Hamlet. Excellent, i' faith : *of* the chameleon's dish."

Hamlet, iii. 2. 98.

(*b*) "To appeal each other *of* high treason."—*Rich. II.* i. 1. 27.

"*Of* capital treason we arrest you here."—*Ib.* iv. 1. 151.

(*c*) "So then you hope *of* pardon from Lord Angelo?"

M. for M. iii. 1. 1.

"I will hope *of* better deeds to-morrow."—*A. and C.* i. 1. 62.

The *of* after "to like" is perhaps a result of the old impersonal use of the verb, "me liketh," "him liketh," which might seem to disqualify the verb from taking a direct object. Similarly "it repents me *of*" becomes "I repent *of;*" "I complain myself *of*" becomes "I complain *of.*" So in E. E. "it marvels me *of*" becomes "I marvel *of.*" Hence—

"It was a lordling's daughter that liked *of* her master."

P. P. 16.

"Thou dislikest *of* virtue for the name."—*A. W.* ii. 3. 131.

"I am a husband if you like *of* me."—*M. Ado*, v. 4. 59.

So *L. L. L.* i. 1. 107; iv. 3. 158; *Rich. III.* iv. 4. 354.

"To like *of* nought that would be understood."

BEAUMONT on B. J.

178. Of naturally followed a verbal noun. In many cases we should call the verbal noun a participle, and the *of* has become unintelligible to us. Thus we cannot now easily see why Shakespeare should write—

"Dick the shepherd *blows* his nail."—*L. L. L.* v. 2. 923.

and on the other hand—

"The shepherd *blowing of* his nails."—3 *Hen. VI.* ii. 5. 3.

But in the latter sentence *blowing* was regarded as a noun, the prepositional "a," "in," or "on" being omitted.

"The shepherd was a-blowing *of* his nails."

In the following instances we should now be inclined to treat the verbal as a present participle because there is no preposition before it :

"Here stood he (*a-*)mumbling *of* wicked charms."—*Lear*, ii. 1. 41.
"We took him (*a-*)setting *of* boys' copies."—2 *Hen. VI.* iv. 2. 96.
"And then I swore thee, (*a-*)saving *of* thy life."—*J. C.* v. 3. 38.
"Here was he merry (*a-*)hearing *of* a song."—*A. Y. L.* ii. 7. 4.

where "hear *of*" does not mean, as with us, "hear *about*." So *Lear*, v. 3. 204. In all the above cases the verbal means "in the act of."

In most cases, however, a preposition is inserted, and thus the substantival use of the verbal is made evident. Thus :

"So find we profit *by* losing *of* our prayers."—*A. and C.* ii. 1. 8.
"Your voice *for* crowning *of* the king."

Rich. III. iii. 4. 29 ; *Hamlet*, i. 5. 175 ; *Lear*, i. 3. 1.

"*With* halloing and singing *of* anthems."—2 *Hen. IV.* i. 2. 213.
"What, threat you me *with* telling *of* the king?"

Rich. III. i. 3. 113.

"*About* relieving *of* the sentinels."—1 *Hen. VI.* ii. 1. 70 ; iii. 4. 29.

If it be asked why "the" is not inserted before the verbal,— *e.g.* "about *the* relieving of the sentinels,"—the answer is that relieving is already defined, and in such cases the article is generally omitted by Shakespeare. (See 89.)

When the object comes before the verbal, *of* must be omitted :

> "   *Ophelia.* Hamlet . . . shaking *of* mine arm
> And thrice *his head thus waving.*"—*Hamlet*, ii. 1. 92.

The reason is obvious.   We can say " in shaking of mine arm,"
but not " in his head thus waving."

Compare *C. of E.* v. 1. 153 ; *A. Y. L.* ii. 4. 44, iv. 3. 10 ; *W. T.* iii.
3. 69 ; 1 *Hen. IV.* ii. 4. 166 ; *R. and J.* v. 1. 40.

"Yet the mother, if the house hold *of* our lady."—ASCH. 40.

" Hold," by itself, would mean " actually hold " (capiat).   " Hold
of " means " be of such a nature as to hold " (capax sit), "hold-
ing *of*."

179. Of is sometimes redundant before relatives and relatival
words in dependent sentences, mostly after verbs intransitive.

> " Make choice *of which* your highness will see first."
> *M. N. D.* v. 1. 43.

> " What it should be . . . I cannot dream *of*."
> *Hamlet*, ii. 2. 10.

> " Making just report
> *Of how* unnatural and bemadding sorrow
> The king hath cause to plain."—*Lear*, iii. 2. 38.

> " He desires to know of you *of whence* you are,"
> *P. of T.* ii. 3. 80.

where, however, " whence " is, perhaps, loosely used for " what
place," and *of* strictly used for " from."

The redundant and appositional *of*, which we still use after
" town," " city," " valley," &c., is used after " river " (as sometimes
by Chaucer and Mandeville) in

> " The *river of* Cydnus."—*A. and C.* ii. 2. 192.

180. On, upon (interchanged in E. E. with " an "), represents
juxtaposition of any kind, metaphorical or otherwise.   It was in
Early English a form of the preposition "an " which is used as an
adverbial prefix (see **141**) ; and as late as Ascham we find—

> " I fall *on* weeping."—ASCH. iii. 4.

> " For sorrow, like a heavy-hanging bell
> Once set *on* ringing, with his own weight goes."—*R. of L.* 1494.

Compare also our *a-head* with

" Hereupon the people ran *on-head* in tumult together."—N. *P.* 191.
" Why runnest thou thus *on head* ?"—*Homily on Matrimony.*

The metaphorical uses of this preposition have now been mostly divided among *of,* *in,* and *at,* &c.   We still, however, retain the phrase, "*on* this," "*on* hearing this," &c. where *on* is "at the time of," or "immediately after."   But we could not say —

"Here comes (333) the townsmen *on* (in) procession."
2 *Hen. VI.* ii. I. 68.

"Read *on* (in) this book."—*Hamlet,* iii. I. 44.   So Mon-
TAIGNE, 227 : "To read *on* some book."

"Blushing *on* (at) her."—*R. of L.* st. 453.

"*On* (at) a moderate pace."—*T. N.* ii. 2. 3.

"The common people being set *on* a broile."—N. *P.* 190.
(Comp. our "set *on* fire.")

"Horses *on* ('in' or 'of') a white foam."—N. *P.* 186.

"*On* (of) the sudden."—*Hen. VIII.* iv. 2. 96.

"And live to be revenged *on* ('for' or 'about') her death."
R. of L. 1778.

"Be not jealous *on* (of) me."

"Fond *on* her."—*M. N. D.* ii. I. 266.

"Nod *on* (at) him."—*J. C.* i. 2. 118.

"Command *upon* me."—*Macbeth,* iii. I. 17.

On, like "upon," is used metaphorically for "in consequence of" in

"Lest more mischance
On plots and errors happen."—*Hamlet,* v. 2. 406 ;

for "in dependence on" in

"I stay here *on* my bond."—*M. of V.* iv. I. 242.

In "She's wandering to the tower
On pure heart's love to greet the tender princes,'
Rich. III. iv. I. 4.

there is a confusion between "*on* an errand of love" and "out of *heart's love.*"

181. On is frequently used where we use "of" in the sense of "about," &c.   Thus above, "jealous *on,*" and in *Sonn.* 84, "Fond *on* praise."   In Early English (Stratmann) we have "*On* witch-craft I know nothing."   "What shall become *on* me?"   "Denmark won nothing *on* him."   Compare—

"Enamour'd *on* his follies."—I *Hen. IV.* v. 2. 71.

"His lands which he stood seized *on.*"*—*Hamlet,* i. I. 88.

* Globe, "of."

"Or have we eaten *on* the insane root?"—*Macbeth*, i. 3. 84.

"He is so much made *on* here."—*Coriol.* iv. 5. 203.

"What think you *on't.*"—*Hamlet*, i. 1. 55.

Note the indifferent use of *on* and "of" in

"God have mercy *on* his soul
And *of* all Christian souls."—*Hamlet*, iv. 5. 200.

The use of *on* in

"Intended or committed was this fault?
If *on* the first,—I pardon thee,"—*Rich. II.* v. 3. 34.

is illustrated by

"My gracious uncle, let me know my fault,
On what condition stands it."—*Ib.* ii. 3. 107.

182. On, being thus closely connected with "of," was frequently used even for the possessive "of," particularly in rapid speech before a contracted pronoun.

"One *on's* ears."—*Coriol.* ii. 2. 85.   So *Coriol.* i. 3. 72 ; ii. 1. 202.

"The middle *on's* face."—*Lear*, iv. 5. 20.

"Two *on's* daughters."—*Ib.* i. 4. 114.

"Two *on's.*"—*Cymb.* v. 5. 311.

"My profit *on't.*"—*Temp.* i. 2. 365, 456.

"You lie out *on't*, sir."—*Hamlet*, v. 1. 132 ; *Lear*, iv. 1. 52.

"He shall hear *on't.*"—B. J. *E. in &c.*

"I am glad *on't.*"—*J. C.* i. 3. 137.

In the two last examples *on* may perhaps be explained as meaning "concerning," without reference to "of."

The explanation of this change of "of" to "on" appears to be as follows. "Of" when rapidly pronounced before a consonant became "o'."

"Body *o'* me."—*Hen. VIII.* v. 2. 22.

"*O'* nights."—*T. N.* i. 3. 5.

Hence the *o'* became the habitual representative of "of" in colloquial language, just as "a-" became the representative of "on" or "an." But when *o'* came before a vowel, what was to be done? Just as the "a-" was obliged to recur to its old form "an" before a vowel or mute *h* (compare *Hamlet*, i. 4. 19, "to stand *an-end*," and see 24), so before a vowel *o'* was forced to assume a euphonic *n.* (Compare the Greek custom.)

And even when the pronoun is not contracted, we find in *Coriol.* iv. 5. 174, the modern vulgarism—

"Worth six *on* him."

"To break the pate *on* thee."—1 *Hen. IV.* ii. 1. 34.

183. Out (out from) is used as a preposition like *forth.*

" You have push'd *out* your gates the very defender of them."
Coriol. v. 2. 41.

(Early Eng. " Come *out* Ireland," " *Out* this land.")

" *Out* three years old."—*Temp.* i. 2. 41, " *beyond* three years."

Explained by Nares, " completely."

From out. See 157.

184. Till is used for *to :*

"From the first corse *till* he that died to-day,"
Hamlet, i. 2. 105.

where probably *till* is a preposition, and "he" for "him." See **He.**

"Lean'd her breast up *till* a thorn."—*P. P.* st. 21.

Early Eng. "He said thus *til* (to) him," and, on the other hand, " *To* (till) we be gone." So "unto" in Chaucer for "until."

"I need not sing this them *until* (for '*unto* them')."
HEYWOOD.

" We know where*until* (whereto) it doth amount."
L. L. L. v. 2. 494.

" And hath shipped me in*til* (into) the land."—*Hamlet,* v. 1. 81.

185. To* (see also **Verbs, Infin.**). Radical meaning *motion towards.* Hence *addition.* This meaning is now only retained with verbs implying motion, and only the strong form " *too* " (comp. *of* and *off*) retains independently the meaning of addition. But in Elizabethan authors *too* is written *to,* and the prepositional meaning "in addition to" is found, without a verb of motion, and sometimes without any verb.

" But he could read and had your languages
And *to't* as sound a noddle," &c.—B. J. *Fox,* ii. 1.

"If he . . . *to* his shape, were heir of all this land."
K. J. i. 1. 144.

* Comp. πρός throughout.

" And to that dauntless temper of his mind
He hath a wisdom that doth guide his valour."

Macbeth, iii. 1. 52.

i.e. "*in addition to* that dauntless temper." *To*, in this sense, has been supplanted by "beside." Compare also

" Nineteen more, *to* myself."—B. J. *E. in &c.* iv. 5.

To is used still adverbially in "*to* and fro," and nautical expressions such as "heave *to*," "come *to*." This use explains "Go *to*," *M. of V.* ii. 2. 169. "Go" did not in Elizabethan or E. E. necessarily imply motion *from*, but motion generally. Hence "go *to*" meant little more than our stimulative " come, come."

186. To hence means motion, "with a view to," "for an end," &c. This is of course still common before verbs, but the Elizabethans used *to* in this sense before nouns.

"He which hath no stomach *to* this fight."—*Hen. V.* iv. 3. 35.

" For *to* that (to that end)
The multiplying villanies of Nature
Do swarm upon him."—*Macbeth*, i. 2. 10.

"Prepare yourself *to* death."—*W. T.* iii. 1. 167.

"Arm you *to* the sudden time."—*K. J.* v. 6. 26.

" The impression of keen whips I 'ld wear as rubies
And strip myself *to* (for) death as *to* a bed."

M. for M. ii. 4. 102.

"Giving to you no further personal power
To (for the purpose of) business with the king."

Hamlet, i. 2. 37.

"Pawn me *to* this your honour."—*T. A.* i. 1. 147.

"Few words, but, *to* effect, more than all yet."

Lear, iii. 1. 52.

"He is frank'd up *to* fatting for his pains."

Rich. III. i. 3. 314.

Hence it seems used for *for* in

"Ere I had made a prologue *to* my brains
They had begun the play."—*Hamlet*, v. 2. 30

And perhaps in

"This is a dear manakin *to* you, Sir Toby."—*T. N.* iii. 2. 57.

But see 419a, for this last example.

187. To hence, even without a verb of motion, means " motion to the side of." Hence "motion to and consequent rest near," as in

" Like yourself
Who ever yet have stood *to* charity."—*Hen. VIII.* ii. 4. 86.
" *To* this point I stand."—*Hamlet*, iv. 5. 187.
"I beseech you, stand *to* me."—*2 Hen. IV.* ii. 1. 70.

i.e. " Come and stand by me, help me."

Motion *against* in :

"The lady Beatrice hath a quarrel *to* you."—*M. Ado*, ii. 1. 44.
So *T. N.* iii. 4. 248 ; *Coriol.* iv. 5. 113.

Motion *to meet:*

" *To* her doom she dares not stand."—B. and F. *Fair Sh.* v. 1.

Motion *toward:*

"What wouldst thou have *to* Athens ?"—*T. of A.* iv. 3. 287.
" *To* Milan let me hear from thee by letters."
T. G. of V. i. 1. 57.

Hence "by the side of," "in comparison with."

"Impostors *to* true fear."—*Macb.* iii. 4. 64.

i.e. "Impostors when brought to the side of, and compared with, true fear."

" There is no woe *to* his correction,
Nor *to* his service no such joy on earth."
T. G. of V. ii. 4. 138, 139.
"The harlot's cheek, beautied with plastering art,
Is not more ugly *to* the thing that helps it
Than is my deed *to* my most painted word."
Hamlet, iii. 1. 51–53.

In " Treason can but peep *to* what it would,
Acts little of his will,"—*Ib.* iv. 5. 125.

either *to* means " towards," an unusual construction with " peep,"
or the meaning is " treason can do nothing more than peep in
comparison with what it wishes to do."

" Undervalued *to* tried gold."—*M. of V.* ii. 7. 53.

Hence " up to," "in proportion to," "according to."

" The Greeks are strong and skilful *to* their strength."
Tr. and Cr. i. 1. 7.
"That which we have we prize not *to* the worth."
M. Ado, iv. 1. 220.
" *To's* power he would
Have made them mules."—*Coriol.* ii. 1. 262.

"Perform'd to point the tempest that I bade thee."
              Temp. i. 2. 194.

"He needs not our mistrust, since he delivers
Our offices and what we have to do
To the direction just."—*Macb.* iii. 3. 4.

Hence "like."

"My lady, *to* the manner of the days,
In courtesy gives undeserving praise."—*L. L. L.* v. 2. 365.
                    "Looked it of the hue
To such as live in great men's bosoms?"—B. J. *Sejan.* v. 1.
"This is right *to* (exactly like) that (saying) of Horace."
              B. J. *E. out &c.* ii. 1.

To seems to mean "even up to" in

"And make my senses credit thy relation
To points that seem unpossible."—*P. of T.* v. 2. 125.

188. To is sometimes used without any sense of motion for
"near."
              "It would unclog my heart
Of what lies heavy *to 't.*"—*Coriol.* iv. 2. 48.
"Sits smiling *to* my heart."—*Hamlet,* i. 2. 124.

for "by" in

"Where . . . the best of all her sex
Doth only *to* her worthy self abide."—B. and F. *F. Sh.* ii. 1.

In the difficult passage (*W. T.* iv. 4. 550) :

"But, as the unthought on accident is guilty
To what we wildly do."

"Guilty" seems used for "responsible," and chance "is said to be
"responsible *to*" rashness (personified). (Or is *to* "as *to*," *i.e.* as
regards?)

In N. *P.* 175 there is "*to* the contrary," (but this is a translation
of "au contraire,") for "on the contrary."

To is inserted after "trust" (whereas we have rejected it in
parenthetical phrases, probaby for euphony's sake).

              "And, trust *to* me, Ulysses,
Our imputation will be oddly poised."—*Tr. and Cr.* i. 3. 339.

To seems "up to," "as much as," in

"I'll part sooner with my soul of reason than yield *to* one foot
of land."—B. and F. *Elder Brother,* iii. 5.

188a. "To," with Adjectives signifying obedience, &c.
To is still used in the sense of "towards" after some adjectives, such
as (1) "gentle," (2) "disobedient," (3) "open." But we could
not say

(1) "If thou dost find him *tractable to* us."—*Rich. III.* iii. 1. 174.
(2) "A will most *incorrect* (unsubmissive) to heaven."
Hamlet, i. 2. 95.
"The queen is *stubborn to* justice."—*Hen. VIII.* ii. 4. 122.
(3) "*Penetrable to* your kind entreats."—*Rich. III.* iii. 7. 225.
"Vulgar *to* sense." *—*Hamlet*, i. 2. 99.

i.e. "open to ordinary observation."
Similarly *to* is used after nouns where we should use "against,"
"in the sight of :"

"Fie ! 'tis a fault *to* heaven,
A fault against the dead, a fault *to* nature,
To reason most absurd."—*Hamlet*, i. 2. 103.

189. To, from meaning "like," came into the meaning of
"representation," "equivalence," "apposition." (Comp. Latin
"Habemus Deum amico.")

"I have a king here *to* my flatterer."—*Rich. II.* iv. 1. 306.
"To crave the French king's sister
To wife for Edward."—3 *Hen. VI.* iii. 1. 31.
"Now therefore would I have thee *to* my tutor."
T. G. of V. iii. 1. 84.
"Destiny . . . that hath *to* instrument this lower world."
Temp. iii. 2. 54.
"And with her *to* dowry some petty dukedoms."
Hen. V. iii. Prol. 31.
"Lay their swords *to* pawn."—*M. W. of W.* iii. 1. 113.
"Had I admittance and opportunity *to* friend."—*Cymb.* i. 4. 118.
"Tunis was never graced before with
Such a paragon *to* their queen."—*Temp.* ii. 1. 75.

Compare also *Macb.* iv. 3. 10 ; *J. C.* iii. 1. 143.

"The king had no port *to* friend."—CLARENDON, *Hist.* 7.
"A fond woman *to* my mother (*i.e.* who was my mother)
taught me so."—WAGER.

Thus "*to* boot" means "*by way of*, or for, addition." So in E. E.
"*to* sooth" is used for "forsooth."

* So "retentive *to*," *J. C.* i. 3. 95.

190. To, in the phrase "I would *to* God," may mean "near," "in the sight of;" or there may be a meaning of motion : "I should desire (even carrying my desire) *to* God." In the phrase "He that is cruel *to* halves" (B. J. *Disc.* 759), *to* means, perhaps, "up to the limit of." Possibly, however, this phrase may be nothing but a corruption of the more correct idiom "Would God that," which is more common in our version of the Bible than "I would." The *to* may be a remnant and corruption of the inflection of "would," "wol*de*;" and the *I* may have been added for the supposed necessity of a nominative. Thus

"Now wol*de* God that I might sleepen ever."
CHAUCER, Monke's Tale, 14746.

So "thou wert best" is a corruption of "it were best for thee."

This theory is rendered the more probable because, as a rule, in Wickliffe's version of the Old Testament, "Wolde God" is found in the older MSS., and is altered into "we wolden" in the later. Thus *Genesis* xvi. 3; *Numbers* xx. 3; *Joshua* vii. 7; *Judges* ix. 29; 2 *Kings* v. 3 (Forshall and Madden, 1850). However, Chaucer has "I hoped *to* God" repeatedly.

To was used, however, without any notion of "motion toward the future" in *to-night* (*last* night).

"I *did* dream *to-night*."—*M. of V.* ii. 5. 18 ; 2 *Hen. VI.* iii. 2. 31.

So in E. E. "*to* year" for "this year," "*to* summer," &c. Perhaps the provincial "I will come *the* night, *the* morn," &c. is a corruption of this "to." It is, indeed, suggested by Mr. Morris that *to* is a corruption of the demonstrative. On the other hand, *to* in E. E. was "often used with a noun to form adverbs."—LAYAMON (*Glossary*).

"He aras *to* þan mid-nihte,"—LAYAMON, i. 324.
is used for "he arose *in* the midnight."

Unto, like **To,** 185, is used for "in addition to :"

"*Unto* my mother's prayers I bend my knee."
Rich. II. v. 3. 97.

191. Upon ("for the purpose of") is still used in "*upon* an errand," but not, as in

"*Upon* malicious bravery dost thou come ?"—*Othello*,. i. 1. 100.

We should use "over" in

"I have no power *upon* you,"—*A. and C.* i. 3. 23.

and we should not use *upon* in

"And would usurp *upon* my watery eyes."—*T. A.* iii. 1. 269.
"Let your highness
Command *upon* me."—*Macbeth*, iii. 1. 17.

though after "claim" and "demand" *upon* is still used. So "an attack upon" is still English, but not

"I have o'erheard a plot of death *upon* him."—*Lear*, iii. 6. 96.

nor "I am yours . . . *upon* your will to suffer."—*A. W.* iv. 4. 30.

i.e. "in dependence on." It would seem that the metaphorical use of *upon* is now felt to be too bold unless suggested by some strong word implying an actual, and not a possible influence. Thus "claim" and "demand" are actual, while "power" may, perhaps, not be put in action. So "attack" and "assault" are the actual results of "plot." Yet the variable use of prepositions, and their close connection with particular words, is illustrated by the fact that we can say, "I will wait *upon* him," but not

"I thank you and will stay *upon* your leisure."—*A. W.* iii. 5. 48.

Even here, however, our "wait *upon*" means, like "call *upon*," an actual interview, and does not, like "stay *upon*," signify the "staying in hope of, or on the chance of, audience."

Upon also means "in consequence of."

"When he shall hear she died *upon* (*i.e.* not 'after,' but 'in consequence of ") his words."—*M. Ado*, iv. 1. 225.

"And fled is he *upon* this villany."—*Ib.* v. 1. 258.

"Break faith *upon* commodity."—*K. J.* ii. 1. 597.

"Thy son is banish'd *upon* good advice."—*Rich. II.* i. 3. 233.

In "You have too much respect *upon* the world,"
M. of V. i. 1. 74.

there is an allusion to the literal meaning of "respect." "You *look* too much *upon* the world." The *upon* is connected with "respect," and is not used like our "for" in "I have no respect *for* him."

The use of "upon" to denote "at" or "immediately after" is retained in "*upon* this;" but we could not say

"You come most carefully *upon* your hour."—*Hamlet*, i. 1. 6.

192. Upon is often used like *on* adverbially after the verb "look."

"Nay, all of you that stand and *look upon*."—*Rich. II.* iv. 1. 237.

"Why stand we like soft-hearted women here
And *look upon*, as if," &c.—3 *Hen. VI.* ii. 3. 27.

"Strike all that *look upon* with marvel, come."—*W. T.* v. 3. 100.

"Near *upon*" is adverbial in

"And very *near upon*
The duke is entering."—*M. for M.* iv. 6. 14.

"Indeed, my lord, it followed hard *upon*."—*Hamlet,* i. 2. 179.

Upon, from meaning superposition, comes to mean "in accordance with" (like "after"):

"*Upon* my power I may dismiss this court."
M. of V. iv. 1. 104.

193. With (which, like "by," signifies juxtaposition) is often used to express the juxtaposition of cause and effect.

"I live *with* (on) bread like you."—*Rich. II.* iii. 2. 175.

We could say "he trembles *with* fear," "fear" being regarded as *connected with* the trembler, but not

"My inward soul
With nothing trembles : at something it grieves
More than *with* parting from my lord the king."
Rich. II. ii. 2. 12, 13.

"As an unperfect actor on the stage
Who *with* his fear is put besides his part."—*Sonn.* 23.

We should say "*in* his fear" (or "*by* his fear," personifying Fear) ; or append the clause to the verb, "put beside his part *with* fear."

"It were a better death than die *with* mocks,
Which is as bad as die *with* tickling."—*M. Ado*, iii. 1. 79, 80.

"Another choaked *with* the kernell of a grape, and an emperour die by the scratch of a combe, and Aufidius *with* stumbling against the doore, and Lepidus *with* hitting his foot."—Montaigne, 32.

Here the use of "by" seems intended to distinguish an external from an internal cause.

We say "so far gone in fear," but not

"*Thus* both are gone *with* conscience and remorse."
Rich. III. iv. 3. 20.

"This comes *with* seeking you."—*T. N.* iii. 4. 366.

"I feel remorse in myself *with* his words."—*2 Hen. VI.* iv. 7. 111.

More rarely, *with* is used with an agent :

" Rounded in the ear
With that same purpose-changer, that sly devil."—*K. J.* ii. 1. 567.

" We had like to have had our two noses snapped off *with* two old men without teeth."—*M. Ado,* v. 1. 116.

" Boarded *with* a pirate."—*2 Hen. VI.* iv. 9. 33.

" He was torn to pieces *with* a bear."—*W. T.* v. 2. 66.

" Assisted *with* your honoured friends."—*Ib.* v. 1. 13.

This explains

" Since I am crept in favour *with* myself
I will maintain it with some little cost."—*Rich. III.* i. 2. 260.

The obvious interpretation is, " since I have crept into the good graces of myself ;" but the second line shows the "I" to be superior to "myself," which is to be maintained by the "I." The true explanation is, " since I have crept into (Lady Anne's) favour *with the aid of* my personal appearance, I will pay some attention to my person." Add, probably, *Hamlet,* iii. 2. 207.

This meaning is common in E. E. :

" He was slayn *wyþ* (by) Ercules."
R. OF BRUNNE, *Chron.* i. 12. 340.

With = " by means of."

" He went about to make amends *with* committing a worse fault." —N. *P.* 176, where the French is "par une autre." So N. *P.* 176.

With = " in addition to," even when there are not two nouns to be connected together :

"Very wise and *with* his wisdome very valiant."—N. *P.* 664.

With is, perhaps, used for " as regards," "in relation to," as in our modern " this has not much weight *with* me," in

" Is Cæsar *with* Antonius priz'd so slight ?"—*A. and C.* i. 1. 56.

though here, perhaps, as above, *with* may mean "by." At all events the passage illustrates the connection between "with" and "by." Compare

" His taints and honours
Wag'd equal *with* (*i.e.* in) him."—*A. and C.* v. 1. 31.

"So fond *with* gain."—*R. of L.* 134.

194. With is hence loosely used to signify any connection with an action, as in "to change *with*" (MONTAIGNE, 233), where we should say "to exchange *for*." So, though we still say "I parted *with* a house," or "*with* a servant (considered as a chattel)," we could not say

> "When you parted *with* the king."—*Rich. II.* ii. 2. 2.

> "As a long-parted mother *with* her child."
>
> > *Ib.* iii. 2. 8 ; *Rich. III.* i. 4. 251.

where *with* is connected with parting.   See 419a.   So

> "I rather will suspect the sun *with* cold
> Than thee *with* wantonness."—*M. W. of W.* iv. 4. 5.

as we say "I charge him *with*."

> "Next them, *with* some small distance, follows a gentleman bearing the purpose."—*Hen. VIII.* ii. 4, *stage direction.*

> "Equal *with*," 3 *Hen. VI.* iii. 2. 137, is like our "level *with*." In

> > "The violence of either grief or joy
> > Their own enactures *with* themselves destroy,"
> >
> > > *Hamlet,* iii. 2. 207.

"*with* themselves" seems to mean "by or of themselves."

Note   "They have all persuaded *with* him."—*M. of V.* iii. 2. 283. *i.e.* "argued with."   So "flatter" is used for "deal flatteringly" in *T. N.* i. 5. 322, and in the first of the following lines :

> "*K. Rich.* Should dying men flatter *with* those that live?
> *Gaunt.* No, no, men living flatter those that die."
>
> > *Rich. II.* ii. 1. 88, 89.

> "(She) married *with* my uncle."—*Hamlet,* i. 2. 151.

> "I will break *with* her."—*M. Ado,* i. 1. 311.

i.e. "open the matter in conversation with."

195. With is used by Ben Jonson for *like.*

> > "Not above a two shilling.
> *B.* 'Tis somewhat *with* the least."—*B. J. E. in &c.* i. 4.

"Something like, very near the least."

"He is not *with* himself."—*T. A.* i. 1. 368. *i.e.* "in his senses."

Ben Jonson also uses *without* in the sense of "unlike," "beyond."

> "An act *without* your sex, it is so rare."—*B. J. Sejan.* ii. 1.

196. Withal, the emphatic form of "with" (see "all"), is used for *with* after the object at the end of a sentence.   Mostly, the object is a relative.

> "These banish'd men *that* I have kept *withal.*"
>
> > *T. G. of V.* v. 4. 152.

i.e.   "With whom I have lived."—*K. J.* iii. 1. 327.

"And this is false you burden me *withal.*"—*C. of E.* v. i. 268.
i.e. "this *with* which you burden me."

" Such a fellow is not to be talk'd *withal.*"—*M. for M.* v. i. 347.

Sometimes "this" is understood after *withal*, so that it means "with all this," and is used adverbially :

" So glad of this as they I cannot be
Who are surprised *withal.*"—*Temp.* iv. i. 217.

i.e. "surprised with, or at, this." Here however, perhaps, and elsewhere certainly, *with* means "in addition to," and "*with*-all (this)" means "besides."

" I must have liberty *withal.*"—*A. Y. L.* ii. 7. 48.
" Adding *withal.*"—*Rich. II.* iv. i. 18, &c.

But in " I came hither to acquaint you *withal*,"—*A. Y. L.* i. i. 139. there is no meaning of "besides," and *withal* means "therewith," "with it."

Withal follows its object, but is (on account of the "all" at the end of the previous verse) not placed at the end of the sentence, in

"Even all I have, yea, and myself and all
Will I *withal* endow a child of thine."—*Rich. III.* iv. 4. 249.

197. Without (used locally for " outside ").

" What seal is that that hangs *without* thy bosom?"
Rich. II. v. i. 56.
" *Without* the peril of the Athenian law."—*M. N. D.* iv. i. 150.
" A mile *without* the town."—*Ib.* i. i. 104.

This explains the pun :

" *Val.* Are all these things perceived in me ?
Speed. They are all perceived *without* ye."—*T. G. of V.* ii. i. 85.

Reversely, " out of" is used metaphorically for "without."

"Neither can anything please God that we do if it be done *out of* charity."—HALLIWELL.

198. Prepositions are frequently omitted after verbs of motion. Motion *in :*

"To *reel* the streets at noon."*—*A. and C.* i. 4. 20.
"She *wander'd* many a wood."—SPENS. *F. Q.* i. 7. 28.
"To *creep* the ground." " *Tower* the sky."—MILTON, *P. L.* vii. 441.

* "To see great Pompey *pass* the streets of Rome."—*J. C.* i. i. 47.

Motion *to* or *from* :

"That gallant spirit hath *aspired* the clouds."
    R. and J. iii. 1. 122.
"Ere we could *arrive* the point proposed."—*J. C.* i. 2. 110.
"*Arrived* our coast."—3 *Hen. VI.* v. 3. 8.
"Some sailors that *escaped* the wreck."—*M. of V.* iii. 1. 110.
"When we with tears *parted* Pentapolis."—*P. of T.* v. 3. 38.
"*Depart* the chamber and leave us."—2 *Hen. IV.* iv. 4. 91.
"To *depart* the city."—N. *P.* 190.
"Since presently your souls must *part* your bodies."
    Rich. II. iii. 1. 3.

We can still say "to descend the hill," but not "to descend the summit," nor

"Some (of her hair) *descended* her sheav'd hat."—*L. C.* 31.

These omissions may perhaps illustrate the idiom in Latin, and in Greek poetry.

Verbs of ablation, such as "bar," "banish," "forbid," often omit the preposition before the place or inanimate object. Thus

"We'll *bar* thee *from* succession."—*W. T.* iv. 4. 440.

Or   "*Of·* succession."—*Cymb.* iii. 3. 102.

becomes   "*Bars* me the right."
    M. of V. ii. 1. 16 ; *Rich. III.* iv. 4. 400 ; *A. Y. L.* i. 1. 20.

Where a verb can take either the person or thing as an object, it naturally takes an indirect object without a preposition. Compare

"Therefore we *banish* you our territories."—*Rich. II.* i. 3. 139.

198 a. The preposition is omitted after some verbs and adjectives that imply "value," "worth," &c.

"The queen is *valued* thirty thousand strong."
    3 *Hen. VI.* v. 3. 14.
"Some precepts *worthy* the note."—*A. W.* iii. 5. 104.

An imitation of this construction is, perhaps, to be traced in

"*Guilty* so great a crime."—B. and F. *F. Sh.* iv. 1.

The omission of a preposition before "good cheap" (A.-S. *ceáp*, "price," "bargain"), 1 *Hen. IV.* iii. 3. 50, may perhaps be thus explained without reference to the French "bon marché." And thus, without any verb or adjective of worth,

"He has disgraced me and hindered me *half a million.*"
    M. of V. iii. 1. 57.

"Semblative" (unless adverbial [1]) is used with the same construction as "like" in

"And all is *semblative* a woman's part."—*T. N.* i. 4. 34.

199. The preposition is also sometimes omitted before the *thing* heard after verbs of hearing :

"To *listen* our purpose."—*M. Ado,* iii. 1. 12.
"*List* a brief tale."—*Lear,* v. 3. 181.

So *J. C.* v. 5. 15 ; *Hamlet,* i. 3. 30 ; *J. C.* iv. 1. 41.

"*Listening* their fear."—*Macbeth,* ii. 2. 28.

Hence in the passive,

"He that no more must say is *listen'd* more."
Rich. II. ii. 1. 9.

"*Hearken** the end."—2 *Hen. IV.* ii. 4. 305 ; *Temp.* i. 2. 122.

200. The preposition is omitted after some verbs which can easily be regarded as transitive. Thus if we can say "plot my death," there is little difficulty in the licence.

"That do *conspire* (for) my death."—*Rich. III.* iii. 4. 62.
"(In) Which from the womb I did *participate.*"—*T.N.* v. 1. 245.
"She *complain'd* (about) her wrongs."—*R. of L.* 1839.
"And his physicians *fear* (for) him mightily."
Rich. III. i. 1. 137.

So 1 *Hen. IV.* iv. 1. 24 ; *T. of A.* ii. 2. 12 ; *T. A.* ii. 3. 305 ; *M. of V.* iii. 2. 29.

This explains

"O, fear *me* not."—*Hamlet,* i. 3. 52 ; iii. 4. 7.
"That he would *labour* (for) my delivery."—*Rich. III.* i. 1. 253.
"To *look* (for) your dead."—*Hen. V.* iv. 7. 76.
"I must go *look* (for) my twigs."—*A. W.* iii. 6. 115.
"He hath been all this day to *look* (for) you."—*A. Y. L.* ii. 5. 34.

And in the difficult passage—

"O, whither hast thou led me, Egypt? See
How I convey my shame out of thine eyes
By *looking* back what I have left behind
'Stroy'd in dishonour."—*A. and C.* iii. 10. 53.

While turning away from Cleopatra, Antony appears to say, that he is *looking back* (for) the fleet that he has left dishonoured and destroyed.

* The Globe inserts "at."

So " *Scoffing* (at) his state."—*Rich. III.* iii. 2. 163.
  " *Smile* you (at) my speeches as I were a fool!"—*Lear*, ii. 2. 88.
  " Thou *swear'st* (by) thy gods in vain."—*Ib.* i. 1. 163.
  " Yet thus far, Griffith, give me leave to *speak* (of) him."
                                        Hen. VIII. iv. 2. 32.

  Both here and in *L. L. L.* v. 2. 349 ; *Macbeth*, iv. 3. 159; *T. N.*
i. 4. 20, "speak" is used for describe. In *Macbeth*, iv. 3. 154, "'tis
spoken" is used for "'tis said."   Again, "said" is used for
"called" in

  " To be *said* an honest man and a good housekeeper."
                        T. N. iv. 2. 10 ; so *Macbeth*, iv. 3. 210.

  " Talking that" is used like " saying that" in *Tempest*, ii. 1. 96.
" Speak," however, in *R. and J.* iii. 1. 158, " *Spake* him fair"
means " speak to :" but in the same expression *M. of V.* iv. 1. 271
it means " speak of."   Similarly, " whisper" is often used without
a preposition before a personal object.

  " He came to *whisper* Wolsey."—*Hen. VIII.* i. 1. 179.
  " They *whisper* one another in the ear."—*K. J.* iv. 2. 189.
  " Your followers I will *whisper* to the business."
                                        W. T. i. 2. 437.

Rarely, " *whisper* her ear."—*M. Ado*, iii. 1. 4.

  In some cases, as in

  " She will *attend* it better,"
                T. N. i. 3. 27, 2. 453; *M. of V.* v. 4. 103.
the derivation may explain the transitive use.

  " *Despair* thy charm,"—*Macbeth*, v. 8. 13.
is, perhaps, a Latinism.   So "sympathise," meaning "suffer with,"
is used thus :
              " The senseless brands will *sympathise*
  The heavy accent of thy moving tongue."
                                        Rich. II. v. 1. 47.

  " Deprive," meaning " take away a thing from a person," like
" rid," can dispense with " of" before the impersonal object.

  " 'Tis honour to deprive dishonour'd life."—*R. of L.* 1186.

This explains how we should understand—

  " Which might deprive your sovereignty of 'reason."
                                        Hamlet, i. 4. 73.

i.e. " which might *take away* your controlling principle of reason."
So, perhaps, " *Frees* all faults."—*Tempest*, Epilogue, 18.

This seems to have arisen from the desire of brevity. Compare the tendency to convert nouns, adjectives, and neuter verbs into active verbs (290).

201. The preposition was also omitted before the indirect object of some verbs, such as "say," "question," just as we still omit it after the corresponding verbs, "tell" and "ask."

" *Sayest* (to) me so, friend?"—*T. of Sh.* i. 2. 190.
" You will *say* (to) a beggar, nay."—*Rich. III.* iii. 1. 119.
" Still *question'd* (of) me the story of my life."—*Othello*, i. 3. 129.
In " *Hear* me a word,"—*Rich. III.* iv. 4. 180.
it must be a question whether *me* or *word* is the direct object. In

"I *cry* thee mercy,"—*Rich. III.* iv. 4. 515.
"mercy" is the direct object. This is evident from the shorter form

"(I) *Cry* mercy."—*Rich. III.* v. 3. 224.
After "give," we generally omit "to," when the object of "to" is a personal noun or pronoun. But we could not write—

" A bed-swerver, even as bad as these
That (to whom) vulgars (the vulgar) give bold'st titles."
W. T. ii. 1. 94.
" Unto his lordship, (to) whose unwished yoke
My soul consents not to give sovereignty."—*M. N. D.* i. 1. 81.
Somewhat similar is

" This 'longs the text."—*P. of T.* ii. Gower, 40.
for "belongs (to) the text."

202. Preposition omitted in adverbial expressions of time, manner, &c.

"Forbear to sleep *the nights*, and fast *the days*."
Rich. III. iv. 4. 118.
This is illustrated by our modern

" (Of) *What kind* of man is he ?"—*T. N.* i. 5. 159.
" But wherefore do not you *a mightier way*
Make war upon this bloody tyrant, time?"—*Sonn.* 16.
" My poor country
(Shall) More suffer, and *more sundry ways*, than ever."
Macbeth, iv. 3. 48 ; so *Ib.* i. 3. 154.
" Revel *the night*, rob, murder, and commit
The newest sins *the newest kind of ways*."—*2 Hen. IV.* iv. 5. 126.

"And ye sad hours that move *a sullen pace.*"
B. and F. *F. Sh.* iv. 1.

"I will a round unvarnish'd tale deliver
Of my whole course of life ; *what drugs, what charms,
What conjuration, and what nightly magic*
(For such proceeding I am charg'd withal)
I won his daughter."—*Othello,* i. 3. 91.

"How many would the peaceful city quit
To welcome him ! Much more, and *much more cause,**
Did they this Harry."—*Hen. V.* v. Prol. 34.

" To keep Prince Harry in continual laughter *the wearing out of
six fashions,* which is four terms."—2 *Hen. IV.* v. 1. 84.

"Why hast thou not served thyself into my table *so many meals?*"
—*Tr. and Cr.* ii. 3. 45 : *i.e.* "*during* so many meals."

"To meet his grace *just distance* 'tween our armies."
2 *Hen. IV.* iv. 1. 225.

"That I did suit me *all points* like a man."—*A. Y. L.* i. 3. 118.

"But were I not *the better part* made mercy."—*Ib.* iii. 1. 2.

"And when *such time* they have begun to cry."—*Coriol.* iii. 3. 19.

"Where and *what time* your majesty shall please."
Rich. III. iv. 4. 450.

"*What time* we will our celebration keep."—*T. N.* iv. 3. 30.

"Awhile they bore her up,
Which time she chanted snatches of old tunes."—*Ham.* iv. 7. 178.

In the following cases it would seem that a prepositional phrase is
condensed into a preposition, just as "by the side of" (Chaucer,
"*byside* Bathe") becomes "be-side," and governs an object.

"*On this side* Tiber."—*J. C.* iii. 2. 254.

"Fasten'd ourselves *at either end* the mast."—*C. of E.* i. 1. 86.

"A sheet of paper writ o' *both sides the leaf.*" —*L. L. L.* v. 2. 8.

"*On each side her* the Bishops of London and Winchester."
Hen. VIII. iv. 1 (*order of coronation*).

"She is as forward of our breeding as
She is *in the rear* our birth."—*W. T.* iv. 4. 522.

" Our purpose " seems to mean " for our purpose," in

"Not to know what we speak to one another, so we seem to
know, is to know straight, *our purpose:* chough's language, gabble
enough and good enough."—*A. W.* iv. 1. 21.

This seems the best punctuation. " Provided we *seem* to know
what we say to one another, ignorance is exactly as good as knowledge, for our purpose."

* But "and (there was) much more cause " may be a parenthesis.

Hence the use of *this* for "in this way" or "thus" is not so bold as it seems :

> "What am I that thou shouldst contemn me *this* ?
> What were thy lips the worse for one poor kiss?"
>
> *V. and A.* 203.

Perhaps, however, "contemn" is confused with "refuse." But *this* is used for "thus" in E. E.

All constantly repeated adverbial expressions have a tendency to abbreviate or lose their prepositions. Compare "alive " for "on live," "around " for "in round," "chance" for "perchance," "like " for "belike," &c. In some adverbial expressions the preposition can be omitted when the noun is qualified by an adjective, but not otherwise. Thus we can use "yester-day," "last night," "this week," adverbially, but not "day," "night," "week," because in the latter words there is nothing to indicate *how* time is regarded. In O. E. the inflections were sufficient to justify an adverbial use, "day*es*," "night*es*." (Compare νυκτός.) But the inflections being lost, the adverbial use was lost with them.

203. Prepositions: transposed. (See also **Upon.**) In A.-S. and E. E. prepositions are often placed after their objects. In some cases the preposition may be considered as a separable part of a compound transitive verb. Thus in

> " Ne how the Grekes with a huge route
>   Three times *riden* all the fire *aboute*,"—CHAUC. *C. T.* 2954.

"ride about" may be considered a transitive verb, having as its object "fire." Naturally, emphatic forms of prepositions were best suited for this emphatic place at the end of the sentence ; and therefore, though "to," "tyll," "fro," "with," "by," "fore," were thus transposed, yet the longer forms, "untylle," "before," "behind," "upon," "again," were preferred. Hence in the Elizabethan period, when the transposition of the weaker prepositions was not allowed, except in the compound words "whereto," "herewith," &c. (compare "se-cum, quo-cum") the longer forms are still, though rarely, transposed.

For this reason, "with," when transposed, is emphasized into "withal." The prepositions "after," "before," and "upon," are thus transposed by Shakespeare :

> " God *before*."—*Hen. V.* i. 2. 307 ; iii. 6. 55, for "'fore God."
> " Hasten your generals *after*."—*A. and C.* ii. 4. 2.

So "I need not sing this them *until* (unto)."—HEYWOOD.

"For fear lest day should look their shames *upon*."
M. N. D. iii. 2. 385.

"That bare-foot plod I the cold ground *upon*."—*A. W.* iii. 4. 6.

"For my good will is to't,
And yours it is *against*."—*Tempest,* iii. 1. 31.

The use of prepositions after the relative, which is now somewhat avoided, but is very common in E. E., is also common in Shakespeare, and is evidently better adapted to the metre than the modern idiom, as far as regards the longer forms. "Upon which" is not so easily metricized as

"Ten thousand men *that* fishes gnawed *upon*."—*Rich. III.* i. 4. 25.

"The pleasure *that* some fathers feed *upon*."—*Rich. II.* ii. 1. 79.

204. Prepositions transposed. "It stands me upon." This phrase cannot be explained, though it is influenced, by the custom of transposition. Almost inextricable confusion seems to have been made by the Elizabethan authors between two distinct idioms : (1) "it stands on" (adv.), or "at hand," or "upon" (comp. "instat," προσήκει), *i.e.* "it is of importance," "it concerns," "it is a matter of duty ;" and (2) "I stand upon" (adj.), *i.e.* "I *in-sist* upon."

In (1) the full phrase would be, "it stands on, upon, to me," but, *owing to the fact that " to me" or " me" (the dative inflection) is unemphatic, and " upon" is emphatic and often used at the end of the sentence,* the words were transposed into "it stands me *upon*." "Me" was thus naturally mistaken for the object of *upon*.

Hence we have not only the correct form—

"It stands *me* (dative) much *upon* (adverb)
To stop all hopes."—*Rich. III.* iv. 2. 59.

(So *Hamlet,* v. 2. 63, where it means "it is imperative on me." But also the incorrect—

"It stands your grace *upon* to do him right."
Rich. II. ii. 3. 138.

"It only stands
Our lives *upon* to use our strongest hands."—*A. and C.* ii. 1. 51.

where "grace" and "lives" are evidently intended to be the objects of "upon," whereas the Shakespearian use of "me" (220) renders it possible, though by no means probable, that "me," in the first of the above examples, was used as a kind of dative.

Hence by analogy—

"It lies you *on* to speak."—*Coriol.* iii. 2. 52.

The fact that this use of *upon* in "stand *upon*" is not a mere poetical transposition, but a remnant of an old idiom imperfectly understood, may be inferred from the transposition occurring in Elizabethan prose :

"Sigismund sought now by all means (*as it stood him upon*) to make himself as strong as he could."—NARES.

Perhaps this confusion has somewhat confused the meaning of the personal verb "I stand on." It means "I trust in" (*M. W. of W.* ii. 1. 242), "insist on" (*Hen. V.* v. 2. 93), and "I depend on" (*R. and J.* ii. 2. 93), and in

"The moist star
Upon whose influence Neptune's empire stands."

Hamlet, i. 1. 119.

PRONOUNS.

205. Personal, Irregularities of (omission of, insertion of , see **Relative** and **Ellipses**). The inflections of Personal Pronouns are frequently neglected or misused. It is perhaps impossible to trace a law in these irregularities. Sometimes, however, euphony and emphasis may have successfully contended against grammar. This may explain *I* in "and *I*," "but *I*," frequently used for *me.* "'Tween you and *I*" seems to have been a regular Elizabethan idiom. The sound of *d* and *t* before *me* was avoided. For reasons of euphony also the ponderous *thou* is often ungrammatically replaced by *thee*, or inconsistently by *you*. This is particularly the case in questions and requests, where, the pronoun being especially unemphatic, *thou* is especially objectionable. To this day many of the Friends use *thee* invariably for *thou*, and in the Midland and North of England we have "wilta ?" for "wilt *thou* ?" Compare E. E. "wiltow ?" for "wilt thou ?" "þinkestow ?" for "thinkest thou ?" and similarly, in Shakespeare, *thou* is often omitted after a questioning verb. Again, since *he* and *she* could be used (see below) for "man" and "woman," there was the less harshness in using *he* for *him* and *she* for *her*. Where an objective pronoun is immediately followed by a finite verb, it is sometimes treated as the subject, as below, "no man *like he* doth grieve."

206. He for **him :**

> "Which of *he* or Adrian, for a good wager, begins to crow ?"
> *Tempest,* ii. 1. 28.

Some commentators insert "them" after "which of." (See 408.)

> "I would wish me only *he.*"—*Coriol.* i. 1. 236.

> "And yet no man like *he* doth grieve my heart."
> *R. and J.* iii. 5. 84.

> "From the first corse till *he* that died to-day."—*Ham.* i. 2. 104.

where "till" is a preposition. See **Prepositions, Till,** 184.

207. He for **him** *precedes* its governing verb in the following examples :

> "Thus *he* that over-ruled I over-sway'd."—*V. and A.* 109.

> "And *he* my husband best of all affects."—*M. W. of W.* iv. 4. 87.

So probably *he* depends upon "within" in

> "'Tis better thee without than *he* within."—*Macbeth,* iii. 3. 14.

208. Him for **he.**

Him is often put for "he," by attraction to "whom" understood, for "he whom."

> "*Him* (he whom) I accuse
> By this the city ports hath enter'd."—*Coriol.* v. 6. 6.

> "Ay, better than *him* (he whom) I am before knows me."
> *A. Y. L.* i. 1. 46.

> "When *him* (whom) we serve's away."—*A. and C.* iii. 1. 15.

> "Your party in converse, *him* (whom) you would sound,
> He closes with you," &c.—*Hamlet,* ii. 1. 42.

Sometimes the relative is expressed :

> "His brother and yours abide distracted—but chiefly *him that* you term'd Gonzalo."—*Temp.* v. i. 14.

Sometimes *he* is omitted :

> "*Whom* I serve above is my master."—*A. W.* ii. 3. 26.

> "To (him to) *whom* it must be done."—*J. C.* ii. 2. 331.

In   "Damn'd be *him,*"—*Macbeth,* v. 8. 34.

perhaps *let,* or some such word, was implied.

209. I for **me** (for euphony : see 205) :

> "Here's none but thee and *I.*"—*2 Hen. VI.* i. 2. 69.

> "All debts are cleared between you and *I.*"—*M. of V.* iii. 2. 321.

"You know my father hath no child but *I*."—*A. Y. L.* i. 1. 46.

"Unless you would devise some virtuous lie
And hang some praise upon deceased *I*."—*Sonn.* 72.

The rhyme is an obvious explanation of the last example. But, in all four, *I* is preceded by a dental.

So "Which may make this island
Thine own for ever, and *I*, thy Caliban,
For aye thy foot-licker."—*Temp.* iv. 1. 217.

210. Me for I :

"No mightier than thyself or *me*."—*J. C.* i. 3. 76.

"Is she as tall as *me*?"—*A. and C.* iii. 3. 14.

Probably *than* and *as* were used with a quasi-prepositional force.

211. She for her :

"Yes, you have seen Cassio and *she* together."—*O.* iv. 2. 3.

"So saucy with the hand of *she* here—what's her name?"

A. and C. iii. 13. 98.

She was more often used for "woman" than "he" for "man." Hence, perhaps, *she* seemed more like an uninflected noun than "he" and we may thus extenuate the remarkable anomaly

"Praise *him* that got thee, *she* that gave thee suck."

Tr. and Cr. ii. 3. 252.

212. Thee for thou.

Verbs followed by *thee* instead of *thou* have been called reflexive. But though "haste *thee*," and some other phrases with verbs of motion, may be thus explained, and verbs were often thus used in E. E., it is probable that "look *thee*," "hark *thee*," are to be explained by euphonic reasons. *Thee*, thus used, follows imperatives which, being themselves emphatic, require an unemphatic pronoun. The Elizabethans reduced *thou* to *thee*. We have gone further, and rejected it altogether. (See 205.)

"Blossom, speed *thee* well."—*W. T.* iii. 3. 46.

"Look *thee* here, boy."—*Ib.* 116.

"Run *thee* to the parlour."—*M. Ado*, iii. 1. 1.

"Haste *thee*."—*Lear*, v. 3. 251.

"Stand *thee* by, friar."—*M. Ado*, iv. 1. 24.

"Hark *thee* a word."—*Cymb.* i. 5. 32.

"Look *thee*, 'tis so."—*T. of A.* iv. 3. 530.

"Come *thee* on."—*A. and C.* iv. 7. 16.

"Now, fellow, fare *thee* well."—*Lear*, iv. 6. 41.
"Hold *thee*, there's my purse."—*A. W.* iv. 5. 46; *J. C.* v. 3. 85.
"Take *thee* that too."—*Macbeth*, ii. 1. 5.

In the two latter instances *thee* is the dative.

Thee is probably the dative in

"Thinkst *thee* ?"—*Hamlet*, v. 2. 63.

or, at all events, there is, perhaps, confusion between "Thinks it *thee ?*" *i.e.* "does it (E. E.) seem to *thee?*" and "thinkst *thou ?*" Very likely "thinkst" is an abbreviation of "thinks it." (See 297.) Compare the confusion in

"Where it *thinkst* best unto your royal selfe."
Rich. III. iii. 1. 63 (Folio).

213. Thee for thou is also found after the verb to be, not merely in the Fool's mouth :

"I would not be *thee*, nuncle."—*Lear*, i. 4. 204.

but also Timon :

"I am not *thee*."—*T. of A.* iv. 3. 277.

and Suffolk :

"It is *thee* I fear."—*2 Hen. VI.* iv. 1. 117.

where *thee* is, perhaps, influenced by the verb, "I fear," so that there is a confusion between "It is *thou* whom I fear" and "*Thee* I fear." In these cases *thee* represents a person not regarded as acting, but about whom something is predicated. Hence *thou* was, perhaps, changed to *thee* according to the analogy of the sound of *he* and *she*, which are used for "man" and "woman."

214. Them for they:

"Your safety, for the which myself and *them*
Bend their best studies."—*K. J.* iv. 2. 50.

Perhaps *them* is attracted by "myself," which naturally suggests the objective "myself and (they) *them*(selves)."

215. Us for we in "shall*'s*." "Shall" (315), originally meaning necessity or obligation, and therefore not denoting an *action* on the part of the subject, was used in the South of England as an impersonal verb. (Compare Latin and Greek.) So Chaucer, "*us* oughte," and we also find "as *us* wol," *i.e.* "as it is pleasing to us." Hence in Shakespeare

" Say, where shall'*s* lay him ?"—*Cymb.* iv. 3. 233.
"Shall'*s* have a play of this?"—*Ib.* v. 5. 28.
"Shall'*s* attend you there?"—*W. T.* i. 2. 178.
"Shall'*s* to the Capitol?"—*Coriol.* iv. 6. 148.

216. After a conjunction and before an infinitive we often find
I, thou, &c., where in Latin we should have "me," "te,"
&c. The conjunction seems to be regarded as introducing a new
sentence, instead of connecting one clause with another. Hence the
pronoun is put in the nominative, and a verb is, perhaps, to be
supplied from the context.

" What he is indeed
More suits you to conceive *than I* (find it suitable) to speak of."
A. Y. L. i. 2. 279.
i.e. "than that I should speak of it."

" A heavier grief could not have been imposed
Than I to speak my griefs unspeakable."—*C. of E.* i. 1. 33.
" The soft way which thou dost confess
Were fit for thee to use *as they* to claim."—*Coriol.* iii. 2. 83.
" Making night hideous, *and we* fools of nature
So horridly to shake our disposition."—*Hamlet,* i. 4. 54.
"Heaven would that she these gifts should have,
And I to live and die her slave."—*A. Y. L.* iii. 2. 162.

Sometimes the infinitive is implied, but not expressed:

" To beg of thee it is my more dishonour
Than thou of them."—*Coriol.* iii. 2. 125.

I, thou, and *he,* are also used for *me, thee,* and *him,* when they
stand quasi-independently at some distance from the governing verb
or preposition.

" But what o' that ? Your majesty and *we* that have free souls,
it touches us not."—*Hamlet,* iii. 2. 252.
"I shall think the better of myself and thee during my life ; *I*
for a valiant champion, and *thou* for a true prince."—1 *Hen. IV.*
ii. 4. 300.
" (God) make me that nothing have with nothing griev'd,
And *thou* with all pleas'd that hast all achieved."
Rich. II. iv. 1. 217.
" With that same purpose-changer, that sly devil,
That daily break-vow, *he* that wins of all."—*K. J.* ii. 1. 568.

> "Now let me see the proudest,
> *He* that dares most, but wag his finger at thee."
>   *Hen. VIII.* v. 3. 131.

(To punctuate, as in the Globe, "the proudest *he*," is intolerably harsh.)

> "Justice, sweet prince, against that woman there,
> *She* whom thou gavest to me to be my wife,
> That hath abused and dishonour'd me."—*C. of E.* v. 1. 198.

> "Why, Harry, do I tell *thee* of my foes
> Which art my near'st and dearest enemy,
> *Thou* that art like enough," &c.?—1 *Hen. IV.* iii. 2. 123.

217. His was sometimes used, by mistake, for *'s*, the sign of the possessive case, particularly after a proper name, and with especial frequency when the name ends in *s*. This mistake arose in very early times. The possessive inflection *'s* (like the dative plural inflection *um*) was separated by scribes from its noun. Hence after the feminine name "Guinivere," we have in the later text of LAYA-MON, ii. 511, "for Gwenayfer *his* love." The *h* is no more a necessary part of this separate inflection than it is of "his," the third pers. sing. indic. pres. of "beon" ("be"). "His" is constantly found for "is" in Layamon. No doubt the coincidence in sound between the inflection *'s* and the possessive "his" made the separation seem more natural, and eventually confused *'s* with *his*.

> "Mars *his* sword . . . nor Neptune's trident nor Apollo's bow."
>   B. J. *Cy.'s Rev.* i. 1.

Also, by analogy,

> "Pallas *her* glass."—BACON, *Adv. of L.* 278.

This is more common with monosyllables than with dissyllables, as the *'s* in a dissyllable is necessarily almost mute. Thus

> "The count *his* gallies."—*T. N.* iii. 3. 26.

> "Mars *his* true moving."—1 *Hen. VI.* i. 2. 1.

So *Tr. and Cr.* iv. 5. 176, 255, &c.

> "Charles *his* gleeks."—1 *Hen. VI.* iii. 2. 123.

but never, or very rarely, "Phœbus *his*."

The possessive inflection in dissyllables ending in a sibilant sound is often expressed neither in writing nor in pronunciation.

> "Marry, my uncle *Clarence* (Folio) angry ghost."
>   *Rich. III.* iii. 1. 144; ii. 1. 137.

"For *justice* sake."—*J. C.* iv. 3. 19.

"At every *sentence* end."—*A. Y. L.* iii. 2. 144.

"Lewis" is a monosyllable in

"King *Lewis his* satisfaction all appear."—*Hen. V.* i. 2. 88.

His is used like "hic" (in the antithesis between "hic . . . ille").

"Desire *his* (this one's) jewels and this other's house."*
Macb. iv. 3. 80 ; *M. of V.* iii. 2. 54-5 ; *Sonn.* xxix. 5, 6.

This explains

"And, at our stamp, here o'er and o'er one falls :
He murder cries, and help from Athens calls."
M. N. D. iii. 1. 25.

His, being the old genitive of *it*, is almost always used for *its*.

218. His, her, &c. being the genitives of *he, she* (*she* in E. E.
had, as one form of the nom., "heo," gen. "hire"), &c. may stand
as the antecedent of a relative. Thus :

"In *his* way *that* comes in triumph over Pompey's blood."
J. C. i. 1. 55.

i.e. "in the way *of him* that comes."

"Love make *his* heart of flint that you shall love."—*T. N.* i. 5. 305.

"Unless *her* prayers *whom* heaven delights to hear."—*A. W.*iii.4.27.

"If you had known . . . *her* worthiness that gave the ring."
M. of V. v. 1. 200.

"Armies of pestilence, and they shall strike
Your children yet unborn and unbegot
That lift your vassal hands against my head."
Rich. II. iii. 2. 89.

i.e. "the children *of you* who lift your hands."

"Upon *their* woes whom fortune captivates."
3 *Hen. VI.* i. 4. 115.   So *Lear*, v. 3. 2.

"And turn our impress'd lances in *our* eyes
Which do command them."—*Lear*, v. 3. 50.

In "Alas, *their* love may be call'd appetite,
No motion of the liver, but the palate,
That suffer surfeit, cloyment and revolt,"—*T. N.* ii. 4. 100–2.

it seems better to take *that* as the relative to "them," implied in
"their (of them)," rather than to suppose "suffer" to be the subjunctive singular (367), or *that* to be the relative to "liver" and
"palate" by confusion. It is true *that* is not often so far from its
antecedent, but the second line may be treated as parenthetical.

* "Condemning some to death, and some to exile ;
Ransoming *him*, or pitying, threatening the other."—*Coriol.* l. 6. 36.

This is perhaps not common in modern poetry, but it sometimes occurs :

> " Poor is *our* sacrifice *whose* eyes
> Are lighted from above."—NEWMAN.

219. Your, our, their, &c., are often used in their old signification, as genitives, where we should use " of *you*," &c.

> "We render you (Coriolanus) the tenth to be ta'en forth
> At . . . *your only* choice."—*Coriol.* i. 9. 36.

i.e. " at the choice *of you alone.*"

> "To all *our* lamentation."—*Coriol.* iv. 6. 34.

i.e. " to the lamentation *of us all.*"

> " Have I not *all their* letters to meet me in arms ?"
> 1 *Hen. IV.* ii. 3. 28.

i.e. " letters *from them all.*"

220. Me, thee, him, &c. are often used, in virtue of their representing the old dative, where we should use *for me, by me,* &c. Thus:

> "I am appointed (by) *him* to murder you."—*W. T.* i. 2. 412.
> "John lays *you* plots."—*K. J.* iii. 4. 145.

This is especially common with *me.*

Me is indirect object in

> " But hear *me* this."—*T. N.* v. 1. 123.
> " What thou hast promis'd—which is not yet perform'd *me.*"
> *Tempest,* i. 2. 244.

We say "do *me* a favour," but not "to do *me* business."—*Tempest,* i. 2. 255.

> " Give *me* your present to one Master Bassanio."
> *M. of V.* ii. 2. 115.

> " Who does *me* this ?"—*Hamlet,* ii. 2. 601.
> " Sayest thou *me* so ?"—2 *Hen. VI.* ii. 1. 109.

Me seems to mean " from me " in

> " You'll bear *me* a bang for that."—*J. C.* iii. 2. 20.

" with me " in

> " And hold *me* pace in deep experiment."—1 *Hen. IV.* iii. 1. 48.

Me means " to my injury " in

> " See how this river comes *me* cranking in,
> And cuts *me,* from the best of all my land,
> A huge half-moon."—1 *Hen. IV.* iii. 1. 100.

" at my cost " and " for my benefit " in

> " The sack that thou hast drunk *me* could have bought *me* lights

as good cheap at the dearest chandler's in Europe."—1 *Hen. IV.* iii. 3. 50.

Me in narrative stands on a somewhat different footing :

"He pluck'd *me* ope his doublet."—*J. C.* i. 2. 270.

"He steps *me* to her trencher."—*T. G. of V.* iv. 4. 9.

"The skilful shepherd peel'd *me* certain wands."
M. of V. i. 3. 85.

"He presently, as greatness knows itself,
Steps *me* a little higher than his vow."—1 *Hen. IV.* iv. 3. 75.

Falstaff, when particularly desirous of securing the attention of the Prince ("Dost thou hear me, Hal?"), indulges twice in this use of *me*.

"I made *me* no more ado, . . . I followed *me* close."
1 *Hen. IV.* ii. 4. 233, 241.

Here, however, the verbs are perhaps used reflexively, though this would seem to be caused by the speaker's intense desire to call attention to *himself*. So in

"Observe me judicially, sweet sir ; they had planted *me* three demi-culverins,"—B. J. *E. in &c.* iii. 2.

the *me* seems to appropriate the narrative of the action to the speaker, and to be equivalent to "mark *me*," "*I* tell you." In such phrases as

"Knock *me* here,"—*T. of Sh.* i. 2. 8.

the action, and not merely the narrative of the action, is appropriated.

You is similarly used for "look you :"

"And 'a would manage *you* his piece thus, and come *you* in and come *you* out."—2 *Hen. IV.* iii. 2. 304.

In "Study *me* how to please the eye indeed
By fixing it upon a fairer eye,"—*L. L. L.* i. 1. 80.

me probably means "for me," "by my advice," *i.e.* "*I* would have you study thus." Less probably, "study" may be an active verb, of which the passive is found in *Macb.* i. 4. 9.

There is a redundant *him* in

"The king, by this, is set *him* down to rest."—3 *Hen. VI.* iv. 3. 2.

where there is, perhaps, a confusion between "has set him(self) down" and "is set down."

Her seems used for "of her," "at her hands," in

"I took *her* leave at court."—*A. W.* v. 3. 79.

i.e. "I bade her farewell."

Us probably is used for "to *us*" in

" She looks *us* like
A thing made more of malice than of duty."—*Cymb.* iii. 5. 32.

But possibly as "look" in *Hen. V.* iv. 7. 76, *A. and C.* iii. 10. 53, is used for "look for," so it may mean "look at." So

"Twa brooks in which I *look* myself."—B. J. *Sad Sh.* ii. 1.

i.e. "I view myself."

Us seems equivalent to "for us" in

" We have not spoke *us* yet of torch-bearers."

M. of V. ii. 4. 5.

i.e. "spoken for ourselves about torch-bearers."

221. Your, like "me" above (Latin, *iste*), is used to appropriate an object to a person addressed. Lepidus says to Antony:

"*Your* serpent of Egypt is lord now of *your* mud by the operation of *your* sun : so is *your* crocodile."—*A. and C.* ii. 7. 29.

Though in this instance the *your* may seem literally justified, the repetition of it indicates a colloquial vulgarity which suits the character of Lepidus. So Hamlet, affecting madness :

"*Your* worm is *your* only emperor for diet ; *your* fat king and *your* lean beggar is but variable service."—*Hamlet,* iv. 3. 24.

Compare

" But he could read and had *your* languages."—B. J. *Fox,* ii. 1.

i.e. " the languages which you know are considered important."

So : "I would teach these nineteen the special rules, as *your* punto, *your* reverso, *your* stoccata, *your* imbroccato, *your* passada, *your* montanto."—*Bobadil,* in B. J. *E. in &c.* iv. 5.

Hence the apparent rudeness of Hamlet is explained when he says to the player :

"But if you mouth it as many of *your* players do."—*Ham.* iii. 2. 3.

i.e. " the players whom you and everybody know."

222. Our is used, like " my," vocatively :

" *Our* very loving sister, well be-met."—*Lear,* v. 1. 20.
" Tongue-tied *our* queen, speak thou."—*W. T.* i. 1. 27.
" *Our* old and faithful friend, we are glad to see you."

M. for M. v. 1. 2.

In all these cases *our* is used in the royal style, for " my," by a single speaker referring merely to himself.

223. Him, her, me, them, &c. are often used in Elizabethan, and still more often in Early English, for *himself, herself,* &c.

" How she opposes *her* (sets *herself*) against my will."
T. G. of V. iii. 2. 26.

" My heart hath one poor string to stay *it* by."—*K. J.* v. 6. 55.

" And so I say I'll cut the causes off
Flattering *me* with impossibilities."—3 *Hen. VI.* iii. 2. 143.

224. He and **she** are used for " man " and " woman."

" And that *he*
Who casts to write a living line must sweat."
B. J. on Shakespeare.

" I'll bring mine action on the proudest *he*
That stops my way in Padua."—*T. of Sh.* iii. 2. 236.

" Lady, you are the cruellest *she* alive."—*T. N.* i. 5. 259.

" I think my love as rare
As any *she* belied with false compare."—*Sonn.* 130.

" That *she* belov'd knows nought that knows not this."
Tr. and Cr. i. 2. 314.

" With his princess, *she*
The fairest I have yet beheld."—*W. T.* v. 1. 86.

" Betwixt two such *shes.*"—*Cymb.* i. 6. 40 ; *ib.* i. 3. 29.*

This makes more natural the use of " he that," with the third person of the verb, in

" Are not you *he*
That *frights* the maidens?"—*M. N. D.* ii. 1. 34.

So *A. Y. L.* iii. 2. 411.

225. Pronoun for pronominal adjective. The pronominal adjectives *his, their,* being originally possessive inflections of *he, they,* &c., were generally used in E. E. possessively or subjectively, *i.e.* " *his* wrongs " would naturally mean then " the wrongs done by him," not " to him." Hence, for objective genitives, " of " was frequently introduced, a usage which sometimes extended to subjective genitives. Hence

" The kindred *of him* hath been flesh'd upon us."—*Hen. V.* ii. 4. 50.

" Tell thou the lamentable tale *of me.*"—*Rich. II.* v. 1. 44.

" The native mightiness and fate *of him.*"—*Hen. V.* ii. 4. 64.

" Against the face *of them.*"—*Psalm* xxi. 12.

* Hence a " lady-*she,*" *W. T.* i. 2. 44, means " a well-born woman."

It is used, perhaps, for antithesis in

> " Let her be made
> As miserable by the death *of him*
> As I am made by my poor lord and thee."
>
> *Rich. III.* i. 2. 21.

> " O world, thou wast the forest to this heart,
> And this indeed, O world, the heart *of thee.*"
>
> *J. C.* iii. 1. 208.

226. It is sometimes used indefinitely, as the object of a verb, without referring to anything previously mentioned, and seems to indicate a pre-existing object in the mind of the person spoken of.

> " Courage, father, fight *it* out."—3 *Hen. VI.* i. 4. 10.

i.e. " the battle."

> " *Ber.* She never saw it.
> *King.*   Thou speak'st *it* falsely."—*A. W.* v. 3. 113.

i.e. " what thou sayest."

> " Dangerous peer,
> That smooth'st *it* so with king and commonweal."
>
> 2 *Hen. VI.* ii. 1. 22.

where *it* = " matters."

> "To revel *it* with him and his new bride." (So *C. of E.* iv. 4. 66.)
> —3 *Hen. VI.* iii. 3. 225.

i.e. " to take part in the intended bridal revels."

> " I cannot daub *it* further."—*Lear*, iv. 1. 54.

i.e. " continue my former dissembling."

But *it* is often added to nouns or words that are not generally used as verbs, in order to give them the force of verbs.

> " *Foot* it."—*Tempest*, i. 2. 380.
> "To *queen* it."—*Hen. VIII.* ii. 3. 37.
> "To *prince* it."—*Cymb.* iii. 4. 85.
> " Lord Angelo *dukes it* well."—*M. for M.* iii. 2. 100.

And, later,

> " Whether the charmer *sinner it* or *saint it,*
> If folly grow romantic, I must paint it."
>
> Pope, *Moral Essays*, ii. 15.

The use of *it* with verbs is now only found in slang phrases.

227. It is sometimes more emphatically used than with us. We have come to use *it* so often superfluously before verbs that the emphatic use of *it* for " that " before " which " is lost.

> " There was *it*
> For which my sinews shall be stretched upon him. "
> > *Coriol.* v. 6. 44.

> " That's *it* that always makes a good voyage of nothing. "
> > *T. N.* ii. 4. 80.

> " An if *it* please me which thou speak'st."—*T. A.* v. 1. 59.

> " *It* holds current *that* I told you of."—1 *Hen. IV.* ii. 1. 59.

So *Isaiah* (A. V.) li. 9 : " Art thou not *it that* hath cut Rahab ? "

Perhaps we must explain it as the antecedent of " what " (and not as in 226) in

> " Deign *it*, Goddess, from my hand
> To receive *whate'er* this land
> From her fertile womb doth send."—B. and F. *Fair Sh.* i. 1.

228. Its was not used originally in the Authorized Version of the Bible, and is said to have been rarely used in Shakespeare's time. It is, however, very common in Florio's Montaigne. *His* still represented the genitive of *It* as well as of *He*. *Its* is found, however, in *M. for M.* i. 2. 4, where it is emphatic ; in *W. T.* i. 2 (three times, 151, 152, 266) ; *Hen. VIII.* i. 1. 18 ; *Lear*, iv. 2. 32, and elsewhere. Occasionally *it*, an early provincial form of the old genitive, is found for *its*, especially when a child is mentioned, or when any one is contemptuously spoken of as a child. Ben Jonson (*Sil. Wom.* ii. 3) uses both forms—

> " Your knighthood shall come on *its* knees. "

And then, a few lines lower down—

> " *It* knighthood shall fight all *it* friends. "

Comp. *W. T.* iii. 2. 109 :

> " The innocent milk in *it* most innocent mouth. "

> " The hedge-sparrow fed the cuckoo so long,
> That it's had *it* head bit off by *it* young."—*Lear*, i. 4. 235.

But also of an unknown person :

> " The corse they follow did with desperate hand
> Fordo *it* own life."—(Folio.) *Hamlet*, v. 1. 245.

> " Woman *it* pretty self."—(Folio.) *Cymb.* iii. 4. 160.

And of the ghost :

"It lifted up *it* head."—(Folio.)   *Hamlet,* i. 2. 216.

Perhaps the dislike of *its*, even in the eighteenth century, aided the adoption of the French idiom "lever la tête."

"Where London's column, pointing at the skies,
  Like a tall bully lifts *the* head and lies."
                    POPE, *Moral Essays,* iii. 340.

"*It*-selfe" is found referring to "who."   (See 264.)

"The world who of *it*-selfe is peised well."—*K. J.* ii. 1. 575.

229. Her is very often applied by Shakespeare to the mind and soul.

"Whose soul is that which takes *her* heavy leave?"
                            3 *Hen. VI.* ii. 6. 42.

"Since my dear soul was mistress of *her* choice."
                            Hamlet, iii. 2. 68.

So *Rich. III.* iii. 5. 28 ; *Hamlet,* ii. 2. 580.

            "Our mind partakes
Her private actions to your secrecy."—*P. of T.* i. 1. 153.

So Montaigne, 117.

The former passage from Hamlet shows the reason of this. The soul, when personified, is regarded as feminine, like Psyche. The body of a woman is also thus personified in

            "And made thy body bare
Of *her* two branches, those sweet ornaments."—*T. A.* ii. 4. 18.

Milton occasionally uses *its;* often *her* for *its;* seldom, if ever, *his* for *its.*

            "His form had not yet lost
All *her* original brightness."—MILTON, *P. L.* i. 592.

In this, and some other passages, but not in all, Milton may have been influenced by the Latin use of the feminine gender. "Form" represents "forma," a feminine Latin noun.

Personification will explain

"That Tiber trembled underneath *her* banks."
                            J. C. i. 1. 50.

230. Ungrammatical remnants of ancient usage. In Chaucer and earlier writers, preference is expressed, both by our modern "I had, or would, rather (*i.e.* sooner)," and by "(To) me (it) were lever (German *lieber*)," *i.e.* "more pleasant." These two idioms are confused in the following example :

> "*Me rather had* my heart might feel your love."
> > *Rich. II.* iii. 3. 192.

In the earliest writers "woe!" is found joined with the dative inflection of the pronoun, "woe is (to) us," "woe is (to) me."

> "Wa worthe (betide) *than* monne (the man, dat.)."
> > LAYAMON, i. 142.

As early as Chaucer, and probably earlier, the sense of the inflection was weakened, and "woe" was used as a predicate : "I am woe," "we are woe," &c. Hence Shakespeare uses "sorrow" thus. Similarly our "I am well" is, perhaps, an ungrammatical modification of "well is me," *Ps.* cxxviii. 2 (Prayer-book). In Early English both constructions are found. In Anglo-Saxon, Mätzner "has only met with the dative construction."

> "*I am sorrow* for thee."—*Cymb.* v. 5. 297.
> "*I am woe* for't, sir."—*Temp.* v. 1. 139.
> "*Woe is my heart.*"—*Cymb.* v. 5. 2.
> "*Woe, woe are we,* sir."—*A. and C.* iv. 14. 133.

On the other hand,

> "*Woe is me.*"—*Hamlet*, iii. 1. 168.
> "*Woe me.*"—*M. for M.* iv. 1. 26.

Similarly, the old "'(to) me (it) were better," being misunderstood, was sometimes replaced by "I were better."

> "*I were better* to be eaten to death."—*2 Hen. IV.* i. 2. 245.
> "I *were best* to leave him."—*1 Hen. VI.* v. 3. 82.
> "Poor lady, *she were better* love a dream."—*T. N.* i. 2. 27.
> "*Thou'rt best.*"—*Tempest*, i. 2. 366.

And when the old idiom is retained, it is generally in instances like the following :

> "Answer truly, *you were best.*"—*J. C.* iii. 3. 15.
> "Madam, *you're best* consider."—*Cymb.* iii. 2. 79.

where *you* may represent either nominative or dative, but was almost certainly used by Shakespeare as nominative.

231. Thou and You.* *Thou* in Shakespeare's time was, very much like "du" now among the Germans, the pronoun of (1)

---

* The Elizabethan distinction between *thou* and *you* is remarkably illustrated by the usage in E. E., as detailed by Mr. Skeat in *William of Palerne*, Preface, p. xli.

affection towards friends (2) good-humoured superiority to servants, and (3) contempt or anger to strangers. It had, however, already fallen somewhat into disuse, and, being regarded as archaic, was naturally adopted (4) in the higher poetic style and in the language of solemn prayer.

(1) This is so common as to need no examples. It should be remarked, however, that this use is modified sometimes by euphony (the ponderous *thou*, *art*, and terminations in *est* being avoided) and sometimes by fluctuations of feeling. Thus in the *T. G. of V.* Valentine and Proteus in the first twenty lines of earnest dialogue use nothing but *thou*. But as soon as they begin to jest, "thou art" is found too seriously ponderous, and we have (i. 1. 25) "*you* are over boots in love," while the lighter *thee* is not discarded in (i. 1. 28) "it boots *thee* not." So in the word-fencing of lines 36–40, *you* and *your* are preferred, but an affectionate farewell brings them back again to *thou*. The last line presents an apparent difficulty :

> " *Proteus.* All happiness bechance to thee in Milan !
> *Valentine.* As much to *you* at home, and so farewell."
> *T. G. of V.* i. 1. 61-2.

But while *thee* applies to the single traveller, *you* is better *suited* to *Proteus and his friends* at home. It may be added, that when the friends meet after their long parting, there is a certain coldness in the frequent *you*. (*T. G. of V.* ii. 5. 120.)

Fathers almost always address their sons with *thou;* sons their fathers with *you*. Thus in the dialogue between Henry IV. and the Prince (1 *Hen. IV.* iii. 2), line 118, "What say *you*?" is perhaps the only exception to the rule. So in the dialogue between Talbot and his son (1 *Hen. VI.* iv. 5) before the battle. In the ex-citement of the battle (1 *Hen. VI.* iv. 6. 6–9) the son addresses his father as *thou:* but such instances are very rare. (*A. Y. L.* ii. 3. 69 is a rhyming passage, and impassioned also.) A wife may vary between *thou* and *you* when addressing her husband. Lady Percy addresses Hotspur almost always in dialogue with *you:* but in the higher style of earnest appeal in 1 *Hen. IV.* ii. 3. 43–67, and in the familiar "I'll break *thy* little finger, Harry," *ib.* 90, she uses *thou* throughout.

In the high Roman style, Brutus and Portia use *you*.

Hotspur generally uses *thou* to his wife, but, when he becomes serious, rises to *you*, dropping again to *thou*.

" *Hotspur.* Come, wilt *thou* see me ride?
And when I am o' horse-back, I will swear
I love *thee* infinitely——But hark *you*, Kate ;
I must not have *you* henceforth question me :
This evening must I leave *you*, gentle Kate.
I know *you* wise ; but yet no further wise
Than Harry Percy's wife: constant *you* are,
But yet a woman: and for secrecy
No lady closer—— For I well believe
Thou wilt not utter what *thou* dost not know;
And so far will I trust *thee*, gentle Kate."

1 Hen. IV. ii. 3. 103-115.

Mark the change of pronoun as Bassanio assumes the part of a friendly lecturer :

"*Gra.* I have a suit to you.
  Bass.   *You* have obtain'd it.
Gra. You must not deny me ; I must go with you to Belmont.
Bass. Why, then *you* must.—But hear *thee*, Gratiano ;
Thou art too wild, too rude and bold of voice," &c.

M. of V. ii. 2. 187–90.

232. Thou is generally used by a master to a servant, but not always. Being the appropriate address to a servant, it is used in confidential and good-humoured utterances, but a master finding fault often resorts to the unfamiliar *you* (much as Cæsar cut his soldiers to the heart by giving them the respectful title of Quirites). Thus Valentine uses *you* to Speed in *T. G. of V.* ii. 1. 1-17, and *thou*, *Ib.* 47–69. Compare

" *Val.* Go to, *sir:* tell me, do *you* know madam Silvia ?"—*Ib.* 14.

with

" *Val.* But tell me: dost *thou* know my lady Silvia ?"—*Ib.* 44.

Similarly to the newly-engaged servant Julia, who says "I'll do what I can," Proteus blandly replies :

 " I hope *thou* wilt. [To *Launce.*] How now, *you* whore-
  son peasant,
 Where have *you* been these two days loitering ?"

T. G. of V. iv. 4. 48.

When the appellative " sir " is used, even in anger, *thou* generally gives place to *you.*

 "And what wilt *thou* do ? Beg, when that is spent?
 Well, *sir*, get *you* in."—*A. Y. L.* i. 1. 79, 80.

"Ay, ay, *thou* wouldst begone to join with Richmond :
    I will not trust *you*, sir."—*Rich. III.* iv. 4. 492.

Compare   "Speak, what trade art *thou ?*"—*J. C.* i. 1. 5.

with   "You, *sir*, what trade are *you ?*"—*Ib.* 9.

This explains the change from *thou* to *you* in *Tempest*, i. 2. 443.
Throughout the scene Prospero, addressing Ferdinand as an im-
postor, "speaks ungently" with *thou*. In *Tempest*, v. 1. 75–79,
Prospero, who has addressed the worthy Gonzalo in the friendly
thou, and the repentant Alonso in the impassioned *thou*, turning to
his unnatural brother says,

> "Flesh and blood
> *You brother mine*,"

but, on pronouncing his forgiveness immediately afterwards, he says,

> "I do forgive *thee*,
> Unnatural though *thou* art."

So   "For *you*, most wicked *sir*, whom to call brother
> Would even infect my mouth, I do forgive
> *Thy* rankest fault."—*Tempest*, v. 1. 230–2.

"Worthy *sir*, *thou* bleed'st."—*Coriol.* i. 5. 15.

is easily explained by the admiring epithet "worthy." Compare
Ib. 24 : "*Bold gentleman*, prosperity be *thy* page."

The difference between *thou* and *you* is well illustrated by the
farewell addressed by Brutus to his *schoolfellow* Volumnius, and his
servant Strato :

> "Farewell to *you ;* and *you ;* and *you*, Volumnius ;
> Farewell to *thee*, too, Strato."—*J. C.* v. 5. 33.

Compare also the farewell between the noble Gloucester and Edgar
"dressed like a peasant :"

> "*Edg.* Now fare *you* well, good *sir*."—*Lear*, iv. 6. 32.

> "*Glouc.* Now, *fellow*, fare *thee* well."—*Ib.* 41.

It may seem an exception that in sc. iv. 1, Edgar uses *thou* to
Gloucester, but this is only because he is in the height of his assumed
madness, and cannot be supposed to distinguish persons. Afterwards, in sc. vi., he invariably uses *you*—a change which, together
with other changes in his language, makes Gloucester say :

> "Thou speak'st
> In better phrase and manner than *thou* didst."—*Lear*, iv. 6. 8.

It may be partly this increased respect for Edgar, and partly
euphony, which makes Gloucester use *you* in *ll.* 10 and 24.

Thus Clarence to the Second Murderer :

> "*Clar.* Where art *thou,* keeper? Give me a cup of wine.
> *Sec. Murd. You* shall have wine enough, my lord, anon.
> *Clar.* In God's name, what art *thou?*
> *Sec. Murd.* A man, as *you* are.
> *Clar.* How darkly and how deadly dost *thou* speak!
> *Your* eyes do menace me : why look *you* pale?
> Who sent *you* hither? Wherefore do *you* come?"
>
> *Rich. III.* i. 4. 167–176.

The last two lines seem discrepant : but they are not. Clarence is addressing *both* murderers, and *both* reply :

> "*Both.* To, to, to——
> *Clar.* To murder me?
> *Both.* Ay, ay."

Afterwards, when the murderers reproach Clarence with his faults, they address him as *thou.*

233. Thou towards strangers who were not inferiors was an insult. "If thou *thouest* him some thrice, it shall not be amiss," (*T. N.* iii. 2. 48,) is the advice given to Sir Andrew Aguecheek when on the point of writing a challenge.

In addressing Angelo, whose seat he occupies, the Duke in the following passage begins with ironical politeness, but passes into open contempt :

> " *Duke* (to *Escalus*). What *you* have spoke I pardon; sit *you* down;
> We'll borrow place of him. (To *Angelo.*) Sir, by *your* leave,
> Hast *thou* or word or wit or impudence,
> That now can do *thee* office?"—*M. for M.* v. 1. 358.

Thou is also used in a contemptuous "aside."

> " *Hastings.* 'Tis like enough for I stay dinner there.
> *Buckingham* (aside). And supper too, although *thou* know'st
> it not.
> Come, will *you* go?"—*Rich. III.* iii. 2. 122.

And, where there is no contempt, Cassius passes into *thou* when he addresses Brutus absent, whereas in his presence he restricts himself to *you* (*J. C.* i. 2. 311). The former is the rhetorical, the latter the conversational pronoun. So

> "Be *thou* my witness,
> *You* know that I held Epicurus strong."—*J. C.* v. 1. 74–7.

This explains the apparent liberty in

> "O wise young judge, how I do honour *thee!* "
>
> *M. of V.* iv. 1. 224.

234. Thou is often used in statements and requests, while *you* is used in conditional and other sentences where there is no direct appeal to the person addressed. Similarly the somewhat archaic *ye* is distinguished by Shakespeare from *you* by being used in rhetorical appeals. (See **Ye,** 236.)

> Come *thou* on my side, and entreat for me
> As *you* would beg, were *you* in my distress."
> > *Rich. III.* i. 4. 273.

> "But tell me now
> My drown'd queen's name, as in the rest *you* said
> *Thou* hast been god-like perfect."—*P. of T.* v. 1. 208.

> "I go, and if *you* plead as well to them
> As I can say nay to *thee* for myself."—*Rich. III.* iii. 7. 52.

> "Give me *thy* hand, Messala;
> Be *thou* my witness that against my will, &c.
> *You* know that I held Epicurus strong."—*J. C.* v. 1. 74–7.

235. Thou. Apparent exceptions.

> "If he be leaden, icy-cold, unwilling,
> Be *thou* so too, and so break off *your* talk."
> > *Rich. III.* iii. 1. 177.

Here "*your* talk" means the talk between "*thee* and him."

In *Hamlet,* i. 2. 41–49, the King, as he rises in his profession of affection to Laertes, passes from *you* to *thou*, subsequently returning to *you*.

In the following instance a kiss induces the speaker to pass from *your* to *thou*:

> "   *Goneril.* Decline *your* head. (*Kisses* Edmund.) This kiss,
> if it durst speak,
> Would raise *thy* spirits up into the air."—*Lear*, iv. 2. 23.

The most difficult passage is :

> "If *thou* beest not immortal, look about *you*."—*J. C.* ii. 3. 8, 9.

In this short scene Cæsar is six times addressed by the soothsayer in the solemn and prophetic *thou* and *thee*, but once, as above, *you*. I can only suggest that "look about *you*" may mean "look about you *and your friends*."

In almost all cases where *thou* and *you* appear at first sight indiscriminately used, further considerations show some change of thought, or some influence of euphony sufficient to account for the change of pronoun.

The French Herald addresses Henry V. as *thou*, not for dis-
courtesy (*Hen. V.* iv. 7. 74), but in the "high style" appropriate
between heralds and monarchs. Few *subjects* would address their
lords as *thou*. Only a Caliban addressing his Stephano would in
the ordinary language say :

"Good my lord, give me *thy* favour still."— *Temp.* iv. 1. 204.

Caliban almost always *thou's unless he is cursing* (*Temp.* i. 2. 363),
or when he is addressing more than one person.

236. Ye. In the original form of the language *ye* is nominative,
you accusative. This distinction, however, though observed in our
version of the Bible, was disregarded by Elizabethan authors, and
ye seems to be generally used in questions, entreaties, and rhetorical
appeals. Ben Jonson says : " The second person plural is for reve-
rence sake to some singular thing." He quotes—

> " O good father dear,
> Why make *ye* this heavy cheer ? "—GOWER.

Compare :

> " I do beseech *ye*, if *you* bear me hard."—*J. C.* iii. 1. **157.**
> "*You* taught me how to know the face of right,
> And come *ye* now to tell me John hath made
> His peace with Rome ? "—*K. J.* v. 2. 91.
> " The more shame for *ye;* holy men I thought *ye.*"
> *Hen. VIII.* iii. 1. 102.
> " Therein, *ye* gods, *you* make the weak most strong."
> *J. C.* i. 3. 91.
> "I' the name of truth,
> Are *ye* fantastical ? . . . My noble partner
> *You* greet with present grace."—*Macbeth,* i. 3. 53–55.

Ye and *your* seem used indiscriminately in *Temp.* v. 1. 33–8, " *Ye*
elves . . . and *ye* that . . . *you* demi-puppets . . . and *you* whose
pastime is, &c."

The confusion between *you* and *ye* is illustrated by the irregularity
of the following:

"What mean *you* . . . do *ye* not know ? . . . If, therefore, at the
first sight *ye* doe give them to understand that *you* are come hither
. . . do *you* not think ? Therefore, if *you* looke . . ."—N. *P.* 170.

Sometimes *ye* seems put for *you* when an unaccented syllable is
wanted :

> "I never loved *you* much ; but I ha' prais'd *ye.*"
> *A. and C.* ii. 6. **78.**

and perhaps in

"*Ye* shall, my lord,"—*Rich. III.* iv. 2. 86.

the "shall" being emphatic, and *ye* unemphatic, but the Folio varies here, as frequently in this play.

237. Mine, my. Thine, thy. The two forms, which are interchangeable in E. E. both before vowels and consonants, are both used by Shakespeare with little distinction before vowels.

Though there are probably many exceptions, yet the rule appears to be that *mine* and *thine* are used where the possessive adjective is to be unemphatic, *my* and *thy* in other cases.

Mine is thus used before words to which it is so frequently prefixed as to become almost a part of them, as "*mine host*" (*M. W. of W.* i. 3. 1), but *my* in the less common

"Unto *my* hostess of the tavern."—1 *Hen. IV.* i. 2. 53.

So we have almost always "*mine* honour," the emphatic

"By *my* honour
He shall depart untouched,"—*J. C.* iii. 1. 141.

being an exception. *Mine* is almost always found before "eye," "ear," &c. where no emphasis is intended. But where there is antithesis we have *my, thy:*

"*My* ear should catch your voice, *my* eye your eye."
M. N. D. i. 1. 188.

and also in the emphatic

"To follow *me* and praise *my* eyes and face."—*M. N. D.* iii. 2. 223.

Euphony would dictate this distinction. The pause which we are obliged to make between *my, thy,* and a following vowel, serves for a kind of emphasis. On the other hand, *mine,* pronounced "min," glides easily and unemphatically on to the following vowel.

238. Mine, hers, theirs, are used as pronominal adjectives *before* their nouns. That *mine* should be thus used is not remarkable, as in E. E. it was interchangeable with *my,* and is often used by Shakespeare where we should use *my.*

"*Mine* and my father's death come not upon thee."
Hamlet, v. 2. 341.

"The body is dead upon *mine* and my master's false accusation."
—*M. Ado,* v. 1. 249. So *P. of T.* i. 2. 92; *Cymb.* v. 5. 230.

In the following, *mine* is only separated by an adjective from its noun : " And his and *mine* lov'd darling."—*Tempest,* iii. 3. 93.

More remarkable are

" What to come is *yours* and my discharge."—*Temp.* ii. 1. 253.
" By *hers* and mine adultery."—*Cymb.* v. 5. 186.
' Even in *theirs* and in the commons' ears."—*Coriol.* v. 6. 4.

It is felt that the ear cannot wait till the end of the sentence while so slight a word as *her* or *their* remains with nothing to depend on. The same explanation applies to *mine,* which, though unemphatic immediately before its noun, is emphatic when separated from its noun.

239. This of yours is now, as in E. E., generally applied to one out of a class, whether the class exist or be imaginary. We could say "this coat of yours," but not (except colloquially) "this head of yours." It is, however, commonly used by Shakespeare where even the conception of a class is impossible.

" Nor scar that whiter skin *of hers* than snow."—*Othello,* v. 2. 4.
" Will not a calf-skin stop that mouth *of thine ?*"—*K. J.* iii. 1. 299.

" This of hers, thine," &c. seem used as an adjective, like the Latin "iste." "This mouth of you" was felt to be harsh, the "you" being too weak to stand in such a position. "This your mouth" requiring a forced and unnatural pause after "this," was somewhat more objectionable to Shakespeare,* than to the Latin style of Milton and Addison. Hence "this of you" was used but modified. It is rare that we find such a transposition as

' O then advance *of yours* that phraseless hand."—*L. C.* 225.

240. Pronouns transposed. A feeling of the unemphatic nature of the nominatives *we* and *they* prevents us from saying "all we."

" Into the madness wherein now he raves
And *all we* mourn for."—*Hamlet,* ii. 2. 151.

So "all we" in the A. V. of the Bible, and "all they," *Mark* xii. 44.

" Find out" is treated as a single word in

" *Cass.* Cinna, where haste you so?
Cinna. To *find-out* you."—*J. C.* i. 3. 134.

---

* See, however— " How many ages hence
Shall *this our* lofty scene be acted over !"—*J. C.* ii. 1. 112.

So   "To *belch-up* you."—*Tempest*, iii. 3. 56.
    "And *leave-out* thee."—*Rich. III.* i. 3. 216.
        " *Both they* (*i.e.* both of them)
    Match not the high perfection of my loss."—*Ib.* iv. 4. 65.

No modern poet would be allowed to write, for the sake of rhyme,

    " All days are nights to see till I see thee,
    And nights bright days when dreams do show *thee me.*"
                               Sonn. 43.

We could only say "give him me," when we meant "give him, not to so-and-so, but to *me*," emphatically, which is not the meaning here.

241. Omission of Thou. (See also 399, 402.) After a verb ending with the second person singular inflection, the *thou* is sometimes omitted in questions, as :

    "*Didst* not mark that ?"—*Othello*, ii. 1. 260.
    " How *dost* that pleasant plague infest ? "—DANIEL.
    "*Wilt* dine with me, Apemantus ?"—*T. of A.* i. 1. 206.

Thou is often omitted after " wouldst," or perhaps merged, in the form " woo't," as " wilt thou " becomes " wilta."

    " Noblest of men, *woo't* die ?"—*A. and C.* iv. 15. 59.
    "*Woo't* weep ? *Woo't* fight ?. . . I'll do it."—*Hamlet*, v. 1. 299.

Sometimes *thou* is inserted :

    " *Woo't thou* fight well ?"—*A. and C.* iv. 2. 7.

242. Insertion of Pronoun. When a proper name is separated by an intervening clause from its verb, then for clearness (see 248) the redundant pronoun is often inserted.

    " Sueno, albeit he was of nature verie cruell, yet qualified *he* his
        displeasure."—HOLINSHED, *Duncane.*
    " Demeratus—when on the bench he was long silent . . . one
        asking him . . . *he* answered."—B. J. *Disc.* 744.
    " For the nobility, though they continued loyal unto him, yet
        did *they* not co-operate with him."—B. *E.*

243. Insertion of Pronoun. Even where there is no intervening conjunctional clause, the pronoun is frequently inserted after a proper name as the subject. More rarely, the subject is a common noun. Still more rarely, the pronoun is inserted after the *object.*

The subject or object stands first, like the title of a book, to call the attention of the reader to what may be said about it. In some passages the transition may be perceived from the exclamatory use

" O thy vile lady !
She has robbed me of my sword,"—*A. and C.* iv. 14. 22.

to the semi-exclamation :

" For God *he* knows."—*Rich. III.* iii. 7. 236 ; 1. 10 ; 1. 26.
" Where Heaven *he* knows how we shall answer him."
K. J. v. 7. 59.

(So *T. G. of V.* iv. 4. 112, and

"God, I pray *him.*"—*Rich. III.* i. 3. 212.

The object (as in the last example) precedes in

" My sons, God knows what has bechanced *them.*"
3 *Hen. VI.* i. 4. 6.
"Senseless trees *they* cannot hear thee,
Ruthless beasts *they* will not cheer thee."—*P. P.* 393.)

and hence to passages of simple statement :

"The skipping king *he* ambled up and down."
1 *Hen. IV.* iii. 2. 60.
" Of six preceding ancestors that gem
Conferr'd by testament to the sequent issue
Hath *it* been owed and worn."—*A. W.* v. 3. 198.
"But this same Cassio, though he speak of comfort
Touching the Turkish loss, yet *he* looks sadly."
Othello, ii. 1. 31.

But many such passages of simple statement may be regarded as abridgments of the construction with " for," " of," or some other preposition :

" *For* your intent . . . *it* is most retrograde to our desires."
Hamlet, i. 2. 112.
" *For* my voice, I have lost *it* with halloing and singing of anthems."—2 *Hen. IV.* i. 2. 213.

So " *For* (as regards) your brother, he shall go with me," might become

"Your brother *he* shall go along with me."
A. W. iii. 6. 117 ; *Rich. II.* ii. 2. 80 ; 1 *Hen. IV.* ii. 4. 442.
So "Of Salisbury, who can report of him ?"—2 *Hen. VI.* v. 3. 1.

RELATIVE PRONOUNS.

244. Omission of the Relative. The relative is frequently omitted, especially where the antecedent clause is emphatic and evidently incomplete. This omission of the relative may in part have been suggested by the identity of the demonstrative *that* and the relative *that* :—

> " We speak *that* (dem.) *that* (rel.) we do know,"

may naturally be contracted into—

> " We speak *that* we do know."

Thus—

> " And that (*that*) most deeply to consider is
> The beauty of his daughter."—*Temp.* iii. 2. 106.
>   " Thy honourable metal may be wrought
> From that (*to which*) it is disposed."—*J. C.* i. 2. 314.
> " Now follows that (*that*) you know, young Fortinbras," &c.
>   *Hamlet,* i. 2. 17.
> " And that (*that*) is worse—the Lords of Ross are fled."
>   *Rich. II.* ii. 2. 52.

i.e. " which is worse." So often in the A. V. of the Bible, " *that* is, being interpreted," means " *which* is" (as the Greek shows), though a modern reader would suppose *that* to be the demonstrative.

In many cases the antecedent immediately precedes the verb to which the relative would be the subject.

> " I have a brother (*who*) is condemned to die."
>   *M. for M.* ii. 2. 33 ; *C. of E.* v. 1. 283.
> " I have a mind (*which*) presages."—*M. of V.* i. 1. 175.
> " The hate of those (*who*) love not the king."
>   *Rich. II.* ii. 2. 128.
> " In war was never lion (*that*) raged more fierce."
>   *Ib.* ii. 1. 173.
> " And sue a friend (*who*) 'came debtor for my sake."
>   *Sonn.* 139.
> " What wreck discern you in me (*that*)
> Deserves your pity ?"—*Cymb.* i. 6. 84 ; *W. T.* iv. 4. 378, 512.
>   " You are one of those (*who*)
> Would have him wed again."—*W. T.* v. 1. 23.
> " I'll show you those (*who*) in troubles reign,
> Losing a mite, a mountain gain."—*P. of T.* ii. Gower, 8.

"Of all (*who* have) 'say'd (tried) yet, may'st thou prove prosperous."—*P. of T.* i. 1. 59.

"And they are envious (*that*) term thee parasite."—B. J. *Fox*, i. 1.

"For once (*when*) we stood up about the corn, he himself stuck not to call us the many-headed multitude."

Coriol. ii. 3. 16.

i.e. "On one occasion (*on which*) we stood up," &c. Compare—

"Was it not yesterday (*on which*) we spoke together?"

Macbeth, iii. 1. 74.

"Off with his head,
And rear it in the place (*in which*) your father's stands."

3 *Hen. VI.* ii. 6. 86.

"Declare the cause
(*for which*) My father, Earl of Cambridge, lost his head."

1 *Hen. VI.* ii. 5. 55.

"O that forc'd thunder (*that*) from his breath did fly !—
O that sad breath (*that*) his spongy lungs bestow'd ! "

L. C. 46.

"And being frank she lends to these (*who*) are free."

Sonn. 4.

So explain :

"To me (*whom*) you cannot reach you play the spaniel."

Hen. VIII. v. 2. 126.

"That's to you sworn (*that*) to none was ever said."

L. C. 25. So *M. for M.* iii. 2. 165.

Most of these examples (except those in which *when* and *why* are omitted) omit the nominative. Modern usage confines the omission mostly to the objective. "A man (*whom*) I saw yesterday told me," &c. We must either explain thus :

"Myself and Toby
Set this device against Malvolio here (*which device*),
Upon some stubborn and discourteous parts,
We had conceiv'd against him,"—*T. N.* v. 1. 370.

or suppose (more probably), that there is some confusion between "conceiving enmity" and "disliking parts."

In "To her own worth
She shall be prized : but *that* you say 'Be 't so,'
I'll speak it in my spirit and honour 'No.'"

Tr. and Cr. iv. 4. 136.

that probably means "as to that which."

Other instances are :

"My sister . . . a lady, sir (*who*), though it was said she much resembled me, was yet of many accounted beautiful."—*T. N.* ii. 1. 27.

" What should I do (*that*) I do not?"—*A. and C.* i. 3. 8.

" Of every virtue (*that*) gives renown to men."—*P. of T.* i. 1. 13.

Either a relative or a nominative (see 399) is omitted in

> " These are my mates that make their wills their law
> (*Who*) have some unhappy passenger in chace."
>   *T. G. of V.* v. 4. 15.

In   " And curse that justice did it,"—*Coriol.* i. 1. 179.

either the relative is omitted after "justice," or "that" is used for "because" (284).

So, after disobeying King Cymbeline by allowing Posthumus to speak to the King's daughter, the Queen, while purposing to betray Posthumus, says aside :

> " Yet I'll move him (the king)
> To walk this way : I never do him (the king) wrong
> But he (*who*, like Posthumus) does buy my injuries to be friends,
> Pays dear for my offences."—*Cymb.* i. 1. 105.

The relative adverb *where* is omitted in

> " From that place (*where*) the morn is broke
> To that place (*where*) day doth unyoke."—B. and F. *F. Sh.* i. 1.

That, meaning " when," is omitted after "now."   (See 284.)

245. The Relative is omitted (as well as the verb "is," "are," &c.) between a pronominal antecedent and a prepositional phrase, especially when *locality is predicated.*

> " And *they in France* of the best rank and station."
>   *Hamlet,* i. 3. 129.

" He made *them of Greece* (*i.e.* the Grecians) to begin warre."
—N. *P.* 175.

So   " What is *he* at the gate ?"—*T. N.* i. 5. 125.

So in Early English and Anglo-Saxon.   We make the same omission, but only after nouns : "The babes in the wood."

246. The Relative is omitted in the following example, and the antecedent is attracted into the case which the relative, if present, would have :

> " *Him* (he *whom*) I accuse,
> By this, the city ports hath enter'd."—*Coriol.* v. 6. 6.

Apparently there is an ellipsis of "*that* (relative) is" before participles in the following :

" Not that devour'd, but that which doth devour,
    Is worthy blame,"—*R. of L.* 451.

where "that devour'd" seems used for "that *that* is devour'd."

" Why have you not proclaim'd Northumberland,
    And all the rest (that are) revolted, faction-traitors?"
                                        Rich. II. ii. 2. 57.

And in

"I hate the murderer, love him murdered,"
                                        Rich. II. v. 5. 40.

the meaning seems to be, not "I love the fact that he is murdered,"
but "I love him (who is) murdered." Compare the harsh construction in

" But you must know your father lost a father,
    That father (who was) lost, lost his."—*Hamlet,* i. 2. 90.
" A little riper and more lusty red
    Than that (which is) mixed in his cheek."
                                        A. Y. L. iii. 5. 222.

The relative is attracted to a subsequent implied object in the
following :

" Thou shalt not lack
    The leaf of eglantine, *whom* not to slander,
    Outsweetened not thy breath."—*Cymb.* iv. 2. 223.

i.e. "the leaf *which*, not to slander *it*, would not outsweeten," &c.

247. The Relative (perhaps because it does not signify by
inflection any agreement in number or person with its antecedent)
frequently (1) takes a *singular* verb, though the antecedent be
plural, and (2) the verb is often in the *third* person, though the
antecedent be in the *second* or *first*.

(1) " All things *that belongs*" (so Folio ; Globe, *belong*).—*T. of Sh.*
    ii. 1. 357.
            " Whose *wraths* to guard you from,
    Which here in this most desolate isle else *falls*
    Upon your head."—*Temp.* iii. 2. 80.
" Contagious fogs *which* falling on our land
    Hath every pelting river made so proud."—*M. N. D.* ii. 1. 91.
This, however, might be explained by 337.
" 'Tis not the many oaths *that makes* the truth."
                                        A. W. iv. 2. 21 ; *K. J.* ii. 1. 216.
" With sighs of love *that costs* the fresh blood dear."
                                        M. N. D. iii. 2. 97.

" My observations
Which with experimental seal *doth* warrant
The tenour of my book."—*M. Ado,* iv. 1. 168.

" 'Tis your graces *that charms.*"—*Cymb.* i. 6. 117.

" So, so, so : they laugh *that wins*" (Globe, *win*).
Othello, iv. 1. 125.

" So are those crisped snaky golden locks
Which makes."—*M. of V.* iii. 2. 92.

" Those springs
In chalic'd flowers *that lies.*"—*Cymb.* ii. 3. 24.

" Each substance of a grief hath twenty shadows
Which shows like grief itself."—*Rich. II.* ii. 2. 15.

" It is not words, *that shakes* me thus."—*Othello,* iv. 1. 43.

" But most miserable
Is the desires *that's* glorious."   (Globe, " desire.")
Cymb. i. 6. 6.

" 'Tis such fools as you
That makes the world full of ill-favour'd children."
A. Y. L. iii. 5. 53.

" (The swords) *That makes* such waste in brief mortality."
Hen. V. i. 2. 28.

" There are some shrewd contents in yon same paper
That steals the colour from your cheeks."—*M. of V.* iii. 2. 246.

" Is kindling coals *that fires* all my heart."—*3 Hen. VI.* ii. 1. 83.

" With such things else of quality and respect
As doth import you."—*Othello,* i. 3. 283.

" Such commendations *as becomes* a maid."—*1 Hen. VI.* v. 3. 177.

" Such thanks *as* fits a king's remembrance."—*Hamlet,* ii. 2. 26.

" Like monarch's hands *that lets* not bounty fall."
L. C. 41 (Globe, *let*).

" If it be you (you gods) *that stirs* these daughters' hearts."
Lear, ii. 4. 275 (Globe, *stir*).

" To be forbod the sweets *that seems* so good."
L. C. 164 (Globe, *seem*).

The distance of the relative from the antecedent sometimes makes
a difference, as in

" I *that please* some, try all, both joy and terror
Of good and bad, *that makes and unfolds* error."
W. T. iv. 1. 2.

This construction is found as late as **1671** :

" If it be true that monstrous births presage
The following mischiefs *that afflicts* the age."
The Rehearsal, Epilogue.

(2) " Antiochus, I thank *thee who hath* taught."—*P. of T.* i. 1. 41.

" Casca, *you* are the first *that rears your* hand."—*J. C.* iii. 1. 30

"*Rears his*" or "*rear your*" would be right.

" To make *me* proud *that jests*."—*L. L. L.* v. 2. 66.

" For it is *you that puts* us to our shifts."—*T. A.* iv. 2. 176.

So *Temp.* v. 1. 79.

" *O Lord, that lends* me life !"—*2 Hen. VI.* i. 1. 9.

" They do but greatly chide *thee who confounds*."—*Sonn.* 8.

The last two examples may also be explained (see 340) by the northern inflection of *s* for *st :* and the examples in (1) might come under the cases of plural nominative with apparently singular inflection considered in 333. But taking all the examples of (1) and (2) we are, I think, justified in saying that the relative was often regarded like a noun by nature third person singular, and, therefore, uninfluenced by the antecedent.

On the other hand, the verb is irregularly attracted into the second person in

" That would I learn of *you*
As *one that are* best acquainted with her person."
Rich. III. iv. 4. 268.

248. Relative with Supplementary Pronoun. With the Germans it is still customary, when the antecedent is a pronoun of the first or second person, to repeat the pronoun for the sake of defining the person, because the relative is regarded as being in the third person. Thus "Thou *who thou* hearest," &c. The same repetition was common in Anglo-Saxon (and in Hebrew) for all persons. " *That* (rel.) through *him* " = " through *whom*," " a tribe *that they* can produce " = " a tribe *who* can produce," &c.

Hence in Chaucer, Prol. 43–45 :

" A knight ther was, and that a worthy man,
That, from the tymë that he first began
To ryden out, *he* lovede chyvalrye ; "

and in the same author " *that his* "=" *whose*," " *that him* "=" *whom*," &c.

In the same way in Elizabethan authors, when the interrogative *who* (251) had partially supplanted *that* as a relative, we find *who his* for *whose, whom him* for *whom, which it* for *which,* &c.

The following is probably not a case of the supplementary pronoun :

"Bardolph and Nym had ten times more valour than this roaring
devil i' the old play, *that* every one may pare his nails with a wooden
dagger."—*Henry V.* iv. 4. 76.

That . . . his is not elsewhere used in Shakespeare, that I know
of. The above probably means "than this (fellow, who is) a mere
devil-in-the-play, so that every one may beat him."

249. The Supplementary Pronoun is generally confined to
cases (as above, 242) where the relative is separated from its verb by
an intervening clause, and where on this account clearness requires
the supplementary pronoun.

" *Who*, when he lived, *his* breath and beauty set
  Gloss on the rose, smell on the violet."—*V. and A.*
" *Which*, though it alter not love's sole effect,
  Yet doth *it* steal sweet hours from love's delight."
                                                    Sonn. 36.
" And *who*, though all were wanting to reward,
  Yet to himself *he* would not wanting be."—B. J. *Cy.'s Rev.*
      " *Whom*,
  Though bearing misery, I desire my life
  Once more to look on *him*."—*W. T.* v. 1. 138.
" (The queen) *whom* Heavens in justice both on *her* and hers
  Have laid most heavy hand."—*Cymb.* v. 5. 464.

Here the construction is further changed by the addition of "both
. . . and hers."

" You are three men of sin *whom* Destiny
  (That hath to instrument this lower world,
  And what is in't) the never-surfeited sea
  Hath caused to belch up *you*."—*Temp.* iii. 2. 53.

In the following passage the *which* may almost with better right
be regarded as supplementary than the noun which follows :

" Our natural goodness
  Imparts this ; *which* if you or stupified
  Or seeming so in skill, cannot or will not
  Relish *a truth* like us, inform yourselves
  We need no more of your advice."—*W. T.* ii. 1. 165.

Here *which* means "as regards *which*," and in this and in other
places it approximates to that vulgar idiom which is well known to
readers of "Martin Chuzzlewit." (See 272.)

The following seems at first as though it could be explained thus ;
but "who" is put for "whom" (see 274), and "exact the penalty" is
regarded as a transitive verb :

" *Who,* if *he* break, thou may'st with better face
Exact the penalty."—*M. of V.* i. 3. 137.

Or this may be an imitation of the Latin idiom which puts the relative before the conjunction, thus :

" *Who,* when *they* were in health, I tell thee, herald,
I thought upon one pair of English legs
Did walk three Frenchmen."—*Hen. V.* iii. 6. 157.

250. Which that.

"Spite of his spite *which that* in vain
Doth seek to force my fantasy."—INGELEND (A.D. 1560).

This use of *which that* consecutively is common in Chaucer, but not in Elizabethan authors. When it is remembered that *which* was originally an interrogative, it is easier to understand how *that* may have been added to give a relative force to *which.*

251. Who and what.

In Early English *who* was the masc. or fem. and *what* the neut. interrogative (or used as the indefinite relative *who-so, what-so*), *that* being both the demonstrative and relative, except in the oblique cases.

The transition of the interrogative to the relative can easily be explained. Thus, the sentence

" O now *who* will behold
The royal captain of this ruin'd band?
Let *him* cry ' Praise and glory on his head,' "
Hen. V. iv. Prologue.

may easily become "now let *him who* will behold," &c.

We can now only use *who-ever* in this sense, but the Germans still use their interrogative (*wer*) thus. In such cases the *who* mostly retains a trace of its interrogative meaning by preceding the antecedent clause :

" *Who* steals my purse (he) steals trash,"—*Othello,* iii. 3. 157.

and hence referring to a definite past :

" *Who* was the thane (he) lives yet."—*Macbeth,* i. 3. 109.

In this and other examples (as in Greek) the antecedent pronoun is often omitted owing to the emphatic position of the relative.

" *Whom* we raise we will make fast."—2 *Hen. VI.* i. 4. 25.
" Is proclamation made that *who* finds Edward
Shall have a high reward ?"—3 *Hen. VI.* v. 3. 9.

" Fixing our eyes on *whom* our care was fixed."
C. of E. i. 1. 85.

" We are going to *whom* it must be done."—*J. C.* ii. 1. 331.

252. What, being simply the neuter of the interrogative *who,*
ought consistently to be similarly used. As, therefore, *who* is used
relatively, we may expect *what* to be used so likewise. And so it
is ; but, inasmuch as the adjective *which* very early took the force
of the relative pronoun, *what* was supplanted by *which,* and is
rarely used relatively. Even when it is thus used, it generally stands
before its antecedent (like the transitional use of *who* above), thereby
indicating its interrogative force, though the position of the verb is
altered to suit a statement instead of a question.

" *What* our contempt doth often hurl from us
   We wish *it* ours again."—*A. and C.* i. 2. 127. So *Rich. II.* i. 1. 87.

" *What* you have spoke *it* may be so perchance."
Macbeth, iv. 3. 11.

" Look, *what* I speak, my life shall prove *it* true."
Rich. II. i. 1. 87.

" It is true that *what* is settled by custom, though it be not
   good, yet at least *it* is fit."—B. *E.* 99

An unemphatic antecedent precedes *what* in

" And I do fearfully believe '*tis* done
   What we so feared he had a charge to do."—*K. J.* iv. 1. 75.

I cannot remember any instance where *what* has for its antecedent
a noun, as in the modern vulgarism, " The man *what* said." In

" And let us once again assail your ears,
   That are so fortified against our story,
   What we have two nights seen."—*Hamlet,* i. 1. 33.

What depends on a verb of speech, implied either in "assail your
ears" or in "story," *i.e.* "let us tell you *what* we have seen," or
"our story describing *what we* have seen."

The antecedent was mostly omitted :

" *What* is done (that) cannot be undone."—*Macb.* v. 1. 74.

This use is common now, but we could not say

" To have his pomp and all *what* (that which) state compounds."
T. of A. iv. 2. 35.

The following is a curious use of *what :*

" That Julius Cæsar was a famous man :
   With what his valour did enrich his wit
   He did set down to make his valour live."
Rich. III. iii. 1. 85 : *i.e.* " (that) with *which.*"

253. What is used for "for what," "why" (quid), as in

" *What* (why) shall I don this robe and trouble you?"

Cymb. iii. 4. 34.

" *What* need we any spur but our own cause?"

J. C. ii. 1. 123.

" *What* shall I need to draw my sword?"—*T. A.* i. 1. 189.

" *What* should I stay?"—*A. and C.* v. 2. 317.

and in some other passages where the context shows this to be the meaning:

" *Falstaff.* This apoplexy is, as I take it, a kind of lethargy.
Justice. *What* tell you me of it: be it as it is."

2 Hen. IV. i. 2. 130.

The following use of *what* for "in what state," *i.e.* "how far advanced," should be noticed:

" *M.*   *What* is the night?
Lady M. Almost at odds with morning, which is which."

Macbeth, iii. 4. 126.

These adverbial uses of *what* are illustrated by

" His equal mind I copy *what* I can
And, as I love, would imitate the man."

POPE, *Imit. Hor.* ii. 131.

254. What = "whatever."

" *What* will hap more to-night, safe scape the king,"

Lear, iii. 6. 121.

where the construction may be "Happen what will," a comma being placed after "will," or "Whatever is about to happen." Probably the former is correct and "will" is emphatic, "hap" being optative.

What = "whoever."

" There's my exchange.   *What* in the world he is
That names me traitor, villain-like he lies."—*Lear*, v. 3. 97.

What is often used apparently with no sense of "of what kind or quality" where we should use *who*, especially in the phrase "*what* is he?"

" *Chief Justice. What's* he that goes there?
Servant. Falstaff, an't please your lordship."

2 Hen. IV. i. 2. 66.

" *What's* he that wishes so? My cousin Westmoreland?"

Hen. V. iv. 3. 18.

" *Ros. What* is he that shall buy his flock and pasture?
Cor. That young swain."—*A. Y. L.* ii. 4. 88–9.
" *Captain.* He did see the love of fair Olivia !
Vio. What's she?
Captain. A virtuous maid, the daughter of a count."
T. N. i. 2. 35 ; *ib.* i. 5. 124.

So *Lear*, v. 3. 125 ; *Macbeth*, v. 7. 2; *Rich. II.* v. 5. 69.

But in the Elizabethan and earlier periods, when the distinction
between ranks was much more marked than now, it may have
seemed natural to ask, as the first question about anyone, " of what
condition or rank is he?" In that case the difference is one of
thought, not of grammar.

255. What hence in elliptical expressions assumes the meaning
" any."
" I love thee not a jar of the clock behind
What lady-she (224) her lord."—*W. T.* i. 2. 44.

i.e. " less than any lady whatsoever loves her lord." So
"With promise of his sister and *what* else."
3 *Hen. VI.* iii. 1. 51 ; *Tempest*, iii. 1. 72.

i.e. " whatever else may be conceived," or " everything else."

" *What* not " is still used in this sense, as
" He that dares approach
On him, on you, *who not ?* I will maintain
Mine honour firmly."—*Lear*, v. 3. 100: *i.e.* " on everybody."

Like the Latin " qua—qua," so " what—what " is used for
" partly—partly," mostly joined to " with." In this collocation
perhaps the alliteration of the two *w*'s has had some influence : for
what is not thus used except before "with."

" And such a flood of greatness fell on you
What with our help, *what* with the absent king,
What with the injuries of a wanton time."
1 *Hen. IV.* v. 1. 50.

So *Tr. and Cr.* v. 1. 103.

Originally this may have been " considering *what* accrued from
our help, *what* from the king's absence," &c. but " what " is used
by Spenser in the sense of " part," " her little *what*." (See p. 5.)

256. What is sometimes used before a noun without the appended indefinite article in exclamations. (See **Article**, 86.) It is
also used without a noun in this sense :

' O father Abram, *what* these Christians are !"

M. of V. i. 3. 162.

" *What* mortality is !"—*Cymb.* iv. 1. 16.

i.e. "what a thing mortality is !"

257. Who for *any one :*

"The cloudy messenger turns me his back
And hums *as who should say,* 'You'll rue the time
That clogs.me with this answer.'"—*Macbeth,* iii. 6. 42.

" He doth nothing but frown, *as who should say,* 'If you will
not have me, choose.'"—*M. of V.* i. 2. 45.

Comp. *M. of V.* i. 1. 93, *Rich. II.* v. 4. 8. In these passages it is possible to understand an antecedent to 'who,' "as, or like (one) who should say." But in the passages

"Timon surnamed Misantropos (as *who* should say Loup-
garou, or the man-hater)."—*N. P.* 171.

" She hath been in such wise daunted
That they were, *as who saith,* enchanted."

GOWER, *C. A.* 1. (quoted by Clarke and Wright).

it is impossible to give this explanation. And in Early Eng. (Morris, Specimens, p. xxxii.) "als *wha* say " was used for "as *any one* may say." Comp. the Latin *quis* after *si, num,* &c. Possibly an *if* is implied after the *as* by the use of the subjunctive. (See 107.)

Littré explains " comme qui dirait " by supplying " celui." " Il portait sur sa teste comme qui dirait un turban ; c'est-à-dire, il portait, comme dirait celui qui dirait un turban." But this explanation seems unsatisfactory, in making a likeness to exist between " carry-ing" and " saying." But whatever may be the true explanation of the original idiom, Shakespeare seems to have understood *who* as the relative, for the antecedent can be supplied in all passages where he uses it, as *J. C.* i. 2. 120, "*As who* goes farthest."

258. That, which, who, difference between. Whatever rule may be laid down for the Elizabethan use of the three relative forms will be found to have many exceptions. Originally *that* was the only relative ; and if Wickliffe's version of the New Testament be compared with the versions of the sixteenth century and with that of 1611, *that* will be found in the former replaced by *which* and *who* in the latter, *who* being especially common in the latest, our Authorized Version. Even in Shakespeare's time, however, there is great diversity of usage. Fletcher, in the *Faithful Shepherdess*

(with the exception of a few lines containing the plot, and probably written by Beaumont), scarcely uses any relative but the smooth *that* throughout the play (in the first act *which* is only used once) ; and during the latter half of the seventeenth century, when the language threw off much of its old roughness and vigour, the fashion of Wickliffe was revived. *That* came into favour not because, as in Wickliffe's time, it was the old-established relative, but because it was the smoothest form : the convenience of three relative forms, and the distinctions between their different shades of meaning, were ignored, and *that* was re-established in its ancient supremacy. Addison, in his "Humble Petition of Who and Which," allows the petitioners to say : "We are descended of ancient families, and kept up our dignity and honour many years, till the jack-sprat *That* supplanted us." But the supplanting was a restoration of an incapable but legitimate monarch, rather than a usurpation. Since the time of Addison a reaction has taken place ; the convenience of the three distinct forms has been recognized, and we have returned somewhat to the Elizabethan usage.

259. As regards the Shakespearian use, the following rules will generally hold good :—

(1) **That** is used as a relative (*a*) after a noun preceded by the article, (*b*) after nouns used vocatively, in order to complete the description of the antecedent by adding *some essential characteristic of it.*

(2) **Who** is used (*a*) as the relative to introduce a *fact* about the antecedent. It may often be replaced by "and he," "for he," "though he," &c. (*b*) It is especially used after antecedents that are lifeless or irrational, when personification is employed, but not necessarily after personal pronouns.

(3) **Which** is used (*a*) in cases where the relative clause varies between an essential characteristic and an accidental fact, especially where the antecedent is preceded by *that ;* (*b*) where the antecedent is repeated in the relative clause ; (*c*) in the form "the which," where the antecedent is repeated, or where attention is expressly called to the antecedent, mostly in cases where there is more than one possible antecedent and care is required to distinguish the real one ; (*d*) where "which" means "a circumstance which," the circumstance being gathered from the previous sentence.

260. That. (*a*) Since *that* introduces an essential characteristic without which the description is not complete, it follows that, even where this distinction is not marked, *that* comes generally nearer to the antecedent than *who* or *which*.

> "To think of the teen *that* I have turn'd you to
> *Which* is from my remembrance !"—*Temp.* i. 2. 65.
> I to the world am like a drop of water
> *That* in the ocean seeks another drop,
> *Who* falling there to seek his fellow forth,
> Unseen, inquisitive, confounds himself."—*C. of E.* i. 2. 37.
> "You have oft enquired
> After the shepherd *that* complain'd of love,
> *Who* you saw sitting by me on the turf."—*A. Y. L.* iii. 4. 52.
> "And here's a prophet *that* I brought with me
> From forth the streets of Pomfret, *whom* I found
> With many hundreds treading on his heels."—*K. J.* iv. 2. 148.

The same order is preserved in *A. Y. L.* iii. 5. 13 ; *2 Hen. IV.* i. 3. 59 ; *Lear*, iii. 4. 134–139 ; *2 Hen. VI.* iv. 1. 3 ; *Lear*, iv. 2. 51–53 (where we find *that, who, that*, consecutively) ; *Lear*, iii. 7. 89, 90 ; *1 Hen. IV.* ii. 1. 80 (*that, the which, that*) ; *Tempest*, iv. 1. 76.
The distinction between *that* and *which* is preserved in

> "It is an heretic *that* (by nature, of necessity) makes the fire,
> Not she *which* (as an accidental fact) burns in it."
> > *W. T.* ii. 3. 115.
> "And he doth sin *that* doth belie the dead,
> Not he *which* (as you do) says the dead is not alive."
> > *2 Hen. IV.* i. 1. 99.

In the latter passage "he *that*" = "who-so," and refers to a *class*, "he which" to the *single person* addressed. Thus Wickliffe (*Matt.* xxiii. 21) has "he *that* sweareth," whereas the other versions have "whoso" or "whosoever sweareth."

That is generally used after *he, all, aught*, &c. where a *class* is denoted. This is so common as not to require examples, and it is found even where *that* is objective.

> "He *that* a fool doth very wisely hit."—*A. Y. L.* ii. 7. 53.

In   "The great globe itself,
> Yea, all *which* it inherit,"—*Temp.* iv. 1. 154.
euphony perhaps will not allow "*that* it." (See **Which**, 265.)
The following is not an exception :

> "It was the swift celerity of his death,
> *Which* I did think with slower foot came on,
> *That* brain'd my purpose."—*M. for M.* v. 1. 400.

for here *which* is used parenthetically (see 271). So *Rich. II.* iii. 4. 50.

In   " He *that* no more must say is listen'd more
        Than they *whom* youth and ease have taught to glose."
                                        Rich. II. ii. 1. 9, 10.

a distinction appears to be drawn between the singular nominative represented by the uninflected *that*, and the objective plural represented by the inflected *whom*.

261. That. (*b*) After nouns used vocatively.

" Hail, many-coloured messenger ! *that* ne'er
  Dost disobey the wife of Jupiter :
  Who with thy saffron wings upon my flowers
  Diffusest honey-drops, refreshing showers."
                                        Temp. iv. 1. 76–79.

" Hast thou conspired with thy brother, too,
  That for thine own gain shouldst defend mine honour?"
                                        K. J. i. 1. 242.

" Yon brother mine, *that* entertain'd ambition,
  Expell'd remorse and nature ; *who* with Sebastian
  Would here have kill'd your king."
                                        Tempest, v. 1. 79 ; 33–9.

This close dependence of *that* on the antecedent, wherein it differs from *who* and *which*, is a natural result of its being less emphatic, and therefore less independent, than the two other forms. When the relative is necessarily emphatic, as at the end of a verse, we may sometimes expect *that* to be replaced by *which*, for that and no other reason.

" Sometimes like apes *that* mow and chatter at me,
  And after bite me ; then like hedgehogs *which*
  Lie tumbling in my bare-foot way."—*Temp.* ii. 2. 10.

262. That is sometimes, but seldom, separated from the antecedent, like *who*. (See 263.)

" As if it were Cain's jawbone *that* did the first murder."
                                        Hamlet, v. 1. 85.

It is perhaps not uncommon after the possessive case of nouns and pronouns. (See 218.) The antecedent pronoun is probably to be repeated immediately before the relative.

" Cain's jawbone, (him) *that* did," &c.

Less commonly as in
> "They know the corn
> Was not our recompense, resting well assured
> *That* ne'er did service for it."—*Coriol.* iii. 1. 122.

The use of *that* for *who* = "and they" is archaic. Acts xiii. 43:
"They sueden Paul and Barnabas *that* spakun and counceileden hym." Tyndale, Cranmer, and Geneva have *which;* Rheims and A. V. *who.*

263. Who (a) for "and he," "for he," &c.

> "Now presently I'll give her father notice
> Of their disguising and pretended flight;
> *Who* (and he), all enraged, will banish Valentine."
> *T. G. of V.* ii. 6. 38.

> "My name is Thomas Mowbray, duke of Norfolk,
> *Who* (and I) hither come engaged by my oath
> Against the duke of Norfolk *that* (because he) appeals me."
> *Rich. II.* i. 3. 17.

> "Caius Ligarius doth bear Cæsar hard
> *Who* (since he) rated him for speaking well of Pompey."
> *J. C.* ii. 1. 216.

Hence *who* is often at some distance from the antecedent.

> "*Archbishop.* It was young Hotspur's case at Shrewsbury.
> *Lord Bardolph.* It was, my lord : *who* (for he) lined himself
> with hope."—2 *Hen. IV.* i. 3. 27.

> "To send the old and miserable king
> To some retention and appointed guard,
> *Whose* (for his) age has charms in it."—*Lear,* v. 3. 48.

"I leave him to your gracious acceptance ; *whose* (for his) trial shall better publish his commendation."—*M. of V.* iv. 1. 165.

> "In Ephesus I am but two hours old,
> As strange unto your town as to your talk,
> *Who* (and I), every word by all my wit being scann'd,
> Want wit, in all, one word to understand."
> *C. of E.* iii. 2. 153.

So *Temp.* iii. 1. 93 ; *A. and C.* i. 3. 29 ; *Hen. V.* i. Prologue, 33.

264. Who personifies irrational antecedents. (b) *Who* is often used of animals, particularly in similes where they are compared to men.

> "I am the cygnet to this pale faint swan,
> *Who* chants a doleful hymn to his own death."—*K. J.* v. 7. 22.

> "Or as a bear encompass'd round with dogs,
> *Who* having pinch'd a few and made them cry."
> 3 *Hen. VI.* ii. 1. 16.

So 1 *Hen. IV.* v. 2. 10 ; 2 *Hen. VI.* iii. 1. 253, v. 1. 153 ; but also in other cases where action is attributed to them, *e.g.*

"A lion *who* glared."—*J. C.* i. 3. 21.
"A lioness *who* quickly fell before him."—*A. Y. L.* iv. 2. 13.

Who is also used of inanimate objects regarded as persons.

"The winds
Who take the ruffian billows by the tops."—*2 Hen. IV.* iii. 1. 22.

So *R. and J.* i. 1. 119 ; i. 4. 100 : "The winds . . . *who.*"

"Rotten opinion, *who* hath writ me down
After my seeming."—*2 Hen. IV.* v. 2. 128.
"Night . . . *who.*"—*Hen. V.* iv. Prol. 21.
"Your anchors, *who*
Do their best office if they can but stay you."—*W. T.* iv. 4. 581.
"A queen
Over her passion, *who* most rebel-like
Sought to be queen o'er her."—*Lear*, iv. 2. 16.

So probably in

"Your eye
Who hath cause to wet the grief on 't."—*Tempest*, ii. 1. 127.

i.e. "your eye which has cause to give tearful expression to the sorrow for your folly."

"My arm'd knee
Who bow'd but in my stirrups."—*Coriol.* iii. 2. 119.

But is *who* the antecedent here to "me" implied in "my?" (See 218.)

"The heart
Who great and puff'd up with this retinue."
2 *Hen. IV.* iv. 3. 120.

So *V. and A.* 191 and 1043, "her heart . . . *who;*" *T. A.* iii. 2. 9, "my breast . . . *who.*"

The slightest active force, or personal feeling, attributed to the antecedent, suffices to justify *who*. Thus :

"The dispers'd air *who answer'd.*"—*R. of L.* 1805.
"Applause
Who like an arch *reverberates.*"—*Tr. and Cr.* iii. 3. 120.
"Therefore I tell my sorrows to the stones
Who though they cannot *answer,*" &c.—*T. A.* iii. 1. 38.
"Bushes,
As *fearful of him, part,* through *whom* he rushes."
V. and A. 630.

So "her body . . . *who*," *R. of L.* 1740; "the hairs *who* wave,"
V. and A. 306; "lips *who* . . . still blush," *R. and J.* iii. 3. 38;
"sighs *who*," *R. and J.* iii. 5. 136; "mouths *who*," *P. of T.* i. 4.
33; "palates *who*," *P. of T.* i. 4. 39; "her eyelids *who* like sluices
stopped," *V. and A.* Sometimes *who* is used where there is no
notion of personality:

"The world, *who* of itself is peised well,"—*K. J.* ii. 1. 575.
where perhaps *who* is used because of the pause after "world," in
the sense "though it." (See 263.) If there had been no comma between "world" and the relative, we should have had *that* or *which*.

Perhaps in this way we may distinguish in

"The first, of gold, *who* this inscription bears;
The second, silver, *which* this promise carries."
M. of V. ii. 7. 4.

i.e. "the first of gold, *and it* bears this inscription; the second,
(silver,) *which* carries," &c. In the first the *material*, in the second
the *promise*, is regarded as the *essential quality*. [Or does euphony
prefer *which* in the accented, *who* in the unaccented syllables?]

In almost all cases where *who* is thus used, an action is implied,
so that *who* is the subject.

Whom is rare.
"The elements
Of *whom* your swords are temper'd."—*Temp.* iii. 2. 62.

**265. Which (E. E. adj. hw-ilc, "wh(a)-like") is used inter-
changeably with Who and That.** It is interchanged with *who*
in

"Then Warwick disannuls great John of Gaunt,
Which did subdue the greatest part of Spain;
. . . .
And, after that wise prince, Henry the Fifth,
Who by his power conquered all France."
3 *Hen. VI.* iii. 3. 87.

Like *who* (263), *which* implies a cause in

"Deposing thee before thou wert possess'd,
Which (for thou) art possess'd now to depose thyself."
Rich. II. ii. 1. 108.

It is often used for *that* (see 261), where the personal antecedent
is vocatively used or preceded by the article:

"*The* mistress *which* I serve."—*Temp.* iii. 1. 6.

So *M. for M.* v. 1. 305; *W. T.* i. 2. 455, v. 2. 60.

> " Abhorred slave,
> *Which* any point of goodness will not take."—*Temp.* i. 2. 352.
> " And thou, great goddess Nature, *which* hast made it."
> *W. T.* ii. 3. 104.

So in our version of the Lord's Prayer.

266. Which, like *that,* is less definite than *who. Who* indicates an individual, *which* a " kind of person ;" *who* is " qui," *which* " qualis."

> " I have known those *which* (*qualis*) have walked in their sleep
> *who* (and yet they, 263) have died holily in their beds."—*Macb.*
> v. 1. 66.

> "For then I pity those I do not know
> *Which* (unknown persons) a dismiss'd offence would after gall."
> *M. for M.* ii. 2. 102.

> "They have—as who have not, that their great stars
> Throned and set high ?—servants, *who* seem no less,
> *Which* are to France the spies and speculations
> Intelligent of our state."—*Lear*, iii. 1. 24.

Here "*who* seem no less" is parenthetical, and for *who* might be written "they." *Which* means " of such a kind that." Where "so dear," "such," &c. is implied in the antecedent, we may expect the corresponding *which* (278) in the relative :

> " Antonio, I am married to a wife
> *Which* is as dear to me as life itself."—*M. of V.* iv. 1. 283.

When the antecedent is personal and *plural, which* is generally preferred to *who. Which*, like *that* (260), often precedes *who.*

> " I am Prospero, and that very duke
> *Which* was thrust from Milan, *who*," &c.—*Tempest*, v. 1. 160.

267. The . . . that; that . . . which. In A.-S. "þe" (the) was the relative and "se" the article. When the form "þe" (the) became the article, "that" became the relative. In the same way it perhaps arises that when *that* was applied to the antecedent, the relative form preferred by Shakespeare was *which.* " *The* man *that* says " = "whoever says," and the indefinite *that* is sufficient ; but "*that* man," being more definite, requires a more definite relative. After a proper name, *who* would answer the purpose ; but after "*that* man," *that* being an adjective, "*which* man" was the natural expression, *which* being originally also an adjective. Hence the marked change in

" If he sees *aught* in you *that* makes him like
    That anything he sees *which* moves his liking."—*K. J.* ii. **1**. 52.
" When living blood doth in *these* temples beat
    Which owe *the* crown *that* thou o'er-masterest."—*Ib.* ii. **1**. 109.

Possibly "that" is a demonstrative, and "he" is used for "man"
in the following, which will account for the use of *which ;* but more
probably *which* is here used for *that,* and there is a confusion of
constructions.

    " Rather proclaim it, Westmoreland, through our host,
      That he *which* hath no stomach to this fight,
    Let him depart."—*Hen. V.* iv. 3. 34.*

268. Which more definite than That. Generally it will be
found that *which* is more definite than *that. Which* follows a name,
that a pronoun :

"Here's the Lord Say *which* sold the towns in France ; he *that*
made us pay one-and-twenty fifteens." —*2 Hen. VI.* iv. 5. 23.

Sometimes *which* is used in this sense to denote an individual
or a defined class, while *that* denotes a hypothetical person or an
indefinite class. Hence

" And such other gambol faculties a' has, *that* show a weak mind
and an able body, for *the which* the Prince admits him."—*2 Hen.
IV.* ii. 4. 74.

And compare

    "She *that* was ever fair and never proud, &c.
    She was a wight, *if ever such wight were.*"—*Othello,* ii. **1**. 149.
with   " I find that she *which* late
    Was in my nobler thoughts most base, is now
    The praised of the king : *who* (263), so ennobled,
    Is as 'twere born so."—*A. W.* ii. 3. 179.
" It is a chance *which* does redeem all sorrows
    That I have ever felt."—*Lear,* v. 3. 266.

Which states a fact, *that* a probability, in

    " Why, Harry, do I tell thee of my foes,
      Which art my near'st and dearest enemy ?
    Thou *that* art like enough."—*1 Hen. IV.* iii. 2. 124.

In " Cut off the heads of too fast growing sprays
    That look too lofty in our commonwealth :
    You thus employ'd, I will go root away
    The noisome weeds *which*, without profit, suck
    The soil's fertility from wholesome flowers."—*Rich. II.* iii 4.37.

    * See 415 and compare *T. A.* iii. **1**. 151 ; *Lear,* ii. **1**. 63.

We must explain " all the heads *that may happen* to look too lofty, and the weeds *which,* as a fact, suck the fertility," &c.

So *that* introduces an essential, and *which* an accidental, or at all events a less essential quality, in the two following passages :—

> "(Thou) commit'st thy anointed body to the cure
> Of those physicians *that* first wounded thee."
>
> *Rich. II.* ii. 1. 99.

> " Now for our Irish wars.
> We must supplant those rough, rug-headed kerns,
> *Which* live like venom where no venom else,
> But only they, have privilege to live." —*Ib.* 157.

That may state a fact with a notion of purpose :

> " Now, sir, the sound *that* tells (*i.e.* to tell) what hour it is
> Are clamorous groans *which* strike upon my heart,
> *Which* is the bell."—*Rich. II.* v. 5. 57.

269. Which with repeated antecedent. *Which* being an adjective frequently accompanies the repeated antecedent, where definiteness is desired, or where care must be taken to select the right antecedent.

> "   *Salisbury.* What other harm have I, good lady, done
> But spoke the harm *that* is by others done ?
> *Constance. Which harm* within itself so heinous is—"
>
> *K. J.* iii. 1. 39.

> "And, if she did play false, the fault was hers,
> *Which fault* lies," &c.—*K. J.* i. 1. 119 ; *Rich. II.* i. 1. 104.

This may sometimes explain why *which* is used instead of *that,* and why *that* is preferred after pronouns :

> " Let my revenge on her *that* injured thee
> Make less a fault *which* I intended not."—*F. Sh.* v. 1.

An antecedent noun ("fault") can be repeated, and therefore can be represented by the relative *which ;* an antecedent pronoun "her" cannot.

Sometimes a noun of similar meaning supplants the antecedent :

> " Might'st bespice a cup
> To give mine enemy a lasting wink,
> *Which draught* to me were cordial."—*W. T.* i. 2. 318

270. The which. The above repetition is, perhaps, more common with the definite "the *which*" :

> " The better part of *valour* is *discretion ;* in *the which better part*
> I have saved my life."—1 *Hen. IV.* v. 4. 125.

Sometimes the noun qualified by *which* is not repeated, and only slightly implied in the previous sentence :

"Under an oak . . . to *the which place.*"—*A. Y. L.* ii. 1. 33.

"Let gentleness my strong enforcement be,
In the which hope I blush."—*Ib.* ii. 7. 119.

The question may arise why "the" is attached to *which* and not to *who.* (The instance

"Your mistress from *the whom* I see
There's no disjunction,"—*W. T.* iv. 4. 539.

is, perhaps, unique in Shakespeare.) The answer is, that *who* is considered definite already, and stands for a noun, while *which* is considered as an indefinite adjective ; just as in French we have "*le*quel," but not "*le*qui." "The *which*" is generally used either as above, where the antecedent, or some word like the antecedent, is repeated, or else where such a repetition could be made if desired. In almost all cases there are two or more possible antecedents from which selection must be made. (The use of "*le*quel" is similar.)

"To make a *monster of the multitude,* of the *which* (multitude) we being members should bring ourselves to be monstrous members."
—*Coriol.* ii. 3. 10.

"Lest your *justice*
Prove *violence,* in *the which* (violence) three great ones suffer."
W. T. ii. 1. 128.

"Eight hundred *nobles*
In name of *lendings* for your highness' *soldiers,*
The which (nobles) he hath detain'd for lewd employments."
Rich. II. i. 1. 90.

"The *which*" is also naturally used after a previous "which."

"The present business
Which now's upon us : without *the which* this story
Were most impertinent."—*Temp.* i. 1. 138.

"The chain
Which God he knows I saw not, for *the which*
He did arrest me."—*C. of E.* v. 1. 230.

271. Which for "which thing," often parenthetically.

"Camillo,
As you are certainly a gentleman, thereto
Clerk-like experienced, *which* no less adorns
Our gentry, than our parents' noble names."—*W. T.* i. 2. 392.

Very often the "thing" must be gathered not from what precedes but from what follows, as in

"And, *which* became him like a prince indeed,
He made a blushing 'cital of himself."—1 *Hen. IV.* v. 2. 62.

"And, *which* was strange, the one so like the other
As could not be distinguished."—*C. of E.* i. 1. 53.

That is rarely thus used by Shakespeare :

"And, *that* is worse,
The Lord Northumberland, his son young Henry Percy,
With all their powerful friends, are fled to him."
Rich. II. ii. 2. 55.

Often, however, in our A. V. *that* in "*that* is, being interpreted," is the relative, though a modern reader would not perceive it.

"I was never so berhymed since Pythagoras' time that (when) I was an Irish cat, *which* I can hardly remember."—*A. Y. L.* iii. 2. 188.

"I'll resolve you,
Which to you shall seem probable, of every
These happen'd accidents."—*Temp.* v. 1. 249.

i.e. "I will explain to you (*and the explanation* shall seem probable) every one of these accidents."

"My honour's at the stake, *which* (danger) to defeat
I must produce my power."—*A. W.* ii. 3. 156.

"Even as I have tried in many other occurrences, *which* Cæsar affirmed (ce que dit César), that often," &c.—MONTAIGNE, 36.

272. Which for "as to which." Hence *which* and "the *which*" are loosely used adverbially for "as to which." So in Latin, "quod" in "quod si."

"Showers of blood,
The which how far off from the mind of Bolingbroke
It is such crimson tempest should bedew," &c.
Rich. II. iii. 3. 45.

"With unrestrained loose companions—
Even such, they say, as stand in narrow lanes,
And beat our watch, and rob our passengers ;
Which he, young, wanton, and effeminate boy,
Takes on the point of honour, to support
So dissolute a crew."—*Rich. II.* v. 3. 10.

"But God be thanked for prevention ;
Which I in sufferance heartily will rejoice."
Hen. V. ii. 2. 159.

273. Which. It is hard to explain the following :

" A mote will turn the balance *which* Pyramus *which* Thisbe is the better."—*M. N. D.* v. 1. 325.

unless *which* is used for the kindred " whether."

In " My virtue or my plague, be it either *which*,"

Hamlet, iv. 7. 13.

there is perhaps a confusion between "be it either" and "be it whichever of the two." Perhaps, however, "either" may be taken in its original sense of "one of the two," so that "either which" is "which-one-so-ever of the two."

274. Who for *whom.* The inflection of *who* is frequently neglected.

" *Who* I myself struck down."—*Macbeth,* iii. 1. 123.

" *Who* does the wolf love ? The lamb."—*Coriol.* ii. 1. 8.

Compare *W. T.* iv. 4. 66, v. 1. 109.

Apparently it is not so common to omit the *m* when the *whom* is governed by a preposition whose contiguity demands the inflection:

" There is a mystery with *whom* relation
Durst never meddle."—*Tr. and Cr.* iii. 3. 201.

Compare especially,

" Consider *who* the king your father sends,
To *whom* he sends."—*L. L. L.* ii. 1. 2.

The *interrogative* is found without the inflection even after a preposition :

" *C.* Yield thee, thief.
Gui. To *who ?* "—*Cymb.* iv. 2. 75 ; *Othello,* i. 2. 52.
" With *who ?*"—*Othello,* iv. 2. 99.

And in a dependent question :

" The dead man's knell
Is there scarce asked for *who.*"—*Macbeth,* iv. 3. 171.

In the following, *who* is not the object of the preposition :

" This is a creature . . . might make proselytes
Of who she but bid follow."—*W. T.* v. 1. 109.

RELATIVAL CONSTRUCTIONS.

275.—So as. Bearing in mind that *as* is simply a contraction for " all-so" ("alse," "als," "as"), we shall not be surprised at some interchanging of *so* and *as.*

We still retain "*as . . . so*". "*As* I had expected *so* it happened," but seldom use "*so . . . as*," preferring "*as . . . as;*" except where *so* (as in the above phrase) requires special emphasis. The Elizabethans frequently used *so* before *as*.

> "*So* well thy words become thee *as* thy wounds."
> > *Macbeth*, i. 2. 43.

> "Look I *so* pale, Lord Dorset, *as* the rest?"
> > *Rich. III.* ii. 1. 83.

> "And with a look *so* piteous in purport
> *As* if he had been loosed out of hell."—*Hamlet*, ii. 1. 82.

> " Thou art *so* full of fear·
> *As* one with treasure laden."—*V. and A.*

> "Fair and fair and twice *so* fair
> *As* any shepherd may be."—PEELE.

> "All *so* soon *as*."—*R. and J.* i. 1. 140.

This is not very common in Shakespeare. Nor is it common to find *so* for *as* where the clause containing the second *as* is implied but not expressed.

> "Make us partakers of a little gain,
> That now our loss might be ten times *so* much."
> > 1 *Hen. VI.* ii. 1. 53.

If the relatival *as* precedes, *so*, not *as*, must follow as the demonstrative. The exception below is explicable as being a repetition of a previous *as* used demonstratively :

> "As little joy, my lord, as you suppose
> You should enjoy, were you this country's king,
> *As* little joy may you suppose in me
> That I enjoy."—*Rich. III.* i. 3. 153.

"That" is the relative.

Ben Jonson (p. 789) writes as follows on *so* and *as* : " When the comparison is in quantity, then *so* goeth before and *as* followeth.

> 'Men wist in thilk time none
> *So* fair a wight *as* she was one.'—GOWER, lib. 1.

But if the comparison be in quality, then it is contrary.

> 'For, *as* the fish, if it be dry,
> Mote, in default of water dye :
> Right *so* without air or live,
> No man ne beast might thrive.'—GOWER."

So as is frequently used for *so that*. (See 109.)

This construction is generally found with the past and future indicative, but we sometimes find "*so as* he may see," for "*so that* he may see." "*So as*" is followed by the subjunctive in

"And lead these testy rivals *so* astray
As one *come* not within another's way."—*M. N. D.* iii. 2. 359.

Compare the use of ὡς with the subjunctive in Greek. There is no more reason for saying, "I come *so that* (i.e. in which way) I may see," than for saying, "I come *so as* (i.e. in which way) I may see." We sometimes find *so as that* for *so as* in this sense.

The *so* is omitted after *as* in the adjurations

"*As* ever thou wilt deserve well at my hands, (so) help me to a candle,"—*T. N.* iv. 2. 86.
where *as* means "in which degree," and *so* "in that degree." Hence *as* approximates to "if."

It would seem that "*as* . . . *so*" are both to be implied from the previous verse in

"Had you been as wise as bold,
(*As*) young in limbs, (*so*) in judgment old."
M. of V. ii. 7. 71.

276. As . . . as. The first *As* is sometimes omitted :

"A mighty and a fearful head they are
As ever offered foul play in a state."—1 *Hen. IV.* iii. 2. 168.
"He pants and looks (*as*) pale *as* if a bear were at his heels."
T. N. iii. 4. 323; *Tempest*, v. 1. 289.

In the expression "old *as* I am," &c. we almost always omit the first *as*. Shakespeare often inserts it :

"*As* near the dawning, provost, *as* it is."—*M. for M.* iv. 2. 97.
"But I believe, *as* cold a night *as* 'tis, he could wish himself in Thames up to the neck."—*Hen. V.* iv. 1. 118.

The expression is elliptical : "(be it) *as* cold *as* it is."

277. That . . . that, that . . . (as) to. *That* is still used provincially for *such* and *so:* e.g. "He is *that* foolish *that* he understands nothing." So

"From me whose love was of *that* dignity
That it went hand in hand even with the vow
I made to her in marriage."—*Hamlet*, i. 5. 48.

That is more precise than "of that kind" or "such."

That, meaning "such," is used before the infinitive where we use the less emphatic "the."

"Had you *that* craft to reave her
Of what should stead her most?"—*A. W.* v. 3. 86.

So *T. N.* i. 1. 33 ; *Rich. III.* i. 4. 257 ; and *Macbeth*, iv. 3. 374 :

"There cannot be
That vulture in you to devour so many."

This omission of "as" after *that* meaning "so," is illustrated by the omission of "as" after "so" (281).

278. Such which. *Such* (in Early English, "swulc," "suilc," "suilch," "sich") was by derivation the natural antecedent to *which; such* meaning* "so-like," "so-in-kind ;" *which* meaning "what-like," "what-in-kind ?" Hence—

"*Such* sin
For *which* the pardoner himself is in."—*M. for M.* iv. 2. 111.

"There rooted between them *such* an affection *which* cannot choose but branch now."—*W. T.* i. 1. 26.

So *W. T.* iv. 4. 788; *Coriol.* iii. 2. 105.

Compare   "Duty *so* great *which* wit *so* poor *as* mine
May make seem bare."—*Sonn.* 26.

Similarly *which* is irregularly used after "too :"

"And salt *too* little *which* may season give
To her foul-tainted flesh."—*M. Ado*, iv. 1. 144.

Whom follows *such* in

"*Such* I will have *whom* I am sure he knows not."
A. W. iii. 6. 24.

279. Such that; so . . . that (rel.); such . . . where.
Hence *such* is used with other relatival words :

"*Such* allowed infirmities *that* honesty
Is never free of."—*W. T.* i. 2. 263.

"To *such* a man
That is no flaming tell-tale."—*J. C.* i. 3. 116.

"For who *so* firm *that* cannot be seduced."—*J. C.* i. 2. 316.

"His mother was a witch, and one *so* strong
That could control the moon."—*Temp.* v. 1. 270 ; *ib.* 315

"But no perfection is *so* absolute
That some impunity doth not pollute."—*R. of L.*

"Who's *so* gross
That seeth not this palpable device ?"—*Rich. III.* iii. 6. 11.

"*Such* things were
That were most precious to me."—*Macbeth*, iv. 3. 222.

* Hence "*such*-like" (*Temp.* iii. 3. 59) is a pleonasm.

> "For no man well of *such* a salve can speak
> *That* heals the wound and cures not the disgrace."
>
> *Sonn.* 34.

Coriol. iii. 2. 55; *T. G. of V.* iv. 4. 70; *A. W.* i. 3. 221; *Lear,* ii. 2. 127; *Othello,* iii. 3. 417.

Hence it seems probable that *that* is the relative, *having for its antecedent the previous sentence,* in the following passages from Spenser:—

> "Whose loftie trees yclad with summer's pride
> Did spred *so* broad *that* heaven's light did hide."—*F. Q.* i. 1. 7.
> "(He) Shook him *so* hard *that* forced him to speak."—*Ib.* 42.

Similarly "And the search *so* slow
Which could not trace them."—*Cymb.* i. 1. 65.

The licence in the use of these words is illustrated by—

> "In me thou seest the twilight of *such* day
> *As*, after sunset, fadeth in the west,
> *Which* by and by black night doth take away.
> In me thou seest the glowing of *such* fire
> *That* on the ashes of his youth doth lie
> *As* on the death-bed."—*Sonn.* 73.

In the first case *such as* is used, because *which* follows; in the second, *such that,* because *as* follows. So *Hamlet,* iii. 4. 41–46:

> "*Such* an act *that* .... *such* a deed *as*."

Such, so, where:

> "*Soch* a schoole *where* the Latin tonge were properly and perfitlie spoken."—ASCH. 45.
> "In no place *so* unsanctified
> *Where* such as thou mayest find him."—*Macbeth,* iv. 2. 81.
> "*So* narrow *where* one but goes abreast."
>
> *Tr. and Cr.* iii. 3. 155.

280. That as. We now use only *such* with *as*, and only *that* with *which*. Since, however, *such* was frequently used with *which*, naturally *that* was also used with *as* (*in which way*) used for *which*. Thus *as* approaches the meaning of a relative pronoun.

> "I have not from your eyes *that* gentleness
> *As* I was wont to have."—*J. C.* i. 2. 33.
> "Under *these* hard conditions *as* this time
> Is like to lay upon us."—*Ib.* 174.

> " *Those* arts they have *as* I could put into them."
> > *Cymb.* v. 5. 338.

> "Methinks the realms of England, France, and Ireland
> Bear *that* proportion to my flesh and blood
> *As* did the fatal brand Althea burned
> Unto the prince's heart at Calydon."—2 *Hen. VI.* i. 1. 233.

> " With *that* ceremonious affection *as* you were wont."
> > *Lear,* i. 4. 63.

So after *this* :

> " I beseech you do me *this* courteous office *as* to know what my offence is."—*T. N.* iii. 4. 278.

Similarly

> " With hate in *those where* I expect most love."
> > *Rich. III.* ii. 1. 33.

Either (1) the nominative is omitted (see 399), or (2) *as* is put for *who,* the relative to an implied antecedent, in :

> "Two goodly sons,
> And, which was strange, the one so like the other
> *As* could not be distinguish'd but by names."
> > *C. of E.* i. 1. 52.

i.e. (1) "so like that (they) could not be," *as* being used for *that* (see 109) ; or (2) " the one so like the other," &c. is loosely used for "the two so like each other *as* could not be distinguished."

Similarly *as* is used as a relative after an antecedent implied, but not expressed, by *so* with an adjective :

> " I cannot but be sad, so heavy-sad
> *As* . . . makes me faint."—*Rich. II.* ii. 2. 31.

i.e. " I feel such sadness *as.*"

281 So (as). Under the **Relative** we have seen that sometimes the antecedent, sometimes the relative, is omitted, without injury to the sense. Similarly in relatival constructions, e.g. *so . . . as, so . . . that,* &c. one of the two can be omitted.

The *as* is sometimes omitted :

> " I wonder he is *so* fond
> (as) To trust the mockery of unjust slumbers."
> > *Rich. III.* ii. 3. 26.

> "*So* fond [*i.e.* foolish] (as) to come abroad."
> > *M. of V.* iii. 3. 10.

> " *No* woman's heart
> So big (as) to hold so much."—*T. N.* ii. 4. 99.

" Shall I *so* much dishonour my fair stars
(as) On equal terms to give him chastisement ? "
Rich. II. iv. **1. 21.**
R. and J. ii. 3. 91 ; *Macbeth,* ii. 3. 55 ; *Rich. II.* iii. 3. 12.

As or *who* is omitted in :

" And while it is so, none *so* dry or thirsty
Will deign to sip or touch one drop of it."—*T. of Sh.* v. 2. 144.

i.e. " None is so thirsty (who) will deign " where we should say " as
to deign." Less probably, " none (be he how) *so* (ever) dry."

So and *as* are both omitted in :

" Be not (*so*) fond
(*As*) To think that Cæsar bears such rebel blood."—*J. C.* iii. 1. 40.

282. So (that). The *that* is sometimes omitted.

" I am *so* much a fool (that) it would be my disgrace."
Macb. iv. 2. 27.

283. (So) that. *So* before *that* is very frequently omitted :

" *Ross.* The victory fell on us. *Dunc.* Great happiness !
Ross. (So) *that* now Sueno, the Norway's king, craves composition."—*Macbeth,* i. 2. 59.

Compare *Macb.* i. 7. 8, ii. 2. 7, ii. 2. 24 ; *J. C.* i. 1. 50.

In all these omissions the missing word can be so easily supplied
from its correspondent that the desire of brevity is a sufficient
explanation of the omission.

" A sheet of paper
Writ o' both sides the leaf, margent and all,
That he was fain to seal on Cupid's name."—*L. L. L.* v. 2. 9.

284. That, for *because, when.* Since *that* represents different
cases of the relative, it may mean " in *that,*" " for *that,*" " because "
(" quod "), " or at *which* time " (" quum ").

In, or *for that :*

" Unsafe the while *that* we must lave our honours," &c.
Macbeth, iii. 2. 32.

" O, spirit of love ! How quick and fresh art thou
That (in that), . . . nought enters there but," &c.
T. N. i. 1. 10.

" Like silly beggars
Who sitting in the stocks refuge their shame,
That (because) many have and others must sit there,
And in this thought they find a kind of ease."
Rich. II. v. 5. 27.

At which time ; when .

> "In the day *that* thou eatest thereof."—*Gen.* ii. 17.

> "Now it is the time of night
> *That* the graves all gaping wide,
> Every one lets forth his sprite."—*M. N. D.* v. 1. 387.

> "So wept Duessa until eventyde,
> *That* shynyng lamps in Jove's high course were lit."
> SPENS. *F. Q.* i. 5. 19.

> "Is not this the day
> *That* Hermia should give answer of her choice?"
> *M. N. D.* iv. 1. 133.

> "So, till the judgment *that* yourself arise,
> You live in this and dwell in lovers' eyes."—*Sonn.* 55.

Compare "Then *that*," apparently "then *when*." (2 *Hen. IV.* iv. 1. 117.)

These uses of *that* are now superseded by the old interrogatives *why* and *when*, just as, even in Shakespeare's time, many of the uses of *that* had been transferred to the interrogatives *who* and *which*.

> "Albeit I will confess thy father's wealth
> Was the first motive *that* I wooed thee, Anne."
> *M. W. of W.* iii. 4. 14.

i.e. "*for which*, or *why*, I wooed thee."

The use of *that* for *when* is still not uncommon, especially in the phrase "now *that* I know," &c. It is omitted after "now" in

> "But now (*that*) I am return'd, and that war thoughts
> Have left their places vacant, in their rooms
> Come thronging soft and delicate desires."—*M. Ado*, i. 1. 303.

So *Rich. III.* i. 2. 170 ; *M. N. D.* iv. 1. 67, 109.

That = "in which" in

> "Sweet Hero, now thy image doth appear
> In the sweet semblance *that* I loved it first."—*M. Ado*, v. 1. 260.

285. That omitted and then inserted. The purely conjunctional use of *that* is illustrated by the Elizabethan habit of omitting it at the beginning of a sentence, where the construction is obvious, and then inserting it to connect a more distant clause with the conjunction on which the clause depends. In most cases the subjects of the clauses are different.

> "Though my soul be guilty and *that* I think," &c.
> B. J. *Cy.'s Rev.* iii. 2.

"Were it not thy sour leisure gave sweet leave,
And *that* thou teachest."—*Sonn.* 39.

"If this law
Of nature be corrupted through affection,
And *that* great minds, of partial indulgence
To their benumbed wills, resist the same."

Tr. and Cr. ii. 2. 179.

This may explain (without reference to "but that," 122):

"If frosts and fasts, hard lodging and thin weeds
Nip not the gaudy blossoms of your love,
But *that* it bear this trial."—*L. L. L.* v. 2. 813.

For "if *that*," see 287.

"Think I am dead, and *that* even here thou takest,
As from my death-bed, my last living leave."

Rich. II. v. 1. 38.

So *T. N.* v. 1. 126; *W. T.* i. 2. 84; *A. and C.* iii. 4. 31; *P. of T.* i. Gower, 11.

"I love and hate her, for she's fair and royal,
And *that* she hath all worthy parts more exquisite."

Cymb. iii. 5. 71.

i.e. "*for that*" or "because."

"She says I am not fair, *that* I lack manners ;
She calls me proud, and *that* she could not love me."

A. Y. L. iv. 2. 16.

In the above example the *that* depends upon a verb of speech implied in "calls." This construction is still more remarkable in—

"But here's a villain that would face me down
He met me on the mart, and *that* I beat him."—*C. of E.* iii. 1. 7.

Compare the French use of "que" instead of repeating "si," "quand," &c.

286. Whatsoever that. In the following there is probably an ellipsis :

"This and *what* needful else (there be)
That calls upon us."—*Macbeth*, v. 8. 72.

"Till *whatsoever* star (*it be*) *that* guides my moving
Points on me graciously with fair aspect."—*Sonn.* 26.

"As if that *whatsoever* god (*it be*) *who* leads him
Were slily crept into his human powers."—*Coriol.* ii. 1. 235.

In the latter, *that* is probably the demonstrative. It might, however, be the conjunctional *that.* See "if *that*," 287.

287. That as a conjunctional affix.   Just as *so* and *as* are affixed
to *who* (whoso), *when* (whenso), *where* (whereas, whereso), in order
to give a relative meaning to words that were originally interrogative,
in the same way *that* was frequently affixed.*

> "*When that* the poor have cried."
>
> > *J. C.* iii. 2. 96 ; *T. N.* v. 1. 398.
>
> "*Why that.*"—*Hen. V.* v. 2. 34.
>
> "You may imagine him upon Blackheath,
> *Where that* his lords desire him to have borne
> His bruised helmet and his bended sword
> Before him through the city."—*Hen. V.* v. Prologue, 17.

So *A. Y. L.* ii. 7. 75 ; iv. 3. 117.   This, with the above, explains

> "*Edmund. When* by no means he could.
> *Gloucester.* Pursue him, ho ! go after.   By no means what ?
> *Edmund.* Persuade me to the murder of your lordship,
> But *that* I told him," &c.—*Lear,* ii. 1. 47.

Gradually, as the interrogatives were recognized as relatives, the
force of *that, so, as,* in "when *that,*" "when *so,*" "when *as,*"
seems to have tended to make the relative more general and indefinite ; "who so" being now nearly (and once quite) as indefinite as "whosoever."   The "ever" was added when the "so" had
begun to lose its force.   In this sense, by analogy, *that* was attached
to other words, such as "if," "though," "why," &c.

> "*If that* the youth of my new interest here
> Have power to bid you welcome."—*M. of V.* iii. 2. 224.

Compare

> "*If that* rebellion
> Came like itself, in base and abject routs."
>
> > 2 *Hen. IV.* iv. 1. 32 ; *T. N.* i. 5. 324, v. 1. 375.

So *Lear,* v. 3. 262 ; *Rich. III.* ii. 2. 7.

The fuller form is found, CHAUC. *Pard. Tale,* 375 : "*If* so were
that I might;" and Lodge writes, "*If* so I mourn."   Similarly, "If
so be thou darest."—*Coriol.* v. 14. 98.

Compare :

> "*While that.*"—*Hen. V.* v. 2. 46.
>
> "*Though that.*"
>
> > *Coriol.* i. 1. 144 ; *Lear,* iv. 6. 219 ; *T. N.* i. 3. 48.
>
> "*Lest that.*"—*Hen. V.* ii. 4. 142; *T. N.* iii. 4. 384.
>
> "*Whether that.*"—1 *Hen. VI.* iv. 1. 28.

* St. Mark iii. 35.   Where our Version has "Who*soever* shall do the will of my
Father," Wickliffe has "*Who that* doth."

"*So as that,*" frequently found.

"*Since that.*"—*Macb.* iv. 3. 106; *Rich. III.* v. 3. 202.

"*How that*" is also frequent. We also find *that* frequently affixed to prepositions for the purpose of giving them a conjunctival meaning: "*For that*" (*Macb.* iv. 3. 185); "*in that;*" "*after that,*" &c.

The Folio has

"Your vertue is my priuiledge : *for that*
It is not night when I doe see your face.
Therefore I thinke I am not in the night."

M. N. D. ii. 1. 220.

The Globe omits the full stop after "face," making "for that" (because) answer to "therefore." Others remove the stop after "privilege" and place it after "for that."

Hence we find "but *that*" where we should certainly omit *that*

"The breath no sooner left his father's body
But *that* his wildness, mortified in him,
Seem'd to die too."—*Hen. V.* i. 1. 26.

288. That, origin of. Is *that,* when used as above, demonstrative or relative? The passage quoted above from Chaucer,* "*If* so were *that,*" renders it probable that a similar ellipsis must be supplied with the other conjunctions: "*Though* (it be) *that,*" "*Since* (it is) *that,*" &c. With prepositions the case is different, *e.g.* "for *that,*" "in *that,*" "after *that.*" For this use of *that* can be traced to A.-S., where we find "for þam þe," *i.e.* "for this purpose that," "after þam þe," &c. Here "þam" is more emphatic than "þe," and evidently gave rise to the English *that.* But "þam" was the A.-S. demonstrative. It follows that the *that* is (by derivative use, at all events) demonstrative in "for *that,*" or, perhaps we should say, stands as an abridgment for "*that* (demonst.) *that* (rel.)." In fact, we can trace the A.-S. "after þam þe" to the E. E. "after *that* that," and so to the later "after *that.*" Hence we must explain

"The rather

For that I saw the tyrant's power afoot."—*Macb.* iv. 3. 185.

as "for *that* (that), *i.e.* for *that,* because, I saw." It would be wrong, however, to say that *that* in "since *that*" is, by derivative use, demonstrative. On the contrary, "since" in itself (siþ-þan) contains the demonstrative, and "since *that*" corresponds to "siþ-þan þat" where *that* (þat) is relative. And similarly "though *that*" corresponds to the A.-S. "þeah þe," where *that* (þe) is the relative. The *that* in

* Compare "If so be that."

"*after that*," "*before that*," invites comparison with the "quam" in "postquam" and "antequam," though in the Latin it is the antecedent, not the relative, that is suppressed. The tendency of the relative to assume a conjunctional meaning is illustrated by the post-classical phrase, "dico *quod* (or *quia*) verum est," in the place of the classical "dico id verum esse." Many of the above Elizabethan phrases, which are now disused, may be illustrated from French : "*Since that*," "puisque ;" "*though that*," "quoi que ;" "*before that*," "avant que," &c. Instead of "*for that*," we find in French the full form, "par ce que," *i.e.* "by *that* (dem.) *that* (rel.)." It is probable that Chaucer and Mandeville, if not earlier writers, were influenced in their use of the conjunctional *that* by French usage. Even in the phrase "I say *that* it is true," *that* may be explained as having a relatival force (like ὅτι, "quod," and the French "que"), meaning, "I say *in what way, how that*, it is true." In the phrase, "I come *that* (*in the way in which ;* 'ut,' ὡς, 'afin que') I may see," the relatival force of *that* is still more evident.

289. As is used in the same way as a conjunctional affix.   Thus "*while as :*"

> "Pirates . . . still revelling like lords till all be gone
> *While as* the silly owner of the goods
> Weeps over them."—2 *Hen VI.* i. 1. 225.

"*When as :*"

> "*When as* the enemy hath been ten to one."—3 *Hen VI.* i. 2. 75.
> "*When as* the noble Duke of York was slain."—*Ib.* ii. 1. 46.

So *Ib.* v. 7. 34.

"*Where as*" is used by us metaphorically.   But Shakespeare has

> "Unto St. Alban's,
> *Where as* the king and queen do mean to hawk."
> 2 *Hen VI.* i. 2. 57.

> "They back retourned to the princely Place,
> *Whereas* an errant knight . . . they new arrived find."
> SPENS. *F. Q.* i. 4. 38.

So "there *as*" is used in earlier English.   "There that" is also found in Chaucer in a local sense.

Of course the "so" in "when*so*," "where*so*" &c., is nearly the same in meaning, just as it is the same in derivation, with the *as* in "when*as*," &c.

VERBS, FORMS OF.

290. Verbs, Transitive (formation of). The termination *en* (the infinitive inflection) is sufficient to change an English monosyllabic noun or adjective into a verb. Thus "heart" becomes "heart*en;*" "light," "light*en;*" "glad," "gladd*en*," &c. The licence with which adjectives could be converted into verbs is illustrated by

"Eche that enhauncith hym schal be *lowid,* and he that *mekith* hymself shall be *highid.*"—WICKLIFFE, *St. Luke* xiv. 11.

In the general destruction of inflections which prevailed during the Elizabethan period, *en* was particularly discarded. It was therefore dropped in the conversion of nouns and adjectives into verbs, except in some cases where it was peculiarly necessary to distinguish a noun or adjective from a verb. (So strong was the discarding tendency that even the *e* in "owen," "to possess," was dropped, and Shakespeare continually uses "owe" for "owen" or "own"* (*T. N.* i. 5. 329; *Rich. II.* iv. 1. 185). The *n* has now been restored.) But though the infinitive inflection was generally dropped, the converting power was retained, undiminished by the absence of the condition. Hence it may be said that any noun or adjective could be converted into a verb by the Elizabethan authors, generally in an active signification, as—

"Which *happies* (makes happy) those that pay the willing lover."
Sonn. 11.

"Time will *unfair* (deface) that (which) fairly doth excel."—*Ib.* 5.
So :

Balm'd (healed).—*Lear,* iii. 6. 105.

Barn.—"*Barns* a harvest."—*R. of L.*

Bench (sit).—*Lear,* iii. 6. 40.

Bold (embolden).—"Not *bolds* the king."—*Lear,* v. 1. 26.

Brain. "Such stuff as madmen
Tongue and *brain* not."—*Cymb.* v. 4. 147.

  i.e. "such stuff as madmen use their tongues in, but not their brains."

Child.—"*Childing* autumn."—*M. N. D.* ii. 1. 112: *i.e.* "autumn producing fruits as it were children."

Climate.—"*Climates* (neut.) [lives] here."—*W. T.* v. 1. 170.

Cowarded.—"That hath so *cowarded* and chased your blood."—*Hen. V.* ii. 2. 75.

* Compare "The gates are *ope,*" *Coriol.* i. 4. 43.

Coy (to be coy).—"Nay, if he *coy'd.*"—*Coriol.* v. 1. 6.

Disaster (make disastrous-looking).—" The holes where eyes should be which pitifully *disaster* the cheeks."—*A. and C.* ii. 7. 18.

False.—"Has *falsed* his faith."—SPENS. *F. Q.* i. 19. 46.

Fame.—"*Fames* his wit."—*Sonn.* 84.

Fault.—"Cannot *fault* (neut.) twice."—N. *P.* Pref.; B. J. *Alch.* iii. 1.

Feeble.—"And *feebling* such as stand not in their liking."
                                                    Coriol. i. 1. 199.

Fever (give a fever to).—" The white hand of a lady *fever* thee,
        Shake thou to look on't."—*A. and C.* iii. 13. 138.

Fond.   " My master loves her truly,
        And I, poor monster, *fond* as much on him."—*T. N.* ii. 2. 35.

Fool (stultify).   " Why, that's the way
        To *fool* their preparations."—*A. and C.* v. 2. 225.

This explains

        " Why old men *fool* and children calculate."—*J. C.* i. 3. 65.

Foot.—"*Foots*" (kicks).—*Cymb.* iii. 5. 148.   On the other hand, in
" A power already *footed* " (*Lear,* iii. 2. 14), it means "set on
foot ;" and in " the traitors late *footed* in the kingdom" (*Ib.*
iii. 7. 45), it means "that have obtained a footing."

Force (to urge forcibly).—"Why *force* you this ?"—*Coriol.* iii. 2. 51.
Also (to attach force to, regard) :

        " But ah ! who ever shunn'd by precedent
          The destin'd ills she must herself assay,
          Or *forced* examples 'gainst her own content,
          To put the by-past perils in her way ?"—*L. C.* 157.

    i.e. " whoever regarded examples."   So *L. L. L.* v. 2. 441.

Furnace.—"*Furnaces* sighs."—*Cymb.* i. 6. 66.

Gentle.—"This day shall *gentle* his condition."—*Hen. V.* iv. 3. 63.

God.—"He *godded* me."—*Coriol.* v. 3. 11.

Honest.—"*Honests* (honours) a lodging."—B. J. *Sil. Wom.* i. 1.

Inherit (make an inheritor).   "That can *inherit* us
        So much as of a thought of ill in him."—*Rich. II.* ii. 1. 85.

Knee (kneel).—"Knee the way."—*Coriol.* v. 1. 5.

Lesson (teach).—"*Lesson* me."—*T. G. of V.* ii. 7. 5; *Rich. III.* i. 4. 246.

Linger (make to linger).   " Life
        Which false hope *lingers* in extremity."
                            Rich. II. ii. 2. 72 ; *M. N. D.* i. 1. 4.

Mad.—" *Mads* " (makes angry).—*Rich. II.* v. 5. 61.

Mellow (ripen, trans.).—*T. N.* i. 3. 43.

Mist (cover with mist).—" If that her breath will *mist* or stain the stone."—*Lear*, v. 3. 262.

Malice.—" *Malices* " (bears malice to).—N. P.

Pale (make pale).—" And 'gins to *pale* his uneffectual fire."
Hamlet, i. 5. 90.

Panging (paining).   " 'Tis a sufferance *panging*
As soul and body's severing."—*Hen. VIII.* ii. 3. 15.

Path (walk).—" For if thou *path* (neuter), thy native semblance on."—*J. C.* ii. 1. 83.

Plain (make plain).—" What's dumb in show I'll *plain* in speech."
P. of T. iii. Gower, 14.

Property (treat as a tool).—" They have here *propertied* me."
T. N. iv. 2. 100 ; *K. J.* v. 2. 79.

Rag'd (enraged).—There is no corruption (though the passage is marked as corrupt in the Globe) in

" For young colts being *rag'd* do rage the more."
Rich. II. ii. 1. 70.

Safe.—" And that which most with you should *safe* my going,
Fulvia is dead."—*A. and C.* i. 3. 55.

i.e. " make my departure unsuspected by you of dangerous consequences."

Scale (weigh, put in the scale).—" *Scaling* his present bearing with his past."—*Coriol.* ii. 3. 257.

Stage (exhibit).—" I do not like to *stage* me to their eyes."
M. for M. i. 1. 69.

Stock (put in the stocks).—" *Stocking* his messenger."
Lear, ii. 2. 139.

Stream (unfurl).—" *Streaming* the ensign."—*Rich. II.* iv. 1. 94.

Toil (give labour to).—Probably in

" Why this same toil and most observant watch
So nightly *toils* the subject of the land."—*Hamlet*, i. 1. 72.

So " toil'd," passive.—*Rich. II.* iv. 1. 96.

Tongue.—" How might she *tongue* me?"—*M. for M.* iv. 4. 28.

i.e. " speak of, or accuse, me." " Tongue " means " speak " in

" Such stuff as madmen
Tongue, and *brain* not."—*Cymb.* v. 4. 147.

Trifle.—"*Trifles* (renders trifling) former knowing."—*Macb.* ii. 4. 4.

Undeaf.—"My death's sad tale may yet *undeaf* his ear."
                                                    Rich. II. ii. 1. 6.

Verse (expressing in verse).—"*Versing* love."—*M. N. D.* ii. 1. 67.

Violent (act violently).—"And *violenteth* in a sense as strong."
                                                    Tr. and Cr. iv. 4. 4.

Wage (pay : so E. E.).—"He *waged* me."—*Coriol.* v. 6. 40.

Womb (enclose).—"The close earth *wombs* or the profound sea hides."
                                                    W. T. iv. 4. 501.

Worthied (ennobled).—"That *worthied* him."—*Lear,* ii. 2. 128.

The dropping of the prefix *be* was also a common licence. We
have recurred to "*be*witch" and "*be*late," but Shakespeare wrote—

"And *witch* the world with noble horsemanship."
                                                    1 *Hen. IV.* iv. 1. 110.

"Now spurs the *lated* traveller apace."—*Macbeth,* iii. 3. 6.

"Disorder, that hath spoil'd us, *friend* us now."
                                                    Hen. V. iv. 5. 17.

291. Sometimes an intransitive verb is converted into a transitive verb.

Cease.—"Heaven *cease* this idle humour in your honour !"
                                                    T. of Sh. Ind. 2. 13. So *Cymb.* v. 5. 255.

Expire.—Time "*expires* a term."—*R. and J.* i. 4. 109.

Fall.—An executioner "*falls* an axe."—*A. Y. L.* iii 5.5 and probably (though *fall* may be the subjunctive) in

"Think on me, and *fall* thy edgeless axe."—*Rich. III.* v. 3. 135.

Peer.—"*Peers* (causes to peer) his chin."—*R. of L.*

Perish.—"Thy flinty heart . . . might *perish* (destroy) Margaret."
                                                    2 *Hen. VI.* iii. 2. 100.

Quail (make to quail).—"But when he meant to *quail* and shake
the orb."—*A. and C.* v. 1. 85.

Relish.—"*Relishes* (makes acceptable) his nimble notes to pleasing
ears."—*R. of L.*

Remember (remind : so Fr.).—"Every stride I take
Will but *remember* me what," &c.—*Rich. II.* i. 3. 269.

Retire (so Fr.).—"That he might have *retired* his power"
                                                    Rich. II. ii. 2. 46.

Shine.—"God doth not *shine* honour upon all men equally."—B.*E.*45.

Squint.—"*Squints* the eye and makes the harelip."—*Lear,* iii. 4. 122.
  i.e. "makes the eye squint."

Fear. This word is not in point. It had the signification of "frighten" in A.-S. and E. E. Hence,

> "Thou seest what's past : go *fear* thy king withal."
>
> 3 *Hen. VI.* iii. 3. 226.

> "This aspect of mine hath *fear'd* the valiant."
>
> *M. of V.* ii. 1. 9.

So in Spenser, "Words *fearen* babes."

The same remark applies to "learn," which meant "teach."

> "The red plague rid you
> For *learning* me your language."—*Tempest*, i. 2. 365.

292. The licence in the formation of verbs arose partly from the unfixed nature of the language, partly from the desire of brevity and force. Had it continued, it would have added many useful and expressive words to the language. In vigorous colloquy we still occasionally use such expressions as—

> "*Grace* me no grace, nor *uncle* me no uncles."—*Rich. II.* ii. 3. 87.
> "*Thank* me no thankings, nor *proud* me no prouds."
>
> *R. and J.* iii. 5. 153.

As it is, we can occasionally use the termination *-fy*, as in "stultify," and sometimes the suffix *-en* or the prefix *be-*. But for the most part we are driven to a periphrasis.

293. Transitive verbs are rarely used intransitively.

Eye (appear).   "But, sir, forgive me
Since my becomings kill me, when they do not
Eye well to you."—*A. and C.* i. 3. 97.

Lack (to be needed).—"And what so poor a man as Hamlet is
May do to express his love and friending to you,
God willing, shall not *lack*."—*Hamlet*, i. 5. 186. So E. E.

Need (to be needed).—"These ceremonies *need* not."
>
> B. J. *E. in &c.* iii. 2.

This is perhaps a remnant of the ancient love for impersonal verbs. Such verbs would be appropriate to express "need." Hence in *Matt.* xix. 20, *Mark* x. 21, Wickliffe has "faileth to me" and "to thee," where the A. V. has "what do I lack" and "thou lackest." Similarly, Milton (*Areopagitica*) uses "what *wants* there?" for "what is needed?" and this use still exists in conversation. So often Shakespeare, *e.g.*

> "There *wanteth* now our brother Gloucester here."
>
> *Rich. III.* ii. 1. 43.

Show (like our "look :" compare German "schauen ").

> " Each substance of a grief hath twenty shadows
> Which *shows* like grief itself.*"—Rich. II.* ii. 2. 15.

294. Verbs Passive (formation of). Hence arose a curious use of passive verbs, mostly found in the participle. Thus "*famous'd* for fights" (*Sonn.* 25) means "made famous ;" but in

> "Who, young and simple, would not be so *lover'd?"—L. C.*

lover'd means "gifted with a lover." And this is the general rule. A participle formed from an adjective means "made (the adjective)," and derived from a noun means "endowed with (the noun)." On the other hand, *stranger'd* below means, not "gifted with a stranger," but "made a stranger." This use will be best illustrated by the following examples :—

Childed (provided with children).—" He *childed* as I *father'd."*
Lear, iii. 6. 117.

Faith'd (believed).—" Make thy words *faith'd."—Ib.* ii. 1. 72.

Father'd (provided with a father). See above, *Lear,* iii. 6. 117.

Feebled (enfeebled).—*K. J.* v. 2. 146.

Fielded (encamped in the field).—" Our fielded friends."
Coriol. i. 4. 12.

Grav'd (entomb'd).—" *Grav'd* in the hollow ground."
Rich. II. iii. 2. 140.

Guiled (deceitful).—"A *guiled* shore."—*M. of V.* iii. 2. 97.

> Compare : " *Beguiled (i.e.* made plausible)
> With outward honesty, but yet defiled
> With inward vice."—*R. of L.*

Inhabited (made to inhabit).—" O, knowledge ill-*inhabited,* worse than Jove in a thatch'd house."—*A. Y. L.* iii. 3. 10.

King'd (ruled).—" *King'd* of our fears, until our fears, resolv'd, Be by some certain king purged and deposed."—*K. J.* ii. 1. 371.

i.e. "ruled by our fears."

Look'd (looking).—"Lean-*look'd* prophets."—*Rich. II.* ii. 4. 11.

Lorded (made a lord).—" He being thus *lorded."— Tempest,* i. 2. 97.

Contrast this with " king'd " above, which means not "made a king," but " ruled as by a king."

Meered. " When half to half the world opposed, He being the *meered* question."—*A. and C.* iii. 13. 10.

The word "meered" is marked as corrupt by the Globe : but perhaps it is the verb from the adj. "meere" or "mere," which in Elizabethan English means "entire." Hence, "he being the *entire* question," *i.e.* "Antony, being the sole cause of the battle, ought not to have fled."

Million'd.—"The *million'd* accidents of time."—*Sonn.* 115.

Mouthed.—"*Mouthed* graves."—*Ib.* 77.

Necessited.—"I bade her, if her fortunes ever stood
    Necessited to help, that by this token
    I would relieve her."—*A. W.* v. 3. 85.

  i.e. "made necessitous."

Nighted (benighted).—"His *nighted* life."—*Lear*, iv. 5. 13 ; "Thy *nighted* colour."—*Hamlet*, i. 2. 68 : *i.e.* "thy night-like colour."

Paled.—"*Paled* cheeks."—*L. C.* 28.

Pensived.—*Ib.* 31.

Pined.—"His *pined* cheek."—*Ib.* 5.

Practised (plotted against).—"The *death-practised* duke."
                                   Lear, iv. 6. 284.

Servanted (made subservient).—*Coriol.* v. 2. 89.

Slow'd (retarded).—"I would I knew not why it should be *slow'd*."
                               R. and J. iv. 1. 16.

Stranger'd (made a stranger).—"Dower'd with our curse, and *stranger'd* with our oath."—*Lear*, i. 1. 207.

Toil'd.—"I have been so *toil'd*."—B. J. *E. out &c.* iii. 1.

Traded.—"*Traded* pilots."—*Tr. and Cr.* ii. 2. 64.

Unlook'd (unlooked for).—*Rich. III.* i. 3. 214 : compare *look* (seek).
                                Hen. V. iv. 7. 76.

Unsured (unassured).—"Thy now *unsured* assurance to the crown."
                                K. J. ii. 1. 471.

Vouchsafed (?).—"To your most pregnant and *vouchsafed* ear."
                                T. N. iii. 1. 190.

  i.e. capable of conceiving and graciously bestowed.

Window'd (placed in a window).

  "Wouldest thou be *window'd* in great Rome."
                              A. and C. iv. 14. 72.

Woman'd (accompanied by a woman).

    "To have him see me *woman'd*."—*Othello*, iii. 4. 195.

Year'd.—"*Year'd* but to thirty."—B. J. *Sejan.* i. 1.

In many cases a participle seems preferred where an adjective would be admissible, as "million'd." So in *Tempest*, v. 1. 43, "the *azured* vault."

295. Verbs Passive.

With some few intransitive verbs, mostly of motion, both *be* and *have* are still used. "He *is* gone," "he *has* gone." The *is* expresses the present state, the *has* the activity necessary to cause the present state. The *is* is evidently quite as justifiable as *has* (perhaps more so), but it has been found more convenient to make a division of labour, and assign distinct tasks to *is* and *has*. Consequently *is* has been almost superseded by *has* in all but the passive forms of transitive verbs. In Shakespearian English, however, there is a much more common use of *is* with intransitive verbs.

"My life *is run* his compass."—*J. C.* v. 3. 25.

"Whether he *be scaped*."—3 *Hen. VI.* ii. 1. 2.

"*Being sat*."—*L. C.* st. x.

"*Being* deep *stept* in age."—ASCH. 189.

"An *enter'd* tide."—*Tr. and Cr.* iii. 3. 159.

"I *am arrived* for fruitful Lombardy."—*T. of Sh.* i. 1. 3.

"Pucelle *is entered* into Orleans."

1 *Hen. VI.* i. 5. 36 ; *Cymb.* v. 4. 120.

"Five hundred horse . . . *are marched* up."

2 *Hen. IV.* ii. 1. 186.

"The king himself *is rode* to view their battle."

Hen. V. iv. 3. 1.

"His lordship *is* walk'd forth."—2 *Hen. IV.* i. 1. 3.

"The noble Brutus *is* ascended."—*J. C.* iii. 2. 11.

"You now *are mounted*
Where powers are your retainers."—*Hen. VIII.* ii. 4. 112.

"*I am descended* of a gentler blood."—1 *Hen. VI.* v. 4. 8.

"Through his lips do throng
Weak words, so thick *come* (particip.) in his poor heart's aid."

R. of L. 1784.

Compare our "welcome."

"How now, Sir Proteus, *are* you *crept* before us?"

T. G. of V. iv. 1. 18.

So *Rich. III.* i. 2. 259.

"Prince John *is* this morning secretly *stolen* away."

M. Ado, iv. 2. 63.

This idiom is common with words of "happening:"
> "And bring us word . . . how everything *is chanced.*"
>> *J. C.* v. 4. 32; 2 *Hen. IV.* i. 1. 87.
> "Things since then *befallen.*"—3 *Hen. VI.* ii. 1. 106.
> "Of every one these *happen'd* accidents."—*Temp.* v. 1. 249.
> "Sad stories *chanced* in the days of old."—*T. A.* iii. 2. 83.

Hence a participial use like "departed" in
> "The treachery of the *two fled* hence."—*W. T.* ii. 1. 195.

In some verbs that are both transitive and intransitive this idiom is natural:
> "You were *used* to say."—*Coriol.* iv. 1. 3.

Perhaps this is sometimes a French idiom. Thus, "I *am* not *purposed*" (MONTAIGNE, 38), is a translation of "je ne suis pas délibéré."

This constant use of "be" with participles of verbs of motion may perhaps explain, by analogy, the curious use of "being" with the present participle in
> "To whom *being going.*"—*Cymb.* iii. 6. 63.

As above mentioned, the tendency to invent new active verbs increased the number of passive to the diminution of neuter verbs:
> "Poor knave, thou *art overwatch'd.*"—*J. C.* iv. 3. 241.
> "Be *wreak'd* (*i.e.* avenged) on him."—*V. and A.* So, N. *P.* 194.

"Possess" was sometimes used for to "put in possession," as in "*Possess* us, *possess* us" (*T. N.* ii. 3. 149) : *i.e.* "inform us." So *M. of V.* iv. 1. 35. Hence the play on the word.
> "Deposing thee before thou wert *possess'd* (of the throne),
> Which art *possessed* (with a spirit of infatuation) to destroy thyself."—*Rich. II.* ii. 1. 107–8 ; *M. of V.* i. 3. 65.

We still say a man "is well read." But in *Macb.* i. 4. 9, there is—
> "As one that had *been studied* in his death."
> "For Clarence is *well-spoken.*"—*Rich. III.* i. 3. 348.
> "I *am declined* into the vale of years."—*Othello*, iii. 3. 265.
> "How comes it, Michael, you *are* thus *forgot?*"
>> *Ib.* ii. 3. 188.

i.e. "you have forgotten yourself."
> "If I had been *remembered.*"—*Rich. III.* ii. 4. 22.

We still say "well-behaved," but not
> "How have I *been behaved.*"—*Othello*, iv. 2. 108.

It was perhaps already considered a vulgarity, for Dogberry says (*M. Ado*, iv. 2. 1) :

> " *Is* our whole *dis*sembly *appear'd* ? "

and in a prose scene (*Coriol.* iv. 3. 9)—

> " Your favour is well *appear'd* (fol.) by your tongue."

Perhaps, however, *appear* was sometimes used as an active verb. See *Cymb.* iv. 2. 47, iii. 4. 148, quoted in 296.

296. Verbs Reflexive.

The predilection for transitive verbs was perhaps one among other causes why many verbs which are now used intransitively, were used by Shakespeare reflexively. Many of these were derived from the French.

> " *Advise you.*"—*T. N.* iv. 2. 102.
> " Where then, alas! may I *complain myself?*"—*Rich. II.* i. 2. 42.
> " *Endeavour thyself* to sleep."—*T. N.* iv. 2. 104.
> " I do *repent me.*"—*Ib.* v. 3. 52.
> " *Repose you.*"—*Ib.* ii. 3. 161.
> " He . . . *retired himself.*"—*Rich. II.* iv. 2. 96 ; *Coriol.* i. 3. 30,

which is in accordance with the original meaning of the word.

It has been shown above that "fear" is used transitively for "frighten." Hence, perhaps, as in Greek φοβοῦμαι,

> " I *fear me.*"—2 *Hen. VI.* i. 1. 150.

Appear is perhaps used reflexively in

> " No, no ; we will hold it as a dream till it *appear itself.*"
> *M. Ado,* i. 2. 22.
>   " If you could wear a mind
> Dark as your fortune is, and but disguise
> That which *to appear itself* must not yet be."—*Cymb.* iii. 4. 148.

i.e. "that which, as regards showing itself, must not yet have any existence." Though these passages might be perhaps explained without the reflexive use of *appear*, yet this interpretation is made more probable by

> " Your favour *is* well *appear'd.*"—*Coriol.* iv. 3. 9.

297. Verbs Impersonal.

An abundance of Impersonal verbs is a mark of an early stage in a language, denoting that a speaker has not yet arrived so far in development as to trace his own actions and feelings to his own agency. There are many more impersonal verbs in Early English than in Elizabethan, and many more in Elizabethan than in modern English. Thus—

" *It yearns* me not."—*Hen. V.* iv. 3. 26.

" *It* would *pity* any living eye."—SPENS. *F. Q.* i. 6. 43.

Comp. 2 Maccabees iii. 21 : " *It* would have *pitied* a man."

" *It dislikes* me."—*Othello*, ii. 3. 49.

So " it *likes* me," " me*seems*," " me*thinks*," &c.

" Which *likes* me."—*Hen. V.* iv. 3. 77.

And therefore *like* is probably (not merely by derivation, but consciously used as) impersonal in

" So *like* you, sir."—*Cymb.* ii. 3. 59.

Want is probably not impersonal but intransitive, " is wanting," in

" There *wants* no diligence in seeking him?"*—*Cymb.*iv. 2. 20.

The singular verb is quite Shakespearian in

" Though bride and bridegroom *wants* (are wanting)
For to supply the places at the table."—*T. of Sh.* iii. 2. 248.

So in " *Sufficeth* my reasons are both good and weighty."—*Ib.* i. 1. 252.

" *Sufficeth* I am come to keep my word."—*Ib.* iii. 2. 108.

the comma after " sufficeth " is superfluous ; " that I am come to keep my word *sufficeth*."

In " And so *betide* to me
As well I tender you and all of yours,"—*Rich. III.* ii. 4. 71.

betide may be used impersonally. But perhaps *so* is loosely used as a demonstrative for " such fortune," in the same way in which *as* (280) assumes the force of a relative. If *betide* be treated as impersonal, *befal* in " fair *befal* you " may be similarly treated, and in that case " fair " is an adverb. But see (5). The supposition that " betide " is impersonal and " fair " an adverb is confirmed by " Well *be* (it) with you, gentlemen."—*Hamlet*, ii. 2. 398.

The impersonal *needs* (which must be distinguished from the adverbial genitive *needs*) often drops the *s ;* partly, perhaps, because of the constant use of the noun *need*. It is often found with " what," where it is sometimes hard to say whether " what " is an adverb and *need* a verb, or " what " an adjective and *need* a noun.

" *What need* the bridge much broader than the flood ?"
M. Ado, i. 1. 318.

either " *why need* the bridge (be) broader?" or " *what need* is there (that) the bridge (be) broader ?"

See 293.

Comp. the old use of "thinketh" (seemeth):

"Where *it thinks* best unto your royal self."—*Rich. III.* iii. 1. 63.

The Folio has *thinkst:* and perhaps this is the true reading, there being a confusion between "it *thinks*" and "*thinkest* thou." Compare "*thinkst* thee" in

"Doth it not, *thinkst thee*, stand me now upon?"—*Hamlet*, v. 2. 63.

The impersonal and personal uses of *think* were often confused. Chapman (Walker) has "*methink.*" *S* seems to have been added to assimilate the termination to that of "methinks" in "methought*s*" (*W. T.* i. 2. 154; *Rich. III.* i. 4. 9).

It is not easy, perhaps not possible, to determine whether, in the phrase "so *please* your highness," *please* is used impersonally or not; for on the one hand we find, "So *please him* come,"

(*J. C.* iii. 1. 140);

and on the other,

"If *they please.*"—*W. T.* ii. 3. 142.

"I do repent: but *Heaven hath pleased* it so."—*Ham.* iii. 4. 173.

VERBS, AUXILIARY.

298. Be, Beest, &c., was used in A.-S. (beon) generally in a future sense. Hence, since the future and subjunctive are closely connected in meaning, *be* assumed an exclusively subjunctive use; and this was so common, that we not merely find "if it *be*" (which might represent the proper inflected subjunctive of *be*), but also "if thou *beest*," where the indicative is used subjunctively.

"If, after three days' space, thou here *beest* found."

2 *Hen. VI.* iii. 2. 295.

"*Beest* thou sad or merry,
The violence of either thee becomes."—*A. and C.* i. 5. 59.

And (Mätzner, vol. i. p. 367), *bee, beest, bee,* pl. *bee,* is stated by Wallis to be the regular form of the subjunctive. Hence, from the mere force of association, *be* is often used (after *though, if,* and other words that often take the subjunctive) without having the full force of the subjunctive. Indeed any other verb placed in the same context would be used in the indicative. Thus:

"*Though* Page *be* a secure (careless) fool, and *stands* so firmly on his wife's frailty."—*M. W. of W.* ii. 1. 242.

"If Hamlet from himself *be* ta'en away
And, when he's not himself, *does wrong* Laertes."—*Ham.* v. 2. 245.

" If he *be* a whoremonger and *comes* before him,
He were as good go a mile on his errand."—*M. for M.* iii. 2. 38.

299. Be in questions and dependent sentences.

So, as a rule, it will be found that *be* is used with some notion of doubt, question, thought, &c.; for instance, (*a*) in questions, and (*b*) after verbs of thinking.

(*a*) " *Be* my horses ready?"—*Lear*, i. 5. 36.
" *Be* the players ready?"—*Hamlet*, iii. 2. 111.

This is especially frequent in questions of appeal :
" Where *be* his quiddities?"—*Hamlet*, v. 1. 107.
" Where *be* thy brothers?"—*Rich. III.* iv. 4. 92.
" Where *be* the bending knees that flatter'd thee?
Where *be* the thronging troops that follow'd thee?"
Ib. iv. 4. 95-6.

And in questions implying doubt, *e.g.* " where can they be?"
" Where *be* these bloody thieves?"—*Othello*, v. 1. 64.

Partly, perhaps, by attraction to the previous *be*, partly owing to the preceding *where*, though not used interrogatively, we have
" Truths would be tales,
Where now half-tales *be* truths."—*A. and C.* ii. 2. 137.

(*b*) " I *think* it *be*, sir ; I deny it not."—*C. of E.* v. 1. 379.
" I *think* this Talbot *be* a fiend of hell."—1 *Hen. VI.* ii. 1. 46.
" I *think* he *be* transformed into a beast."—*A. Y. L.* ii. 7. 1.
" I think it *be* no other but even so."—*Hamlet*, i. 1. 108.
So 1 *Hen. IV.* ii. 1. 12 ; *T. G. of V.* ii. 3. 6.

Be expresses more doubt than *is* after a verb of thinking. In the following, the Prince thinks it *certain* that it is past midnight, the Sheriff thinks it *may possibly be* two o'clock :
" *Prince.* I think it *is* good morrow, is it not?
Sheriff. Indeed, my lord, I think it *be* two o'clock."
1 *Hen. IV.* ii. 4. 573.

Very significant is this difference in the speech of the doubtful Othello—
" I *think* my wife *be* honest, and *think* she *is* not,"
Othello, iii. 3. 384.

where the *is* is emphatic and the line contains the extra dramatic syllable. *Be* is similarly used by a jealous husband after " hope:"
" *Ford.* Well, I *hope* it *be* not so."—*M. W. of W.* ii. 1. 113.

where the hope is mixed with a great deal of doubt.

> " I kissed it (the bracelet):
> I *hope* it *be* not gone to tell my lord
> That I kiss aught but he,"—*Cymb.* ii. 3. 153.

where, though the latter part is of course fanciful, there is a real
fear that the bracelet may be lost.

Also, in a dependent sentence like the following :

> " Prove true
> That I, dear brother, *be* now ta'en for you."—*T. N.* iii. 4. 410.

Be follows " when," as " where " above, especially where *when*
alludes to a future possibility.

> " Haply a woman's voice may do some good
> *When* articles too nicely urged *be* stood on."—*Hen. V.* v. 2. 93.

In   " Alas, our frailty is the cause, not we,
> For such as we are made, of such we *be*,"—*T. N.* ii. 2. 33.

it can scarcely be asserted that "for" is "for that" or "because."
It is more probable that the scene originally ended there, and that
Shakespeare used *be* in order to get the rhyme, which so often termi-
nates a scene.

300. Be is much more common with the plural than the singular.
Probably only this fact, and euphony, can account for

> " When blood *is* nipp'd and ways *be* foul."—*L. L. L.* v. 2. 926.

In " When he sees reason of fears, as we do, his fears out of
doubt *be* of the same relish as ours,"—*Hen. V.* iv. 1. 113.
the *be* may partly be explained as not stating an independent fact,
but a future event, dependent on the clause " when," &c.   Partly,
perhaps, " out of doubt " is treated like " there is no doubt that,"
and *be* follows in a kind of dependent clause.

Be is also used to refer to a number of persons, considered not
individually, but as a kind or class.

> "O, there *be* players that I have seen play, and heard others
> praise, and that highly, that," &c.—*Hamlet*, iii. 2. 32 ; *ib.* 44.

> " There *be* some sports are painful."—*Tempest*, iii. 1. 1.

But it cannot be denied that the desire of euphony or variety
seems sometimes the only reason for the use of *be* or *are*.

> "Where *is* thy husband now ?   Where *be* thy brothers ?
> Where *are* thy children ?"—*Rich. III.* iv. 4. 92.

301. Were.   What has been said above of *be* applies to *were*,
that it is often used as the subjunctive where any other verb would

not be so used, and indeed where the subjunctive is unnecessary or wrong, after "if," "though," &c., and in dependent sentences.

In early authors there seems to have been a tendency to use *should* for *shall*, and *were* for *be* after "that" in subordinate sentences : "Go we fast that we *were* there." "Let us pray that he *would*." "My will is that it *were* so." In these sentences a wish is implied, and *were*, perhaps, indicates the desire that the wish should be fulfilled, not hereafter, but at once, as a thing of the past.

"I am a rogue, *if I were* not at half-sword with a dozen of them two hours together."—1 *Hen. IV.* ii. 4. 182.

"If there *were* anything in thy pocket but tavern reckonings, I am a villain."—1 *Hen. IV.* iii. 3. 180.

"What if we do omit
This reprobate till he *were* well inclined?"—*M. for M.* iv. 3. 78.

In some of these passages there may be traced, perhaps, a change of thought : "I am a rogue (that is, I should be), if it *were* true that I was not," &c. "What if we omit (what if we were to omit) this reprobate till he *were* well inclined?"

"*Duchess.* I pray thee, pretty York, who told thee this ?
York. Grandam, his nurse.
Duchess. His nurse ! Why, she was dead ere thou wert born.
York. If '*twere* not she, I cannot tell who told me."
Rich. III. ii. 4. 34.

"If ever Bassianus, Cæsar's son,
Were gracious in the eyes of royal Rome,
Keep then this passage to the Capitol."—*T. A.* i. 1. 11.

Comp. 2 *Hen. IV.* v. 2. 85 ; *A. and C.* i. 3. 41.

"No marvel, then, though he *were* ill-affected."—*Lear*, ii. 1. 100.

where the meaning is : "It is no wonder, then, that he *was* a traitor," and no doubt or future meaning is implied.

Somewhat similar is an idiom common in good authors even now : "It is not strange that he should have succeeded," for the shorter and simpler, "It is not strange that he succeeded."

"Lamachus, . . . whom they sent hither, though he *were* waxen now somewhat old."—N. *P.* 172.

So, but with a notion of concession,

"And *though* (granting that) he *were* unsatisfied in getting,
Which *was* a sin, yet in bestowing, madam,
He was most princely."—*Hen. VIII.* iv. 2. 55.

"If it *were* so it *was* a grievous fault."—*J. C.* iii. 2. 84.

So, beginning with certainty :

"She *that was* ever fair and never proud."—*Othello,* ii. 1. 149.

and ending with doubt :

"She was a wight, *if* ever such wight *were.*"—*Ib.* ii. 1. 159.

In dependent sentences even after "know," as well as "think :"

"I would I had thy inches : thou shouldst *know*
There *were* a heart in Egypt."—*A. and C.* i. 3. 41.

"Which of your friends have I not strove to love,
Although I *knew* he *were* mine enemy."—*Hen. VIII.* ii. 4. 31.

"*Imagine* 'twere the right Vincentio."—*T. of Sh.* iv. 4. 12.

"As who should *say* in Rome no justice *were.*"—*T. A.* iv. 3. 20.

"But that it eats our victuals, I should *think*
Here *were* a fairy."—*Cymb.* iii. 6. 42.

"He will lie, sir, with such volubility that you would *think* truth *were* a fool."—*A. W.* iv. 3. 285.*

302. Were is used after "while" in

"If they would yield us but the superfluity *while* it *were* wholesome."—*Coriol.* i. 1. 18.

and, still more remarkably, after "until," referring to the past, in

"It hath been taught us from the primal state
That he which is, was wish'd *until* he *were.*"
A. and C. i. 4. 42.

The following is contrary to our usage, though a natural attraction :

"And they it *were* that ravished our sister."—*T. A.* v. 3. 99.

for "it was they."   See 425 at end.

Can. See **May,** 307.

303. Do, Did: original use. In Early as in modern English, the present and past indefinite of the indicative were generally represented by inflected forms, as "He comes," "He came," without the aid of *do* or *did.* *Do* was then used only in the sense of "to cause," "to make," &c. ; and in this sense was followed by an infinitive.

* In this and many other instances the verb in the second clause may be attracted into the subjunctive by the subjunctive in the first clause.

"They have *done* her understonde."—GOWER.*

i.e. "they have caused her to understand."

Similarly it is used like the French "faire" or "laisser" with the ellipsis of the person who is "caused" to do the action, thus—

> "*Do* stripen me and put me in a sakke,
> And in the nexte river *do* me drenche."
>
> CHAUCER, *Marchante's Tale*, 10,074.

i.e. "cause (some one) to strip me—to drench me."

In the same way "let" is repeatedly used in Early English :

> "He *let* make Sir Kay seneschal of England."—*Morte d'Arthur.*

where a later author might have written "he *did* make."

Gradually the force of the infinitive inflection *en* was weakened and forgotten ; thus "*do* stripen" became "*do* strip," and *do* was used without any notion of causation. †

Sometimes *do* is reduplicated, as :

"And thus he *did do* slen hem alle three."—CHAUCER, *C. T.* 7624.

or used with "let," as in

> "He *let* the feste of his nativitee
> *Don* crien."—CHAUCER, *C. T.* 10,360.

The verb was sometimes used transitively with an objective noun, as :

> "He *did* thankingys."—WICKLIFFE, *St. Matt.* xv. 36.

and so in Shakespeare in

> "*Do* me some charity."—*Lear*, iii. 4. 61.
>
> "This fellow *did* the third (daughter) a blessing."
>
> *Lear*, i. 4. 115.
>
> "*Do* my good-morrow to them."—*Hen. V.* iv. 1. 26.
>
> "To *do* you salutation from his master."
>
> *J. C.* iv. 2. 5 ; *Rich. III.* v. 3. 210.
>
> "After the last enchantment you *did* here."—*T. N.* iii. 1. 123.

and in the words "to don," *i.e.* "put on," and "dout," *i.e.* "put out."

But as a rule *do* had become a mere auxiliary, so that we even find it an auxiliary to itself, as in

> "Who *does do* you wrong?"—*T. N.* v. 1. 143.

---

* Quoted from Richardson's Dictionary.

† The question may arise why *do* was preferred to *let* as an auxiliary verb. Probably the ambiguity of *let*, which meant both "suffer" and "hinder," was an obstacle to its general use.

304. Do, did. How used by Shakespeare? In *St. Matt.*
xv. 37, Wickliffe has "and alle eten;" Tyndal, &c., "all *dia*
eat." It is probable that one reason for inserting the *did* here was
the similarity between the present and past of "eat," and the desire
to avoid ambiguity. In the following verse, however, Wickliffe has
"etun," Tyndal "ate," and the rest "did eat." This shows how
variable was the use of *did* in the sixteenth century, and what slight
causes determined its use or non-use. The following passage in
connection with the above would seem to show that *did* was joined
to *eat* to avoid ambiguity, and when it was not joined to other
verbs :

"And the Peloponnesians *did eat* it up while the Byzantines
died."—N. *P.* 180.

It can hardly be denied that in such lines as

"It *lifted* up it (so Folio) head, and *did* address
Itself to motion,"—*Hamlet*, i. 2. 216.

the *did* is omitted in the first verb and inserted in the second simply
for the sake of the metre. *Did* is commonly used in excited
narrative :

"Horses *did* neigh, and dying men *did* groan,
And ghosts *did* shriek and squeal about the streets."
J. C. ii. 2. 23.
"The sheeted dead
Did squeak and gibber in the Roman streets."
Hamlet, i. 1. 116.

But in both the above passages the inflection in -*ed* is also used.

305. Verbs: "Do" omitted before "Not." In Early
English the tenses were represented by their inflections, and there
was no need of the auxiliary "do." As the inflections were disused, "do" came into use, and was frequently employed by Elizabethan authors. They, however, did not always observe the modern
rule of using the auxiliary whenever *not* precedes the verb. Thus—

"I not doubt."—*Temp.* ii. 1. 121.
"Whereof the ewe not bites."—*Ib.* v. 1. 38.
"It not belongs to you."—2 *Hen. IV.* iv. 1. 98.
"It not appears to me."—*Ib.* 107.
"Hear you bad writers and though you not see."
BEAUMONT *on B. J.*

"On me whose all not equals Edward's moiety."

Rich. III. i. 2. 259.

"Neat Terence, witty Plautus, now not please."

B. J. *on Shakespeare.*

Less commonly in a subordinate sentence

"I beseech you . . . that you not delay."—*Coriol.* i. 6. 60.

Later, a rule was adopted that either the verb, or the auxiliary part of it, must precede the negative : "I doubt not," or "I do not doubt." Perhaps this may be explained as follows. The old English negative was "ne." It came before the verb, and was often supplemented by a negative adverb "nawicht," "nawt," "noht" (which are all different forms of "no whit" or "naught"), coming after the verb.

"His hors was good, but he *ne* was *not* gaie."

CHAUCER, *C. T.* 74.

(Compare in French "ne . . . pas," in Latin, "non (nenu)," *i.e.* "ne . . . unum.") In the fifteenth century (Mätzner) this reduplication began to pass out of fashion. In Shakespeare's time it had been forgotten ; but, perhaps, we may trace its influence in the double negative "*nor* will *not*," &c., which is common in his works.

"Vex not yourself, *nor* strive *not* with your breath."

Rich. II. ii. 1. 3.

Possibly the idiom now under consideration is also a result of the Early English idiom. The *not*, which had ousted the old dual negative "ne" . . . "not," may have been thought entitled to a place either before or after the verb. Latin, moreover, would tend in the same direction. It must further be remembered that *not* is now less emphatic than it was, when it retained the meaning of "naught" or "no-whit." We can say, "I *in-no-way* trust you," or, perhaps, even "I *no-whit* trust you," but *not* is too unemphatic to allow us to say "I *not* trust you." Hence the "do" is now necessary to receive a part of the emphasis.

Not is sometimes found in E. E. and A.-S. between the subject and the verb, especially in subordinate sentences where the *not*, "no-whit," is emphatic.

306. Do, Did, omitted and inserted. In modern English prose there is now an established rule for the insertion and omission of *do* and *did*. They are inserted in negative and interrogative sentences, for the purpose of including the "not" or the subject of the interrogation between the two parts of the verb, so as to avoid ambiguity. Thus: "*Do* our subjects revolt?" "*Do* not forbid him." They are not inserted except for the purpose of unusual emphasis in indicative sentences such as "I remember." In Elizabethan English no such rule had yet been established, and we find—

"Revolt our subjects?"—*Rich. II.* iii. 2. 100.
"Forbid him not."—*Mark* ix. 39. E. V.

On the other hand—

"I *do* remember."—*T. N.* iii. 3. 48.

This licence of omission sometimes adds much to the beauty and vigour of expression.

"Gives not the hawthorn-bush a sweeter shade?"
3 Hen. VI. ii. 5. 42.

is far more natural and vigorous than

"*Does* not the hawthorn-bush give sweeter shade?"

307. Can, May, Might. *May* originally meant "to be able" (E. E. "mag;" A.-S. "magan;" German "mögen"). A trace of this meaning exists in the noun "might," which still means "ability." Thus we find

"I am so hungry that I *may* (can) not slepe."
CHAUCER, *Monke's Tale*, 14,744.
"Now help me, lady, sith ye *may* and can."
Knighte's Tale, 2,314.

In the last passage *may* means "can," and "ye can" means "ye have knowledge or skill." This, the original meaning of "can," is found, though very rarely, in Shakespeare :

"I've seen myself and served against the French,
And they *can* well on horseback."—*Hamlet*, iv. 7. 85.

i.e. "they are well skilled."

"And the priest in surplice white
That defunctive music *can*."—*Phœnix and Turtle*, 14.

And perhaps in

"The sum of all I *can*, I have disclosed ;
Why or for what these nobles were committed
Is all un*known* to me, my gracious lady."
Rich. III. ii. 4. 46.

"The strong'st suggestion
Our worser genius *can* "—*Tempest*, iv. 1. 27.

A trace of this emphatic use of *can* is found in

"What *can* man's wisdom
In the restoring his bereaved sense ?"—*Lear,* iv. 4. 8.

But, as "can" (which even in A.-S. meant "I know how to" and therefore "I am able ") gradually began to encroach on *may*, and to assume the meaning "to be able," *may* was compelled to migrate from "ability" to "possibility" and "lawfulness." Thus "mögen" signifies moral, "können" physical, possibility. In the following passage :

"From hence it comes that this babe's bloody hand
May not be cleansed with water of this well,"—*F. Q.* ii. 10.

it is not easy at once to determine whether *may* means "can " or "is destined," "must," "ought." Hence we are prepared for the transition which is illustrated thus by Bacon :*

"For what he *may* do is of two kinds, what he *may* do as *just* and what he *may* do as *possible.*"

308. May in "I *may* come" is therefore ambiguous, since it may signify either "lawfulness," as in "I *may* come if I like," or "possibility," as in "I *may* come, but don't wait for me." In the latter sentence the "possibility" is transposed so as to include the whole sentence "it is possible that I may come," just as—

"He needs not our mistrust,"—*Macb.* iii. 3. 2.

means "it is not necessary that we should mistrust him."

309. May is used with various shades of the meaning of "permission," "possibility," &c. :

"He shall know you better, sir, if I *may* live to report you. "
M. for M. iii. 2. 172.

i.e. "if I am *permitted* by heaven to live long enough."

It is a modest way of stating what ought to be well known, in

"If you *may* please to think I love the king."—*W. T.* iv. 4. 532.

"A score of ewes *may* be worth ten pounds."—*2 Hen. IV.* iii. 2.57.

i.e. "is *possibly* worth ten pounds." "*May* be" is often thus used almost adverbially for possibly.

In   "Season your admiration for awhile
Till I *may* deliver,"—*Hamlet,* i. 2. 193.

may means "can," "have time to."

"*May* (can) it be possible ?"—*Hen. V.* ii. 2. 100.

* Quoted from Todd's "Johnson."

310. May with a Negative. Thus far Elizabethan and modern English agree ; but when a negative is introduced, a divergence appears.

In "I *may* not-come" *may* would with us mean "possibility," and the "not" would be connected with "come" instead of *may ;* "my not-coming is a possibility." On the other hand, the Elizabethans frequently connect the "not" with *may,*[*] and thus with them "I *may*-not come" might mean "I can-not or must-not come." Thus *may* is parallel to "must" in the following passage :—

> "Yet I must not,
> For certain friends that are both his and mine,
> Whose loves I *may* not drop."—*Macb.* iii. 1. 122.

Probably this disuse of *may* in "may not" (in the sense of "must not") may be explained by the fact that "may not" implies compulsion, and *may* has therefore been supplanted in this sense by the more compulsory "must."

311. May used for the old subjunctive in the sense of purpose.

If we compare Wickliffe's with the sixteenth-century Versions of the New Testament, it appears that, in the interval, the subjunctive had lost much of its force, and consequently the use of auxiliary verbs to supply the place of the subjunctive had largely increased.

In 1 *Cor.* iv. 8, Wickliffe has, "And I wold that ye regne, that also we *regnen* with you," where the later Versions, "And I would to God that ye did reign, that we also *might reign.*" So also *Col.* i. 28 : "Techynge eche man in al wisdom ; that we *offre* eche man perfight," where the rest have "*that we may* offer" or "*to* offer." So *ib.* 25, "that I *fille* the word of God" for "that I may fulfil." But *may* is found very early used with its modal force

The subjunctive of purpose is found in—

> "Go bid thy mistress . . . she strike upon the bell."—*Macb.* ii. 1. 31.
> "Sir, give me this water that I thirst not."—*St. John* iv. 15.
> "He wills you, in the name of God Almighty,
> That you divest yourself."—*Hen. V.* ii. 4. 78.

But it was not easy to distinguish the subjunctive representing an

---

* So in ante-Elizabethan English, and in Spenser, we find "nill," "not," for "will not," "wot not," "nam" for "am not," &c. "Cannot" is also a trace of the close connection between the verb and the accompanying negative.

object, from the indicative representing a fact, since both were used after "that," and there was nothing but their inflections (which are similar in the plural) to distinguish the two. The following is an instance of the indicative following "that :"—

> "But freshly looks and over-bears attaint
> With cheerful semblance and sweet majesty,
> *That* every wretch pining and pale before,
> Beholding him, plucks comfort from his looks."
>
> *Hen. V.* iv. Prologue, 39.

Hence arose the necessity, as the subjunctive inflections lost their force, of inserting some word denoting "possibility" or "futurity" to mark the subjunctive of purpose. "Will" is apparently used in this sense as follows :—

> "Therefore in fierce tempest is he coming,
> In thunder and in earthquake like a Jove,
> That, if requiring fail, he *will* compel."—*Hen. V.* ii. 4. 99.

But, as a rule, *may* was used for the present subjunctive and *might* for the past, according to present usage. "That" is omitted in

"Direct mine arms I *may* embrace his neck."—1 *Hen. VI.* ii. 5. 37.

i.e. "that I may embrace."

In "Lord marshal, command our officers at arms
Be ready to direct these home alarms,"—*Rich. II.* i. 1. 204–5.

it is doubtful whether "be" is the subjunctive or the infinitive with "to" omitted (349). I prefer the former hypothesis, supplying "that" after "command." Compare

> "Some one take order Buckingham *be* brought
> To Salisbury."—*Rich. III.* iv. 4. 539.

So "that" is omitted before "shall :"

> "The queen hath heartily consented he *shall espouse* Elizabeth."
> *Rich. III.* iv. 5. 18.

312. Might, the past tense of *may*, was originally used in the sense of "was able" or "could."

"He was of grete elde and *might* not travaile."—R. BRUNNE.

So "That *mought* not be distinguish'd."—3 *Hen. VI.* v. 2. 45.

> "So loving to my mother,
> That he *might* not beteem the winds of heaven
> Visit her face too roughly."—*Hamlet*, i. 2. 141.

i.e. "*could* not bring himself to allow the winds," &c.

It answers to "can" in the following :—

> "*Ang.* Look, what I will not that I *can*not do.
> *Isab.* But *might* you do't, and do the world no wrong?"
>
> *M. for M.* ii. 2. 52.

> "*Might* you not know she would do as she has done?"
>
> *A. W.* iii. 4. 2.

i.e. "*Could* you not know."

> "I *might* not this believe
> Without the sensible and true avouch
> Of mine own eyes."—*Hamlet,* i. 1. 56.

"But I *might* see young Cupid's fiery shaft quench'd in the chaste beams of the wat'ry moon."—*M. N. D.* ii. 1. 161.

> "In that day's feats,
> When he *might* act the woman in the scene,
> He proved best man i' the field."—*Coriol.* ii. 2. 100.

i.e. "when he was young enough *to be able* to play the part of a woman on the stage."

Might naturally followed *may* through the above-mentioned changes. Care must be taken to distinguish between the indicative and the conditional use of *might.* "How *might* that be?" (indicative) would mean "How was it possible for that to take place?" On the other hand, "How *might* that be?" (subjunctive) would mean "How would it be possible hereafter that this should take place?" The same ambiguity still attends "could." Thus "How *could* I thus forget myself yesterday!" but "How *could* I atone to-morrow for my forgetfulness yesterday?"

313. May, Might, like other verbs in Elizabethan English, are frequently used optatively. We still use *may* thus, as in "May he prosper!" but seldom or never *might.* But it is clear that—

> "Would I *might*
> But ever see that man,"—*Temp.* i. 2. 168.

naturally passes into "*Might* I but see that man," Thus we have—

> "Lord worshipped *might* he be."—*M. of V.* ii. 2. 98.

314. Must (E. E. *moste*) is the past tense of the E. E. present tense *mot,* which means "he is able," "he is obliged." From meaning "he had power to do it," or "might have done it," the word came to mean "ought," and it is by us generally used with a notion of compulsion. But it is sometimes used by Shakespeare to mean no more than definite futurity, like our "is to" in "He *is to* be here to-morrow."

"He *must* fight singly to-morrow with Hector, and is so prophetically proud of an heroical cudgelling that he raves in saying nothing."—*Tr. and Cr.* iii. 3. 247.

So, or nearly so, probably in

> "Descend, for you *must* be my sword-bearer."
> *M. of V.* ii. 6. 40.

And somewhat similar, without the notion of compulsion, is the use in *M. of V.* iv. 1. 182 ; *M. N. D.* ii. 1. 72.

It seems to mean "is, or was, destined" in

> "And I *must* be from thence."—*Macbeth,* iv. 3. 212.

So　　　　　　　　 "A life which *must* not yield
> To one of woman born."—*Ib.* v. 8. 12.

315. Shall. *Shall* for *will. Shall* meaning "to owe" is connected with "ought," "must,"* "it is destined."

Thus,

> "If then we *shall* shake off our slavish yoke,
> Imp out our drooping country's broken wing,
> Away with me."—*Rich. II.* ii. 2. 291.

i.e. "if we are to, ought to."

> "Fair Jessica *shall* be my torch-bearer."—*M. of V.* ii. 4. 40.

i.e. "is to be."

Hence *shall* was used by the Elizabethan authors with all three persons to denote inevitable futurity without reference to "will" (desire).

> "If much you note him,
> You *shall* offend him and extend his passion."—*Macb.* iii. 4. 57.

i.e. "you *are sure* to offend him."

So probably,

> "Nay, it *will* please him well, Kate, it *shall* (is sure to) please him."
> *Hen. V.* v. 2. 369.

> "My country
> *Shall* have more vices than it had before."—*Macb.* iv. 3. 47.

> "And, if I die, no man *shall* pity me."—*Rich. III.* v. 3. 201.

i.e. "it is certain that no man will pity me."

* "Thou *shalt* not," &c.

There is no notion of compulsion on the part of the person speaking in

> "They *shall* (are sure to) be apprehended by and by."
> > *Hen. V.* ii. 2. 2.

> "If they do this (conquer),
> As, if please God, they *shall* (are destined to do)."
> > *Hen. V.* iv. 3. 120.

The notion of necessity, *must*, seems to be conveyed in

> "He that parts us *shall* bring a brand from heaven,
> And fire us hence like foxes."—*Lear*, v. 3. 22.

In　　"He *shall* wear his crown,"—*J. C.* i. 3. 87.

shall means "is to." So in

> "Your grace *shall* understand."—*M. of V.* iv. 1. 149.
> "What is he that *shall* (is to) buy?"—*A. Y. L.* ii. 4. 88.
> "Men *shall* deal unadvisedly sometimes."
> > *Rich. III.* iv. 4. 292.

i.e. "men cannot help making mistakes."

> "He that escapes me without some broken limb *shall* (must, will have to), acquit him well."—*A. Y. L.* i. 1. 134.

> "*K.*　Desire them all to my pavilion.
> *Glost.* We *shall*, my lord."—*Hen. V.* iv. 1. 27.

In the last passage, "I *shall*" has a trace of its old meaning, "I ought:" or perhaps there is a mixture of "I am bound to" and "I am sure to." Hence it is often used in the replies of inferiors to superiors.

> "　*King Henry.* Collect them all together at my tent:
> I'll be before thee.
> *Erpingham.* I *shall* do't, my lord."—*Hen. V.* iv. 1. 305.
> "Fear not, my lord, your servant *shall* do so."
> > *M. N. D.* ii. 1. 268.

So *A. W.* v. 3. 27; *A. and C.* iii. 12. 36, iv. 6. 3, v. 1. 3; *Hen. V.* iv. 3. 126; *M. for M.* iv. 4. 21; *A. and C.* v. 1. 68.

"You *shall* see, find," &c., was especially common in the meaning "you may," "you will," applied to that which is of common occurrence, or so evident that it *cannot but be* seen.

> "You *shall* mark
> Many a duteous and knee-crooking slave,
> That, doting on his own obsequious bondage,
> Wears out his time.　Whip me such honest knaves."
> > *Othello*, i. 1. 440.

Shall is sometimes colloquially or provincially abbreviated into *se, s:*

"Thou'*s* hear our counsel."—*R. and J.* i. 3. 9.
"I'*se* try."—*Lear,* iv. 6. 246. (See 461.)

316. Will. You will. He will. Later, a reluctance to apply a word meaning necessity and implying compulsion* to a person addressed (second person), or spoken of (third person), caused post-Elizabethan writers to substitute *will* for *shall* with respect to the second and third persons, even where no *will* at all, *i.e.* no purpose, is expressed, but only futurity. Thus *will* has to do duty both as *will* proper, implying purpose, and also as *will* improper, implying merely futurity. Owing to this unfortunate imposition of double work upon *will,* it is sometimes impossible to determine, except from emphasis or from the context, whether *will* signifies purpose or mere futurity. Thus (1) "He *will* come, I cannot prevent him," means "He *wills* (or is determined) to come ;" but (2) "He *will* come, though unwillingly," means "His coming is certain."

Will is seldom used without another verb :

"I *will* no reconcilement."—*Hamlet,* v. 2. 258.
So in "I *will* none of it." (See 321.)

317. Shall. You shall. He shall. On the other hand *shall,* being deprived by *will* of its meaning of futurity, gradually took up the meaning of compulsory necessity imposed by the first person on the second or third. Thus : "You *shall* not go," or even "You *shall* find I am truly grateful." (Not "you *will* find," but "I will so act that you *shall* perforce find," &c.)

The prophetic *shall* ("it *shall* come to pass ") which is so common in the Authorized Version of the Bible, probably conveyed to the original translators little or nothing more than the meaning of futurity. But now with us the prophetic *shall* implies that the prophet identifies himself with the necessity which he enunciates. Thus the Druid prophesying the fall of Rome to Boadicea says—

"Rome *shall* perish."—COWPER.

* *Coriol.* iii. 1. 90, "Mark you his *absolute 'shall.'"* A similar feeling suggested the different methods of expressing an imperative in Latin and Greek, and the substitution of the optative with ἄν for the future in Greek.

318. Shall. I shall. When a person speaks of *his own* future actions as inevitable, he often regards them as inevitable only because fixed by *himself.* Hence "I *shall* not forgive you" means simply, "*I* have fixed not to forgive you ;" but "I *shall* be drowned," "*My drowning* is fixed." (See 315.)

319. Will. "*I will.*" Some passages which are quoted to prove that Shakespeare used *will* with the first person without implying *wish, desire,* &c., do not warrant such an inference.

In *Hamlet,* v. 2. 183, " I will win for him, if I can ; if not, I *will* gain nothing but my shame and the odd hits," the *will* is probably used by attraction with a jesting reference to the previous "*will :*" "My purpose is to win if I can, or, if not, to gain shame and the odd hits."

"   There is no hope that ever I *will* stay
    If the first hour I shrink and run away."—I *Hen. VI.* iv. 5. 30.

i.e. " There is no hope of my ever being willing to stay."

    "I'*ll* do well yet."—*Coriol.* iv. I. 21.

i.e. " I *intend* to do well yet."

    " I will not reason what is meant hereby,
    Because I *will* (desire to) be guiltless of the meaning."
                                            Rich. III. i. 4. 95.

In " I *will* sooner have a beard grow in the palm of my hand than he shall get one on his cheek," —2 *Hen. IV.* i. 2. 23. there is a slight meaning of purpose, as though it were, "I *will* sooner make a beard grow," derived from the similarity in sound of the common phrase " I *will* sooner die, starve, than, &c."

In " Good argument, I hope, we *will* not fly,"—*Hen. V.* iv. 3. 113. the meaning appears to be "good argument, I hope, that we have no intention of flying."

There is a difficulty in the expression "perchance I *will ;*" but, from its constant recurrence, it would seem to be a regular idiom. Compare the following passages :—

    "*Perchance,* Iago, I *will* ne'er go home."—*Othello,* v. 2. 197.
    "*Perchance* I *will* be there as soon as you."—*C. of E.* iv. I. 39.
    "*Perhaps* I *will* return immediately."—*M. of V.* ii. 5. 52.

In all these passages "perchance" precedes, and the meaning seems to be in the last example, for instance : " My purpose may, perhaps, be fulfilled," and "my purpose is to return immediately," or, in other words, "If possible, I intend to return immediately." In all these cases, the "perhaps" stands by itself. It does not qualify "will," but the whole of the following sentence.

In "I *will* live to be thankful to thee for't,"—*T. N.* iv. 2. 88.

the *will* refers, not to live, but to "live-to-be-thankful," and the sentence means "I *purpose* in my future life to prove my thankfulness."

320. Will is sometimes used with the second person (like the Greek optative with ἄν) to signify an imperative. It is somewhat ironical, like our "You *will* be kind enough to be quiet." Perhaps originally an ellipsis, as in Greek, was consciously understood, "You *will* be quiet (if you are wise)," &c.

"You'*ll* leave your noise anon, ye rascals."—*Hen. VIII.* v. 4. 1.

In "Gloucester, thou *wilt* answer this before the pope,"
                                                    1 *Hen. VI.* i. 3. 52.

there is no imperative, but there is irony.

On the other hand, "you *will*," perhaps, means "you are willing and prepared" in :

"*Portia.* You know I say nothing to him : he hath neither Latin, French, nor Italian, and you *will* come into court and swear that I have a poor pennyworth in the English."—*M. of V.* i. 2. 75.

321. Will, with the third person.   Difficult passages.

The following is a perplexing passage :—

"If it *will* not be (*i.e.* if you will not leave me) I'll leave you."—*M. Ado,* ii. 1. 208.

Here the meaning seems to be "if it is not to be otherwise," and in Elizabethan English we might expect *shall.* But probably "it" represents fate, and, as in the phrase, "come what *will*," the future is personified : "If fate *will* not be as I would have it." And this explains

"What *shall* become of (as the result of) this? What *will* this do?"—*M. Ado,* iv. 1. 211.

The indefinite unknown consequence is not personified, the definite project is personified. "What *is destined to result* from this project? What does this project *intend to do* for us?"

"My eye *will* scarcely see it,"—*Hen. V.* ii. 2. 104.

means "can scarcely be *induced* to see it."

" He *will*" means "he will have it that," "he pretends," in

" This is a riddling merchant for the nonce ;
  He *will* be here, and yet he is not here."—1 *Hen. VI.* ii. 3. 58.

In   " She'*ll* none of me,"—*T. N.* i. 3. 113.

"will" means "desires," "none" "nothing," and "of" "as regards" (173), "to do with."

322. Should. *Should* is the past tense of *shall*, and underwent the same modifications of meaning as *shall*. Hence *should* is not now used with the second person to denote mere futurity, since it suggests a notion, if not of compulsion, at least of bounden duty. But in a conditional phrase, "If you *should* refuse," there can be no suspicion of compulsion. We therefore retain this use of *should* in the conditional clause, but use *would* in the consequent clause :

" If you *should* refuse, you *would* do wrong."

On the other hand, Shakespeare used *should* in both clauses :

" You *should* refuse to perform your father's will if you *should*
  refuse to accept him."—*M. of V.* i. 2. 100.

And *should* is frequently thus used to denote contingent futurity.

" They told me here, at dead time of the night,
  Ten thousand swelling toads, as many urchins,
  Would make such fearful and confused cries,
  As any mortal body hearing it
  Should straight fall mad."—*T. A.* ii. 3. 102, 104.

" Would " = "were in the habit." Comp. ἐφίλουν.

" (In that case) Strength *should* be lord of imbecility,
  And the rude son *should* strike the father dead ;
  Force *should* be right."—*Tr. and Cr.* i. 3. 114.

323. Should for ought. *Should*, the past tense, not being so imperious as *shall*, the present, is still retained in the sense of *ought*, applying to all three persons. In the Elizabethan authors, however, it was more commonly thus used, often where we should use *ought :*

" You *should* be women ;
  And yet your beards forbid me to interpret
  That you are so."—*Macbeth*, i. 3. 45.

" So *should* he look that seems to speak things strange."
                                                     Ib. i. 2. 46.

" I *should* report that which I say I saw,
  But know not how to do it."—*Ib.* v. 5. 31.

" Why 'tis an office of discovery, love,
    And I *should* be obscured."—*M. of V.* ii. 6. 44.

i.e. " A torch-bearer's office reveals (439) the face, and mine *ought to* be hidden."

324. Should is sometimes used as though it were the past tense of a verb " shall," meaning " is to," not quite " ought." Compare the German " sollen."

" About his son that *should* (was to) have married a shepherd's daughter."— *W. T.* iv. 4. 795.

" The Senate heard them and received them curteously, and the people the next day *should* (were to) assemble in counsell to give them audience."—N. *P. Alcibiades,* 170.

In the following, *should* is half-way between the meaning of " ought " and " was to." The present, *shall,* or " am to," might be expected ; but there is perhaps an implied past tense, " I (you said) *was to* knock you."

"   *Petruchio.* And rap me well, or I'll knock your knave's pate.
    Grumio. My master is grown quarrelsome : I *should* knock you,
And then I know after who comes by the worse."

T. of Sh. i. 1. 131.

325. Should was hence used in direct questions about the past, where *shall* was used about the *future.* Thus, " How *shall* the enemy break in ?" *i.e.* " How *is the* enemy to break in ?" became, when referred to the past, " How *was* the enemy *to* break in ?"

" I was employ'd in passing to and fro
    About relieving of the sentinels.
    Then how or which way *should* they first break in ?"

1 *Hen. VI.* ii. 1. 71.

" What *should* this mean ?"—*Hen. VIII.* iii. 2. 160.

i.e. " what *was* this (destined, likely) to mean ?" It seems to increase the emphasis of the interrogation, since a doubt about the past (time having been given for investigation) implies more perplexity than a doubt about the future. So we still say, " Who *could* it be ?" " How old *might* you be ?"

" What *should* be in that Cæsar ?"—*J. C.* i. 2. 142.

i.e. " what *could* there be," " what *might* there be." " Shall," " may," and the modern " can," are closely connected in meaning.

" Where *should* he have this gold ?"—*T. of A.* iv. 3. 398.

In the following instance, *should* depends upon a verb in the present ; but the verb follows the dependent clause, which may, therefore, be regarded as practically an independent question.

"What it *should* be . . . I cannot dream of."—*Hamlet*, ii. 2. 7.

But also

"Put not yourself into amazement how *should* these things be."
M. for M. iv. 2. 220.

326. Should was used in a subordinate sentence after a simple past tense, where *shall* was used in the subordinate sentence after a simple present, a complete present, or a future. Hence we may expect to find *should* more common in Elizabethan writers than with us, in proportion as *shall* was also more common. We say "I will wait till he comes," and very often, also, "I intended to wait till he came." The Elizabethans more correctly, "I will wait till he *shall* come ;" and therefore, also, "I intended to wait till he *should* come." Thus, since it was possible to say "I *ask* that I *shall* slay him," Wickliffe could write "They *axeden* of Pilate that thei *schulden* sle hym" (*Acts* xiii. 28); "They *aspiden* hym that thei *schulden* fynde cause" (*Luke* vi. 7). In both cases we should now say "might."

So   "She replied,
It *should* be better he became her guest."—*A. and C.* ii. 2. 226.
                          "Thou knew'st too well
My heart was to thy rudder tied by the strings,
And thou *shouldst* tow me after."—*Ib.* iii. 11. 58.

The verb need not be expressed, as in

"A lioness lay crouching . . . with cat-like watch,
When that the sleeping man *should* stir."—*A. Y. L.* iv. 2. 117.

"She has a poison which *shall* kill you," becomes

                          "She did confess she had
For you a mortal mineral, which being took
Should by the minute feed on life."—*Cymb.* v. 5. 51.

This perhaps explains

"Why, 'tis well known that whiles I was protector,
Pity was all the fault that was in me,
For I *should* melt at an offender's tears,
And lowly words were ransom for their fault."
2 Hen. VI. iii. 1. 126.

" All my fault is that I *shall* melt (am sure to melt)," would become " all my fault was that I *should* melt ;" " for " meaning " for
that " or " because."

> " And (Fol.) if an angel should have come to me,
> And told me Hubert *should* put out mine eyes,
> I would not have believed him."—*K. J.* iv. 1. 68 -70.

Here, since the Elizabethans could say "Hubert *shall*," they can
also say " he told me Hubert *should*."

So since the Elizabethans could say " To think that deceit *shall*
steal such gentle shapes," they could also say, regarding the subordinate clause as referring to the past,

> " Oh, that deceit *should* steal such gentle shapes !"
> > *Rich. III.* ii. 2. 27.

> " Good God, (to think that) these nobles *should* such stomachs
> bear!"—1 *Hen. VI.* i. 3. 90.

327. " Should have " with the second and third persons.
The use of "*should* have " with the second and third persons is to be
noted. It there refers to the past, and the *should* simply gives a
conditional force to "have." It is incongruous to use *should* in connection with the past, and hence we now say " If an angel had come"
in this sense. When we use "*should* have," it refers to *a question
about the past* which is to be *answered in the future*. " If he *should
have* forgotten the key, how should we get out," *i.e* "if, when he
comes, it should turn out that he had forgotten." Compare, on the
other hand, the Shakespearian usage.

> " Gods, if you
> *Should have* ta'en vengeance on my faults, I never
> Had lived to put on this."—*Cymb.* v. 1. 8.

In *M. Ado*, ii. 3. 81, the " should have " is inserted, not in the
conditional clause, but in a dependent relative clause. " If it had
been a dog that *should have howled* thus, they would have killed
him."

328. " Should," denoting a statement not made by the
speaker. (Compare "sollen" in German.) There is no other
reason for the use of *should* in

> " But didst thou hear without wonder how thy name *should* be so
> hanged and carved about these trees."—*A. Y. L.* iii. 2. 182.

Should seems to indicate a false story in George Fox's Journal :

"From this man's words was a slander raised upon us that the Quakers *should* deny Christ," p. 43 (Edition 1765). "The priest of that church raised many wicked slanders upon me : 'That I rode upon a great black horse, and that I *should* give a fellow money to follow me when I was on my black horse.'"

"Why should you think that I *should* woo in scorn?"

M. N. D. iii. 2. 122.

329. Would for **will, wish, require.** *Would,* like *should, could, ought,* (Latin* "potui," "debui,") is frequently used conditionally. Hence "I *would* be great" comes to mean, not "I wished to be great," but "I wished (subjunctive)," *i.e.* "I should wish." There is, however, very little difference between "thou wouldest wish" and "thou wishest," as is seen in the following passage :—

> "Thou *wouldst* (wishest to) be great,
> Art not without ambition, but without
> The illness *should* (that *ought* to) attend it : what thou
>   *wouldst* highly
> That thou *wouldst* holily, *wouldst* not play false,
> And yet *wouldst* wrongly win."—*Macbeth,* i. 5. 20.

As *will* is used for "*will* have it," "pretends," so *would* means "pretended," "*wished* to prove."

"She that *would* be your wife."—*C. of E.* iv. 4. 152.

i.e. "She that wished to make out that she was your wife."

So "One that *would* circumvent God."—*Hamlet,* v. 1. 87.

Applied to inanimate objects, a "wish" becomes a "requirement:"

> "I have brought
> Golden opinions from all sorts of people,
> Which *would* (require to) be worn now in their newest gloss."
> *Macbeth,* i. 7. 32.

> "Words
> Which *would* (require to) be howled out in the desert air."
> *Ib.* iv. 3. 194.

> "And so he goes to heaven,
> And so am I revenged. That *would* (requires to) be scann'd."
> *Hamlet,* iii. 3. 75.

"This *would* (requires to) be done with a demure abasing of your eye sometimes."—B. *E.* 92.

---

* Madvig, 348. 1.

It is a natural and common mistake to say, "*Would* is used for *should*, by Elizabethan writers."

Would is not often used for "desire" with a noun as its object :

"If, duke of Burgundy, you *would* the peace."

Hen. V. v. 2. 68.

330. Would often means "liked," "was accustomed." Compare ἐφίλει.

"A little quiver fellow, and a' would manage his piece thus : and a' *would* about and about, and come you in and come you out ; rah-tah-tah *would* a' say, bounce *would* a' say : and away again *would* a' go, and again *would* a' come."—2 *Hen. IV.* iii. 2. 200.

"It (conscience) *was wont to* hold me only while one *would* tell twenty."—*Rich. III.* i. 4. 122.

"But still the house affairs *would* draw her hence."

Othello, i. 3. 147.

So, though more rarely, *will* is used for "is accustomed."

"Sometimes a thousand twangling instruments
Will hum about mine ears."—*Tempest*, iii. 2. 147.

331. "Would" not used for "should." Would seems on a superficial view to be used for *should*, in

"You amaze me ; I *would* have thought her spirit had been invincible against all assaults of affection."—*M. Ado*, ii. 3. 119.

But it is explained by the following reply : "I *would* have sworn it had," *i.e.* "I was ready and willing to swear." So, "I was willing and prepared to think her spirit invincible."

So in "What power is in Agrippa,
If I *would* say, 'Agrippa, be it so,'
To make this good?"—*A. and C.* ii. 2. 144.

'If I *would* say" means "If I wished, were disposed, to say."

"Alas, and *would* you take the letter of her?"—*A. W.* iii. 4. 1.

i.e. "Were you willing," "Could you bring yourself to."

To take *would* for *should* would take from the sense of the following passage :

"For I mine own gain'd knowledge should profane
If I *would* time expend with such a snipe,
But for my sport and profit."—*Othello*, i. 3. 390.

i.e. "If I *were willing* to expend."

Would probably means "wish to" or "should like to," in

"You could, for a need, study a speech which I *would* set down and insert in't, could you not?"—*Hamlet*, ii. 2. 567.

> In "*Prince.* What wouldest thou think of me, if I should weep?
> *Poins.*   I *would* think thee a most princely hypocrite."
>
>   2 *Hen. IV*. ii. 2. 59.

the second *would* is attracted to the first, and there is also a notion of determination, and voluntary "making up one's mind" in the reply of Poins.

So "be triumphant" is equivalent to "triumph," in which willingness is expressed, in

> "Think you, but that I know our state secure,
>   I *would be* so *triumphant* as I am?"—*Rich. III*. iii. 2. 84.

i.e. "think you I *would* triumph as I do?"

In "I *would* be sorry, sir, but the fool should be as oft with your master as with my mistress,"—*T. N.* iii. 1. 44.

it must be confessed there seems little reason for *would*. Inasmuch, however, as the fool is speaking of something that depends upon himself, *i.e.* his presence at the Count's court, it may perhaps be explained as "I *would* not willingly do anything to prevent," &c., just as we can say "I *would* be loth to offend him," in confusion between "I *should* be loth to offend him" and "I *would* not willingly, or I *would* rather not, offend him."

> In   "And how unwillingly I left the ring,
>   When nought *would* be accepted but the ring,"
>
>   *M. of V.* v. 1. 197.

there seems, as in our modern "nothing *would* content him but," some confusion between "he *would* accept nothing" and "nothing could make itself acceptable."

VERBS, INFLECTIONS OF.

332. Verbs: Indicative Present, old forms of the Third Person Plural. There were three forms of the plural in Early English—the Northern in *es*, the Midland in *en*, the Southern in *eth*: "they hop-*es*," "they hop-*en*," "they hop-*eth*." The two former forms (the last in the verbs "doth," "hath," and possibly in others) are found in Shakespeare. Sometimes they are used for the sake of the rhyme; sometimes that explanation is insufficient:

En.—" Where, when men be-*en*, there's seldom ease."

Pericles, ii. Gower, 28.

" O friar, these are faults that are not seen,
Ours open and of worst example be-*en*."—B. J. *S Sh.* i. 2.

" All perish*en* of men of pelf,
Ne aught escap*en* but himself."—*Pericles*, ii. Gower, 36.

" As fresh as *bin* the flowers in May."—PEELE.

" Words fear*en* (terrify) babes."—SPENS. *F. Q.*

" And then the whole quire hold their hips and laugh,
And *waxen* in their mirth."—*M. N. D.* ii. 1. 56.

This form is rarely used by Shakespeare, and only archaically. As an archaic form it is selected for constant use by Spenser.

333. Third person plural in -s. This form is extremely common in the Folio. It is generally altered by modern editors, so that its commonness has not been duly recognized. Fortunately, there are some passages where the rhyme or metre has made altera-tion impossible. In some cases the subject-noun may be con-sidered as singular in *thought*, e.g. "manners," &c. In other cases the quasi-singular verb *precedes* the plural object; and again, in others the verb has for its nominative two singular nouns or an antecedent to a plural noun (see 247). But though such instances are not of equal value with an instance like "his tears *runs* down," yet they indicate a general predilection for the inflection in -*s* which may well have arisen from the northern E. E. third person plural in -*s*.

" The venom clamours of a jealous woman
Poisons more deadly than a mad dog's tooth."

C. of E. v. 1. 69.

" The great man down, you mark his favourites *flies*,
The poor advanced makes friends of enemies."

Hamlet, iii. 2. 214–5.

Here the Globe reads "favourite;" completely missing, as it seems to me, the intention to describe the *crowd* of favourites *scattering in flight* from the fallen patron.

" The extreme parts of time extremely *forms*
All causes to the purpose of his will."—*L. L. L.* v. 2. 750.

" Manners " is, perhaps, used as a singular in

" What manners *is* in this ?"—*R. and J.* v. 3. 214.

" Which very manners *urges*."—*Lear*, v. 3. 234.

So   " Whose church-like humours *fits* not for a crown."

2 *Hen. VI.* i. 1. 247.

" Riches" may, perhaps, be considered a singular noun (as it is by derivation, " richesse ") in

"The riches of the ship *is* come ashore."—*Othello*, ii. 1. 83.

But not

"My old bones *aches*" (Globe, *ache*).—*Tempest*, iii. 2. 2.
"His tears *runs* down his beard like winter-drops" (Globe, *run*).
Ib. v. 1. 16.

"We poor unfledg'd
Have never wing'd from view o' the nest, nor *knows* not
What air's from home " (Globe, *know*).—*Cymb.* iii. 3. 27.

"And worthier than himself'
Here *tends* (Globe and Quarto, *tend*) the savage strangeness he
puts on,
Disguise the holy strength of *their* command," &c.
Tr. and Cr. ii. 3. 135.

"These naughty times
Puts (Globe, *put*) bars between the owners and their rights."
M. of V. iii. 2. 19.

"These high wild hills and rough uneven ways
Draws out our miles, and *makes* them wearisome."
Rich. II. ii. 3. 5.

"Not for all the sun sees, or
The close earth wombs, or the profound seas *hides.*"
(Globe, *sea.*)—*W. T.* iv. 4. 501.

"The imperious seas *breeds* monsters" (Globe, *breed*).
Cymb. iv. 2. 35.

"Untimely storms *makes* men expect a dearth " (Globe, *make*).
Rich. III. ii. 3. 33.

Numbers, perhaps, sometimes stand on a different footing :

"Eight yards of uneven ground *is* three score and ten miles
afoot with me."—1 *Hen. IV.* ii. 2. 28.
i.e. "A distance of eight yards ;" and compare

"Three *parts* of him *is* ours already."—*J. C.* i. 3. 154.
"*Two* of both kinds *makes* up four."—*M. N. D.* iii. 2. 438.

But no such explanation avails in

"She lifts the coffer-lids that close his eyes,
Where, lo ! two lamps burnt out in darkness *lies.*"
V. and A. 1128.

"Whose own hard dealings *teaches* them suspect
The deeds of others."—*M. of V.* i. 3. 163.

"Those pretty wrongs that liberty commits
Thy beauty and thy years full well *befits.*"—*Sonn.* 41.

There is some confusion in

> " Fortune's blows
> When most struck home, being gentle wounded *craves*
> A noble cunning."—*Coriol*. iv. 4. 8.

On the whole, it is probable that though Shakespeare intended to make "blows" the subject of "craves," he afterwards introduced a new subject, "being gentle," and therefore "blows" must be considered nominative absolute and "when" redundant: "Fortune's blows (being) struck home, to be gentle then requires a noble wisdom."

> " Words to the heat of deeds too cold breath *gives*,"
> *Macbeth*, ii. 1. 61.

in a rhyming passage.

It is perhaps intended to be a sign of low breeding and harsh writing in the play of Pyramus and Thisbe.

> "Thisbe, the flowers of odours *savours* sweet."
> *M. N. D.* iii. 1. 84.

334. Third person plural in -th.

> "Those that through renowne *hath* ennobled their life."
> MONTAIGNE, 32.

See, however, **Relative,** 247.

"Their encounters, though not personal, *hath* been royally encountered" (Globe, *have*).—*W. T.* i. 1. 29.

"Where men enforced *doth* speak anything."—*M. of V.* iii. 2. 33.

"*Hath* all his ventures fail'd?" (Globe, *have*.)—*Ib.* iii. 2. 270.

This, however, is a case when the verb precedes the subject. (See below, 335.)

335. Inflection in -s preceding a plural subject.

Passages in which the quasi-singular verb *precedes* the plural subject stand on a somewhat different footing. When the subject is as yet future and, as it were, unsettled, the third person singular might be regarded as the normal inflection. Such passages are very common, particularly in the case of " There is," as—

"There *is* no more such masters."—*Cymb.* iv. 2. 371.

"There *was* at the beginning certaine light suspitions and accusations put up against him."—N. *P.* 173.

"Of enjoin'd penitents there's four or five."—*A. W.* iii. 5. 98.

"The spirit upon whose weal *depends* and *rests*
The lives of many."—*Hamlet*, iii. 3. 14.

"Then what *intends* these forces thou dost bring?"
2 *Hen. VI.* v. 1. 60.

"There *is* no woman's sides can," &c.—*T. N.* ii. 4. 96.

"*Is* there not charms?"—*Othello,* i. 1. 172.

"*Is* all things well?"—2 *Hen. VI.* iii. 2. 11.

"*Is* there not wars? Is there not employment?"
2 *Hen. IV.* i. 2. 85.

So 1 *Hen. VI.* iii. 2. 123; *R. and J.* i. 1. 48; 2 *Hen. IV.* iii. 2. 199; 1 *Hen. VI.* iii. 2. 9.

"Here *comes* the townsmen."—2 *Hen. VI.* ii. 1. 68.

"Here *comes* the gardeners" (Globe, *come*).—*Rich. II.* iii. 4. 24.

"There *comes* no swaggerers here."—2 *Hen. IV.* ii. 4. 83.

This, it is true, comes from Mrs. Quickly, but the following are from Posthumus and Valentine:

"How *comes* these staggers on me?"—*Cymb.* v. 5. 233.

"Far behind his worth

Comes all the praises that I now bestow."—*T. G. of V.* ii. 4. 72.

And in the *Lover's Complaint,* where the rhyme makes alteration impossible:

"And to their audit *comes*

Their distract parcels in combined sums."—*L. C.* 230.

"What *cares* these roarers for the name of king?"—*Temp.* i. 1. 17.

"There *grows* all herbs fit to cool looser flames."
B. and F. *F. Sh.* i. 1.

"There *was* the first gentlemanlike tears that ever we shed."
W. T. v. 2. 155.

"*Has* his daughters brought him to this pass?" (Globe, *have.*)
Lear, iii. 4. 65.

"What *means* your graces?" (Globe, *mean.*)—*Ib.* iii. 7. 30.

"But most miserable

Is the desires that's (247) glorious" (Globe, *desire*).—*Cymb.* i. 6. 6.

("Few" and "more" might, perhaps, be considered nouns in

"Here's a few flowers."—*Cymb.* iv. 2. 283.

"There *is* no more such masters."—*Ib.* iv. 2. 371.

A sum of money also can be considered as a singular noun:

"For thy three thousand ducats here *is* six."—*M. of V.* iv. 1. 84.)

"There *lies*

Two kinsmen (who) digged their graves with weeping eyes."
Rich. II. iii. 3. 168.

"Sir, there *lies* such secrets in this fardell and box."
> *W. T.* iv. 4. 783.

> "At this hour
> *Lies* at my mercy all mine enemies" (Globe, *lie*).
> *Tempest*, iv. 1. 264.

336. Inflection in "s" with two singular nouns as subject.

The inflection in *s* is of frequent occurrence also when two or more singular nouns precede the verb :

> "The heaviness and guilt within my bosom
> *Takes* off my manhood."—*Cymb.* iv. 2. 2.

> "Faith and troth *bids* them."—*Tr. and Cr.* iv. 5. 170.

> "Plenty and peace *breeds* cowards."—*Cymb.* iii. 5. 21.

> "For women's fear and love *holds* quantity."—*Hamlet*, iii. 2. 177.

> "Where death and danger *dogs* the heels of worth."
> *A. W.* iii. 4. 15.

> "Scorn and derision never *comes* (Globe and Quarto, *come*) in tears."—*M. N. D.* iii. 2. 123.

> "Thy weal and woe are both of them extremes,
> Despair and hope *makes* thee ridiculous."—*V. and A.* 988.

> "My hand and ring *is* yours."—*Cymb.* ii. 4. 57.

> "O, Cymbeline, heaven and my conscience *knows*."
> *Ib.* iii. 3. 99.

> "Hanging and wiving *goes* by destiny."—*M. of V.* ii. 9. 83.

> "The which my love and some necessity
> Now *lays* upon you."—*M. of V.* iii. 4. 34.

337. Apparent cases of the inflection in "s."

Often, however, a verb preceded by a plural noun (the apparent nominative) has for its real nominative, not the noun, but the noun clause.

> "The combatants being kin
> Half *stints* their strife before they do begin."—*Tr. and Cr.* iv. 5. 93.

i.e. "The fact that the combatants are kin."

> "Wherein his brains still beating *puts* him thus
> From fashion of himself."—*Hamlet*, iii. 1. 182.

i.e. "The beating of his brains on this."

> "And our ills told us
> *Is* as our earing."—*A. and C.* i. 2. 115.

i.e. "The telling us of our faults is like ploughing us."

> " And great affections wrestling in thy bosom
>   *Doth* make an earthquake of nobility."—*K. J.* v. 2. 42.

> " To know our enemies' minds we 'ld rip their hearts :
>   (To rip) Their papers *is* more lawful."—*Lear*, iv. 6. 266.

So in   " Blest be those,
>   How mean soe'er, that have their honest wills,
>   Which *seasons* comfort,"—*Cymb.* i. 6. 8.

"which" has for its antecedent "having one's honest will."

Conversely, a plural is implied, and hence the verb is in the plural, in

> " Men's flesh preserv'd so whole *do* seldom win."
>   2 *Hen. VI.* iii. 1. 301.

i.e. " when men are too careful about their safety they seldom win."

> " Smile heaven (the gods, or the stars) upon this fair conjunction,
>   That long *have* frowned upon their enmity."—*Rich. III.* v. 5. 21.

It may be conjectured that this licence, as well as the licence of using the *-s* inflection where the verb precedes, or where the noun clause may be considered the nominative, would in all proba-bility not have been tolerated but for the fact that *-s* was still recognized as a provincial plural inflection.

The following is simply a case of transposition :

> "Now, sir, the sound that tells what hour it is
>   *Are* clamorous groans."—*Rich. II.* v. 5. 56.

338. S final misprinted. Though the rhyme and metre establish the fact that Shakespeare used the plural verbal inflection in *s*, yet it ought to be stated that *-s* final in the Folio is often a misprint. Being indicated by a mere line at the end of a word in MS., it was often confused with the comma, full stop, dash or hyphen.

> " *Comes* (,) shall we in ?"—*T. of A.* i. 1. 284.

> " At that that I have kil'd my lord, a *Flys*."—*T. A.* iii. 2. 53.

> " Good man, these joyful tears show thy true *hearts*."
>   *Hen. VIII.* v. 3. 175.

Conversely, in one or two places the dash or hyphen has usurped the place of the *s*.

> " Unkle, what *newe*— ?"—1 *Hen. IV.* v. 2. 30.

> " With gobbets of thy *Mother-bleeding* heart."
>   2 *Hen. VI.* iv. 1. 85.

Sometimes (even without the possibility of mistake for a comma) the *-s* is inserted :

" Sir Protheus, your *Fathers* call's for you."—*T. G. of V.* i. 3. 88.
" Sawcie Lictors
Will catch at us like Strumpets, and scald Rimers
Ballads us out of tune."—*A. and C.* v. 2. 216.

Yet in many passages the -*s* is probably correct, though we should now omit it, especially at the end of nouns. As we still use "riches," "gains," almost as singular nouns, so Shakespeare seems to have used "lands," "wars," "stones," "sorrows," "flatteries," "purposes," "virtues," "glories," "fortunes," "things," "attempts," "graces," "treasons," "succours," "behaviours," "duties," "funerals," "proceedings," &c. as collective nouns.

In other cases there seems at least a *method* in the error. The -*s* is added to *plural adjectives* and to adjectives or nouns *dependent upon nouns inflected in* "*s*," as

"The letters *patents*."—*Rich. II.* ii. 1. 202 (Folio).

It is common in E. E. for plural adjectives of Romance origin to take the plural inflection. But see 430. The Globe reads "*patents*" in *Rich. II.* ii. 3. 130.

The following are selected, without verification, from Walker:

"*Kings* Richards throne."—*Rich. II.* i. 3.
"Smooth and *welcomes* newes."—1 *Hen. IV.* i. 1.
"*Lords* Staffords death."—*Ib.* v. 3.
"The *Thicks-lips*."—*Othello*, i. 1.

A word already plural sometimes receives an additional plural inflection :

"Your *teethes*."—*J. C.* v. 1.
"*Others* faults."—1 *Hen. IV.* v. 2.
"Men look'd . . . each at *others*."—*Coriol.* v. 5.
"*Boths*."—*T. A.* ii. 4. "On *others* grounds."—*Othello*, i. 1.

339. Past indicative forms in u are very common in Shakespeare. Thus, "sang" does not occur, while "sung" is common as a past indicative. "Sprang" is less common as a past tense than "sprung" (2 *Hen. IV.* i. 1. 111). "Begun" (*Hamlet*, iii. 2. 220) is not uncommon for "began," which is also used. We also find

"I *drunk* him to his bed."—*A. and C.* i. 5. 21.

Past indicative tenses in *u* were common in the seventeenth century, but the irregularity dates from the regular Early English idiom.

In A.-S. the second person singular, and the three plural persons of some verbs, *e.g.* "singan," had the same vowel *u*, while the first and third persons singular had *a*. Hence, though the distinction was observed pretty regularly in E. E., yet gradually the *u* and *a* were used indiscriminately in the past tense without distinction of person.

340. Second Person Singular in -ts. In verbs ending with -*t*, -*test* final in the second person sing. often becomes -*ts* for euphony. Thus: "Thou *torments,*" *Rich. II.* iv. 1. 270 (Folio); "Thou *requests,*" *Rich. III.* ii. 1. 98 (Folio); "*revisits,*" *Hamlet,* i. 4. 53; "*splits,*" *M. for M.* ii. 2. 115; "*exists,*" *Ib.* iii. 1. 20 (Folio); "*solicites,*" *Cymb.* i. 6. 147 (Folio); "*refts,*" *Cymb.* iii. 3. 103 (Folio). "Thou *fleets,*" *Sonn.* 19; this is marked in

> "What art thou call'*st* . . . and affright*s*?"
>
> B. and F. *F. Sh.* iv. 1.

This termination in -*s* contains perhaps a trace of the influence of the northern inflection in -*s* for the second pers. sing.

341. Past Indicative: -t for -ted. In verbs in which the infinitive ends in -*t*, -*ed* is often omitted in the past indicative for euphony.

> "I *fast* and prayed for their intelligence."—*Cymb.* iv. 2. 347
> "There they *hoist* us."—*Tempest,* i. 2. 147.
> "Plunged in the foaming brine and *quit* the vessel."—*Ib.* 211.
> "When service *sweat* for duty, not for meed."—*A. Y. L.* ii. 3. 58.
> "Stood Dido . . . and *waft* her love
> To come again to Carthage."—*M. of V.* v. 1. 10.

Compare *Hen. VIII.* ii. 1. 33; *M. of V.* iii. 2. 205.

We find "bid" for "bided," *i.e.* "endured," in

> "Endured of (by) her for whom you *bid* like sorrow."
>
> *Rich. III.* iv. 4. 304.

This is, of course, as natural as "chid," "rid," &c., which are recognized forms. On the other hand, the termination in -*ed* is sometimes used for a stronger form:

> "I *shaked.*"—*Tempest,* ii. 1. 319.

342. Participle: -ed omitted after d and t. Some verbs ending in -*te*, -*t*, and -*d*, on account of their already resembling participles in their terminations, do not add -*ed* in the participle. The same rule, naturally dictated by euphony, is found in E. E. "If the root of a verb end in -*d* or -*t* doubled or preceded by another consonant, the -*de* or -*te* of the past tense, and -*d* or -*t* of the past participle, are omitted." * Thus—

Acquit.—"Well hast thou *acquit* thee."—*Rich. III.* v. 5. 3.

Addict.—*Mirror for Magistrates* (NARES).

Articulate.—"These things indeed you have *articulate*."
                                               1 *Hen. IV.* v. 1. 72.

Betid.—*Tempest,* i. 2. 31.

Bloat(*ed*).—"Let the *bloat* king tempt you."—*Hamlet,* iii. 4. 182.

Contract.—"He was *contract* to lady Lucy."—*Rich. III.* iii. 7. 179.

Degenerate.—"They have *degenerate*."—B. E. 38.

Deject.—"And I of ladies most *deject* and wretched."
                                               Hamlet, iii. 1. 163.

Devote.—*T. of Sh.* i. 1. 32.

Disjoint for *disjointed.*—*Hamlet,* i. 2. 20.

Enshield.—"An *enshield* beauty."—*M. for M.* ii. 4. 80.

Exhaust.—"Their means are less *exhaust*."—B. E. 16.

Graft.—"Her noble stock *graft* with ignoble plants."
                                               Rich. III. iii. 7. 127.

   Compare "An *ingraft* infirmity."—*Othello,* ii. 3. 144.

Heat.—"The iron of itself, though *heat* red-hot."—*K. J.* iv. 1. 61.

Hoist.—"For 'tis the sport to have the enginer
           Hoist with his own petard."—*Hamlet,* iii. 4. 207.

Infect.—"Many are *infect*."—*Tr. and Cr.* i. 3. 188.

Quit.—"The very rats instinctively have *quit* it."—*Temp.* i. 2. 147.

Suffocate.—"Degree is *suffocate*."—*Tr. and Cr.* i. 3. 125.

Taint.—"Unspotted heart never yet *taint* with love."
                                               1 *Hen. VI.* v. 3. 183.

Wed.—*Hen. VIII.* ii. 1. 141.

Waft.   "A braver choice of dauntless spirits
       Than now the English bottoms have *waft* o'er."—*K. J.* ii. 1. 73.

Wet.—*Rich. III.* i. 2. 216.

Whist (for "whisted," which is used by Surrey in the indicative).

       "The wild waves *whist*."—*Tempest,* i. 2. 379.

---

* Morris, Specimens of Early English, xxxv.

i.e. "being *unmade* or made silent." So, in imitation,

> " The winds, with wonder *whist*,
> Smoothly the waters kist."—MILTON, *Hymn on the Nativity.*

Words like "miscreate," *Hen. V.* i. 2. 16 ; "create," *M. N. D.* v. 1. 412, "consecrate," *Ib.* 422, being directly derived from Latin participles, stand on a different footing, and may themselves be regarded as participial adjectives, without the addition of *d.*

343. Participles, Formation of. Owing to the tendency to drop the inflection *en,* the Elizabethan authors frequently used the curtailed forms of past participles which are common in Early English : " I have spoke, forgot, writ, chid," &c.

> "Have you *chose* this man ?"—*Coriol.* ii. 3. 163.

Where, however, the form thus curtailed was in danger of being confused with the infinitive, as in "taken," they used the past tense for the participle :

Arose.—"And thereupon these errors are *arose.*"—*C. of E.* v. 1. 388.

Drove for *driven.*—*2 Hen. VI.* iii. 2. 84.

Eat.—"Thou . . . hast *eat* thy bearer up."—*2 Hen. IV.* iv. 5. 165 ; *M. Ado,* iv. 1. 196.

Froze for *frozen.*—*C. of E.* v. 1. 313 ; *2 Hen. IV.* i. 1. 199.

Holp.—"We were . . . *holp* hither."—*Temp.* i. 2. 63.

> (In this case, however, the *en* is merely dropped.)

Took.—"Where I have *took* them up."—*J. C.* ii. 1. 50.

Mistook.—"Then, Brutus, I have much *mistook* your passion."
> *Ib.* i. 2. 48.

Rode for *ridden.*—*2 Hen. IV.* v. 3. 98 ; *Hen. V.* iv. 3. 2.

Smit for *smitten.*—*T. of A.* ii. 1. 123.

Smote for *smitten.*—*Coriol.* iii. 1. 319.

Strove for *striven.*—*Hen. VIII.* ii. 4. 30.

Writ.—*Rich. II.* ii. 1. 14.

Wrote for *written.*—*Lear,* i. 2. 93 ; *Cymb.* iii. 5. 21.

Or sometimes the form in *ed :*

> " O, when degree is *shaked.*"—*Tr. and Cr.* i. 3. 101.

So *Hen. V.* ii. 1. 124 ; *Temp.* ii. 1. 39 ; *1 Hen. IV.* iii. 1. 17. But *shook* for *shaken* is also common.

> " The wind-*shaked* surge."—*Othello,* ii. 1. 13.

"Ope" in "The gates are *ope*," *Coriol.* i. 4. 43, seems to be the adjective "open" without the -*n*, and not a verb.

344. Irregular participial formations. The following are irregular :—

"You have *swam.*"—*A. Y. L.* iv. 1. 38.

"I have *spake.*"—*Hen. VIII.* ii. 4. 153.

"*Misbecomed.*"—*L. L. L.* v. 2. 778.

"*Becomed.*"—*Cymb.* v. 5. 406.

"Which thou hast perpendicularly *fell.*"—*Lear*, iv. 6. 54.

"We had *droven* them home."—*A. and C.* iv. 7. 5.

"*Sawn*" for "seen" is found as a rhyme to "drawn," *L. C.* 91.

"*Strucken.*"—*C. of E.* i. 1. 46 ; *L. L. L.* iv. 3. 224 ; *J. C.* iii. 1. 209.

"When they are *fretten* with the gusts of heaven."

M. of V. iv. 1. 77.

"*Sweaten.*"—*Macbeth*, iv. 1. 65. (So Quartos.)

Caught seems to be distinguished as an adjective from the participle *catch'd* in

"None are so surely *caught* when they are *catch'd*
As wit turned fool."—*L. L. L.* v. 2. 69.

The following are unusual :—

"*Splitted.*"—*C. of E.* i. 1. 105, v. 1. 308 ; *A. and C.* v. 1. 24.

"*Beated.*"—*Sonn.* 62.

The following are archaic :—

"Marcus, unknit that *sorrow-wreathen* knot."—*T. A.* iii. 2. 4.

"*Foughten.*"—*Hen. V.* iv. 6. 18.

345. The participial prefix y- is only two or three times used in Shakespeare's plays : "y-clept," "y-clad," "y-slaked." In E. E. *y-* is prefixed to other forms of speech beside participles, like the German *ge-*. But in Elizabethan English the *y-* was wholly disused except as a participial prefix, and even the latter was archaic. Hence we must explain as follows :

"The sum of this
Brought hither to Pentapolis
Yravished the regions round."—*P. of T.* iii. Gower, 35.

Shakespeare was probably going to write (as in the same speech, line 1, "*yslaked* hath") "*yravished* the regions hath," but the necessity of the rhyme, and the diminished sense of the grammatical force of the participial prefix, made him alter the construction.

The *y-* is used by Sackville before a present participle, "*y*-causing." In *M. of V.* ii. 9. 68, and elsewhere, we find "I wiss" apparently for the old "y-wiss."

VERBS, MOODS AND TENSES.

346. Indicative simple present for complete present with adverbs signifying "as yet," &c.

This is in accordance with the Latin idiom, "jampridem opto," &c., and it is explicable on the ground that, when an action continued up to the present time is still continuing, the speaker may prefer the verb to dwell *simply* on the fact that the action is present, allowing the adverb to express the past continuousness :

" That's the worst tidings that *I hear of yet.*"

1 Hen. IV. iv. 1. 127.

"*How does* your honour *for this many a day?*"—*Hamlet*, iii. 1. 91.

347. Simple past for complete present with "since," &c.

This is in accordance with the Greek use of the aorist, and it is as logical as our more modern use. The difference depends upon a difference of thought, the action being regarded *simply* as *past* without reference to the present or to *completion.*

" I *saw* him not *these many years*, and yet
I know 'tis he."—*Cymb.* iv. 2. 66.

"I *saw* not better sport these seven years' day."—2 *Hen. VI.* ii. 1. 3.

"*Since* death of my dear'st mother
It *did not speak* before."—*Cymb.* iv. 2. 190.

" I *did* not see him *since.*"—*A. and C.* i. 3. 1.

" I *was* not angry *since* I came in France
Until this instant."—*Hen. V.* iv. 7. 58.

"I can tell you strange news that you *yet dreamed* not of."—*M. Ado*, i. 2. 4.

It will be noticed that the above examples all contain a negative. The *indefinite* tense seems to have peculiar propriety when we are denying that an action was performed at *any time whatever*. Hence the contrast :

"Judges and senates *have been* bought with gold,
Esteem and love *were never* to be sold."

POPE, Essay on Man, iv. 187.

But we have also, without a negative,

> " And *since* I *saw* thee,
> The affliction of my mind amends."—*Tempest*, v. 1. 114.

The simple present is in the following example incorrectly combined with the complete present. But the two verbs are so far apart that they may almost be regarded as belonging to different sentences, especially as "but" may be regarded as semi-adversative.

> "And never since the middle summer's spring
> *Met we . . .* but . . . thou *hast disturbed* our sport."
> > *M. N. D.* ii. 1. 83–7.

On the other hand, the complete present is used remarkably in—

> "*D. Pedro.* Runs not this speech like iron through your blood?
> *Claud.* I *have drunk* poison whiles he utter'd it."
> > *M. Ado*, v. 1. 253.

This can only be explained by a slight change of thought : "I have drunk poison (and drunk [339] poison all the) while he spoke."

348. Future for Subjunctive and Infinitive. The future is often used where we should use the infinitive or subjunctive.

A comparison of Wickliffe with the versions of the sixteenth century would show that in many cases the Early English subjunctive had been replaced by the Elizabethan "shall."

> "And I will sing that they *shall* hear I am not afraid."
> > *M. N. D.* iii. 1. 126.
> "That you *shall* surely find him
> Lead to the Sagittary the raised search."—*Othello*, i. 1. 158.
> "That thou *shalt* see the difference of our spirits,
> I pardon thee thy life before thou ask it."—*M. of V.* iv. 1. 368.
> "Therefore in fierce tempest is he coming
> That, if requiring fail, he *will* compel."—*Hen. V.* ii. 4. 101.

Here, however (283), "so" may be omitted before "that," *i.e.* "so that he purposes compulsion if fair means fail."

> "Reason with the fellow,
> Lest you *shall chance* to whip your information."
> > *Coriol.* iv. 6. 53.
> "If thou *refuse* and *wilt encounter* with my wrath."
> > *W. T.* ii. 3. 138.
> "The constable desires thee *thou wilt mind*
> Thy followers of repentance."—*Hen. V.* iv. 3. 84.
> "Will you permit that I *shall* stand condemn'd?"
> > *Rich. II.* ii. 3. 119.

So with "for" used for "because" (117) in the sense of "in order that."

> " And, *for* the time *shall* not seem tedious,
>   I'll tell thee what befel me."—3 *Hen. VI.* iii. 1. 10.

As in Latin, the future is sometimes correctly and logically used with reference to future occurrences ; but we find it side by side with the incorrect and modern idiom.

> " Farewell till we *shall* meet again."—*M. of V.* iii. 4. 40.
> " He that *outlives* this day and *comes* safe home,
>   He that *shall live* this day and *see* old age."
>   *Hen. V.* iv. 3. 40.
> " All France will be replete with mirth and joy,
>   When they *shall* hear how we have play'd the men."
>   1 *Hen. VI.* i. 6. 16.
> "When they *shall* know."—*Rich. II.* i. 4. 49.
> " If you *shall* see Cordelia."—*Lear,* iii. 1. 46.
> " Till your strong hand *shall* help to give him strength."
>   *K. J.* ii. 1. 133.

The future seems used (perhaps with reference to the original meaning of "shall") to signify *necessary and habitual recurrence* in

> " Good Lord, what madness rules in brain-sick men
>   When for so slight and frivolous a cause
>   Such factious emulations *shall* arise."—1*Hen. VI.* iv. 1. 113.
>
> So   " Men *shall* deal unadvisedly sometimes."
>   *Rich. III.* iv. 4. 293.

349. Infinitive. " To " omitted and inserted. In Early English the present infinitive was represented by -*en* (A.-S. -*an*), so that " to speak " was " spek*en*," and " he is able to speak " was " he can spek*en*," which, though very rare, is found in *Pericles,* ii. Prologue, 12. The -*en* in time became -*e,* and the -*e* in time became mute ; thus reducing " sing-*en* " to " sing." When the *en* dropped into disuse, and *to* was substituted for it, several verbs which we call auxiliary, and which are closely and commonly connected with other verbs, retained the old licence of omitting *to,* though the infinitival inflection was lost. But naturally, in the Elizabethan period, while this distinction between auxiliary and non-auxiliary verbs was gradually gaining force, there was some difference of opinion as to which verbs did, and which did not, require the " *to,*" and in Early English there is much inconsistency in this respect. Thus in consecutive lines "ought" is used without, and "let" with, "*to*."

> "And though we *owe* the fall of Troy requite,
> Yet *let* revenge thereof from gods *to* light."
>
> *Mirror for Magistrates* (quoted by Dr. GUEST).

"You ought not walk."—*J. C.* i. 1. 3.

"Suffer him speak no more."—B. J. *Sejan.* iii. 1.

"If the Senate still command me serve."—*Ib.* iii. 1,

"The rest I wish thee gather."—1 *Hen. VI.* ii. 5. 96.

"You were wont be civil."—*Othello,* ii. 3. 190.

"I list not prophesy."—*W. T.* iv. 1. 26.

"He thought have slaine her:"—SPENS. *F. Q.* i. 1. 50.

"It forst him slacke."—*Ib.* 19.

"Stay" is probably a verb in

> "How long within this wood intend you (to) stay?"
> *M. N. D.* ii. 1. 138.

"Desire her (to) call her wisdom to her."—*Lear,* iv. 5. 35.

> "As one near death to those that wish him (to) live."
> *A. W.* ii. 1. 134.

> "What might'st thou do that honour would (wished) thee (to)
> do?"—*Hen. V.* Prologue, 18.

> "That wish'd him in the barren mountains (to) starve."
> 1 *Hen. IV.* i. 3. 159.

So *M. for M.* iv. 3. 138; *M. Ado,* iii. 1. 42. Hence "overlook" is probably not the subjunctive (see however 369) but the infinitive in

> "Willing you (to) overlook this pedigree."—*Hen. V.* ii. 4. 90.

So after "have need :"

"Thou *hadst need* send for more money."—*T. N.* ii. 3. 99.

"Vouchsafe me speak a word."—*C. of E.* v. 1. 282.

"To come view fair Portia."—*M. of V.* ii. 7. 43.

"We'll come dress you straight."—*M. W. of W.* iv. 2. 80.

"I will go seek the king."—*Hamlet,* ii. 1. 101.

We still retain a dislike to use the formal *to* after "go" and "come," which may almost be called auxiliaries, and we therefore say, "I will come *and* see you."

We cannot reject now the *to* after "know" (though after this word we seldom use the infinitive at all, and prefer to use the conjunction "that"), but Shakespeare has

"Knowing thy heart (to) torment me with disdain."—*Sonn.* 132.

A similar omission is found in

> " That they would suffer these abominations
> By our strong arms from forth her fair streets (to be) chased."
> — *R. of L.* 1634.

So   " Because, my lord, we would have had you (to have) heard
       The traitor speak."—*Rich. III.* iii. 5. 56.

To is inserted after "let" both in the sense of "suffer" and in that of "hinder."

> " And *let* (suffer) no quarrel nor no brawl *to* come."
> — *T. N.* v. i. 364.
> " If nothing *lets* (prevents) *to* make us happy both."—*Ib.* 256.

On the other hand, *to* is omitted after "beteem" in the sense of "suffer :"

> " He might not beteem the winds of heaven
> Visit her face too roughly."—*Hamlet*, i. 2. 141.

After "durst :"

> " I *durst*, my lord, *to* wager she is honest."—*Othello*, iv. 2. 11.

The *to* is often inserted after verbs of perceiving,—"feel," "see," "hear," &c.

> " Who heard me *to* deny it ?"—*C. of E.* v. i. 25.
> " Myself have heard a voice *to* call him so."
> — 2 *Hen. VI.* ii. i. 94.
> " Whom when on ground she grovelling saw *to* roll."
> — Spens. *F. Q.* v. 7. 32.
> " Methinks I feel this youth's perfections
> *To* creep in at mine eyes."—*T. N.* i. 5. 317.
> " I had rather hear you *to* solicit that."—*Ib.* iii. i. 120.
> " To see great Hercules *whipping* a gig,
> And profound Solomon *to tune* a jig,
> And Nestor *play* at push-pin with the boys."
> — *L. L. L.* iv. 3. 167–9.

This quotation shows that, after "see," the infinitive, whether with or without "to," is equivalent to the participle. "Whipping," "to tune," and "play," are all co-ordinate. The participial form is the most correct : as in Latin, "Audivi illam canentem ;" modern English, "I heard her *sing ;*" Elizabethan English, "I heard her *to sing.*" The infinitive with *to* after verbs of perception occurs rarely, if ever, in Early English (Mätzner quotes Wickliffe, *St. John* xii. 18, but ?). It seems to have been on the increase towards the end of the sixteenth century, for whereas Wickliffe (*St. Matt.* xv. 31) has "The puple wondride seynge dumb men spekynge and crokid men goynge, blynde men seyinge," Tyndale (1534) has "The people wondred to se the domme speak, the maymed whole, the halt *to* go, and the blynde *to* se ;" and the A. V. (1611) has *to* throughout. This idiom is also very common in North, and Florio's "Montaigne." We have recurred to the idiom of Early English.

Compare William of Palerne, l. 871 : "and whan he sei╡ þat semly *sitte* him bi-fore," *i.e.* "and when he saw her in her beauty *sit* before him." In this quotation we might render "sitte " by the participle "sitting," as the girl is regarded as "in the state of sitting." This opens the question of the origin of the phrase "to see great Hercules *whipping.*" Is "whipping," by derivation, a verbal abbreviated for "a-whipping," as in 93, or a present participle? The common construction after "see" and "hear" in Layamon and William of Palerne seems to be neither the participle nor the verbal, but the infinitive in *-e* or *-en*. Probably, when the infinitive inflection died out, it was felt that the short uninflected form was not weighty enough to express the emphatic infinitive, and recourse was had to the present participle, a substitution which was aided by the similarity of the terminations *-en* and *-ing*. This is one of the many cases in which the terminations of the infinitive and present participle have been confused together (93), and the *-ing* in this construction represents the old infinitive inflection *-en*. This may explain :

"I my brother know
Yet *living* (to live) in my glass."—*T. N.* iii. 4. 415.

i.e. "that my brother lives."

Hence, perhaps, also *-ing* was added as a reminiscence of the old gerundive termination *-ene*, in such expressions as

"Put the liveries to *making.*"—*M. of V.* ii. 2. 124.

Similarly we find, side by side, in Selden's "Table Talk," "He fell to *eating*" and he "fell to *eat.*"

350. "To" omitted and inserted in the same sentence.

The *to* is often omitted in the former of two clauses and inserted in the latter, particularly when the finite principal verb is an auxiliary, or like an auxiliary.

" Whether *hadst* thou rather be a Faulconbridge
And, like thy brother, *to* enjoy thy land."—*K. J.* i. 1. 134.
" I *would* no more
Endure this wooden slavery than *to* suffer
The flesh-fly blow my mouth."—*Tempest,* iii. 1. 62.
" Who *would* be so mock'd with glory, or *to* live
But in a dream of friendship?"—*T. of A.* iv. 2. 33.

So *K. J.* v. 2. 138-9 ; *J. C.* iv. 3. 73 ; *T. N.* v. 1. 346.

" Sir, I *desire* you (*to*) do me right and justice,
And *to* bestow your pity on me."—*Hen. VIII.* ii. 4. 14.
" *Bids* you
Deliver up the crown and *to* take pity."—*Hen. V.* ii. 4. 104.
" *Makes* both my body pine and soul *to* languish."
P. of T. i. 1. 31.
" *Make* thy two eyes like stars start from their spheres,
Thy knotted and combined locks *to* part."—*Hamlet,* i. 4. 18.
" Brutus *had* rather be a villager
Than *to* repute himself a son of Rome."—*J. C.* i. 2. 173.
" She tells me she'*ll* wed the stranger knight,
Or never more *to* view nor day nor night."—*P. of T.* ii. 5. 17.
" Some pagan shore,
Where these two Christian armies *might* combine
The blood of malice in a vein of league,
And not *to* spend it so unneighbourly."—*K. J.* v. 2. 39.

Thus probably we must explain :

" And *let* them all encircle him about,
And fairy-like *to* pinch the unclean knight."
M. W. of W. iv. 4. 57.

The common explanation "to-pinch," attributes to Shakespeare
an archaism which is probably nowhere found in his works (not
even in *P. of T.* iii. 2. 17). See **All to, 28.**

It is a question how to explain

" She is abus'd, stol'n from me and corrupted
By spells and medicines bought of mountebanks :
For nature so preposterously *to* err,
Being not deficient, blind or lame of sense,
Sans witchcraft *could* not."—*Othello,* i. 3. 62.

Here, either as above, (1) "*to* err" depends on "could," *i.e.*
"Nature was not able *to* err ;" or (2) "could not" might perhaps
stand for "could not be," "was impossible," having for its subject
"Nature to err." (See 354.) In (2) "for" may be either (*a*) a con-

junction, or (*b*) a preposition : "It was not possible for Nature thus to err." I prefer (1).

> In   "For little office
> The hateful commons will perform for us
> Except, like curs, *to* tear us all to pieces," *Rich. II.* ii. 2. 139.

"to tear" may be considered as a noun, the object of "except."

351. It were best (to). *To* is often omitted after "best" in such phrases as "it were best," "thou wert best," &c. Perhaps there is in some of these cases an unconscious blending of two constructions, the infinitive and imperative, exactly corresponding to the Greek οἶσθ' οὖν ὃ δρᾶσον.

> "'Tis best put finger in the eye."—*T. of Sh.* i. 1. 78.
> "I were best not call."—*Cymb.* iii. 6. 19.
> "'Twere best not know myself."—*Macbeth,* i. 2. 73.
> "Best draw my sword."—*Cymb.* iii. 6. 25.

In most of these cases the speaker is speaking of himself : but often it is impossible, without the context, to tell whether the verb is in the infinitive or imperative. Thus in

> "Better be with the dead,"—*Macbeth,* iii. 2. 20.

it is only the following line,

> "Whom we, to gain our peace, have sent to peace,"

that shows that *be* is infinitive. When we now use this idiom, we generally intend the verb to be used imperatively.

352. I were best (to). The construction

> "*Thou wert better* gall the devil."—*K. J.* iv. 3. 94.
> "*I were best* leave him."—1 *Hen. VI.* v. 3. 82.
> "Madam, *you're best* consider."—*Cymb.* iii. 2. 79.

like the modern construction "if you please," (in which we should now say, and be correct in saying, that "you" is the subject, though it was originally the object, of "please,") represents an old impersonal idiom : "Me were liefer," *i.e.* "it would be more pleasant to me ;" "Me were loth ;" "Him were better." Very early, however, the personal construction is found side by side with the impersonal. The change seems to have arisen from an erroneous feeling that "Me were better" was ungrammatical. Sometimes the *to* is inserted :

> "You were best *to* go to bed."—2 *Hen. VI.* v. 1. 196.
> "You were best *to* tell Antonio what he said."—*M. of V.* ii. 8. 33.

353. "To" omitted after Conjunctions.

Where two infinitives are coupled together by a conjunction, the *to* is still omitted in the former, *where the latter happens to be nearer to the principal verb*, e.g. after "rather than." "Rather than see himself disgraced, he preferred to die." But we could not say

"Will you be so good, scauld knave, *as eat* it ?"—*Hen. V.* v. 1. 31.

This is probably to be explained, like the above, as a blending of two constructions—the infinitive, "Will you be so good as *to* eat it ?" and the imperative, "Eat it, will you be so good ?"

In "Under the which he shall not choose *but fall.*"

Hamlet, iv. 7. 66.

"Nay then, indeed she cannot choose *but hate* thee."

Rich. III. iv. 4. 289.

"Thou shalt not choose *but go.*"—*T. N.* iv. 1. 61.

the obvious and grammatical construction is "he shall not choose anything except (to) fall ;" "she cannot choose anything except (to) hate thee ;" but probably (contrary to Mätzner's view, iii. 18) the explanation of the omission is, that Shakespeare mentally supplies "shall," "can," &c. "He shall not choose anything else, but (shall) fall." This is supported by

"Who . . . cannot choose but *they must* blab."—*Othello,* iv. 1. 28.

354. Noun and infinitive used as subject or object.

It might be thought that this was a Latinism. But a somewhat similar use of the infinitive with a noun in impersonal sentences is often found in E. E. and, though rarely, in A.-S.

"No wondur is a lewid man *to ruste.*"—CHAUCER, *C. T.* 504.

"It is ful fair *a man to bear* him even."—*Ib.* 1525.

"It spedith one man *for to die* for þe puple."—WICKLIFFE, *St John* xviiii. 14.

(So Mätzner, but Bagster has "that o man,") *i.e.* "that one man should die."

"It is the lesser fault, modesty finds,
Women to change their shapes than men their minds."

T. G. of V. v. 4. 109.

"As in an early spring
We see the appearing buds *which to prove* fruit
Hope gives not so much warrant as despair
That frosts will bite them."—2 *Hen. IV.* i. 3. 39.

"*This to prove* true
I do engage my life."—*A. Y. L.* v. 4. 171.

> " Be then desir'd
> A little to disquantity your train,
> And the remainder that shall still depend
> *To be* such men that shall besort your age."—*Lear*, i. 4. 272.

In the following instance " brags of " is used like " boasts :"

> " Verona brags of him
> *To be* a virtuous and well-govern'd youth."—*R. and J.* i. 5. 70.
> " I have deserv'd
> *All tongues to talk* their bitterest."—*W. T.* iii. 2. 217.
> " (This) is all as monstrous to our human reason
> As *my Antigonus to break* his grave."—*Ib.* v. 1. 42.
> " O that self-chain about his neck
> *Which* he foreswore most monstrously *to have.*"
> C. *of E.* v. 1. 11 ; *Rich. III.* iv. 4. 337.

Add perhaps   " The duke
> Will never grant *this forfeiture to hold,*"—*M. of V.* iii. 3. 25.

though "forfeiture" may be personified, and "grant" used like "allow." We retain this use, but transpose "for" in "*for to*" (see the example from Wickliffe above) and place it before the **noun or pronoun** :

> "*For me to put* him to his purgation would perhaps plunge him into far more choler."—*Hamlet*, iii. 2. 317.

355. The Infinitive used as a Noun. This use is still retained when the Infinitive is the subject of a verb, as " To walk is pleasant ; " but we should not now say—

> " What's sweet to do *to do* will aptly find."—*L. C.* 13.
> " My operant powers their functions leave *to do.*"
> *Hamlet*, iii. 2. 184 ; *ib.* iii. 4. 66.
> " Have not *to do* with him."—*Rich. III.* i. 3. 292.

So 3 *Hen. VI.* iv. 5. 2.

> " Metaphors far-fet hinder *to be understood.*"—B. J. *Disc.* 757.

Apparently *to* is omitted in the following curious passage :—

> " For to (*to*) *have* this absolute power of Dictator they added never *to* be afraid to be deposed."—N. *P.* 611.

It is doubtful whether the infinitive is a noun in the objective in

> " Nor has he with him *to supply* his life."—*T. of A.* iv. 1. 46.

i.e. "the power of supplying ; " or whether "anything" is understood : "He has not anything to supply his livelihood."

We can say " I was denied my rights," but not

"I am denied *to sue* my livery here."—*Rich. III.* ii. 3. 129.

356. Infinitive, indefinitely used. *To* was originally used not with the infinitive but with the gerund in -*e*, and, like the Latin "*ad*" with the gerund, denoted a purpose. Thus "*to love*" was originally "*to lovene*," *i.e.* "*to* (or *toward*) loving" (ad amandum). Gradually, as *to* superseded the proper infinitival inflection, *to* was used in other and more indefinite senses, "for," "about," "in," "as regards," and, in a word, for any form of the gerund as well as for the infinitive.

"*To* fright you thus methinks I am too savage."—*Macb.* iv. 2. 70.

Not "too savage *to* fright you," but "*in* or *for* frighting you."

"I was too strict *to* make mine own away."—*Rich. II.* i. 3. 243.

i.e. "I was too severe to myself *in sacrificing* my son."

"Too proud *to* be (of being) so valiant."—*Coriol.* i. 1. 263.

"I will not shame myself *to* give you (by giving you) this."
M. of V. iv. 1. 431.

"Make moan *to* be abridged."—*Ib.* i. 1. 126.

Not, "*in order to be*," but, "*about being* abridged."

"Who then shall blame
His pester'd senses *to* recoil and start."—*Macb.* v. 2. 22.

i.e. "for recoiling." Comp. *T. of Sh.* iii. 2. 27 ; *A. Y. L.* v. 2. 110.

"O, who shall hinder me *to* wail and weep ?"
Rich. III. ii. 2. 27.

i.e. "as regards, or from, wailing."

"But I shall grieve you *to* report (by reporting) the rest."
Rich. II. ii. 2. 95.

"You might have saved me my pains *to* have taken away the ring."
T. N. ii. 2. 6.

i.e. "by having taken away."

"I the truer, so *to* be (for being) false with you."
Cymb. i. 5. 44.

"Lest the State shut itself out *to* take any penalty for the same."—*B. E.* 158.

i.e. "as regards taking any penalty." We still say, "I fear *to* do it," where "to" has no meaning of purpose ; but Bacon wrote—

"Young men care not *to* innovate."—*B. E.* 161.

"are not cautious *about innovating*." So *Tr. and Cr.* v. 1. 71.

This gerundive use of the infinitive is common after the verb "to mean :"

> "What mean these masterless and gory swords
> *To lie* discolour'd by this place of peace ?"—*R. and J.* v. 3. 143.
>   "What mean you, sir,
> *To give* them this discomfort ?"—*A. and C.* iv. 1. 34.

So *Tr. and Cr.* v. 1. 30.

> "To weep *to have* that which it fears to lose."—*Sonn.* 64.

i.e. "to weep *because of having, because-it has.*"

We say, "I took eleven hours to write it," or "I spent eleven hours *in writing,*" not

> "Eleven hours I spent *to write* it over."
>   *Rich. III.* iii. 6. 5 ; *M. of V.* i. 1. 154.
>   "But thou strik'st me
> Sorely, *to say* (in saying) I did."—*W. T.* v. 1. 18.
> "You scarce can right me throughly then *to say*
> You did mistake."—*Ib.* ii. 1. 99.

i.e. "by saying."

> "I know not what I shall incur *to pass* it."—*Ib.* ii. 2. 57.

i.e. "I know not what penalty I shall incur as the consequence of, or *for,* letting it pass."

> "You're well *to live.*"—*W. T.* iii. 3. 121.

i.e. "You are well off *as regards living,*" resembles our modern, "You are well *to do.*" The infinitive thus used is seldom preceded by an object :

> "So that, *conclusions to be* as kisses, if your (221) four negatives
> Make your two affirmatives, why then," &c.—*T. N.* v. 1. 22.
> "What ! *I,* that kill'd her husband and his father,
> *To take* her in her heart's extremest hate !"
>   *Rich. III.* i. 2. 231-2.

From 216 it will be seen that the English pronoun, when it represents the Latin accusative before the infinitive, is often found in the nominative. The following is a curious instance of the ambiguity attending this idiom :—

>   "I do beseech your grace
> *To have* some conference with your grace alone."
>   *Rich. II.* v. 3. 27.

i.e. "about having some conference," and here, as the context shows, "that I may have some conference."

Equally ambiguous, with a precisely opposite interpretation, is

> "Sir, the queen
> Desires your visitation, and *to be*
> Acquainted with this stranger."—*Hen. VIII.* v. 1. 169.

i.e. "and that you will become acquainted."

> "Of him I gather'd honour
> Which he *to seek* (seeking) of me again perforce
> Behoves me keep at utterance."—*Cymb.* iii. 2. 73.

Probably we must thus explain :

> "Thou'lt torture me *to leave* unspoken that
> Which, *to be spoke*, would torture thee."—*Ib.* v. 5. 139.

i.e. "You wish to torture me *for leaving* unspoken that which, *by being spoken*, would torture you."

> "Foul is most foul being foul *to be* a scoffer,"
>   *A. Y. L.* iii. 5. 62.

seems to mean "foulness is most foul when its foulness consists *in being* scornful."

357. "To" frequently stands at the beginning of a sentence in the above indefinite signification. Thus *Macb.* iv. 2. 70, quoted above, and—

> "*To* do this deed,
> Promotion follows."—*W. T.* i. 2. 356.

> "*To* know my deed, 'twere best not know myself."
>   *Macbeth*, ii. 2. 73.

> "*To* say to go with you, I cannot."—B. J. *E. out &c.* iv. 6.

> "*To* belie him I will not."—*A. W.* iv. 3. 299.

> "Other of them may have crooked noses, but *to owe* (as regards owning) such straight arms, none."—*Cymb.* iii. 1. 38.

> "For of one grief grafted alone,
> *To* graft another thereupon,
> A surer crab we can have none."—HEYWOOD.

> "*To* lack or lose that we would win
> So that our fault is not therein,
> What woe or want end or begin?"—*Ib.*

> "*To sue* to live, I find I seek to die,
> And *seeking* death find life,"—*M. for M.* iii. 1. 43.

where "*to sue* to live" means "*as regards suing* to live," and corresponds to "*seeking* death."

This indefinite use of the infinitive in a gerundive sense seems to be a continuation of the old idiom which combined *to* with the gerund.

Less frequently the clause depends on " that :"

" But *that* I'll give my voice on Richard's side,
God knows I will not do it."—*Rich. III.* iii. 1. 53.

358. For to. When the notion of purpose is to be brought out, *for to* is often used instead of *to*, and in other cases also. Similarly the Danish and Swedish languages (Mätzner) have "for at," and the old French has "por (pour) à," with the infinitive. *For to* is still more common in Early English than in Elizabethan.

359. Infinitive active is often found where we use the passive, as in

" Yet, if men moved him, was he such a storm
As oft 'twixt May and April is *to see*."—*L. C.* 102.

This is especially common in "what's *to do*" (*T. N.* iii. 3. 18; &c.) for " what's *to be done*." See **Ellipses**, 405, and compare

"Savage, extreme, rude, cruel, not *to trust*."—*Sonn.* 129.

i.e. "not to be trusted."

360. Infinitive, complete Present. It is now commonly asserted that such expressions as " I hoped *to have seen* him yester-day" are ungrammatical. But in the Elizabethan as in Early English authors, after verbs of *hoping*, *intending*, or verbs signifying that something *ought* to *have* been done but was not, the Complete Present Infinitive is used. We still retain this idiom in the expression, " I *would* (i.e. *wished to*) *have* done it." " I ought (*i.e.* was *bound*) *to have* done it." But we find in Shakespeare—

" I hoped thou *shouldst have been* my Hamlet's wife;
I thought thy bride-bed *to have deck'd*, sweet maid."
Hamlet, v. 1. 268.

" Thought *to have* begg'd."—*Cymb.* iii. 6. 48.

In " Levied an army weening to redeem,
And *have install'd* me in the diadem,"—1 *Hen. VI.* ii. 5. 89,

it is difficult to explain the juxtaposition of the simple present with an apparently complete present infinitive. Probably *have* is here used in the sense of "cause," *i.e.* "thinking to redeem me and to have me install'd," "to cause me to be install'd." So in

> " Ambitious love hath so in me offended
> That barefoot plod I the cold ground upon
> With sainted vow my faults *to have amended,*"
>
> *A. W.* iii. 4. 7.

"to have amended" seems to mean "to cause to be amended."
But possibly there is no need for this supposition of transposition.
The thought of *unfulfilment* and disappointment growing on the
speaker might induce her to put the latter verb in the complete
present infinitive.

> "Pharnabazus came thither thinking *to have* raised the siege."—
> N. *P.* 179.

Sometimes the infinitive is used without a verb of "thinking," to
imply an unfulfilled action.

> "I told him of myself, which was as much
> As *to have ask'd* him pardon."—*A. and C.* ii. 2. 79.

But often it seems used by attraction to "have," expressed or
implied in a previous verb.

> "She would *have* made Hercules *to have turned* spit."
>
> *M. Ado,* ii. 1. 261.

> "I had not (*i.e.* should not *have*) been persuaded *to have hurled*
> These few ill-spoken lines into the world."
>
> BEAUMONT *on Faithful Shepherdess.*

So Milton : " He trusted *to have equall'd* the Most High."

The same idiom is found in Latin poetry (Madvig, 407. Obs. 2)
after verbs of *wishing* and *intending.* The reason of the idiom
seems to be a desire to express that the object wished or intended is
a completed fact, that has happened contrary to the wish and cannot
now be altered.

361. Subjunctive, simple form. See also **Be, Were, An,
But, If,** &c. The subjunctive (a consequence of the old inflectional
form) was frequently used, not as now with *would, should,* &c., but
in a form identical with the indicative, where nothing but the
context (in the case of past tenses) shows that it is the subjunctive,
as :

> " But, *if* my father *had* not scanted me,
> Yourself, renowned prince, then *stood* as fair."
>
> *M. of V.* ii. 1. 17.

> " Preferment goes by letter and affection,
> And not by old gradation where each second
> *Stood* heir to the first."—*Othello,* i. 1. 38.

If it be asked what is the difference between "stood" here and "would have stood," I should say that the simple form of the subjunctive, coinciding in sound with the indicative, implied to an Elizabethan more of *inevitability* (subject, of course, to a condition which is not fulfilled). "Stood" means "would certainly have stood." The possibility is regarded as *an unfulfilled fact*, to speak paradoxically. Compare the Greek idiom of *ἵνα* with the indicative.

"If he *did* not care whether he had their love or no, he *waived* indifferently 'twixt doing them neither good nor harm; but he seeks their hate with greater devotion than they can render it him."— *Coriol.* ii. 2. 17.

> "If they
> Should say, 'Be good to Rome,' they *charged* him even
> As those should do," &c.—*Coriol.* iv. 6. 112.

"(If I rebuked you) then I *check'd* my friends."
> *Rich. III.* iii. 7. 150.

"Till" is used varyingly with the indicative present, future, and the subjunctive.

The subjunctive is found after "so" in the sense of "so (that)," *i.e.* "(if it be) so (that)."

> "I will . . . endow a child of thine,
> *So* in the Lethe of thy angry soul
> Thou *drown* the sad remembrance of these wrongs."
> *Rich. III.* iv. 4. 251.

Sometimes the presence of the subjunctive, used conditionally (where, as in the case of *did*, the subjunctive and indicative are identical in inflections), is indicated by placing the verb before the subject :

> "*Did I* tell this . . . who would believe me ?"
> *M. for M.* ii. 4. 171.
> "*Live* Roderigo,
> He calls me to a restitution."—*Othello*, v. 1. 14.
> " *Live* a thousand years,
> I shall not find myself so fit to die."—*J. C.* iii. 1. 159.
> "*Live thou*, I live."—*M. of V.* iii. 2. 61.

Where we should say, "*Should I* tell, live," &c.

The indicative is sometimes found where the subjunctive **might** be expected:

> "*Pleaseth* you walk with me down to his house,
> I will discharge my bond,"—*C. of E.* iv. 1. 12.

where the first clause might be taken interrogatively, "Is it your pleasure to walk with me? In that case I will," &c. *So* 2 *Hen. IV.* iv. 1. 225.   Perhaps we may thus explain the so-called imperative in the first person plural:

> "Well, *sit we* down,
> And let us hear Bernardo speak of this."—*Hamlet*, i. 1. 33.

i.e. "suppose we sit down?" "what if we sit down?"   Compare *Ib.* 168.

So   "*Alcib.* I'll take the gold thou giv'st me, not all thy counsel.
> *Timon. Dost thou, or dost thou not*, Heaven's curse upon
>   thee!"—*T. of A.* iv. 3. 131.

So "willy-nilly" and

> "He left this ring behind him, *would I or not.*"—*T. N.* i. 5. 321.

"Please" is, however, often found in the subjunctive, even interrogatively.

> "*Please* it you that I call?"—*T. of Sh.* iv. 4. 1.

It then represents our modern "may it please?" and expresses a modest doubt.

The subjunctive is also found, more frequently than now, with *if*, *though*, &c.   The subjunctive "he dare" is more common than "he dares" in the historical plays, but far less common in the others.   The only difference between the two is a difference of *thought*, the same as between "he *can* jump six feet" and "he could jump six feet," *i.e.* if he liked.

Compare   "For I know thou *darest*,
> But this thing *dare* not." *—Tempest*, iii. 2. 62–3.

i.e. "would not dare on any consideration:" stronger than "dares."

The indiscriminate use of "dare" and "dares" (regulated, perhaps, by some regard to euphony) is illustrated by

> "Here boldly spread thy hands, no venom'd weed
> *Dares* blister them, no slimy snail *dare* creep."
>   B. and F. *F. Sh.* iii. 1.

362. Subjunctive auxiliary forms.   The simple form of the subjunctive is sometimes interchanged and co-ordinate with the auxiliary form.

"If thou wert the ass, thy dulness *would* torment thee, and still thou *livedst* but as a breakfast to the wolf; if thou wert the wolf, thy greediness *would afflict* thee, and oft thou *shouldst hazard* thy life for a dinner; wert thou a horse, thou *wouldest be seized* by

---

* "This thing" means "this creature Trinculo," and is antithetical to "thou."

the leopard ; wert thou a leopard, thou wert german to the lion."—
T. of A. iv. 3. 385–94.

Note here that "livedst" and "shouldst" imply inevitability and compulsion. "Wouldest" is used in the passive because the passive in itself implies compulsion. "Would" is used after "dulness" and "greediness" because they are quasi-personified as *voluntary* persecutors. Why not "hazardedst" as well as "livedst?" Perhaps to avoid the double *d.*

"Do," "did," are often used with verbs in the subjunctive :

"Better far, I guess,
That we *do make* our entrance several ways."—1 *Hen. VI.* ii. 1. 30.
"Lest your retirement *do amaze* your friends."—1 *Hen. IV.* v. 4. 5.

363. The Subjunctive is replaced by the Indicative after "if," where there is no reference to futurity, and no doubt is expressed, as in "if thou lovest me."

"O Nell, sweet Nell, *if* thou *dost* love thy lord,
Banish the cankers of ambitious thoughts."
1 *Hen. VI.* i. 2. 17.
"*An* thou *canst* not smile as the wind sits, thou'lt catch cold shortly."—*Lear*, i. 4. 112.
"Ah, no more of that, Hal, *an* thou *lovest* me."—1 *Hen. IV.* ii. 4. 312.

In the last example Falstaff is assuming the Prince's love as a *present fact* in order to procure the immediate cessation of ridicule. But in the following he asks the Prince to do him a favour regarded as *future*, and as somewhat more *doubtful :*—

"*If* thou *love* me, practise an answer."—1 *Hen. IV.* ii. 4. 411.
Incredulity is expressed in

"*If* thou *have* power to raise him, bring him hither."
Ib. iii. 1. 60.
In "*If* thou *dost* nod thou *break'st* thy instrument,"
J. C. iv. 3. 271.
the meaning is "you are sure to break," and the present indicative being used in the consequent, is also used in the antecedent. So in

"I *am* quickly ill and well
So (almost 'since') Antony *loves*."—*A. and C.* i. 3. 73.
In "It (my purpose) is no more
But that your daughter, ere she seems as won,
Desires this ring,"—*A. W.* iii. 7. 32.

the purpose is regarded graphically as a *fact* in the act of being completed. However, the indiscriminate use of the indicative and subjunctive at the beginning of the seventeenth century is illustrated by the A. V. *St. Matt.* v. 23 :

> "Therefore, if thou *bring* thy gift to the altar, and there *rememberest.*"

364. Subjunctive used optatively or imperatively. This was more common then than in modern poetry.

> "Who's first in worth, the same *be* first in place."
> > B. J. *Cy.'s Rev.* v. 1.

> (May) "Your own good thoughts *excuse* me, and farewell."
> > *L. L. L.* ii. 1. 177.

> "O heavens, that they *were* living both in Naples,
> The king and queen there! (provided) that they *were*, I wish
> Myself were mudded in the oozy bed."—*Tempest*, v. 1. 150.

> "No man *inveigh* against the wither'd flower,
> But *chide* rough winter that the flower hath kill'd."
> > *R. of L.*

> "In thy fats our cares *be* drowned,
> With thy grapes our hairs *be* crowned."—*A. and C.* ii. 7. 122.

The juxtaposition of an imperative sometimes indicates the imperative use.

> "Touch you the sourest points with sweetest terms,
> Nor (let) curstness *grow* to the matter."—*A. and C.* ii. 2. 25.

> "Good now, sit down, and *tell* me *he* that knows," &c.
> > *Hamlet*, i. 1. 70.

> "*Take* Antony Octavia to *his* wife."—*A. and C.* ii. 2. 129.

> "*Run* one before, and let the queen know."—*Ib.* iv. 8. 1.

> "Thus time we waste, and longest leagues make short ;
> Sail seas in cockles, *have* an wish but for 't."
> > *F. of T.* iv. 4. Gower, 2.

i.e. "Let any one but wish it, and we will sail seas in cockles."

Sometimes only the context shows the imperative use :

> "For his passage,
> (See that) The soldiers' music and the rites of war
> *Speak* loudly for him."—*Hamlet*, v. 2. 411.

The "and" is superfluous, or else "question" is imperative, in

> "*Question*, your grace, the late ambassadors,
> And you shall find."—*Hen. V.* ii. 4. 31.

So in   "*Hold out* my horse and I will first be there."
> *Rich. II.* ii. 1. 300.

"Then (see that) every soldier *kill* his prisoners."
> *Hen. V.* iv. 6. 37.

On the other hand, "prove" is conditional (or "and" is omitted) in

> "O my father !
> *Prove* you that any man with me conversed,
> Refuse me, hate me, torture me to death."
> > *M. Ado*, iv. 1. 182–6.

Often it is impossible to tell whether we have an imperative with a vocative, or a subjunctive used optatively or conditionally.

> "*Melt* Egypt into Nile, and kindly creatures
> *Turn* all to serpents."—*A. and C.* ii. 5. 78.
> > "That I shall clear myself,
> *Lay* all the weight ye can upon my patience,
> I make as little doubt as," &c.—*Hen. VIII.* v. 1. 66.

"Now to that name my courage *prove* my title."
> *A. and C.* v. 2. 291.

"Sport and repose *turn* from me day and night."
> *Hamlet*, iii. 2. 218.

365. This optative use of the subjunctive dispensing with "let," "may," &c. gives great vigour to the Shakespearian line :

> "*Judge* me the world."—*Othello*, i. 2. 72.

i.e. "let the world judge for me."

> "Disorder, that hath spoil'd us, *friend* us now."
> > *Hen. V.* iv. 5. 17.

> "Long *die* thy happy days before thy death."
> > *Rich. III.* i. 3. 207.

> "The worm of conscience still *begnaw* thy soul."—*Ib.* 222.

The reader of Shakespeare should always be ready to recognize the subjunctive, even where the identity of the subjunctive with the indicative inflection renders distinction between two moods impossible, except from the context.   Thus :

> "Therefore take with thee my most heavy curse,
> Which in the day of battle *tire* thee more
> Than all the complete armour that thou wear'st !
> My prayers on the adverse party *fight*,
> And there the little souls of Edward's children
> *Whisper* the spirits of thine enemies,
> And *promise* them success and victory."—*Rich. III.* iv. 4. 190.

Here, in the second line, "tire," necessarily subjunctive, impresses upon the reader that the co-ordinate verbs, "fight," &c., are also subjunctive. But else, it would be possible for a careless reader to take "fight," &c. as indicative, and ruin the passage.

This optative or imperative use of the subjunctive, though common in Elizabethan writers, had already begun to be supplanted by auxiliaries. Thus Wickliffe has (*Coloss.* ii. 16) "No man *juge* you," while all the other versions have "*Let* no man judge you."

366. Subjunctive, complete present. (See Should for "if he should have.") The subjunctive with "have" is not very frequent. It is used where a past event is not indeed denied, but qualified conditionally, in an argumentative manner :

> "If, sir, perchance
> She *have* restrain'd the riots of your followers,
> 'Tis on such ground . . . as clears her from all blame."
> *Lear*, ii. 4. 145.

i.e. "If it should hereafter be proved that she *have*," "if so be that she *have*."

So "If this young gentleman *have* done offence."
> *T. N.* iii. 4. 344.

"Though it *have*" is somewhat similarly used to express a concession for the sake of argument, not a fact.

> "For though it *have* holp madmen to their wits."
> *Rich. II.* v. 5. 62.

367. Subjunctive used indefinitely after the Relative.

> "In her youth
> There is a prone and speechless dialect
> *Such as move* men."—*M. for M.* i. 2. 189

> "And the stars *whose* feeble light
> *Give* a pale shadow."—B. and F.

> "But they *whose* guilt within their bosom *lie*
> Imagine every eye beholds their blame."—*R. of L.* ii. 1344.

> "Thou canst not die, *whilst* any zeal *abound.*"
> DANIEL (quoted by WALKER).

> "I charge you to like as much of this play *as please* you."
> *A. Y. L.* Epilogue.

> "And may direct his course *as please* himself."
> *Rich. III.* ii. 2. 129.

Perhaps (but see 218)

> "Alas, their love may be called appetite,
> No motion of the liver, but the palate
> That *suffer* surfeit."—*T. N.* ii. 4. 102.

In the subordinate clauses of a conditional sentence, the relative is often followed by the subjunctive :

> "A man *that were* to sleep your sleep."—*Cymb.* v. 4. 179.

i.e. "If there were a man who was destined to sleep your sleep."

> "If they would yield us but the superfluity *while* it *were* wholesome."—*Coriol.* i. 1. 18.

368. Subjunctive in a subordinate sentence. The subjunctive is often used with or without "that," to denote a purpose (see above, **That**). But it is also used after "that," "who," &c. in dependent sentences where no purpose is implied, but only futurity.*

> "Be it of less expect
> *That* matter needless of importless burden
> *Divide* thy lips."—*Tr. and Cr.* i. 3. 71.

No "purpose" can be said to be implied in "please," in the following :—

> "May it please you, madam,
> *That* he *bid* Helen come to you."—*A. W.* i. 3. 71.

> "Yet were it true
> To say this boy *were* like me."—*W. T.* i. 2. 135.

> "Thou for whom Jove would swear
> Juno but an Æthiop *were*."—*L. L. L.* iv. 3. 118.

> "Would you not swear that she *were* a maid?"
> *M. Ado*, iv. 1. 40.

> "One would think his mother's milk *were* scarce out of him."
> *T. N.* i. 5. 171.

In the last four passages the second verb is perhaps attracted to the mood of the first.

> "*Proteus.* But she is dead.
> *Silv.*   Say that she *be:* yet," &c.
> *T. G. of V.* iv. 2. 109.

> "With no show of fear,
> No, with no more than if we heard that England
> *Were* busied with a Whitsun Morris-dance."
> *Hen. V.* ii. 4. 25.

---

* I have found no instance in Shakespeare like the following, quoted by Walker from Sidney's *Arcadia :*

> "And I think there she *do* dwell."

"I pray (hope) his absence *proceed* by swallowing that."
> *Cymb.* iii. 5. 58.

"If it be proved against an alien
That by direct or indirect attempt
He *seek* the life of any citizen."—*M. of V.* iv. 1. 351.

"One thing more rests that thyself *execute.*"—*T. of Sh.* i. 1. 251.

where, however, "that" may be the relative, and "execute" an imperative.

I know of no other instance in Shakespeare but the following, where the subjunctive is used after "that" used for "so that," of a fact:

"Through the velvet leaves the wind
All unseen can passage find,
That the lover sick to death
Wish himself the heaven's breath."—*L. L. L.* iv. 3. 108.

The metre evidently may have suggested this licence: or -*es* or -*d* may have easily dropped out of "wish*es*" or "wish'*d.*"

The subjunctive is used where we should use the future in

"I doubt not you (will) *sustain* what you're worthy of by your attempt."—*Cymb.* i. 4. 125.

"Think" seems used subjunctively, and "that" as a conjunction in

"And heaven defend (prevent) your good souls that you
(should) *think*
I will your serious and great business scant
For (because) she is with me."—*Othello*, i. 3. 267.

The "that" is sometimes omitted:

"It is impossible they *bear* it out."—*Ib.* ii. 1. 19.

Here "bear" is probably the subjunctive. The subjunctive is by no means always used in such sentences. We may contrast

"No matter then *who see* it."—*Rich. II.* v. 2. 59.

"I care not *who know* it."—*Hen. V.* iv. 7. 118.

with

"I care not *who knows* so much."—*T. N.* iii. 4. 300.

369. The Subjunctive after verbs of command and entreaty is especially common; naturally, since command implies a *purpose.*

"We enjoin thee that thou *carry.*"—*W. T.* ii. 3. 174.

"I conjure thee that thou *declare.*"—*Ib.* i. 2. 402.

So *M. for M.* v. 1. 50.

> "Tell him from me
> He *bear* himself with honourable action."
> > *T. of Sh.* Ind. i. **1**. 110.

> "Thy dukedom I resign, and do entreat
> Thou *pardon* me my wrongs."—*Temp.* v. **1**. 119.

So after "forbid."

> "Fortune forbid my outside *have* not charmed her."
> > *T. N.* ii. **2**. 19.

Sometimes an auxiliary is used :

> "I do beseech your majesty *may salve.*"—1 *Hen. IV.* iii. 2. 155.

Hence in such passages as

> "Go charge my goblins that they *grind* their joints,"
> > *Temp.* iv. **1**. 259.

the verb is to be considered as in the subjunctive.

After a past tense "should" is used :

> "She bade me . . . I *should* teach him."—*Othello*, i. **3**. 165.

370. Irregular sequence of tenses. Sometimes the sequence of tenses is not observed in these dependent sentences :

> "Therefore they *thought* it good you *hear* a play."
> > *T. of Sh.* Ind. 2. 136.

> "'*Twere* good you *do* so much for charity."—*M. of V.* iv. **1**. 261.

In both cases a present is implied in the preceding verb : "They thought and think," "It were and is good."

Reversely in

> > "But do not stain
> The even virtue of our enterprise
> To think that or our cause or our performance
> *Did need* an oath."—*J. C.* ii. **1**. 136.

"Did need" means "ever could need," and is stronger than "need" or "can need."   In

> "Is it not meet that I *did* amplify my judgment?"—*Cymb.* i. **5**. 17.

as in "It is time he *came*," the action is regarded as one "meet" in time past, as well as in the future.

> "It hath been taught us from the primal state
> That he which is *is wished* until he *were.*"—*A. and C.* i. **3**. 42.

Here "were" is used partly for euphony and alliteration, partly because the speaker is speaking of the past, "is and was always wished until he were."

371. Conditional sentences. The consequent does not always answer to the antecedent in mood or tense. Frequently the irregularity can be readily explained by a change of thought.

> "And that I'*ll* prove on better men than Somerset,
> (Or rather, I would) *Were* growing time once ripen'd to
> my will."—I *Hen. VI.* ii. 4. 98.

So 3 *Hen. VI.* v. 7. 21.

> "If we *shall* stand still
> (Or rather, if we should, for we shall not) We *should* take root."
> *Hen. VIII.* i. 2. 86.

> "I *will* find
> Where truth is hid, (and I would find it) though it *were* hid
> indeed
> Within the centre."—*Hamlet,* ii. 2. 157–8.

Compare *Ezek.* xiv. 14, A. V. :

> "Though these three men, Noah, Daniel, and Job, *were* in it, they
> *should* deliver but their own souls."

with *ib.* 20, "they *shall* deliver."

> "But if the gods themselves *did see* her then
>   *   *   *   *   *   *   *
> (If they had seen her) The instant burst of clamour that she
> made
> *Would have made* milch the burning eyes of heaven."
> *Hamlet,* ii. 2. 535-40.

> "Till I *know* 'tis done,
> Howe'er my hopes (might be), my joys *were* ne'er begun."
> *Ib.* iv. 3. 70.

Sometimes the consequent is put graphically in the present merely for vividness :

> "If he *should* do so,
> He *leaves* his back unarm'd ; . . . never fear that."
> 2 *Hen. IV.* i. 3. 80.

Or else the speaker rises in the tone of confidence :

> "I am assured, if I *be* measured rightly,
> Your majesty *hath* no just cause to hate me."—*Ib.* v. 2. 66.

PARTICIPLES.

372. Participles, Active. Our termination *-ing* does duty for (1) the old infinitive in *-an ;* (2) the old imperfect participle in *end, ende, ande ;* and (3) a verbal noun in *-ung.* Hence arises great con-

fusion. It would sometimes appear that Shakespeare fancied that
-*ing* was equivalent to -*en*, the old affix of the Passive Participle.
Thus—

> " From his *all-obeying* breath
> I hear the doom of Egypt."—*A. and C.* iii. 13. 77.

i.e. " obeyed by all."

> " Many a dry drop seemed a *weeping* tear."—*R. of L.* i. 1375.

So " His *unrecalling* crime " (*R. of L.*) for " unrecalled."

(In " Many excesses which are *owing* a man till his age,"—*B. E.* 122.
i.e. " *own*, or, belonging to a man," *owing* is not a participle at all,
but an adjective, " agen," " âwen," " ôwen," " owenne," " owing;"
which was mistaken for a participle.

> " There is more *owing* her than is paid."—*A. W.* i. 3. 107.

" Wanting," as in *Coriol.* ii. 1. 217, " One thing is *wanting*," can be
explained from the use of the verb *wanteth* in the following passage :

> " There *wanteth* now our brother Gloucester here
> To make the period of this perfect peace."—*R. III.* ii. 1. 43.)

The same explanation may apply to " I am much *beholding* to
you," which is sometimes found for " beholden," *Rich. III.* ii. 1. 129,
J. C. iii. 2. 70-3, and even to

> " Relish your nimble notes to *pleasing* ears."—*R. of L.*

In the following, -*ing* might be supplanted, without altering the
sense, by the infinitive or the verbal preceded by *a-* :*

> " Women are angels, *wooing* :
> Things won are done."—*Tr. and Cr.* i. 2. 312.

i.e. " women are considered angels *to woo*, or *a-wooing*," where
wooing, if treated as an ordinary present participle, would give the
opposite to the intended meaning. Probably in the above, as in
the following, *a-* is omitted.

> " Be brief, lest that the process of thy kindness
> Last longer (a-, or in) *telling* than thy kindness date."
> *Rich. III.* iv. 4. 254.

The " in " is inserted in

> " Pause a day or two
> Before you hazard ; for *in* choosing wrong I lose your com-
> pany."—*M. of V.* iii. 2. 2.

---

* Comp. " Return*ing* were as tedious as (to) go o'er,"—*Macb.* iii. 4. 138.
in which the *ing* perhaps qualifies " go" as well as " return," and might be supplanted by " to."

i.e. "in the event of *your* choosing wrong, *I* lose your company."
The two constructions occur together in

> "Come, come, *in wooing* sorrow let's be brief,
> Since, (a-)*wedding* it, there is such length in grief."
>
> *Rich. II.* v. 3. 72.

It is perhaps a result of this confusion between the verbal and the infinitive that, just as the infinitive with "to" is used independently at the beginning of a sentence (357) in a gerundive signification, so is the infinitive represented by *-ing*:

> "Why, were thy education ne'er so mean,
> *Having* thy limbs, a thousand fairer courses
> Offer themselves to thy election."—B. J. *E. in &c.* ii. 1.

i.e. "since thou hast thy limbs." This explains the many instances in which present participles appear to be found agreeing with no noun or pronoun.

Part of this confusion may arise from the use of the verbal in *-ing* as a noun in compounds. We understand at once that a "knedyng trowh" (CHAUCER, *C. T.* 3548) means "a trough for kneading;" but "spending silver" (*Ib.* 12946) is not quite so obviously "money for spending." Still less could we say

> "Sixth part of each! A *trembling* contribution."
>
> *Hen. VIII.* i. 2. 95.

Somewhat different is

> "Known and *feeling* sorrows,"—*Lear*, iv. 6. 226.

where "feeling" seems to be used like "known," passively, "known and realized sorrows."

So "loading" is used for "laden," BACON, *Essays*, p. 49 (Wright).

> "Your *discontenting* father,"—*W. T.* iv. 4. 543.

may perhaps be explained by the use of the verb "content you;" "I discontent (me)" meaning "I am discontented."

373. The Verbal differs in Elizabethan usage from its modern use. (*a*) We do not employ the verbal as a noun followed by "of," unless the verbal be preceded by "the," or some other defining adjective. But such phrases as the following are of constant occurrence in Elizabethan English :

> "To disswade the people from *making of* league."—N. *P.* 170.
> "He was the onely cause of *murdering of* the poor Melians."
>
> *Ib.* 171.

" By *winning* only *of* Sicilia."—N. *P.* 171.

" Enter Clorin the Shepherdess, *sorting* of herbs."

B. and F. *F. Sh.* ii. 1.

i.e. "a-sorting, or in sorting of herbs."

For instances from Shakespeare, see 178 and 93.

(*b*) On the other hand, when the verbal is constituted a noun by the dependence of "the," or any other adjective (except a possessive adjective) upon it, we cannot omit the *of.* The Elizabethans can.

" To plague thee for thy *foul misleading* me."

3 *Hen. VI.* v. 1. 97.

We should prefer now to omit the "thy" as well as "foul," though we have not rejected such phrases as

" Upon *his leaving* our house."—*Goldsmith.*

For instances of "of" omitted when "the" precedes the verbal, see Article, 93. In this matter modern usage has recurred to E. E.

374. Participles, Passive. It has been shown (294) that, from the licence of converting nouns, adjectives, and neuter verbs into active verbs, there arose an indefinite and apparently not passive use of Passive Participles. Such instances as

" Of all he dies *possess'd* of,"—*M. of V.* v. 1. 293.

(*possess* being frequently used as an active verb,) may thus be explained.

Perhaps,

" And, gladly *quaked* (made to quake), hear more,"

Coriol. i. 9. 6.

may be similarly explained. Compare also :

" All the whole army stood *agazed* on him."

1 *Hen. VI.* i. 1. 126.

But, in the following, we can only say that, in the excessive use of this licence, *-ed* is loosely employed for *-ful, -ing,* or some other affix expressing connection.

" Revenge the jeering and *disdain'd* contempt."

1 *Hen. IV.* i. 3. 183.

" *Brooded*-watchful day."—*K. J.* iii. 3. 52.

As we talk of "watching (during) the night," this may explain

" The weary and all-*watched* night."—*Hen. V.* iv. Prologue, 38.

But more probably "all-watched" (like "o'er-watched," *J. C.* iv. 3. 241) resembles "weary," and means "tired with watching." For this use of adjectives see 4.

> " Grim-*look'd* night."—*M. N. D.* v. 1. 171.
> " The *ebbed* man."—*A. and C.* i. 4. 43.

It is perhaps still not unusual to say "the tide *is* ebbed."

> " A *moulten* raven."—1 *Hen. IV.* iii. 1. 152.
> " With *sainted* vow."—*A. W.* iii. 4. 7. (= saintly).
> " And at our more *considered* time we'll read."—*Hamlet*, ii. 2. 81.
> " *Unconstrained* gyves."—*L. C.* 242.

Sometimes passive participles are used as epithets to describe the state which would be the result of the active verb. Thus:

> " Why are you *drawn?*"—*Temp.* ii. 1. 308; *M.N.D.* iii. 2. 402.

i.e. " Why do I find you with your swords drawn?"

> " Under the blow of *thralled* discontent."—*Sonn.* 124.

"The *valued* file" (*Macb.* iii. 1. 95) perhaps means "the file or catalogue to which values are attached."

375. The Passive Participle is often used to signify, not that which *was* and *is*, but that which *was*, and therefore *can be hereafter*. In other words, *-ed* is used for *-able*.

> " Inestimable stones, *unvalued* jewels."—*Rich. III.* i. 4. 27.

i.e. "invaluable."

> " All *unavoided* is the doom of destiny."—*Ib.* iv. 4. 217.

i.e. "inevitable." So

> " We see the very wreck that we must suffer,
> And *unavoided* is the danger now."—*Rich. II.* ii. 2. 268.
> " With all *imagined* (imaginable) speed."—*M. of V.* iii. 4. 52.
>   "The murmuring surge
> That on the *unnumber'd* idle pebbles chafes."—*Lear*, iv. 6. 21.

So, probably, Theobald is right in reading

> " The twinn'd stone upon th' *unnumber'd* beach,"
>   *Cymb.* i. 6. 36.

though the Globe retains "number'd."

" Unprized " in

> "This *unprized* precious maid,"—*Lear*, i. 1. 262.

may mean " unprized by others, but precious to me."

" There's no *hoped for* mercy with the brothers."

3 *Hen. VI.* v. 4. 35.

i.e. " to be hoped for."

It has been conjectured that " deli ;hted" means " capable of being delighted " in

> " This sensible warm motion to become
> A *kneaded* clod, and the *delighted* spirit
> To bathe in fiery floods."—*M. for M.* iii. 1. 121.

More probably, " delighted " here means the spirit " that once took its delight in this world ; " but " knead*ed* " seems used for " knead*able.* "

376. Participle used with a Nominative Absolute. In

Anglo-Saxon a dative absolute was a common idiom. Hence, even when inflections were discarded, the idiom was retained ; and indeed, in the case of pronouns, the nominative, as being the normal state of the pronoun, was preferred to its other inflections. The nominative absolute is much less common with us than in Elizabethan authors. It is often used to call attention to the object which is superfluously repeated. Thus in

> " *The master and the boatswain,*
> *Being awake,* enforce them to this place,"—*Temp.* v. 1. 100.

there is no need of " them." So " he " is superfluous in

> " Why should he then protect our sovereign,
> *He* being of age to govern of himself ? "—*2 Hen. VI.* i. 1. 166.

It is common with the relative and relative adverbs.

> " Then Deputy of Ireland ; *who remov'd,*
> Earl Surrey was sent thither."—*Hen. VIII.* ii. 1. 42.
> " My heart,
> *Where the impression* of mine eye *infixing,*
> Contempt his scornful perspective did lend me."
> *A. W.* v. 3. 47.
> " Thy currish spirit
> Govern'd a wolf, *who hang'd for human slaughter,*
> Even from the gallows did his fell soul fleet."
> *M. of V.* iv. 1. 134.
> " Emblems
> Laid nobly on her ; *which perform'd,* the choir
> Together sung ' Te Deum.' "—*Hen. VIII.* iv. 1. 91.

The participle with a nominative originally intended to be absolute seems diverted into a subject in

> " *The king* . . . *aiming* at your interior hatred
> Makes him send."—*Rich. III.* i. 3. 65-8.

i.e. " the fact that the king guesses at your hatred makes him send."

377. The Participle is often used to express a condition
where, for perspicuity, we should now mostly insert "if."

> " Requires to live in Egypt, *which not granted,*
> He lessens his requests."—*A. and C.* iii. 12. 12.

> " That whoso ask'd her for his wife,
> *His riddle told not,* lost his life."—*P. of T.* i. Gower, 38.

> " For I do know Fluellen valiant,
> And, *touch'd with choler,* hot as gunpowder."
> > *Hen. V.* iv. 7. 188.

> " *Your honour not o'erthrown* by your desires,
> I am friend to them and you."—*W. T.* v. 1. 230.

"Admitted " is probably a participle in

> " This is the brief of money, plate and jewels
> I am possess'd of : 'tis exactly valued,
> *Not petty things admitted.*"—*A. and C.* v. 1. 146.

i.e. " exactly, if petty things be excepted."

The participle is sometimes so separated from the verb that it seems to be used absolutely.

> " Resolve me with all modest haste which way
> *Thou* might'st deserve, or they impose this usage,
> *Coming* from us."—*Lear,* ii. 4. 27.

i.e. " since thou comest."

> " But *being* moody give him line and scope."
> > 2 *Hen. IV.* iv. 4. 39.

"And " is sometimes joined to a participle or adjective thus used. See **And,** 95.

> " What remains
> But that I seek occasion how to rise,
> *And* yet the king *not privy* to my drift."—3 *Hen. VI.* i. 2. 47.

> " But when the splitting wind
> Makes flexible the knees of knotted oaks,
> *And flies* (being) *fled* under shade."—*Tr. and Cr.* i. 3. 51.

i.e. "the flies also being (295) fled."

378. Participle without Noun. This construction is rare in earlier English.

" My name is gret and meiveylous, treuly you telland."—*Cov. Myst.* (Mätzner).

Here again, as in 93, we must bear in mind the constant confusion between the infinitive, the present participle, and the verbal. In the above example we should expect the infinitive, "to tell you the truth," and perhaps "telland" is not exactly used for, but confused with, "tellen." *

It is still a usual idiom with a few participles which are employed almost as prepositions, *e.g.* "touching," "concerning," "respecting," "seeing." "Judging" is also often thus incorrectly used, and sometimes "considering ;" but we could scarcely say—

" Or in the night *imagining* (if one imagines) some fear,
    How easy is the bush suppos'd a bear."—*M. N. D.* v. 1. 21.

" Here, as I point my sword, the sun arises,
    Which is a great way growing on the south,
    Weighing the youthful season of the year."—*J. C.* ii. 1. 108.

Note especially—

" I may not be too forward,
    Lest (I) *being seen* thy brother, tender George,
    Be executed."—*Rich. III.* v. 3. 95.

" (It must be done) something from the palace, always *thought*
    That I require a clearness."—*Macbeth*, iii. 1. 132.

i.e. " it being always borne in mind."

" (Death sits) infusing him (man) with self and vain conceit,
    And, (man having been) *humour'd* thus,
    (Death) comes at the last."—*Rich. II.* iii. 2. 168.

This use is common in prose.

" He was presently suspected, *judging* (since men judged) the ill success not in that he could not, but . . . for that he would not."— N. P. 182.

So "being," *i.e.* " it being the fact," is often used where we use " seeing."

" You loiter here too long, *being* you are to take soldiers up in counties as you go."—*2 Hen. IV.* ii. 1. 200 ; *M. Ado*, iv. 1. 51.

" Though I with death and with
    Reward did threaten and encourage him,
    Not *doing* 't and (it) *being* done."—*W. T.* iii. 2. 166.

* It would be interesting to trace the corresponding process in French by which the gerund "dicendo" and the participle "dicens" were blended in "disant." It was not till the beginning of the eighteenth century that the Academy definitely pronounced "La règle est faite. On ne fera plus accorder les participes présents." But from the earliest times the *d* of the gerund became *t.*

i.e. "I threatened him, not doing it, with death, and encouraged him with reward, (it) being done;" a specimen of irregular terseness only to be found in Elizabethan authors and in Mr. Browning's poems.

The context often suggests a noun or pronoun :

"If not that, I being queen, you bow like subjects,
Yet that, (I being) by you *deposed*, you quake like rebels."
Rich. III. i. 3. 162.

"But her eyes—
How could he see to do them ? *Having made* one,
Methinks it should have power to steal both his."
M. of V. iii. 2. 125.

i.e. "when he had made one."

"*Had*, having, and in quest to have, extreme."—*Sonn.* 129.

i.e. "when an object is *had*, possessed," unless it is still more irregularly used for "having had."

This irregularity is perhaps in some cases explained by 372.

379. Participle with Pronoun implied. Sometimes a pronoun on which a participle depends can be easily understood from a pronominal adjective. Compare

"*Nostros* vidisti *flentis* ocellos."

So "Not *helping*, death's *my* fee."—*A. W.* ii. 1. 192.

i.e. "death is the fee *of me* not helping."

"Men
Can counsel speak and comfort to that grief
Which they themselves not feel ; but, *tasting* it,
Their counsel turns to passion."—*M. Ado*, v. 1. 22.

"She dares not look, yet, *winking*, there appears
Quick-shifting antics ugly in *her* eye."—*R. of L.* 458.

"*Coming* (as we came) from Sardis, on *our* former ensign
Two mighty eagles fell."—*J. C.* v. 1. 80.

380. Instead of the Participle an Adjective is sometimes found.

"I would not seek an absent argument
Of my revenge, *thou present*."—*A. Y. L.* iii. 1. 4.

"And (she), her *attendants absent*, swallowed fire."—*J. C.* iv. 3. 156.

"*Joy absent*, grief is present for that time."—*Rich. II.* i. 3. 259.

Sometimes the adjective depends on an implied pronoun :

" Thy word is current with him for my death,
But *dead*, thy kingdom cannot buy *my* breath."

Rich. II. i. 3. 232.

i.e. "the breath of me when dead."

" It is an obvious conjecture from this use of "absent," "present,"
"dead," that their quasi-participial terminations favoured this participial use. But add

"Thence,
A prosperous south-wind friendly, we have cross'd."

W. T. v. 1. 161.

381. The Participle is sometimes implied in the case of
a simple word, such as "being."

" I have heard him oft maintain it to be fit that *sons* (being) *at
perfect age* and fathers declining, the father should be as ward to the
son."—*Lear*, i. 2. 77.

"And be well contented
To make your house our tower. *You* (being) *a brother* of us,
It fits we thus proceed, or else no witness
Would come against you."—*Hen. VIII.* v. 1. 106.

i.e "Since you are our brother." (Or (?) "though you were our
brother, it [would be and] is fit to proceed thus.")

"(Those locks are) often known
To be the dowry of a second head,
The skull that bred them (being) in the sepulchre."

M. of V. iii. 2. 96.

We retain this use in antithetical phrases, such as "face to face,"
"sword against sword," but we should rarely introduce an adjective
into such an antithetical compound. Shakespeare, however, has

"And answer me *declined* sword 'gainst sword."

A. and C. iii. 13. 27.

ELLIPSES.

382. Several peculiarities of Elizabethan language have already
been explained by the desire of brevity which characterised the
authors of the age. Hence arose so many elliptical expressions that
they deserve a separate treatment. The Elizabethan authors objected to scarcely any ellipsis, provided the deficiency could be easily
supplied from the context.

" Vouchsafe (to receive) good-morrow from a feeble tongue."
J. C. ii. 1. 313.

" When shall we see (one another) again ?"
Cymb. i. 1. 124 ; *Tr. and Cr.* iv. 4. 59.

Just so we still use "meet."

" You and I have known (one another), sir."
A. and C. ii. 6. 86 ; *Cymb.* i. 4. 36.

" On their sustaining garments (there is) not a blemish,
But (the garments are) fresher than before."
Tempest, i. 2. 219.

Thus also, as in Latin, a verb of speaking can be omitted where it is implied either by some other word, as in

" She *calls* me proud, and (says) that
She could not love me."—*A. Y. L.* iv. 3. 16.

" But here's a villain that would *face me down*
He met me on the mart."—*C. of E.* iii. 1. 7.

i.e. "maintain to my face that he met me ;" or by a question as in

" What are you?
(I ask) Your name and quality ; and why you answer
This present summons."—*Lear,* v. 3. 120.

(The Globe inserts a note of interrogation after quality.)

" Enforce him with his envy to the people,
And (say) that the spoil got on the Antiates
Was ne'er distributed."—*Coriol.* iii. 3. 4.

Thus, by implying from "forbid" a word of speaking, "bid," and not by a double negative, we should perhaps explain

" You may as well forbid the mountain pines
To wag their high tops and (bid them) to make no noise."
M. of V. iv. 1. 76.

Thus   " I know not whether to depart in silence
Or bitterly to speak in your reproof
Best fitteth my degree or your condition.
If (I thought it fittest) not to answer, you might haply
think," &c.—*Rich. III.* iii. 7. 144.

After " O !" "alas !" and other exclamations, a verb of surprise or regret is sometimes omitted.

" *O* (it is pitiful) that deceit should steal such gentle shapes."
Rich. III. ii. 2. 27.

"Good God ! (I marvel that) these nobles should such stomachs bear :
I myself fight not once in forty year."—1 *Hen. VI.* i. 3. 90.

Sometimes no exclamation is inserted :

> "Ask what thou wilt. (I would) That I had said and done."
> > 2 *Hen. VI.* i. 3. 31.

Ellipses in Conjunctional Sentences. The Elizabethans seem to have especially disliked the repetition which is now considered necessary, in the latter of two clauses connected by a relative or a conjunction.

383. And:

> "Have you
> Ere now denied the asker, *and* now again
> Of him that did not ask but mock (do you) bestow
> Your sued-for tongues?"—*Coriol.* ii. 3. 213.

Here in strictness we ought to have "bestowed," or "do you bestow."

An ellipse must be supplied proleptically in

> "(Beggars) Sitting in the stocks refuge their shame,
> That (*i.e.* because) many have (sat), *and* many must sit
> there."—*Rich. II.* v. 5. 27.
>
> "Of (such) dainty *and* such picking grievances."
> > 2 *Hen. IV.* iv. 1. 196.
>
> "It (*i.e.* love) shall be (too) sparing *and* too full of riot."
> > *V. and A.* 1147.
>
> "It shall be (too) merciful *and* too severe."—*Ib.* 1155.

384. As:

> "His ascent is not so easy *as* (the ascent of) those who," &c.
> > *Coriol.* ii. 2. 30.
>
> "Returning were *as* tedious as (to) go o'er."—*Macb.* iii. 4. 138.
>
> "They boldly press so far *as* (modern Eng. *that*) further none
> (press)."—B. J. *Cy.'s Rev.* v. 3.
>
> > "O, 'tis sweating labour
> To bear such idleness so near the heart
> *As* Cleopatra (bears) this."—*A. and C.* i. 3. 95.
>
> "And I, that haply take them from him now,
> May yet ere night yield both my life and them
> To some man else, *as* this dead man doth (to) me."
> > 3 *Hen. VI.* ii. 5. 60.
>
> "Return those duties back *as* (they) are most fit (to be returned)."
> > *Lear,* i. 1. 99.

As can scarcely, in the above, be taken for "which."

" This is a strange thing (as strange) *as* e'er I look'd on."

Temp. v. i. 289.

385. But (after *but* the finite verb is to be supplied *without* the negative) :

"The tender nibbler would not take the bait
But (would) smile and jest."—*P. P.* 4.

"To be thus is nothing,
But to be safely thus (is something)."—*Macbeth,* iii. i. 47.

"And though I could
With barefaced power sweep him from my sight
And bid my will avouch it, yet I must not,
(For certain friends that are both his and mine,
Whose loves I may not drop,) *but* (I must) wail his fall
Who I myself struck down."—*Macbeth,* iii. i. 119.

Sometimes *but* itself is omitted :

"'Tis not my profit that doth lead mine honour,
(*But* it is) Mine honour (that doth lead) it (*i.e.* profit)."

A. and C. ii. 7. 83.

Sometimes the repeated varies slightly from the original proposition :

"'Tis not enough to help the feeble up,
But (it is necessary) to support him after."—*T. of A.* i. i. 107.

In the following, the negative is *implied* in the first verb through *the question,* " Why need we ?" *i.e.* " We need not." The second verb *must not be taken interrogatively,* and thus it omits the negative.

"Why, what need we
Commune with you of this, *but* rather follow
Our forceful indignation ?"—*W. T.* ii. i. 162.

i.e. " Why need we commune with you? we need rather follow our own impulse." Else, if both verbs be taken interrogatively, " but " must be taken as " and *not :*" " Why need we commune with you, and *not* follow our own impulse ?"

Where the negative is part of the subject, as in " none," a new subject must be supplied :

" God, I pray him
That *none* of you may live your natural age
But (each of you) by some unlook'd accident cut off."

Rich. III. i. 3. 214.

386. Ere:

" The rabble should have first unroof'd the city
Ere (they should have) so prevail'd with me."—*Coriol.* i. i. 223.

" I'll lean upon one crutch and fight with the other
  Ere (I will) stay behind this business."—*Coriol.* i. 1. 246.

387. If:

" I am more serious than my custom ; you
  Must be so too, if (*you must* or *intend to*) heed me."
  Temp. ii. 1. 220.

See "must," 314.

" I yet beseech your majesty
  If (it is) for (*i.e.* because) I want that glib and oily art
  . . . That you make known," &c.—*Lear*, i. 1. 227.

"   O, if (you be) a virgin
  And your affection (be) not gone forth, I'll make you
  The queen of Naples."—*Tempest*, i. 2. 447–8.

" Haply you shall not see me more, or *if* (you see me),
  (You will see me) A mangled shadow."—*A. and C.* iv. 1. 27.

This is a good Greek idiom.   So

" Not like a corse : or *if*, not to be buried,
  But quick, and in mine arms."—*W. T.* iv. 4. 131.

In the following hypothetical sentence there is a curious ellipsis :

" Love, loving not itself, none other can."—*Rich. II.* v. 2. 88.

i.e. " if a man does not love his own flesh and blood he cannot (love)
a stranger."

388. Like (*i.e.* resembling) :

"But you *like* none, none (like) you, for constant heart."—*Sonn.*

388a. Or :

" For women's fear and love holds quantity ;
  In neither (is) aught, or (it is) in extremity."
  Hamlet, iii. 2. 178.

i.e. " women's fear and love vary together, are proportionable : they
either contain nothing, or what they contain is in extremes."

389. Since :

"Be guilty of my death *since* (thou art guilty) of my crime."
  R. of L.

390. Than :

" To see sad sights moves more *than* (to) hear them told."
  R. of L. 451.

"It cost more to get *than* (was fit) to lose in a day."*
B. J. *Poetaster.*

" Since I suppose we are made to be no stronger
  Than (that) faults may shake our frames."
M. for M. ii. 4. 133.

"But I am wiser *than* (I should be were I) to serve their
  precepts."—B. J. *E. out &c.* i. 1.
" My form
Is yet the cover of a fairer mind
Than (that which is fit) to be butcher of an innocent child."
K. J. iv. 2. 258.

"This must be known ; which being kept close might move
 More grief to hide, *than* hate to utter (would move) love."
Hamlet, i. 1. 108–9.

i.e. "this ought to be revealed, for it (273), by being suppressed,
might excite more grief in the king and queen by the hiding (356)
of the news, than our unwillingness to tell bad news would excite
love."

"What need we any spur but our own cause
 To prick us to redress ?   What other bond
 Than (that of) secret Romans?"—*J. C.* ii. 1. 125.

As in the case of "but " (385), so in the following, the verb must
be repeated without its negative force :

"I heard you say that you had rather refuse
 The offer of an hundred thousand crowns
 Than (have) Bolingbroke's return to England."
Rich. II. iv. 1. 17.

Here, perhaps, the old use of the subjunctive "had " for "would
have " exerts some influence.

The word "rather" must be supplied from the termination *er* in

" The rar*er* action is
In virtue (rather) than in vengeance."—*Temp.* v. 1. 28.

"You are well understood to be a perfect*er* giber for the table
than a necessary bencher in the Capitol."—*Coriol.* ii. 1. 91.

391. Though:

" Saints do not more, *though* (saints) grant for prayers' sake."
R. and J. i. 5. 107.

" I keep but two men and a boy (as) yet, till my mother be dead.
  But what *though ?*   Yet I live like a poor gentleman Lorn."
M. W. of W. i. 1. 287.

---

* Compare the Greek idiom.—*Jelf,* ii. 863. 2. 2.

392. Till :

    "He will not hear till (he) feel."—*T. of A.* ii. 2. 7.

393. Too . . . . to :

    "His worth is *too* well known (for him) *to* be forth-coming."
                     B. J. *E. out &c.* v. 1.

394. Relative. (In relative sentences the preposition is often not repeated.)

    "Most ignorant of *what* he's most assured (ot)."
                     M. for M. ii. 2. 119.
    "A gift of all (of *which*) he dies possess'd."—*M. of V.* iv. 1. 389.
    "Err'd in this point (in) *which* now you censure him."
                     M. for M. ii. 1. 15.
    "For that (for) *which*, if myself might be his judge,
    He should receive his punishment in thanks."—*Ib.* i. 4. 28.
    "I do pronounce him in that very shape
    (In *which*) He shall appear in proof."—*Hen. VIII.* i. 1. 196.
    "As well appeareth by the cause (for *which*) you come."
                     Rich. II. i. 1. 26.
    "In this (in or of) *which* you accuse her."—*W. T.* ii. 1. 133.
    "In that behalf (in) *which* we have challenged it."
                     K. J. ii. 1. 264.
    "To die upon the bed (upon *which*) my father died."
                     W. T. iv. 4. 466.
    "In such a cause as fills mine eyes with tears,
    And stops my tongue *while* (my) heart is drown'd in cares."
                     3 *Hen. VI.* iii. 3. 14.

There is a proleptic omission in

    "Or (upon) *whom* frown'st thou *that* I do fawn upon."
                     Sonn. 149.

395. Antithetical sentences frequently do not repeat pronouns, verbs, &c.

    "What most he should dislike seems pleasant to him,
    What (he should) like, (seems) offensive."—*Lear,* iv. 2. 10.

Sometimes the verb has to be repeated in a different tense.

    "To know our enemies' minds we 'ld rip their hearts:
    (To rip) Their papers is more lawful."—*Lear,* iv. 6. 266.
    "To be acknowledg'd, madam, is (to be) overpaid."
                     Ib. iv. 7. 4.

The antithesis often consists in the opposition between past and present time.

> " I meant to rectify my conscience, which
> I *then did feel* full sick, and *yet* (do feel) not well."
> > *Hen. VIII.* ii. 4. 204.

> " And may that soldier a mere recreant prove
> That means not (to be), hath not (been), or is not in love."
> > *Tr. and Cr.* i. 3. 288.

> " She *was* beloved, she *loved;* she *is* (beloved) and *doth* (love)."
> > *Ib.* iv. 5. 292.

396. Ellipsis of Neither before Nor, One before Other.

> " (Neither) He *nor* that affable familiar ghost."—*Sonn.* 86.

> "But (neither) my five wits *nor* my five senses can
> Dissuade one foolish heart from seeing thee."—*Ib.* 141.

> " A thousand groans . . .
> Came (one) on an*other's* neck."—*Ib.* 131.

> " *Pomp.* You will not bail me then, sir.
> *Lucio.* (Neither) Then, Pompey, *nor* now."
> > *M. for M.* iii. 2. 86.

397. Ellipsis of Adverbial and other Inflections.

> " The duke of Norfolk sprightfully and bold(ly)."
> > *Rich. II.* i. 3. 3.

> " Good gentlemen, look fresh(ly) and merrily."—*J. C.* ii. 1. 224.

> " Apt(ly) and willingly."—*T. N.* v. 1. 135.

> " With sleided silk, feat(ly) and affectedly."—*L. C.* 48.

> " His grace looks cheerfully and smooth(ly) this morning."
> > *Rich. III.* iii. 4. 50.

> " And she will speak most bitterly and strange(ly)."
> > *M. for M.* v. 1. 36.

> " How honourable(y) and how kindly we
> Determine."—*A. and C.* v. 1. 58.

> " And that so lamely and unfashionable(y)."—*Rich. III.* i. 1. 22.

It will not escape notice (1) that in all but two of these instances the *-ly* is omitted after *monosyllabic* adjectives, which can be more readily used as adverbs without change ; (2) that "honourable," "unfashionable," &c., in their old pronunciation would approximate to "honourably," "unfashionably," and the former is itself used as an adverb. (See 1.) Nevertheless it seems probable that this, like the following idiom, and like many others, arises partly from the readiness with which a compound phrase connected by a conjunction is regarded as one and inseparable. Compare

" Until her husband('s) and my lord's return."—*M. of V.* iii. 4. 30.

" As soul('s) and body's severing."—*Hen. VIII.* ii. 3. 16.

where " soul-and-body " is a quasi-noun.

" Shall be your love('s) and labour's recompense."

Rich. II. ii. 3. 62.

398. Ellipsis of Superlative Inflection.

" The *generous* and gravest citizens."—*M. for M.* iv. 6. 13.

" Only the *grave* and wisest of the land."—HEYWOOD (Walker).

" The *soft* and sweetest music."—B. J. (*Ib.*).

" The *vain* and haughtiest minds the sun e'er saw."

GOFFE (*Ib.*).

" To mark the *full*-fraught man and best endued."

Hen. V. ii. 2. 139.

" The *humble* as the proudest sail doth bear."—*Sonn.* 80.

The *est* of the second adjective modifies the first.

Reversely we have—

"The best condition'd and unwearied spirit,"—*M. of V.* iii. 2. 295.

where " best " modifies the second adjective.

" Call me the *horrid'st* and *unhallow'd* thing
That life and nature tremble at."—MIDDLETON (Walker).

In " I took him for the plainest harmless creature,"

Rich. III. iii. 4. 25.

though the meaning may be "the plainest, (the most) harmless creature," it is more likely a compound word, "plainest-harmless" (see 2).

399. Ellipsis of Nominative. Where there can be no doubt what is the nominative, it is sometimes omitted.

" It was upon this fashion bequeathed me by will, but poor a thousand crowns, and as thou sayest *charged* my brother, on his blessing, to breed me well."—*A. Y. L.* i. 1. 3.

" They call him Doricles : and *boasts* himself
To have a worthy feeding."—*W. T.* iv. 4. 168.

" Who loved her so, that speaking of her foulness
(He) *Washed* it with tears."*—*M. Ado,* iv. 1. 156.

" (It) shall not be long but I'll be here again."

Macbeth, iv. 2. 23.

" Nor do we find him forward to be sounded,
But with a crafty madness *keeps* aloof."—*Hamlet,* iii. 1. 8.

* "That" might (but for, 260) be treated as a relative pronoun.

This explains *K. J.* ii. 1. 571, and

> "When I am very sure, if they should speak,
> (They) *Would* almost damn those ears which," &c.
>
> *M. of V.* i. 1. 97.

Compare

> "Come, fortune's a jade, I care not who tell her,
> (Who, *i.e.* since she) *Would* offer to strangle a page of the
> cellar."—B. and F.

> "The king must take it ill
> That he's so slightly valued in his messenger,
> (*That he* or ? *you*) *Should* have him thus restrained."
>
> *Lear*, ii. 2. 154.

So *Hen. VIII.* i. 2. 197.

The following might be explained by transposition, "may all" for "all may:" but more probably "they" is implied :

> "That he awaking when the other do,
> May all to Athens back again repair."
>
> *M. N. D.* iv. 1. 72.   See also *Ib.* v. i. 98.

400. The omission of the Nominative is most common with "has," "is," "was," &c.

"He has" is frequently pronounced and sometimes written "has," and "he" easily coalesces with "was,"* "will," &c.   Hence these cases should be distinguished from those in the preceding paragraph.

> "And to the skirts of this wild wood he came,
> Where, meeting with an old religious man,
> After some question with him *was* converted."
>
> *A. Y. L.* v. 4. 167.

"This young gentlewoman had a father whose skill was almost as great as his honesty : had it stretch'd so far, *would* have made nature immortal."—*A. W.* i. 1. 20.

> "*Hero.* I'll wear this.
> *Marg.* By my troth, *'s* not so good."—*M. Ado*, iii. 4. 9 and 18.

> "For Cloten
> There wants no diligence in seeking him,
> And (he) *will* no doubt be found."—*Cymb.* iv. 3. 21.

> "For I do know Fluellen valiant.
> And, touch'd with choler, hot as gunpowder ;
> And quickly *will* return an injury."—*Hen. V.* iv. 7. 188.

> "This is that banish'd haughty Montague,
> And here *is* come."—*R. and J.* v. 3. 52.

* See 461.

" As for Cromwell,
Beside that of the jewel-house, (he) *is* made master
O' the rolls."—*Hen. VIII.* v. i. 34 ; 50.
" I know the gentleman ; and, as you say,
There (he) *was* a' gaming."—*Hamlet,* ii. 1. 58.
" Bring him forth ; *has* sat in the stocks all night," &c.
A. W. iv. 3. 116.
So *Ib.* 114, 298 ; *T. N.* i. 5. 156.
" 'Tis his own blame : *hath* put himself from rest."
Lear, ii. 4. 293.
Ib. iii. 1. 5 ; *Othello,* iii. 1. 67 ; *T. of A.* iii. 2. 39, iii. 3. 23, iv.
3. 463.   This omission is frequent after appellatives or oaths.
" *Poor jade, is* wrung in the withers out of all 'cess."
1 *Hen. IV.* ii. 1. 6.
" *Poor fellow,* never *joyed* since the price of oats rose."—*Ib.* 11.
" *Richard.*   Send for some of them.
Ely.   Marry, and *will,* my lord, with all my heart."
Rich. III. iii. 4. 36.
In   " And the fair soul herself,
Weigh'd between loathness and obedience, at
Which end o' the beam *should* bow,"—*Tempest,* ii. 1. 131.
either " she " is omitted, or "should" is for "she would," or " o' "
has been inserted by mistake.

401. A Nominative in the second person plural or first person
is less commonly omitted.

" They all rush by
And leave you hindermost ;
Or like a gallant horse, fall'n in first rank,
(You) *Lie* there for pavement to the abject rear."
Tr. and Cr. iii. 3. 162.
" They . . . gave me cold looks,
And, meeting here the other messenger,
Having more man than wit about me, (I) drew."
Lear, ii. 4. 42.
The *I* before " pray thee," "beseech thee," is constantly omitted.
(*Tempest,* ii. 1. 1.)
" Good-morrow, fair ones ;
(I) pray you if you know."—*A. Y. L.* iv. 3. 76.
i.e. " I ask you whether you know."
The inflection of the second person singular allows the nominative
to be readily understood, and therefore justifies its omission.

"*Art* any more than a steward?"—*T. N.* ii. 3. 122.
" It was she
First told me thou wast mad; then (thou) *cam'st* in smiling."
Ib. v. i. 357.

402. Ellipsis of Nominative explained. This ellipsis of
the nominative may perhaps be explained partly (1) by the lingering
sense of inflections, which of themselves are sometimes sufficient to
indicate the person of the pronoun understood, as in Milton—

"Thou art my son beloved : in him *am* pleased ;"

partly (2) by the influence of Latin ; partly (3) by the rapidity of
the Elizabethan pronunciation, which frequently changed "he" into
" 'a" (a change also common in E. E.),

" 'a must needs,"—2 *Hen. VI.* iv. 2. 59.

and prepared the way for dropping "he" altogether.   Thus perhaps
in   "Who if *alive* and ever dare to challenge this glove, I have
sworn to take him a box o' th' ear,"—*Hen. V.* iv. 7. 132.

we should read "'a live and ever dare."   In the French of Rabelais
the pronouns are continually dropped : but the fuller inflections in
French render the omission less inconvenient than in English.   In
the following instance there is an ambiguity which is only removed
by the context :—

"We two saw you four set on four ; and (you) bound them
and were masters of their wealth."—1 *Hen. IV.* ii. 4. 278.

403. Ellipsis of It is, There is, Is.
" So beauty blemish'd once (is) for ever lost."—*P. P.* 13.
" I cannot give guess how near (it is) to day."—*J. C.* ii. 1. 2.
" Seldom (is it) when
The steeled gaoler is the friend of men."
M. for M. iv. 2. 90.
" And (it is) wisdom
To offer up a weak poor innocent lamb."—*Macb.* iv. 3. 16.
" Since [there is neither (163)] brass nor stone nor earth nor
boundless sea,
But sad mortality o'ersways their power."—*Sonn.* 64.
"'Tis certain, every man that dies ill, the ill (is) upon his
own head."—*Hen. V.* iv. 1. 197.
" Many years,
Though Cloten (was) then but young, you see, not wore him
From my remembrance."—*Cymb.* iv. 4. 23.

So *Hen. V.* iv. 7. 132 (quoted in 402), if the text be retained.
It is a question whether "are" is omitted, or whether (less probably) (**And,** 95) "and" is used for "also" with a nom. absolute, in

"But 'tis not so above ;
There is no shuffling, there the action lies
In his true nature : and we ourselves (? are) compelled
To give in evidence."—*Hamlet*, iii. 3. 62 ; *T. N.* i. 1. 38 ;
Hen. V. i. 1. 57.

"Which I did store to be my foster-nurse,
When service should in my old limbs lie lame,
And unregarded age (? should be) in corners thrown."
A. Y. L. ii. 2. 42.

As the verb is omitted by us constantly after "whatever," *e.g.* "anything whatever," so Shakespeare could write,

"Beyond all limit of *what else* (is) in the world."
Temp. iii. 1. 172.

Thus also "however" is for "however it may be," *i.e.* "in any case :"

"If haply won perhaps a hapless gain ;
If lost, why then a grievous labour won ;
However (*it be*), but a folly bought with wit."
T. G. of V. i. 1. 34.

We have passed in the use of "however" from the meaning "in spite of what *may happen* in the *future*," to "in spite of what *happened* in the *past*," *i.e.* "nevertheless."

"There is" is often omitted with "no one but," as

"(There is) *no one* in this presence
But his red colour hath forsook his cheeks."
Rich. III. ii. 1. 84.

"Who is" (244) is omitted in

"Here's a young maid (who is) with travel much oppressed,
And faints for succour."—*A. Y. L.* ii. 4. 75.

Otherwise the nominative (399) is omitted before "faints."

404. Ellipsis of It and There.

"Whose wraths to guard you from,
Which here in this most desolate isle else falls
Upon your head, (there) is nothing but heart-sorrow,
And a clear life ensuing."—*Temp.* iii. 2. 82.

"Satisfaction (there) can be none but by pangs of death."
T. N. iii. 4. 261

" *D. Pedro.* What ! sigh for the toothache?
Leon. Where (there) is but a humour or a worm."
M. Ado, iii. 2. 27 ; *Ib.* ii. 2. 20.
" At the Elephant (it) is best to lodge."—*T. N.* iii. 3. 40.
" Be (it) what it is."—*Cymb.* v. 4. 149.
" The less you meddle with them the more (it) is for your
honesty."—*M. Ado,* iii. 3. 56.

The omission is common before "please."

" So *please* (it) him (to) come unto this place."—*J. C.* iii. 1. 140.
" Is (*it*) then unjust to each his due to give ?"
SPENS. *F. Q.* i. 9. 38.
" (*It*) remains
That in the official marks invested you
Anon do meet the Senate."—*Coriol.* ii. 3. 147.

This construction is quite as correct as our modern form with
"*it.*" The sentence "That in . . . . Senate," is the subject to
" remains." So—

" And that in Tarsus (*it*) was not best
Longer for him to make his rest."—*Pericl.* ii. Gower, 25.
" Happiest of all is (*it* or *this*), that her gentle spirit
Commits itself to you to be directed."—*M. of V.* iii. 2. 166.

We see how unnecessary and redundant our modern " it " is from
the following passage :—

" Unless self-charity be sometimes a vice,
And to defend ourselves *it* be a sin."—*Othello,* ii. 3. 203.

This is (if the order of the words be disregarded) as good English as
our modern " Unless *it* be a sin to defend ourselves." The fact is,
this use of the modern "it" is an irregularity only justified by the
clearness which it promotes. "It" at the beginning of a sentence
calls attention to the real subject which is to follow. "*It* is a sin,
viz. to defend oneself."

The sentence is sometimes placed as the object, "it" being
omitted.

" But long she thinks (*it*) till he return again."—*R. of L.* 454.

"Being" is often used for "it being," or "being so," very much
like ὄν and its compounds in Greek.

" That Lepidus of the triumvirate
Should be deposed ; and, (it) *being* (so), that we detain
All his revenue."—*A. and C.* iii. 6. 30.

" I learn you take things ill which are not so
Or, *being* (so), concern you not."—*A. and C.* ii. 2. 30.

405. Ellipses after will and is.

"I *will*," i.e. "I purpose," when followed by a preposition of
motion, might naturally be supposed to mean "I *purpose* motion."
Hence, as we have

"He *purposeth* to Athens,"—*A. and C.* iii. 1. 35.

so   "*I'll to* him."—*R. and J.* iii. 2. 141.

"*Will* you *along?*"—*Coriol.* ii. 3. 157.

"Now we'*ll* together."—*Macbeth*, iv. 3. 136.

"I *will* to-morrow,
And betimes I *will*, *to* the weird sisters."—*Ib.* iii. 4. 133.

"Strange things I have in head that *will to* hand."
Ib. iii. 4. 139.

Compare

"Give these fellows some means (of access) *to* the king."
Hamlet, iv. 6. 13.

Similarly, as we have

"I *must* (go) to Coventry."—*Rich. II.* i. 2. 56.

"I *must* (go) a dozen mile to-night."—*2 Hen. IV.* iii. 2. 310.

so   "And he to England *shall* along with you."—*Hamlet*, iii. 3. 4.

We still say, " He *is* (journeying) for Paris," but not

" He *is* (ready) for no gallants' company without them."
B. J. *E. out &c.* i. 1.

"Any ordinary groom *is* (fit) for such payment."
Hen. VIII. v. 1. 174.

So *T. N.* iii. 3. 46 ; *A. W.* iii. 6. 109.

"I *am* (bound) to thank you for it."—*T. of A.* i. 2. 111.

Such an ellipsis explains

"Run from her guardage to the sooty bosom
Of such a thing as thou, (a thing *fit*) to fear (*act.*), not to
delight."—*Othello*, i. 2. 71.

Again, we might perhaps say, "This *is* not a sky (fit) to walk
under," but not

"This sky *is* not (fit) to walk in."—*J. C.* i. 3. 39.

The modern distinction in such phrases appears to be this : when
the noun follows *is*, there is an ellipse of " fit," "worthy :" when
the noun precedes *is*, there is an ellipse of "intended," "made."

Thus : "this *is* a book to read" means "this *is* a book *worthy* to read ;" but, "this book *is* to read and not to tear," means "this book *is intended* or made for the purpose of reading." This distinction was not recognized by the Elizabethans. When we wish to express "worthy" elliptically, we insert *a:* "He *is a* man to respect," or we use the passive, and say, "He *is* to be respected." Shakespeare could have written "He *is* to respect" in this sense. The Elizabethans used the active in many cases where we should use the passive. Thus—

> "Little is *to do.*"—*Macbeth,* v. 7. 28.
> "What's more *to do.*"—*Ib.* v. 8. 64; *A. and C.* ii. 6. 60;
>   *J. C.* iii. 1. 26 ; 2 *Hen. VI.* iii. 2. 3.

Hence "This food is not to eat" might in Shakespeare's time have meant "This food is not *fit* to eat;" now, it could only mean "*intended* to eat." Similarly "videndus" in Cicero meant "one who *ought* to be seen," "*worthy* to be seen ;" but in poetry and in later prose it meant "one who *may* be seen," "visible."

The following passages illustrate the variable nature of this ellipsis :—   "I have been a debtor to you

> For curtesies which I *will be* ever to pay you,
> And yet pay still."—*Cymb.* i. 4. 39.

i.e. "kindnesses which I *intend* to be always *ready* to pay you, and yet to go on paying."

We still retain an ellipsis of "under necessity" in the phrase

> "I *am* (yet) to learn."—*M. of V.* i. 1. 5.

But we should not say :

> "That ancient Painter who *being* (under necessity) to represent

the griefe of the bystanders," &c.—MONTAIGNE, 3.

We should rather translate literally from Montaigne : "Ayant à représenter."

In   "I *am* to break with thee of some affairs,"

>   *T. G. of V.* iii. 1. 59.

the meaning is partly of desire and partly of necessity: "I want."

So Bottom says to his fellows :

> "O, masters, I *am* (ready) to discourse wonders."
>   *M. N. D.* iv. 2. 29.

The ellipsis is "sufficient" in

> "Mark Antony is every hour in Rome
> Expected ; since he went from Egypt '*tis*
> A space (sufficient) for further travel."—*A. and C.* ii. 1. 31.

IRREGULARITIES.

406. Double Negative.—Many irregularities may be explained by the desire of emphasis which suggests repetition, even where repetition, as in the case of a negative, neutralizes the original phrase :

> "First he *denied* you had in him *no* right."
>
> > *C. of E.* iv. 2. 7.
>
> "You may *deny* that you were *not* the cause."
>
> > *Rich. III.* i. 3. 90.
>
> "*Forbade* the boy he should *not* pass these bounds."—*P. P.* 9.
>
> "*No* sonne, were he* never so old of yeares, might *not* marry."—ASCH. 37.

This idiom is a very natural one, and quite common in E. E.

Double Comparative and Superlative. See Adjectives, 11.

407. Double Preposition. Where the verb is at some distance from the preposition with which it is connected, the preposition is frequently repeated for the sake of clearness.

> "And generally *in* all shapes that man goes up and down in, from fourscore to thirteen, this spirit walks *in*."
>
> > *T. of A.* ii. 2. 119.
>
> "For *in* what case shall wretched I be *in*."—DANIEL.
>
> "But *on* us both did haggish age steal *on*."—*A. W.* i. 2. 29.
>
> "The scene where*in* we play *in*."—*A. Y. L.* ii. 7. 139.
>
> "*In* what enormity is Marcius poor *in ?*"—*Coriol.* ii. 1. 18.
>
> "*To* what form but that he is, should wit larded with malice, and malice forced with wit, turn him *to?*"—*Tr. and Cr.* v. 1. 63.

408. "Neither ... nor," used like "Both ... and," followed by "not."

> "Not the king's crown *nor* the deputed sword,
> The marshal's truncheon *nor* the judge's robe,
> *Become* them," &c.—*M. for M.* ii. 2. 60.

---

* The use of "never so" is to be explained (as in Greek, θαυμαστὸν ὅσον) by an ellipsis. Thus—

"Though *ne'er so* richly parted (endowed)."—*E. out &c.* iii. 1.

means—"Though he were endowed richly—though *never* a man were endowed *so* richly."

This very natural irregularity (natural, since the *unbecomingness* may be regarded as predicated *both* of the "king's crown," the "deputed sword," *and* the "marshal's truncheon") is very common.

> "He *nor* that affable familiar ghost
> That nightly gulls him with intelligence
> As *victors* of my silence çannot (406) boast."—*Sonn.* 86.

The following passage may perhaps be similarly explained :

> "He* waived indifferently '*twixt* doing them *neither* good *nor* harm."—*Coriol.* ii. 2. 17.

But it is perhaps more correct to say that there is here a confusion of two constructions, "He waived 'twixt good and harm, doing them neither good nor harm." The same confusion of two constructions is exemplified below in the use of the superlative.

409. Confusion of two Constructions in Superlatives.

> "This is the *greatest* error *of all the rest.*"—*M. N. D.* v. 1. 252.
> "*Of all other* affections it is the most importune."—B. *E. Envy.*
> "York is *most unmeet* of any man."—*2 Hen. VI.* i. 3. 167.
> "*Of all men else* I have avoided thee."—*Macbeth*, v. 8. 4.
> "He hath simply the *best wit of any handicraft-man* in Athens."
> *M. N. D.* iv. 2. 9.
> "To try whose right,
> *Of thine or mine,** is *most* in Helena."—*Ib.* iii. 2. 337.
> "I do not like the tower *of any place.*"—*Rich. III.* iii. 1. 68.

This (which is a thoroughly Greek idiom, though independent in English) is illustrated by Milton's famous line—

> "The *fairest of her daughters* Eve."

The line is a confusion of two constructions, "Eve fairer *than* all her daughters," and "Eve fairest *of* all women." So "I dislike the tower *more than any place,*" and "*most of all places,*" becomes "*of any place.*"

Our modern "He is the best man that I have ever seen," seems itself to be incorrect, if "that" be the relative to "man." It may, perhaps, be an abbreviation of "He is the best man of the men that I have ever seen."

---

* Comp. if the reading be retained—
> "Which, of he *or* Adrian, begins to crow?"—*Temp.* i. 1. 29.

410. Confusion of two constructions with "whom."

"Young Ferdinand *whom* they suppose *is drown'd*."

Temp. iii. 2. 92.

"Of Arthur *whom* they say *is killed* to-night."—*K. J.* iv. 2. 165.

"The nobility . . . *whom* we see *have sided*."—*Coriol.* iv. 2. 2.

So in *St. Matt.* xvi. 13, all the versions except Wickliffe's have "*Whom* do men say that I, the son of man, *am?*" Wickliffe has "*Whom* seien men *to be* mannes sone?"

The last passage explains the idiom. It is a confusion of two constructions, *e.g.* "Ferdinand *who*, they suppose, *is drowned*," and "*whom* they suppose *to be drowned*."

411. Other confusions of two constructions.

"Why I do trifle thus with his despair
Is done to cure it,"—*Lear*, iv. 6. 33.

combines "*Why* I trifle is *to cure*" and "*My trifling is done* to cure." In itself it is illogical.

"The battle done, *and* they within our power
Shall never see his pardon,"—*Lear*, v. 1. 67.

is a confusion of "*let* the battle *be* done, *and* they" and "the battle (being) done, they."

"I saw not better sport *these seven years day*."—2 *Hen. VI.* ii. 1. 3.
A combination of "since *this* day seven years" and "during *these* seven years."

"Out of all 'cess (excess),"—1 *Hen. IV.* ii. 1. 6.
is a confusion of "to *excess*," or "in *excess*," and "*out of* all bounds." "So late ago," *T. N.* v. 1. 22, seems a combination of "*so lately*" and "*so* short a time *ago*,"

"Marry that, I think, *be* young Petruchio,"—*R. and J.* i. 5. 133.
is a confusion of "That, I think, *is*" and "I think that that *be*." For the subjunctive after "think," see **Subjunctive**, 368 and 299.
So, perhaps,

"This youth, howe'er distressed, *appears* he *hath had*
Good ancestors,"—*Cymb.* iv. 2. 47.

is a confusion of "He hath had, (it) appears, good ancestors," and "He appears to have had." This is, perhaps, better than to take "appears" as an active verb. See 295. Precisely similar is :

"Let what is meet be said, it must be meet."—*Coriol.* iii. 1. 170.

combining "Let what is meet be said *to be*" and "Let it be said (that) what is meet must be meet."

Compare 353, and add, as a confusion of the infinitive and imperative,

"There is no more but (*to*) *say* so."—*Rich. III.* iv. 2. 81.

In "We would have had you *heard*," *Ib. III.* iii. 5. 56, there may be some confusion between "you should have heard" and "we would have had you hear;" but more probably the full construction is "We would have had you (to have) heard (360)," and "to have" is omitted through dislike of repetition. So *Coriol.* iv. 6. 35 (415):
"We should . . . *found* it so."

Compare also

"He would have had me (to have) *gone* into the steeple-house."
Fox's *Journal* (ed. 1765), p. 57.

"He would have had me (to have) *had* a meeting."—*Ib.* p. 60.

412. Confusion of proximity. The following (though a not uncommon Shakespearian idiom) would be called an unpardonable mistake in modern authors :—

"The *posture* of your *blows are* yet unknown."—*J. C.* v. 1. 33.

"Whose *loss* of his most precious *queen* and *children*
Are even now to be afresh lamented."—*W. T.* iv. 1. 26.

"Which now the loving *haste* of these dear *friends*
Somewhat against our meaning *have* prevented."
Rich. III. iii. 5. 56.

"The *venom* of such *looks*, we fairly hope,
Have lost their quality."—*Hen. V.* v. 2. 19.

"But yet the *state* of *things require*."—DANIEL, *Ulysses and Siren.*

"The *approbation* of *those* . . . *are*," &c.—*Cymb.* i. 4. 17.

"How the *sight*
Of those smooth rising *cheeks renew* the story
Of young Adonis."—B. F. *F. Sh.* i. 1.

"*Equality* of two domestic *powers*
Breed scrupulous faction."—*A. and C.* i. 3. 48.

"The *voice* of all the *gods*
Make heaven drowsy."—*L. L. L.* iv. 3. 345.

Here, however, "voice" may be (471) for "voices."

"Then know
The *peril* of our *curses* light on thee."—*K. J.* iii. 1. 295.

> "The very *thought* of my *revenges* that way
> Recoil upon myself."—*W. T.* ii. 3. 20.
>> "More than the *scope*
>> Of these delated *articles allow.*"—*Hamlet*, i. 2. 38.

The subjunctive is not required, and therefore "have" is probably plural, in

> "If the *scorn* of your bright *eyne*
> *Have* power to raise such love in mine."—*A. Y. L.* iv. 3. 51.

In these cases the proximity of a plural noun seems to have caused the plural verb, contrary to the rules of grammar. The two nouns together connected by "of" seem regarded as a compound noun with plural termination. So

> "*These kind*-of-*knaves.*"—*Lear*, ii. 2. 107.
> "*Those* blest-*pair*-of-fixed-*stars.*"—B. and F. *F. Sh.* ii. 1.
> "*These* happy-*pair* of *lovers meet* straightway."—*Ib.*

Similarly—

> "Where *such* as *thou mayest* find him."—*Macbeth*, iv. 2. 81.

In the following instance the plural nominative is implied from the previous singular noun—

> "As *every* alien pen hath got my use,
> And under thee their poesy *disperse.*"—*Sonn.* 78.

In "And the stars whose feeble light
> *Give* a pale shadow to the night,"—B. and F. *F. Sh.* iii. 1.

perhaps "give" may be subjunctive after the relative. (See 367.)

413. Implied nominative from participial phrases. Sometimes a nominative has to be extracted ungrammatically from the *meaning* of a sentence. This is often the case in participial phrases:

> "*Beaten for loyalty*
> Excited me to treason."—*Cymb.* v. 5. 343.

i.e. "my having been beaten."

> "*The king* of his own virtuous disposition,
> *Aiming* belike at your interior hatred,
> Which in your outward actions shews itself,
> *Makes* him to send."—*Rich. III.* i. 2. 63.

i.e. "the fact that the king aims makes him to send."

414. The redundant Object. Instead of saying "I know what you are," in which the object of the verb "I know" is the clause "what you are," Shakespeare frequently introduces before the dependent clause another object, so as to make the dependent clause a mere explanation of the object.

"I know *you* what you are."—*Lear*, i. 1. 272.

"I see *you* what you are."—*T. N.* i. 4. 269.

"Conceal *me* what I am."—*Ib.* i. 2. 53.

"You hear *the learn'd Bellario* what he writes."
M. of V. iv. 1. 167.

"We'll hear *him* what he says."—*A. and C.* v. 1. 51.

"To give *me* hearing what I shall reply."
1 *Hen. VI.* iii. 1. 28.

"But wilt thou hear *me* how I did proceed?"
Hamlet, v. 2. 27.

"March on and mark *King Richard* how he looks."
Rich. II. iii. 3. 61; *Ib.* v. 4. 1.

"Sorry I am my noble cousin should
Suspect *me* that I mean no good to him."
Rich. III. iii. 7. 89.

"See the dew-drops, how they kiss
Every little flower that is."—B. and F. *F. Sh.* ii. 1.

Hence in the passive :

"The queen's in labour,
(They say in great extremity) and fear'd
She'll with the labour end,"—*Hen. VIII.* v. 1. 19.

where the active would have been "they fear the queen that she will die." For "fear" thus used, see **Prepositions**, 200.

So "no one asks about the dead man's knell for whom it is" becomes in the passive

"The dead man's knell
Is there scarce asked, for *who*,"—*Macbeth*, iv. 3. 171.

and "about which it is a wonder how his grace should glean it" becomes

"Which is a wonder *how his grace should glean it.*"
Hen. V. i. 1. 53.

This idiom is of constant occurrence in Greek ; but it is very natural after a verb of observation to put, first the primary object of observation, *e.g.* "King Richard," and then the secondary object, viz. "King Richard's looks." There is, therefore, no reason whatever for supposing that this idiom is borrowed from the Greek. After a verb of commanding the object cannot always be called redundant, as in

> "(She) bade *me*, if I had a friend that loved her,
> I should but teach him how to tell my story."
> *Othello*, i. 3. 165.

i.e. "she commanded me (that) I should," &c. But it is redundant in

> "The constable desires *thee* thou wilt mind
> Thy followers of repentance."—*Hen. V.* iv. 3. 85.

> "He wills *you* . . . that you divest yourself."—*Ib.* ii. 4. 77–8.

Compare

> "Belike they had some notice of (about) *the people*
> How I had moved them."—*J. C.* iii. 2. 275.

A somewhat different case of the redundant object is found in

> "Know you not, master, to some kind of men
> Their graces serve *them* but as enemies?
> No more do yours,"—*A. Y. L.* ii. 3. 10.

where the last line means, "your graces are not more serviceable to you."

415. Construction changed by change of thought.

"One of the prettiest touches was *when*, at the relation of the queen's death, . . . *how* attentiveness wounded his daughter."—*W. T.* v. 2. 94.

The narrator first intends to narrate the point of time, then diverges into the manner, of the action.

> "Purpose is but the slave to memory,
> Which now, like fruit unripe, *sticks* on the tree,
> But *fall* unshaken when they mellow be."—*Hamlet*, iii. 2. 201.

The subject, which is singular, is here confused with, and lost in, that to which it is compared, which is plural. Perhaps this explanation also suits:

> "And then our *arms*, like to a muzzled *bear*,
> Save in aspect *hath* all offence sealed up,"—*K. J.* ii. 1. 250.

though this may be a case of plural nominative with singular verb. (See 334.)

In the following, Henry V. begins by *dictating* a proclamation, but under the influence of indignation passes into the *imperative* of the proclamation itself:

> "Rather proclaim it, Westmoreland, through our host
> *That* he which hath no stomach to this fight
> *Let* him depart."—*Hen. V.* iv. 3. 35–6.

This is more probable than that " he " (224) is used for " man."

" Should " is treated as though it were " should have " (owing to the introduction of the conditional sentence with " had ") in the following anomalous passage :

> " We *should* by this to all our lamentation,
> If he had gone forth consul, *found* it so."—*Coriol*. iv. 6. 35.

So *Rich. III*. iii. 5. 56 (411).

The way in which a divergence can be made from the subject to *the thing compared with the subject* is illustrated by

> " So the proportions of defence are filled :
> *Which*, of a weak and niggardly projection,
> *Doth, like a miser, spoil his coat* with scanting
> A little cloth."—*Hen. V*. ii. 4. 46.

> " Whose *veins, like a dull river* far from spring
> *Is still the same*, slow, heavy, and unfit
> For stream and motion, though the strong winds hit
> With their continual power upon his sides."
> B. and F. *F. Sh*. i. 1.

> " But, good my brother,
> Do not, as some ungracious pastors do,
> Show me the steep and thorny way to heaven,
> Whiles, like a puffed and reckless libertine,
> *Himself* the primrose path of dalliance *treads*."
> *Hamlet*, i. 3. 50.

instead of " whiles you tread." But in

> " Those sleeping stones
> That, as a waist, *doth* girdle you about,
> Had been dishabited,"—*K. J*. ii. 1. 216.

" doth," probably, has " that " for its subject. See **Relative,** 247.

In

> " Are not you he
> That *frights* the maidens of the villagery,
> *Skim* milk, and sometimes *labour* in the quern
> And bootless *make* the breathless housewife churn?"
> *M. N. D*. ii. 1. 35-9.

the transition is natural from " Are not you the person who?" to " Do not you ?"

416. Construction changed for clearness. (See also 285.)

Just as (285) *that* is sometimes omitted and then inserted to connect a distant clause with a first part of a sentence, so sometimes "*to*" is inserted apparently for the same reason—

> "That God forbid, that made me first your slave,
> I *should* in thought control your times of pleasure,
> Or at your hand the account of hours *to* crave."—*Sonn.* 58.

Here "to" might be omitted, or "should" might be inserted instead, but the omission would create ambiguity, and the insertion would be a tedious repetition.

> "Heaven would that she these gifts *should* have,
> And I *to* live and die her slave."—*A. Y. L.* iii. 2. 162.

> "Keep your word, Phœbe, *that* you'*ll* marry me,
> Or else, refusing me, *to* wed this shepherd."
>
> *Ib.* v. 4. 21–2.

> "But on this condition, *that* she *should* follow him, and he not *to* follow her."—BACON, *Adv. of L.* 284.

> "The punishment was, *that they should be* put out of commons and not *to* be admitted to the table of the gods."—*Ib.* 260.

> "That we make a stand upon the ancient way, and look about us and discover what is the straight and right way, and so *to* walk in it."—B. *E.* 100.

In the following, the infinitive is used in both clauses, but the "*to*" only in the latter :—

> "In a word, a man were better relate himself to a Statue or Picture, than *to* suffer his thoughts to pass in smother."
>
> B. *E.* 103.

417. Noun Absolute. See also Redundant Pronoun, 243.

Sometimes a noun occurs in a prominent position at the beginning of a sentence, to express the subject of the thought, without the usual grammatical connection with a verb or preposition. In some cases it might almost be called *a vocative,* only that the third person instead of the second is used, and then the pronoun is not redundant. Sometimes the noun seems the real subject or object of the verb, and the pronoun seems redundant. When the noun is the object, it is probably governed by some preposition understood, "as for," "as to."

> "*My life's foul deed,* my life's fair end shall free it."—*R. of L.*
> "*The prince* that feeds great natures, they will slay him."
>
> B. J. *Sejanus,* iii. 3.

> "But *virtue,* as it never will be moved,
> So lust," &c.—*Hamlet,* i. 5. 53.

"Look when I vow, I weep; and *vows so born,*
   In their nativity all truth appears."—*M. N. D.* iii. 2. 124.
But this may be explained by 376.

"'Tis certain, *every man that dies ill,* the ill upon his own head."
—*Hen. V.* iv. 1. 197.

"But if I thrive, *the gain of my attempt*
   The least of you shall share his part thereof."
                                          Rich. III. v. 3. 267.

" *That thing* you speak of I took it for a man."—*Lear,* iv. 6. 77.

The following may be thus explained :—

"Rather proclaim it, Westmoreland, through our host,
   That *he* which hath no stomach to this fight,
   Let him depart."—*Hen. V.* iv. 3. 34.

"That can we not . . . but *he* that proves the king
   To him will we prove loyal."—*K. J.* ii. 1. 271.

" He" being regarded as the normal form of the pronoun, is appropriate for this independent position. So

"But I shall laugh at this a twelve-month hence,
   That *they* who brought me in my master's hate
   I live to look upon their tragedy."—*Rich. III.* iii. 2. 57.

These three examples might, however, come under the head of
Construction changed, 415, as the following (which closely
resembles the first) certainly does :
                     " My lord the emperor,
   Sends thee this word *that,* if thou love thy son,
   Let Marcius, Lucius, or thyself, old Titus,
   Or any one of you, chop off your hand."—*T. A.* iii. 1. 151
In this, and perhaps in the first example, the " that," like ὅτι in
Greek, is equivalent to inverted commas.

"May it please your grace, *Antipholus, my husband,*
   Whom I made lord of me, . . . this ill day
   A most outrageous fit of madness took him."
                                          C. of E. v. 1. 138.
" *The trumpery in my house,* go bring it hither."—*Temp.* iv. 1. 186.

It is, of course, possible to have an infinitive instead of a noun :

" *To strike him dead,* I hold it not a sin."—*R. and J.* i. 4. 61.

For the noun absolute with the participle, see **Participle,** 376.

418. Foreign Idioms. Several constructions in Bacon, Ascham,
and Ben Jonson, such as " ill," for " ill men " (Latin ' mali '),
" without *all* question " (' sine omni dubitatione '), seem to have been

borrowed from Latin. It is questionable, however, whether there
are many Latinisms in *construction* (Latinisms in the formation of
words are of constant occurrence) in Shakespeare. We may
perhaps quote—

> " Those dispositions that *of late transform* you
> From what you rightly are."—*Lear*, i. 4. 242.

Compare

> " He *is* ready to cry all this day,"—B. J. *Sil. Wom.* 4.

as an imitation of the Latin use of " jampridem " with the present
in the sense of the perfect. But it is quite possible that the same
thought of *continuance* may have prompted the use of the present,
both in English and Latin. " He is and has been ready to cry," &c.
The use of " more better," &c., the double negative, and the infinitive
after ' than," are certainly of English origin. The following—

> " Whispering fame
> Knowledge and proof doth to the jealous give,
> Who *than to fail* would their own thought believe," —
>
> > B. J. *Sejan.* 2.

in the omission of "rather" after "would," reminds us of the omission of "potius" after "malo." Perhaps also

> " Let that be mine,"—*M. for M.* ii. 2. 12.

is an imitation of "meum est," "It is my business."

The following resembles the Latin idiom, "post urbem conditam,"
except that there is also an ellipsis of a pronoun :

> " 'Tis our hope, sir,
> *After* (our being) *well enter'd* (as) *soldiers,* to return
> And find your grace in health."—*A. W.* ii. 1. 6.

I cannot recall another such an instance, and it is doubtful whether "after" does not here mean "hereafter :" "It is our hope
to return hereafter well-apprenticed *soldiers.*" But such participial
phrases preceded by prepositions seem to be of classical origin, as
in Milton :

> " Nor delay'd
> The winged saint *after his charge received.*"
>
> > MILTON, *P. L.* v. 248.

> " He, *after Eve seduced*, unminded slunk
> Into the wood fast by."—*Ib.* 332.

and even, contrary to the particular Latin idiom :

> " They set him free *without his ransom paid.*"—1 *Hen. VI.* iii. 3. 72.

The following resembles the Latin use of "qui si," for the English "and if he."

> "Which parti-coated presence of loose love
> Put on by us, if in your heavenly eyes
> Have misbecomed our oaths and gravities."—*L. L. L.* v. 2. 778.

419. Transposition of Adjectives.

The adjective is placed after the noun :

(1) In legal expressions in which French influence can be traced :

> "*Heir apparent.*"—1 *Hen. IV.* i. 2. 65.
> "*Heir general.*"—*Hen. V.* i. 2. 66.
> "Thou cam'st not of the *blood-royal.*"—*Ib.* 157.
> "In the *seat royal.*"—*Rich. III.* iii. 1. 164.
> "*Sport royal.*"—*T. N.* ii. 3. 187.
> "Or whether that the *body public* be a horse."
> > *M. for M.* i. 2. 163.
> "My *letters patents* (Fol.) give me leave."—*Rich. II.* ii. 3. 130.

(2) Where a relative clause, or some conjunctional clause, is understood between the noun and adjective :

> "Duncan's horses,
> (Though) *Beauteous and swift,* the minions of their race,
> Turned wild in nature."—*Macbeth,* ii. 4. 15.
> "Filling the whole realm . . . with new opinions
> (That are) *Divers and dangerous.*"—*Hen. VIII.* v. 3. 18.

Hence, where the noun is unemphatic, as "thing," "creature," this transposition may be expected :

> "In killing *creatures* (that were) *vile.*"—*Cymb.* v. 5. 252.
> "He look'd upon *things* (that are) *precious* as they were
> The common muck of the world."—*Coriol.* ii. 2. 129.

Hence, after the name of a class, the adjective is more likely to be transposed than in the case of a proper name. Thus

> "*Celestial* Dian, goddess *argentine.*"—*P. of T.* v. 2. 251.

i.e. "goddess (*that* bearest) the silver bow." The difference between a mere epithet *before* the noun, and an additional statement conveyed by an adjective *after* the noun, is illustrated by

> "If yet your *gentle* souls fly in the air
> And be not fix'd in (a) doom (that is) *perpetual.*"
> > *Rich. III.* iv. 4. 11, 12.

Similarly in

> "With eyes *severe,* and beard of formal cut."—*A. Y. L.* ii. 7. 155.

"My presence like a robe *pontifical.*"—1 *Hen. IV.* iii. 2. 56.

"eyes" and "a robe" are unemphatic, their existence being taken for granted, and the essence of the expression is in the transposed adjective.

The "three" is emphatic, and the divorcing of *some* "souls and bodies" is taken as a matter of course, in

"*Souls and bodies* hath he divorced *three.*"—*T. N.* iii. 4. 260

Somewhat similar—

"*Satisfaction* there can be *none.*"—*Ib.* 262.

This relative force is well illustrated by

"*Prince.* I fear no *uncles dead.*
Glou.   Nor *none that live,* I hope."
                              Rich. III. iii. 1. 146.

(3) Hence participles (since they imply a relative), and any adjectives that from their terminations resemble participles, are peculiarly liable to be thus transposed.

Similarly adjectives that end in *-ble*, *-ite*, and *-t*, *-ive*, *-al*, are often found after their nouns, *e.g.* "unspeakable," "unscaleable," "impregnable;" "absolute," "devout," "remote," "infinite" (often), "past," "inveterate;" "compulsative," "invasive," "defective;" "capital," "tyrannical," "virginal," "angelical," "unnatural."

(4) Though it may be generally said that when the noun is unemphatic, and the adjective is not a mere epithet but essential to the sense, the transposition may be expected, yet it is probable that the influence of the French idiom made this transposition especially common in the case of some words derived from French. Hence, perhaps, the transposition in

"Of *antres vast* and deserts idle."—*Othello,* i. 1. 140.

And, besides "apparent" in the legal sense above, we have

"As well the fear of harm as harm *apparent.*"
                              Rich. III. ii. 2. 130.

Hence, perhaps, the frequent transposition of "divine," as

"By Providence *divine.*"—*Tempest,* i. 2. 158.

So   "Ful wel sche sang the service *devyne.*"
                              CHAUCER, *C. T.* 122.

"*Men devout.*"—*Hen. V.* i. 1. 9.

"Unto the appetite and *affection common.*"—*Coriol.* i. 1. 108

Latin usage may account for some expressions, as
" A *sectary astronomical.*"—*Lear,* i. 2. 164.

419 a. Transposition of adjectival phrases.

It has been shown above (419), that when an adjective is not a
mere epithet, but expresses something essential, and implies a relative, it is often placed after the noun.   When, however, connected
with the adjective, *e.g.* "whiter," there is some adverbial phrase,
e.g. "than snow," it was felt that to place the adjective after the
noun might sometimes destroy the connection between the noun and
adjective, since the adjective was, as it were, drawn forward to the
modifying adverb.   Hence the Elizabethans sometimes preferred to
place the adjectival part of the adjective before, and the adverbial
part after, the noun.   The noun generally being unemphatic caused
but slight separation between the two parts of the adjectival
phrase.   Thus "whiter than snow," being an adjectival phrase,
"whiter" is inserted before, and "than snow" after, the noun.

> " Nor scar that [whiter] skin-of-hers [than snow]."
> > *Othello,* v. 2. 4.

> "So much I hate a [breaking] cause to be
> [Of heavenly oaths]."—*L. L. L.* v. 2. 355.

So   " A [promising] face [of manly princely virtues]."
> > B. and F. (Walker).

> " As common
> As any [the most vulgar] thing [to sense]."—*Ham.* i. 2. 99.

i.e. "anything the most commonly perceived."

> " I shall unfold [equal] discourtesy
> [To your best kindness]."—*Cymb.* ii. 3. 101.

> " The [farthest] earth [removed from thee]."—*Sonn.* 44.

> " Bid these [unknown] friends [to us], welcome."
> > *W. T.* iv. 3. 65.

> " Thou [bloodier] villain [than terms can give thee out]."
> > *Macbeth,* v. 8. 7.

> " A [happy] gentleman [in blood and lineaments]."
> > *Rich. II.* iii. 1. 9.

> " As a [long-parted] mother [with her child]."
> > *Ib.* iii. 2. 8.   (See 194.)

> ' Thou [little better] thing [than earth]."—*Ib.* iii. 4. 77.

> ' You have won a [happy] victory [to Rome]."
> > *Coriol.* v. 3. 186.

Hence, even where the adjective cannot immediately precede the noun, yet the adjective comes first, and the adverb afterwards.

"That were to enlard his *fat-already-pride.*"
Tr. and Cr. ii. 2. 205.

"May soon return to this our [suffering] country
[Under a hand accurst]."—*Macbeth*, iii. 6. 48.

"The [appertaining] rage
[To such a greeting]."—*R. and J.* iii. 1. 66.

"With [declining] head [into his bosom]."—*T. of Sh.* Ind. 1. 119.

So probably

"Bear our [hack'd] targets [like the men that owe them]."
A. and C. iv. 8. 31.

This is very common in other Elizabethan authors :

"The [stricken] hind [with Shaft]."—LORD SURREY (Walker).

"And [worthie] work [of infinite reward]."
SPENSER, *F. Q.* iii. 2. 21.

"Of that [too wicked] woman [yet to die]."
B. and F. (Walker).

"Some sad [malignant] angel [to mine honour]."—*Ib.*

which perhaps explains

"Bring forth that [fatal] screech-owl [to our house]."
3 Hen. VI. ii. 6. 56.

So   "Thou [barren] thing [of honesty] and honour !"—B. and F.
perhaps explains

"Thou perjur'd and thou [simular] man [of virtue]."
Lear, iii. 2. 54.

"Bring me a [constant] woman [to her husband]."
Hen. VIII. iii. 1. 134.

"O, for my sake do you with fortune chide,
The [guilty] goddess [of my harmful deeds]."—*Sonn.* 111.

"To this [unworthy] husband [of his wife]."—*A. W.* iii. 4. 30.

"A [dedicated] beggar [to the air]."—*T. of A.* iv. 2. 13.

This transposition extends to an adverb in

"And thou shalt live [as freely] as thy lord
[To call his fortunes thine]."—*T. N.* i. 4. 39, 40.

i.e. "as free to use my fortune as I am."

Unless "to " is used loosely like "for," the following is a case of transposition :

"This is a [dear] manakin [to you], Sir Toby."
T. N. iii. 2. 57.

420. Transposition of Adverbs. The Elizabethan authors allowed themselves great licence in this respect.

We place adverbial expressions that measure excess or defect before the adjective which they modify, "twenty times better," &c. This is not always the case in Shakespeare :

> "Being *twenty times* of better fortune."—*A. and C.* iv. 1. 3.

> "Our spoils (that) we have brought home
> Do more than counterpoise, *a full third part*,
> The charges of the action."—*Coriol.* v. 6. 77.

> "I am solicited *not* by a few,
> And those of true condition."—*Hen. VIII.* i. 2. 18.

For *not* transposed, see also 305.

> "Like to a harvest man that's task'd to mow
> *Or* all, or lose his hire."—*Coriol.* i. 3. 40.

In "All good things vanish *less* than in a day" (Nash), there is, perhaps, a confusion between "less long-lived than a day" and "more quickly than in a day." At all events the emphatic use of "less" accounts for the transposition.

Such transpositions are most natural and frequent in the case of adverbs of limitation, as *but* (see **But**, 54), *only*, *even*, &c.

> "*Only* I say,"—*Macbeth*, iii. 6. 2.

for "I *only* say."

> "*Only* I yield to die."—*J. C.* v. 4. 12.

for "I yield *only* in order to die,"

> "And I assure you
> *Even* that your pity is enough to cure me,"—B. J.

for "that *even* your pity."

> "He did it to please his mother and to be *partly* proud,"
> *Coriol.* i. 1. 40.

for "and *partly* to be proud."

Somewhat similar is

> "Your single bond,"—*M. of V.* i. 3. 146.

for "the bond of you alone."

421. Transposition of Adverbs. When an adverb is transposed to the beginning for emphasis, it generally transposes the subject after the verb, but adverbs are sometimes put at the beginning of a sentence without influencing the order of the other words.

" *Seldom* he smiles."—*J. C.* i. 2. 205.

" For *always* I am Cæsar."—*Ib.* i. 2. 212.

" *No more* that thane of Cawdor shall deceive."

Macbeth, i. 2. 63.

" Of something *nearly* that concerns yourselves."

M. N. D. i. 1. 126.

422. Transposition of Article. In Early English we some-times find " *a* so new robe." The Elizabethan authors, like our-selves, transposed the *a* and placed it after the adjective : " so new *a* robe." But when a participle is added as an epithet of the noun, *e.g.* "fashioned," and the participle itself is qualified by an adjective used as an adverb, *e.g.* " new," we treat the whole as one adjective, thus, " so new-fashioned *a* robe." Shakespeare on the contrary writes—

" So new *a* fashion'd robe."—*K. J.* iv. 2. 27.

" So fair *an* offer'd chain."—*C. of E.* iii. 2. 186.

" Or having sworn too hard *a* keeping oath."

L. L. L. i. 1. 65.

" So rare *a* wonder'd father and *a* wife."

Temp. iv. 1. 123.

" I would have been much more *a* fresher man."

Tr. and Cr. v. 6. 20.

We still say, "too great *a* wit," but not with Chaucer, *C. T.* :

" For when a man hath overgret *a* wit,"

possibly because we regard " overgreat" as an adjective, and "too great" as a quasi-adverb. Somewhat similar is :

" On *once-a-flock-bed*, but repair'd with straw,
With tape-ty'd curtains never meant to draw."

POPE, *Moral E.* iii. 301.

So we can say " how poor *an* instrument," regarding "how" as an adverb, and "how poor" as an adverbialized expression, but not

" What poor *an* instrument,"—*A. and C.* v. 2. 236.

because " what" has almost lost with us its adverbial force.

" So brave(ly) *a* mingled temper saw I never."

B. and F. (Walker).

" Chaucer, who was so great(ly) *a* learned scholar."

KINASTON (Walker)

The *a* is used even after the comparative adjective in

> "If you should need a pin,
> You could not with more tame *a* tongue desire it."
>
> *M. for M.* ii. **2**. **46**.

423. Transpositions in Noun-clauses containing two nouns connected by "of."

It has been observed in **412** that two nouns connected by "of" are often regarded as one. Hence sometimes pronominal and other adjectives are placed before the whole compound noun instead of, as they strictly should be, before the second of the two nouns.

> "Yet that *thy brazen* gates of heaven may ope."
>
> 3 *Hen. VI.* ii. 3. 40.

> "*My pith of business.*"—*M. for M.* i. 4. 70.

> "The tribunes have pronounced
> *My everlasting doom of banishment.*"—*T. A.* iii. 1. 51.

> "Let it stamp wrinkles in *her brow of youth.*"
>
> *Lear,* i. 4. 306.

> "*My latter part of life.*"—*A. and C.* iv. 6. 39.

> "*My whole course of life.*"—*Othello,* i. 3. 91.

> "I will presently go learn *their day of marriage.*"
>
> *M. Ado,* ii. 2. 57.

> "*Thy bruising irons of wrath.*"—*Rich. III.* v. 3. 110.

> "*Thy ministers of chastisement.*"—*Ib.* 113.

> "*In my prime of youth.*"—*Ib.* 119.

> "*Thy heat of lust.*"—*R. of L.* 1473.

> "*My home of love.*"—*Sonn.* 109.

> "And punish them to *your height of pleasure.*"
>
> *M. for M.* v. 1. 240.

> "*His means of death,* his obscure funeral."
>
> *Hamlet,* iv. 5. 213.

i.e. "the means of his death."

> "What is *your cause of distemper ?*"—*Hamlet,* iii. 2. 350.

> "*Your sovereignty of reason.*"—*Ib.* i. 4. 73. (See **200**.)

> "*My better part of man.*"—*Macbeth,* v. 7. 18.

> "*His chains of bondage.*"—*Rich. II.* i. 3. 89.

> "*Your state of fortune* and *your due of birth.*"
>
> *Rich. III.* iii. 7. 127.

This is perhaps illustrated by

> "What *country-man ?*"— *T. N.* v. 1. 238; *T. of Sh.* i. 2. 190.

for "a man of what country?"

The possessive adjective is twice repeated in

"*Her* attendants *of* her chamber."—*A. Y. L.* ii. 2. 5.

So "*This cause of Rome*,"—*T. A.* i. 1. 32.

does not mean "*this* cause as distinguished from *other* causes of Rome," but "this, the Roman cause." Somewhat similar is

"*Your reproof*
Were well deserv'd *of rashness*,"—*A. and C.* ii. 2. 124.

where we should say "the reproof of your rashness" (unless "of" here means "about," "for").

"The idea of her life shall sweetly creep
Into *his study of imagination*."—*M. Ado,* iv. 2. 27.

i.e. "the study of his imagination."

"Our raiment and *state of bodies*."—*Coriol.* v. 3. 95.

"More than ten criers, and *six noise of trumpets*."
B. J. *Sejan.* v. 7.

The compound nature of these phrases explains, perhaps, the omission of the article in

"Hath now himself met with the fall-of-leaf."
Rich. II. iii. 4. 49.

424. Transposition of Prepositions in Relative and other clauses. We now dislike using such transpositions as

"The late demand *that* you did sound me in."—*Rich. III.* iv. 2. 87.

"Betwixt that smile we would aspire *to*."—*Hen. VIII.* iii. 2. 368.

"A thousand men *that* fishes gnawed *upon*."—*Rich. III.* i. 4. 25.

"Found thee a way out of his wreck to rise *in*."
Hen. VIII. iii. 2. 438.

But it may be traced to E. E. (203), and is very common in Shakespeare, particularly in *Hen. VIII.*, where we even find

"Where no mention
Of me must more be heard *of*."—*Hen. VIII.* iii. 2. 435.

It has been said above (203) that the dissyllabic forms of prepositions are peculiarly liable to these transpositions. Add to the above examples :

"Like *a falcon* towering in the skies,
Coucheth the fowl *below*."—*R. of L.* 506.

425. Transposition after Emphatic Words. The influence of an emphatic word at the beginning of a sentence is shown in the transposition of the verb and subject. In such cases the last as well as the first word is often emphatic.

" *In dreadful secrecy* impart they *did.*"—*Hamlet,* i. 2. 207.

" And *so have I* a noble father *lost,*
A sister driven into desperate terms."—*Ib.* iv. 7. 25.

Here note, that though the first line could be re-transposed and Laertes could naturally say "I have lost a father," on the other hand he could not say "I have driven a sister" without completely changing the sense. " Have " is here used in its original sense, and is equivalent to "I find." When "have" is thus used without any notion of action, it is separated from the participle passive.

" But *answer* made it *none.*"—*Hamlet,* i. 2. 216.

" *Pray* can I *not.*"—*Ib.* iii. 3. 38.

" *Supportable*
To make the dear loss *have I means much weaker.*"
Temp. v. 1. 146.

The influence of an emphatic adverbial expression preceding is shown in the difference between the order in the second and the first of the two following lines :—

" As every alien pen *hath got my use,*
And *under thee their poetry disperse.*"—*Sonn.* 78.

" *I did,* my lord,
But *loath am* to produce so bad an instrument."
A. W. v. 3. 201.

" *Before the time* I did Lysander see,
Seem'd Athens as a paradise to me."—*M. N. D.* i. 1. 205.

When the adverbs "never," "ever," are emphatic and placed near the beginning of a sentence, the subject often follows the verb, almost always when the verb is "was," &c. We generally write now "never was," but Shakespeare often wrote " (there) was never."

" Was never *widow* had so dear a loss."—*Rich. III.* ii. 2. 77.

Sometimes a word is made emphatic by repetition :

" *Sec. O.* Peace ! We'll hear him.
Third O. Ay, *by my beard will we.*"—*T. G. of V.* iv. 1. 10.

" *Hamlet.* Look you, these are the stops.
Guild. But *these* cannot I *command.*"—*Hamlet,* iii. 3. 377.

Or partly by antithesis, as well as by its natural importance :

" *I your* commission will forthwith despatch,
And *he* to *England* shall along with you."

Hamlet, iii. 3. 3, 4.

" *My* soul shall *thine* keep company to heaven."

Hen. V. iv. 6. 16.

The following is explained by the omission of "there :"

" I am question'd by my fears . . . that (there) *may blow*
No sneaping winds at home."—*W. T.* i. 2. 13.

There seems a disposition to place participles, as though used absolutely, before the words which they qualify.

"And these news,
Having been well, that would have made *me* sick,
Being sick, have in some measure made *me* well."

2 Hen. IV. i. 1. 138.

It is rare to find such transpositions as

" Then the rich jewell'd coffer of Darius,
Transported shall be at high festivals."—1 *Hen. VI.* i. 6. 26.

Transpositions are common in prose, especially when an adverb precedes the sentence.

" *Yet hath Leonora, my onely daughter, escaped.*"

MONTAIGNE (Florio), **225.**

" And, *therefore, should not we marry* so young."—*Ib.*

" Now, sir, the sound that tells what hour it is
Are clamorous groans,"—*Rich. II.* v. 5. 56.

is rather a case of " confusion of proximity " ("are" being changed to "is") than transposition.   (See 302.)

426. Transposition after Relative. The relative subject, possibly as being somewhat unemphatic itself, brings forward the object into a prominent and emphatic position, and consequently throws a part of the verb to the end, not however (as in German) the auxiliary.

" By Richard *that dead is*."—1 *Hen. IV.* i. 3. 146.

" But chide rough winter *that the flower hath killed*."—*R. of L.*

" *That heaven's light did hide*."—SPENS. *F. Q.* i. 1. 7.

427. Other Transpositions. In the second of two passive clauses when the verb "is" is omitted, the subject is sometimes transposed, perhaps for variety.

" When liver, heart, and brain,
These sovereign thrones, are all supplied, and filled
(Are) Her sweet perfections with one self king."
T. N. i. 1. 39.
" Since his addiction was to courses vain,
And never (was) noted in him any study."—*Hen. V.* i. 1. 57.

It is not probable that "perfections" and "study" are here absolutely used with the participle. See, however, **And**, 95.

In "By *such two* that would by all likelihood have confounded each other" (*Cymb.* i. 4. 53), "two" is emphatic, like "a pair." So "we" is emphatic in, "all *we* like sheep have gone astray," and in *Hamlet*, ii. 2. 151, in both cases, because of antithesis.

" Into the madness wherein now *he* raves
And *all we* mourn for."—*Hamlet*, ii. 2. 151.   (See 240.)

COMPOUND WORDS.

428. Hybrids. The Elizabethans did not bind themselves by the stricter rules of modern times in this respect. They did not mind adding a Latin termination to a Teutonic root, and *vice versâ*. Thus Shakespeare has "increaseful," "bodement," &c. Holland uses the suffix *-fy* after the word "fool" (which at all events does not come to us direct from the Latin), "foolify," where we use "stultify." The following words illustrate the Elizabethan licence :—

" Bi-fold."—*Tr. and Cr.* v. 2. 144.
" Out-cept."—B. J. (Nares).
" Exteriorly."—*K. J.* iv. 2. 257.
" Sham'st thou not, knowing whence thou art *extraught?* "
3 *Hen. VI.* ii. 2. 142.
where there is a confusion between the Latin "extracted" and the English "raught," past part. of "reach." Compare Pistol's "exhale," *Hen. V.* ii. 1. 66, *i.e.* "ex-haul," "draw out," applied to a sword.

There was also great licence in using the foreign words which were pouring into the language.

" And quench the *stelled* fires."—*Lear*, iii. 7. 61.
" Be *aidant* and remediate."—*Ib.* iv. 4. 17.
" *Antres* vast and deserts idle."—*Othello*, i. 3. 140.

429. Adverbial Compounds.

" Till Harry's *back-return.*"—*Hen. V.* v. Prologue, 41.

"Thy *here-approach,*" *Macb.* iv. 3. 133, 148 ; " Our *hence-going,*" *Cymb.* iii. 2. 65 ; " *Here-hence,*" B. J. *Poetast.* v. 1 ; "So that men are punish'd for *before-breach* of the king's laws in *now-the-king's-quarrel,*" *Hen. V.* iv. 1. 179, *i.e.* "the king's now (present) quarrel." This last extraordinary compound is a mere construction for the occasion, to correspond antithetically to "before-breach," but it well illustrates the Elizabethan licence.

" The *steep-up* heavenly hill."—*Sonn.* 7.

" I must *up-fill* this osier cage of ours."—*R. and J.* ii. 3. 7.

" *Up-hoarded.*"—*Hamlet,* i. 1. 136.

"With hair *up-staring.*"—*Tempest,* i. 2. 213.

430. Noun-Compounds.
Sometimes the first noun may be treated as a genitive used adjectively. (See 22.) Thus, "thy *heart-blood*" (*Rich. II.* iv. 1. 38) is the same as "thy *heart's blood;*" "*brother-love*" (*Hen. VIII.* v. 3. 73), i.e. *brother's love.*

So " *Any-moment-leisure.*"—*Hamlet,* i. 3. 133.

" This *childhood*-proof."—*M. of V.* i. 1. 144.

" *Childhood*-innocence."—*M. N. D.* iii. 2. 202.

" All the *region-kites.*"—*Hamlet,* ii. 2. 607.

" A *lion-fell.*"—*M. N. D.* v. 1. 227, *i.e.* "a lion's skin."

So probably

" *Faction-traitors.*"—*Rich. II.* ii. 2. 57.

" Self " is used as a compound noun in "self-conceit," and this explains

"Infusing him with *self-and-vain-conceit.*"—*Rich. II.* iii. 2. 166.

"Every *minute-while,*"—1 *Hen. VI.* i. 4. 54.

where " while " has its original force as a noun = "time."

But often when a noun is compounded with a participle, some preposition or other ellipse must be supplied, as "like" in our "*stone-still,*" &c., and the exact meaning of the compound can only be ascertained by the context.

" *Wind-changing* Warwick."—3 *Hen. VI.* v. 1. 57.

" My *furnace-burning* heart."—*Ib.* ii. 1. 80.

i.e. "burning *like* a furnace."

" *Giant-rude,*" *A. Y. L.* iv. 3. 34 ; "*marble-constant,*" *A. and C.* v. 2. 240 ; "*honey-heavy-dew,*" *J. C.* ii. 1. 230 ; so "*flower-*

"ソft hands," *A. and C.* ii. 1. 215, "*multi-pale* peace," *Rich. II.*
iii. 3. 98 ; "an orphan's *water-standing* eye," 3 *Hen. VI.* v. 6. 40,
i.e. "standing *with* water;" "*weeping-ripe,*" *L. L. L.* v. 2. 274,
"ripe *for* weeping;" "*thought-sick,*" *Hamlet,* iii. 4. 51, *i.e.* "as
i.e. the result of thought ;" so "*lion-sick,*" *Tr. and Cr.* ii. 3. 13, is
explained lower down, "sick *of* proud heart ;" "*pity-pleading*
eyes," *R. of L.* 561, *i.e.* "pleading *for* pity ;" "*peace-parted* souls,"
Hamlet, v. i. 261, *i.e.* "souls *that have* departed in peace ;"
"*fancy-free,*" *M. N. D.* ii. 1. 164, *i.e.* "free *from* fancy (love) ;"
"*child-changed* father," *Lear.* iv. 7. 17, *i.e.,* "changed *to* a child."

Or the noun is put for a passive participle or an adjective.

"Upon your sword sit *laurel*(led) victory."—*A. and C.* i. 3. 100.
"The honey of his *music*(al) vows."—*Hamlet,* iii. 1. 164.
"The *venom*(ous) clamours of a jealous woman."
C. of E. v. 1. 69; so *R. of L.* 850.
"The *Carthage* queen."—*M. N. D.* i. 1. 173.
"Your *Corioli* walls."—*Coriol.* i. 1. 8 ; ii. 1. 180.
"Our *Rome* gates."—*Ib.* iii. 3. 104.

For similar examples, see 22.

Sometimes the genitive is used :

"I'll knock your *knave's* pate."
T. of Sh. i. 2. 12 ; *C. of E.* iii. 1. 74.

431. Preposition-Compounds.

"An *after-dinner's* (comp. 'afternoon's') breath."
Tr. and Cr. ii. 3. 120.
"At *after-supper.*"—*Rich. III.* iv. 3. 31 ; *M. N. D.* v. i. 34.
"At *over-night.*"—*A. W.* iii. 4. 23.
"The *falling-from* of his friends."—*T. of A.* iv. 3. 400.

The preposition usually attached to a certain verb is sometimes
appended to the participle of the verb in order to make an adjective.

"There is no *hoped-for* mercy."—3 *Hen. VI.* v. 4. 35.
"Some *never-heard-of* torturing pain,"—*T. A.* ii. 3. 285.
for "unheard-of."

"Your *sued-for* tongues."—*Coriol.* ii. 3. 216.
"*Bemock'd-at* stabs."—*Temp.* iii. 3. 63.
"The *unthought-on* accident."—*W. T.* iv. 4. 549.
"Your *unthought-of* Harry."—1 *Hen. IV.* iii. 2. 141.

432. Verb-Compounds. Verbs were compounded with their objects more commonly than with us.

> " Some *carry-tale*, some *please-man*, some slight zany,
> Some *mumble-news*."—*L. L. L.* v. 2. 463–4.

> " All *find-faults*."—*Hen. V.* v. 2. 398.

We still use "mar-plot" and "spoil-sport." Such compounds seem generally depreciatory. "Weather-fend" in

> " In the lime grove which *weather-fends* your cell,"
> > *Temp.* v. 1. 10.

means "defend *from* the weather," and stands on a somewhat different footing.

One is disposed to treat "wilful-blame" as an anomalous compound in

> " In faith, my lord, you are too *wilful-blame*."
> > 1 *Hen. IV.* iii. 1. 177.

like   " A *false-heart* traitor."—2 *Hen. VI.* v. 1. 143.

But "heart" is very probably a euphonious abbreviation of "hearted." The explanation of "too *wilful-blame*" is to be sought in the common expression "I am *too* blame," *Othello*, iii. 3. 211, 282 ; *M. of V.* v. 1. 166. "I am *too too* blame," is also found in Elizabethan authors. It would seem that, the "to" in "I am to blame" being misunderstood, "blame" came to be regarded as an adjective, and "to" (which is often interchanged in spelling with "too") as an adverb. Hence "blame," being regarded as an adjective, was considered compoundable with another adjective.

433. Participial Nouns. A participle or adjective, when used as a noun, often receives the inflection of the possessive case or the plural.

> " His *chosen's* merit."—B. and F. *F. Sh.* iii. 1.

> " All *cruels* else subscribed."—*Lear*, iii. 7. 65.

i.e. "All cruel acts to the contrary being yielded up, forgiven." Compare for the meaning *Lear*, iv. 7. 36, and for " subscribe," *Tr. and Cr.* iv. 5. 105. Another explanation is, "all other cruel animals being allowed entrance."

So "*Vulgars*," *W. T.* ii. 1. 94 ; " *Severals*," *Hen. V.* i. 1. 86, *i.e.* "details."

> " Yon equal *potents*."—*K. J.* ii. 1. 357.

> > " To the ports
> The *discontents* repair."—*A. and C.* i. 4. 39.

" Lead me to the *revolts* (revolters) of England here."
K. *J.* v. 4. 7 : so *Cymb.* iv. 4. 6.

Add, if the text be correct :

" The *Norways'* king."—*Macbeth,* i. 2. 59.

i.e. " the king of the Norwegians."

It would appear as though an adjective in agreement with a plural noun received a plural inflection in

" Letters-*patents.*"—*Hen. VIII.* iii. 2. 249 ; *Rich. II.* ii. 1. 202 (Folio), 3. 130.

More probably the word was treated by Shakespeare as though it were a compound noun. But in E. E. adjectives of Romance origin often take the plural inflection.

" Lawless *resolutes.*"—*Hamlet,* i. 1. 98.
" Mighty *opposites.*"—*Ib.* v. ii. 62.

434. Phrase-Compounds. Short phrases, mostly containing participles, are often compounded into epithets.

" The *always-wind-obeying* deep."—*C. of E.* i. 1. 64.
" My *too-much-changed* son."—*Hamlet,* ii. 2. 36.
" The *ne'er-yet-beaten* horse of Parthia."—*A. and C.* iii. 1. 33.
" Our *past-cure* malady."—*A. W.* ii. 1. 124.
" A *past-saving* slave."—*Ib.* iv. 3. 158.
" The *none-sparing* war."—*Ib.* iii. 2. 108.
" A jewel in a *ten-times-barred-up* chest."—*Rich. II.* i. 1. 180.
" A *too-long-wither'd* flower."—*Ib.* ii. 1. 134.
" Tempt him not so *too-far.*"—*A. and C.* i. 3. 11.
" The *to-and-fro-conflicting* wind."—*Lear,* iii. 1. 11.
" You that have turn'd off a *first-so noble* wife."
A. W. v. 3. 220.
" Of this *yet-scarce-cold* battle."—*Cymb.* v. 5. 469.
" A cunning thief, or *a-that-way-accomplished* courtier."
Ib. i. 4. 101.
" In this *so-never-needed* help."—*Coriol.* v. 1. 34.
" A *world-without-end* bargain."—*L. L. L.* v. 2. 799.

See *Sonn.* 5.

" Our *not-fearing* Britain."—*Cymb.* ii. 4. 191.
" The *ne'er-lust-wearied* Antony."—*A. and C.* ii. 1. 38.
" A *twenty-years-removed* thing ."—*T. N.* v. i. 92.

435. Anomalous Compounds. We still, though rarely, abbreviate "the other" into "t'other," but we could not say

> " The *t'other*."—B. J. *Cy's. Rev.* iv. 1 ; v. 1 (a corruption
> of E. E. þet oþer).

> " Yea, and furr'd moss when winter flowers are none,
> To *winter-ground* thy corpse."—*Cymb.* iv. 2. 229.

i.e. perhaps "to inter *during winter*." So "to winter-rig" is said (Halliwell) to mean " to fallow land during winter."

"And" is omitted in

> " At this *odd-even* and dull watch of the night."
> *Othello*, i. 1. 124.

Cicero says, that the extreme test of a man's honesty is that you can play at odd and even with him in the dark. And perhaps "odd-(and-)even" here means, a time when there is no distinguishing between *odd* and *even*.

As there is a noun "false-play," there is nothing very remarkable in its being converted thus into a verb :

> " Pack'd cards with Cæsar and *false-played* my glory."
> *A. and C.* iv. 14. 19.

A terse compound is often invented for special use, made intelligible by the context. Thus, the profit of excess is called

> " *Poor-rich* gain."—*R. of L.* 140.
> "Where shall I *live* now Lucrece is *unlived*."—*Ib.* 1754.

PREFIXES.

A-. See 24.

436. All-to (see 28) is used in the sense of "completely asunder" as a prefix in

> " And *all-to*-brake his skull."—*Judges* ix. 53.

"Asunder" was an ordinary meaning of the prefix "to" in E. E. It must be borne in mind that *all* had no necessary connection with *to*, till by constant association the two syllables were corrupted into a prefix, *all-to*, which was mistaken for *altogether* and so used. Hence, by corruption, in many passages, where *all-to* or *all-too* is said to have the meaning of "asunder," it had come to mean "altogether," as in

> " Mercutio's ycy hand had *al-to* frozen mine."—HALLIWELL.

It has been shown (73) that *too* and *to* are constantly interchanged in Elizabethan authors. Hence the constant use of *all too* for "quite," "decidedly too," as in *Rich. II.* iv. 1. 28, "*all* too base," may have been encouraged by the similar sound of *all-to.* Shakespeare does not use the archaic *all-to* in the sense of "asunder," nor does Milton probably in

> "She plumes her feathers and lets grow her wings,
> That in the various bustle of resort
> Were *all too* ruffled."—MILTON, *Comus,* 376.

437. At- in "attask'd," *Lear,* i. 4. 366 ("task'd," "blamed"), perhaps represents the O.E. intensive prefix "of," which is sometimes changed into "an-," "on-," or "a-." But the word is more probably a sort of imitation of the similar words "attach" and "attack."

438. Be. The prefix *be* is used, not merely with verbs of colouring, "smear," "splash," &c., to localize and sometimes to intensify action, but also with nouns and adjectives to convert the nouns into verbs :

> "*Be*monster."—*Lear,* iv. 2. 63.
> "*Be*-sort."—*Ib.* i. 4. 272.
> "All good *be*-fortune you."—*T. G. of V.* iv. 3. 41.
> "*Be*madding."—*Lear,* iii. 1. 38.

It is also used seemingly to give a transitive signification to verbs that, without this prefix, mostly require prepositions :

> "*Be*gnaw."—*Rich. III.* i. 3. 221.
> "*Be*howls the moon."—*M. N. D.* v. 1. 379.
> "*Be*speak " and "address" in *Hamlet,* ii. 2. 140.
> "*Be*weep."—*Rich. III.* ii. 2. 49 ; *Lear,* i. 4. 324.

In participles, like other prefixes, it is often redundant, and seems to indicate an unconscious want of some substitute for the old participial prefix.

> "Well *be*-met."—*Lear,* v. 1. 20.

But the theory that *be-* in "become," "believe," "belove," &c., represents the old *ge-*, does not seem to be sound.

439. Dis- was sometimes used in the sense of un-, to mean "without," as

> "*Dis*companied," *Cy.'s Rev.* iii. 3, for "unaccompanied,"
> *i.e.* "without company."

"A little to *dis*quantity your train."—*Lear*, i. 4. 270.

"*Dis*habited," *K. J.* ii. 1. 220, = "Caused to migrate."

"*Dis*lived," CHAPMAN, = "Deprived of life."

"*Dis*natured," *Lear*, i. 4. 305, for "Unnatural."

"*Dis*noble," HOLLAND ; "*Dis*temperate," RALEIGH ; for "ignoble" and "intemperate."

"Being full of supper and *dis*tempering draughts."
Othello, i. 1. 99.

"*Dis*covery" is often used for "uncovering," *i.e.* "unfold," whether literally or metaphorically. "So shall my anticipation prevent your *discovery*," *Hamlet*, ii. 2. 305, *i.e.* "render your *dis*closure needless by anticipation." So *Rich. III.* iv. 4. 240.

440. En- was frequently used, sometimes in its proper sense of enclosing, as "*en*closed," "*en*guard," *Lear*, i. 4. 349 ; "*en*cave," *Othello*, iv. 1. 82 ; "How dread an army hath *en*rounded him," *Hen. V.* iv. Prol. 36 ; "*en*wheel thee round," *Othello*, ii. 1. 87 ; "*en*fetter'd," *ib.* ii. 3. 351 ; "*en*mesh," *ib.* 368 ; "*en*rank," 1 *Hen. VI.* i. 1. 115 ; "*en*shelter'd and *em*bay'd," *Othello*, ii. 1. 18 ; "*en*steep'd," *ib.* 70 ; "*en*gaol'd," *Rich. II.* i.`3. 166 ; "*en*scheduled," *Hen. V.* v. 2. 73 ; "*en*shelled," *Coriol.* iv. 6. 45. So "*em*bound," "*en*vassell'd," DANIEL on Florio ; "*em*battle" (to put *in* battle array) ; "*en*free" (to place *in* a state of freedom) ; "*en*tame," *A. Y. L.* iii. 5. 48 (to bring *into* a state of tameness). But the last instances show that the locative sense can be metaphorical instead of literal, and scarcely perceptible. There is little or no difference between "free" and "*en*free." So "the *en*ridged sea," *Lear*, iv. 6. 71 ; "the *en*chafed flood," *Othello*, ii. 1. 17, are, perhaps, preferred by Shakespeare merely because in participles he likes some kind of prefix as a substitute for the old participial prefix. In some cases the *en-* or *in-* seems to take a person as its object, "*en*dart," *R. and J.* i. 3. 98 ("to set darts *in*," not "*in* darts"). So "*en*pierced," *R. and J.* i. 4. 19 ; and so, perhaps, "*em*poison." The word "*im*pale" is used by Shakespeare preferably in the sense of "surrounding :"

"*Im*pale him with your weapons round about,"
Tr. and Cr. v. 7. 5.
means "hedge him round with your weapons." So

"Did I *im*pale him with the regal crown."—3 *Hen. VI.* iii. 3. 189.

441. For- is used in two words now disused :

"*For*slow no longer."—3 *Hen. VI.* ii. 3. 56.

"She *for*did herself."—*Lear*, v. 3. 255 ; *M. N. D.* v. 1. 381.

In both words the prefix has its proper sense of "injury."

442. Un- for modern **in-**; **in-** for **un-**. (**Non-** only occurs twice in all the plays of Shakespeare, and in *V. and A.* 521.)

> *In*charitable, *in*fortunate, *in*certain, *in*grateful, *in*civil, *in*substantial.

> *Un*possible, *un*perfect, *un*provident, *un*active, *un*expressive, *un*proper, *un*respective, *un*violable, *un*partial, *un*fallible, *un*dividable, *un*constant, *un*curable, *un*effectual, *un*measurable, *un*disposed, *un*vincible (N. *P.* 181), *un*reconcil*i*able (*A. and C.* v. 1. 47).

We appear to have no definite rule of distinction even now, since we use *un*grateful, *in*gratitude ; *un*equal, *in*equality.* *Un*- seems to have been preferred by Shakespeare before *p* and *r*, which do not allow *in*- to precede except in the form *im*-. *In*- also seems to have been in many cases retained from the Latin, as in the case of "*in*gratus," "*in*fortunium," &c. As a general rule, we now use *in*- where we desire to make the negative a part of the word, and *un*- where the separation is maintained—"*un*true," "*in*firm." Hence *un*- is always used with participles—"*un*tamed," &c. Perhaps also *un*- is stronger than *in*-. "*Un*holy" means more than "not holy," almost "the reverse of holy." But in "*in*attentive," "*in*temperate," *in*- has nearly the same meaning, "the reverse of."

> "You wrong the reputation of your name
> In so *unseeming* to confess receipt."—*L. L. L.* ii. 1. 156.

Here "unseeming" means "the reverse of seeming" more than "not seeming" (like οὐ φημί) : "in thus making us as though you would not confess."

SUFFIXES.

443. -Er is sometimes appended to a *noun* for the purpose of signifying an agent. Thus—

> "A Roman sword*er*."—2 *Hen. VI.* iv. 1. 135.

---

* This however is perhaps explained below. *In*- is a part of the *noun* "*in*gratitude ;" *un*- in the *adjective* "*un*grateful" means "not."

"O most gentle pulpit*er*."—*A. Y. L.* iii. 2. 163.
"A moral*er*."—*Othello*, ii. 3. 301.
"Homag*er*."—*A. and C.* i. 1. 31. (O. Fr. "homagier.")
"Justic*ers*."—*Lear*, iv. 2. 79. (Late Lat. "justitiarius.")

In the last two instances the *-er* is of French origin, and in many cases, as in "enchant*er*," it may seem to be English, while really it represents the French *-eur*.

"Joind*er*," *T. N.* v. 1. 160, perhaps comes from the French "joindre."

The *-er* is often added to show a masculine agent where a noun and verb are identical :

"Trust*er*."—*Hamlet*, i. 2. 172.
"The paus*er* reason."—*Macbeth*, ii. 3. 117.
"Caus*er*."—*Rich. III.* iv. 4. 122.
"To you, my origin and end*er*."—*L. C.* ii. 22.

Note the irregular, "Precurrer" (for "precursor").—*P. P.*

We have "windring" from "wind*er*," *Tempest*, iv. 1. 128, formed after the analogy of "wand*er*," "clamb*er*," "wav*er*," the *er* having apparently a frequentative force.

444. **-En**, *made of* (still used in gold*en*, &c.), is found in—
"Her thread*en* fillet."—*L. C.* 5.
"A twigg*en* bottle."—*Othello*, iii. 3. 152.

445. **-Ive, -ble.** (See 3.) *-Ive* is sometimes used in a passive instead of, as now, in an active signification. Thus : "Incomprehens*ive* depths ;" "plau*sive*," "worthy to be applauded ;" "direc*tive*," "capable of being directed ;" "insuppress*ive* metal ;" "the fair, the inexpress*ive* she" (similarly used by Milton in the Hymn on the Nativity). On the other hand, *-ble* is sometimes used actively, as in "medicina*ble*" (which is also used passively), and in "un-merita*ble*."

"This is a slight unmeritable man."—*J. C.* iv. 1. 12.
So "defensible," "deceivable," "disputable," and "tenable."

In "Inten*ible* sieve," *A. W.* i. 2. 208, not only does *-ble* convey an active meaning, but Shakespeare uses the Latin instead of the English form of the termination, just as we still write "ter*ri*ble," not "ter*ra*ble." I imagine we have been influenced in our *-able* by the accidental coincidence of meaning between the word "able" and the termination *-ble.* But French influence must have had some weight.

446. -Less. Sometimes found with adjectives, as "busy*less*," "sick*less*," "modest*less*."

-Less used for "not able to be."

> "That phrase*less* hand."—*L. C.* 225 ; *i.e.* " in-describable."
> "That term*less* skin."—*Ib.* 94.
> "Sum*less* treasuries."—*Hen. V.* i. 2. 165.
> "My care*less* crime."—*R. of L.* 771.
> "Your great oppose*less* wills."—*Lear*, iv. 6. 38.

It is commonly used with words of Latin or Greek origin, as above. Add "reason*less*," *Hen. V.* v. 4. 137 ; "crime*less*," 2 *Hen. VI.* ii. 4. 63.

447. -Ly found with a noun, and yet not appearing to convey an adjectival meaning. "Anger-*ly*," *Macb.* iii. 5. 1 ; *T. G. of V.* i. 2. 62. Compare "wonder-*ly*" in the *Morte d'Arthur*, and "cheer-*ly*," *Tempest*, i. 1. 6. This is common in E. E.

The *-ly* represents "like," of which it is a corruption. Compare :

> "*Villain-like* he lies."—*Lear*, v. 3. 97.

So "master*ly*," adv., *W. T.* v. 3. 65 ; *Othello*, i. 1. 26 ; "hunger*ly*," adv., *ib.* iii. 4. 105 ; "exterior*ly*," adv., *K. J.* iv. 2. 257 ; "silver*ly*," adv., *ib.* v. 2. 46. "Fellow*ly*," *Temp.* v. 1. 64, and "traitor*ly*," *W. T.* iv. 4. 822, are used as adjectives. Perhaps a vowel is to be supplied in sound, though omitted, in "unwield(i)*ly*," *Rich. II.* iv. 1. 205 ; "need(i)*ly*," *R. and J.* iii. 2. 117 ; and they may be derived from "unwieldy" and "needy." Add "orderly," *Rich. II.* i. 3. 9 ; "manly," *Macbeth*, iv. 3. 235.

448. -Ment. We seldom use this suffix except where we find it already existing in Latin and French words adopted by us. Shakespeare, however, has "intend*ment*," "supply*ment*," "design*ment*," "denote*ment*," and "bode*ment*."

449. -Ness is added to a word not of Teutonic origin :

> "Equal*ness*."—*A. and C.* v. 1. 47.

450. -Y is found appended to a noun to form an adjective.

> "Slumber*y* agitation."—*Macbeth*, v. 1. 12.
> "Unheed*y* haste."—*M. N. D.* i. 1. 237.

In "Bat*y* wings," *M. N. D.* iii. 2. 365, "bat*ty*" seems to mean
"*like* those of bats." "Worm*y* beds," *ib.* iii. 2. 384, is "worm-*filled.*"
"Vast*y*," in "the vast*y* fields of France," *Hen. V.* Prologue, 12 ;
1 *Hen. IV.* iii. 1. 52, is perhaps derived from the noun "vast,"
Tempest, i. 2. 327 ; *Hamlet,* i. 2. 198.   " Womb*y* vaultages,"
Henry V. ii. 4. 124 : *i.e.* "womb-like."

Y appended to adjectives of colour has a modifying force like -*ish* :

"Their pal*y* flames."—*Hen. V.* iv. Prol. 8.

"His browny locks."—*L. C.* 85.

451. Suffixes were sometimes influenced by the Elizabethan
licence of converting one part of speech into another.   We should
append -*ation* or -*ition*, -*ure* or -*ing*, to the following words used by
Shakespeare as nouns: "solicit," "consult," "expect," &c. ; "my
depart," 2 *Hen. VI.* i. 1. 2 ; 3 *Hen. VI.* iv. 1. 92, ii. 1. 110 ; "un-
curable *discomfort*," 2 *Hen. VI.* v. 2. 86 ; "make *prepare* for war,"
3 *Hen. VI.* iv. 1. 131 ; "a smooth *dispose*," *Othello,* i. 3. 403 ; "his
repair," 3 *Hen. VI.* v. 1. 20 ; "deep *exclaims*," *Rich. III.* i. 2. 52,
iv. 4. 135 ; "his brow's *repine*," *V. and A.* 490 ; "a sweet *retire*,"
Hen. V. iv. 3. 86 ; "false *accuse*," 2 *Hen. VI.* iii. 1. 160 ; "your
ladyship's *impose*," *T. G. of V.* iv. 3. 8 ; "the sun's *appear*," B. and
F. F. Sh. v. 1 ; "from *suspect*," 2 *Hen. VI.* iii. 2. 139 ; "*manage*,"
M. of V. iii. 4. 25 ; "*commends*," *ib.* ii. 1. 90 ; "the boar's *annoy*,"
Rich. III. v. 3. 156 ; "the *disclose*," *Hamlet,* iii. 1. 174 ; "*com-
mends*," *Rich. II.* iii. 3. 126.

Almost all of these words come to us through the French.

Note "O heavenly *mingle*."—*A. and C.* i. 5. 59.

"*Immoment* toys."—*Ib.* v. 1. 106.

PROSODY.

452. The ordinary line in blank verse consists of five feet of two syllables each, the second syllable in each foot being accented.

" We bóth | have féd | as wéll, | and wé | can bóth
Endúre | the wínt | er's cóld | as wéll | as hé."

J. C. i. 2. 98–9.

This line is tóo monotonous and formal for frequent use. The metre is therefore varied, sometimes (1) by changing the position of the accent, sometimes (2) by introducing trisyllabic and monosyllabic feet. These licences are, however, subject to certain laws. It would be a mistake to suppose that Shakespeare in his tragic metre introduces the trisyllabic or monosyllabic foot at random. Some sounds and collections of sounds are peculiarly adapted for mono-syllabic and trisyllabic feet. It is part of the purpose of the following paragraphs to indicate the laws which regulate these licences. In many cases it is impossible to tell whether in a tri-syllabic foot an unemphatic syllable is merely slurred or wholly suppressed, as for instance the first *e* in " diff*e*rent." Such a foot may be called either dissyllabic or *quasi-trisyllabic*.

453. The accent after a pause is frequently on the first syllable. The pause is generally at the end of the line, and hence it is on the first foot of the following line that this, which may be called the "pause-accent," is mostly found. The first syllable of initial lines also can, of course, be thus accented. It will be seen that in the middle of the line these pause-accents generally follow *emphasized monosyllables*. (See 480–6.)

" *Cómfort*, | my liége ! | why loóks | your gráce | so pále ? "

Rich. II. iii. 2. **75.**

Examples of the "pause-accent" not at the beginning.

(1) " Feéd and | regárd | him nót. | *Aré you* | a mán ? "

Macbeth, iii. 4. 58.

Sometimes the pause is slight, little more than the time necessary for recovery after an *emphatic monosyllable.*

(2) " Be ín | their flów | ing cúps | *fréshly* | remémber'd."

Hen. V. iv. 3. 55.

So arrange

" And thése | *flátter* | *ing* stréams, | and máke | our fáces."

Macbeth, iii. 2. 33.

"These " may be emphasized. (See 484.)

(3) " Whó would | beliéve | me. O'! | *péril* | ous móuths."

M. for M. ii. 4. 172.

(4) " Afféc | tion, poóh! | You spéak | —*like a* | green gírl."

Hamlet, i. 3. 101.

"Wé shall | be cáll'd | —*púrgers*, | not múr | derérs."

J. C. ii. 1. 180.

(5) "The lífe | of cóm | fort. Bút | for thée, | *féllow.*"

Cymb. iv. 3. 9.

The old pronunciation " fellów " is probably not Shakespearian.

In (3) (4) and (5) " O," "speak," "call'd," and "thee" may, perhaps, be regarded as dissyllables (see 482–4), and the following foot a quasi-trisyllabic one. There is little practical difference between the two methods of scansion.

(6) " Sénseless | *línen!* | Háppier | thereín | than I."

Cymb. i. 3. 7.

Here either there is a pause between the epithet and noun, or else "senseless" may possibly be pronounced as a trisyllable, " *Sénse* (486) | less línen." The line is difficult.

" *Therefóre,* | *mérchant,* | I'll lím | it thée | this dáy,"

C. of E. i. 1. 151.

seems to begin with two trochees, like Milton's famous line :

" *U'ni* | *vérsal* | reproách | far wórse | to béar."—*P. L.* vi. 34.

But " therefore" may have its accent, as marked, on the last syllable.

The old pronunciation "merchánt" is not probable. Or "there " may be one foot (see 480) : " Thére | fore mérchant | ."

(7) "*Ant.* Obéy | it ón | all cáuse. |

Cleop.   Párdon, | párdon.

A. and C. iii. 11. 68.

is, perhaps, an instance of two consecutive trochees. (There seems no ground for supposing that " pardon " is to be pronounced as in

French.) But if the diphthong "cause" be pronounced as a dis-syllable (see 484), the difficulty will be avoided.

We find, however, a double trochee (unless "my" has dropped out) in

> " *Sec. Cit.* Cæ'sar | has hád | great wróng. |
> *Third Cit.*   IIás he, | másters ?"
> *J. C.* iii. 2. 115.

Even here, however, " wrong" may be a quasi-dissyllable (486).

(8) Between noun and participle a pause seems natural. Often the pause represents "in" or "a-" (178).

> "Thy knée | *bússing* | the stónes."—*Coriol.* iii. 2. 75.
> "The smíle | *mócking* | the sígh."—*Cymb.* iv. 2. 54.
> "My wínd | *cóoling* | my bróth."—*M. of V.* i. 1. 22.

In these lines the foot following the emphasized monosyllable may (as an alternative to the "pause-accent") be regarded as quasi-trisyl-labic.

453 a. Emphatic Accents. The syllable that receives an accent is by no means necessarily emphatic. It must be emphatic *relatively to the unaccented syllable or syllables in the same foot*, but it may be much less emphatic than other accented syllables in the same verse. Thus the last syllable of "injuries," though accented, is unemphatic in

> "The ín | jur*íes* | that théy | themsélves | procúre."
> *Lear,* ii. 4. 303.

Mr. Ellis (Early English Pronunciation, part i. p. 334) says that "it is a mistake to suppose that there are commonly or regularly five stresses, one to each measure." From an analysis of several tragic lines of Shakespeare, taken from different plays, I should say that rather less than one of three has the full number of five emphatic accents. About two out of three have four, and one out of fifteen has three. But as different readers will emphasize differently, not much importance can be attached to such results. It is of more importance to remember, (1) that the first foot almost al ways has an emphatic accent ; (2) that two unemphatic accents rarely, if ever, come together ("for" may perhaps be emphatic in

> "Heár it | not, Dún | can ; fór | it ís | a knéll."
> *Macbeth,* ii. 1. 63) ;

and (3) that there is generally an emphatic accent on the third *or* fourth foot.

The five emphatic accents are common in verses that have a pause-accent at the beginning or in the middle of the line.

> "*Náture* | seems déad, | and wíck | ed dréams | abúse."
> *Macbeth*, ii. 1. 50.
> "The hánd | le tóward | my hánd. | *Cóme, let* | me clútch thee."—*Ib.* ii. 1. 34.

And in antithetical lines :

> "I *háve* | thee nót, | and yét | I *sée* | thee stíll."
> *Macbeth*, ii. 1. 35.
> "Bríng with | thee *aírs* | from *héaven* | or *blásts* | from *héll.*"
> *Hamlet*, i. 4. 41.

454. An extra syllable is frequently added before a pause, especially at the end of a line :

> (*a*) "'Tis nót | alóne | my ínk | y clóak, | good móther."
> *Hamlet*, i. 2. 77.

but also at the end of the second foot :

> (*b*) "For míne | own sáfe*ties ;* | you máy | be ríght | ly júst."
> *Macbeth*, iv. 3. 30.

and, less frequently, at the end of the third foot :

> (*c*) "For góod | ness dáres | not chéck *thee ;* | wear thoú | thy wróngs."—*Macbeth*, iv. 3. 33.

and, rarely, at the end of the fourth foot :

> (*d*) "With áll | my hón | ours ón | my bróth*er :* | whereón."
> *Temp.* i. 2. 127.

But see 466.

> "So déar | the lóve | my peó | ple bóre *me :* | nor sét."
> *Ib.* i. 2. 141.

455. The extra syllable is very rarely a monosyllable, still more rarely an emphatic monosyllable. The reason is obvious. Since in English we have no enclitics, the least emphatic monosyllables will generally be prepositions and conjunctions. These carry the attention *forward* instead of *backward*, and are therefore inconsistent with a *pause*, and besides to some extent emphatic.

The fact that in *Henry VIII.*, and in no other play of Shakespeare's, *constant exceptions are found to this rule*, seems to me a sufficient proof that Shakespeare did not write that play.

> "Go gíve | 'em wél | come ; yóu | can spéak | the Frénch tongue."—*Hen. VIII.* i. 4. 57.
> "Féll by | our sérv | ants, by | those mén | we lóv'd *most.*"
> *Ib.* ii. 1. 122.

"Be súre | you bé | not lóose ; | for thóse | you máke
    friends."—Hen. VIII. ii. 1. 127.
"To sí | lence én | vious tóngues. | Be júst | and feár not."
    Ib. iii. 2. 447.

So Hen. VIII. ii. 1. 67, 78, 97 ; and seven times in iii. 2. 442–451 ;
eight times in iv. 2. 51–80.

Even where the extra syllable is not a monosyllable it occurs
so regularly, and in verses of such a measured cadence, as almost
to give the effect of a trochaic* line with an extra syllable at the
beginning, thus :

"In ‖ áll my | míser | íes ; but | thóu hast | fórced me
    Out ‖ óf (457 a) thy | hónest | trúth to | pláy the | wóman.
    Let's ‖ drý our | éyes : and | thús far | héar me, | Crómwell :
    And ‖ whén 1 | ám for- | gótten, | ás I | sháll be,
    And ‖ sléep in | dúll cold | márble | whére no | méntion
    Of ‖ mé must | móre be | héard of, | sáy I | táught thee.
    Say, ‖ Wólsey, | thát once | tród the | wáys of | glóry
    And ‖ sóunded | áll the | dépths and | shóals of | hónour,
    Found ‖ thée a | wáy, out | óf (457 a) his | wréck, to | ríse in
    A ‖ súre and | sáfe one, | thóugh thy | máster | míssed it."
    Hen. VIII. iii. 2. 430–9.

It may be safely said that this is not Shakespearian.

"Boy" is unaccented and almost redundant in

"I párt | ly knów | the mán : | go cáll | him hither, boy."
    (Folio) Rich. III. iv. 2. 41.

(Hither, a monosyllable, see 189.) And even here the Globe is,
perhaps, right in taking "Boy exit" to be a stage direction.

In "Bíd him | make háste | and meét | me át | the Nórth
    gate,"—T. G. of V. iii. 1. 258.

"gate" is an unemphatic syllable in "Nórthgate," like our "Néw-
gate." So

"My mén | should cáll | me lórd : | I ám | yoúr good-man."
    T. of Sh. Ind. 2. 107.

"A hált | er grát | is : nó | thing élse, | for God's-sake."
    M. of V. iv. 1. 379.

"Parts," like "sides," is unemphatic, and "both" is strongly
emphasized, in

"Ráther | to shów | a nób | le gráce | to bóth parts."
    Coriol. v. 3. 121.

---

* The words "trochaic" and "iambic" are of course used, when applied to
English poetry, to denote accent, not quantity.

So "out" is emphatic in
> " We'll háve | a swásh | ing ánd | a márt | ial *oútside*."
> *A. Y. L.* i. 3. 122.

The *'s* for "is" is found at the end of a line in
> "Perceive I speak sincerely, and high note *'s*
> Ta'en of your many virtues."—*Hen. VIII.* ii. 3. 59.

456. Unaccented Monosyllables. Provided there be only one accented syllable, there may be more than two syllables in any foot. "It is he" is as much a foot as "'tis he;" "we will serve" as "we'll serve;" "it is over" as "'tis o'er."

Naturally it is among pronouns and the auxiliary verbs that we must look for unemphatic syllables in the Shakespearian verse. Sometimes the unemphatic nature of the syllable is indicated by a contraction in the spelling. (See 460.) Often, however, syllables must be dropped or slurred in sound, although they are expressed to the sight. Thus in
> "Províde *thee* | two próp | er pál | freys, bláck | as jet,"
> *T. A.* v. 2. 50.

"thee" is nearly redundant, and therefore unemphatic.

"If" and "the" are scarcely pronounced in
> "And ín *it* | are *the* lórds | of Yórk, | Bérkeley, | and Séy-
> mour."—*Rich. II.* ii. 3. 55.
> " *Mir.* I év | er sáw | so nóble. |
> *Prosp.*   *It* goes ón, | I sée."—*Temp.* i. 2. 419.
> "Bút that | the séa, | moúnting | to *the* wél | kin's chéek."
> *Ib.* i. 2. 4.

("The" need not be part of a quadrisyllabic foot, nor be suppressed in pronouncing
> " *The* cúr | iósi | ty of ná | tions tó | depríve me."
> *Lear*, i. 2. 4.

Compare, possibly,
> "But I have ever had that *cúriós(i)ty*."—B. and F. (Nares).)

So "to," the sign of the infinitive, is almost always unemphatic, and is therefore slurred, especially where it precedes a vowel. Thus :
> "*In* séeming | *to* augmént | it wástes | it. Bé | advís'd."
> *Hen. VIII.* i. 1. 145.

where "in" before the participle is redundant and unemphatic.
> "For trúth | to (*t'*) over(*o'er*)péer. | Ráther | than fóol | it só."
> *Coriol.* ii. 3. 128.

So the "l" before "beseech" (which is often omitted, as *Temp.*
ii. I. 1), even when inserted, is often redundant as far as sound goes.

"(*I*) beseéch | your májes | ty, gíve | me léave | to gó."
2 *Hen. VI.* ii. 3. 20.

"(*I*) beséech | your grác | es bóth | to pár | don mé."
Rich. III. i. I. 84. So *Ib.* 103.

Perhaps

"(*I*) pray thee (*prithee*) stáy | with ús, | go nót | to Wítt | enbérg,"
Hamlet, i. 2. 119.

though this verse may be better scanned

"I práy | thee stáy | with us, | go nót | to Wíttenberg." See 469.

"Let *me* sée, | let *me* sée ; | ís not | the léaf | turn'd dówn ?"
J. C. iv. 3. 273.

So (if not 501)

"And I' | will kíss | thy fóot : | (*I*) prithee bé | my gód."
Temp. ii. 2. 152.

"With you" is "wi' you" (as in "good-bye" for "God be
with you") ; "the" is *th'*, and "of" is slurred in

"Two nó | ble párt | ners *with you;* | *the* old dúch | ess
of Nórfolk."—*Hen. VIII.* v. 3. 168.

To write these lines in prose, as in the Folio and Globe, makes
an extraordinary and inexplicable break in a scene which is wholly
verse.

For the quasi-suppression of *of* see

"The bás | tard *of* O'r | leáns | with hím | is joín'd,
The dúke | *of* Alén | çon flí | eth tó | his síde."
1 *Hen. VI.* i. I. 92, 93.

In the *Tempest* this use of unaccented monosyllables in trisyllabic
feet is very common.

"Go máke | thysélf | like *a* nýmph | o' *the* séa; | be súbject
To *no* síght | but thíne | and míne."—*Temp.* i. 2. 301.

Even in the more regular lines of the *Sonnets* these superfluous
syllables are allowed in the foot. Thus :

"Excúse | not sí | lence só ; | for *'t* lies | in thée."—*Sonn.* 101.

And even in rhyming lines of the plays :

"Cáll them | agaín, | sweet prínce, | accépt | their suít ;
I'f you | dený | them, áll | the lánd | will rúe *'t.*"
Rich. III. iii. 7. 221.

This sometimes modifies the scansion. "Hour" is a dissyllable,
and *'t* is absorbed, in

"You knów | I gáve '*t* | you hálf | an *hoú* | *r* sínce."
C. of E. iv. I. 65.

Almost any syllables, however lengthy in pronunciation, can be used as the unaccented syllables in a trisyllabic foot, provided they are unemphatic. It is not usual, however, to find two such unaccented syllables as

" *Which most* gíb | inglý, | ungráve | ly hé | did fáshion."
Coriol. ii. 3. 233.

457. Accented monosyllables. On the other hand, sometimes an unemphatic monosyllable is allowed to stand in an emphatic place, and to receive an accent. This is particularly the case with conjunctions and prepositions at the end of the line. We still in conversation emphasize the conjunctions "but," "and," "for," &c. before a pause, and the end of the line (which rarely allows a final monosyllable to be light, *unless it be an extra-syllable*) necessitates some kind of pause. Hence

" This my mean task
Would be as heavy to me as odious, *but*
The mistress which I serve quickens what's dead."

Temp. iii. I. 5.

"Or ere
It should the good ship so have swallow'd *and*
The fraughting souls within her."—*Ib.* i. 2. 12.

" Freed and enfranchised, not a party *to*
The anger of the king, nor guilty *of*
(If any be) the trespass of the queen."—*W. T.* ii. 2. 62, 63.

So *Temp.* iii. 2. 33, iv. I. 149 ; *W. T.* i. 2. 372, 420, 425, 432, 449, 461, &c.

The seems to have been regarded as capable of more emphasis than with us :

" Whose shadow *the* dismissed bachelor loves."—*Temp.* iv. I. 67.

" With silken streamers *the* young Phœbus fanning."
Hen. V. iii. Prol. 6.

" And your great uncle's, Edward *the* Black Prince."
Ib. i. I. 105, 112.

" And Prosp'ro (469) *the* prime duke, being (470) so reputed."—*Temp.* i. 2. 72.

"Your breath first kindled *the* dead coal of war."—*K. J.* v. 2. 83.

" Omitting *the* sweet benefit of time."—*T. G. of V.* ii. 4. 65.

" So doth the woodbine, *the* sweet honeysuckle."
M. N. D. iv. 1. 47.

" Then, my queen, in silence sad,
Trip we after *the* night's shade."—*Ib.* iv. 1. 101.

" His brother's death at Bristol *the* Lord Scroop."
1 *Hen. IV.* i. 3. 271.

" So please you something touching *the* Lord Hamlet."
Hamlet, i. 3. 89.

" Thou hast affected *the* fine strains of honour."
Coriol. v. 3. 149, 151.

In most of these cases *the* precedes a monosyllable which may be lengthened, thus :

" Your bréath | first kíndled | the déa | d (484) cóal | of wár."
So *Temp.* i. 2. 196, 204 ; ii. 2. 164 ; iv. 1. 153.

Compare

" Oh, weep for Adonais. *The* quick dreams."
SHELLEY, *Adonais,* 82.

But this explanation does not avail for the first example, nor for

" That heals the wound and cures not *the* disgrace."—*Sonn.* 34.

" More needs she *the* divine than the physician."—*Macb.* v. 1. 82.

(Unless, as in *Rich. II.* i. 1. 154, " physician " has two accents :

" More néeds she | the divíne | thán the | physí | cián.")

On the whole there seems no doubt that " the " is sometimes allowed to have an accent, though not (457 a) an emphatic accent.

Scan thus :

" A dévil (466), | *a* bór | n (485) dév | il (475), ón | whose nature."—*Tempest,* iv. 1. 188.

avoiding the accent on *a*.

The in

" Then méet | and jóin. | Jove's líght | nings, *thé* | precúrsors,"
Tempest, i. 2. 201.

seems to require the accent. But " light(e)nings " is a trisyllable before a pause in *Lear,* iv. 7. 35 (see 477), and perhaps even the slight pause here may justify us in scanning—

" Jove's líght | (e)níngs, | the precúrsors."

457 a. Accented Monosyllabic Prepositions. Walker
(*Crit.* on Shakespeare, ii. 173-5) proves conclusively that " of " in " out *of*" frequently has the accent. Thus :

" The fount out *of* which with their holy hands."—B. and F.

" Into a relapse ; or but suppose out *of.*"—MASSINGER.

" Still walking like a ragged colt,
And oft out *of* a bush doth bolt."—DRAYTON.

Many other passages quoted by Walker are doubtful, but he brings forward a statement of Daniel, who, remarking that a trochee is inadmissible at the beginning of an iambic verse of four feet, instances :

" Yearly out *of* his wat'ry cell,"

which shows that he regarded " out óf" as an iambus. Walker conjectures " that the pronunciation (of monosyllabic prepositions) was in James the First's time beginning to fluctuate, and that Massinger was a partisan of the old mode." Hence, probably, the prepositions received the accent in

" Such mén | as hé | be né | ver *át* | heart's éase."
J. C. i. 1. 208.

" Therefóre (490), | out *óf* | thy lóng | expér | ienc'd tíme."
R. and J. iv. 1. 60 ; *Coriol.* i. 10. 19.

" Vaunt cóur | iers *tó* | oak-cléav | ing thún | der-bólts."
Lear, iii. 2. 5.

So *Hen. VIII.* iii. 2. 431, 438.

" To bríng | but fíve | and twén | ty ; *tó* | no móre."
Lear, ii. 4. 251.

" *Lor.* Who únd | ertákes | you *tó* | your end. |
Vaux. Prepáre there."—*Hen. VIII.* ii. 2. 97.

For this reason I think it probable that " to " in " in-*to*," "un-*to*," sometimes receives the accent, thus :

" That év | er lóve | did máke | thee rún | *intó.*"
A. Y. L. ii. 4. 35.

" Came thén | *intó* | my mínd, | and yét | my mínd."
Lear, iv. 1. 36.

" Fán you | *intó* | despáir. | Have the pów | er stíll."
Coriol. iii. 3. 127.

"I had thóught, | by mák | ing thís | well knówn | *untó* you."
Lear, i. 4. 224 ; *M. of V.* v. 1. 169.

" By thís | vile cón | quest sháll | attaín | *untó.*"
J. C. v. 5. 38 ; *Rich. III.* iii. 5. 109.

" Discúss | *untó* | me. A'rt | thou óff | icér ?"
Hen. V. iv. 1. 38. (But this is Pistol.)

With in " *with*out " seems accented in

"That wón | you *with* | out blóws."—*Coriol.* iii. 3. 133.

458. Two extra syllables are sometimes allowed, if unemphatic, before a pause, especially at the end of the line. For
the details connected with this licence see 467-9, and 494, where
it will be seen that verses with six accents are very rare in Shakespeare, and that therefore the following lines are to be scanned with
five accents.

"Perúse | this létter. | Nóthing | almóst | sees *míracles.*"
                                                    Lear, ii. 2. 172.

"Múst be | a fáith | that réa | son wíth | out *míracle.*"
                                                    Ib. i. 1. 225.

"Like óne | that méans | his pró | per hárm | in *mánacles.*"
                                                    Coriol. i. 9. 57.

"Was dúke | dom lárge | enóugh : | of témp(o) | ral
    róyalties."—*Tempest,* i. 2. 110.

"I dáre | avóuch | it, sír. | What, fíf | ty *fóllowers!*"
                                                    Lear, ii. 4. 240.

"You fóol | ish shép | herd, whére | fore dó | you *fóllow*
    her?"—*A. Y. L.* iii. 5. 49.

"Of whóm | he's chíef, | with áll | the síze | that *vérity.*"
                                                    Coriol. v. 2. 18.

"*Ely.* Inclíne | to ít, | or nó. |
 Cant.   He séems | *indífferent.*"—*Hen. V.* i. 1. 72.

"As íf | I lóv'd | my lítt | le shóuld | be *díeted.*"
                                                    Coriol. i. 9. 52.

"Why, só | didst thóu. | Come théy | of nó | ble *fámily ?*"
                                                    Hen. V. ii. 2. 129.

"That né | ver máy | ill óff | ice ór | fell *jéalousy.*"
                                                    Ib. v. 2. 491.

"That hé | suspécts | none ; ón | whose fóol | ish *hónesty.*"
                                                    Lear, i. 2. 197.

"Withín | my tént | his bónes | to-níght | shall líe
Most líke | a sóld | ier, órd | er'd *hón* | (ou)*rably.*"
                                                    J. C. v. 5. 79.

Compare

"Young mán, | thou cóuld'st | not díe | more *hón* | (ou)*rable.*"
                                                    Ib. v. 1. 60.

If "ily" were fully pronounced in both cases, the repetition would
be intolerable in the following :—

" *Cor.* But whát | is líke | me fór | merlý. |
Men. That's *wórthily.*"—*Coriol.* iv. 1. 53.
"The rég | ion óf | my héart : | beKént | *unmánnerly.*"
Lear, i. 1. 147.
"Lóok, where | he cómes! | Not póp | py nór | *man-drágora.*"—*Othello,* iii. 3. 330.
" A's you | are óld | and *réverend,* | you shóuld | be wíse."
Lear, i. 4. 261.
" To cáll | for *récompense :* | appeár | it tó | your mínd."
Tr. and Cr. iii. 3. 8.
"Is nót | so *ést* | *imable,* próf | itáb | le neíther."
M. of V. i. 3. 167.
"Agé is | *un-néc* | *essary;* ón | my knées | I bég."
Lear, ii. 4. 157.
" Our múst | y *sú* | *perflúity.* | Sée our | best élders."
Coriol. i. 1. 230.

459. The spelling (which in Elizabethan writers was more influenced by the pronunciation, and less by the original form and derivation of the word, than is now the case) frequently indicates that many syllables which we now pronounce were then omitted in pronunciation.

460. Prefixes are dropped in the following words :—

'bolden'd for " embolden'd."—*Hen. VIII.* i. 2. 55.
'bove for "above."—*Macbeth,* iii. 5. 31.
'bout for "about."—*Temp.* i. 2. 220.
'braid for "upbraid."—*P. of T.* i. 1. 93.
'call for "recall."—B. and F.
'came for "became."—*Sonn.* 139.
'cause for "because."—*Macbeth,* iii. 6. 21.
'cerns for "concerns."
"What 'cerns it you."—*T. of Sh.* v. 1. 77.
'cide for "decide."—*Sonn.* 46.
'cital for "recital."
"He made a blushing *'cital* of himself."—1 *Hen.IV.*v.2.62.
'collect for "recollect."—B. J. *Alch.* i. 1. ‹
'come for "become."
"Will you not dance?
How *'come* you thus estranged ?"—*L. L. L.* v. 2. 213.
'coraging for "encouraging."—ASCH. 17.

'count for "account."

"Why to a public *'count* I might not go."

Hamlet, iv. 7. 17.

'dear'd for "endear'd."—*A. and C.* i. 4. 44.

'fall for "befall."—*Ib.* iii. 7. 40.　So in O. E.

'friend for "befriend."—*Hen. V.* iv. 5. 17.

'gain-giving for "against-giving," like our "misgiving."—
Hamlet, v. 2. 226.

'gave for "misgave."—*Coriol.* iv. 5. 157 (perhaps).

So "My minde *'gives* me that all is not well" (Nares).　But the
dropping of this essential prefix seems doubtful.　"Gave" would
make sense, though not such good sense.　In

"Then sáy | if théy | be trúe. | This (mis-)shá | pen knáve,"

Temp. v. 1. 268.

Walker with great probability conjectures "*mís-shap'd.*"　In

"Told thee no lies, made thee no mistakings, serv'd,"

Temp. i. 2. 248.

it is more probable that the second "thee," not *mis-,* is slurred.

'get for "beget."—*Othello,* i. 3. 191.

'gree for "agree."—*M. of V.* ii. 2. 108 ; *T. G. of V.* ii. 4.
183 ; *A. and C.* ii. 6. 38.

'haviour for "behaviour."—*Hamlet,* i. 2. 81.

'joy for "enjoy."—*2 Hen. VI.* iii. 2. 365.

'larum for "alarum."

"Then shall we hear their *'larum* and they ours."

Coriol. i. 4. 9.

Folio, "their *Larum.*"

'las for "alas."—*Othello,* v. 1. 111.

'lated for "belated."—*A. and C.* iii. 11. 3.

'less for "unless."—B. J. *Sad Sh.* iii. 1.

'longs for "belongs."—*Per.* ii. Gow. 40.

'longing for "belonging."—*Hen. VIII.* i. 2. 32 ; *W. T.*
iii. 2. 104 ; *Hen. V.* ii. 4. 80.

'miss for "amiss."—*V. and A.*

'mong (pronounced) for "among."

"Be bríght | and jóv | ial amóng | your gúests | to-níght."

Macbeth, iii. 2. 28.

" *Cel.* That líved | amongst mén. |

Oliv. And wéll | he míght | do só."

A. Y. L. iv. 3. 124.

'nighted for "benighted."—*Lear,* iv. 5. 13.

'nointed for "anointed."—*W. T.* iv. 4. 813.

'noyance for "annoyance."—*Hamlet,* iii. 3. 13.

'pairs for "impairs."—B. *E.* 91. So in O. E.

'pale* for "impale," "surround."

> "And will you *'pale* your head in Henry's glory,
> And rob his temples of the diadem."—3 *Hen. VI.* i. 4. 103.

'parel for "apparel."—*Lear,* iv. 1. 51.

'plain for "complain." (Fr. plaindre.)

> "The king hath cause to *plain.*"
> > *Lear,* iii. 1. 39 ; *Rich. II.* i. 3. 175.

'rag'd for "enraged."—*Rich. II.* ii. 1. 70.

'ray for "array."—B. J. *Sad Sh.* ii. "Battel *ray.*"
> > N. *P.* 180. O. E.

'rested for "arrested."—*C. of E.* iv. 2. 42. Dromio uses whichever form suits the metre best.

> "I knów | not át | whose súit | he ís | arrés | ted wéll ;
> But hé's | in a súit | of búff | which résted | him, thát can |
> I téll."—*C. of E.* iv. 2. 43.

So should be read

> "*King.* Or yield up Aquitaine.
> *Princess.*   We (*ar*)*rest* your word."
> > *L. L. L.* ii. 1. 160.

It has been objected that *'rested* is a vulgarism only fit for a Dromio.
But this is not the case. It is used by the master Antipholus E. (*C.
of E.* iv. 4. 3).

'say'd for "assay'd."—*Per.* i. 1. 59. Comp. B. J. *Cy.'s Rev.* iv. 1.

'scape for "escape" freq.

'scuse for "excuse."—*Othello,* iv. 1. 80 ; *M. of V.* iv. 1. 444.

'stall'd apparently for "forestalled."—B. J. *Sejan.* iii. 1 ; for
"install'd."—*Rich. III.* i. 3. 206.

'stonish'd for "astonish'd."

> "Or *'stonish'd* as night-wanderers often are."—*V. and A.* 825.

'stroy'd for "destroy'd."

> "'*Stroy'd* in dishonour."—*A. and C.* iii. 11. 54.

'tend for "attend."—*Hamlet,* iv. 3. 47.

'turn for "return;" *'lotted* for "allotted."

unsisting for "unresisting" (explained in the Globe Glossary
as "unresting").

---

* "Did I *impale* him with the regal crown?"—3 *Hen. VI.* iii. 3. 189.

"That wounds the *unsisting* postern with these blows."
M. for M. iv. 2. 92.

This explains how we must scan

"Prevént | it, resíst (*'sist*) | it, lét | it nót | be só."
Rich. III. iv. 1. 148.

"A sóoth | sayer bíds | you bewáre (*'ware*) | the ídes | of Márch." *J. C.* i. 2. 19.

"Envíron'd (*'viron'd*) | me abóut | and hów | led ín | mine éars."—*Rich. III.* i. 4. 59.

"At án | y tíme | have, recóurse (*'course*) | untó | the prínces."—*Ib.* iii. 5. 109.

"Lest I' | revenge (*'venge*)—whát? | Mysélf | upón | mysélf?"—*Ib.* v. 3. 185.

The apostrophe, which has been inserted above in all cases, is only occasionally, and perhaps somewhat at random, inserted in the Folio. It is therefore not always possible to tell when a verb is shortened, as "comes" for "becomes," or when a verb may, perhaps, be invented. For instance, "dear'd" may be a verbal form of the adjective "dear," or a contraction of the verb "endear'd."

"*Comes* (becomes) *dear'd* (endear'd) by being lack'd."
A. and C. i. 4. 44.

Sometimes, perhaps, the prefix, though written, ought scarcely to be pronounced:

"How fáres | the kíng | and 's fóllow | ers? (Con) | fíned | togéther."—*Temp.* v. 1. 7.

"O (de)spiteful love! unconstant womankind,"
T. of Sh. iv. 2. 14.

unless the "O" stands by itself. (See 512.)

"(Be)lónging | to a mán. | O bé | some óth | er mán."
R. and J. ii. 2. 42.

461. Other Contractions are:

Barthol'mew (*T. of Sh.* Ind. i. 105); *Ha'rford* for "Haverford" (*Rich. III.* iv. 5. 7); *dis'ple* for "disciple" (B. J. *Fox*, iv. 1; so SPENSER, *F. Q.* i. 10. 27); *ignomy* for "ignominy" (*M. for M.* ii. 4. 111, 1 *Hen. IV.* v. 4. 100 [Fol.]; *genman* (UDALL); *gentl'man* (*Ham.* [1603] i. 5); *gent* (SPENSER) freq. for "gentle" (so in O. E.); *easly* (CHAPMAN, *Odyss.*) for "easily;" *par'lous* for "perilous" (*Rich. III.* ii. 4. 35); *inter'gatories* for "interrogatories" (*M. of V.* v. 1. 298); *canstick* for "candlestick,"—

"I had rather hear a brazen *canstick* turned."
I *Hen. IV.* iii. 1. 131.

Marle (B. J. *E. out &c.* v. 4) for "marvel;" *whe'er* for "whether" (O. E.); and the familiar contraction *good-bye,* "God be with you," which enables us to scan *Macbeth,* iii. 1. 44. We also find *in's* for "in his;" *th'wert* for "thou wert;" *you're* for "you were;" *h'were* for "he were." So "she were" is contracted in pronunciation:

> "'Twere goód | *she were* spó | ken wíth: | for shé | may
> stréw."—*Hamlet,* iv. 5. 14.

Y'are for "you are;" *this'* for "this is:"

> "O *this'** the poison of deep grief; it springs
> All from her father's death."—*Hamlet,* iv. 5. 76.

> "*This'* a | good blóck."—*Lear,* iv. 6. 187.

So we ought to scan

> "*Lear. Thís is a* | dull síght. | Aré you | not Ként? |
> *Kent.* The sáme."—*Lear,* v. 3. 282.
> "Sir, *thís is* | the gént | lemán | I tóld | you óf."
> *T. of Sh.* iv. 4. 20.
> "Sir, *thís is* | the hoúse. | Pléase it | you thát | I cáll?"
> *Ib.* 1.

This, for "this is," is also found in *M. for M.* v. 1. 131 (Fol. *this 'a*); *Temp.* iv. 1. 143; *T. of Sh.* i. 2. 45. Many other passages, such as *T. G. of V.* v. 4. 93, *M. for M.* iv. 2. 103, *T. of Sh.* iii. 2. 1, require *is* to be dropped in reading. This contraction in reading is common in other Elizabethan authors; it is at all events as early as Chaucer, *Knighte's Tale,* 233.

Shall is abbreviated into *'se* and *'s* in *Lear,* iv. 6. 246; *R. and J.* i. 3. 9. In the first of these cases it is a provincialism, in the second a colloquialism. A similar abbreviation "I'st," for "I will," "thou'st" for "thou wilt," "thou shalt," &c., seems to have been common in the early Lincolnshire dialect (Gill, quoted by Mr. Ellis). Even where not abbreviated visibly, it seems to have been sometimes audibly, as,

> "If thát | be trúe | I *shall* sée | my bóy | agáin."
> *K. J.* iii. 4. 78.

> "I *shall* gíve | worse páy | ment."—*T. N.* iv. 1. 21.

> "He ís, | Sir Jóhn: | I féar | we *shall* stáy | too lóng."
> I *Hen. IV.* iv. 2. 83.

---

* Globe, "this is."

With seems often to have been pronounced *wi'*, and hence combined with other words. We have "*w'us*," (B. and F. *Elder Brother*, v. 1) for "with us," and "take me *w' ye*" (*ib.*) for "with ye."

Beside the well-known "doff" "do-off," and "don" "do-on," we also find "dout" for "do-out" (*Hamlet*, iv. 7. 192); "probal" for "probable" (*Othello*, ii. 3. 344).

WORDS CONTRACTED IN PRONUNCIATION.

462. Sometimes the spelling does not indicate the contracted pronunciation. For instance, we spell *nation* as though it had three syllables, but pronounce it as though it had two. In such cases it is impossible to determine whether two syllables coalesce or are rapidly pronounced together. But the metre indicates that one of these two processes takes place.

Syllables ending in vowels are also frequently elided before vowels in reading, though not in writing. Thus :

> "*Prosp.* Against | what should | ensúe. |
> *Mir.* How cáme | we ashóre ?"
> *Temp.* i. 2. 158.

> "You gíve | your wífe | *too* unkínd | a cáuse | of grief."
> *M. of V.* v. 1. 175.

> "No (i)mpéd | imént | betwéen, | bút that | you múst."
> *Coriol.* ii. 3. 236.

> "There wás | a yíeld | ing ; thís | admíts | no (e)xcúse."
> *Ib.* v. 6. 69.

Here even the Folio reads "excuse."

> "It ís | too hárd | a knót | for mé | *to* untíe."
> *T. N.* ii. 2. 42.

The is often elided before a vowel, and therefore we may either pronounce *this is, this'* (461), or write *th'* for *the*, in

> "O worthy Goth, *this is the* incarnate devil."—*T. A.* v. 1. 40.

Remembering that "one" was pronounced without its present initial sound of *w*, we shall easily scan (though "the" is not elided in many modern texts)—

> "*Th' one* swéet | ly flátt | ers, *th'* óth | er féar | eth hárm."
> *R. of L.* 172.

> "One hálf | of mé | is yóurs, | *th' óther* | half yóurs."
> *M. of V.* iii. 2. 16.

"Ránsom | ing hím (217) | or píty | ing, thréate | ning
th' other."—*Coriol.* i. 6. 36.

And this explains

" And óf | his óld | expér(i) (467) | ence *th(e)* ón | ly dárling."
A. W. ii. 1. 110.

" Has shóok | and trém | bled át | *the* ill néigh | bourhóod."
Hen. V. i. 2. 154.

" Whére should | this mú | sic bé? | *I'* the áir, | or *the éarth?*"
Temp. i. 2. 387, 389.

(Folio " i' th' air, or th' earth.")

463. R frequently softens or destroys a following vowel (the vowel being nearly lost in the burr which follows the effort to pronounce the *r*).

" Whén the | *alárum* | were strúck | than í | dly sít."
Cor. ii. 2. 80.

" *Ham.* Perchánce | t'will wálk | agáin.
Hor. I *wárrant* | it will."—*Hamlet*, i. 2. 3.

" I' have | cast óff | for éver; | thou shált, | I *wárrant* thee."
Lear, i. 4. 332.

" I bét | ter broók | than *flourish* | *ing* péo | pled tówns."
T. G. of V. v. 4. 3.

" Whiles I | in Ire | land *nóurish* * | a míght | y bánd."
2 Hen. VI. iii. 1. 348.

" Place *bárrels* | of pítch | upón | the fát | al stáke."
1 Hen. VI. v. 4. 57.

" 'Tis *márle* | he stább' | d you nót."
B. J. E. out &c. v. 4 ; *Rich. III.* i. 4. 64.

" A *bárren* | detést | ed vále | you sée | it is."
T. A. ii. 3. 92 ; *2 Hen. VI.* ii. 4. 3.

So " quarrel," *Rich. III.* i. 4. 209.

This is very common with "spirit," which softens the following *i*, or sometimes the preceding *i*, in either case becoming a mono-syllable.

" And thén, | they sáy, | no *spírit* | dares stír | abróad."
Hamlet, i. 1. 161.

So scan

" Hów now, | *spírit*, whither | wánder | you?"—*M. N. D.* ii. 1. 1.

(" Whither" is a monosyllable. See 466.)

---

* Compare *nourrice, nurse.*

This curtailment is expressed in the modern "sprite." So in Lancashire, "brid" for "bird." Hence we can scan

"In aíd | whereóf, | wé of | the *spírit* | *ualty*."

Hen. V. i. 2. 132.

Instances might be multiplied.

464. R often softens a preceding unaccented vowel.

This explains the apparent Alexandrine

"He thínks | me nów | incáp | ablé ; | conféd(e)rales."

Temp. i. 2. 111, iv. 1. 140.

465. Er, el, and le final dropped or softened, especially before

vowels and silent *h*.* The syllable *er*, as in *letter*, is easily interchangeable with *re*, as *lettre*. In O. E. "bettre" is found for "better." Thus words frequently drop or soften *-er ;* and in like manner *-el* and *-le*, especially before a vowel or *h* in the next word :

(1) " Repórt | should rénd | *er* him hoúr | ly tó | your eár."

Cymb. iii. 4. 153.

"Intó | a góod | ly búlk. | Good tíme | encoúnt*er* her."

W. T. ii. 1. 20.

"This létt | *er* he eár | ly báde | me gíve | his fáther."

R. and J. v. 3. 275.

"You'll bé | good cómpany, | my síst | *er* and yoú."

MIDDLETON, *Witch*, ii. 2.

"Than e'ér | the mást | *er* of árts | or gív | *er* of wít."

B. J. *Poetast.*

(2) " Tráv*el* you | far ón, | or áre | you át | the fárthest?"

T. of Sh. iv. 2. 73.

(3) " That máde | great Jóve | to húmb | *le* him tó | her hánd."

Ib. i. 1. 174.

" Gént*le*men | and friénds, | I thánk | you fór | your páins."

Ib. iii. 2. 186.

" I' am | a gént*le* | man óf | a cóm | paný."

Hen. V. iv. 1. 39, 42.

"Needle," which in Gammer Gurton rhymes with "feele," is often pronounced as a monosyllable.

" Deep clerks she dumbs, and with her need*le* (Folio) composes."

P. of T. v. Gower, 5; *Cymb.* i. 1. 168.

---

* The same tendency is still more noticeable in E. E. See Essay on the Metres of Chaucer, by the Rev. W. W. Skeat (Aldine Series).

" Or when she would with sharp need*le* (Folio) wound
The cambric which she made more sound
By hurting it."—*P. of T.* iv. Gower, 23.

In the latter passage "needle wóund" is certainly harsh, though
Gower does bespeak allowance for his verse. Mr. A. J. Ellis
suggests "'ld" for "would," which removes the harshness.

" And gríp | ing ít | the néed*le* | his fíng | er pricks."
R. of L. 319.

" Their néed*les* | to lán | ces, ánd | their gént | le héarts."
K. J. v. 2. 157.

" To thréad | the póst | ern óf | a smáll | need*le's* éye."
Rich. II. v. 5. 17.

" Needle's " seems harsh, and it would be more pleasing to modern
ears to scan "the póst | ern óf a | small née | dle's éye." But this
verse in conjunction with *P. of T.* iv. Gower, 23, may indicate that
"needle" was pronounced as it was sometimes written, very much
like "neeld," and the *d* in "neeld" as in "vild" (vile) may have
been scarcely perceptible.

" A sámp*le* | to the yoúng | est, tó | the móre | matúre."
Cymb. i. 1. 48.

" The cómm | on peóp*le* | by númb | ers swárm | to ús."
3 *Hen. VI.* iv. 2. 2 ; *T. A.* i. 1. 20.

And, even in the *Sonnets :*

" And troúb*le* | deaf heáv | en wíth | my bóot | less críes."
Sonn. 29.

" Unc*le* Már | cus, sínce | it ís | my fá | ther's mínd."
T. A. v. 3. 1.

" *Duke F.* And gét | you fróm | our cóurt. |
Ros.   Me, unc*le?* |
Duke F.   You, cóusin ? "
A. Y. L. i. 3. 44.

466. Whether and **ever** are frequently written or pronounced
whe'r or **where** and **e'er.** The **th** is also softened in **either,
hither, other, father,** &c., and the **v** in **having, evil,** &c.

It is impossible to tell in many of these cases what degree of
"softening" takes place. In "other," for instance, the *th* is so
completely dropped that it has become our ordinary "or," which
we use without thought of contraction. So "whether" is often
written "wh'er" in Shakespeare. Some, but it is impossible to say
what, degree of "softening," though not expressed in writing,
seems to have affected *th* in the following words :—

Brother.

"But fór | our trúst | y *bróther* | -in-láw, | the ábbot."
Rich. II. v. 3. 137.

Either.

"*Either* léd | or drív | en ás | we póint | the wáy."
J. C. iv. 1. 23; *Rich. III.* i. 2. 64, iv. 4. 82.

"Are híred | to béar | their stáves; | *either* thóu, | Macbéth."
Macbeth, v. 7. 18; *M. N. D.* ii. 1. 32.

Further.

"As íf | thou never (*né'er*) | walk'dst *fúrther* | than Fins | bury."
1 *Hen. IV.* iii. 1. 257.

Hither.

"'Tis hé | that sént us ('s) | *hither* nów | to slaúght | er thée."
Rich. III. i. 4. 250.

So the Quartos. The Folio, which I have usually followed in other plays, differs greatly from the Quartos in *Rich. III.* Its alterations generally tend to the removal of seeming difficulties.

Neither.

"*Neither* háve | I món | ey nór | commód | itý."
M. of V. i. 1. 178.

Rather.

"*Ráther* than | have máde | that sáv | age dúke | thine héir."
3 *Hen. VI.* i. 1. 224. So *Othello,* iii. 4. 25; *Rich. II.* iv. 1. 16.

Thither.

"*Thither* gó | these néws | as fást | as hórse | can cárry 'em."
2 *Hen. VI.* i. 4. 78.

Whether.

"Good sír, | say *whéther* | you'll áns | wer mé | or nó."
C. of E. iv. 1. 60.

Perhaps "Which hé | desérves | to lóse. | *Whether* he wás (h' was: 461) | combíned."—*Macbeth,* i. 3. 111.

"But sée, | *whether* Brút | us bé | alíve | or déad."
J. C. v. 4. 30; *Rich. III.* iv. 2. 120.

"A héart | y wélcome. | *Whether* thóu | beest hé | or nó."
Tempest, v. 1. 111.

Whither.

"What meáns | he nów? | Go ásk | him *whither* | he góes."
1 *Hen. VI.* ii. 3. 28.

" *Glouc.* The kíng | is ín | high rágc. |
" *Corn.*   *Whither* is | he góing?"—*Lear,* ii. 4. 299.

So scan

"Hów now, | spírit ! *whither* | wánder | yoú ? "
M. N. D. ii. 1. 1.

This perhaps explains :

> "To fínd | the (462) *other* fórth, | and bý | advént | uring
> bóth."—*M. of V.* i. 1. 143.

But see 501.

Having.

> "Hów could | he sée | to dó | them? *Háving* | made óne."
> *M. of V.* iii. 2. 124.

> "*Having* lóst | the faír | discóv | ery óf | her wáy."
> *V. and A.* 828.

> "Our grán | dam éarth | *having* thís | distémp | eratúre."
> 1 *Hen. IV.* iii. 1. 34.

So *Rich. III.* i. 2. 235 ; *T. of A.* v. 1. 61 ; *A. W.* v. 3. 123 ; *Cymb.* v. 3. 45.

In all of these verses it may seem difficult for modern readers to understand how the *v* could be dropped. But it presents no more difficulty than the *v* in "ever," "over."

Evil.

It is also dropped in "evil" and "devil" (Scotch "de'il").

> "The *évils* | she hátch'd | were nót | efféct | ed, só."
> *Cymb.* v. 5. 60.

> "Of hórr | id héll | can cóme | a *dévil* | more dámn'd."
> *Macbeth,* iv. 3. 56.

> "*Evil*-éyed | untó | you ; y' áre (461) | my príson | er, bút."
> *Cymb.* i. 1. 72.

So *Rich. III.* i. 2. 76. Of course, therefore, the following is not an Alexandrine :

> "Repróach | and díss | olú | tion háng | eth óver him."
> *Rich. II.* ii. 1. 258.

Similarly the *d* is dropped in "ma*d*am," which is often pronounced "ma'am," a monosyllable.

The *v* is of course still dropped in *hast* for *havest*, *has* for *haveth* or *haves*. In the Folio, *has* is often written *ha's*, and an omission in other verbs is similarly expressed, as "sit's" for "sitteth" (*K. J.* ii. 1. 289).

467. I in the middle of a trisyllable, if unaccented, is frequently dropped, or so nearly dropped as to make it a favourite syllable in trisyllabic feet.

> (1) "Judí | cious *púnish* | ment! 'Twás | this flésh | begót."
> *Lear,* iii. 4. 76 ; *M. for M.* i. 3. 39.

"Our rév | (e)rend *cárdi* | *nal* cárried. | Líke it, | your gráce."—*Hen. VIII.* i. 1. 100, 102, 105, &c.

"With whóm | the Ként | ishmén | will *wlll* | *ingly* ríse."
3 *Hen. VI.* i. 2. 41.

"Which áre | the móv | ers óf | a *lánguish* | *ing* déath."
Cymb. i. 5. 9.

"My thóught | whose múr | der yét | is bút | *fantástical*."
Macbeth, i. 3. 139.

"That lóv'd | your fáther: | the *rési* | *due* óf | your fórtune."
A. Y. L. ii. 7. 196.

"*Prómising* | to bríng | it tó | the Pór | pentíne."
C. of E. v. 1. 222.

So 1 *Hen. VI.* iv. 1. 166.

(2) Very frequently before *ly*:

"The méa | sure thén | of óne | is *éasi* | *ly* tóld."
L. L. L. v. 2. 190.

"His shórt | thick néck | cannót | be *eás* | *ily* hármed."
V. and A. 627.

"*Préttily* | methóught | did pláy | the ór | atór."
1 *Hen. VI.* iv. 1. 175.

(3) And before *ty*:

"Such bóld | *hostíli* | *ty*, téach | ing his ('s) dú | teous lánd."
1 *Hen. IV.* iv. 3. 44.

"Of gód- | like *ámi* | *ty*, whích | appéars | most stróngly."
M. of V. iii. 4. 3.

"A·riel | and áll | his *quáli* | *ty*.
"*Prosp.*   Hást | thou, spírit?"—*Tempest*, i. 2. 193.

"Of smóoth | *civíli* | *ty* yét | am I ín | land bréd."
A. Y. L. ii. 7. 96.

Compare BUTLER, *Hudibras*, part ii. cant. 3. 945:

"Which ín | their dárk | *fatál* | '*ties* lúrk | ing
At dés | tin'd pér | iods fáll | a-wórk | ing."

This explains the apparent Alexandrines:

"Thóu wilt | prove hís. | Táke him | to prí | son, *ófficer*."
M. for M. iii. 2. 32.

"Some trícks | of dés | perát | ion, áll | but *máriners*."
Temp. i. 1. 211.

"One dówle | that's ín | my plúme, | my féll | ow * mínisters*."
Temp. iii. 2. 65, v. 1. 28 ; *M. for M.* iv. 5. 6 ; *Macb.* i. 5. 49.

"Thís is | the gént | lemán | I tóld | your *ládyship*."
T. G. of V. ii. 4. 87.

" A vírt | uous gént | lewóm | an, míld | and *beaútiful.*"
T. G. of V. iv. 4. 184.

" And té | d*i*ousnéss | the límbs | and oút | ward *flóurishes.*"
Hamlet, ii. 2. 91.

Sometimes these contractions are expressed in writing, as
"par'lous," *Rich. III.* ii. 4. 35. This is always a colloquial form.

468. Any unaccented syllable of a polysyllable (whether
containing *i* or any other vowel) may sometimes be softened and
almost ignored. Thus—

a " Hóld thee, | from thís, | for éver. | The bárb | *a*rous
Scýthian."—*Lear,* i. 1. 118.

" Sáy by | this tó | ken I' | desíre | his cómp*a*ny."
M. for M. iv. 3. 144.

ed " With thém | they thínk | on. Thíngs | withoút | all
rém*e*dy."—*Macbeth,* iii. 2. 11.

" *Men.* Yoú must | retúrn | and ménd | it.
Sen. Thére's | no rém*e*dy."
Coriol. iii. 2. 26 ; *T. N.* iii. 4. 367.

em " All bró | ken ímpl*e* | *m*ents óf | a rú | ined hóuse."
T. of A. iv. 2. 16.

"Joín'd with | an én*e*my | procláim'd ; | and fróm | his cóffers."
Hen. V. ii. 2. 168; *M. for M.* ii. 2. 180; *Macb.* iii. 1. 105.

en " The méss | *en*gers fróm | our sís | ter ánd | the kíng."
Lear, ii. 2. 54.

" 'Tis dóne | alréa | dy, ánd | the méss | *en*ger góne."
A. and C. iii. 6. 31 ; *A. W.* iii. 2. 111.

Passenger is similarly used.

er " In oúr | last cónfer*e*nce, | páss'd in | probá | tion with
you."—*Macbeth,* iii. 1. 80.

es " This ís | his máj | *e*sty, sáy | your mínd | to hím."
A. W. ii. 1. 98.

" I thát | am rúde | ly stámped, | and wánt | love's máj*e*sty."
Rich. III. i. 1. 16.

Majesty is a quasi-dissyllable in *Rich. III.* i. 3. 1, 19, ii. 1. 75 ;
Rich. II. ii. 1. 141, 147, iii. 2. 113, v. 2. 97, 3. 35 ; *Macbeth,*
iii. 4. 2, 121.

ess " Our púr | pose néc | *ess*ary ánd | not én | vious."
J. C. ii. 1. 178.

i " Lét us | be sácr*i*fic | ers ánd | not bút | chers, Caíus."
Ib. ii. 1. 166.

"The ínn | ocent mílk | in ít | most ínn | ocent moúth."
                                        W. T. iii. 2. 101.

"There táke | an ín | ventorý | of áll | I háve."
                                        Hen. VIII. iii. 2. 452.

ua   "Go thóu | to sánct*ua* | ry [sanctu'ry or sanct'ry], ánd | good
       thóughts | posséss thee." —*Rich. III.* iv. 1. 94.

"Shall flý | out óf (457 a) | itsélf; | nor sléep | nor *sánctuary.*"
                                        Coriol. i. 10. 19.

"Some réad | Alvár | ez' Hélps | to Gráce,
 Some Sánct*ua* | ry óf | a tróub | led sóul."
                        Colvil's *Whig Supplication,* i. 1186 (Walker).

u   "When lív | ing líght | should kíss | it ; 'tís | unnát*u*ral."
                        Macbeth, ii. 4. 10; *Hen. V.* iv. 2. 13.

"Thoughts spéc*u* | latíve | their ún | sure hópes | reláte."
                                        Macbeth, v. 4. 19.

"And né | ver líve | to shów | the incréd*u* | lous wórld."
                                        2 Hen. IV. iv. 5. 153.

"Hów you | were bórne | in hánd, | how cróss'd, | the ín-
strúments."—*Macbeth,* iii. 1. 81, iv. 3. 239.

**469. Hence polysyllabic names often receive but one
accent at the end of the line in pronunciation.**

Proper names, not conveying, as other nouns do, the origin and
reason of their formation, are of course peculiarly liable to be
modified ; and this modification will generally shorten rather than
lengthen the name.

"To yoúr | own cón | science, sír, | befóre | *Políxenes.*"
                                        W. T. iii. 2. 47.

"That ére | the sún | shone bríght | on. O'f | *Hermíone.*"
                                        Ib. v. 1. 95.

"The rár | est óf | all wó | men. Gó, | *Cleómenes.*"
                                        Ib. 112.

"To oúr | most fáir | and prínce | ly cóus | in *Kátharine.*"
                                        Hen. V. v. 2. 4.

"My bróth | er ánd | thy ún | cle, cálled | *António.*"
                                        Temp. i. 2. 66.

"My lórd | Bassán | io, sínce | you have fóund | *António.*"
                        M. of V. i. 1. 59 : so often in this play.

"Then all | a-fíre | with mé | ; the kíng's | son *Férdinand.*"
                                        Temp. i. 2. 212.

"I rát | ifý | thís my | rich gíft. | O *Férdinand.*"—*Ib.* iv. 1. 8.

"Then pár | don mé | my wróngs. | But hów | should
Próspero ?"—*Ib.* v. 1. 119.

" I'll áf | ter, móre | to bé | revenged | on *E'glamour.*"
T. G. of V. v. 2. 51.

"Whát it | contáins. | I'f you | shall sée | *Cordélia.*"
Lear, iii. 1. 46.

" Upón | such sácr | ifíc | es, mý | *Cordélia.*"
Ib. v. 3. 20, 245.

So throughout the play.

"Whẹn thóu | liest hów | ling. Whát! | the faír | *Ophélia.*"
Hamlet, v. 1. 265.

" At Gré | cian swórd | contémn | ing. Téll | *Valéria.*"
Coriol. i. 3. 46.

" Here, íf | it líke | your hón | our. Sée | that *Cláudio.*"
M. for M. ii. 1. 33, iii. 1. 48.

" So thén | you hópe | of pár | don fróm | lord *A'ngelo ?*"
Ib. iii. 1. 1, iv. 3. 147, i. 4. 79.

" I sée | my són | Antíph | olús | and *Drómio.*"
C. of E. v. 1. 196.

" The fórm | of déath. | Meantíme | I writ | to *Rómeo.*"
R. and J. v. 3. 246.

" Lóoks it | not líke | the kíng? | Márk it, | *Horátio.*"
Hamlet, i. 1. 43.

" They lóve | and dóte | on ; cáll | him boúnt | (e)ous *Búck-ingham."—Hen. VIII.* ii. 1. 52; *Rich. III.* iv. 4. 508, ii. 2. 123.

" *Vaux.* The greát | ness óf | his pér | son.
Buck. Náy, | Sir *Nícolas.*"
Hen. VIII. ii. 1. 100.

" But I' | beséech | you, whát's | becóme | of *Kátharine ?*"
Ib. iv. 1. 22.

" Sáw'st thou | the mél | anchól | y Lórd | *Northúmber-land?"—Rich. III.* v. 3. 68.

" Thérefore | presént | to hér, | as sóme | time *Márgaret.*"
Ib. iv. 4. 274.

" And yóu | our nó | less lóv | ing són | of *A'lbany.*"
Lear, i. 1. 43.

" Exásp | erátes, | makes mád | her sís | ter *Góneril.*"
Ib. v. 1. 60.

" As fít | the bríd | al. Beshréw | me múch, | *Emília.*"
Othello, iii. 4. 150.

" Is cóme | from Cæ's | ar ; thére | fore héar | it, *A'ntony.*"
A. and C. i. 1. 27, i. 5. 21, &c.

" Than Clé | opátr | a, nór | the quéen | of *Ptólemy.*"
Ib. i. 4. 6.

"With thém, | the twó | brave beárs, | Wárwick | and
Móntague."—3 Hen. VI. v. 7. 10.

Less frequently in the middle of the line :

"My lórd | of Búckingham, | if mý | weak ór | atóry."
Rich. III. iii. 1. 37.

"Cóusin | of Búck | ingham ánd | you ságe, | grave mén."
Ib. iii. 7. 217.

"Lóoking | for A'ntony. | But áll | the chárms | of lóve."
A. and C. ii. 1. 20.

"Did sláy | this Fórtinbras ; | who, bý | a seál'd | compáct
(490)."—Hamlet, i. 1. 86.

"Thrift, thríft, | Horátio, | the fú | nerál | bak'd méats."
Ib. i. 2. 180.

"He gáve | to Alexánder ; | to Ptólem | y hé | assígned."
Ib. iii. 6. 15.

"Thou árt | Hermíone ; | or ráth | er, thoú | art shé."
W. T. v. 3. 25.

"To sóft | en A'ngelo, | and thát's | my píth | of búsiness."
M. for M. i. 4. 70.

Enobárbus in *A. and C.* has but one accent, wherever it stands
in the verse :

"Bear háte | ful mémo | ry, póor | Enobár | bus did."
A. and C. iv. 9. 9, &c.

"Of yóur | great pré | decéssor, | King E'dward | theThírd."
Hen. V. i. 2. 248.

It may here be remarked that great licence is taken with the
metre wherever a list of names occurs :

"That Harry duke of Hereford, Rainold lord Cobham,
Sir Thomas Erpingham, Sir John Ramston,
Sir John Norbery, Sir Robert Waterton, and Francis Quoint."
Rich. II. ii. 1. 279, 283, 284.

"The spirits
Of valiant Shirley, Stafford, Blunt, are in my arms."
1 Hen. IV. v. 4. 4.

"Whither away, Sir John Falstaffe, in such haste?"
1 Hen. IV. iii. 2. 104.

"John duke of Norfolk, Walter Lord Ferrers."
Rich. III. v. 5. 13.

"Lord Cromwell of Wingfield, Lord Furnival of Sheffield."
Ib. iv. 7. 166.

"Sir Gilbert Talbot, Sir William Stanley."—Ib. iv. 5. 10.

In the last examples, and in some others, the pause between two names seems to license either the insertion or omission of a syllable.

470. Words in which a light vowel is preceded by a heavy vowel or diphthong are frequently contracted, as *power, jewel, lower, doing, going, dying, playing, prowess,* &c.

"The whích | no sóon | er hád | his prówe*ss* | confírm'd."
Macbeth, v. 8. 41.

Comp. "And he that routs most pigs and cows,
The fórm | idáb | lest mán | of prówe*ss.*"
Hudib. iii. 3. 357.

Perhaps

"Which bóth | thy dú | ty ówes | and óur | *power* cláims."
A. W. ii. 3. 168.

(This supposes "our" emphasized by antithesis, but "and our pów | er cláims" (ELLIS) may be the correct scanning.)

Being.—"That wíth | his pér | emptór | y "sháll" | *being* pút."
Coriol. iii. 1. 94, 2. 81.

"The sóv | ereigntý | of eí | ther *béing* | so great."
R. of L. 69.

This explains the apparent Alexandrines :

"And *béing* | but a tóy | that ís | no gríef | to gíve."
Rich. III. ii. 1. 114.

"Withóut | a párall | el, thése | *being* áll | my stúdy."
Tempest, i. 2. 74.

Doing.—"Can láy | to béd | for éver : | whiles yóu, | *doing* thús."
Ib. ii. 1. 284.

Seeing.—"Or *séeing* | it óf | such chíld | ish fríend | linéss."
Coriol. ii. 3. 183.

"I'll in | mysélf | to sée, | and in thée | *seeing* íll."
Rich. II. ii. 1. 94.

"That yóu | at súch | times *séeing* | me né | ver sháll."
Hamlet, i. 5. 173.

-ying.—"And *próph* | es*ýing* | with ác | cents tér | rible."
Macbeth, ii. 3 62.

This may explain

"Lóck'd in | her món(u) [468] | ment. Shé'd | a *préph(e)-* | s*ying* féar."—*A. and C.* iv. 14. 120.

So with other participles, as

"They, *knówing* | dame E'l | eanór's | aspír | ing húmour."
2 Hen. VI. i. 2. 97.

The rhythm seems to demand that "coward" should be a quasi-monosyllable in

> "Wrong ríght, | base nóble, | old yoúng, | *coward* vál | iánt."
> *T. A.* iv. 1. 29.

"Noble" a monosyllable.   (See 465.)

> "Yét are | they páss | ing *cówardly*. | But I' | beséech you."
> *Coriol.* i. 1. 207.

471. The plural and possessive cases of nouns in which the singular ends in s, se, ss, ce, and ge, are frequently written, and still more frequently pronounced, without the additional syllable :

> "A's the | dead *cár* | *casses* óf | unbúr | ied mén."
> *Coriol.* iii. 3. 122.

> "Thínking | upón | his *sér* | *vices* tóok | from yóu."
> *Ib.* ii. 2. 231.

> "Their *sénse* | *are* [Fol. sic] shút."—*Macbeth,* v. 1. 29.

> "My *sénse* | *are* stópped."—*Sonn.* 112.

> "These *vérse.*"—DANIEL.

> "I'll tó | him; hé | is híd | at *Láwr* | *ence*' céll."
> *R. and J.* iii. 2. 141.

> "Great kings of France and England ! That I have laboured,
> Your *míght* | *inéss* | on bóth | parts bést | can wítness."
> *Hen. V.* v. 2. 28.

"Place" is probably used for "places" in

> "The frésh | springs, bríne- | pits, bár | ren *pláce* | and
> fértile."—*Tempest,* i. 2. 338.

> "These twó | *Antíph* | *olús* [Folio], | these twó | so líke."
> *C. of E.* v. 1. 357.

> "Are there *balance ?*"—*M. of V.* iv. 1. 255.

> "(Here) have I, thy schoolmaster,, made thee more profit
> Than óth | er *prín* | *cess* [Folio] cán | that háve | more
> tíme."—*Temp.* i. 2. 173.

> "Sits on his *horse* back at mine *hostess* door."
> *K. J.* ii. 1. 289 (Folio).

> "Looked pále | when théy | did héar | of *Clár* | *ence* (Folio)
> déath."—*Rich. III.* ii. 1. 137, iii. 1. 144.

Probably the *s* is not sounded (*horse* is the old plural) in

> "And Duncan's *horses* (a thing most strange and certain)."
> *Macbeth,* ii. 4. 14.

> "Lies in their *purses*, and whoso empties them."
> *Rich. II.* ii. 2. 130.

Even after *ge* the *s* was often suppressed, even where printed.
Thus :

    " How many ways shall *Carthage's* glory grow !"
                 SURREY'S *Æneid IV.* (Walker).

But often the *s* was not written. So
    " In violating *marriage* sacred law."
                 Edward III. (1597 A.D.) (LAMB.)

The *s* is perhaps not pronounced in

    " Conjéct | (u)ral *márr* | *iage*(*s*) ; mák | ing párt | ies stróng."
                         Coriol. i. 1. 198.

    " Are brá | zen *ím* | *ages* óf | canón (491) | iz'd sáints."
                       2 *Hen. VI.* i. 3. 63.

    " The *ím* | *ages* óf | revólt | and flý | ing óff !"
                       Lear, ii. 4. 91.

    " O'ff with | his són | *George's* héad."—*Rich. III.* v. 3. 344.

    " Létters | should nót | be knówn, | *riches* póv | ertý."
                       Tempest, ii. 1. 150.

This may perhaps explain the apparent Alexandrines :

    " I próm | is'd yóu | redréss | of thése | same *griévances.*"
                      2 *Hen. IV.* iv. 2. 113.

    " This déi | ty in | my bós | om twén | ty *cónsciences.*"
                      Temp. ii. 1. 278.

    " And stráight | discláim | their tóngues ? | Whát are | your
        óffices ?"—*Coriol.* iii. 1. 85.

    " Popíl | ius Lé | na spéaks | not óf | our *púr* | *poses.*"
                      J. C. iii. 1. 23.

    " She lév | ell'd át | our *púr* | *poses,* ánd | being (470) róyal,"
                      A. and C. v. 2. 339.

(or " | our *púrpose*(*s*), | and bé | ing róyal.")

    " A thíng | most brú | tish, I' | endówed | thy *púrposes.*"
                      Tempest, i. 2. 357.

    " Nor whén | she *púrposes* | retúrn. | Beséech | your híghness."
                      Cymb. iv. 3. 15.

    " As blánks, | *benévo* | *lences* ánd | I wót | not whát."
                      Rich. II. ii. 1. 250.

    " My *sérv* | *ices* whích | I have ('ve) dóne | the Sígn | iorý."
                      Othello, i. 2. 18.

    " These pípes | and thése | *convéy* | *ances* óf | our blóod."
                      Coriol. v. 1. 54.

    " *Profésses* | to persuáde | the kíng | his són's | alíve."
                      Temp. ii. 1. 236.

Either " whom I" is a detached foot (499) or *s* is mute in
" Whom I', | with this | obéd | ient stéel, | three ínches of it
(inch of 't)."—*Tempest,* ii. 1. 285.

**472. Ed following d or t is often not written (this
elision is very old: see 341, 342), and, when written,
often not pronounced.**

" I hád | not quót*ed* him. | I féar'd | he díd | but trífle."
Hamlet, ii. 1. 112.
" *Reg.*   That ténd*ed* (Globe, ' tend') | upón | my fáther.
Glou. I knów | not, mádam."—*Lear,* ii. 1. 97.
" Since nót | to bé | avóid*ed* | it fálls | on mé."
1 *Hen. IV.* v. 4. 13.
" But júst | ly ás | you háve | excéed*ed* | all prómise."
A. Y. L. i. 2. 156.
" For tréas | on éxe | cut*ed* ín | our láte | king's dáys."
1 *Hen. VI.* ii. 4. 91.
" And só, | rívet*ed* | with faíth | untó (457) | your flésh."
M. of V. v. 1. 169.
" Be sóon | colléct | *ed* and áll | things thóught | upón."
Hen. V. i. 2. 305.
" I's to | be fríght*ed* | out of féar : | and ín | that móod."
A. and C. iii. 13. 196.
" Was ápt | ly fítt*ed* | and nát | (u)rally | perfórm'd."
T. of Sh. Ind. 1. 87.
" Is nów | convért*ed* : | but nów | I wás | the lórd."
M. of V. iii. 2. 169.
" Which I' | mistrúst*ed* | not : fáre | well thére | fore, Héro."
M. Ado, ii. 1. 189.
" All ún | avóid*ed* | is the dóom | of dést | iný."
Rich. III. iv. 4. 217.

but here "destiny" (467) may be a dissyllable, and -*ed* sonant.

This explains the apparent Alexandrine :

" I thús | negléct | ing wórld | ly énds | all *dédicated.*"
Temp. i. 2. 89.
" Shóuting | their ém | ulá | tion. Whát | is *gránted* them ? "
Coriol. i. 1. 218.

So strong was the dislike to pronouncing two dental syllables
together, that "it" seems nearly or quite lost after "set" and
"let" in the following :

" I húmb | ly *sét it* | at your wíll ; | but fór | my místress."
Cymb. iv. 3. 9.

" To hís | expér | ienced tóngue ; | yet *lét it* | please bóth."
Tr. and Cr. i. 3. 68.
" Yóu are a | young húnt | sman, Már | cus : *lét it* alone."
T. A. iv. 2. 101.
" You sée | is kíll'd | in hím : | and *yét it* | is dánger."
Lear, iv. 7. 79.
So perhaps " Of éx | cellént | dissémb | ling ; ánd | *let it* lóok."
A. and C. i. 3. 79.
But more probably, " dissémbling ; | and lét | it lóok."

**473. Est in superlatives is often pronounced st after
dentals and liquids.** A similar euphonic contraction with respect
to *est* in verbs is found in E. E. Thus "bindest" becomes "binst,"
"eatest" becomes "est." Our "best" is a contraction for "bet-est."
" Twó of | the swéet'*st* | compán | ions ín | the wórld."
Cymb. v. 5. 349.
" At yóur | *kind'st* léisure."—*Macbeth*, ii. 1. 24.
" The *stérn'st* | good níght."—*Ib.* ii. 2. 4.
" *Secret'st.*"—*Ib.* iii. 4. 126.
" Thís is | thy *éld'st* | son's són."—*K. J.* ii. 1. 177.
So *Temp.* v. 1. 186.
" Since déath | of mý | *dear'st* móth | er."—*Cymb.* iv. 2. 190.
" The *lóy* | *al'st* hús | band thát | did é'er | plight tróth."
Ib. i. 1. 96.
A. W. ii. 1. 163, "*great'st.*" " The *sweet'st, dear'st.*"—*W. T.*
iii. 2. 202. " *Near'st.*"—*Macb.* iii. 1. 118. " *Unpleasant'st.*"—
M. of V. iii. 2. 254. "*Strong'st.*"—*Rich. II.* iii. 3. 201. "*Short'st.*"
—*Ib.* v. 1. 80. "*Common'st.*"—*Ib.* v. 3. 17. "*Faithfull'st.*"—
T. N. v. 1. 117.
This lasted past the Elizabethan period.
" Know there are rhymes which fresh and fresh apply'd
Will cure the *arrant'st* puppy of his pride."
POPE, *Imit. Hor. Epist.* i. 60.
The Folio reads "stroakst," and "made" in
" Thou *stróakedst* | me ánd | *madest* múch | of mé, | *would'st*
gíve me."—*Tempest*, i. 2. 333.
But the accent on "and" is harsh. Perhaps "and má | dest."

VARIABLE SYLLABLES.

**474. Ed final is often mute and sonant in the same
line.** Just as *one* superlative inflection -*est* does duty for two closely
connected adjectives (398) :

" The generous and grav*est* citizens."—*M. for M.* iv. 6. 13.
and the adverbial inflection *ly* does duty for two adverbs (397) :

" And she will speak most bitter*ly* and strange."
M. for M. v. 1. 36.

so, when two participles ending in -*ed* are closely connected by
"and," the *ed* in one is often omitted in pronunciation.

" *Despís'd*, | *distréss* | *ed*, hát | ed, márt | yr'd, kílled."
R. and J. iv. 5. 59.

" We have wíth | a *léav* | *en'd* ánd | *prepár* | *ed* chóice."
M. for M. i. 1. 52.

" To thís | *unlóok'd* | for, *ún* | *prepár* | *ed* pómp."
K. J. ii. 1. 560.

In the following the -*ed* sonant precedes :

" That wére | *embátt* | *ailéd* | and *ránk'd* | inKént." ·
K. J. iv. 2. 200.

" We áre | *impréss* | *ed ánd* | *engág'd* | to fíght."
1 *Hen. IV.* i. 1. 21.

" For thís | they háve | *engróss* | *ed* ánd | pil'd úp."
2 *Hen. IV.* iv. 5. 71.

" Thou *cháng* | *ed* ánd | *self-cóv* | *er'd* thíng, | for sháme."
Lear, iv. 2. 62.

At the end of a line *ed* is often sounded after *er :*

" Which hís | hell-góv | ern'd árm | hath *bútc* | *heréd.*"
Rich. III. i. 2. 74.

See *J. C.* ii. 1. 208 ; iii. 1. 17 ; iii. 2. 7, 10 ; iv. 1. 47; v. 1. 1.
So *Rich. III.* iii. 7. 136 ; iv. 3. 17 ; v. 3. 92 ; *M. N. D.* iii. 2. 18,
&c.   This perhaps arises in part from the fact that " er " final in
itself (478) has a *lengthened* sound approaching to a dissyllable.

Ed is very frequently pronounced in the participles of words
ending in *fy,* "glori*fy*," &c.

" Most *pút* | *rifí* | *ed* córe, | so fáir | withóut."
Tr. and Cr. v. 9. 1.

" My *mórt* | *ifí* | *ed* spírit. | Now bíd | me rún."
J. C. ii. 1. 324.

" Váughan | and áll | that háve | *miscárr* | *iéd.*"
Rich. III. v. 1. 5.

" The Frénch | and E'ng | lish thére | *miscár* | *riéd.*"
M. of V. ii. 8. 29.

" That cáme | too lág | to sée | him *bú* | *riéd.*"—*Ib.* ii. 1. 90.

So frequently in other Elizabethan authors.   Also when preceded
by *rn, rm,* "tu*rn*ed," "confi*rm*ed," &c., and in "followed : "

" As théy | us tó | our trénch | es *fóll* | *owéd.*"
Coriol. i. 4. 42.

On the other hand, *-ed* is mute in

" By whát | by-páths | and ín | diréct | *crook'd* wáys."
2 *Hen. IV.* iv. 5. 185.

In " *Warder.* We dó | no óth | erwíse | than wé | are *will'd.*
Glou. Who *will* | *ed* yóu? | Or whóse | will stánds |
but míne,"—1 *Hen. VI.* i. 3. 11.

it would seem that the latter "willed" is the more emphatic of the two, and it will probably be found that in many cases where two participles are connected, the more emphatic has *ed* sonant. Thus the former "banished" is the more emphatic of the two in

"Hence *bán* | *ishéd* | is *bánish'd* fróm | the wórld."
R. and J. iii. 3. 19.

475. A word repeated twice in a verse often receives two accents the first time, and one accent the second, when it is less emphatic the second time than the first. Or the word may occupy the whole of a foot the first time, and only part of a foot the second. Thus in

" *Fáre* (480) | well, gen | tle mís | tress : *fáre* | *well,* Nán."
M. W. of W. iii. 4. 97.

" *Fáre* (480) | *well,* gén | tle cóus | in. Cóz, | *farewéll.*"
K. J. iii. 2. 17.

" Of gréat | est júst | ice. *Wrí* | *te* (484), *write,* | Rináldo."
A. W. iii. 4. 29.

"These *ví* | *olént'*| desíres | have *vío* | *lent* énds."
R. and J. ii. 6. 9.

" With hér | that *hát* | *eth* thée | and *hátes* | us áll."
2 *Hen. VI.* ii. 4. 52.

Here the emphasis is on "ends" and "us all."

" *Duke. Stíll* (486) | so crú | el?
Oliv. *Stíll* | so cón | stant, lórd."—*T. N.* v. 1. 113.

" *Com. Knów* (484), | I práy | you.
Coriol. I' | 'll *knów* | no fúrther."—*Coriol.* iii. 3. 87.

" *Déso* | *late, dés* | *olate,* wíll | I hénce | and díe."
Rich. II. i. 2. 73.

The former "Antony" is the more emphatic in

"But wére | I Brútus
And Brú | tus *A'n* | *tonŷ,* | thére were | an *A'ntony.*"
J. C. iii. 2. 231.

So, perhaps, the more emphatic verb has the longer form in

"He róus | *eth* úp | himsélf | and mák*es* | a páuse "

R. of L. 541.

This is often the case with diphthongic monosyllables.   See 484.
Compare

" *Nów* | it schéy | neth, *nów* | it réyn | eth fáste."

CHAUCER, *C. T.* 1537.

476. On the other hand, when the word increases in emphasis, the converse takes place.

"And lét | thy blóws, | *dóubly* | *redóub* | (*e*)*léd*."

Rich. II. i. 3. 80.

" *Virg.* O, *héavens,* | O, *héav* | *ens.*
  Coriol.   Náy, | I prí | thee, wóman."

Coriol. iv. 1. 12.

"Wás it | his *spírit* | by *spír* | *its* táught | to wríte?"

Sonn. 86.

" And wíth | her *pérson* | *age,* hér | tall *pér* | *sonáge.*"

M. N. D. iii. 2. 292.

" *Március* | would háve | all fróm | you—*Már* | *ciús,*
  Whom láte | you have námed | for cónsul."

Coriol. iii. 1. 95.

Even at the end of the verse Marcius has but one accent, as a rule. But here it is unusually emphasized.

" And *whé'r* | he rún | or flý | they knów | not *whéther.*"

V. and A. 304.

" *King.* Be *pát* | *ient,* gént | le quéen, | and I' | will stáy.
  Queen. Whó can | be *pát* | *iént* | in thése | extrémes."

3 *Hen. VI.* i. 1. 215–6.

" *Yield,* my lórd | protéct | or, *yí* | *eld,* Wínch | estér."

1 *Hen. VI.* iii. 1. 112.

" *Citizens. Yield,* Már | cius, *yí* | *eld.*
  Men.   Hé | *ar* (480) mé, | one wórd."

Coriol. iii. 1. 215.

" A *dévil* (466), | a bór | n (485) *dé* | *vil,* ín | whose náture."

Tempest, iv. 1. 188.

So arrange   "You héavens (512), |
  Gíve me | that *pát* | *ience, pát* | *iénce* | I néed."

Lear, ii. 4. 274.

("Patient" was treated as a trisyllable by the orthoepists of the time.)

"*Being* hád, | to trí | umph *bé* | *ing* (on the other hand)
láck'd, | to hópe."—*Sonn.* 52.

Similarly "Which árt | my *néar'st* | and *déar* | *est* én | emý."
1 *Hen. IV.* iii. 2. 123.

On the other hand, perhaps, "sire," and not "cówards," is a dissyllable in

"Cowards fá | ther cówards, | and báse | things *sí* | *re* base."
Cymb. iv. 2. 26.

So, perhaps, "Pánting | he lí*es* | and bréath | *eth* ín | her fáce."
V. and A. 62.

Here "lies" is unemphatic, "breatheth" emphatic.

For diphthongic monosyllables see 484.

The same variation is found in modern poetry. In the following line there is, as it were, an antithetical proportion in which the two middle terms are emphatic, while the extremes are unemphatic :

"*Tówer* be | yond *tów* | *er*, *spí* | *re* bé | yond *spíre.*"—Tennyson.

LENGTHENING OF WORDS.

477. R, and liquids in dissyllables, are frequently pronounced as though an extra vowel were introduced between them and the preceding consonant :

"The párts | and grá | ces óf | the wrés | t(*e*)lér."
A. Y. L. ii. 2. 13.
"In séc | ond ácc | ent óf | his órd | (*i*)nánce."
Hen. V. ii. 4. 126.

The Folio inserts *i* here, and *e*, *Ib.* iii. Prologue, 26. In the latter passage the word is a dissyllable.

"If yóu | will tár | ry, hó | ly pílg | (*e*)rím."—*A. W.* iii. 5.43.
"While shé | did cáll | me rás | cal fíd | d(*e*)lér."
T. of Sh. ii. 1. 158.
"The lífe | of hím. | Knów'st thou | this cóun | t(*e*)rý ?"
T. N. i. 2. 21. So *Coriol.* i. 9. 17; 2 *Hen. VI.* i. 1. 206.
"And thése | two Dróm | ios, óne | in sémb | (*e*)lánce."
C. of E. v. 1. 358; *T. G. of V.* i. 3. 84.
"Yóu, the | great tóe | of thís | assémb | l(*e*)ý."
Coriol. i. 1. 158.
"*Cor.* Be thús | to thém. |
Patr. You dó | the nó | b(*e*)lér."—*Ib.* iii. 2. 6.
"*Edm.* Sír, you | speak nó | b(*e*)lý. |
Reg. Whý is | this réason'd ? "—*Lear*, v. 1. 28.

(?) " Go séarch | like nó | b(*e*)lés, | like nó | ble súbjects."
P. of T. ii. 4. 50.

The *e* is actually inserted in the Folio of *Titus Andronicus* in
"brethren :"

"Give Mú | cius búr | ial wíth | his bréth | *e*rén."
T. A. i. 1. 347.

And this is by derivation the correct form, as also is " child*e*ren."

"These áre | the pár | ents óf | these chíl | d(*e*)rén."
C. of E. v. 1. 360.

"I gó. | Wríte to | me vér | y shórt | (*e*)lý."
Rich. III. iv. 4. 428.

" A rót | ten cáse | abídes | no hánd | (*e*)líng."
2 *Hen. IV.* iv. 1. 161.

"The fríends | of Fránce | our shróuds | and táck | (*e*)língs."
3 *Hen. VI.* v. 3. 18.

" Than Ból | ingbróke's | retúrn | to E'ng | (*e*)lánd."
Rich. II. iv. 1. 17.

"And méan | to máke | her quéen | of E'ng | (*e*)lánd."
Rich. III. iv. 4. 263.

So in E. E. "Eng*e*land."

" To bé | in án | ger ís | impí | etý ;
But whó | is mán | that ís | not án | g(*e*)rý?"
T. of A. iii. 5. 56.

in which last passage the rhyme indicates that *angry* must be pronounced as a trisyllable.

" And stréngth | by límp | ing swáy | disá | b(*e*)léd."—*Sonn.* 66.

So also in the middle of lines—

"Is Cáde | the són | of Hén | (*e*)rý | the Fífth?"
2 *Hen. VI.* iv. 8. 36.

This is common in *Hen. VI.*, but not I think in the other plays—
not for instance in *Rich. II.*

"That cróaks | the fá | tal én | t(*e*)ránce | of Dúncan."
Macbeth, i. 5. 40.

"Cárries | no fá | vour ín't | but Bért | (*e*)rám's."
A. W. i. 1. 94.

" O mé! | you júgg | (*e*)lér! | you cán | ker blóssom."
M. N. D. iii. 2. 282.

"'Tis mónst | (*e*)róus. | Iá | go, whó | begán it ?"
Othello, ii. 3. 217.

" And thát | hath dázz | (*e*)léd | my réa | son's líght."
T. G. of V. ii. 4. 210.

"Béing | so frús | t(e)ráte. | Téll him | he mócks."

A. and C. v. 1. 2.

"Lord Dóug | (e)lás, | go yóu | and téll | him só."

1 *Hen. IV.* v. 2. 83.

"Gráce and | remém | b(e)ránce | be tó | you bóth."

W. T. iv. 4. 76.

"Of quíck | cross líght | (e)ning? | To wátch, | poor pérdu."

Lear, iv. 7. 35.

"Thou kíll'st | thy míst | (e)réss : | but wéll | and frée."

A. and C. ii. 5. 27.

"To táunt | at sláck | (e)néss. | Caníd | ius wé."

Ib. iii. 7. 28.

So also probably "sec(e)ret," "monst(e)rous" (*Macbeth*, iii. 6. 8), "nob(e)ly," "wit(e)ness," *T. G. of V.* iv. 2. 110, and even "cap(i)tains" (French "capitaine :" *Macbeth*, i. 2. 34, 3 *Hen. VI.* iv. 7. 32, and perhaps *Othello*, i. 2. 53).

Spenser inserts the *e* in some of these words, as "hand*e*ling," *F. Q.* i. 8. 28; "ent*e*rance," *ib.* 34.

478. Er final seems to have been sometimes pronounced with a kind of "burr," which produced the effect of an additional syllable ; just as "Sirrah" is another and more vehement form of "Sir." Perhaps this may explain the following lines, some of which may be explained by 505–10, but not all :

" *Corn.* We'll téach | you——
Kent.　　　　　　　　　*Sír*, | 'I'm | too óld | to léarn."

Lear, ii. 2. 135.

(But? " I' am.")

" Lénds the | tongue vóws ; | these blá | zes dáugh | *tér.*"

Hamlet, i. 3. 117.

" And thére | upón, | gíve me | your *dáugh* | *tér.*"

Hen. V. v. 2. 475.

" *Bru.* Spread fúr | *thér.* |
Menen.　　　　　　One wó | rd (485) móre, | one wórd."

Coriol. iii. 1. 311.

" Líke a | ripe sís | *tér :* | the wóm | an lów."

A. Y. L. iv. 3. 88.

" Of óur | dear sóuls. | Meantíme, | sweet sís | *tér.*"

T. N. v. 1. 393.

" I práy | you, úncle (465), | gíve me | this dág | *gér.*"

Rich. III. iii. 1. 110.

" A bróth | er's múr | *dér.* | Práy can | I nót."

Hamlet, iii. 3. 38.

"Frighted | each óth | *ér.* | Why should | he fóllow ?"
A. and C. iii. 13. 6.

"And só | to árms, | victór | ious fá | *thér.*"
2 *Hen. VI.* v. 1. 211.

"To céase. | Wast thóu | ordáin'd, | dear fá | *thér ?*"
Ib. v. 2. 45.

" *Corn.* Whére hast | thou sént | the kíng? |
Glouc. To *Dó* | *vér.*"—*Lear*, iii. 7. 51.

"Will I' | first wórk. | Hé's for | his más | *tér.*"—*Cymb.* i. 5. 28.

" *Lear.* Thán the | sea-móns | *tér.* |
Alb. Práy, sir, | be pátient."—*Lear*, i. 4. 283.

But perhaps "patient" may have two accents. In that case "ter"
is a pause-extra syllable.

In the two following lines *s* follows the *r :*

"To spéak | of hór | *rórs,* | he cómes | befóre me."
Hamlet, ii. 1. 84.

"Públius, | how nów ? | How nów, | my más | *térs ?*"
T. A. iv. 3. 35; and perhaps *Macbeth*, iii. 4. 133.

"And gíve | him hálf : | and fór | thy víg | *our.*"
Tr. and Cr. ii. 2. 272.

"Téll me, | how fáres | our lóv | ing móth | *er ?*"
Rich. III. v. 3. 82.

" *Cass.* Good níght, | my lórd. |
Brut. Good níght, | good bróth | *er.*"
J. C. iv. 3. 237.

"He whóm | my fáth | er námed? | Your E'd | *gár.*"
Lear, ii. 1. 94.

(? " *ná*(484) | *med ? You* | *r* (480) E'dgar.")

"I'll fól | low yóu | and téll | what án | *swér.*"
3 *Hen. VI.* iv. 3. 55.

"I have síx | ty sáil : | Cæ'sar | none bét | *tér.*"
A. and C. iii. 7. 50.

"This woód | en slá | very, thán | to súff | *er.*"
Temp. iii. 1. 62.

Sometimes this natural burr on *r* influences the spelling. In
Genesis and Exodus (Early English Text Society, Ed. Morris) we
have "coren" for "corn," "boren" for "born." Thus the E. E.
"thurh" is spelt "thorugh" by early writers, and hence even by
Shakespeare in

"The fálse | revólt | ing Nór | mans *thó* | *rough* thée."
2 *Hen. VI.* iv. 1. 87.

So *M. N. D.* ii. 1. 3, 5; *Coriol.* v. 3. 115.

In the following difficult lines it may be that *r* introduces an extra syllable :

> "I'gnomy | in rán | som ánd | free *pá* | *rdón*
> A're of | two hóu | ses, láw | ful *mé* | *rcý.*"
> > *M. for M.* ii. 4. 111, 112.

It would of course save trouble to read "ignominy," against the Folio. But compare

> "Thy *íg* | *nomý* (Fol.) | sleep wíth | thee ín | thy gráve."
> > 1 *Hen. IV.* v. 4. 100.
> "Hence, brók | er láck | ey ! *I'g* | *nomý* | and sháme."
> > *Tr. and Cr.* v. 11. 33.

and in *T. A.* iv. 2. 115 (where the Folio reads "ignominy") the *i* is slurred.

> "No mán | knows whíther. | I crý | thee *mé* | *rcý.*"
> > *Rich. III.* iv. 4. 515.
> "It ís | my són, | young Hár | ry *Pé* | *rcý.*"
> > *Rich. II.* ii. 3. 21.
> "Thou, Rích | ard, shált | to the dúke | of *Nór* | *fólk.*"
> > 3 *Hen. VI.* i. 2. 38.

So we sometimes find the old comparative "near" for the modern "nearer."

> "Bétter | far óff | than néar | be né'er | the *néar.*"
> > *Rich. II.* v. 1. 88.
> > "The *néar* | in blóod |
> The néar | er blóody."—*Macbeth,* ii. 3. 146.
> "Nor *near* nor *farther* off . . . than this weak arm."
> > *Rich. II.* iii. 2. 64.

And "far" for "farther," the old "ferror."

> "*Fár* than | Deucá | lion óff."—*W. T.* iv. 4. 442.

479. The termination "ion" is frequently pronounced as two syllables at the end of a line.   The *i* is also sometimes pronounced as a distinct syllable in *soldier, courtier, marriage, conscience, partial,* &c. ;   less frequently the *e* in *surgeon, vengeance, pageant, creature, pleasure,* and *treasure.*

The cases in which *ion* is pronounced in the middle of a line are rare.   I have only been able to collect the following :

> "With ób | servá | *tión* | the whích | he vénts."
> > *A. Y. L.* ii. 7. 41.

"Of Hám | let's tráns | formá | tión : | so cáll it."
Hamlet, ii. **2. 5.**

"Be chósen | with pró | clamá | *tións* | to-dáy."
T. A. i. **1.** 190.

Gill, 1621, always writes "ti-on" as two syllables. But there is some danger in taking the books of orthoepists as criteria of popular pronunciation. They are too apt to set down, not what is, but what ought to be. The Shakespearian usage will perhaps be found a better guide.

Tión, when preceded by *c,* is more frequently prolonged, perhaps because the *c* more readily attracts the *t* to itself, and leaves *ion* uninfluenced by the *t.*

"It wére | an hón | est áct | *ión* | to sáy so."
Othello, ii. 3. 145 ; *Tr. and Cr.* i. 3. 340.

"Her swéet | perféct | *ións* | with óne | self kíng."
T. N. i. **1.** 39.

"Yet háve | I fiérce | afféct | *ións* | and thínk."
A. and C. i. 5. 17.

"With sóre | distráct | *ión* | what I' | have dóne."
Hamlet, v. 2. 241.

"To ús | in oúr | eléct | *ión* | this dáy."—*T. A.* i. 1. 235.

In "That shall | make áns | wer tó | such quést | *ións.*
  It is enóugh. | I'll thínk | upón | the quést | *ións,*"
2 *Hen. VI.* i. 2. 80, 82.

it seems unlikely that "questions" is to be differently scanned in two lines so close together. And possibly, "it is (it's) enóugh," is one foot. Still, if "questions" in the second verse be regarded as an unemphatic (475) repetition, it might be scanned :

"It ís | enóugh. | I'll thínk | upón | the quéstions."

The Globe has

"Jóin'd in | *commíss* | ion wíth him ; | but éither (466) |
  Had bórne ‖ the action of yourself, or else
  To him ‖ had left it solely."—*Coriol.* iv. 6. 14.

But better arrange as marked above, avoiding the necessity of laying two accents on "commission." So Folio—which, however, is not of much weight as regards arrangement.

I is pronounced in "business" in

"To sée | this bús | inéss. | To-mór | row néxt."
Rich. II. ii. 1. 217 ; *Rich. III.* ii. 2. 144; *M. of V.* iv. 1. 127 ; *Coriol.* v. 3. 4.

"Divín | est *cré* | *atúre,* | Astræ' | a's dáughter."

1 Hen. VI. i. 6. 4.

So probably

"Than thése | two *cré* | *atŭres.* | Whích is | Sebástian ? "

T. N. v. 1. 231.

"But hé's | a tríed | and vál | iant *sóld* | *iér.*"—*J. C.* iv. 1. 28.

"Your sís | ter ís | the bét | ter *sól* | *diér.*"—*Lear,* iv. 5. 3.

"Máking | them wóm | en óf | good *cárr* | *iáge.*"

R. and J. i. 4. 94.

" *Márri* | *age* ís | a mát | ter óf | more wór | th."

1 Hen. VI. v. 5. 55, v. 1. 21.

"To wóo | a máid | in wáy | of *márr* | *iáge.*"

M. of V. ii. 9. 13.

" While I' | thy *ám* | *iá* | *ble* chéeks | do cóy."

M. N. D. iv. 1. 2.

"Young, *vál* | *iánt,* | wíse, and, | no dóubt, | right róyal."

Rich. III. i. 1. 245; Tempest, iii. 2. 27.

" With th' *án* | *ciént* | of wár | on óur | procéedings."

Lear, v. 1. 32.

"You have dóne | our *plé* | *asúres* | much gráce, | fair ládies."—*T. of A.* i. 2. 151.

So   "Táke her | and úse | her át | your *plé* | *asúre.*"

B. and F. (Walker).

" We'll léave | and thínk | it ís | her *plé* | *asúre.*"—*Ib.*

" But 'tís | my lórd | th' Assíst | ant's *plé* | *asúre.*"—*Ib.*

" He dáre | not sée | you. A't | his *plé* | *asúre.*"—*Ib.*

"Yóu shall | have ránsom. | Lét me | have *súr* | *geóns.*"

Lear, iv. 6. 196.

" If ón | ly to gó | ' (484) wárm | were *górg* | *eóus.*"

Ib. ii. 4. 271.

"Your mínd | is tóss | ing ón | the *ó* | *ceán.*"

M. of V. i. 1. 8 ; Hen. V. iii. 1. 14.

"The néw | est státe. | Thís is | the *sér* | *geánt.*"

Macbeth, i. 2. 3.

Similarly "But théy | did sáy | their *práy* | *ers* ánd | addréss'd them."—*Ib.* ii. 2. 25; *Coriol.* v. 3. 105.

"Hath túrn'd | my féign | ed *práy* | *er* ón | my héad."

Rich. III. v. 1. 21, ii. 2. 14.

Even where " prayer " presents the appearance of a monosyllable, the second syllable was probably slightly sounded.

For *i* and *e* sonant in " -ied," see 474.

479 a. Monosyllabic feet in Chaucer. Mr. Skeat (Essay on Metres of Chaucer, Aldine Edition, 1866) has shown that Chaucer often uses a monosyllabic foot, but the instances that have been pointed out are restricted to the first foot.

" *May*, | with all thyn floures and thy greene."—*C. T.* 1512.
" *Til* | that deeth departe schal us twayne."—*Ib.* 1137.
" *Ther* | by aventure this Palamon."—*Ib.* 1518.
" *Now* | it schyneth, now it reyneth fast."—*Ib.* 1537.
" *Al* | by-smoterud with his haburgeon."—*Ib.* 77.

It will be shown in paragraphs 480–6 that Shakespeare uses this licence more freely, but not without the restrictions of certain natural laws.

480. Fear, dear, fire, hour, your, four, and other monosyllables ending in r or re, preceded by a long vowel or diphthong, are frequently pronounced as dissyllables. Thus "fire" was often spelt and is still vulgarly pronounced "fier." So "fare" seems to have been pronounced "fa-er;" "ere," "e-er;" "there," "the-er," &c.

It is often emphasis, and the absence of emphasis, that cause this licence of prolongation to be adopted and rejected in the same line :

Fair.—" *Ferd.* Or níght | kept cháin'd | belów. |
    Prosp.   Fáir | ly spóke."
                                 Tempest, iv. 1. 31.

(or perhaps (484) " belów. | ' Fáir | ly spóke.")

Fare.—" Póison'd, | ill *fá* | *re,* déad, | forsóok, | cast óff."
                                K. J. v. 7. 35.

"Lóath to | bid *fá* | *re*wéll, | we táke | our léaves."
                             P. of T. ii. 5. 13.

"Lúcius, | my gówn. | *Fáre* | well, góod | Méssala."
                             J. C. iv. 3. 231.

"Died év | ery dáy | she lív'd (Fol.). | *Fáre* | thee wéll."
                             Macbeth, iv. 3. 111.

" *Fáre* | well, kíns | man ! I' | will tálk | with yóu."
                          1 *Hen. IV.* i. 3. 234.

"For wórms, | brave Pér | cy. *Fá* | *re*wéll (so Folio), | great héart."—*Ib.* v. 4. 87.

"Why thén | I *wí* | *ll* (483). *Fá* | *re*wéll, | old Gáunt."
                          Rich. II. i. 2. 44.

So *J. C.* iv. 3. 231; 1 *Hen. IV.* iv. 3. 111 (Folio); *M. W. of W.* iii. 4. 97 ; *K. J.* iii. 2. 17. (See 475.)

Ere.—"For I' | inténd | to háve | it *ér* | *e* (é-er) lóng."
1 Hen. VI. i. 3. 80.

I should prefer to prolong the emphatic *here*, rather than "our," in

"What shóuld | be spók | en *hé* | *re* (hé-er) whére | our fáte."
Macbeth, ii. 3. 128.

Mere.—The pause after "night" enables us to scan thus :
    "They have tráv | ell'd áll | the níght (484). | '*Mé* | *re* fétches."—*Lear,* ii. 4. 90.

There.—"Hath déath | lain wíth | thy wífe. | *Thére* | she líes."
R. and J. iv. 5. 36.

"Towards Cálais ; | now gránt | him *thé* | *re, thé* | *re* seen."
Hen. V. v. Prol. 7.

(I have not found a Shakespearian instance of "Caláis." Otherwise at first sight it is natural to scan "Towárds | Caláis.")

    "*Exe.* Like mú | sic.
    Cant.   *Thé* | refóre | doth héav'n | divíde."
Hen. V. i. 2. 183.

Where.—"I knów | a bánk, | *whére* | the wíld | thyme blóws."
M. N. D. ii. 1. 249.

    "*Hor. Whére,* | my lórd ? |
    Ham.   I'n my | mind's eýe, | Horátio."
Hamlet, i. 2. 185.

(But Folio inserts "Oh" before "where.")

Rarely.—"I's not | this búck | led wéll? | *Ráre* | *ly,* rárely."
A. and C. iv. 4. 11.

(The first "rarely" is the more emphatic : or? (483), "well.")

Dear.—"As dóne : | persév | eránce, | *déar* | my lórd."
Tr. and Cr. iii. 3. 150.

    "*Déar* | my lórd, | íf you, | in yóur | own próof."
M. Ado, iv. 1. 46.

    "The kíng | would spéak | with Córnwall : | the *dé* | *ar* fáther."—*Lear,* ii. 4. 102.

    "*Oliv.* Than mú | sic fróm | the *sphé* | *res.*
    Viol.   *Dé* | *ar* lády."
T. N. iii. 1. 1-1.

Fear. —"*Féar* | me nót, | withdráw, | I héar | him cóming."
Hamlet, iii. 4. 7.

Hear.—"Hear, Ná | ture, *hé* | *ar, dé* | *ar* Gód | dess, *héar.*"
Lear, i. 4. 297.

(The emphasis increases as the verse proceeds.)

Near.—"*Néar,* | why thén | anóth | er tíme | I'll héar it."
T. of A. i. 2. 184.

Tears.—"*Auf.* Náme not | the Gód, | thou bóy | of *té* | *ars.*
    Coriol.   Há !"
                                         Coriol. v. 6. 101.
" *Téar* | for téar, | and lóv | ing kíss | for kíss."
                                       T. A. v. 3. 156.

Year.—"Twelve *yé* | *ar* sínce, | Mirán | da, twélve | year sínce."
                                      Tempest, i. 2. 59.

(The repeated "year" is less emphatic than the former.)
And, perhaps, if the line be pronounced deliberately,

    "Mány | yéars | of háp | py dáys | befál."—*Rich.II.* i. 1. 21.

It might be possible to scan as follows :

    "Well strúck | in *yé* | *ars, fá* | *ir* ánd | not jéalous."
                                   Rich. III. i. 1. 92.

But the Folio has "jealious," and the word is often thus written
(Walker) and pronounced by Elizabethan authors.
Their (?).—If the text be correct, in.

    " The commons hath he pill'd with grievous taxes,
    And quite lóst | their héarts. | The nó | bles háth | he fín'd
    For án | cient quárrels (463), | and quíte | lost *thé* | *ir*
    hearts,"—*Rich. II.* ii. 1. 247–8.

it is almost necessary to suppose that the second *their* is more
emphatic than the first. Else the repetition is intolerable. See
475, 476. But even with this scansion the harshness is so great as
to render it probable that the text is corrupt.
Hire.—"A shíp | you sént | me fór | to *hí* | *re* wáftage."
                                    C. of E. iv. 1. 95.
Sire.—"And ís | not líke | the *sí* | *re:* hón | ours thríve."
                                    A. W. ii. 3. 142.
Door.—" And wíth | my swórd | I'll kéep | this *dó* | *or* sáfe."
                                    T. A. i. 1. 288.
More.—"If móre, | the *mó* | *re* hást | thou wróng'd | (èd) mé."
                                    Lear, v. 3. 168.

(The second "more" is the more emphatic.)

    " As máy | compáct | it *mó* | *re.* Gét | you góne."
                                    Ib. i. 4. 362.

    " Who hádst | desérv | ed *mó* | *re* thán | a príson."
                                    Temp. i. 2. 362.

Our (perhaps).— "To líst | en *óu* | *r* púr | pose. Thís is (461) | thy
    óffice."—*M. Ado,* iii. 1. 12.

("This is" is a quasi-monosyllable. See 461.)

"And bý | me, hád | not *óu* | *r* háp | been bád."

C. *of E.* i. 1. 39.

" *First Sen.* Which wé | devíse | him.

Corn. O'*u* | *r* spóils | he kíck'd at."

Coriol. ii. 2. 128.

" First " requires emphasis in

" *Sic.* In *óu* | *r* fírst | way.

Men. I' | 'll bríng | him tó you.

Ib. iii. 1. 334.

Hour (often).—" A't the | sixth hóu | r, át | which tíme | my lórd."

Tempest, v. 1. 4.

Your.—" And só, | though *yóu* | *rs,* nót | yours*—próve | it só."

M. of V. iii. 2. 20.

" *Lart.* My hórse | to *yóu* | *rs,* nó! |

Mart. 'Tis dóne! |

Lart. Agréed."

Coriol. i. 4. 2.

"And pún | ish thém | to *yoú* | *r* héight | of pléasure."

M. for M. v. i. 240.

Unless "pleasure" is a trisyllable. (See 479.)

" Is he párd | on'd ánd | for *yóu* | *r* lóve | ly sáke."—*Ib.* 496.

There is an emphatic antithesis in

"Whó is | lost tóo. | Take *yóu* | *r* pá | tience tó you,
And *I'll* say nothing."—*W. T.* iii. 2. 232.

"And shállǀ have *yóu* | *r* wíll, | becáuse | our kíng."

3 *Hen. VI.* iv. 1. 17.

481. Monosyllables which are emphatic either (1) from their meaning, as in the case of exclamations, or (2) from their use in antithetical sentences, or (3) which contain diphthongs, or (4) vowels preceding *r,* often take the place of a whole foot. This is less frequent in dissyllabic words. In (1) and (2) as well as (3) the monosyllables often contain diphthongs, or else long vowels.

In many cases it is difficult, perhaps impossible, to determine whether a monosyllable should be prolonged or not. Thus, in

" On thís | unwórth | y scáff | old *tó* | *bring* fórth,"

Hen. V. Prologue, 10.

many may prefer to scan " | -old to *brí* | *ng fórth,*" and to prolong the following monosyllable rather than to accent "to ;" and in

" Came póur | ing líke | the *tíde* | *intó* | a bréach,"

Hen. V. i. 2. 149.

* It is a matter of taste which *yours* should receive the emphasis.

it is possible to prolong the preceding monosyllable, "the *tí* | *de* in | to a bréach." Such cases may often be left to the taste of the reader (but for the accent of "into" see 457*a*). All that can safely be said is, that when a very unemphatic monosyllable, as "at," "and," "a," "the," &c. has the accent, it is generally preceded or followed by a very strongly accented monosyllable, as

"Assume the port of *Mars*; and *at* his heels."
Hen. V. Prologue, 6.

It is equally a matter of taste whether part of the prolonged monosyllable should be considered to run on into the following foot, or whether a pause be supposed after the monosyllable, as

"Gírding | with gríev | ous *síege* | cástles | and tówns."
Hen. V. i. 2. 152.

"As *knóts* | bý the | conflúx | of méet | ing sáp."
Tr. and Cr. i. 3. 7.

482, Monosyllabic exclamations.

Ay.—" *Polon.* Whérefore | should yóu | do thís? |
    Reg.   *A'y*, | my lórd?"
Hamlet, ii. 1. 36.

  "*King.* Wíll you | be rúled | by mé? |
    Laert.   *A'y*, | my lórd."
Ib. iv. 7. 60.

  "*A'y*, | what élse? | And bút | I bé | decéiv'd."
T. of Sh. iv. 4. 2.

  "*Vol.* That bróught | thee tó | this wórld. |
    Vir.   *A'y*, | and míne."
Coriol. v. 3. 125.

  "*Corn.* I's he | pursú | ed (474)?
    Glou.   *A'* | *y*, mý | good lórd."
Lear, ii. 1. 111.

Nay.—"What sáys | he? *Ná* | *y*, nó | thing; áll | is sáid."
Rich. II. ii. 1. 148.

  "*Cor.* How, trái | tor !
    Com.   *Ná* | *y*, tém | p(e)ratelý ; | your prómise."
Coriol. iii. 3. 67.

Stay.—"*Stáy*, | the kíng | hath thrówn | his wárd | er dówn."
Ib. i. 3. 118.

Yea.—"*Yéa*, | my lórd. | How bróoks | your gráce | the aír?"
Ib. iii. 2. 2.

Hail.—"'Gaínst mý | captív | itý. | *Háil*, | brave fríend."
Macbeth, i. 2. 5.

O.—" *Cass. O^t*, | 'tis trúe. |
   Hect.   Ho ! bíd | my trúm | pet sóund."
                                       Tr. and Cr. v. 3. 13.
  " *Cleo.*   *O^t*, | 'tis tréa | son.
    Charm.   Mádam, | I trúst | not só."
                                          A. and C. i. 5. 7.
  " To híde | the sláin. | *O^t*, | from thís | time fórth."
                                        Hamlet, iv. 4. 65.
  " *Mir. O^t*, | good sír, | I dó. |
    Prosp.   I práy | thee, márk me."
                                      Tempest, i. 2. 80.

Perhaps "*Pol.* The dévil | himsélf. |
    King.   *O^t*, | 'tis (it ís) | too trúe."
                                         Ib. iii. 1. 49.
  " Sélf a | gainst sélf. | *O^t*, | prepós | teróus."
                                       Rich. III. ii. 4. 63.
  " Their cléa | rer réa | son. O^t, | ` góod | Gonzálo."
                                       Temp. v. 1. 68.

I have not found "reason" a trisyllable in Shakespeare.
  " *O^t*, | my fóllies ! | Then E'd | gar wás | abúsed."
                                       Lear, iii. 7. 91.
  " *O^t*, | the díff | erénce | of mán | and mán."
                                       Ib. iv. 2. 26.
? " The héart | of wó | man ís. | *O^t*, | (453) Brútus."
                                       J. C. ii. 4. 40.
  " Struck Cæ' | sar ón | the néck. | *O^t*, | you flátterers."
                                       Ib. v. 1. 44.

Soft.—" But *só* | *ft!* cóm | paný | is cóm | ing hére."
                                       T. of Sh. iv. 5. 26.

Come.—" *Cóme*, | good féll | ow, pút | mine ír | on ón."
                                       A. and C. iv. 4. 3.

What.—" Whére be | these knáves? | *Whát*, | no mán | at dóor !"
                                     T. of Sh. iv. 1. 125.
  " *Whát*, | unjúst ! | Bé not | so hót ; | the dúke."
                                       M. for M. v. 1. 315.

Well.—" *Wéll*, | gíve her | that ríng, | and thére | withál."
                                       T. G. of V. iv. 4. 89.
  " *Gon.* Rémem | ber whát | I téll | you.
    Osw.   *Wé* | *ll*, mádam."
                                       Lear, i. 3. 21.

483. Monosyllables emphasized by position or anti-thesis. A conjunction like "yet" or "but," implying hesitation, may naturally require a pause immediately after it ; and this pause may excuse the absence of an unaccented syllable, additional stress being laid on the monosyllable.

But.—" Of góod | ly thóus | ands. *Bú | t,* fór | all thís."
Macbeth, iv. 3. 44.

" The Góde | rebúke | me *bu | t* ĭt | ĭs tídings."
A. and C. v. 1. 27.

Yet.—" Thóugh I | condémn | not, *yé | t,* ún | der párdon."
Lear, i. 4. 365.

" *Yét* (as yet), | I thínk, | we áre | not bróught | so lów."
T. A. iii. 2. 76.

" *Brut.* When Cǽ's | ar's héad | is óff. |
Cass. *Yét |* I féar him."
J. C. ii. 1. 183.

Pronouns emphasized by antithesis or otherwise, sometimes dispense with the unaccented syllable.

" Shów | men dú | tifúl?
Why, só | didst *thó | u.* Séem | they gráve | and léarned?
Why, só | didst thóu."—*Hen. V.* ii. 2. 128.

(Possibly, however, "seem" may be prolonged instead of "thou.")

" When yóu | shall pléase | to pláy | the thíeves | for wíves.
I'll wátch | as lóng | for *yó | u* thén. | Appróach."
M. of V. ii. 6. 24.

" Were *yó | u* ín | my stéad, | would yóu | have héard ?"
Coriol. v. 3. 192.

You is emphatic from Desdemona to Othello in

" *Othello.* 'Tís a | good hánd,
A fránk | one.
Desd. *Yó | u* máy | indéed | say só."
Othello, iii. 4. 44.

So in " Hów in | my stréngth | you pléase. | For *yó | u,* E'dmund."
Lear, ii. 1. 114.

and in the retort of Brutus on Cassius,

" Lét me | tell *yó | u,* Cáss | ius, yóu | yoursélf
Are múch | condémn'd | to háve | an ítch | ing pálm."
J. C. iv. 3. 9.

Perhaps aware of Ferdinand's comment on his emotion, "your father's in some passion," Prospero turns to Ferdinand and says, " it is *you* who are moved" in

" *Yo'u |* do lóok, | my són, | ín a | mov'd sórt."
Temp. iv. 1. 146.

Otherwise the reading of the line so as to avoid accenting "my" seems difficult.

There is no prolongation, though there is antithetical emphasis, in

"Lóok up | on *hím*, | love hím, | he wór | ships yóu."
A. Y. L. v. 2. 88.

The repeated "thence" seems to require a pause in

" Thénce to | a wátch, | *thénce* | intó (457*a*) | a wéakness."
Hamlet, ii. 1. 148.

But possibly, like " ord(i)nance," "light(*e*)ning" (see 477), so "weakness" may be pronounced a trisyllable.

484. Monosyllables containing diphthongs and long vowels, since they naturally allow the voice to rest upon them, are often so emphasized as to dispense with an unaccented syllable. When the monosyllables are imperatives of verbs, as "speak," or nouns used imperatively, like "peace," the pause which they require after them renders them peculiarly liable to be thus emphasized. Whether the word is dissyllabized, or merely requires a pause after it, cannot in all cases be determined. In the following examples the scansion is marked throughout on the former supposition, but it is not intended to be represented as necessary.

A (long). " Júst as | you léft | them, *á* | *ll* prís | 'ners, sír."
Temp. v. 1. 8.

"Try mán | y, *á* | *ll* góod, | serve trú | ly néver."
Cymb. iv. 2. 373.

" Yea, lóok'st | thou *pá* | *le?* Lét | me sée | the wríting."
Rich. II. v. 2. 57.

" *Duke.* Líke the | old *á* | *ge.*
Clown. A're | you réad | y, sír?"
T. N. ii. 4. 50.

"Yéa, his | dread trí | dent sháke. | My *brá* | *ve* spírit."
Temp. i. 2. 206.

Ai. " 'Gainst mý | captív | itý. | *Háil,* | brave fríend."
Macbeth, i. 2. 5.

" I'll bé | with (wi') you *strái* | *ght.* Gó | a líttle | befóre."
Hamlet, iv. 4. 31.

I should prefer to avoid laying an accent on " the " in

" To *fá* | *il* ín the | dispós | ing óf | these chánces."
Coriol. iv. 7. 40.

" Which ís | most *fá* | *int.* Nów | 'tis trúe
I múst | be hére | confín'd | by yóu."—*Temp.* Epilogue, 3.

Ay. " *Sáy* | agáin, | whére didst | thou léave | these várlets?"
Temp. iv. 1. 170.

So in the dissyllable " payment."

" He húmb | ly práys | you spéed | y *páy* | *mént.*"
T. of A. ii. 2. 28.

Perhaps

" What *sá* | *y* yóu, | my lórd? | Aré you | contént."
1 *Hen. VI.* iv. 1. 70.

Perhaps

E. " *Senators.* Wé | 'll súre | ty him.
  Com.   A'g | ed sír, | hands óff."
Coriol. iii. 1. 178.

" *Men.* The cón | sul Córi | olán | us——
  Bru.   Hé | ' cónsul!"—*Ib.* iii. 1. 280.

Ea. " *Péace,* | I sáy. | Good é | ven tó | you, fríend."
A. Y. L. ii. 3. 70.

" Antón | ius *dé* | *ad!* I'f | thou sáy | so, víllain."
A. and C. ii. 5. 26.

" *Doct.* But, thóugh | slow, *dé* | *adlý.* |
  Queen.   I wón | der, dóctor."
Cymb. i. 5. 10.

" Whý dost | not spéak? | What, *dé* | *af:* nót | a wórd?"
T. A. v. 1. 46.

" *Spéak,* | Lavín | ia, whát | accúrs | ed hánd?"
Ib. iii. 1. 66.

" Which wás | to *plé* | *ase.* Nów | I wánt
  Spírits to | enfórce, | nót to | enchánt."
Temp. Epilogue, 13.

" Eárth's in | *créase,* | fóison | plénty,
  Bárns and | gárners | néver | émpty."—*Ib.* iv. 1. 110.

Perhaps " *Glou.* Aláck, | the níght | comes ón, | and the (457)
  blé | *ak* wínds."—*Lear,* ii. 4. 303.

Perhaps " Trúly | to *spé* | *ak,* ánd | with nó | addítion,"
Hamlet, iv. 4. 17.

or " Trúly | to spéak, | and with nó | addít | ión."
" Be frée | and *hé* | *althfúl.* | So tárt | a fávour."
A. and C. ii. 5. 38.

" The safety and health of this whole state,"
Hamlet, i. 3. 21.

could not be scanned without prolonging both " health " and
" whole." Such a double prolongation is extremely improbable,
considering the moderate emphasis required. More probably

"sanity" should be read, as has been suggested, for "sanctity," the reading of the Folio.

Ee. "Fórward, | not pér | manént, | *swéet*, | not lásting."
Hamlet, i. 3. 8.

"*Séek* | me óut, | and thát | way I' | am wífe in."
Hen. VIII. iii. 1. 39.

"The cúrt | ain'd *slé* | *ep* wítch | craft cél | ebrátes."
Macbeth, ii. 1. 51.

"Doth cóm | fort thée in | thy *slé* | *ep ;* líve, | and flóurish."
Rich. III. v. 3. 130.

"This íg | norant prés | ent ánd | I *fé* | *el* nów."
Ib. i. 5. 58.

"Enóugh | to fétch | him ín. | *Sée* | it dóne."
A. and C. iv. 1. 14.

"Yét but | *thrée.* | Cóme one | móre,
Twó of | bóth kinds | máke up | fóur."
M. N. D. iii. 2. 437.

"When *sté* | *el* gróws | sóft as | the pára | site's sílk."
Coriol. i. 9. 45.

"Soft" is emphasized as an exclamation (see 481), but perhaps on the whole it is better to emphasize "steel" here.

"*Ferd.* Makes thís | place Pár | adíse.
"*Prosp.*   *Swéet* | now, sílence."
Temp. iv. 1. 124.

Eo. The *eo* in the foreign-derived word "leopard" stands on a different footing :

"Or hórse | or óx | en fróm | the *lé* | *opárd*."
1 *Hen. VI.* i. 5. 31.

So, often, in Elizabethan authors.

I. "Mén for | their *wí* | *ves :* wí | ves fór | their húsbands."
3 *Hen. VI.* v. 6. 41.

"Of gréat | est júst | ice. *Wrí* | *te,* wríte, | Rináldo."
A. W. iii. 4. 29.

"Hórri | ble *sí* | *ght!* Nów | I sée | 'tis trúe."
Macbeth, iv. 1. 122.

"Full fíf | teen húndred, | *besí* | *des* cóm | mon mén."
Hen. V. iv. 8. 84.

I know of no instance where "hundred," like (477) "Henry," receives two accents. Else the "be-" in "besides" might (460) be dropped, and the verse might be differently scanned.

"Each mán's | like *mĺ* | ne. yóu | have shéwn | all Héctors."
A. and C. iv. 8. 7.
"At a póor | man's hóuse : | he ús'd | me *kĺ* | ndlý."
Coriol. i. 9. 83.   But see 477.

Ie.   Possibly "friends" may require to be emphasized, as its
position is certainly emphatic, in

"Till déath | unlóads | thee.   *Frĺ* | ends hást | thou nóne."
M. for M. iii. 1. 28.
"No, sáy'st | me só, | *frĺend?* | What cóun | trymán ?"
T. of Sh. i. 2. 190.
"Yield, my lórd, | protéct | or *yĺ* | eld, Wín | chestér."
1 Hen. VI. iii. 1. 112.
("My" is dropped, 497.)
"Mórt de | ma *vĺ* | e! I'f | they ríde | alóng."
Hen. V. iii. 5. 11.

O.   "Dríve him | to *Ró* | me: 'tís (ít | is) tíme | we twaín."
A. and C. i. 4. 73.
"Card. Róme | shall réme | dy thís. |
Glou.   Roam thí | ther, thén."
1 Hen. VI. iii. 1. 51.
"While hé | himsélf | kéeps in | the *có* | ld fíeld."
3 Hen. VI. iv. 3. 14.
"Tóad that | únder | *cóld* | stóne
Dáys and | níghts has | thírty | óne."—Macbeth, iv. 1. 6.
So scan " Go tó the | creáting | a *whó* | le tríbe | of fóps."
Lear, i. 2. 14.

Oa.   "Is *gó* | ads, *thó* | rns (485), nét | tles, táils | of wásps."
W. T. i. 2. 329.

Oi.   "*Jóint* | by jóint, | but wé | will knów | hïs púrpose."
M. for M. v. 1. 314.
"What whéels, | racks, fíres? | What fláy | ing, *bó* | ilĺng?"
W. T. iii. 2. 177.
"God sáve | you, sír. | Where have yóu | been *bró* | ilĺng ?"
Hen. VIII. iv. 1. 56.
"Of théir | own *chó* | ice: óne | is Jún | ius Brútus."
Coriol. i. 1. 220.
"What sáy | you, *bó* | ys ?   Wíll | you bíde | with hím?"
T. A. v. 2. 13.

Oo.   "Than ín | my thóught | it líes. | *Góod* | my lórd."
A. W. v. 3. 184.

It might be thought that in the above the prolongation rests on
lies (lieth), but that we have also

" *Góod* | my lórd, | gíve me | thy fáv | our stíll."
Temp. iv. 1. 204.

"The *gó* | *od* góds | will móck | me prés | entlý."
A. and C. iii. 4. 15.

"He stráight | declín | ed, *dró* | *op'd,* tóok | it déeply."
W. T. ii. 3. 14.

"Tó it, | boy! Már | cus, *ló* | *ose* whén | I bíd."
T. A. iv. 3. 58.

"Hours, mín | utes, *nó* | *on,* míd | night, ánd | all eýes."
W. T. i. 2. 290.

"But *ró* | *om,* fái | ry, hére | comes O'b | erón."
M. N. D. ii. 1. 58.

" *Bóot* | *less* hóme | and wéath | er-béat | en báck."
1 *Hen. IV.* iii. 1. 67.

" Pull óff | my *bó* | *ot :* hárd | er, hárd | er, só."
Lear, iv. 6. 177.

"But *mó* | *ody* | and *dú* | *ll* mél | anchóly."
C. of E. v. 1. 79.

Some may prefer to read "dull" as a monosyllable ; but I can
find no instance of "meláncholý" to justify such a scansion.

In " *Lear.* To thís | detést | ed *gró* | *om.*
Gon. A't | your chóice, sir,'
Lear, ii. 4. 220.

either "groom" or "your" should be dissyllabized.

"I' do | wánder | évery | whére
Swífter | thán the | *móon's* | sphére."—*M. N. D.* ii. 1. 7.
Ou. "Which élse | would frée | have *wró* | *ught.* A'll | is wéll."
Macbeth, ii. 1. 19.

In "Should drínk | his blóod— | *móunts* | up tó | the áir."
MARLOW, *Edw. II.*

Collier (Hist. of British Stage, vol. iii.) thinks "mounts" the
emphatic word to be dwelt on for the length of a dissyllable.

Ow. "Own" is perhaps emphasized by repetition (or "Are" is a
dissyllable, as "fare," "ere," "where," 480) in

"*Hel.* Mine ówn | and nót | mine *ó* | *wn.*
Dem. A're | you súre?"
M. N. D. iv. 1. 189.

Oy. The last syllable of "destroy" seems prolonged in

"To fríght | them ére | *destró* | *y.* Bút | come ín."
Coriol. iv. 5. 149.

U. It may be that "fume" is emphasized in

"She's tíck | led nów. | Her *fú* | *me* néeds | no spúrs."
2 Hen. VI. i. 3. 153.

(Unless "needs" is prolonged either by reason of the double vowel
or because "needs" is to be pronounced "needeth.")

" *Trúe* | nobíl | ity ís | exémpt | from féar."
2 Hen. VI. iv. 1. 129.

Titania speaks in verse throughout, and therefore either "and"
must be accented and "hoard" prolonged, or we must scan as
follows :

" The squír | rel's hóard, | and fétch | thee *néw* | ' núts."
M. N. D. iv. 1. 40.

" *Cord.* That wánts | the méans | to léad it. |
Mess.   *Néws,* | mádam."
Lear, iv. 4. 20.

485. Monosyllables containing a vowel followed by "r"
are often prolonged.

A.   " *Thyr.* Héar it | *apár* | *t.*
Cleo.   Nóne | but friends : | say bóldly."
A. and C. iii. 13. 47.

" Hó | ly séems | the quárrel
Upón | his grá | ce's *pá* | *rt;* bláck | and féarful
O'n the | oppó | ser."—*A. W.* iii. 1. 5.

" Well fítt(ed) | in *á* | *rts,* gló | rióus | in árms."
L. L. L. ii. 1. 45.

" Stríkes his | breast *há* | *rd,* ánd | anón | he cásts."
Hen. VIII. iii. 2. 117.

" But cóuld | be wílling | to *má* | *rch* ón | to Cálais."
Hen. V. iii. 6. 150.

" *Hárk* | ye, lórds, | ye sée | I have gíven | her phýsic."
T. A. iv. 2. 162.

" Lóok how | he mákes | to Cæ's | ar, *már* | *k* hím."
J. C. iii. 2. 18.

Ei.   " I dréamt | last níght | óf the | three *wé* | *ird* sísters."
Macbeth, ii. 1. 20 (Folio, " weyard").

" A'nd be | times I' | will tó | the *wé* | *ird* sísters."
Ib. iii. 4. 133, iv. 1. 136.

Or "will" is perhaps emphasized and the prefix in "betimes"
ignored.   In either case "weird" is a dissyllable.

" The *wé* | *ird* sís | ters hánd | in hánd."—*Macbeth,* i. 3. 32.

I.   "A *thí* | *rd* thínks | withóut | expénse | at áll."

                 1 *Hen. VI.* i. 1. 76.

    "Of Líon | el dúke | of Clárence, | the *thí* | *rd* són."

                 Ib. ii. 5. 75.

    "To kíng | Edwárd | the *thí* | *rd,* whére | as hé."—*Ib.* 76.

O.   "*Bru.* Spread fúr | thér (478).

    Men.   One *wó* | *rd* móre, | one wórd."

                 Coriol. iii. 1. 311.

    "Máke the | prize líght. | One *wór* | *d* móre, | I chárge thee."—*Temp.* i. 2. 452.

    "*Ham.* One *wór* | *d* móre, | good lády. |

    Queen.   Whát shall | I dó ?"

                 Hamlet, iii. 4. 180.

    "Do móre | than thís | in *spó* | *rt;* fá | ther, fáther ! "

                 Lear, ii. 1. 37.

    "*Wórse* | and wórse ! | She wíll | not cóme ! | O, víle !"

                 T. of Sh. v. 2. 93.

    "Nót in | the *wó* | *rst* ránk | of mán | hood, sáy't."

                 Macbeth, iii. 1. 103.

    "Why só, | brave *ló* | *rds,* whén | we joín | in léague."

                 T. A. iv. 2. 136.

    "My *ló* | *rd,* wíll | it pléase | you páss | alóng."

                 Rich. III. iii. 1. 110.

    "Of góod | old A' | brahám. | *Lórds* | appéllants."

                 Rich. II. iv. 1. 104.

("A'ppellants " is not Shakespearian.)

    "But téll | me, ís | young *Geór* | *ge* Stán | ley líving?"

                 Ib. v. 5. 9.

or, possibly,

    "But téll me, |
    Is yóung | George Stán | ley líving? "

Ou.   "Henry doth claim the crown from John of Gaunt,
    The *fóu* | *rth* són : | York cláims | it fróm | the thírd."

                 2 *Hen. VI.* ii. 2. 55.

So, perhaps,

    "And lóng | live Hén | ry *fóu* | *rth* óf | that náme."

                 Rich. II. iv. 1. 112.

("Four" was often spelt "fower."   "Henry" is not pronounced "Hén(e)rý " in *Richard II.*)

    "Heart," not "you," ought to be emphatic in

    "Nót by | the mát | ter whích | your *héar* | *t* prómpts you."

                 Coriol. iii. 2. 54.

Probably we ought to arrange the difficult line, *Macbeth*, iv. 1.
105, thus :

"A'nd an | etérn | al *cú* | *rse* fáll | on yóu.
Let me knów.
Why sínks," &c. ?

486. Monosyllables are rarely prolonged except as in the
above instances.   In some cases, however, as in "bath," "dance,"
a vowel varies very much in its pronunciation, and is often pronounced (though the incorrectness of the pronunciation would now
be generally recognized) in such a way as to give a quasi-dissyllabic
sound.

"Yóu and | your *crá* | *fts*, yóu | have cráft | ed fáir."
                                        Coriol. iv. 6. 118.
" I'f that | yóu will | *Fránce* | wín,
    Thén with | Scótland | first be | gín."—*Hen. V.* i. 2. 167.

In a few other cases monosyllables are, perhaps, prolonged :

"You sháll | read ús | the *wi* | *ll.*   Cæ's | ar's wíll !"
                                        J. C. iii. 2. 153.
" *Cas.* Cícer | o *ón* | *e?*
  Mes.   Cíc | eró | is déad."—*Ib.* iv. 3. 179.

" I' will | éver | bé your | héad,
  Só be | *góne;* | yóu are | spéd."—*M. of V.* ii. 9. 72.

" Then sháll | the réalm | of A'lb | ión
  Cóme | to gréat | confús | ión."—*Lear*, iii. 2. 92.

"For óur | best áct. | I'f we | shall *stá* | *nd* still."
                                        Hen. VIII. i. 2. 85.

(Can "all" have dropped out after "shall?")

" The thánk | ings óf | a *kí* | *ng.*   I' | am, sír."
                                        Cymb. v. 5. 407.

" Hére she | *cómes,* | cúrst and | sád :
  Cúpid | ís a | knávish | lád."—*M. N. D.* iii. 2. 439.

"Well" (481) is prolonged as an exclamation, and perhaps
there is a prolongation of the same sound in

" *Mélt* | *ed* ás | the snów | séems to | me nów."
                                        M. N. D. iv. 1. 163.

So, in " The gó | ds, nót | the patríc | ians, máke | it, ánd,"
                                        Coriol. i. 1. 75.

"gods" is probably prolonged by emphasis, and the second "the"
is not accented.   So "most" in

"With Tí | tus Lárcius, | a *mó* | *st* vál | iant Róman."
Coriol. i. 2. 14.

"Larcius" has probably but one accent. However, "a" appears sometimes to have the accent.
So, perhaps,

"*Ang.* Where práy | ers *cró* | *ss.*
Isab. A't | what hóur | to-mórrow?"
M. for M. ii. 2. 159.

"Drachm" (Folio "Drachme") is a dissyllable in

"A't a | crack'd *drách* | *m!* Cúsh | ions, léad | en spóons."
Coriol. i. 5. 6.

487. E mute pronounced. This is a trace of the Early English pronunciation.

Es, s. "Your gráce | misták | *es:* ón | ly tó | be bríef."
Rich. II. iii. 3. 9.

"Who's thére, | that knóck | (e)*s* só | impér | iouslý?"
1 *Hen. VI.* i. 3. 5.

"Well, lét | them rést : | come híth | er, Cát | *es*bý."
Rich. III. iii. 1. 157.

"Here cómes | his sérv | ant. Hów | now, Cát | *es*bý.?"
Ib. 7. 58.

"Till áll | thy bónes | with ách | *es* máke | thee róar."
Temp. i. 2. 370.

"A'ch*es* | contráct, | and stárve | your súp | ple jóints."
T. of A. i. 1. 257, v. 1. 202.

But this word seems to have been pronounced, when a noun, "aatch." At least it is made by Spenser, *Sh. Cal.* Aug. 4, to rhyme with "matche."

"Send Có | *le*víle | with hís | conféd | erátes."
2 *Hen. IV.* iv. 3. 79.

So "Wórc*es* | ter, gét | thee góne! | For I' | do sée."
1 *Hen. IV.* i. 3. 15, iii. 1. 5, v. 5. 14 (Fol. omits "thee").

"We háve ; | whereupón (497) | the éarl | of Wórc | *es*tér."
Rich. II. ii. 2. 58.

So "Glóuc*es*tér," 1 *Hen. VI.* i. 3. 4, 6, 62, and

"O lóv | ing úncle (465), | kind dúke | of Glóu | *ces*tér."
1 *Hen. VI.* iii. 1. 142.

"This is the flower that smiles on every one
To shów | his téeth | as whíte | as whá | *le's* bóne."
L. L. L. v. 2. 332.

So, in a rhyming passage,

> "Whose shád | ow thé | dismíss | ed báche | lor lóves
> Béing | lass-lórn ; | thy póle | -clipt vín | e-yárd
> And thý | sea-márge, | stérile | and róck | y-hárd."
>> *Temp.* iv. 1. 69.

> "She név | er hád | so swéet | a cháng | eling."
>> *M. N. D.* ii. 1. 23.

Perhaps "*Fran.* They ván | ish'd stráng | ely.

> *Seb.*   No mát | ter, sínce."
>> *Temp.* iii. 3. 40.   But see 506.

Possibly "cradles" may approximate to a trisyllable, "crad(e)les" (so "jugg(e)ler," &c. 477), in

> "Does thóughts | unvéil | in théir | dumb *crá* | *dlés.*"
>> *Tr. and Cr.* iii. 3. 200.

The *e* is probably not of French but of Latin origin in "statue :"

> "She dréamt | to-níght | she sáw | my *stát* | *ué.*"
>> *J. C.* ii. 2. 76.

> "E'ven at | the báse | of Póm | pey's *stát* | *ué.*"
>> (Folio) *Ib.* iii. 2. 192.

Globe "statua."

So in the plural :

> "But líke | dumb *stát* | *ués* | of bréath | ing stónes."
>> *Rich. III.* iii. 7. 25.

Globe, "*statuas.*"

> "No marble *statua* nor high
> Aspiring pyramid be raised."—HABINGTON (Walker).

488. The "e" in commandment, entertainment, &c., which originally preceded the final syllable, is sometimes retained, and, even where not retained, sometimes pronounced.

> "Be vál | ued 'gáinst | your wífe's | commánd | (*e*)mént."
>> *M. of V.* iv. 1. 451.

> "From hím | I háve | expréss | commánd | (*e*)mént."
>> 1 *Hen. VI.* i. 3. 20.

The *e* is inserted in

> "If to women he be bent
> They have at command*e*ment."—*P. P.* 418.

> "Good sír, | you'll gíve | them én | tertáin | (*e*)mént."
>> B. J. *Fox,* iii. 2.

Perhaps an *e* is to be sounded between *d* and *v* in

"A'nton | y Wóod | (*e*)vílle, | her bróth | er thére."
Rich. III. i. 1. 67.

489. E final in French names is often retained in sound as well as spelling :

"The mél | anchól | y *Jáq* | *ues* gríeves | at thát."
A. Y. L. ii. 1. 26.

"O mý | *Paróll* | *es*, théy | have márr | ied mé."
A. W. ii. 3. 289.

"His gráce | is át | *Marséill* | *es*, tó | which pláce."
Ib. iv. 3. 9 ; *T. of Sh.* ii. 1. 377.

"Dáughter | to *Chár* | *lemáin*, | who wás | the són."
Hen. V. i. 2. 75.

"Guiénne, | *Champág* | *ne*, Rhé | ims, O'r | leáns."
1 *Hen. VI.* i. 1. 60.

"This prínce | *Montáig* | *ne*, íf | he bé | no móre."
"He cán | not sáy | but thát | *Montáig* | *ne* yét."
DANIEL (on Florio).

"Now *E'sp* | *eránc* | *e*, Pér | cy, ánd | set ón."
1 *Hen. IV.* v. 2. 97.

"Cáll'd the | brave lórd | Pónton | de *Sáu* | *traillés*."
1 *Hen. VI.* i. 4. 28.

"Díeu de | *battái* | *lles!* Whére | have théy | this méttle?"
Hen. V. iii. 5. 15.

So in "Vive :"

"'*Víve* | le roí,' | as I' | have bánk'd | their tówns."
K. J. v. 2. 104.

Thus, perhaps, we may explain the apparent trisyllabic "marshal" by a reference to "mareschal :"

"Great már | (e)shál | to Hén | (e)rý (477) | the Síxth."
1 *Hen. VI.* iv. 7. 70.

"With wíng | ed háste | tó the | lord már | (e)shál."
1 *Hen. IV.* iv. 4. 2.

On the other hand, the influence of the *r* (see 463) seems to make "marshall" a quasi-monosyllable in

"Lord *márshal,* | commánd | our óff | icérs | at árms."
Rich. II. i. 1. 204.

The *i* in the French "capitaine" is invisibly active in

"A wíse | stout cáp | (*i*)táin, | and sóon | persuáded."
3 *Hen. VI.* iv. 7. 30 ; *Macbeth,* i. 2. 34.

ACCENT.

490. Words in which the accent is nearer the end than with us.

Many words, such as "édict," "outrage," "contract," &c., are accented in a varying manner. The key to this inconsistency is, perhaps, to be found in Ben Jonson's remark that all dissyllabic nouns, *if they be simple,* are accented on the first. Hence "edict" and "outrage" would generally be accented on the first, but, when they were regarded as *derived from verbs,* they would be accented on the second. And so, perhaps, when "exile" is regarded as a person, and therefore a "simple" noun, the accent is on the first; but when as "the state of being exiled," it is on the last. But naturally, where the difference is so slight, much variety may be expected. Ben Jonson adds that "all verbs coming from the Latin, either of the supine or otherwise, hold the accent as it is found in the first person present of those Latin verbs ; as from *célebro, célebrate.*" Without entering into the details of this rule, it seems probable that "edíct," "precépt," betray Latin influence. The same fluctuation between the English and French accent is found in CHAUCER (Prof. Child, quoted by Ellis, *E. E. Pronunc.* i. 369), who uses "batáille," *C. T.* 990, and "bátail," *ib.* 2099 : "Fortúne," *ib.* 917, and "fórtune," *ib.* 927 ; " daungér," and " dáunger."

Abjéct (Latin).—"Wé are | the quéen's | abjécts, | and múst | obéy."
Rich. III. i. 1. 106.

But if the monosyllable "queen" be emphasized, we may scan
" Wé are | the qué | en's *ábjects,* | and múst | obéy."

Accéss (Latin).—*W. T.* v. 1. 87.

Aspéct (Latin).—*A. and C.* i. 5. 33 ; *T. N.* i. 4. 28.

Charácters.—"I sáy | without | charác | ters fáme | lives lóng."
Rich. III. iii. 1. 81 ; *Hamlet,* i. 3. 59.

Comméndable.

"Thanks fáith, | for sílence | is ónly | comménd | ablé
In a néat's | tongue dríed | and a máid | not vénd | iblé."
M. of V. i. 1. 111.

This shows how we must scan

"'Tis swéet and (497) | comménd | able ín | your ná | ture,
Hámlet."—*Hamlet,* i. 2. 87.

But, on the other hand,

> " And pówer, | untó | itsélf | most cóm | mendáble."
>
> > *Coriol.* iv. 7. 51.

Commérce (Latin).—So arrange

> "Péaceful | *commérce* | from dí | vidá- | ble shóres."
>
> > *Tr. and Cr.* i. 3. 105.

Confíscate (Latin).—*C. of E.* i. 1. 21 ; but " cónfiscáte," *ib.* i. 2. 2.

Consórt (Latin).—"What sáy'st | thou? Wílt | thou bé | of óur |
consórt?"—*T. G. of V.* iv. 1. 64.

> " *Edmund.* Yes, madam,
> He wás | of thát | consórt.
> *Reg.* No már | vel, thén."
>
> > *Lear*, ii. 1. 99.

Contráry (Latin).—" Our wílls | and fátes | do só | contrá | ry rún."
> > *Hamlet*, iii. 2. 221.

Contráct (Latin).

> "Márk our | contráct. | Márk your | divórce, | young sír."
> *W. T.* iv. 4. 428 ; *A. W.* ii. 3. 185 ; 1 *Hen. VI.* iii.
> 1. 143, v. 4. 156 ; *Rich. III.* iii. 7. 5, 6 ; *Temp.*
> ii. 1. 151.

Compáct (Latin, noun).—*Rich. III.* ii. 2. 133 ; *J. C.* iii. 1. 215.

Différent (Latin).—" And múch | *differ* | ent fróm | the mán | he
wás."—*C. of E.* v. 1. 46.

Here, however, by emphasizing the monosyllable "much," the
word "different" may be pronounced in the usual way.

Edíct (Latin).—2 *Hen. VI.* iii. 2. 258, and

> "It stánds | as án | *edíct* | in dés | tiný."
> > *M. N. D.* i. 1. 151.

Effígies (Latin unaltered).

> " And ás | mine éye | doth hís | *effí* | *gies* wítness."
> > *A. Y. L.* ii. 7. 193.

Envý (verb ; noun, *énvy*).

> "I's it | for hím | you dó | *envý* | me só?"—*T. of Sh.* ii. 1. 18.

Execútors.—*Hen. V.* i. 2. 203 is not an instance, for it means
"executioners." In its legal sense, *Ib.* iv. 2. 51, it is accented as
with us.

Exíle (Latin).—*R. and J.* v. 3. 211 (frequent).

Instínct (noun, Latin).

> "Háth, by | *instínct*, | knówledge | from óth | ers' éyes."
> > 2 *Hen. IV.* i. 1. 86.

" Bý a | divine | *instinct* | men's minds | mistrúst."
                    Rich. III. ii. 3. 42 ; *Coriol.* v. 3. 85.

Intó.—See 457 *a*.

Miséry.—Some commentators lay the accent on the penultimate in

" Of súch | *misér* | *y* dóth | she cút | me óff,"
                                    M. of V. iv. 1. 272.

but much more probably "a" has dropped out after "such."
The passage

" And búss | thee ás | thy wífe. | Míser | y's lóve,"
                                    K. J. iii. 4. 35.

proves nothing.   The pause-accent is sufficient to justify "mísery."

Nothíng.—See *Something*, below.

Obdúrate (Latin).—3 *Hen. VI.* i. 4. 142 ; *M. of V.* iv. 1. 8 ; *T. A.*
ii. 3. 160 ; *R. of L.* 429.

" A'rt thou | *obdú* | *rate*, flín | ty, hárd | as stéel?"
                                    V. and A. 198.

Oppórtune (Latin).—"And móst | *oppórt* | *une* tó | our néed |
                    I háve."—*W. T.* iv. 4. 511.

" The móst | oppórt | une pláce, | the stróng'st | suggéstion."
                                    Temp. iv. 1. 26.

Outráge.—1 *Hen. VI.* iv. 1. 126.

Perémptory (perhaps).

" Yea, mís | tress, áre | you só | perémp | tóry ? "
                                    P. of T. ii. 5. 73.

This accentuation is not found elsewhere in Shakespeare : but the
author of *Pericles of Tyre* may have used it.   It is possible, however,
to scan

" Yea, mís | t(e)réss (477), | are you | so pé | rempt(o)rý ? "

Porténts.—"Thése are | *porténts :* | but yét | I hópe, | I hópe."
                                    Othello, v. 2. 45.

So 1 *Hen. IV.* ii. 3. 65 ; *Tr. and Cr.* i. 3. 96.

Hence "fear" is not a dissyllable in

" A pród | igý | of féar, | ánd a | *portén .*"
                                    1 *Hen. IV.* v. 1. 20.

If "and" is correct, we must probably scan as follows :

" And thése | doth she applý | for wárn | ings ánd | *porténts.*"
                                    J. C. ii. 2. 80.

Precépts (Latin).—*Hen. V.* iii. 3. 26 ; but "précepts," *Hamlet*,
ii. 2. 142.

Prescíence retains the accent of science, indicating that the word was not familiar enough as yet to be regarded as other than a compound :

"Forestáll | *prescí* | ence ánd | estéem | no áct."
Tr. and Cr. i. 3. 199.

Recórd (noun, Latin).—*Rich. III.* iii. 1. 72, iv. 4. 28 ; *T. N.* v. 1. 253.

Sepúlchre (Latin).—"Bánish'd | this fráil | *sepúl* | *chre* óf | our flésh."—*Rich. II.* i. 3. 194.

"Or, át | the léast, | in hérs | *sepúl* | *chre* thíne."
T. G. of V. iv. 2. 118.

"May líke | wise bé | *sepúl* | *chred* ín | thy sháde."
R. of L. 805 ; and, perhaps, *Lear*, ii. 4. 134.

Siníster (Latin).—"'Tis nó | *sinís* | *ter* nór | no áwk | ward cláim."
Hen. V. ii. 4. 85.

So, but comically, in

"And thís | the crán | ny ís, | ríght and | *siníster*,
Through whích | the féar | ful lóv | ers áre | to whísper."
M. N. D. v. 1. 164.

Sojóurn'd (perhaps) in

"My héart | to hér | but ás | guest-wíse | *sojóurn'd.*"
Ib. iii. 2. 171,

But (?) emphasize "her," and scan

"My héart | to hér | ' bút | as gúest- | wise *sójourn'd.*"

Somethíng (sometimes perhaps). "My ínward | sóul
At nó | thing trémb | les : át | *somethíng* | it gríeves."
Rich. II. ii. 2. 12.

Compare perhaps

"And I' | *nothíng* | to báck | my súit | at áll."
Rich. III. i. 1. 236.

But, if "I" be emphasized, "nothing" may be pronounced as usual.

" I féar | *nothíng* | what máy | be sáid | agáinst me."
Hen. VIII. i. 2. 212.

But "fear" may be a dissyllable, 480.

Sweethéart.—*Hen. VIII.* i. 4. 94 : *heart* being regarded as a noun instead of the suffix -*ard*.

Triúmphing (Latin) sometimes.

"As 't wére | *triúmph* | *ing* át | mine én | emíes."
Rich. III. iii. 4. 91.

Untó.—See 457 a.

Welcóme.—"Nor fríends, | nor fóes, | to mé | *welcóme* | you áre."
Rich. II. ii. 3. 170.

This particular passage may be explained by a pause, but "welcóme" is common in other authors.

Wherefóre (in some cases), though it can often be taken as "thérefore," and explained by a preceding pause.

"O'ft have | you (óft | en háve | you thánks | *therefóre*)."
Tr. and Cr. iii. 3. 20.

"And wé | must yéarn | *therefóre.*"—*Hen. V.* ii. 3. 6.

"Hate mé ! | *Wherefóre ?* | O mé ! | what néws, | my lóve."
M. N. D. iii. 2. 272.

Perhaps
"Fór the | sound mán. | Déath on | my státe, | *wherefóre ?* "
Lear, ii. 4. 113.

But better
"Death on my state ! (512)
Whérefore | should hé | sit hére? | This áct | persuádes
me."

491. -Ised, when ending polysyllables, generally has now a certain emphasis. This is necessary, owing to the present broad pronunciation of *i*. Such polysyllables generally have now two accents, the principal accent coming first. But in Shakespeare's time it would seem that the *i* approximated in some of these words to the French *i*, and, the *-ed* being pronounced, the *i* in *-ised* was unemphatic. Hence the Elizabethan accent of some of these words differs from the modern accent.

Advértised.—"As I' | by fríends | am wéll | *advért* | *iséd.*"
Rich. III. iv. 4. 501.

"Wheréin | he míght | the kíng | his lórd | *advértise.*"
Hen. VIII. ii. 4. 178.

"I wás | *advért* | *ised* théir | great gén | eral slépt."
Tr. and Cr. ii. 2. 111.

So *M. for M.* i. 1. 42.

Chástised.—"And whén | this árm | of míne | hath *chás* | *tiséd.*"
Rich. III. iv. 4. 331.

"This cáuse | of Róme, | and *chás* | *tiséd* | with arms."
T. A. i. 1. 32.

This explains :

Canónized.—"Canón | izéd, | and wór | shipp'd ás | a sáint."
K. J. iii. 1. 177.

"Whý thy | *canón* | *iz'd* bónes, | héarsed | in déath."
Hamlet, i. 4. 47.

"Are brá | zen ím | age(s) [471] óf | *canón* | *iz'd* sáints."
2 *Hen. VI.* i. 3. 63.

Authórized.—"*Authór* | *iz'd* bý | her grán | dam. Sháme | itsélf."
Macbeth, iii. 4. 66.

"*Authór* | *izíng* | thy trés | pass wíth | compáre."—*Sonn.* 35.

"His rúde | ness só | with hís | *authór* | *iz'd* yóuth."
L. C. 104.

So once :

Solémnised.—"Of Já | ques Fál | conbrídge | *solém* | *niséd.*"
L. L. L. ii. 1. 42.

But in *M. of V.* "sólemnised."

492. Words in which the accent was nearer the beginning than with us. Ben Jonson (p. 777) says all nouns, both dissyllabic (if they be "simple") and trisyllabic, are accented on the first syllable. Perhaps this accounts for the accent on *cónfessor*, &c. The accent on the first syllable was the proper noun accent ; the accent on the second (which in the particular instance of *conféssor* ultimately prevailed) was derived from the verb.

Archbishop.—"The már | shal ánd | the *árch* | *bishóp* | are stróng."
2 *Hen. IV.* ii. 3. 42, 65.

Cément (noun).

"Your tém | ples búrn | ed ín | their *cé* | *ment* ánd."
Coriol. iv. 6. 85.

So the verb, *A. and C.* ii. 1. 48 ; iii. 2. 29.

Cómpell'd (when used as an adjective).

"This *cóm* | *pell'd* fór | tune, háve | your móuth | fill'd úp."
Hen. VIII. ii. 3. 87.

"I tálk | not of | your sóul : | our *cóm* | *pell'd* síns."
M. for M. ii. 4. 57.

Cómplete.—"A máid | of gráce | and *cóm* | *plete* máj | estý."
L. L. L. i. 1. 137.

So *Hamlet*, i. 4. 52 ; *Hen. VIII.* i. 2. 118 ; *Rich. III.* iii. 1. 189.

Cónceal'd.—"My *cón* | *ceal'd* lá | dy tó | her cán | cell'd lóve."
R. and J. iii. 3. 98.

Cónduct.—The verb follows the noun "safe-cónduct" in

"*Safe-cón* | *ducting* | the réb | els fróm | their shíps."
Rich. III. iv. 4. 483.

But the noun is *condúct* in *T. A.* iv. 3. 65.

Cónfessor.—*Hen. VIII.* i. 2. 149 ; *R. and J.* ii. 6. 21, iii. 3. 49.

"O'ne of | our có (*sic*) | vent ánd | his *cón | fessór.*"
M. *for* M. iv. 3. 133.

Cóngeal'd.—"O'pen | their *cón | geal'd* móuths | and bléed | afrésh."—*Rich. III.* i. 2. 56.

Cónjure (in the sense of "entreat").—*T. G. of V.* ii. 7. 2 ; frequent.

Cónsign'd.—"With *dís | tinct* bréath, | and *cón | sign'd* kíss | es tó them."—*Tr. and Cr.* iv. 4. 47.

See "*distinct*" below.

Córrosive.—"Cáre is | no cúre, | but rá | ther *cór | rosíve.*"
1 *Hen. VI.* iii. 3. 3 ; 2 *Hen. VI.* iii. 2. 403.

Délectable.—"Máking | the hárd | way sóft | and *dé | lectáble.*"
Rich. II. ii. 3. 7.

Détestable.—"And I' | will kíss | thy *dé | testá | ble* bónes."
K. J. iii. 4. 29 ; T. of A. iv. 1. 33.

Dístinct.—"To offénd | and júdge | are *dís | tinct* óff | icés."
M. of V. ii. 9. 61.

See "*cónsign'd*" above.

Fórlorn.—"Now fór | the hón | our óf | the *fór | lorn* Frénch."
1 *Hen. VI.* i. 2. 19.

Húmane.—"It ís | the *húm | ane* wáy, | the óth | er cóurse."
Coriol. iii. 1. 327.

Máintain.—"That hére | you *máin | tain* sév | eral fác | tións."
1 *Hen. VI.* i. 1. 71.

Máture.—So apparently in

"Of múrder | ous léchers : | ánd in | the *má | ture* tíme."
Lear, iv. 6. 228.

This is like "náture," but I know no other instance of "máture."

Méthinks (sometimes).

"So yóur | sweet húe | which *mé | thinks* stíll | doth stánd."
Sonn. 104.

I cannot find a conclusive instance in Shakespeare, but this word is often (Walker) thus accented in Elizabethan writers.

Mútiners.—*Coriol.* i. 1. 492. See *Píoners* below.

Mýself (perhaps, but by no means certainly, in)

"I *mý | self* fíght | not ónce | in fór | ty yéar."
1 *Hen. VI.* i. 3. 91.

But certainly *hímself, mýself,* &c. are often found in Elizabethan authors, especially in Spenser :

"Mourns inwardly and makes to *himselfe* mone."
SPENS. F. Q. ii. 1. 42.

The reason for this is that *self,* being an adjective and not a noun, is not entitled to, and had not yet invariably received, the emphasis which it has acquired in modern times.

And so, perhaps :

"And bánd | ing *thém* | *selves* ín | contrá (490) | ry párts."
1 Hen. VI. iii. 1. 81.

Nórthampton.—"Last níght | I héar | they láy | at *Nórth-* | *amptón*."—*Rich. III.* ii. 4. 1.

O'bscure (adj.; as a verb, *obscúre*).

"To ríb | her cére | cloth ín | the *ób* | *scure* gráve."
M. of V. ii. 7. 51.

"His méans | of déath, | his *ób* | *scure* fú | nerál."
Hamlet, iv. 5. 213.

O'bservant.—"Than twén | ty síll | y dúck | ing *ób* | servánts."
Lear, ii. 2. 109.

Perséver—"Ay, dó, | *persév* | *er,* cóunt | erféit | sad lóoks."
M. N. D. iii. 2. 236 ; A. W. iii. 7. 31 ; K. J. ii. 1. 421 ;
Hamlet, i. 2. 92.

This is the Latin accent in accordance with Ben Jonson's rule.

"Bóunty, | *persév* | (*e*)*rance,* mér | cy, lów | linéss."
Macbeth, iv. 3. 93.

Pérspective.—*A. W.* v. 3. 48 ; *Rich. II.* ii. 2. 18.

The double accent seems to have been disliked by the Elizabethans. They wrote and pronounced "muleters" for "muleteers," "enginer" (*Hamlet,* iii. 4. 206) for "engineer," "pioners" for "pioneers." This explains :

Píoners.—"A wórth | y *pioner.* | Once móre | remóve, | good friends."—*Hamlet,* i. 5. 162.

Plébeians (almost always).

"The *pléb* | *eiáns* | have gót | your fél | low-tríbune."
Coriol. v. 4. 39 ; i. 9. 7, &c.

This explains

"Lét them | have cúsh | ions bý you. | You're *pléb* | *eiáns*."
Ib. iii. 1. 101.

Exceptions : *Hen. V.* v. Chorus, 27 ; *T. A.* i. 1. 231.

So "Epicúrean" in Elizabethan authors and *A. and C.* ii. 1. 24. The Elizabethans generally did not accent the *e* in such words.

Pùrsuit.—"In *púr* | *suit* óf | the thíng | she wóuld | have stáy."
Sonn. 143.

"We trí | fle tíme. | I prí | thee *púr* | *sue* séntence."
M. of V. iv. 1. 298.

Púrveyor.—"To bé | his *púr* | *veyór* : | but hé | rides wéll."
Macbeth, i. 6. 22.

Quíntessence.—"Téaching | áll that | réad to | knów
    The *quínt* | *essénce* | of év | ery spríte."—*A. Y. L.* iii. 2. 147.

Récordér (?).—"To bé | spoke tó | but by | the *ré* | *cordér.*"
Rich. III. iii. 7. 30.

So also Walker, who quotes from DONNE'S *Satires*, v. 248, Ed. 1633 :

    "Recorder to Destiny on earth, and she."

But this line might be scanned otherwise.

Rélapse.—"Kílling | in *ré* | *lapse* óf | mortál | itý."
Hen. V. iv. 3. 107.

Rhéumatic.—"O'erwórn, | despís | ed, *rhéu* | *matic*, | and óld."
V. and A. 135 ; *M. N. D.* ii. 1. 105.

So   "These *prág* | *matíc* | young mén | at théir | own wéapons."
B. J.

Sécure.—"Upón | my *sé* | *cure* hóur | thy ún | cle stóle."
Hamlet, i. 5. 61 ; *Othello*, iv. 1. 72.

Séquester'd.—"Whý are | you *sé* | *questér'd* | from áll | your tráin ?"
T. A. ii. 3. 75.

Súccessor (rare).

    "For béing | not própp'd | by án | cestrý | whose gráce
    Chalks *súcc* | *essórs* | their wáy, | nor cáll'd | upón," &c.
Hen. VIII. i. 1. 60.

Súccessive (rare).—"Are nów | to háve | no *súcc* | *essíve* | degrées."
M. for M. ii. 2. 98.

Tówards (sometimes).

    "And sháll | contín | ue our grác | es *tó* | *wards* hím."
Macbeth, i. 6. 30.

    "I gó, | and *tó* | *wards* thrée | or fóur | o'clóck."
Rich. III. iii. 5. 101.

Compare "Should, líke | a swáll | ow préy | ing *tó* | *wards* stórms."
B. J. *Poetast.* iv. 7.

    "O' the plágue, | he's sáfe | from thínk | ing *tó* | *ward* Lóndon."
B. J. *Alchemist*, i. 1.

So, perhaps,

"I ám | infórmed | that hé | comes *tó* | *wards* Lóndon."
3 Hen. VI. iv. 4. 26.

"And *tó* | *ward* Lón | don théy | do bénd | their cóurse."
Rich. III. iv. 5. 14.

U'tensils (perhaps).

"He has brave *útensils;* for so he calls them."
Temp. iii. 2. 104.

Without.—See 457 *a.*

The English tendency, as opposed to the Latin, is illustrated by the accentuation of the first syllable of "ígnominy," and its consequent contraction into "*ígnomy*" (1 *Hen. IV.* v. 4. 100, &c.).

VERSES.

493. A proper Alexandrine with six accents, such as—
"And nów | by wínds | and wáves | my lífe | less límbs | are tóssed,"—DRYDEN.

is seldom found in Shakespeare.

494. Apparent Alexandrines. The following are Alexandrines only in appearance. The last foot contains, instead of one extra syllable, two extra syllables, one of which is slurred (see 467–9) :—

"The núm | bers óf | our hóst | and máke | *discóvery* (discov'ry)."—*Macbeth*, v. 4. 6.

"He thínks | me nów | incáp | ablé; | *conféderates.*"
Tempest, i. 2. 111.

"In vír | tue thán | in vén | geance : théy | being *pénitent.*"
Ib. v. 1. 28.

"And móre | divérs | itý | of sóunds | all *hórrible.*"—*Ib.* 235.

"In bítt | ernéss. | The cómm | on *éx* | *ecútioner.*"
A. Y. L. iii. 5. 3.

"I sée | no móre | in yóu | than ín | the *órdinary.*"—*Ib.* 42.

" Were rích | and hón | ouráble; | besídes | the *géntlemen.*"
T. G. of V. iii. 1. 64.

"Which sínce | have steád | ed múch; | so, óf | his *géntleness.*"—*Temp.* i. 2. 165 ; *Rich. III.* v. 3. 245 ; *Hen. V.* ii. 2. 71.

For the contraction of "gentleman" to "gentl'man," or even "genman," see 461.

"Are yóu | not gríeved | that A'r | thur ís | his *prísoner* (468)?"—*K. J.* iii. 4. 123.

"And I' | must frée | ly háve | the hálf | of *ánything.*"
                   M. of V. iii. 2. 251.

"To másk | thy mónst | rous vísage. | Seek nóne | *con-spíracy.*"—*J. C.* ii. 1. 01.

"Had hé | been vánq | u(i)sher, ás, | bý the | same *cóve-nant.*"—*Hamlet,* i. 1. 93.

"My lórd, | I cáme | to sée | your fá | ther's *fúneral.*"
                   Ib. i. 2. 176.

"Untáint | ed, ún | exám | in'd, frée, | at *líberty.*"
                   Rich. III. iii. 6. 9.

"And só | doth míne. | I múse | why shé's | at *líberty.*"
                   Ib. i. 3. 305.

So, perhaps,

"From tóo | much lí | bertý, | my Lú | cio, *líberty.*"
                   M. for M. i. 2. 129.

"A'bso | lute Mí | lan. Mé, | poor mán, | my *líbrary.*"
                   Tempest, i. 2. 109.

"Shall sée | advánt | ageá | ble fór | our *dígnity.*"
                   Hen. V. v. 2. 88.

unless "advántage | able fór | ."

495. Sometimes the two syllables are inserted at the end of the third or fourth foot—

"The flúx | of *cómpany.* | Anón | a cáre | less hérd."
                   A. Y. L. ii. 1. 52.

"To cáll | for ré*compense;* | appéar | it tó | your mínd."
                   Tr. and Cr. iii. 3. 3.

"Is nót | so ést*ima* | ble, pró | fitá | ble néither."
                   M. of V. i. 3. 167.

"O'erbéars | your óff*icers;* | the ráb | ble cáll | him lórd."
                   Hamlet, iv. 5. 102.

"To mé | invét*erate,* | héarkens | my bróth | er's súit."
                   Temp. i. 2. 122.

"With áll | preróg*ative.* | Hénce his | ambít | ion grówing."
                   Ib. i. 2. 105.

"In báse | *applíance*(s) (471). | This óut | ward sáint | ed *députy* (468)."—*M. for M.* iii. 1. 89.

"Than wé | bring mén | to cóm*fort them* ('em). | The fáult's | your ówn."—*Tempest,* ii. 1. 134–5.

496. In other cases the appearance of an Alexandrine arises from the non-observance of contractions—

"I dáre | abíde | no lónger (454). | *Whither* (466) should | I flý?"—*Macbeth*, iv. 2. 73.

"She lé | vell'd át | our *púr* | *pose*(*s*) (471), ánd, | *béing* (470) roýal."—*A. and C.* v. 2. 339.

"All mórt | al *cónse* | *quence*(*s*) (471) háve | pronóunced | me thús."—*Macbeth*, v. 3. 5.

"As mís | ers dó | by béggars (454) ; | *neither* (466) gáve | to mé."—*Tr. and Cr.* iii. 3. 142.

497. Apparent Alexandrines. The following can be explained by the omission of unemphatic syllables :—

"*Hor.* Háil to | your lórdship. |
Ham. I am (*I'm*) glád | to sée | you wéll."
Hamlet, i. 2. 160.

"Whereóf | he is the (*he's th'*) héad ; | then íf | he sáys | he lóves you."—*Ib.* i. 3. 24.

"Thou *art* swórn | as déeply | to (*t'*) efféct | what wé | inténd."—*Rich. III.* iii. 1. 158.

"I *had* thóught, | my lórd, | to *have* léarn'd | his héalth | of yóu."—*Rich. II.* ii. 3. 24.

"That tráce him | in his (*in's*) líne. | No bóast | ing líke | a fóol."—*Macbeth*, iv. 1. 153.

"In séeming | *to* augmént | it wástes | it. Bé | advís'd."
Hen. VIII. i. 1. 145.

"When mír(*a*) | cles háve | by *the* gréat | est béen | denéed."
A. W. ii. 1. 144.

"Persuádes | me *it* is (*t's*) óth | erwíse ; | howe'ér | it bé."
Rich. III. ii. 2. 29.

"A wórth | y óff (*i*)*cer* | i' *the* wár, | but ín | solént."
Coriol. iv. 6. 30.

"I prómise | you I' am ('*m*) | afráid | to héar | you téll it."
Ib. i. 4. 65.

"Come, sís | ter, cóusin | I would ('*ld*) sáy, | pray pár | don mé."—*Rich. II.* ii. 2. 105.

"That máde | them dó it ('*t*). | They are ('*re*) wíse | and hón | (*ou*)ráble."—*J. C.* iii. 2. 218.

"With áll | preróg(*a*)tive ; | hénce his | ambít | ion grów-ing."—*Tempest*, i. 2. 105.

"Mine éyes | even sóc | iablé | to *the* shów | of thíne."
Ib. v. 1. 63.

" As gréat | to mé | as láte ; | *and* suppórt | ablé."
Temp. v. 1. 146.

unless " supportable" can be accented on the first.
"Ostentation" is perhaps for " ostention " (Walker), and "the "
is " th'," in
" The *ostentation* of our love which, left unshown."
A. and C. iii. 6. 52.

"Is " ought probably to be omitted in
" With gól | den chéru | bims (*is*) frétted ; | her án | diróns."
Cymb. ii. 4. 88.

" So sáucy | with *the* hánd | of shé | here—whát's | her
náme ?"—*A. and C.* iii. 13. 98.

" Come Lám | mas éve | at níght | *shall* she bé | fourtéen."
R. and J. i. 3. 17.

" Of óffic(467) | er, (465) and óff | ice sét | all héarts | *in the*
(*i' th'*) státe."—*Tempest*, i. 2. 84.

"Uncóup | *le* (465) *in the* (*i' th'*) wést | ern váll | ey, lét | them
gó."—*M. N. D.* iv. 1. 112.

" Cóme to | one márk ; | as mány | ways méet *in* | one
tówn."—*Hen. V.* i. 2. 208.

" Verbátim | to rehéarse | the méth | od óf | my pén."
1 *Hen. VI.* iii. 1. 13.

The following is intended to be somewhat irregular :
" Now bý | mine hón | our, bý | my lífe, | by *my* tróth."
Rich. II. v. 2. 78.

We must probably scan as an ordinary line,
" That séeming | to be móst | which wé | indéed | least áre,"
T. of Sh. v. 2. 175.

since it rhymes with an ordinary line,
" Our stréngth | as weak, | our wéak | ness pást | compáre."

The following can be explained by the quasi-omission of unemphatic syllables :
" Awáy ! | though párt | ing bé | a dréad | ful córr(*o*)sive."
2 *Hen. VI.* iii. 2. 403.

"Córrosive," as in 1 *Hen. VI.* iii. 3. 3, is accented on the first,
and here pronounced " corsive."

" Bút with | a knáve | of cómm | on híre, | a gónd(*o*)lier."
Othello, i. 1. 126.

"Our " is not a dissyllable, but " ag'd " is a monosyllable in
" But lóve, | dear lóve, | and óur | *ag'd* fá | ther's ríght."
Lear, iv. 4. 28.

So perhaps
> " An *ág'd* | intér | pretér | though yóung | in yéars."
> > *T. of A.* v. 3. 6.

498. Alexandrines doubtful. There are several apparent Alexandrines, in which a shortening of a preposition would reduce the line to an ordinary line. "Upon," for instance, might lose its prefix, like "'gainst" for "against."

> " To lóok | *upon* my sóme | time más | ter's róy | al fáce."
> > *Rich. II.* ii. 5. 75.

> " Forbíds | to dwéll *up* | on ; yét | remém | ber thís."
> > *Rich. III.* v. 3. 239.

> " *Upon* óur | house('s) (471) thátch, | whíles a | more fróst | y péople."—*Hen. V.* iii. 5. 24.

> " *Upon* the sís | terhóod, | the vó | tarists óf | St. Cláre."
> > *M. for M.* i. 4. 5.

> " *Brut.* "Is líke | to láy *upon* us (on's). |
> *Cass.*   I'm glád | that mý | weak wórds."
> > *J. C.* i. 2. 176.

> " Is góne | to práy | the hó | ly kíng | *upon* his (on's) áid."
> > *Macbeth*, iii. 6. 30.

So "to" (or "in," 457*a*) in "into" may be dropped in

> " Fall *into* | the cóm | pass óf | a præ' | muníre."
> > *Hen. VIII.* iii. 2. 340.

> "The wátches | on *únto* | mine éyes | the óut | ward wátch."
> > *Rich. II.* v. 4. 52.

>   (?)   " Ráther | a dítch | in E'gypt
> Be géntle | grave *únto* | me. *Ráther* | on Ní | lus' múd."
> > *A. and C.* v. 2. 58.

"Gentle" is a quasi-monosyllable, see 465 ; "rather," see 466.
So Walker reads "to" for "unto" in

> " *Unto* a póor, | but wórth | y gént | lemán. | She's wédded,"—*Cymb.* i. 1. 7.

and observes, " *Unto* and *into* have elsewhere, I think, taken the place of *to*."

Perhaps the second line of the rhyming couplet is purposely lengthened in

> " I' am | for the áir ; | this níght | I'll spénd
> *Un'to* | a dís | mal ánd | a fát | al énd."—*Macb.* iii. v. 21.

In " Better to leave undone, than by our deed
> Acquire too high a fame when him we serve's away,"
> > *A. and C.* iii. 1. 15.

we might arrange

" Better léave | undóne, | than bý | our déed | acqúire."

Or the latter line might be (but there is not pause enough to make it probable) a trimeter couplet. (See 501.)

" At Má | rián | a's hóuse | to-níght. | Her cáuse | and yóurs,"
M. for M. iv. 3. 145.

must be an Alexandrine, unless in the middle of the line "Mariana" can be shortened like "Marian," as "Helena" becomes "Helen" (*M. N. D.* i. 1. 208). Compare

" For Már | iana's sáke : | but ás | he adjúdg'd | your bróther."
M. for M. v. 1. 408.

The following seem pure Alexandrines, or nearly so, if the text be correct :—

" How dáres (499) | thy hársh | rude tóngue | sound thís |
unpléas | ing néws."—*Rich. II.* iii. 4. 74.

" Suspíc | ion, áll | our líves, | shall bé | stuck fúll | of éyes."
1 *Hen. IV.* v. 2. 8.

" A chér | ry líp, | a bón | ny éye, | a páss | ing pléas | ing
tóngue."—*Rich. III.* i. 1. 94.

" Tó the | young Ró | man bóy | she hath sóld | me ánd |
I fáll."—*A. and C.* iv. 12. 48.

" And thése | does shé | applý | for wárn | ings ánd | por-
ténts."—*J. C.* iii. 1. 23.

This is the Shakespearian accent of "portent" (490), but perhaps "and" should be omitted.

" Oút of | a gréat | deal óf | old ír | on I' | chose fórth."
1 *Hen. VI.* i. 2. 101.

It is needless to say that Shakespeare did not write this line, whether it be read thus or

" Oút of | a great déal | of óld | iron I' | chose fórth."

In " 'Tis hé | that sént | us híth | er nów | to slaugh | ter thée,"
Rich III. i. 4. 250.

"hither" (466) may be a monosyllable, and then we can read

" 'Tis hé | that sént us | ."

The latter line in the following couplet seems to be an Alexandrine :

" Of whát | it ís | not : thén, | thrice-grác | ious quéen,
Móre than | your lórd's | depárt | ure wéep | not : móre's
| not séen."—*Rich. II.* ii. 2.˙25, v. 4. 110.

Sometimes apparent Alexandrines will be reduced to ordinary lines, if exclamations such as "O," "Well," &c. be considered (512) as detached syllables.

> " *Vol.* That théy | combíne | not thére. |
> *Cor.* (*Tush, tush!*)
> *Men.* A góod demánd."
> *Coriol.* iii. 2. 45.

> " *Coriol.* The óne | by the óther. |
> *Com.* (*Well,*) | O'n to | the márk | et pláce."
> *Ib.* iii. 1. 112.

> " *Sic.* 'Tis hé, | 'tis hé: | (*O,*) he's grówn | most kínd | of láte."—*Ib.* iv. 6. 11.

> " Upón | the Brít | ish párty. | (*O,*) untíme | ly déath."
> *Lear,* iv. 6. 25.

In the last two examples " O " might coalesce with the following vowel. But see also 503 and 512.

499. Apparent Alexandrines are sometimes regular verses of five accents preceded or followed by a foot, more or less isolated, containing one accent.

> "(Shall I) With bated breath and whispering humbleness
> *Say thís.* ‖ Fair sír, | you spít | on mé | on Wéd | nesday lást."—*M. of V.* i. 3. 126.

> " *Háve I* ‖ No fríend | will ríd | me óf | this lív | ing féar?"
> *Rich. II.* v. 4. 2.

The " No " is emphatic, and there is a slight pause after " I."

> " *Whíp him,* ‖ Were't twén | ty óf | the gréat | est tríb | u- táries."—*A. and C.* iii. 13. 96.

> " *Come, cóme,* ‖ No móre | of thís | unpróf | itá | ble chát."
> 1 *Hen. IV.* iii. 1. 63.

> " There cannot be those numberless offences
> '*Gáinst me,* ‖ that I' | cannót | take péace | with: nó | black énvy."—*Hen. VIII.* ii. 1. 85.

> " A's you | are cért | ainlý | a gén | tlemán, ‖ *theretó,* Clerk-líke | expéri | énced."—*W. T.* i. 2. 391.

> " *Besídes,* ‖ I líke | you nót. | I'f you | will knów | my hóuse."
> *A. Y. L.* iii. 5. 74.

> " Whích to | dený | concérns | móre than | aváils,
> *For ás* ‖ thy brát | hath béen | cast óut | líke to | itsélf."
> *W. T.* iii. 2. 87.

> "Só it | should nów,
> Wére there | necéss | itý | in yóur | requést, ‖ *although* 'Twere néed | ful I' | deníed it."—*Ib.* i. 2. 22.

" Máking | práctis'd | smíles
A's in | a lóok | ing gláss, | and thén | to sígh, ‖ *as 'twére*
The mórt | o' the déer."—*W. T.* i. 2. 117.

The context might perhaps justify a pause after "well" in

" *Flor.* To háve | them ré | compénsed | as thóught | on.
Cam.   Wéll, ‖ *my lórd.*"
                                        W. T. iv. 4. 532.

But better " To have them (*t' have 'em*) ré | compénsed."

" His traín | ing súch
That hé | may fúrn | ish ánd | instrúct | great téachers,
And név | er séek | for áid | óut of | himsélf.
‖ *Yet see,*" &c.—*Hen. VIII.* i. 2. 114.

" Whát, girl ! | though gréy
Do sóme | thing míng | le wíth | our yóung | er brówn,
                                        ‖ *yet há' we*
A bráin," &c.—*A. and C.* iv. 8. 21.

" A cértain númber,
Though thánks | to áll, | múst I | seléct | from áll. ‖ *The
rést*
Shall béar," | &c.—*Coriol.* i. 6. 81 ; i. 7. 2.

" And the buildings of my fancy.
Only—
There's one thing wanting which I doubt not but."
                                        Ib. ii. 1. 216.

Collier transposes "only" and "but" to the respectively following lines.   The line

" So to esteem of us and on our knees we beg,"

ought probably to be arranged thus :

" Só to | estéem | of ús, | and ón | our knées
We bég | as ré | compénse | of óur | dear sérvices (471)."
                                        W. T. ii. 3. 150.

So   " Whom I' | with thís | obé | dient stéel, | three ínches (471)
of it."—*Temp.* ii. 1. 283 ; *i.e.* "three ínch of't."

So transpose "'tis," *i. e.* "it is," to the preceding line in

" *York.* I féar, | I féar,— |
Duch.   What should | you féar? | *It ís*
('Tis) Nothing bút | some bónd | that hé | is ént | er'd
ínto."—*Rich. II.* v. 2. 65.

"I do" must be omitted (456) before "beseech you" in

"(I do) beséech | you, pár | don mé, | I máy | not shów it."
                                        Ib. 70.

So *Cymb.* i. 6. 48.

500. Trimeter Couplet. Apparent Alexandrines are often couplets of two verses of three accents each. They are often thus printed as two separate short verses in the Folio. But the degree of separateness between the two verses varies greatly. Thus perhaps—

"Whére it | may sée | itsélf; || thís is | not stránge | at áll."
Tr. and Cr. iii. 3. 111.

"That hás | he knóws | not whát. || Náture, | what thíngs | there áre."—*Ib.* iii. 3. 127.

And certainly in the following :—

"*Anne.* I wóuld | I knéw | thy héart. || *Glou.* 'Tis fíg | ured ín | my tóngue.
Anne. I féar | me bóth | are fálse. || *Glou.* Then név | er mán | was trúe.
Anne. Well, wéll, | put úp | your swórd. || *Glou.* Say thén | my péace | is máde."—*Rich. III.* i. 2. 193.

"*Jul.* I wóuld | I knéw | his mínd. || *Luc.* Perúse | this pá | per, mádam.
Jul. 'To Jú | lia.' Sáy, | from whóm? || *Luc.* Thát the | conténts | will shéw.
Jul. Say, sáy, | who gáve | it thée?"—*T. G. of V.* i. 2. 33-7.

"*Luc.* Go tó ; | 'tis wéll ; | awáy! || *Isab.* Heaven kéep | your hón | our sáfe."—*M. for M.* ii. 2. 156.

"*Isab.* Sháll I | atténd | your lórdship? || *A.* At án | y tíme | 'fore nóon."—*Ib.* ii. 2. 60; ii. 4. 104, 141.

"*Ros.* The hóur | that fóols | should ásk. || *B.* Now fáir | befáll | your másk.
Ros. Fair fáll | the fáce | it cóvers. || *B.* And sénd | you má | ny lóvers."—*L. L. L.* ii. 1. 123.

"*Ang.* Why dóst | thou ásk | agáin? || *Prov.* Lést I | might bé | too rásh.
Prov. Repént | ed ó'er | his dóom. || *Ang.* Go tó, | let thát | be míne!
Ang. And yóu | shall wéll | be spáred. || *Prov.* I cráve | your hón | our's párdon."—*M. for M.* ii. 2. 9-12 ; *Othello,* iii. 3. 28-31; *Temp.* iii. 1. 31, 59.

Shakespeare seems to have used this metre mostly for rapid dialogue and retort. But in the ghost scene in *Hamlet :*

"*Ghost.* To whát | I sháll | unfóld. ||
Ham.   Speak ; I' | am bóund | to héar."
Hamlet, i. 5. 6.

501. The trimeter couplet, beside being frequent in dialogue, is often used by one and the same speaker, but most frequently in comic, and the lighter kind of serious, poetry. It is appropriate for Thisbe:

> " Most rád | iant Pý | ramús, ‖ most líl | y-whíte | of húe."
> *M. N. D.* iii. 1. 94, 97.

And for Pistol, when he rants:

> " An óath | of míck | le míght; ‖ and fú | ry sháll | abáte."
> *Hen. V.* ii. 1. 70, 44; ii. 3. 4, 64; v. 1. 93.

> " He ís | not vé | ry táll: ‖ yet fór | his yéars | he's táll."
> *A. Y. L.* iii. 5. 118.

> " And 'I'll | be swórn | 'tis trúe: ‖ trávell | ers né'er | did líe."—*Temp.* iii. 2. 26.

> " Coy lóoks | with héart- | sore síghs; ‖ one fád | ing mó· | ment's mírth."—*T. G. of V.* i. 1. 30.

> " He wóuld | have gív'n | it yóu,‖ but I' | being ín | the wáy
> Did ín | your náme | recéive it: ‖ párdon | the fáult, | I práy."—*Ib.* 39, 40.

> " A frée- | stone cól | our'd hánd; ‖ I vér | ilý | did thínk."
> *A. Y. L.* iv. 3. 25.

> " Then lét's | make háste | awáy, ‖ and lóok | untó | the máin."—*2 Hen. VI.* i. 1. 208.

> " Am I' | not wítch'd | like hér? ‖ Or thóu | not fálse | like hím?"—*Ib.* iii. 2. 119.

> " Why ríng | not óut | the bélls ‖ alóud | throughóut | the tówn?"—*1 Hen. VI.* i. 6. 12.

> " As Æ'th | ióp | ian's tóoth, ‖ ór the | fann'd snów | that's bólted."—*W. T.* iv. 4. 375.

> " This páus | inglý | ensúed. ‖ Néither | the kíng | nor's héirs."—*Hen. VIII.* i. 2. 168.

> " The mónk | might bé | decéiv'd; ‖ and thát | 'twas dáng(e) | rous fór him."—*Ib.* 179.

> " Anón | expéct | him hére; ‖ but íf | she bé | obdú- rate (490)."—*Rich. III.* iii. 1. 39.

This metre is often used by the Elizabethan writers in the translation of quotations, inscriptions, &c. It is used for the inscriptions the caskets:

> " Who chóos | eth mé | shall gáin ‖ what mán | y mén | desíre.
> Who chóos | eth mé | must gíve ‖ and ház | ard áll | he háth."—*M. of V.* ii. 7. 5, 9.

In the pause between a comparison and the fact such a couplet
may be expected.

> " A's | Ǽné | as díd
> The óld | Anchí | ses béar, ‖ so fróm | the wáves | of Tíber
> Did I' | the tír | ed Cǽ'sar."—*J. C.* i. 2. 114.

> " To háve | what wé | would háve, ‖ we spéak | not whát | we
>   méan."—*M. for M.* ii. 4. 118.

Sometimes the first trimeter has an extra syllable, which takes the
place of the first syllable of the second trimeter.

> " Shall thére | by bé | the swéet*er*. ‖ Reá | son thús | with
>   lífe."—*M. for M.* iii. 1. 5.

> " Envél | ope yóu, | good Próv*ost!* ‖ Whó | call'd hére | of
>   láte?"—*Ib.* iv. 2. 78.

> " Mátters | of néed | ful vál*ue*. ‖ Wé | shall wríte | to yóu."
>   *Ib.* i. 1. 56.

Sometimes the first trimeter, like the ordinary five-accent verse,
has an extra syllable. In the following examples the two verses are
clearly distinct. They might almost be regarded as separate lines of
three accents rather than as a couplet :

> " Hypér | ion tó | a sát*yr*. | So lóv | ing tó | my móther."
>   *Hamlet,* i. 2. 140.

> " For énd | ing thée | no sóon*er*. ‖ Thou hást | nor yóuth |
>   nor áge."—*M. for M.* iii. 1. 32.

> " That I' | am tóuch'd | with mád*ness*. ‖ Make nót | im-
>   póss | iblé."—*Ib.* v. 1. 51. (But ? 494.)

> " *Ariel.* And dó | my spírit | ing gent*ly*. ‖
> *Prosp.*   Do só, | and áfter | two dáys."
>   *Tempest,* i. 2. 298.

> " Belów | their cób | bled shóes. ‖
>   Théy say | there's gráin | enough."
>   *Coriol.* i. 1. 200.

502. **The comic trimeter.** In the rhyming parts of the
Comedy of Errors and *Love's Labour Lost*, there is often great irregularity in the trimeter couplet. Many of the feet are trisyllabic,
and one-half of the verse differs from the other. Often the first half
is trochaic and the second iambic.

> " *Ant. E.* Whérefore? | fór my | dínner : ‖ I háve | not dín'd
> | to-dáy."—*C. of E.* iii. 1. 40.

> " *Ant. E.* Dó you | héar, you | mínion ? ‖ You'll lét | us ín, |
>   I hópe."—*Ib.* 54.

In the following, the former half is iambic and the latter *anapæstic* :

> " Thou wóuldst | have cháng'd | thy fáce || *for a náme,* | *or thy náme* | *for an áss.*" C. *of E.* iii. I. 47.

And conversely :

> " It *would máke* | *a man mád* | *as a húck* || to bé | so bóught | and sóld."—*Ib.* 72.

There are often only five accents.

> " *Bal.* Gŏod méat, sĭr, | ĭs cómmŏn : | that é | very chúrl | affórds.
> *Ant. E.* And wélcŏme | mŏre cómmŏn ; | for thát | is nóthĭng | but wórds."—*Ib.* iii. I. 24, 25.

Sometimes it is hard to tell whether the verse is trisyllabic with four accents, or dissyllabic with five.

> "Have át | you wíth | a próverb— | Shall I' | set ín | my stáff?"
> *Ib.* 51.

may be scanned with six accents, but the line to which it rhymes seems to have four :

> " And só | tell your máster. | O Lórd, | I must láugh,"
> *Ib.* 50.

and the following line also :

> " Have at yóu | with anóther ; | that's whén | can you téll,"
> *Ib.* 52.

and it is therefore possible that we ought to accent thus :

> " Have at yoú | with a próverb— | Shall I sét | in my stáff?"

503. Apparent trimeter couplets. Some apparent trimeter couplets are really ordinary dramatic lines.

For example, in the last line but two of 501 (*M. for M.* v. i. 51), "impóssible " may easily be one foot with two superfluous syllables. It is often a matter of taste which way to scan a line, but it must be borne in mind, that the trimeter couplet is rarely used to express intense emotion. Hence in an impassioned address like that of Henry V. at Harfleur, we should probably read

> " Defý us | to our wórst : | for ás | I ám | a sóldier,"
> *Hen. V.* iii. 3. 5.

or, better (479), "for as 'I'm | a sól | diér."

> So " And wél | come, Sómerset ; | I hóld | itców | ardíce."
> 2 *Hen. VI.* iv. 2. 7.

Or, less probably, "Sómersét" may have two accents and "cówardice" (470) one.

> "As chíl | dren fróm | a béar, | the Vóls | ces shúnning him."
>
> *Coriol.* i. 3. 34.

> "So tédi*ously* | awáy. | The póor | condém | ned E'nglish."
>
> *Hen. V.* iv. Prol. 221 ; but *ib.* 28 is a trimeter couplet.

> "And húgg'd *me* | *in his* árm | and kínd | ly kíss'd | my chéek."—*Rich. III.* ii. 2. 24.

> "Than thát | míx'd in | his chéek. | 'Twas júst | the díf-f(e)rence."—*A. Y. L.* iii. 5. 122.

> "He is ('s) my bróth | er tóo. | But fítt | er tíme | for thát."
>
> *M. for M.* v. 1. 498.

> "And nót | the pún(i)sh | ment; thérefore, | indéed | my fáther."—*M. for M.* i. 3. 39.

The following are doubtful, but probably ordinary lines :

> "I knów *him* | as *my*sélf, | fór from | our *in* | *fancý*."
>
> *T. G. of V.* ii. 3. 62.

Or "ínfancy" may have only one accent (467).

> "Máy a | free fáce, | put ón, | deríve | a *líberty*."
>
> *W. T.* i. 2. 112.

"Either" may be a monosyllable (see 466) in

> "Your sénse | pursúes | not míne : | *either* yóu | are *ignorant*."
>
> *M. for M.* ii. 4. 74.

> "For ín | equál(i)ty : | but lét | your réa | son sérve."
>
> *Ib.* v. 1. 65.

In "Alexas did revolt ; and went to Jewry on Affairs of Antony,"—*A. and C.* iv. 6. 12.

"on" may be transposed to the second line ; or, considering the licence attending the use of names and the constant dropping of prefixes, we might perhaps read "Aléxas | did (re)vólt | ."

In "Cálls her | a nón | paréil ; | I né | ver sáw | a wóman,"
> *Temp.* iii. 2. 108.

though it is against Shakespearian usage to pronounce "non-pareil" a dissyllable, as in Dorsetshire, "a núnprel apple," yet Caliban here may be allowed to use this form. I believe "nonp'rel type" is still a common expression.

Sometimes an exclamation, as "O," gives the appearance of a trimeter couplet :

> "Fór the | best hópe | I háve. | (O,) do not wísh | one móre."—*Hen. V.* iv. 3. 33.

See also 498 *ad fin.*

504. The verse with four accents is rarely used by Shake-speare, except when witches or other extraordinary beings are intro-duced as speaking.   Then he often uses a verse of four accents with rhyme.

> " Dóuble, | dóuble, | tóil and | trouble,
> Fíre | búrn and | cáuldron | búbble."—*Macbeth*, iv. **1**. 20.

The iambic metre in such lines is often interchanged with the trochaic :

Iambic * { " He whó | the swórd | of héav'n | will béar
          { Should bé | as hó | ly ás | sevére :

Trochaic { Páttern | ín him | sélf to | knów,
         { Gráce to | stánd and | vírtue | gó."

$$\hspace{4cm} M.\ for\ M.\ \text{iii. 2. 274–8.}$$

(The last line means "he ought to have grace for the purpose of standing upright, and virtue [for the purpose of] walking in the straight path."   "Go" is often used for "walk."   "To" is omitted before "go.")

Sometimes in the same couplet we find one line iambic and the other trochaic :

> " And hére | the mái | den sléep | ing sóund
> O'n the | dánk and | dírty | gróund."—*M. N. D.* ii. 2. 74–5.

It would be, perhaps, more correct to say that both lines are trochaic, but in one there is an extra syllable at the beginning, as well as at the end.   So apparently

> " Thís is | hé my | máster | sáid,
> (De)spísed | thé A | thénian | máid."—*M. N. D.* 72–3 :

but the prefix "de-" might (460) be dropped.

So   " (De)spísed | ín na | tív | i | tý
         Shall úp | ón their | chíldren | bé."—*Ib.* v. i. 420.

There is difficulty in scanning

> " Prétty | sóul, she | dúrst not | líe
> Near this lack-love, this kill-courtesy."—*Ib.* 76–7.

It is of course possible that "kill-curt'sy" may have the accent on the first : but thus we shall have to áccent the first "this" and "love" with undue emphasis.   It is also more in Shakespeare's manner to give "courtesy" its three syllables at the end of a line.   I therefore scan

> " (Near this) láck-love, | thís kill | córte | sý."

---

* The words "iambic" and "trochaic" here and elsewhere refer to accent, not quantity.

Perhaps, however, as in *Macbeth*, iii. 5. 34, 35, and ? 21, a verse of five accents is purposely introduced.

505. Lines with four accents are, unless there is a pause in the middle of the line, *very* rare. The following, however, seem to have no more than four accents :

"Let's éach | one sénd | únto | his wífe."—*T. of Sh.* v. 2. 66.
"No wórse | than I' | upon sóme | agreément."—*Ib.* iv. 4. 33.
"He sháll | you fínd | réady | and wílling."—*Ib.* 34.
"The mátch | is máde, | and áll | is dóne."—*Ib.* 46.
"Go fóol, | and whóm | thou kéep'st | commánd."
                                    Ib. ii. 1. 259.

The frequent recurrence of these lines in the *Taming of the Shrew* will not escape notice.

"And pút | yoursélf | únder | his shrówd."   (? corrupt.)
                                    A. and C. iii. 13. 71.
" A lád | of lífe, | an ímp | of fáme."
                                    Hen. V. iv. 1. 45 (Pistol).
            "We knew not
The dóc | trine óf | ill-dóing, | nor dréam'd
That any did."—*W. T.* i. 2. 70.
"Go téll | your cóusin | and bríng | me wórd."
                                    1 *Hen. IV.* v. 1. 109.
"For áught | I knów, | my lórd, | they dó."
                                    Rich. II. v. 1. 53.

But perhaps the lines may be arranged :

"   *Aum.*   For áught | I knów,
My lórd, | they dó. |
   York.   You wíll | be thére, | I knów.
   Aum. If Gód | prevént | (it) nót, | I púrpose | só."

"With" may be, perhaps (457), transposed to the former of the following verses, thus :

" With ád | orá | tions, fér | tile té | ars, (480) *with*
Gróans (484) | that thún | der lóve, | with síghs | of fíre."
                                    T. N. i. 5. 274.

But the *enumerative* character of the verse (509) may justify it as it stands.

It is difficult to scan

"Lock'd in her monument.   She had a prophesying fear,"
                                    A. and C. iv. 14. 120.

without making the latter portion a verse of four accents.

(Perhaps

"Lóck'd in | her món(u) | ment. Shé'd | a próphe | sying féar,"
making "sying" a monosyllable like "being," "doing." See 470.)

"Should fróm | yond cloúd | spéak di | vine thíngs."
Coriol. iv. 5. 110.

But I should prefer

"If Jupiter
Shóuld, from | yond clóud, | spéak di | vine thíngs | *and sáy*
''Tis trúe,'— | (507) I'd nót | belíeve | them móre
Than thée, | all-nó | ble Március."

Shakespeare would have written "things divine," not "divine things" at the end of a verse. (See 419, at end.)

"Is nót | much míss'd | bút with | his fríends."—*Coriol.* iv. 6. 13.
"Befóre | the kíngs | and quéens | of Fránce."
1 *Hen. VI.* i. 6. 27.
"And éven | these thrée | days háve | I wátch'd."
Ib. i. 4. 16.
"Here throúgh | this gáte | I cóunt | each óne."—*Ib.* 60.
"Think nót | the kíng | did bán | ish thée,"
Rich. II. i. 3. 279.

is not found in the Folio, which also varies, *ib.* i. 3. 323; iii. 7. 70.
Perhaps

"They thús | diréct | ed, wé | will fóllow
I'n the | main báttle | whose púissance | on éi | ther
síde."—*Rich. III.* v. 3. 298.

(But the second line is harsh, and perhaps part of it ought to be combined with the first in some way. "Puissance" is a dissyllable generally in Shakespeare, except at *the end of* the line. I know no instance in Shakespeare where, as in Chaucer, "battle" is accented on the last. Remembering that *ed* is often not pronounced after *t* and *d*, we might scan the first line thus, with three accents :

"They thús | diréct(ed), | we'll fóllow.")

If "ed" is not pronounced (472) in "divided," that may explain

"The archdéa | con háth | *divíded* it."—1 *Hen. IV.* iii. 1. 72.

The following may seem a verse of four accents :

"Whereas the contrary bringeth bliss."—1 *Hen. VI.* v. 5. 64.

But "contráry" is found in *Hamlet*, iii. 2. 221. And as "country" (see 477) is three syllables, so, perhaps, "contrary" is four :

"Whereás | the cónt | (e)rár | y bríng | eth blíss."

A verse of four accents is exceedingly discordant in the formal and artificial speech of Suffolk, in which this line occurs.

Somewhat similarly, Shakespeare has "cursoráry" for "cursory :"

"I have but with a *cursorary* eye."—*Hen. V.* v. 2. 77.

In "Anthony Woodville, her brother there,"—*Rich. III.* i. 1. 67. "Woodville" is probably to be pronounced a trisyllable, a semi-vowel inserting itself between the *d* and *v*—"Wood-e-ville." The *e* final (see 488) would not be sounded before "her."

"Valiant" is a trisyllable in

"Young, vál | iánt, | wíse, and | no dóubt | right róyal."
Rich. III. i. 2. 245.

506. Lines with four accents, where there is an interruption in the line, are not uncommon. It is obvious that a syllable or foot may be supplied by a gesture, as beckoning, a movement of the head to listen, or of the hand to demand attention, as in

"He's tá'en. | [*Shóut.*] | And hárk, | they shóut | for jóy."
J. C. v. 3. 32.

"Knéel thou | down, Phílip. | (*Dubs hím knight.*) | But ríse | more gréat."—*K. J.* i. 1. 161.

"Márry | to——(*Enter O'thello.*) | Come, cáp | tain, wíll | you gó?"—*Othello,* i. 2. 53.

Here, however, as in

"A wíse | stout cáp | (i)táin, | and sóon | persuáded."
3 Hen. VI. iv. 7. 32.

"Our cáp | (i)táins, | Macbéth | and Bán | quo? Yés."
Macbeth, i. 2. 34.

we may scan

"Márry | to——Cóme, | cáp(i) | tain, wíll | you gó,"

but very harshly and improbably.

"*Cass.* Flátter | ers!" (*Turns tó Brutus.*) | Now,Brú | tus, thánk | yoursélf."—*J. C.* v. 1. 45.

An interruption may supply the place of the accent :

"And fálls | on th' óth | er——(*Enter Lády Macbeth.*) | How nów, | what néws?"—*Macbeth,* i. 7. 28.

The interval between two speakers sometimes justifies the omission of an accent, even in a rhyming passage of regular lines :

"*Fairy.* Aré not | you hé? | ' *Puck.* | Thou spéak'st | aríght,
I ám | that mér | ry wán | derer óf | the níght."

M. N. D. ii. 1. 42.

"*Mal.* As thóu | didst léave | it. ' *Serg.* | Dóubtful | it stóod."

Macbeth, i. 2. 7.

"*Cass.* Messá | la ! ' *Mess.* | What sáys | my gén | erál?"

J. C. v. 1. 70.

"*Dun.* Who cómes | here? ' *Mal.* | The wórth | y tháne | of
Róss."—*Macbeth* i. 2. 45.

"*Sic.* Withóut | assístance. | | *Men.* I thínk | not só."

Coriol. iv. 6. 33.

The break caused by the arrival of a new-comer often gives rise
to a verse with four accents.

"Than yóur | good wórds. | ' | But whó | comes hére?"

Rich. II. ii. 3. 20.

"Stánds for | my bóunty. | ' | But whó | comes hére?"

Ib. 67.

"Agáinst | their wíll. | ' | But whó | comes | hére?"

Ib. iii. 3. 19.

So, perhaps, arrange

"High be our thoughts !
I know my uncle York hath power enough
To sérve | our túrn. | ' | But whó | comes hére?"

Ib. iii. 2. 90.

It is possible that in some of these lines "comes" should be
pronounced "cometh." "Words," "turn," and "will" might be
prolonged by 485, 486.

**507. Lines with four accents where there is a change
of thought** are not uncommon. In some cases the line is divided
into two of two accents each, or into one line of three accents, and
another of one.

(1) Change of thought from the present to the future :

"Háply | you sháll | not sée | me móre; | or íf,
A máng | led shádow. | ' | Perchánce | *to-mórrow*
You'll sérve | anóther | máster."—*A. and C.* iv. 1. 28.

"I'll sénd | her stráight | awáy. | ' | *To-mórrow*
I'll' to | the wárs : | shé to | her síng | le sórrow."

A. W. ii. 3. 313.

"Fresh kíngs | are cóme | to Tróy. | ' | *To-mórrow*
We múst | with áll | our máin | of pówer | stand fást."

Tr. and Cr. ii. 2. 272.

(2) From a statement to an appeal, or *vice versâ :*

"You háve | not sóught it. | ' | *How* cómes | it thén?"
    1 *Hen. IV.* v. 1. 27.

Unless "comes" is "cometh." See 506 at end.

"Lórd of | his réason. | ' | *Whát* though | you fléd?"
    A. and C. iii. 13. 4.

(I do not remember an instance of "ré | asón." See, however, 479.)

Perhaps "Come híth | er, cóunt. | ' | *Do you* (*d' you*) *knów* |
    these wómen?"—*A. W.* v. 3. 165.

But possibly :

"Come híth | er, cóu | nt (486). Dó | you knów | these
    women?"

"*But stáy.* | Here cómes (Fol.) | the gár | denérs."
    Rich. II. iii. 4. 24.

("gárdeners" may have but one accent.)

"*Néver* | *believe* | *me.* ' | Bóth are | my kínsmen."
    Ib. ii. 2. 111.

The pause may account for

"As hé | would dráw it. | ' | Long stáy'd | he só."
    Hamlet, ii. 1. 91.

(As *ed* is pronounced after *i* and *u,* so it might be after *y* in
"stáyed," but the effect would be painful.)

"Which hás | no néed | of yóu.
Begóne,"

is the best way of arranging *A. and C.* iii. 11. 10.

"And léave | eightéen. | ' | *Alás,* poor | príncess."
    A. and C. ii. 1. 61.

"A prínc | e's cóurage. | ' | *Awáy,* | I príthee."
    Cymb. iii. 4. 187.

"*Lét us* | *withdráw.* | ' | 'Twill bé | a stórm."
    Lear, ii. 4. 290.

(3) Hence after vocatives :

"*Títus,* | ' | I (am)'m cóme | to tálk | with thée."
    T. A. v. 2. 16.

"*Géntle* | *men,* ' | impórt | une mé | no fúrther."
    T. of Sh. i. 1. 48.

"*Géntle* | *men,* ' | that I' | may sóon | make góod."—*Ib.* 74.

"*Géntle* | *men,* ' | contént | ye, 'I'm | resólved."—*Ib.* 90.

"*Géntle* | *men,* ' | wíll you | go mús | ter mén?"
    Rich. II. ii. 2. 108.

" Géntle | men, ' | go mús | ter úp | your mén."

Rich. II. ii. 2. 118

"Good Már | garét. | Rún | thee tó | the párlour."

M. Ado, iii. 1. 1.

Either a pause may explain

"But téll | me, ' | is yóung | George Stán | ley líving?"

Rich. III. v. 5. 9.

or "George" (485) may be a quasi-dissyllable.

508. A foot or syllable can be omitted where there is any marked pause, whether arising from (1) emotion, (2) antithesis, or (3) parenthesis, or (4) merely from the introduction of a relative clause, or even a new statement.

(1)   "Wére't | my fítness
To lét | these hánds | obéy | my blóod, | —' |
They're ápt | enóugh | to dís | locáte | and téar
Thy flésh | and bónes."—Lear, iv. 2. 64.

       "O' | dislóy | al thíng
That shóuld'st | repáir | my yóuth, | —' | thou héap'st
A yéar's | age ón | me."—Cymb. i. 1. 132.

There is an intended solemnity in the utterances of the ghosts in

"Let fáll | thy lánce. | ' | Despáir | and díe."

Rich. III. v. 3. 143.

and "Thínk on | lord Hástings. | ' | Despáir | and díe."—Ib. 148.

(2)   "Scarce án | y jóy
Did év | er só | long líve. | | No sórrow
But kíll'd | itsélf | much sóon | er."—W. T. v. 3. 53.

(3)   "He quít | his fórt | unes hére
(Which yóu | knew gréat) | ' | ánd to | the házard."

Ib. iii. 2. 169.

(4) "Mark whát | I sáy, | ' | which yóu | shall fínd."

M. for M. iv. 3. 130.

Perhaps "Is my kíns | man, ' | whóm | the kíng | hath wróng'd,"

Rich. II. ii. 2. 114.

in a very irregular passage, part of which is nearly prose.

"Í'nto | his títle | which | the | we fínd."

1 Hen. IV. iv. 3. 104.

"That shé | did gíve me, | ' | whose pó | sy wás."

M. of V. v. 1. 148.

"Cáll our | cares féars, | ' | which wíll | in tíme."

Coriol. iii. 1. 137.

" 'Tis súre | enóugh | —án you | knew hów."
T. A. iv. 1. 95.

A pause may, perhaps, be expected before an oath, as in

" As yoú | shall gíve | th' advíce. | Bý | the fíre
That quíck | ens E' | gypt's slíme."—*A. and C.* i. 3. 68.

(But "vice" or "by" may be prolonged.)

" That mý | most jéal | ous ánd | too dóubt | ful héart
May líve | at péace. | ' | He shall | concéal it."
T. N. iv. 3. 28 ; *Macbeth,* i. 5. 6.

"To wátch, | poor pérdu !
With thís | thin hélm. | ' | Mine éne | my's dóg,
Thóugh he | had bít | me, shóuld | have stood | that níght
Agáinst | my fíre."—*Lear,* iv. 7. 36.

" Last níght | 'twas ón | mine árm. | ' | I kíss'd it."
Cymb. ii. 3. 151.

(Certainly not " I kíss | ed ít.")

" Would thén | be nóthing. | ' | Trúths would | be táles."
A. and C. ii. 2. 137.

" Póint to | rich énds. | ' | Thís my | mean tásk."
Temp. iii. 1. 4.

" Must gíve | us páuse (484). | ' | Thére's the | respéct."
Hamlet, iii. 1. 68.

509. Lines with four accents are found where a number
of short clauses or epithets are connected together in one line, and
must be pronounced slowly :

" Earth gapes, hell burns, fiends roar, saints pray."
Rich. III. iv. 4. 75.

" Witty, courteous, liberal, full of spirit."
3 *Hen. VI.* i. 2. 43.

The last line is very difficult. "And," or a pause equal to
" and," after " witty," would remove the difficulty.

It is remarkable that Shakespeare ventures to introduce such
a line even in a rhyming passage :

" *Youth, beauty, wisdom, courage, all*
That happiness and prime can happy call."
M. for M. ii. 1. 184.

" Ho ! héarts, | tongues, fígures, | scribes, bárds, | poéts |
cannót
Think, spéak, | cast, wríte, | sing núm | ber, ho !
His love to Antony."—*A. and C.* iii. 2. 17.

" Is goads, thorns, nettles, tails of wasps."—*W. T.* i. 2. 329.

(Here, however, "goads" and "thorns" may be prolonged. See 484, 485.)

"With thát | harsh, nó | ble, sím | ple— | nóthing."

Cymb. iii. 4. 135.

The following occurs amid regular verse :

"These drums ! these trumpets ! flutes ! what."

A. and C. ii. 7. 138.

" When you do dance, I wish you
A wave of the sea, that you might ever do
Nóthing | but thát; | move stíll, | still só."

W. T. iv. 4. 142.

Here *still,* which means "always," is remarkably emphatic, and may, perhaps, be pronounced as a quasi-dissyllable. So "til" is a monosyllabic foot in CHAUCER, *C. T.* 1137.

510. Apparent lines of four accents can sometimes be explained by giving the full pronunciation to contractions, such as *s* for *eth,* *'d* for *ed,* *'ll* for *will,* *'ve* for *have,* *'t* for *it,* &c. ; or they are lines of three accents with a detached foot.

"*Silv.* Whát's (is) | your wíll? |
Prot.   That I' | may cóm | pass yóurs."

T. G. of V. iv. 2. 92.

"And wére | the kíng | *on't* (of ít), | what wóuld | I dó?"

Temp. ii. 1. 145.

"In whát | you pléase. | T'*ll* (will) | do whát | I cán."

Ib. iv. 4. 47.

" You've ádd | ed *wó* | *rth* (485) ún | to ít | and lústre."

T. of A. i. 2. 154.

" Dríve him | to *Rö* | *me; 't* (it) | is tíme | we twáin."

A. and C. i. 4. 73.

" Whence cóm | *est* thóu? | What wóuld | *est* thóu? | Thy náme?"—*Coriol.* iv. 5. 58.

But the pauses between the abrupt questions may be a sufficient explanation.

"And *ne'er* (név | er) á | true óne. | In súch | a níght."

M. of V. v. 1. 148.

The first "a" may be emphatic, meaning "one." Else 508.

"Our thíghs | páck'*d* (ed) | with wáx, | our móuths | with hóney."—2 *Hen. IV.* iv. 5. 77.

"So múch | as lán | k'*d* (ed) nót. | 'Tis pít | y óf him."

A. and C. i. 4. 71.

" ' s " = "his" in

"Vincént | ió | 's (his) són | brought úp | in Flórence."
T. of Sh. i. 1. 14.

In "*Sal.* My lord, I long to hear it at full,"
2 *Hen. VI.* ii. 2. 6.

"hear" is a dissyllable (485), or "the" omitted after "at." Compare "atte" in E. E. for "at the."

I feel confident that "but would" must be supplied in

" And what poor duty cannot do, noble respect
Takes it in might, not merit,"—*M. N. D.* v. 1. 91.

and we must read :

" And what poor duty cannot do, *but would,*
Noble respect takes *not* in might *but* merit."*

" And, ere our coming, see thou shake the bags
Of hoarding abbots ; imprisoned angels
Set at liberty.   The fat ribs of peace
Must by the hungry now be fed upon,"—*K. J.* iii. 3. 8.

ought probably to be arranged :

"Of hoarding abbots ;
Imprisoned angels set at liberty.
The fat ribs of peace
Must," &c.

Or (Walker) invert "imprisoned angels" and "set at liberty."

Arrange thus :

" Your Coriolanus
Is nót | *much míss'd,*
Bút with | *his friends.* | The cóm | monwéalth | doth stánd,
And só | would dó, | were hé | more áng | ry át it."
Coriol. iv. 6. 13.

Similarly

" *Most cért* | *ain. Síst* | *er, wélcome.*
Práy you | (see 512)
Be év | er knówn | to pát | ience, mý | dear.st síster."
A. and C. iii. 6. 97.

So arrange

"That won you without blows.
Despising (499),
For you, the city, thus I turn my back."
Coriol. iii. 3. 133.

* I think I have met with this conjecture in some commentator.

"   *Cel.* Look, whó | comes hére ? |
     Silv.   *My érr | and ís | to yóu :*
     Fair yóuth (512), |
     My gént | le Phœ' | be bíd | me gíve | you thís."
                                   A. Y. L. iv. 3. 6.

" *Got 'twéen | aslèep | and wáke.*
   Wéll, then (512),
   Legít(i) | mate E'd | gar, I' | must háve | your lánd."
                                   Lear, i. 2. 15.

" *As péarls | from día | monds drópp'd.*
   In brief (511)."—*Lear,* iv. 3. 24.

Hen. V. ii. Prologue, 32, is corrupt.

     " *I live with bread like you :*
     Feel want, taste grief, need friends : subjected thus,
     How can you say to me I am a king?"—*Rich. II.* iii. 2. 175.

511. Single lines with two or three accents are frequently interspersed amid the ordinary verses of five accents.
They are, naturally, most frequent at the beginning and end of
a speech.

These lines are often found in passages of soliloquy where passion
is at its height. Thus in the madness of *Lear,* iv. 6. 112–29, there
are eight lines of three accents, and one of two ; and the passage
terminates in prose. And so perhaps we should arrange

     " Would use his heav'n for thunder ; nothing but thunder !
     Merciful heaven (512),
     Thou rather with thy sharp and sulphurous bolt
     Split'st the unwedgeable and gnarled oak
     Than the soft myrtle.
     But man, proud man,
     Drest in a little brief authority," &c.
                              M. for M. ii. 2. 110–19.

So in the impassioned speech of Silvius :

     " If thou remember'st not the slightest folly
     That ever love did make thee run into,
     Thou hast not loved,"—*A. Y. L.* ii. 4. 36.

which is repeated in l. 39 and 42.

The highest passion of all expresses itself in prose, as in the
earful frenzy of *Othello,* iv. 1. 34–44, and *Lear,* iv. 6. 130.

Rarely we have a short line to introduce the subject.

     "   *York. Then thus :*
     Edward the third, my lords, had seven sons."
                               2 Hen. VI. ii. 2. 9, 10.

" Into his ruin'd ears, and thus deliver :
   '*Henry Bolingbroke,*
   On both his knees,' " &c.—*Rich. II.* iii. 3. 32.
" Ross. (So) *That now*
   Sweno, the Norways' king, craves composition."
                                        Macbeth, i. 2. 59.
" *For Cloten :*
   There wants no diligence in seeking him."—*Cymb.* iv. 3. 19.

Sometimes the verse (which is often written as prose in the Folio) closely resembles prose. It is probable that the letter *J. C.* ii. 3. 1–10 is verse, the last two words, "thy lover, Artemidorus," being irregular. So *A. Y. L.* iii. 2. 268–74.

The irregular lines uttered by Cassius, when he is cautiously revealing the conspiracy to Casca, looking about to see that he is not overheard, and also pausing to watch the effect of his words on Casca, are very natural.

" *Unto some monstrous state.*
   Now could I, Casca, name to thee a man
   Most like this dreadful night,
   That thunders, lightens, opens graves, and roars."
                                        J. C. i. 3. 71–74.

It will also not escape notice that "now could I, Casca," and "that thunders, lightens," are amphibious sections. See 513.

The following pause may be explained by the indignation of Macduff, which Malcolm observes and digresses to appease :

" Why in that rawness left you wife and child
   Without leave-taking ?
   I pray you (512)
   Let not my jealousies be your dishonours."
                                        Macbeth, iv. 3. 28.

A pause is extremely natural before Lear's semi-confession of infirmity of mind :

" *A'nd, to | deal pláinly,*
   I féar | I ám | not ín | my pérf | ect mínd."
                                        Lear, iv. 7. 62.

A stage direction will sometimes explain the introduction of a short line. The action takes up the space of words, and necessitates a broken line, thus :

" *Macb.* This is a sorry sight. [*Looking on his hands.*]
   Lady M. A foolish thought, to say a sorry sight."
                                        Macbeth, ii. 2. 21.

Macbeth may be supposed to draw his dagger after the short line:

"As thís | which nów | I dráw."—*Macbeth*, ii. 1. 41.

So after Lady Macbeth has openly proposed the murder of Duncan in the words—

<blockquote>
"Oh, never
Shall sun that morrow see,"—*Macbeth*, i. 5. 62.
</blockquote>

she pauses to watch the effect of her words till she continues :

"Your face, my thane, is as a book where men," &c.

The irregular lines in the excited narrative of the battle—

<blockquote>
"Like valour's minion, carv'd out his passage
Till he faced the slave,"—*Macbeth*, i. 2. 20 (so *ib*. 51).
</blockquote>

are perhaps explained by the haste and excitement of the speaker. This is illustrated by

<blockquote>
"Except they meant to bathe in reeking wounds,
Or memorize another Golgotha,
I cannot tell.
But I am faint, my wounds cry out for help."
</blockquote>

Macbeth, i. 2. 41.

In "As cannons overcharged with double cracks ; ‖ so they ‖
Doubly redoubled strokes upon the foe,"—*Ib*. i. 2. 37.

there may be an instance of a short line. But more probably we must scan "As cánnons | o'erchárged | ."

Such a short line as

<blockquote>
"Only to herald thee into his sight,
Not pay thee,"—*Macbeth*, i. 3. 103.
</blockquote>

is very doubtful. Read (though somewhat harshly) :

"On'ly | to hér(a)ld (463) | thee ín | to's síght, | not páy thee."

So "Lét's (us) | awáy ; | our téars | are nót | yet bréw'd,"

Macbeth, ii. 3. 129, 130.

and the following lines must be arranged so as to make l. 132 an interjectional line.

There is a pause after "but let" in

<blockquote>
"*But let*—
The fráme | of thíngs | disjóint, | bóth the | worlds súffer."
</blockquote>

Macbeth, iii. 2. 16 ; iv. 3. 97.

and in the solemn narrative preparatory to the entrance of the Ghost :

<blockquote>
"*Last night of all,*
When yond same star that's westward from the pole."
</blockquote>

Hamlet, i. 1. 35.

So "And are upon the Mediterranean flote
　　Bound sadly home for Naples,
　　Supposing that they saw the king's ship wreck'd."
　　　　　　　　　　　　　　　Temp. i. 2. 235.
So *M. N. D.* iii. 2. 49.

　　" *Lastly,*
　　If I do fail in fortune of my choice
　　Immediately to leave you and be gone."—*M. of V.* ii. 9. 14.

　　" *Yet I,*
　　A dull and muddy-mettled rascal, peak."
　　　　　　　　　　　　　　　Hamlet, ii. 2. 593.

　　" I, his sole son, do this same villain send
　　To heaven."—*Ib.* iii. 3. 78.

In　　"Dost thou hear?"—*Temp.* i. 2. 106.

"thou" is unemphatic, and scarcely pronounced.　Or else these
words must be combined with the previous, thus :

　　"Hénce his | ambít | ion grów | —ing—Dóst | thou héar?"

512. Interjectional lines.　Some irregularities may be explained by the custom of placing ejaculations, appellations, &c.
out of the regular verse (as in Greek φεῦ, &c.).

　　" *Yes.* |
　　Has he | affections in him?"—*M. for M.* iii. 1. 107.

　　"*Alack*
　　I love myself.　Wherefore? for any good?"
　　　　　　　　　　　　　　　Rich. III. v. 3. 187.

　　" *What,*
　　Are there no posts despatch'd for (480) Ireland?"
　　　　　　　　　　　　　　　Rich. II. ii. 2. 103.

So arrange
　　"　*North. Why?*
　　I's he | not wíth | the quéen? |
　　　Percy.　　　　　　Nó, my | good lórd."
　　　　　　　　　　　　　　　Ib. ii. 3. 512.

　　" *Fie,*
　　There's no such man ; it is impossible."
　　　　　　　　　　　　　　　Othello, iv. 2. 134.

　　" And such a one do I profess myself,
　　For, sir,
　　It is as sure as you are Roderigo."
　　　　　　　　　　　　　　　Othello, i. 1. 55 ; *Lear,* i. 1. 56.

Perhaps we ought thus to arrange

" *O, sir,*
Your presence is too bold and péremptory."
                                            1 *Hen. IV.* i. 3. 17.

This is Shakespeare's accentuation of "peremptory."

" *Farewell.   [Exit Banquo.]*
Let every man be master of his time."—*Macbeth,* iii. 1. 40.
" *Sir,*
I have upon a high and pleasant hill."—*T. of A.* i. 1. 63.
" *Sirrah,*
Get thee to Plashy, to my sister Gloucester."
                                            Rich. II. ii. 2. 90.

So *Rich. III.* i. 2. 226 ; i. 4. 218.

" *Great king,*
Few love to hear the sin they love to act."—*P. of T.* i. 1. 91.
" My dismal scene I needs must act alone.
Come, vial."—*R. and J.* iv. 3. 20.
" Come, Hastings, help me to my lodging.   O !
Poor Clarence."—*Rich. III.* ii. 1. 133.
" *For Hecuba!*
What's Héc | ubá | to hím, | or he | to Hécuba (469)?"
                                            Hamlet, ii. 2. 584.
" If thou hast any sound or use of voice,
Speak to me."—*Ib.* i. 1. 129.

So *ib.* 132, 135 : and "*O vengeance,*" *ib.* 610 ; "*A scullion!*" *ib.*
616.

So we should read

" I'll wait upon you instantly. (*Exeunt.*) [*To* FLAV.] Come hither.
Pray you,
How goes," &c.—*T. of A.* ii. 1. 36.

Similarly "*Nay, more,*" *C. of E.* i. 1. 16; "*Stay,*" *T. N.* iii. 1.
149; "*Who's there?*" *Hamlet,* i. 1. 1; "*Begone,*" *J. C.* i. 1. 57 ;
"*O, Cæsar,*" *J. C.* iii. 1. 281; "*Let me work,*" *J. C.* ii. 1. 209 ;
"*Here, cousin,*" *Rich. II.* iv. 1. 182; "*What's she?*" *T. N.* i. 2. 35;
"*Draw,*" *Lear,* ii. 1. 32 ; "*Think,*" *Coriol.* iii. 3. 49.

So arrange

" *Viol.* Hold, ‖ there's hálf ⊦ my cóffer. |
Anton.   Wíll you | dený | me nów?"
                                            T. N. iii. 4. 38.
" *So,* ‖ I am sát | isfíed, | gíve me | a bówl | of wíne."
                                            Rich. III. v. 3. 72.

"*Ratcliffe*, ‖ abóut | the míd | of níght | cóme to | my tént."
Rich. III. 77, 209.

The excitement of Richard gives rise to several interjectional lines of this kind in this scene.

A short line sometimes introduces a quotation :

> " If Cæsar hide himself, shall they not whisper,
> *Lo, Cæsar is afraid ?*"—*J. C.* ii. 2. 101.
> " Did scowl on gentle Richard.   No man cried
> ' *God save him.*' "—*Rich. II.* v. 2. 28.

Perhaps we should arrange as follows :

> " He'll spend that kiss
> Which is my heaven to have.
> *Come* [*applying the asp to her bosom*]
> *Thou mortal wretch,*
> With thy sharp teeth this knot intrinsicate
> Of life at once untie."—*A. and C.* v. 2. 306.

This seems better than scanning the words from "which" to " wretch" as one line, either (1) as an ordinary line, with "come, thou mór | tal wretch," or (2) as a trimeter couplet, making "come " a dissyllable.

So it is better to arrange :

> " *Buckingham,*
> *I prithee pardon me*
> That I have giv'n no answer all this while."
> 2 *Hen. VI.* v. 1. 32.

Merely with a special view to mark a solemn pause Shakespeare writes :

> " So, as a painted tyrant Pyrrhus stood,
> And, like a neutral to his will and matter,
> *Did nothing.*
> But, as we often see," &c.—*Hamlet,* ii. 2. 504.

Such irregularities are very rare.

> " *Sirrah,*
> A word with you.   Attend those men our pleasure ?"

is the right way to arrange *Macb.* iii. 1. 45, 46.   Shakespeare could not possibly (as Globe) make " our pleasure " a detached foot.

The ejaculation seems not a part of the verse in

> " Hath séiz'd | the wáste | ful kíng. | [O,] what pít | y ís it."
> *Rich. II.* iii. 4. 55.

" And hé | himsélf | not présent. | [O,] foreférnd | it, Gód !"
                                        Rich. II. iv. 1. 129.

See also 498, at end ; 503.

513. The Amphibious Section. When a verse consists of two parts uttered by two speakers, the latter part is frequently the former part of the following verse, being, as it were, *amphibious*—thus :

" *S.* The E′ng | lish fórce, | so pléase you. ‖
   M. Táke thy | face hénce. ‖ Séyton, | I'm síck | at héart."
                                        Macbeth, v. 3. 19.

" *M.* Néws, my | good lórd, | from Róme. ‖
   Ant.   *Grátes me: | the súm.* ‖
   Cleo. Nay, héar | them, A′n | tonÿ."—*A. and C.* i. 1. 19.

" *B.* Who's thére? |
   M. A fríend. ‖
   B. Whát, sir, | not yét | at rést ? ‖ The kíng's | abéd."
                                        Macbeth, ii. 1. 10.

" *Kent.* This óff | ice tó you. ‖
   Gent.   *I′ will | talk fúr | ther wíth* ‖ *you.* ‖
   Kent.   Nó, | do not."—*Lear*, iii. 1. 42.

" *Gent.* Which twáin | have bróught | her tó. ‖
   Edg.   *Hail, gént | le sír.* |
   Gent. Sir, spéed | you, whát's | your wíll? "
                                        Lear, iv. 6. 212.

" *Prosp.* Agáinst | what shóuld | ensue. ‖
   Mir.   *How cáme | we ashóre?* ‖   •
   Prosp.   By Pró | vidénce | divíne."
                                        Temp. i. 2. 158.

" *Claud.* And húg | it ín | my árms. ‖
   Is. Thére spake | my bró | ther, ‖ thére | my fá | ther's gráve."
                                        M. for M. iii. 1. 86.

" *E.*   How fáres | the prínce? ‖
   Mess. Well, mád | am, ánd | in héalth. ‖ *Duch.* Whát is |
   thy néws, then?"—*Rich. III.* ii. 4. 40.

" *Brut.* That óth | er mén | begín. ‖
   Cas. Then léave | him óut. ‖ *Casca.* Indéed | he ís | not fít."
                                        J. C. ii. 1. 153.

Probably—

" *Macb.* And bréak it | to our hópe. ‖ *I wíll | not fíght | with thée.* ‖
   Macd. Then yíeld | thee, cóward."—*Macbeth*, v. 8. 22.

Compare also *Macbeth*, i. 4. 43, 44 ; ii. 3. 75, 101–2 ; iii. 1. 18 19, 2.
12–13, 4. 12, 15, 20, 151 ; *J. C.* ii. 4. 16, 17 ; *Coriol.* iii. 2. 6 ;
Othello, iii. 3. 282, &c.

In the following instance the first "still" is emphatic :

> "*Oliv.* As hówl | ing áft | er músic.‖
> *Duke.*   Stíll | so crú ‖ el !
> *Oliv.*   Stíll | so cón | stant, lórd."
> *T. N.* v. 1. 113.

Sometimes a section will, on the one side, form part of a regular
line, and, on the other, part of a trimeter couplet.

> "*Hor.* Of míne | own éyes. ‖ *Mar.* I's it | not líke | the kíng? ‖
> *Hor.* As thóu | art tó | thysélf."—*Hamlet*, i. 1. 58, 59.
> "*Ophel.* In hón | ourá | ble fáshion. | *Pol.* Ay, fásh | ion yóu |
> may cáll it. ‖ Go to, go to."—*Ib.* i. 3. 112.
> *Ham.* Nó, it | is strúck. ‖ *Hor.* Indéed, | I héard | it nót ; ‖
> then ít | draws néar | the séason.—*Ib.* i. 4. 4.

In the last example, "indeed," when combined with what *follows*,
is a detached interjection (512).

514. Interruptions are sometimes not allowed to interfere with the completeness of the speaker's verse.

This is natural in dialogue, when the interruption comes from a
third person :

> "*Polon.* Práy you | be róund | with hím. |
> (*Ham.* [*Within*] Mother, mother, mother !)
> *Queen.*   I'll wár | rant yoú."
> *Hamlet*, iii. 4. 5, 6.

Or, when a man is bent on continuing what he has to say :

> "   *Ham.* Rashly—and that should teach us
> There's a divinity that shapes our ends,
> Rough-hew them how we will—
> (*Hor.* That's certain.)
> *Ham.*   Up from my cabin," &c.
> *Hamlet*, v. 2. 11, 12.
> "*Shy.* This is (461) kínd | I óffer—
> (*Bass.* This were kindness.)
> *Shy.*   This kínd | ness wíll | I shów."
> *M. of V.* i. 3. 143.
> "*King R.* Rátcliffe— |
> (*Rat.* My lord.)
> *King R.*   The sún | will nót | be séen | to-day."
> *Rich. III.* v. 3. 281.

"*Brutus.* Awáy, | slight mán. |
    (*Cassius.* Is't possible ?)
Brutus.   Héar me, | for I' | will speak."
                J. C. iv. 3. 37, 38.

Or, when a speaker is pouring forth his words, endeavouring to break through the obstacle of unintelligence, as Kent trying to make himself intelligible to the mad Lear :

   "*Kent.* Nó, my | good lórd ; | I ám | the vér | y mán—
      (*Lear.* I'll see that straight.)
   Kent. Thát from | your fírst | of díf | ference ánd | decáy
    Have fóll | ow'd your | sad stéps, | —
      (*Lear.* You're welcome hither.)
   Kent.   Nor nó | man élse."

i.e. "I and no one else." Then, in despair of making himself understood, Kent continues :

   "All's cheerless, dark, and deadly."

Sometimes the interlocutor's words, *or* the speaker's continuation, will complete the line :

   "*Cæsar.* So múch | as lánk | ed nót. | (Folio has *lank'd.*)
   Lep.   'Tis pít | y óf him.
   Cæsar. Lét his | shames quíckly."—*A. and C.* i. 4. 71.

If there are *two* interlocutors, sometimes *either* interlocution will complete the line :

   "*Gent.* Than ís | his úse. |
   Widow.   Lord, hów | we lóse | our páins !
   Helena.   All's wéll | that énds | well yét."
              A. W. v. 1. 24, 25.

   "*Bru.* Good Márc | ius | hóme | again. |
   Sic.   The vé | ry tríck on't.
   Men.   Thís is | unlíkely."
            Coriol. iv. 6. 71.

515. Rhyme. Rhyme was often used as an effective termination at the end of the scene. When the scenery was not changed, or the arrangements were so defective that the change was not easily perceptible, it was, perhaps, additionally desirable to mark that a scene was finished. The rhyme in *T. N.* ii. 2. 32 is perhaps a token that the scene once concluded with these lines, and that the nine lines that follow are a later addition.

   Rhyme was also sometimes used in the same conventional way, to mark an *aside*, which otherwise the audience might have great difficulty in knowing to be an *aside*. Thus, in a scene where there are no other rhyming lines, Queen Margaret is evidently intended to utter *Rich. III.* iv. 4. 16, 17 ; 20, 21, as *asides*, though there is no notice of it. One of the lines even rhymes with the line of another speaker :

> " *Q. Eliz.* When didst thou sleep, when such a deed was
> done ?
> *Q. Marg.* When holy Harry died, and my sweet son."
>
> *Rich. III.* iv. 4. 24, 25.

Queen Margaret does not show herself till line 35, as also in *Rich. III.* i. 3. till line 157, though in the latter scene the asides do not rhyme.

515 a. Prose. Prose is not only used in comic scenes ; it is adopted for letters (*M. of V.* iv. 1. 149–66), and on other occasions where it is desirable to lower the dramatic pitch : for instance, in the more colloquial parts of the household scene between Volumnia and Virgilia, *Coriol.* i. 3, where the scene begins with prose, then passes into verse, and returns finally to prose. It is also used to express frenzy, *Othello*, iv. 1. 34–44 ; and madness, *Lear*, iv. 6. 130 ; and the higher flights of the imagination, *Hamlet*, ii. 2. 310–20

SIMILE AND METAPHOR.

516. Similarity.—In order to describe an *object* that has not been seen we use the description of some object or objects that have been seen. Thus, to describe a lion to a person who had never seen one, we should say that it had something like a horse's mane, the claws of a cat, &c. We might say, "A lion is like a monstrous cat with a horse's mane." This sentence expresses a likeness of things, or a *similarity.*

517. Simile.—In order to describe some *relation* that cannot be seen, *e.g.* the relation between a ship and the water, as regards the action of the former upon the latter, to a landsman who had never seen the sea or a ship, we might say, "The ship acts upon the water as a plough turns up the land." In other words, "The *relation* between the ship and the sea is *similar* to the *relation* between the plough and the land." This sentence expresses *a similarity of relations*, and is called *a simile.* It is frequently expressed thus :

"As the plough turns up the land, so the ship acts on the sea."

Def. **A Simile is a sentence expressing a similarity of relations.**

Consequently a simile is a kind of rhetorical proportion, and must, when fully expressed, contain four terms :

$$A : B :: C : D.$$

518. Compression of Simile into Metaphor.—A simile is cumbrous, and better suited for poetry than for prose. Moreover, when a simile has been long in use, there is a tendency to consider the assimilated relations not merely as *similar* but as *identical.* The *simile* modestly asserts that the relation between the ship and the sea is *like* ploughing. The *compressed simile* goes further, and asserts that the relation between the ship and the sea *is* ploughing. It is expressed thus : "The ship ploughs the sea."

Thus the relation between the plough and the land is *transferred* to the ship and the sea. A simile thus compressed is called a *Metaphor*, i.e. *transference.*

Def. **A Metaphor is a transference of the relation between one set of objects to another, for the purpose of brief explanation.**

519. Metaphor fully stated or implied.—A metaphor may be either fully stated, as " The ship *ploughs* (or *is the plough of*) *the sea,*" or implied, as " The winds are the horses that draw *the plough of the sea.*" In the former case it is distinctly stated, in the latter implied, that the "plough of the sea" represents a ship.

520. Implied Metaphor the basis of language.—A great part of our ordinary language, all that relates to the relations of invisible things, necessarily consists of *implied metaphors ;* for we can only describe invisible relations by means of visible ones. We are in the habit of assuming the existence of a certain proportion or *analogy* between the relations of the mind and those of the body. This *analogy* is the foundation of all words that express mental and moral qualities. For example, we do not know how a thought suggests itself suddenly to the mind, but we *do* know how an external object makes itself felt by the body. Experience teaches us that anything which *strikes* the body makes itself suddenly felt. Analogy suggests that whatever *is suddenly perceived comes in the same way* into contact with the mind. Hence the simile—"As a stone strikes the body, so a thought makes itself perceptible to the mind." This simile may be compressed into the *full* metaphor thus, "The thought struck my mind," or into the *implied* metaphor thus, " This is a striking thought." In many words that express immaterial objects the implied metaphor can easily be traced through the derivation, as in "excellence," "tribulation," "integrity," "spotlessness," &c.

N.B. The use of metaphor is well illustrated in words that describe the effects of sound. Since the sense of hearing (probably in all nations and certainly among the English) is less powerful and less suggestive of words than the senses of sight, taste, and touch, the poorer sense is compelled to borrow a part of its vocabulary from the richer senses. Thus we talk of "a *sweet* voice," "a *soft* whisper," "a *sharp* scream," "a *piercing* shriek," and the Romans used the expression "a *dark-coloured* voice,"* where we should say "a *rough* voice."

521. Metaphor expanded.—As every *simile* can be *compressed* into a *metaphor*, so, conversely, every *metaphor* can be *expanded* into its *simile*. The following is the rule for expansion. It has been seen above that the simile consists of four terms. In the third term of the simile stands the subject ("ship," for instance) whose unknown predicated relation ("action of ship on water") is to be explained. In the first term stands the corresponding subject ("plough") whose predicated relation ("action on land") is known. In the second term is the known relation. The fourth term is the unknown predicated relation which requires explanation. Thus—

the plough	turns up the land,	so	the ship	acts on the sea.
Known subject.	Known predicate.		Subject whose predicate is unknown.	Unknown predicate.

Sometimes the fourth term or unknown predicate may represent something that has received no name in the language. Thus, if we take the words of Hamlet, "In my mind's eye," the metaphor when expanded would become—

* "Vox *fusca.*"

As	the body	is enlightened by the eye,	so	the mind	is enlightened by a certain perceptive faculty.
	Known subject.	Known predicate.		Subject whose predicate is unknown.	Unknown predicate.

For several centuries there was no word in the Latin language to describe this "perceptive faculty of the mind." At last they coined the word "imaginatio," which appears in English as "imagination." This word is found as early as Chaucer; but it is quite conceivable that the English lan guage should, like the Latin, have passed through its best period without any single word to describe the "mind's eye."

522. The details of the expansion will vary according to the point and purpose of the metaphor. Thus, when Macbeth (act iii. sc. 1) says that he has "given his eternal jewel to the common enemy of man," the point of the metaphor is apparently the pricelessness of a pure soul or good conscience, and the metaphor might be expanded thus—

"As a jewel is precious to the man who wears it, so is a good conscience precious to the man who possesses it."

But in *Rich. II.* i. 1. 180, the same metaphor is expanded with reference to the necessity for its safe preservation :—

"A jewel in a ten-times barr'd-up chest
Is a bold spirit in a loyal breast."

523. Personal Metaphor.—There is a universal desire among men that visible nature, *e.g.* mountains, winds, trees, rivers and the like, should have a power of sympathising with men. This desire begets a kind of poetical belief that such a sympathy actually exists. Further, the vocabulary expressing the variable moods of man is so much richer than that which expresses the changes of nature that the latter bor rows from the former. Hence the *morn* is said to *laugh*, *mountains* to *frown*, *winds* to *whisper*, *rivulets* to *prattle*, *oaks* to *sigh.* Hence arises what may be called Personal Metaphor.

Def. A Personal Metaphor is a transference of personal relations to an impersonal object for the purpose of brief explanation.

524. Personal Metaphors expanded.—The first term will always be "a person;" the second, the predicated relation properly belonging to the person and improperly transferred to the impersonal object; the third, the impersonal object. Thus—

"As a person frowns, so an overhanging mountain (looks gloomy).

"As a child prattles, so a brook (makes a ceaseless cheerful clatter)."

525. Personifications.—Men are liable to certain feelings, such as shame, fear, repentance and the like, which seem *not* to be originated by the *person*, but to come upon him from without. For this reason such *impersonal* feelings are in some languages represented by *impersonal* verbs. In Latin these verbs are numerous, "pudet," "piget," "tædet," "pœnitet," "libet," &c. In Early English they were still more numerous, and even now we retain not only "it snows," "it rains," but also (though more rarely) "methinks," "meseems," "it shames me," "it repents me." Men are, however, not contented with *separating* their feelings from their own *person;* they also feel a desire to account for them. For this purpose they have often imagined as the causes of their feelings, Personal Beings, such as Hope, Fear, Faith, &c. Hence arose what may be called *Personification.*

In later times men have ceased to believe in the personal existence of Hope and Fear, Graces and nymphs, Flora and Boreas ; but poets still use Personification, for the purpose of setting before us with greater vividness the invisible operations of the human mind and the slow and imperceptible processes of inanimate nature.

Def. **Personification is the creation of a fictitious Person in order to account for unaccountable results, or for the purpose of vivid illustration.**

526. Personifications cannot be expanded.—The process of expansion into simile can be performed in the case of a Personal Metaphor, because there is implied a comparison between a Person and an impersonal object. But the process cannot be performed where (as in Personifications) the impersonal object has no material existence, but is the mere creation of the fancy, and presents no point of comparison. "A frowning mountain" can be expanded, because there is implied a comparison between a mountain and a person, a gloom and a frown. But "frowning Wrath" cannot be expanded, because there is no comparison.

It is the essence of a metaphor that it should be literally false, as in "a frowning mountain." It is the essence of a personification that, though founded on imagination, it is conceived to be literally true, as in "pale fear," "dark dishonour." A painter would represent "death" as "pale," and "dishonour" as "dark," though he would not represent a "mountain" with a "frown," or a "ship" like a "plough."

527. Apparent Exception.—The only case where a simile is involved and an expansion is possible is where a person, as for instance Mars, the God of War, is represented as doing something which he is not imagined to do literally. Thus the phrase "Mars mows down his foes" is not literally true. No painter would represent Mars (though he would Time) with a scythe. It is therefore a metaphor and, as such, capable of expansion thus :—

"As easily as a haymaker mows down the grass, so easily does Mars cut down his foes with his sword."

But the phrase "Mars slays his foes" is, from a poet's or painter's point of view, literally true. It is therefore no metaphor, and cannot be expanded.

528. Personification analysed.—Though we cannot expand a Personification into a simile, we can explain the
details of it. The same *analogy* which leads men to find a
correspondence between *visible* and *invisible* objects leads
them also to find a similarity between *cause* and *effect.*
This belief, which is embodied in the line—

> " Who drives fat oxen should himself be fat,"

is the basis of all Personification. Since fear makes men
look pale, and dishonour gives a dark and scowling expression to the face, it is inferred that Fear *is* " pale," and Dishonour " dark." And in the same way Famine is " gaunt ;"
Jealousy " green-eyed ;" Faith " pure-eyed ;" Hope " white-
handed."

529. Good and bad Metaphors.—There are certain laws
regulating the formation and employment of metaphors
which should be borne in mind.

(1.) *A metaphor must not be used unless it is needed for
explanation or vividness, or to throw light upon the thought
of the speaker.* Thus the speech of the Gardener, *Rich. II.*
iii. 4. 33,—

> "Go then, and like an executioner
> Cut off the heads of our fast-growing sprays," &c.

is inappropriate to the character of the speaker, and conveys
an allusion instead of an explanation. It illustrates what is
familiar by what is unfamiliar, and can only be justified by
the fact that the gardener is thinking of the disordered condition of the kingdom of England and the necessity of a
powerful king to repress unruly subjects.

(2.) *A metaphor must not enter too much into detail:* for
every additional detail increases the improbability that the
correspondence of the whole comparison can be sustained.
Thus, if King Richard (*Rich. II.* v. 5. 50) had been content,
while musing on the manner in which he could count time
by his sighs, to say—

> "For now hath Time made me his numbering clock,"

there would have been little or no offence against taste. But when he continues—

> "My thoughts are minutes, and with sighs they jar
> Their watches on unto mine eyes, the outward watch,
> Whereto my finger, like a dial's point,
> Is pointing still, in cleansing them from tears.
> Now, sir, the sound that tells what hour it is
> Are clamorous groans which strike upon my heart,
> Which is the bell,"—

we have an excess of detail which is only justified because it illustrates the character of one who is always " studying to compare,"* and "hammering out" unnatural comparisons.

(3.) *A metaphor must not be far-fetched nor dwell upon the details of a disgusting picture :*

> " Here lay Duncan,
> His *silver* skin *laced* with his *golden* blood ;
> . . . . . there the murderers
> Steep'd in the colours of their trade, *their daggers*
> *Unmannerly breech'd with gore.*"—*Macbeth,* ii. 3. 117.

There is but little, and that far-fetched, similarity between *gold lace* and *blood*, or between *bloody daggers* and *breech'd* legs. The slightness of the similarity, recalling the greatness of the dissimilarity, disgusts us with the attempted comparison. Language so forced is only appropriate in the mouth of a conscious murderer dissembling guilt.

(4.) *Two metaphors must not be confused together, particularly if the action of the one is inconsistent with the action of the other.*

It may be pardonable to *surround*, as it were, one metaphor with another. Thus, fear may be compared to an ague-fit, and an ague-fit passing away may be compared to the overblowing of a storm. Hence, " This ague-fit of fear is overblown " (*Rich. II.* iii. 2. 190) is justifiable. But

> " Was the hope drunk
> Wherein you dressed yourself? Hath it slept since ?"
> *Macbeth,* i. 7. 36.

---

* " I have been *studying how I may compare*
This prison where I live unto the world ;
* * * * *
I cannot do it ; yet I'll *hammer it out*."—*Rich. II.* v. 5. 1.

is, apart from the context, objectionable ; for it makes Hope a person and a dress in the same breath.   It may, however, probably be justified on the supposition that Lady Macbeth is playing on her husband's previous expression—

> " I have bought
> Golden opinions from all sorts of people,
> Which would be worn now in their newest gloss,
> Not cast aside so soon."

(5.) *A metaphor must be wholly false, and must not combine truth with falsehood.*

"A king is the pilot of the state," is a good metaphor. " A careful captain is the pilot of his ship," is a bad one.   So

> " Ere my tongue
> Shall wound mine honour with such feeble wrong,
> Or sound so base a parle,"—*Rich. II.* i. i. 190.

is objectionable.   The tongue, though it cannot "wound," can touch.   It would have been better that "honour's" enemy should be intangible, that thereby the proportion and the perfection of the falsehood might be sustained.   Honour can be wounded intangibly by "slander's venom'd spear" (*Rich. II.* i. i. 171) ; but, in a metaphor, not so well by the tangible tongue.   The same objection applies to

> "Ten thousand bloody crowns of mothers' sons
> Shall ill-become the flower of England's face,
> Change the complexion of her maid-pale peace
> To scarlet indignation, and bedew
> Her pastures' grass with faithful English blood."
>
> *Rich. II.* iii. 3. 96.

If England is to be personified, it is England's blood, not the blood of ten thousand mothers, which will stain her face. There is also a confusion between the blood which mantles in a blush and which is shed ; and, in the last line, instead of "England's face," we come down to the literal "pastures' grass."

(6.) **Personifications** must be regulated by the laws of personality.   No other rule can be laid down.   But exaggerations like the following must be avoided :—

" Comets, importing change of times and states,
 Brandish your crystal tresses in the sky,
 And with them scourge the bad revolting stars."

1 *Hen. VI.* i. 1. 2.

The Furies may be supposed to scourge their prostrate victims with their snaky hair, and comets have been before now regarded as scourges in the hand of God. But the liveliest fancy would be tasked to imagine the stars in revolt, and scourged back into obedience by the crystal hair of comets.

NOTES AND QUESTIONS.*

MACBETH, Act III.

Scene i.

LINE

3. "Thou *play'dst* most foully for't." Expand the metaphor into its simile. (Grammar, 521.)

14. "And *all*-thing unbecoming." See "All" (Grammar). What is there remarkable in this use of all? Comp. iii. 2. 11—
    "Things without *all* remedy."

15. "A *solemn* supper." Modernize. Trace the present meaning from the derivation. Compare
    "A *solemn* hunting is in hand."—*T. A.* ii. 1. 112.

17. "To *the which*." What is the antecedent to *the which*? Why do we say *the which*, but never *the who*? (Grammar, "Which," 270.)

25. "*The better*." When do we add *the* to a comparative? (Grammar, 94.) Can *the* be explained here?

44. "*While* then." (See 137.) Compare
    "He shall conceal it
    Whiles you are willing it shall come to note."
    T. N. iv. 3. 29.
    Illustrate from Greek and Latin.

49. "To be thus thus is nothing but *to be safely thus*." Explain the grammatical construction of the last clause. (See 385.)

51. "Which *would* be feared." Modernize *would*. Explain (Grammar, 329) the Elizabethan usage.

"'Tis much *he dares*." Is there any object to "he dares"? (244.)

* The numbers refer to the paragraphs of the Grammar.

52. "And *to* that dauntless temper of his mind." Meaning of? (See Grammar, " To.")

54. " None *but he.*" Illustrate this construction by Shakespeare's use of *except.* (See Grammar, " But.")

56.
> " . . . And, under him,
> My genius is rebuked ; as, it is said,
> Mark Antony's was by Cæsar."

See *A. and C.* ii. 3. 20—30. Trace the meaning of *genius* from its derivation.

65. " For Banquo's issue have I *filed* my spirit." Meaning of? Give similar instances of the dropping of the prefix. (See Prosody, 460.)

72. " Champion me to the utterance." Meaning of? Trace the meaning of *champion* and *utterance* from the derivation. What historical inference may be drawn from the fact that both these words are derived from the French? Mention a similar inference contained in the dialogue between Gurth and Wamba in " Ivanhoe."

75. " So *please* your highness." Parse *please.* (See 297.)

81. "How you were borne in hand, how cross'd, the instruments." Is this an Alexandrine? (See Prosody, 468 ; and compare

> " My books and instruments shall be my company."
> *T. of Sh.* i. 1. 82.)
> "Like labour with the rest, where the other instruments."
> *Coriol.* i. 1. 104.
> " *I.* But now thou seem'st a coward.
> *P.* Hence, vile instrument."—*Cymb.* iii. 4. 75.

" *Borne in hand.*" Meaning?

> " The Duke
> *Bore* many gentlemen, myself being one,
> *In hand* and hope of action."—*M. for M.* i. 4. 52.

We do not now say "to *bear* in hope," but "to *keep* a person in hope, suspense," &c. So a rich hypocrite, pretending illness to squeeze presents out of his expectant legatees, is said to—

> " Look upon their kindness, and take more
> And look on that, still *bearing them in hand,*
> Letting the cherry knock against their lips."
> B. J. *Fox,* i. 1. *init.*

LINE

We still say, to "bear *in* mind," but we generally use "a hand" in this sense.

83. "To half a soul and to a *notion* crazed." Meaning of *notion* here? Compare

> "His *notion* weakens, his discernings
> Are lethargied."—*Lear*, i. 4. 248.

Trace the double meaning of the word from the derivation.

84. " *M.* Say 'Thus did Banquo.' *Murd.* You made it known to us." Scan. (See 454.)

87. "Your patience so predominant in your nature." Scan.

88. "Are you *so* gospell'd to pray for this good man." Modernize. (See 282.)

91. " *M.* And beggar'd yours for ever. *Murd.* We are men, my liege." Scan.

95. "The *valued file.*" Trace this and other meanings of *file* from the derivation. Explain the meaning and use of *valued* (374). Could we say "a valued catalogue?"

99. " The gift which bounteous nature hath in him *closed.*" Parse *closed.* (See 460.) Compare

> "Dance, sing, and in a well-mixed border
> *Close* this new brother of our order."—ROWLEY.

What is now the difference between "I have him caught," and "I have caught him"? Compare

> "And when they had this done."—*St. Luke* v. 6.

100. "Particular addition *from* the bill that writes them all alike." Meaning of *from?* (See Prepositions.)

103. "Not in the worst rank of manhood, say't." Scan. (See 485.)

108. "Who wear our health but sickly in his life
Which in his death were perfect. *Murd.* I am one, my liege."

What is the antecedent to *which?* Scan the second line.

112. "So weary with disasters, *tugg'd* with fortune." Parse and explain *tugg'd.* How does the meaning differ from the modern meaning? Compare

" Both *tugging* to be victors, *breast to breast.*"
                            3 *Hen. VI.* ii. 5. 12.

and, for the construction :

" And, *toil'd with* works of war, retired himself
  To Italy."—*Rich. II.* iv. 1. 96.

113. "That I would *set* my life on any chance." Expand the
     metaphor. Compare

     " Who *sets* me else ? By heaven I'll throw at all."
                            Rich. II. iv. 1. 57.

116.   " And in such bloody distance,
            That every minute of his being thrusts
            Against my near'st of life."

     Expand the metaphor. What is meant by " my *near'st of
     life ?* " Illustrate by " home-thrust," and οἰκεῖος.

120. "And bid my will *avouch* it." Trace the meaning from the
     derivation.

121. " *For* certain friends." Meaning of *for* here ? How did *for*
     become a conjunction ?

122. " Whose loves I *may* not drop." What is the meaning of
     may ? Derive the modern from the original meaning.

123.   " But wail his fall
            Who I myself struck down."

     What is the antecedent to *who ?* What is there remarkable in
     the sentence ? (Gram. 274.)

127. "Perform what you command us. *First Murd.* Though our
     lives—"

     What do you suppose the First Murderer intended to say ?
     Why did Macbeth interrupt him ?

128. "Your spirits shine through you. Within this hour at most.'
     Scan.

130. "The perfect *spy* of the time." Apparently in this difficult pas-
     sage *spy* is put for "that which is spied," " knowledge."

132. "Always thought." Parse *thought.* Illustrate the construc-
     tion from Greek.*

     " *From* the palace." *From,* how used ?

     * Liddell and Scott: δοκῶ, ii. 4.

LINE
1ʃ0. "I'll come to you anon.   We are resolved, my lord."
Perhaps "t' you anón" is to be considered as one foot.
If not, how can this verse be scanned? (See 500.)   What
is the emphatic word in the Murderer's reply?

SCENE 2.

3. " Say to the king, *I would attend his leisure.*"   Modernize the
latter words.   Trace the different meanings of *attend* from
the derivation.   What is the exact meaning of *would?*

9.   " *Lady M.* 'Tis safer to be that which we destroy
Than by destruction dwell in doubtful joy.

Enter MACBETH.
How now, my lord !   Why do you keep alone?"
Illustrate the character of Lady Macbeth from her words
before and after the entrance of her husband.   Why and
when, for the most part, does Shakespeare use rhyme?

11. " With them they think on.   Things without *all* remedy."
Scan.   What is the object of *on ?*   (See 242.)   How is *all*
used?

16. "But let the frame of things disjoint, both the worlds suffer."
Perhaps a pause is intended after "let :"   "But let—yes,
even the frame," &c.   In that case "But let" is an un-
finished verse, and the rest is a complete verse.   In the
Fol. 1623 the first line ends with "disjoint," containing
four accents.   When does Shakespeare use verses with *four*
accents (505-9)?

19. " That shake us nightly ; better be with the dead."   Scan.
How can you justify an accent on the first syllable in the
foot "bétter?"

21.   " Than *on the torture* of the mind *to lie*
In restless *ecstasy.*   Duncan is in his grave."
What suggested the expression " *to lie on the torture* of the
mind"?   Trace this, as well as the modern, meaning of
ecstasy from the derivation.   Compare

"Where violent sorrow seems
A modern *ecstasy.*"—*Macbeth,* iv. 3. 170.

LINE

Give instances of classical words restricted in meaning by modern, compared with Elizabethan, usage. (See Introduction.) Scan the latter line.

27. "Gentle *my lord.*" Explain and illustrate the position of *my.* (See 13.)

29. "Be bright and *jovial* among your guests to-night." Trace the meaning from the derivation. Give words similarly derived. Scan.

30. "Let your remembrance apply to Banquo." Scan. (See Prosody, 477.)

38. "Nature's copy." Meaning of? Comp. *T. N.* i. 5. 257 :

"'Tis beauty truly blent whose red and white
Nature's own sweet and cunning hand laid on."

40.   "Ere the bat hath flown
His *cloister'd flight.*"

What is alluded to?

42. "The *shard-borne* beetle." *Shard* is *scale.* Ben Jonson talks of "*scaly* beetles with their habergeons." And in *Cymb.* iii. 2. 20, "The *sharded* beetle" is opposed to "the *full-winged* eagle."

46. "*Seeling* night." To *seel* was "to close the eyelids of hawks partially or entirely by passing a fine thread through them ; *siller*, Fr. This was done to hawks till they became tractable."—NARES.

48. "*Cancel* and tear to pieces that great *bond.*" Comp. *Rich. III.* iv. 4. 77 : "*Cancel* his *bond* of life." *Macbeth* iv. 1. 99 : "Shall live the *lease* of nature." And—

"Through her wounds doth fly
Life's lasting date from *cancell'd* destiny."—*R. of L.*

Explain the meaning of the expression here, and trace the meaning of *cancel* from the derivation.

54. "Hold *thee* still." Modernize. (See 20.)

SCENE 3.

3, 4. "*To* the direction just." Meaning of *to?* (See 187.)

5. "Now spurs the *lated* traveller apace." Modernize. Illustrate by similar instances the shortening of the word.

INE

10. "Within the *note* of expectation." This may perhaps mean, "the memorandum or list of expected guests." Compare

"I come by *note*."—*M. of V.* iii. 2. 140.

"That's out of my *note*."—*W. T.* iv. 3. 49.

Otherwise it may mean "the boundary," "limit." Compare

"Within the prospect of belief."—*Macbeth*, i. 3. 74.

SCENE 4.

1.   "Sit down : *at first*
And last the hearty welcome."

Compare 1 *Hen. VI.* v. 5. 102 :

"Ay grief I fear me *both at first and last.*"

Meaning of? What distinction is now made between *first* and *at first, last* and *at last?*

5.   "Our hostess keeps her state, *but* in best time
We will require her welcome."

Show, from the antithesis implied in *but*, what is meant by "*keeping her state.*" Compare

"The king caused the queene to keepe the estate, and then sate the ambassadors and ladies, as they were marshalled by the king, who would not sit, but walked from place to place making cheare."—HOLINSHED, *quoted by* CLARK *and* WRIGHT.

The "state" was used technically to mean "a canopy."

11. "Be *large* in mirth." Modernize. Illustrate from *largess.*

12. "The table round. There's blood upon thy face. *M.* 'Tis Banquo's then." What name has been given, and why, to this arrangement of the parts of verses? Compare lines 15, 20, 51, 69, which are similarly arranged. (See Prosody, 513.)

13. "'Tis better thee without than he within." Meaning? Comment on the syntax. (See 206, 212.)

23. "As broad and *general* as the casing air." Compare 2 *Hen. VI.* v. 2. 43 :

"Now let the *general* trumpet blow his blast."

LINE

Meaning of *general* ? Modernize. What is the difference between " general," " universal," and " common " ?

34.
" The feast is sold
That is not often vouch'd, while 'tis *a-making*,
'Tis given with welcome : to feed were best at home."

Analyse the sentence, and show the confusion of two constructions. Whence arose the use of *a*, as in *a-making ?* (See 140.) Scan the last line.

36. " *From* thence." Meaning of ? (See 158.)

42. " *Who* may I rather challenge for unkindness." Is *who* always used for *whom ?* Whence arises the difference between *may*, in " *may* I challenge," as here, and " I may challenge " ?

57. " You *shall* offend him." Modernize. What is the present rule for the use of *shall* with respect to the second and third persons ? How did the rule arise ? (See 317.)

61. " This is the *very* painting of your fear." Modernize. Trace from the derivation the Elizabethan meaning, and hence the modern meaning, as in " His *very* dog deserted him."

64. "Impostors *to* true fear." Meaning of *to ?* (See 187.)

66. " *Authorized* by her grandam." Compare for the accent—
" His madness so with his authorized youth."—*L. C.* 15.
" *Authorizing* thy trespass with compare."—*Sonn.* 35.*

75. " Ere human statutes purged the *gentle* weal." How is *gentle* used ? If the *weal* was already *gentle,* how did it require to be *purged ?*

79.
"The times have been
That, when the brains were out, the man would die."
Modernize *that.* Illustrate this use. (See 284.)

81. " With *twenty* mortal murders on their crowns." Why *twenty ?* (See above, line 27.)

87. " To those that know me. Come, love and health to all." Scan this and the previous line.

* Neither of these passages is conclusive, as *authorize* coming at the beginning of the verse may have the accent on the first syllable. Add therefore:
" His rudeness so with his *authorized* youth."—*L. C.* 15.

91. " We thirst." *Thirst* is not used elsewhere by Shakespeare in the sense of " drinking a health." [? "first."]

95. "Thou hast no *speculation* in those eyes." Illustrate from this use of *speculation* the general difference between the Elizabethan and the modern use of classical words. (See Introduction.)

98. " *Only.*" Probably transposed. (See Grammar, 420.)

99. " What man *dare.*" Why not *dares?* Compare
> " Let him that *is* no coward
> But *dare* maintain."—1 *Hen. VI.* ii. 4. 32.

(*Dare* occurs thus three times in the unhistorical plays, *dares* thirty times. In the historical plays *dare* eight, *dares* seven times.)

105. " If trembling I *inhabit*, then *protest* me." No other instance has been given where *inhabit* means "linger at home." Shakespeare may, however, have derived this use of the word from οἰκουρεῖν ("to be a stay-at-home" as opposed to "going out to war") through NORTH's *Plutarch*, 190 :—

> " The home-tarriers and house-doves," &c.

Trace this and the modern meaning of *protest* from the derivation. Comp. *M. Ado*, v. 1. 149 :

> " I will *protest* your cowardice."

106. " The baby *of* a girl." *Baby* was sometimes used for " doll : "
> " And now you cry for't
> As children do for *babies* back again."
> B. and F. (HALLIWELL).

109. " You have displaced the mirth, broke the good meeting." What is here contrary to common usage? (See 343.)

112.
> " You make me *strange*
> Even to the disposition that I *owe.*"

Comp. *C. of E.* ii. 2. 151 :

> " As *strange* unto your town as to your talk."

Owe is frequently used for *ow(e)n*, as *ope* for *open*. Comp. *debeo* from *de* and *habeo*.

122. Why does not Lady Macbeth continue her expostulations when she is alone with her husband ?

LINE

124. "Augurs and understood *relations*." Comp. below, iv. 3. 173 :

> "O, *relation*
> Too nice, and yet too true."

The utterances of birds are apparently called *relations*.

126. "*What* is the night?" Illustrate this use of *what*. (See **252**.)

129. "Did you send to him, *sir?*" Why does Shakespeare here make Lady Macbeth thus address her husband?

133. "And betimes I will to the weird sisters." This line must probably be scanned by pronouncing *weird* as two syllables. (See Prosody.) In the Folio *weird* is spelt *weyard*. Comp. ii. 1. 20 :

> "I dreamt last night of the three *weird* sisters."

138. "*Returning* were as tedious as *go* o'er." Parse *returning* and *go*.

141. "You lack the season of all natures, sleep." Illustrate from this and other passages the practical and unimaginative character of Lady Macbeth, as contrasted with her husband. Compare with this v. 1. Compare also ii. 2. 67 : "A little water clears us of this deed ;" and v. 1. 35 : "Yet here's a spot," and, in the same scene, "What, will these hands ne'er be clean?" In what sense may such lines as ii. 2. 67, iii. 4. 141, be called specimens of "irony"?

Compare also Duncan speaking of the *first* (*not of the second*) Thane of Cawdor :

> "There's *no art*
> *To find the mind's construction in the face.*
> He was a gentleman on whom I built
> An absolute trust."—i. 4. 11.

In the same scene, l. 58, Duncan says of Macbeth, "It is a peerless kinsman."

Other instances of Shakespearian "irony" may be found in *Rich. III.* iii. 2. 67 ; *Coriol.* iii. 1. 19 ; 1 *Hen. IV.* ii. 4. 528, compared with 2 *Hen. IV.* v. 5. 51 ; *A. and C.* i. 2. 32, compared with *Ib.* v. 2. 330, *T. of A.* i. 2. 92, *Rich. III.* i. 2. 112, and *Ib.* iv. 1. 82 ; *Macbeth*, ii. 3. 97–100, and *Ib.* v. 2. 22 ; *Rich. III.* iii. 1. 110.

SCENE 5.

1. Why does Shakespeare make the witches speak in a different metre from the rest of the play? Illustrate from the *Midsummer Night's Dream* and the *Tempest*.

7. "*Close* contriver of all harms." Meaning of *close?* Comp. *Cymb.* iii. 5. 85 : "*Close* villain, I'll have thy secret."

11.   "All you have done
Hath been but for *a wayward son.*"

Illustrate this from Lady Macbeth's description of her husband, i. 5. Contrast the character of Macbeth with that of Richard III.

24. "There hangs a vaporous drop *profound.*" Perhaps *mysterious.*

32.   "And you all know *security*
Is mortals' chiefest enemy."

Trace the modern meaning of *security* from the derivation. What does it mean here? Illustrate from Milton's *Allegro.*

SCENE 6.

2. "*Only* I say." Probably transposed as above.

4. "Was pitied of Macbeth." Modernize. Account for this use of *of.*

8. "Who cannot *want* the thought how monstrous." Scan. (See Prosody, 477.) Compare, for the meaning of *want*, *W. T.* iii. 2. 55.

19. "I think . . . they should find." Modernize. Explain the difference between the Elizabethan and the modern *should.* (See 326.)

"*An't* please heaven." Explain *an't.* (See 101.)

21. "He *fail'd* his presence." Comp. *Lear*, ii. 4. 143 :
            "I cannot think my sister in the least
            Would *fail* her obligation."
How is *fail* now used when it takes an object after it?

27. "Received *of* the most pious Edward." (See line 4.)

LINE

30. "Is gone to pray the holy king upon his aid." Unless it can be shown that *upon* is sometimes used for *on*, this line, as it stands, is an Alexandrine.

35. "Free from our feasts and banquets bloody knives." Comp. *Timon of A.* v. 1. :
   "Rid me these villains from your companies."
   Also perhaps *Tempest*, Epilogue : "Prayer which frees all faults."

36. "Do faithful *homage*." Trace the modern and ancient meaning from the derivation.

38. "Hath so *exasperate* the king." Why is the *d* omitted? (See 343.)

40. "And with an *absolute* 'Sir, not I.'" Compare "an absolute 'shall.'"—*Coriol.* iii. 1. Also, " an *absolute* and excellent horse."—*Hen. V.* iii. 7 ; "I am *absolute* 'twas very Cloten."—*Cymb.* iv. 2. Trace the different meanings from the derivation.

42. "*As who* should say." (See 257.)

INDEX TO THE QUOTATIONS

FROM SHAKESPEARE'S PLAYS.

The references are to the numbered paragraphs, and to the scenes and lines of the "Globe" edition.

References marked thus (†) will not be found quoted in the paragraph referred to, but similar references will be found explaining the difficulty of the reference in question.

References in parentheses thus (6) refer to the explanatory notes at the end of the play.

ALL'S WELL THAT ENDS WELL.

ACT I. Sc.	Line	Par.	Sc.	Line	Par.	Sc.	Line	Par.	ACT IV. Sc.	Line	Par.
i.	7	172	i.	192	379	iv.	7	{360 / 374	i.	20	88
i.	94	477	ii.	73	27	iv.	15	336	i.	21	202
ii.	29	407	iii.	131	177	iv.	27	218	ii.	21	247
iii.	71	368	iii.	142	480	iv.	29	484	ii.	30	129
iii.	107	372	iii.	156	271	iv.	30	419a	iii.	9	489
iii.	208	445	iii.	168	470	v.	43	477	iii.	114	400
iii.	221	279	iii.	179	268	v.	48	191	iii.	116	400
iii.	244	81	iii.	185	490	v.	58	1	iii.	158	434
			iii.	223	64	v.	98	335	iii.	285	301
ACT II.			iii.	261	208	v.	103	175	iii.	298	400
i.	6	418	iii.	289	489	v.	104	198a	iii.	299	357
i.	60	97	iii.	313	507	vi.	24	278	iv.	30	{76 / 191
i.	98	468				vi.	27	12	v.	46	212
i.	110	462	**ACT III.**			vi.	109	405	v.	55	87
i.	111	p. 16	i.	5	485	vi.	115	200			
i.	124	434	ii.	108	434	vi.	117	243	**ACT V.**		
i.	134	349	ii.	111	468	vii.	30	128	i.	24	514
i.	144	497	iv.	1	{99 / 331	vii.	31	492	i.	25	514
i.	163	473	iv.	2	312	vii.	32	363			
i.	184	509	iv.	6	203	vii.	30	127			

ANTONY AND CLEOPATRA.

(1) Folio, "and." (2) Compare iv. 1. 20. (3) *Hamlet*, i. 2. 182
(4) "Wearer's" for "weary." (5) *Rich. III.* i. 2. 217. (6) See i. 2. 52
(7) *Rich. II.* v. 5. 55 (8) *Ib.* v. 1. 28. (9) *Macbeth*, iv. 3. 176

COMEDY OF ERRORS.

CORIOLANUS.

Sc.	Line	Par.	Sc.	Line	Par.	Sc.	Line	Par.	Sc.	Line	Par.
i.	54	471	iii.	21	†161	iii.	{143}{144}	†278	vi.	{22}{23}	†244
i.	62	(17)	iii.	35	490				vi.	23	†494
ii.	5	†494	iii.	{54}{73}	†442	iii.	{149}{151}	457	vi.	35	†448
ii.	8	13				iii.	154	†497	vi.	40	29c
ii.	18	458	iii.	82	†p.13	iii.	186	419a	vi.	41	†495
ii.	22	†92	iii.	95	423	iii.	189	†1	vi.	43	†285
ii.	41	183	iii.	96	†490				vi.	44	227
ii.	65	(15)	iii.	100	†349	iii.	192	483	vi.	61	†513
ii.	77	†212	iii.	105	479	iv.	39	492	vi.	69	462
ii.	89	294	iii.	108	†494	iv.	55	†469	vi.	71	†479
ii.	90	†16	iii.	115	478	iv.	64	143	vi.	78	420
ii.	95	†151	iii.	121	455	vi.	4	238	vi.	101	480
iii.	4	479	iii.	125	482	vi.	11	†440	vi.	128	†p.13
iii.	{7}{8}	†279							vi.	138	†457
iii.	11	290									

(1) Folio, "and."
(2) *M. for M.* iv. 6. 13.
(3) *J. C.* iii. 2. 16.
(4) *Othello*, i. 2. 22.
(5) *A. and C.* i. 4. 40.
(6) See above, i. 1. 272.
(7) See *A. Y. L.* ii. 2. 8.
(8) *Hamlet*, v. 2. 95.
(9) *M. of V.* iv. 1. 406.
(10) *Hamlet*, i. 1. 162.
(11) Conversely, 1 *Hen. VI.* v. 4. 7.
(12) *M. of V.* i. 1. 98.
(13) *Tempest*, i. 2. 200. Ref.
(14) Folio, "appeared."
(15) *J. C.* iv. 3. 138.
(16) *J. C.* iii. 3. 22
(17) 3 *Hen. VI.* iii. 2. 46

CYMBELINE.

ACT I.											
i.	24	81	iv.	36	382	v.	44	356	vi.	209	1
i.	48	465	iv.	39	405	vi.	8	337	**ACT II.**		
i.	65	279	iv.	53	427	vi.	36	375	i.	61	507
i.	72	466	iv.	101	434	vi.	40	224	iii.	24	247
i.	96	473	iv.	112	90	vi.	48	499	iii.	29	1
i.	105	244	iv.	118	189				iii.	59	297
i.	124	382	iv.	125	368	vi.	59	{53}{85}	iii.	68	13
i.	132	508	v.	9	467	vi.	66	290	iii.	80	76
i.	168	465	v.	10	484	vi.	84	244	iii.	101	419a
iii.	7	453	v.	17	370	vi.	116	8	iii.	111	148
iii.	29	224	v.	25	93	vi.	117	247	iii.	151	508
iv.	16	158	v.	28	478	vi.(Fol.)147		340	iii.	153	{118}{299}
iv.	17	412	v.	32	212	vi.	165	18	iv.	19	434
			v.	41	93						

(1) *W. T.* v. 2. 82.   (2) *Macbeth*, iii. 1. 15.   (3) *Rich. III.* i. 2. 3.

(4) Folio, "sanctify:" probably "sanity."

(5) Perhaps a corruption arising from a repetition of "oft" misspelt "oft," "ost" most."

(6) *Macbeth*, iii. 5. 32.   (6a) Compare "free," *Hamlet*, iii. 2. 252.

(7) *Macbeth*, iii. 5. 7.   (8) *Macbeth*, iv. 3. 170.   (c) Folio, "hath."

(10) Folio, "favourites."   (11) *Hamlet*, iv. 7. 145.

(12) Folio, "depends and rests."   (13) *Rich. III.* iii. 1. 82.

(14) Folio, "it," not "its."   (15) *L. L. L.* v. 1. 13-4

(16) Above, 283.--*Macbeth*, ii. 2. 56-7.

1 HENRY IV.

2 HENRY IV.

1 HENRY VI.

2 HENRY VI.

HENRY VIII.

(1) 1 *Hen. IV.* iii. 2. 16.   (2) Folio, "and."   (3) *Rich. III.* v. 3. 156
(4) Play on " bond."—*Macbeth* iii. 2. 49 ; *Rich. III.* iv. 4. 77.
(5) *Rich. III.* iv. 4. 444.   (6) *M. of V.* iii. 2. 61.   (7) *A. Y. L.* i. 3. 35
(8) Perhaps i. 2. 156.   (9) Folio, "Pluto's." See Introduction, p. 16, note.
(10) *Tempest,* i. 2. 213.

LEAR.

Sc.	Line	Par.	Sc.	Line	Par.	Sc.	Line	Par.	Sc.	Line	Par.
iii.	2	.†218	iii.	102	.†513	iii.	181	. 199	iii.	247	.†274
iii.	20	. 469	iii.	120	. 382	iii.	202	. 51	iii.	255	. 441
iii.	22	. 315	iii.	125	. 254	iii.	204	. 178	iii.	262	{287/290}
iii.	48	. 263	iii.	138	.†361	iii.	208	.†499	iii.	266	. 268
iii.	50	{218/†159}	iii.	143	.†285	iii.	213	.†223	iii.	274	. 24
iii.	97	. 254	iii.	144	.†397	iii.	222	.|513	iii.	282	. 461
iii.	98	. 447	iii.	{148/149}	{†242 or/†272}	iii.	234	. 333			
iii.	100	. 255	iii.	168	. 480	iii.	239	.†513			
						iii.	245	. 469			

(1) *A. W.* v. 3. 297.   (2) Folio, "too blame."   (3) 1 *Hen. VI.* iii. 3. 10.
(4) Folio, "and" (&) for "an."   (5) Folio, "tended."   (6) *Hen. V.* iv. 3. 35-6.
(7) *Macbeth*, iv. 1. 59.   (8) *Ib.* v. 7. 1, 2.   (9) But Folio, "importuned.

LOVE'S LABOUR LOST.

ACT I.			i.	123	. 500	iii.	219	. 165	ii.	365	. 187
i.	43	. 176	i.	133	. 111	iii.	224	. 344	ii.	440	. 290
i.	65	. 422	i.	156	. 442	iii.	345	. 412	ii.	{463/464}	. 432
i.	80	. 220	i.	160	. 460	**ACT V.**			ii.	494	. 184
i.	86	. 5	i.	174	. 109	i.	152	. 81	ii.	522	. 19
i.	107	. 177	i.	177	. 364	ii.	8	. 202	ii.	750	. 333
i.	137	. 492	**ACT III.**			ii.	9	. 283	ii.	752	. 144
			i.	153	. 13d	ii.	69	. 344	ii.	778	{344/418}
ACT II.			**ACT IV.**			ii.	190	. 467	ii.	799	. 434
i.	2	. 274	iii.	108	. 368	ii.	213	. 460	ii.	813	. 285
i.	28	. 168	iii	118	. 368	ii.	274	. 430	ii.	923	. 178
i.	42	. 491	iii.	150	. 145	ii.	332	. 487	ii.	925	. 90
i.	45	. 485	iii.	{167/-9}	. 349	ii.	349	. 200	ii.	926	. 300
i.	107	. 2				ii.	355	.419a			

MACBETH.

ACT I.			ii.	10	. 186	ii.	43	. 275	ii.	59	. 433
i.	1	.†504	ii.	13	. 171	ii.	45	. 506	ii.	64	.†501
i.	12	.†466	ii.	20	. 511	ii.	46	. 323	iii.	32	. 485
ii.	3	. 479	ii.	34	. 477	ii.	51	. 511	iii.	45	. 323
ii.	5	. 484	ii.	37	. 511	ii.	53	.†460	iii.	{53/55}	. 236
ii.	7	.†506	ii.	41	. 511	ii.	58	{283/†511}	iii.	57	.†283

(1) Compare *Macbeth*, v. 8. 48.
(3) *Lear*, iii. 2. 8.   (4) *Ib.* iii. 7. 54.
(2) *Rich. III.* iv. 4. 77.
(5) Compare ii. 2. 57.

MEASURE FOR MEASURE.

MERCHANT OF VENICE

(1) *Macbeth*, v. 2. 5.   (2) *C. of E.* i. 2. 38.   (3) *P. of T.* iv. Prologue, 45.
(4) *R. and J.* ii. 3. 54.   (5) *Coriol.* i. 1. 16.   (6) *A. Y. L.* ii. 7. 57.
(7) Folio, "and."   (7a) Folio, "puts."   (8) *M. Ado*, iii. 2. 31.
(9) Folio, "makes."   (10) Folio, "masters." So *Tempest*, ii. 1. 5. Compare "Where be thy *mastres*, man? I would speak with *her*."—B. and F. *Coxcomb*, 2. 3 *ad fin*.   (11) Compare "invaluable."   (12) Folio, "and."
(13) *Macbeth*, ii. 3. 2.   (14) *T. A.* v. 3. 70.   (15) Folio, "too blame."

MERRY WIVES OF WINDSOR.

ACT I.			Sc.	Line	Par.	Sc.	Line	Par.	Sc.	Line	Par.
Sc.	Line	Par.	i.	242 .	{204, 298}	iv.	97 .	{475, 480}	iv.	57 .	{28, 350}
i.	287 .	{64, 391}	ii.	50 . .	25	iv.	103 . .	57	iv.	87 . .	207
iii	1 . .	237	ii.	278 . .	41	v.	100 . .	148	v.	26 . .	38
iv	80 . .	175		ACT III.			ACT IV.			ACT V.	
	ACT II.		i.	113 . .	189	ii.	80 . .	349	v.	72 . .	2
i.	113 . .	299	iv.	14 . .	284	iv.	5 . .	194	v.	231 . .	37

MIDSUMMER NIGHT'S DREAM.

ACT I.						ACT II.					
i.	4 . .	290	i.	182 . .	†5				i.	83 . .	347
i.	39 . .	133	i.	184 . .	83				i.	91 .	{(3), 247}
i.	45 .	tp.13	i.	188 . .	237		ACT II.		i.	92 .	tp. 13
i.	69 .	.†466	i.	205 . .	425	i.	7 . .	484	i.	95 .	.†228
i.	71 . .	†90	i.	212 . .	†69	i.	9 .	.†356	i.	105 . .	492
i.	{74, 75}	.†281	i.	225 .	.†365	i.	14 .	.†349	i.	106 .	.†478
i.	76 . .	†1	i.	226 . .	21	i.	19 .	.†369	i.	112 . .	290
i.	81 . .	201	i.	229 .	.†118	i.	21 .	.†287	i.	127 .	.†462
i.	100 .	.†295	i.	231 .	.†178	i.	23 .	. 487	i.	138 . .	349
i.	103 .	.†271	i.	232 . .	(1)	i.	24 .	.†329	i.	146 .	.†405
i.	104 .	.†170	i.	237 .	. 450	i.	30 .	{†121, †283}	i.	149 . .	132
i.	111 .	.†275	i.	245 . .	66	i.	32 .	. 466	i.	160 .	.†107
i.	117 .	.†149	i.	251 .	.†356	i.	34 .	. 224	i.	161 . .	312
i.	123 . .	30	ii.	{2, 93}	.†230	i.	35 .	.†468	i.	164 . .	430
i.	126 . .	421	ii.	25 . .	†1	i.	{35-, 39}	. 415	i.	171 .	.†136
i.	141 .	.†301	ii.	27 . .	†93	i.	42 .	506	i.	179 .	{†242, †244}
i.	151 . .	490	ii.	52 . .	(2)	i.	48 .	. †16	i.	191 .	.†295
i.	156 .	.†469	ii.	{73, 77}	.†283	i.	56 . .	332	i.	201 .	.†406
i.	160 .	tp. 13	ii.	86 . .	104	i.	58 .	. 484	i.	202 .	.†466
i.	164 . .	156	ii.	90 . .	†25	i.	67 . .	290	i.	220 .	. 287
i.	173 . .	430	ii.	95 .	.†221				i.	227	†223
			ii.	105 .	.†492						

(1) *Hamlet*, iii. 2. 177.
(2) Folio, "and."
(3) Folio, "hath."
(4) *A. W.* v. 3. 297.
(5) *Hamlet*, iii. 2. 188.
(6) Folio, "comes.
(7) *L. L. L.* v. 1. 103-4
(8) Folio varies.

MUCH ADO ABOUT NOTHING.

OTHELLO.

PERICLES.

RICHARD II.

(a) Lines 18 and 19 are perhaps to be transposed. Comp., however, *W. T.* iii. 2. 165.

(b) Read "from off a 'nointed ;" or, as Folio, "From an anointed."

(c) Folio, "*and* if."

ACT V.

Sc.	Line	Par.
i.	31	. †356
i.	37	. . 41
i.	38	. . 285
i.	44	. . 225
i.	46	. . 75
i.	47	. . 200
i.	62	. †268
i.	64	. . 52
i.	77	. . 291
i.	80	. . 473
i.	88	. . 478
i.	90	. . 82
i.	91	. †470
i.	94	. . 372
ii.	{12/15}	. †285
ii.	18	. . 80
ii.	28	. . 512
ii.	48	. †406
ii.	53	. . 505
ii.	55 ?	{"it" om.)
ii.	56	. . 197
ii.	57	. . 484
ii.	59	. . 368
ii.	{65/70}	. 499
ii.	75	. . 155
ii.	78	. . 497
ii.	97	. . 468
ii.	99	. . 53
ii.	101	. †512
ii.	115	. . 122
iii.	4	. †190
iii.	5	. . 144
iii.	10	. . 272
iii.	17	. . 473
iii.	21	. †499
iii.	27	. . 356
iii.	34	. . 181
iii.	50	. †349
iii.	52	. . 296
iii.	72	. †372
iii.	88	. . 387
iii.	97	. . 190
iii.	101	{†501 or †497}
iii.	103	. †329
iii.	113	{Fol. "and"} †103
iii.	137	{†149 466}
iv.	1	. . 414
iv.	2	{†244 499}
iv.	8	. . 257
v.	3	. . 151
v.	5	. 529 n.
v.	8	. †69
v.	17	. . 465
v.	18	. †243
v.	22	. †151
v.	25	. †406
v.	27	. . 284
v.	{43/46}	. †343
v.	52	. . 498
v.	54	. . 164
v.	54-7	. {529 268}
v.	56	. . 425
v.	61	. . 290
v.	62	. . 366
v.	64	. †218
v.	66	. . 28
v.	{67/69}	. †506
v.	69	. . 254
v.	70	. †406
v.	75	. . 498
v.	76	. . 297
v.	83	. †275
vi.	6	. †494
vi.	26	. . 460
vi.	27	. . 133
vi.	40	. . 246

RICHARD III.

ACT I.

Sc.	Line	Par.
i.	16	. . 468
i.	22	. . 397
i.	58	. †151
i.	67	. . 505
i.	75	. †494
i.	82	. †287
i.	84	. . 456
i.	92	. p. 372
i.	94	. . 498
i.	103	. . 456
i.	106	. . 490
i.	137	. . 200
i.	157	. †270
ii.	2	. †307
ii.	3	. . (1)
ii.	23	. †490
ii.	26	. p. 449
ii.	27	. . 225
ii.	31	. †69
ii.	52	. †451
ii.	56	. . 492
ii.	67	. . 474
ii.	{68/70}	. †233
ii.	71	. †123
ii.	76	. . 466
ii.	{89/91}	. †500
ii.	117	. †446
ii.	154	. †239
ii.	155	. †490
ii.	{156/165}	. 84
ii.	163	. †283
ii.	166	. †428
ii.	170	. . 284
ii.	179	. . 92
ii.	{193/203}	. 500
ii.	211	. †349
ii.	215	. †468
ii.	216	. . 342
ii.	217	. (1a)
ii.	226	. †512
ii.	232	. . 356
ii.	235	. . 466
ii.	236	. . 490
ii.	245	. . 479
ii.	250	. . 305
ii.	255	. . †1
ii.	259	. {295 193}
ii.	261	. . 159
iii.	1	. . 468
iii.	5	{"live-ly,"} (2)
iii.	6	. . 174
iii.	19	. {(3) 468}
iii	36	{Fol. or 460}
iii.	63	. . †68

(1) *Hamlet*, i. 2. 92.   (1a) *A. Y. L.* iii. 1. 18.   (2) *Cymb.* iv. 4. 132.
(3) "Majesty" when a dissyllable will henceforth not be noticed.
(3a) ? Pun on "noble."   (4) Folio, "Ay, madam."   (5) *Macbeth*, v. 8. 48.
(6) Folio, "an end."   (7) Compare *Hamlet*, v. 1. 1-235.   (8) *J. C.* i. 2. 317.
(9) *M. of V.* v. 1. 77.   (10) Folio omits "weighty."   (11) Folio, "thinks't."
(12) Folio, "and."   (13) Folio, "worshipfully."   (14) *Lear*, iv. 1. 54.
(15) Folio omits "and."   (16) Folio, "King Richard."   (17) *Rich. III.* i. 1. 158.
(18) Folio omits "deep."   (19) Folio omits "my lord."   (20) *Macbeth*, iii. 2. 49.
(21) *A. W.* v. 3. 297.   (22) *J. C.* i. 3. 22.

ROMEO AND JULIET.

TAMING OF THE SHREW.

TEMPEST.

* Read either "let it alone" (472, end) or "let's along" (30)

(1) Folio, "th' outward."   (2) "Impertinent."—*Lear*, iv. 6. 178.
(2a) *J. C.* iv. 3. 280. (3) "Old."—*Macbeth*, ii. 3. 2. (4) "Owes."—*A.W.* v. iii. 97.
(5) "Masters."—*M. of V.* iv. 1. 51. "Mastres" is written for "mistress" in B.
and F. *Coxcomb*, ii. 3.   (6) "Against course and kind."—Munday.
(7) Folio, "and."   (8) See *Tempest*, i. 2. 200.
(9) Theobald, "busy less;" (?) "most busy *least*."   (10) Folio, "lies "

TIMON OF ATHENS.

TITUS ANDRONICUS.

TWELFTH NIGHT.

(a) A pun.

(1) See *K. J.* iii. 4. 81.   (2) See *Macbeth,* . 5. 30.
(3) See below, line 35; *A. Y. L.* ii. 7. 81.   (4) *A. Y. L.* iii. 1. 17.
(5) *J. C.* iii. 1. 207-8.   (6) *K. J.* v. 2. 79.   (7) *K. J.* v. 5. 7.

TWO GENTLEMEN OF VERONA.

(b) Compare " I have *fairly* forgotten it."

VERBAL INDEX.

A

PAR.

Happily = "haply" . . . 42
Happy (verb). 290
Hardy = "bold" 148
Have. "Should *have*" . . 327
  "to *have*" omitted after
    "would have" 411
  "Thought *to have* begged" 360
Hear. "Who *heard* me *to* deny
    it?". 349
Heat (participle) 342
He for "him" . . . 206, 207
  "man" 224
Hence, without verb of motion . 41
Hen(*e*)ry 477
Henry VIII. not written by
    Shakespeare 455
Her, antecedent of relative . . 218
  for "herself" 223
  "its" 229
  "'s" 217
Here. "Thy *here*-approach". 43
Hers, used for "her" adj. . . 238
Him, dative 220
  for "he" 208
  "himself". 223
  = "he whom". . . . 246
Hinder. "Who shall *hinder* me
    to weep?" 349
His, antecedent of a relative . 21
  for "its" 228
  "'s" 217
Hither, without verb of motion . 41
  monosyllable 466
Hitherto, used of space . . 44
Hoist (participle) 342
Holp for "holpen". . . . 343
Homage*r* 443
Home. "Speak him *home*". . 45
Honest (verb) 290
Hour (dissyllable) 480
How. "*How* chance?". . . 37
  for "however," for "as" . 46
However (it be) 403
Hybrid compounds 428

I.

I for "me" 209
  unaccented dropped . . . 461
  "(I) beseech you" . . . 456, 401
  slurred in "min*i*ster," &c. . 467
If. "*If* that" 287

PAR.

Ignomy 478
Impersonal verbs 297
Import*less* 446
-In for "-un," prefix . . . 442
In. "He fell *in* love" . . . 159
  = "*in* the case of". . . 162
  "*In* round" 163
  = during : "*in* night" . . 161
  with the verbal, "*in* sleep-
    ing". 164
Indicative 346–348
  Simple Present for Complete 346
  Simple Past for Complete
    Present 347
  Present, Third Pers. Pl. in *-en* 332
  in *-es, th* 335, 336
  Past in *u* 339
  Second Per. Sing. in *-ts* . 340
  Future for Subjunctive . . 348
  "And thou *lovest* me" . . 363
Infect (participle) 155, 342
Infinitive 349–360
  active for passive 359
  indefinitely used 356
  perfect, "He thought to have
    done it" 360
  used as a noun 355
  "To" omitted ; inserted . 349
  „ omitted and inserted
    after the same verb . 350
  „ with noun, used as
    subject or object . 354
Inflections 332–345
-Ing, termination 372
  confused with the old inflec-
    tion "en" 93, 372
Inhabited = "housed" . . 294
In's for "in his" 461
Interjectional lines 512
Interrogative Pronouns, transi-
    tion from to Relative 251, 252
Into, with verbs of rest . . . 159
  accent of 457*a*
Inward (noun) 77
Irregularities of construction 406–27
Is, ellipses after 405
  ellipse of 403
-Is*é*d final in polysyllables . . 491
It 226–29
  ellipse of 404
  for "its" 228
  "*it* is," ellipse of 166
  "To voice *it* with claims". 226
  emphatic as antecedent . 227
-Ition, -ation, suffix omitted . 451
  Its, post-Shakespearian . . 228
  substitutes for . . . 228, 229
-Ive, suffix passive 3, 445

J.

	PAR.
Jugg(e)ler	477
Just, adj. = "exact", . . .	14
Justicers	443

K.

Know. "I *know* you what you are"	414

L.

Lack = "to be wanting" . .	293
Laid (adjective)	22
Lated (verb)	290
Latinisms	418
Learn (verb act.)	291
Lengthening of words in pronunciation . . .	477–86
Less, suffix	3, 445
Let = "did".	303
Like. "If you *like* of me" .	177
Likes. "It *likes* me" . . .	297
Lines, see Verses.	
Liquids introduce a semi-vowel .	477
List. "*List* a brief tale" . .	199
'Longs for "belongs" . . .	460
Look. "To *look* your dead" .	200
Lover'd	294
-Ly, suffix	447

M.

Mad (verb)	290
Maj(es)ty, (dissyllable) . . .	468
Malice (verb)	290
Many. "*Many* a man" . . .	81
"A *many* men"	87
a noun	87
an adjective adverbially used	81
Mark. "*Mark* King Richard how he looks" . . .	414
Marle for "marvel"	461
May	307–313
"*May* not" = "must not"	310
used for the subjunctive in the sense of purpose .	138(*f*)
Me for "I"	210
= "for *me*," "by *me*" . .	220
= "myself"	223
"Of me" for "my" . . .	225
"*Me* rather had" . . .	230

	PAR.
Mean. "What *mean* ye to weep?".	356
Meered (particip.)	294
Meiny = "train"	87
derivation of	12
-Ment, suffix	448
Mere, adj. = "complete" . .	15
Mered (particip.)	294
Might	307–13
= "could"	312
Million'd (participle passive) .	294
Mine, how differs from "my" .	237
used for "my"	238
Misbecomed for "misbecame".	344
Mistook (participle)	343
Monosyllables accented . . .	457
unaccented	456
prolonged so as to make up a foot . . .	479*a*–486
Monosyllabic prepositions, accent of	457*c*
Moods	346–70
Moral*er*	443
More, most = "greater" "greatest" . . .	17
"*More* better"	11
"*More* fearful"	51
"No *more* but"	127
Most = "greatest"	17
"*Most* best"	11
Mouthed (participle passive) .	294
Much = "great"	51
Must, original use of	314
= "is to"	314
My, how differs from "mine" .	237
"Good *my* lord	13
Myself (derivation of)	20

N.

Names, used as adjectives .	22, 430
polysyllabic, receive but one accent	469
Near for "nearer"	478
Necessited	295
Neck. "In the *neck* of that" .	160
Need (verb intr.)	293
"What *need*?"	297
Needs (adverb)	25
Negative, double	406
Neither, ellipse of, before "nor"	396
a monosyllable	466
used for "both"	408
-Ness, suffix	449
Never. "*Never* so" . . .	52, 406
No. "*No* more but"	127
Nominative absolute . . .	376–381

PAR.

Prepositions omitted before indirect object 201
omitted after verbs of motion, worth, hearing, and other verbs 198-200
omitted in adverbial phrases 202
transposed 203, 424
accent of 457*a*
local and metaphorical meaning 138
restricted in meaning . . 139
transition of into conjunctions 287, 151
Present, Simple for Complete . 346
Presently = "at once" . . . 59
Private (noun) 5
Probable (adj.), active . . . 3
Pronoun, personal . . . 205-243
redundant 242, 243
relative 244-274
omitted 244
anomalies of. 205
between conjunction and infinitive 216
transposed 240
Proper = "own" 16
Prose, when used 515*a*
Prosody 452-515
Prowess, (quasi-monosyllable) . 470

Q.

Quail = "make to quail" . . 291
Quit (participle) 342

R.

R softens or destroys a following or preceding vowel 463, 464
prolongs -*er* 478
when following a vowel prolongs a monosyllable . . 485
-*r* and -*re* final dissyllabize monosyllables . . . 480
after dentals introduces a quasi-vowel 477
Recall. "Unrecalling" for "unrecalled" 372
Relatival constructions . . 275-289
Relative 244-274
with plural antecedent and singular verb 247
omitted 244
with supplementary pronoun {248 {249
See "who," "which," "that."

PAR.

Relish (verb transitive) . . . 291
Remains for "it *remains*" . . 404
Remember = "remind" . . . 291
Rememb(*e*)rance 477
Retire (verb act.) . . . 291, 296
Rhyme, when used 515
Right used for "true" . . . 19
Rode for "ridden" 343
Round = "straightforwardly" 60
Royal, why transposed . . . 419
Run. "Is *run*" 295

S.

'S, adverbial suffix 25
-S final dropped after *se, ce* . . 471
S misprinted in Folio 338
Sanctuary pronounced "sanct'ry" 468
Sat. "Being *sat*" 295
Save. "*Save* he". 118
Sawn for "seen" 344
Say used for "call" 200
'Say'd for "assayed" . . . 460
Scaling = "weighing" . . . 290
'Se for "shall" 461
Se'cure 492
Seldom (adjective) 22
Self (adjective) 20
omitted 223
Semb(*e*)lance 477
Sense for "senses". . . . 471
Several (noun) 5
Severally = "separately" . . 61
Shaked for "shaken" . . . 343
Shall 315-318
"I *shall*, my lord" . . . 315
= "is sure to" . . . 315
"It *shall* come to pass" . 317
"Mark you his absolute *shall*". 316
She for "her" 211
"woman" 224
Shine (verb act.) . . . 291
(verb transitive) . . . 291
Should 322-8
denotes contingent futurity 322
= "ought," "was to" 323, 324
"*should* have" . . . 327
like German "sollen" . . 328
after past, corresponds to "shall" after present . . 326
Show = "appear" . . . 293
Sightless (passive) . . . 3
Since, difference of tenses with . {132 {347
"A year *since*" . . . 62
"*Since* that" 287
= "when" 132

A CATALOG OF SELECTED
DOVER BOOKS
IN ALL FIELDS OF INTEREST

A CATALOG OF SELECTED DOVER
BOOKS IN ALL FIELDS OF INTEREST

CONCERNING THE SPIRITUAL IN ART, Wassily Kandinsky. Pioneering work by father of abstract art. Thoughts on color theory, nature of art. Analysis of earlier masters. 12 illustrations. 80pp. of text. 5⅜ x 8½. 23411-8

ANIMALS: 1,419 Copyright-Free Illustrations of Mammals, Birds, Fish, Insects, etc., Jim Harter (ed.). Clear wood engravings present, in extremely lifelike poses, over 1,000 species of animals. One of the most extensive pictorial sourcebooks of its kind. Captions. Index. 284pp. 9 x 12. 23766-4

CELTIC ART: The Methods of Construction, George Bain. Simple geometric techniques for making Celtic interlacements, spirals, Kells-type initials, animals, humans, etc. Over 500 illustrations. 160pp. 9 x 12. (Available in U.S. only.) 22923-8

AN ATLAS OF ANATOMY FOR ARTISTS, Fritz Schider. Most thorough reference work on art anatomy in the world. Hundreds of illustrations, including selections from works by Vesalius, Leonardo, Goya, Ingres, Michelangelo, others. 593 illustrations. 192pp. 7⅛ x 10¼. 20241-0

CELTIC HAND STROKE-BY-STROKE (Irish Half-Uncial from "The Book of Kells"): An Arthur Baker Calligraphy Manual, Arthur Baker. Complete guide to creating each letter of the alphabet in distinctive Celtic manner. Covers hand position, strokes, pens, inks, paper, more. Illustrated. 48pp. 8¼ x 11. 24336-2

EASY ORIGAMI, John Montroll. Charming collection of 32 projects (hat, cup, pelican, piano, swan, many more) specially designed for the novice origami hobbyist. Clearly illustrated easy-to-follow instructions insure that even beginning papercrafters will achieve successful results. 48pp. 8¼ x 11. 27298-2

THE COMPLETE BOOK OF BIRDHOUSE CONSTRUCTION FOR WOOD-WORKERS, Scott D. Campbell. Detailed instructions, illustrations, tables. Also data on bird habitat and instinct patterns. Bibliography. 3 tables. 63 illustrations in 15 figures. 48pp. 5¼ x 8½. 24407-5

BLOOMINGDALE'S ILLUSTRATED 1886 CATALOG: Fashions, Dry Goods and Housewares, Bloomingdale Brothers. Famed merchants' extremely rare catalog depicting about 1,700 products: clothing, housewares, firearms, dry goods, jewelry, more. Invaluable for dating, identifying vintage items. Also, copyright-free graphics for artists, designers. Co-published with Henry Ford Museum & Greenfield Village. 160pp. 8¼ x 11. 25780-0

HISTORIC COSTUME IN PICTURES, Braun & Schneider. Over 1,450 costumed figures in clearly detailed engravings—from dawn of civilization to end of 19th century. Captions. Many folk costumes. 256pp. 8⅜ x 11¾. 23150-X

ANATOMY: A Complete Guide for Artists, Joseph Sheppard. A master of figure drawing shows artists how to render human anatomy convincingly. Over 460 illustrations. 224pp. 8⅜ x 11¼. 27279-6

MEDIEVAL CALLIGRAPHY: Its History and Technique, Marc Drogin. Spirited history, comprehensive instruction manual covers 13 styles (ca. 4th century through 15th). Excellent photographs; directions for duplicating medieval techniques with modern tools. 224pp. 8⅜ x 11¼. 26142-5

DRIED FLOWERS: How to Prepare Them, Sarah Whitlock and Martha Rankin. Complete instructions on how to use silica gel, meal and borax, perlite aggregate, sand and borax, glycerine and water to create attractive permanent flower arrangements. 12 illustrations. 32pp. 5⅜ x 8½. 21802-3

EASY-TO-MAKE BIRD FEEDERS FOR WOODWORKERS, Scott D. Campbell. Detailed, simple-to-use guide for designing, constructing, caring for and using feeders. Text, illustrations for 12 classic and contemporary designs. 96pp. 5⅜ x 8½. 25847-5

SCOTTISH WONDER TALES FROM MYTH AND LEGEND, Donald A. Mackenzie. 16 lively tales tell of giants rumbling down mountainsides, of a magic wand that turns stone pillars into warriors, of gods and goddesses, evil hags, powerful forces and more. 240pp. 5⅜ x 8½. 29677-6

THE HISTORY OF UNDERCLOTHES, C. Willett Cunnington and Phyllis Cunnington. Fascinating, well-documented survey covering six centuries of English undergarments, enhanced with over 100 illustrations: 12th-century laced-up bodice, footed long drawers (1795), 19th-century bustles, 19th-century corsets for men, Victorian "bust improvers," much more. 272pp. 5⅜ x 8¼. 27124-2

ARTS AND CRAFTS FURNITURE: The Complete Brooks Catalog of 1912, Brooks Manufacturing Co. Photos and detailed descriptions of more than 150 now very collectible furniture designs from the Arts and Crafts movement depict davenports, settees, buffets, desks, tables, chairs, bedsteads, dressers and more, all built of solid, quarter-sawed oak. Invaluable for students and enthusiasts of antiques, Americana and the decorative arts. 80pp. 6½ x 9¼. 27471-3

WILBUR AND ORVILLE: A Biography of the Wright Brothers, Fred Howard. Definitive, crisply written study tells the full story of the brothers' lives and work. A vividly written biography, unparalleled in scope and color, that also captures the spirit of an extraordinary era. 560pp. 6⅛ x 9¼. 40297-5

THE ARTS OF THE SAILOR: Knotting, Splicing and Ropework, Hervey Garrett Smith. Indispensable shipboard reference covers tools, basic knots and useful hitches; handsewing and canvas work, more. Over 100 illustrations. Delightful reading for sea lovers. 256pp. 5⅜ x 8½. 26440-8

FRANK LLOYD WRIGHT'S FALLINGWATER: The House and Its History, Second, Revised Edition, Donald Hoffmann. A total revision–both in text and illustrations–of the standard document on Fallingwater, the boldest, most personal architectural statement of Wright's mature years, updated with valuable new material from the recently opened Frank Lloyd Wright Archives. "Fascinating"–*The New York Times.* 116 illustrations. 128pp. 9¼ x 10¾. 27430-6

PHOTOGRAPHIC SKETCHBOOK OF THE CIVIL WAR, Alexander Gardner. 100 photos taken on field during the Civil War. Famous shots of Manassas Harper's Ferry, Lincoln, Richmond, slave pens, etc. 244pp. 10⅝ x 8¼. 22731-6

FIVE ACRES AND INDEPENDENCE, Maurice G. Kains. Great back-to-the-land classic explains basics of self-sufficient farming. The one book to get. 95 illustrations. 397pp. 5⅜ x 8½. 20974-1

SONGS OF EASTERN BIRDS, Dr. Donald J. Borror. Songs and calls of 60 species most common to eastern U.S.: warblers, woodpeckers, flycatchers, thrushes, larks, many more in high-quality recording. Cassette and manual 99912-2

A MODERN HERBAL, Margaret Grieve. Much the fullest, most exact, most useful compilation of herbal material. Gigantic alphabetical encyclopedia, from aconite to zedoary, gives botanical information, medical properties, folklore, economic uses, much else. Indispensable to serious reader. 161 illustrations. 888pp. 6½ x 9¼. 2-vol. set. (Available in U.S. only.) Vol. I: 22798-7
Vol. II: 22799-5

HIDDEN TREASURE MAZE BOOK, Dave Phillips. Solve 34 challenging mazes accompanied by heroic tales of adventure. Evil dragons, people-eating plants, blood-thirsty giants, many more dangerous adversaries lurk at every twist and turn. 34 mazes, stories, solutions. 48pp. 8¼ x 11. 24566-7

LETTERS OF W. A. MOZART, Wolfgang A. Mozart. Remarkable letters show bawdy wit, humor, imagination, musical insights, contemporary musical world; includes some letters from Leopold Mozart. 276pp. 5⅜ x 8½. 22859-2

BASIC PRINCIPLES OF CLASSICAL BALLET, Agrippina Vaganova. Great Russian theoretician, teacher explains methods for teaching classical ballet. 118 illustrations. 175pp. 5⅜ x 8½. 22036-2

THE JUMPING FROG, Mark Twain. Revenge edition. The original story of The Celebrated Jumping Frog of Calaveras County, a hapless French translation, and Twain's hilarious "retranslation" from the French. 12 illustrations. 66pp. 5⅜ x 8½. 22686-7

BEST REMEMBERED POEMS, Martin Gardner (ed.). The 126 poems in this superb collection of 19th- and 20th-century British and American verse range from Shelley's "To a Skylark" to the impassioned "Renascence" of Edna St. Vincent Millay and to Edward Lear's whimsical "The Owl and the Pussycat." 224pp. 5⅜ x 8½. 27165-X

COMPLETE SONNETS, William Shakespeare. Over 150 exquisite poems deal with love, friendship, the tyranny of time, beauty's evanescence, death and other themes in language of remarkable power, precision and beauty. Glossary of archaic terms. 80pp. 5$\frac{3}{16}$ x 8¼. 26686-9

THE BATTLES THAT CHANGED HISTORY, Fletcher Pratt. Eminent historian profiles 16 crucial conflicts, ancient to modern, that changed the course of civilization. 352pp. 5⅜ x 8½. 41129-X

THE WIT AND HUMOR OF OSCAR WILDE, Alvin Redman (ed.). More than 1,000 ripostes, paradoxes, wisecracks: Work is the curse of the drinking classes; I can resist everything except temptation; etc. 258pp. 5⅜ x 8½.　　20602-5

SHAKESPEARE LEXICON AND QUOTATION DICTIONARY, Alexander Schmidt. Full definitions, locations, shades of meaning in every word in plays and poems. More than 50,000 exact quotations. 1,485pp. 6½ x 9¼. 2-vol. set.
Vol. 1: 22726-X
Vol. 2: 22727-8

SELECTED POEMS, Emily Dickinson. Over 100 best-known, best-loved poems by one of America's foremost poets, reprinted from authoritative early editions. No comparable edition at this price. Index of first lines. 64pp. 5³⁄₁₆ x 8¼.　　26466-1

THE INSIDIOUS DR. FU-MANCHU, Sax Rohmer. The first of the popular mystery series introduces a pair of English detectives to their archnemesis, the diabolical Dr. Fu-Manchu. Flavorful atmosphere, fast-paced action, and colorful characters enliven this classic of the genre. 208pp. 5³⁄₁₆ x 8¼.　　29898-1

THE MALLEUS MALEFICARUM OF KRAMER AND SPRENGER, translated by Montague Summers. Full text of most important witchhunter's "bible," used by both Catholics and Protestants. 278pp. 6⅝ x 10.　　22802-9

SPANISH STORIES/CUENTOS ESPAÑOLES: A Dual-Language Book, Angel Flores (ed.). Unique format offers 13 great stories in Spanish by Cervantes, Borges, others. Faithful English translations on facing pages. 352pp. 5⅜ x 8½.　　25399-6

GARDEN CITY, LONG ISLAND, IN EARLY PHOTOGRAPHS, 1869–1919, Mildred H. Smith. Handsome treasury of 118 vintage pictures, accompanied by carefully researched captions, document the Garden City Hotel fire (1899), the Vanderbilt Cup Race (1908), the first airmail flight departing from the Nassau Boulevard Aerodrome (1911), and much more. 96pp. 8⅞ x 11¾.　　40669-5

OLD QUEENS, N.Y., IN EARLY PHOTOGRAPHS, Vincent F. Seyfried and William Asadorian. Over 160 rare photographs of Maspeth, Jamaica, Jackson Heights, and other areas. Vintage views of DeWitt Clinton mansion, 1939 World's Fair and more. Captions. 192pp. 8⅞ x 11.　　26358-4

CAPTURED BY THE INDIANS: 15 Firsthand Accounts, 1750-1870, Frederick Drimmer. Astounding true historical accounts of grisly torture, bloody conflicts, relentless pursuits, miraculous escapes and more, by people who lived to tell the tale. 384pp. 5⅜ x 8½.　　24901-8

THE WORLD'S GREAT SPEECHES (Fourth Enlarged Edition), Lewis Copeland, Lawrence W. Lamm, and Stephen J. McKenna. Nearly 300 speeches provide public speakers with a wealth of updated quotes and inspiration–from Pericles' funeral oration and William Jennings Bryan's "Cross of Gold Speech" to Malcolm X's powerful words on the Black Revolution and Earl of Spenser's tribute to his sister, Diana, Princess of Wales. 944pp. 5⅜ x 8⅜.　　40903-1

THE BOOK OF THE SWORD, Sir Richard F. Burton. Great Victorian scholar/adventurer's eloquent, erudite history of the "queen of weapons"–from prehistory to early Roman Empire. Evolution and development of early swords, variations (sabre, broadsword, cutlass, scimitar, etc.), much more. 336pp. 6⅛ x 9¼.
25434-8

AUTOBIOGRAPHY: The Story of My Experiments with Truth, Mohandas K. Gandhi. Boyhood, legal studies, purification, the growth of the Satyagraha (nonviolent protest) movement. Critical, inspiring work of the man responsible for the freedom of India. 480pp. 5⅜ x 8½. (Available in U.S. only.) 24593-4

CELTIC MYTHS AND LEGENDS, T. W. Rolleston. Masterful retelling of Irish and Welsh stories and tales. Cuchulain, King Arthur, Deirdre, the Grail, many more. First paperback edition. 58 full-page illustrations. 512pp. 5⅜ x 8½. 26507-2

THE PRINCIPLES OF PSYCHOLOGY, William James. Famous long course complete, unabridged. Stream of thought, time perception, memory, experimental methods; great work decades ahead of its time. 94 figures. 1,391pp. 5⅜ x 8½. 2-vol. set.
Vol. I: 20381-6 Vol. II: 20382-4

THE WORLD AS WILL AND REPRESENTATION, Arthur Schopenhauer. Definitive English translation of Schopenhauer's life work, correcting more than 1,000 errors, omissions in earlier translations. Translated by E. F. J. Payne. Total of 1,269pp. 5⅜ x 8½. 2-vol. set. Vol. 1: 21761-2 Vol. 2: 21762-0

MAGIC AND MYSTERY IN TIBET, Madame Alexandra David-Neel. Experiences among lamas, magicians, sages, sorcerers, Bonpa wizards. A true psychic discovery. 32 illustrations. 321pp. 5⅜ x 8½. (Available in U.S. only.) 22682-4

THE EGYPTIAN BOOK OF THE DEAD, E. A. Wallis Budge. Complete reproduction of Ani's papyrus, finest ever found. Full hieroglyphic text, interlinear transliteration, word-for-word translation, smooth translation. 533pp. 6½ x 9¼. 21866-X

MATHEMATICS FOR THE NONMATHEMATICIAN, Morris Kline. Detailed, college-level treatment of mathematics in cultural and historical context, with numerous exercises. Recommended Reading Lists. Tables. Numerous figures. 641pp. 5⅜ x 8½. 24823-2

PROBABILISTIC METHODS IN THE THEORY OF STRUCTURES, Isaac Elishakoff. Well-written introduction covers the elements of the theory of probability from two or more random variables, the reliability of such multivariable structures, the theory of random function, Monte Carlo methods of treating problems incapable of exact solution, and more. Examples. 502pp. 5⅜ x 8½. 40691-1

THE RIME OF THE ANCIENT MARINER, Gustave Doré, S. T. Coleridge. Doré's finest work; 34 plates capture moods, subtleties of poem. Flawless full-size reproductions printed on facing pages with authoritative text of poem. "Beautiful. Simply beautiful."–*Publisher's Weekly.* 77pp. 9¼ x 12. 22305-1

NORTH AMERICAN INDIAN DESIGNS FOR ARTISTS AND CRAFTSPEOPLE, Eva Wilson. Over 360 authentic copyright-free designs adapted from Navajo blankets, Hopi pottery, Sioux buffalo hides, more. Geometrics, symbolic figures, plant and animal motifs, etc. 128pp. 8⅜ x 11. (Not for sale in the United Kingdom.) 25341-4

SCULPTURE: Principles and Practice, Louis Slobodkin. Step-by-step approach to clay, plaster, metals, stone; classical and modern. 253 drawings, photos. 255pp. 8⅛ x 11. 22960-2

THE INFLUENCE OF SEA POWER UPON HISTORY, 1660–1783, A. T. Mahan. Influential classic of naval history and tactics still used as text in war colleges. First paperback edition. 4 maps. 24 battle plans. 640pp. 5⅜ x 8½. 25509-3

CATALOG OF DOVER BOOKS

THE STORY OF THE TITANIC AS TOLD BY ITS SURVIVORS, Jack Winocour (ed.). What it was really like. Panic, despair, shocking inefficiency, and a little heroism. More thrilling than any fictional account. 26 illustrations. 320pp. 5⅜ x 8½.
20610-6

FAIRY AND FOLK TALES OF THE IRISH PEASANTRY, William Butler Yeats (ed.). Treasury of 64 tales from the twilight world of Celtic myth and legend: "The Soul Cages," "The Kildare Pooka," "King O'Toole and his Goose," many more. Introduction and Notes by W. B. Yeats. 352pp. 5⅜ x 8½.
26941-8

BUDDHIST MAHAYANA TEXTS, E. B. Cowell and others (eds.). Superb, accurate translations of basic documents in Mahayana Buddhism, highly important in history of religions. The Buddha-karita of Asvaghosha, Larger Sukhavativyuha, more. 448pp. 5⅜ x 8½.
25552-2

ONE TWO THREE . . . INFINITY: Facts and Speculations of Science, George Gamow. Great physicist's fascinating, readable overview of contemporary science: number theory, relativity, fourth dimension, entropy, genes, atomic structure, much more. 128 illustrations. Index. 352pp. 5⅜ x 8½.
25664-2

EXPERIMENTATION AND MEASUREMENT, W. J. Youden. Introductory manual explains laws of measurement in simple terms and offers tips for achieving accuracy and minimizing errors. Mathematics of measurement, use of instruments, experimenting with machines. 1994 edition. Foreword. Preface. Introduction. Epilogue. Selected Readings. Glossary. Index. Tables and figures. 128pp. 5⅜ x 8½.
40451-X

DALÍ ON MODERN ART: The Cuckolds of Antiquated Modern Art, Salvador Dalí. Influential painter skewers modern art and its practitioners. Outrageous evaluations of Picasso, Cézanne, Turner, more. 15 renderings of paintings discussed. 44 calligraphic decorations by Dalí. 96pp. 5⅜ x 8½. (Available in U.S. only.)
29220-7

ANTIQUE PLAYING CARDS: A Pictorial History, Henry René D'Allemagne. Over 900 elaborate, decorative images from rare playing cards (14th–20th centuries): Bacchus, death, dancing dogs, hunting scenes, royal coats of arms, players cheating, much more. 96pp. 9¼ x 12¼.
29265-7

MAKING FURNITURE MASTERPIECES: 30 Projects with Measured Drawings, Franklin H. Gottshall. Step-by-step instructions, illustrations for constructing handsome, useful pieces, among them a Sheraton desk, Chippendale chair, Spanish desk, Queen Anne table and a William and Mary dressing mirror. 224pp. 8⅛ x 11¼.
29338-6

THE FOSSIL BOOK: A Record of Prehistoric Life, Patricia V. Rich et al. Profusely illustrated definitive guide covers everything from single-celled organisms and dinosaurs to birds and mammals and the interplay between climate and man. Over 1,500 illustrations. 760pp. 7½ x 10⅛.
29371-8